EMILY

EMILY

Part Three of
THE KIROV SAGA

CYNTHIA HARROD-EAGLES

SIDGWICK & JACKSON
LONDON

First published 1992 by
Sidgwick & Jackson Limited
A division of Pan Macmillan Publishers Limited
Cavaye Place London SW10 9PG
and Basingstoke

Associated companies throughout the world

ISBN 0 283 99822 9

9 8 7 6 5 4 3 2 1

A CIP catalogue record for this book is available from the
British Library

Phototypeset by Intype, London

Printed and bound in Great Britain by
Billing & Sons Ltd, Worcester

AUTHOR'S NOTE

At the time of the action of this novel, Russia was still using the
Julian Calendar while the rest of Europe had changed to the
Gregorian. Therefore, Russia was eleven days behind. Dates
quoted while Emily is in England are according to the Gregorian
Calendar, and while she is in Russia according to the Julian.

For Tony, who bore with me through thin and thin

THE KIROV FAMILY

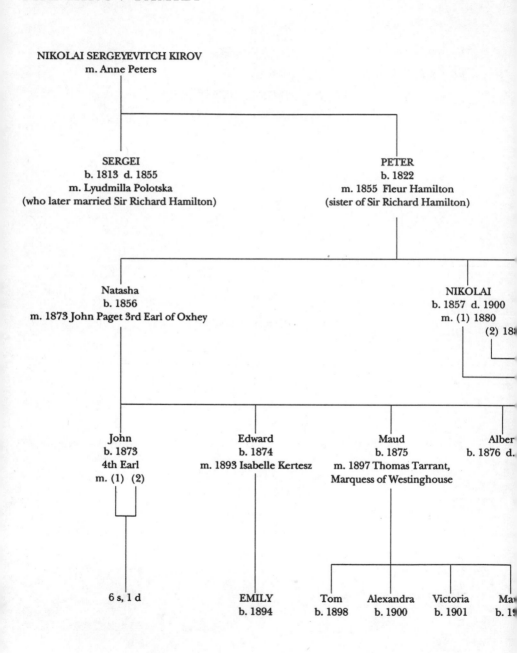

NIKOLAI SERGEYEVITCH KIROV
m. Anne Peters

SERGEI
b. 1813 d. 1855
m. Lyudmilla Polotska
(who later married Sir Richard Hamilton)

PETER
b. 1822
m. 1855 Fleur Hamilton
(sister of Sir Richard Hamilton)

Natasha
b. 1856
m. 1873 John Paget 3rd Earl of Oxhey

NIKOLAI
b. 1857 d. 1900
m. (1) 1880
(2) 18

John
b. 1873
4th Earl
m. (1) (2)

Edward
b. 1874
m. 1893 Isabelle Kertesz

Maud
b. 1875
m. 1897 Thomas Tarrant,
Marquess of Westinghouse

Alber
b. 1876 d.

6 s, 1 d

EMILY
b. 1894

Tom
b. 1898

Alexandra
b. 1900

Victoria
b. 1901

Ma
b. 1

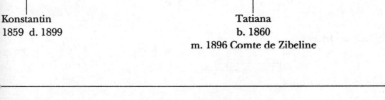

Konstantin
1859 d. 1899

Tatiana
b. 1860
m. 1896 Comte de Zibeline

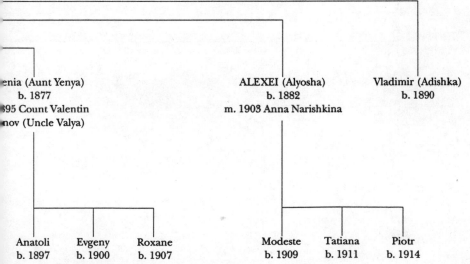

:nia (Aunt Yenya)
b. 1877
395 Count Valentin
nov (Uncle Valya)

ALEXEI (Alyosha)
b. 1882
m. 1903 Anna Narishkina

Vladimir (Adishka)
b. 1890

Anatoli
b. 1897

Evgeny
b. 1900

Roxane
b. 1907

Modeste
b. 1909

Tatiana
b. 1911

Piotr
b. 1914

BOOK ONE

LEARNING

Chapter One

From the row of poplars, the park was almost flat all the way back to the Big House. Emily could just see it nestling on the horizon, improbable and pale against its background of dark trees: Bratton Park, seat of the marquesses of Westinghouse, of the Wiltshire Tarrants, a family noble and numerous enough to have appropriated a county to its name. The present building was less than a hundred years old, but there had always been a house on the site. Blurred by the distance, this one looked like a fairy palace on the stroke of midnight, just making up its mind to disappear.

In the other direction the park sloped suddenly downwards towards its boundary. Emily thought the poplars must have been planted along the crest to stop overheated Tarrants – throughout history they were neck-or-nothing riders – from galloping straight over the edge and coming to grief. From here she could see the high brick wall which marched around three sides of the vast park, and the white streak of the track which led to the West Gate, which was never used because it didn't go anywhere important. At the end of the track, about a quarter of a mile away, she could see the West Gatehouse, always known as The Lodge, which was her home.

She smiled at the sight of it. It was the sort of building you couldn't help smiling at, even if you were Modern, and devoted to Charles Rennie Mackintosh and the Geometricalists. It was a gatehouse that thought it was a Transylvanian castle, and hadn't the least idea how small it was. It had turrets and crenellations and spires, massive oak doors, and a great deal of stained glass in the colours of melting cough drops: camphor red, paregoric yellow, winter green.

There was smoke rising from the kitchen chimney, reminding her that she was hungry; and she had news to tell. She hauled up the heavy serge skirt of her habit, draped it over her arm, and started down the slope as fast as her riding boots, which weren't made for walking, would allow.

Down the side of The Lodge there was a dank stone path which led between the mossy wall and gloomy banks of laurels to the

3

kitchen door. Emily usually went in that way when she came back from riding. The kitchen, although dark because of the laurels and the narrow ecclesiastical windows, was always cosy and full of good smells.

Opening the door, Emily lifted her nose, sniffed, and said rapturously, 'Not steak and kidney pie!'

'Boots?' Penny said sternly, looking over her shoulder from her position in front of the range.

'Clean,' said Emily, twisting one foot up to display the sole. She sniffed again doubtfully. 'Cauliflower?'

'With a cheese sauce,' Penny qualified. 'And roast potatoes,' she added kindly.

'Oh, bliss! You're a wizard, darling old Pen.'

Penny grunted, pleased with the compliment but not wishing to show it. 'Nice ride?'

'Rather! Except that Jacob insisted on coming all the way back to the poplars with me. He complains because it takes him away from his work, but when I tell him he needn't he just says, "Tain't proper for a young lady to ride alone, Miss Emily." There's no arguing with him.'

Emily had a gift for mimicry. Just for a moment she almost looked like her aunt's elderly groom as well as sounding like him. But Penny went on stirring sauce unsmilingly. She had no time for what she called 'silliness'.

Emily remembered her news. 'Oh, and guess what? Jacob says Aunt Maud and Uncle Westie are coming tomorrow morning!'

'That's nice,' said Penny absently. Her sauce was threatening lumps and she wasn't really listening.

'So I'll have the cousins to play with,' Emily persevered. 'For three weeks, nearly, until they all go to Scotland.'

Now Penny looked up, but only to survey Emily critically. 'You're getting too big for playing. You're fifteen – a young lady, really. Time you learned a bit of dignity.'

'Darling Penny, don't you start! It's bad enough with Jacob telling me "what's fitting, miss" all the time.'

'Jacob's right. You must never forget who you are: there are enough who'll try to do it for you. And you never know what Fortune may bring. Suppose one day a prince was to walk in through that door and ask to marry you? You wouldn't want him to know you'd been rushing round unchaperoned like a menagerie, would you?'

4

Emily would have loved to know what Penny thought 'menagerie' meant, but knew better than to ask. 'There's no prince the right age for me. Prince Edward's too young, and you wouldn't want me marrying a foreigner, now would you?'

Penny was not to be drawn. 'Half an hour till luncheon,' she said dismissingly.

'I'll tell Pa, then. Give him time to get back to earth,' Emily said, turning away.

The Lodge, being a gatehouse, had not been designed as a gentleman's residence, but still there were three rooms downstairs, apart from the kitchen. Two of them were the tiny dark dining-room and the even darker and overstuffed sitting-room. The third and largest was the study of Emily's father, the Hon. Edward Paget.

It was the kind of study which in story-books was referred to as the owner's 'sanctum'. Emily had learnt from the moment she first staggered proudly up from all fours onto her hind legs that she must never go into Papa's study without permission. Though age and increasing responsibility had eased the rules a little in her favour, she still approached it with a sense of awe.

It was much the nicest room, having really quite large casement windows which looked out onto the little garden and caught all the sun. Cheddar pinks grew in the bed below them, filling the room with their scent, and a white rambling rose drooped nodding sprays into view from above.

It was simply furnished, with two high-backed armchairs covered in red plush by the fireside, overflowing bookcases against the panelled walls, and on the floor an ancient Turkey carpet whose intricate pattern of red, brown and blue had been rendered almost monochrome by age.

The rest of the room was dominated by the massive desk drawn up near the window, which was covered with a litter of papers, pens, pencils and books. At this desk, seated so that he could see out of the window merely by lifting his eyes, Edward spent every day writing.

He was writing when Emily came in, and didn't turn his head. She walked over to stand behind his chair silently, waiting for him to come to the end of the paragraph. Papa's work was sacrosanct: the worst crime known to their small household was to interrupt his creative flow. Raising herself a little on her toes and craning her neck, Emily could read a few lines of her father's neat handwriting at the top of the current page.

. . . and warming the mellow grey stones of Big School. Spiffy stood four square before his wicket, his bat straight, ready for whatever the demon bowler of St Luke's might send down to him. Twenty to get, and the light fading fast: it all depended on Spiffy now . . .

At last Edward put down his pen and looked up. 'Well?' he said, and made an effort to be cordial. 'Good ride?'

'All right, thanks. Jacob says everyone's coming down tomorrow.'

'Oh, good.'

'Is that for the *Magnet*? Have you nearly finished?'

'*Chums*. And it's quite finished,' Edward said, stretching out his hands and flexing his cramped fingers.

'Did Spiffy make twenty runs and save the honour of the dear old school?'

'Twenty-two. His final shot was a cracking six right over the hedge into the headmaster's garden. Is luncheon ready?'

'As good as.' She stepped aside out of the way as Edward pushed back his chair and stood up, placed the last sheet of paper on the stacked manuscript and patted the pile together. Whatever his next action would be, it would take him out of her presence, and Penny's snub had left Emily hungry for human contact. She searched for something to say.

'How's work? Have you got lots of commissions?'

'Only a Lionheart Lomas story for the *Boy's Own Paper*. Why? Are you afraid I'll join the ranks of the unemployed?'

'Of course not. I just wondered.'

'Chapman at Amalgamated said in his last letter that I ought to have the Telephone installed, so that they could ask me for things at short notice, but I don't think I'd care for that. At the beck and call of an Instrument all day long . . . And just think how quickly bad news would be able to reach you. Imagine being woken in the middle of the night to be told someone had died!'

He spoke lightly, but Emily believed he must be thinking about her mother, who had died when she was born. Emily's warm heart and active imagination always made her quick to sympathise with anyone's troubles but her own. Papa's Broken Heart was legendary. No photograph or portrait existed of Emily's mother, and she and Penny did not even mention her in Edward's presence, for fear of Turning the Knife in the Wound.

'Perhaps you'll have time to get back to your novel tomorrow,'

6

she said gently. Work, she had always been told, was the best antidote to sorrow; and Papa's novel was going to make him rich and famous, if only he ever got time to finish it.

'No, no, something else will come in tomorrow's post,' he said quickly. 'It always does. Hadn't you better go and change out of your habit?'

'I was just going to,' Emily said, accepting the second snub meekly. Owners of broken hearts were entitled to put up Keep Off notices, even to their nearest and dearest.

Upstairs, one of The Lodge's four bedrooms had been sacrificed in the interests of gentlemanly living to make a bathroom. It was an example of her aunt's generosity which Emily never undervalued, for she had been in many a village house, and knew that gracious living stood or fell by its plumbing. Even the vicar spoke of The Lodge bathroom with awe, for it had a 'Deluge' washdown water-closet of the very latest design, as well as a bath and hand-basin.

Washing her hands and face in this Temple of Hygeia, Emily reflected on the business of being a poor relation. She couldn't say she had ever really suffered by it. She had a comfortable home in The Lodge, and when her aunt and uncle were not in residence at Bratton – which was more often than not – she had the whole of the park to wander in.

She also had free access to the vast library up at the Big House. This indigestible collection of books had been assembled by generations of Tarrants with widely varying and often unsuitable tastes. Reading her way through it had provided her with most of her education. She had never had any formal lessons, though the vicar had managed to get some mathematics and less Latin into her head. Her father had taught her French, because he had spoken it at home as a child, and they sometimes conversed in it to keep in practice.

For recreation, Aunt Maud had left orders that Emily was to have the use of the old schoolmaster pony whenever she liked. The animal in question was a twenty-year-old misanthropist with an iron mouth who had been bought to teach the Tarrant children how to fall off without hurting themselves. Only old Jacob had stricter ideas than Sooty about the proper conduct of a lady's ride, but Emily loved him anyway, and coaxed more out of him than anyone else ever had. Once, when his mind had been on other things, she had actually got him to jump two logs, one after the other.

For the rest, the poor relations at The Lodge never went short of food: the Home Farm provided them with milk and eggs, the kitchen gardens up at the Big House sent them fruit and vegetables when the Family didn't want them, and there were occasional gifts of meat and game. They had no rent to pay for the roof over their heads, and most of Penny's and Emily's clothes were hand-me-downs from the Big House, which Penny cleverly made over so that you really wouldn't recognise them.

Edward's earnings from his stories were enough for the rest of their household expenses, for his clothes and tobacco, and for the occasional indulgence of a parcel of wine, sherry and brandy which he had sent up from London. The stationmaster at Hadspent Halt, the nearest station, would bring it round for him on the back of his bicycle, always eager for a chance to do a favour to a member of the Family. Sometimes, to Emily's delight, he also brought copies of magazines that travellers had left in the waiting-room or on the train – *Strand*, or *Punch*, or the *Illustrated London News*.

He had no need to bring them newspapers: *The Times* and the *Telegraph* were sent over from the Big House every afternoon, when everyone had finished with them. When the Marquess and Marchioness were not in residence they were almost pristine, for only Corde the butler read them, and a lifetime's practice allowed him to do it without creasing.

They were also sent the previous day's *Daily Mail* from the servants' hall – ostensibly for Penny, though in reality Edward always grabbed it first and bore it off to his study to read up the murders and scandals, and to chuckle over the unconscious humour provided by its novel journalistic style.

So really, Emily told herself, staring at her reflection, she lacked for nothing: her life was comfortable, and she had everything to be grateful for. It had been an isolated life – her only friends were the characters in books – but she led a rich inner life, and she didn't remember ever feeling really lonely or unhappy.

But today Jacob had said something that had started off a new and unwelcome train of thought. He had been grumbling, not for the first time, that she had grown too big for Sooty.

'Ought to have a proper lady's horse, now you've turned fifteen,' he said. 'I'll speak to her ladyship about it, when she comes down tomorrow.'

Emily was alarmed. 'Oh no, really, you mustn't! It's very kind of Aunt Maud to let me ride at all.'

But Jacob stuck out his jaw. When his own or the Family's dignity was at stake, he could be determined. 'Tain't proper, Miss Emily, now you've growed so much. Look at your foot – touching the ground prac'ly! An' old Sooty ain't up to your weight neether. What with the saddle an' all, 'is legs is buckling. What'd people say'f they seen me ridin' beside you lookin' such a scarecrow? I got my good name to think of.'

He had rumbled on in that way, and she had been forced to distract him at last by reviving the other, older conflict with him, that she didn't need escorting when she was only riding in the park.

But it had started her thinking about her future. It was all very well being a poor relation when you were a child: nobody expected a child to take care of itself or to contribute to its upkeep. But fifteen was nearly grown up. What was to become of her? What had her upbringing and education fitted her for? She couldn't spend the rest of her life here, riding Sooty about the park, walking her uncle's hound puppies, reading her way through the Bratton library, occasionally having tea with the vicar and his wife, and helping the latter with the flowers on Sunday.

A restlessness had begun in her, a feeling as of cramped limbs longing to be stretched, a desire to see more of the world than Bratton Park and the village; most of all a desire to know much, much more, and to know it at firsthand, rather than by reading. She had a feeling like unsatisfied hunger for experience, for knowledge, for people and places and situations.

She dried her hands on the towel and thought that perhaps over luncheon she would float the idea upon a larger sea of speculation, and see what happened. She would see what They thought – Papa and Penny, her own particular arbiters of fate. Then the bell rang downstairs, and Emily's healthy fifteen-year-old body reminded her about steak and kidney pie and roast potatoes, and she rushed for her bedroom to change out of her habit.

By the time she had tidied herself to a sufficient standard to satisfy Penny, she was late, and got into trouble anyway. Penny would not have thought it fitting to scold in Mr Edward's presence, but she gave Emily a look as she served the soup (Scotch broth from yesterday's dinner vegetables) and said, 'Day-dreaming again, I suppose.'

'Sorry, Pen,' Emily said meekly. Penny sniffed, placed the bread on the table, and departed to eat her own soup in the kitchen. She was a stickler for propriety, and would never sit down and eat with them, any more than she would dream of using the bathroom. She lived and ate in the kitchen, used the outside privvy, and took her bath in front of the kitchen fire as she had done all her serving life.

Miss Aveline Pennistone – known as Mrs Pennistone for diplomatic reasons, or more usually just Penny – had gone into service at the age of ten as a sewing-maid, in the household of the old earl, Edward's father. Edward had been a toddler then, very hard on the knees and elbows of his sailor suits, and Penny had sewn love into each triangular rent she repaired, adoring the flaxen-haired, blue-eyed little boy whose ungoverned exuberance created so much work for her.

As time passed, Penny rose through the ranks to upper housemaid. Edward grew to handsome young manhood, and Penny's love grew with him, only the more silent and fierce as he became less and less accessible. She had never read a book in her life, and had no impossible Cinderella fantasies. She dreamed not of his sudden realisation of her beauty, but of somehow being able to do something for him. But what could a mere housemaid do for the wild young scion of a noble house, particularly when he was away at university for half the year?

Then he had made his disastrous marriage to a ballet girl. The fuss and outcry had rocked the house to its foundations, and he and his unsuitable wife had been banished to muddle and poverty in rooms in Paddington. The servants' hall had sucked its combined teeth and shaken its doleful head, and prepared to write Mr Edward out of their lives as the cautionary tale to end all cautionary tales.

Not so Penny. For the first and last time in her life she experienced a surge of determination which overrode humility, obedience, sense of propriety, all the things which had hitherto kept her in her place. With astonishing calmness she gave back her last quarter's wages to the housekeeper in lieu of notice, packed her bag, and begged a lift on Smart's the Carrier's cart up to London. There she presented herself at Mr Edward's door, and, being admitted, had taken over the running of his life from that moment.

It had been an act of insane courage born of love, and if love's desire is to serve, she had been amply rewarded. Penny had washed and cooked and cleaned, first for the young couple, and then, when Mrs Edward died of childbed fever, for Edward and Emily, and all for no wages but the knowledge of being useful. Far from thanking her, Edward had barely seemed to know she existed, but still in the tiny, gloomy flat she had cared for him and his baby, made and mended their clothes, haggled in the market for meat and vegetables when there was money, and done wonders with soup when it was short.

It was Penny, too, who had written at last to Lady Maud when she had made her celebrated marriage to Lord Westinghouse. Penny had pointed out how bad it was for Emily to be growing up in those poky rooms, whose windows were forever blackened with the smoke of the Great Western trains passing just beneath them. Her ladyship had responded with admirable promptness by providing and furnishing the unused West Gatehouse for her disgraced brother's use, and there they had all been ever since.

Mr Edward, Penny knew, would never have thought of asking – not so much because of pride, but because he had retreated from grief into the safe world of the boys' weekly, so far in that he hardly seemed to notice he had changed his surroundings. But asking the Marchioness on his behalf – an act of unspeakable presumption by a former housemaid – had bent Penny so far out of her nature that her reaction had been doubly fierce.

Once at The Lodge – a genteel, if not quite a gentleman's, residence – she had retreated into the kitchen, and insisted on the strictest maintenance of the proper distance between servant and served. Adoring them both, it had been hard to hold herself apart from them; but hers was a love strong enough to do what was good for them, whatever it cost her personally.

Penny had never known or hoped for intimacy with Mr Edward; but it was another matter with Emily. Growing up knowing no mother but Penny, Emily had naturally come to her with kisses and hugs, and it had been agony to Penny to turn them away, and to see the naturally affectionate and demonstrative child learning not to offer them. A grazed knee or a toothache would be attended to with efficiency and sympathy, but there was no cuddle, no kissing away of tears. In time Emily became self-sufficient beyond her years, and Penny developed a gruffness of manner to cover the pain of rebuffing the child she loved as her own.

Still, Penny never ceased to hope that some stroke of Fortune would restore them to their proper place in the world, and she did not mean them to be shamed by any recollection of having demeaned themselves. The time would come, she thought, when they would thank her; or, more realistically, she hoped that one day Emily

11

would appreciate it was through Penny's determination that she had no embarrassing memories to shun, or habits of familiarity to break.

For the moment, Emily, patiently eating soup, understood as little of Penny's motives as of her father's thought processes. He was not a good eating companion: he sat silent and frowning at most meals, not from displeasure, but because he was not really there. The world of Richard 'Lionheart' Lomas – a hero of his own creation whose courage in adversity bordered on the suicidal – was much more exciting than the dining-room of The Lodge.

Emily bore with the silence through the soup and the cold cod that followed. When Penny came in with the main course, however, she felt it was now or never, for it was not often that the three of them were all in the same room at the same time. So she said loudly, 'I've been thinking, Papa.' It was always necessary to attract his attention before you said anything you actually wanted him to hear, for he usually had a long distance to travel back.

'Hmm?' Her father's eyes slowly focused on her. Behind her Penny was unloading the tray onto the sideboard.

'I've been thinking what I ought to do when I grow up.'

'Do? Why should you want to do anything?' her father said vaguely. Penny came into view to put the dishes of roast potatoes and cauliflower on the table and was clearly not listening. It was not a good start.

'Well, I must do something. I can't just live here like this for ever, with you and Penny, can I?' Emily persevered.

'Why not?' Edward said. He hadn't yet understood her point. 'What do you want to do that you can't do here?'

'Oh, it isn't that – it's being a Poor Relation. Living on sufferance – it's a bit hard on Aunt Maud. Besides, there's my whole life to come, and what am I to *do*, you know?'

Penny was behind her again, cutting the pie – Emily smelled the exact moment by the lifting fragrance of glorious gravy – but she knew instinctively that she was listening now.

'I don't see what you can do,' Edward said plainly.

Emily had expected that. Her upbringing might not have fitted her for any other life, but there must be things that she could learn, or that took very little skill. She was quite clever really, though it was never tested.

'I could be a shop girl in a draper's shop. That might be rather jolly: I'd love to work one of those little brass things that whizz about the ceiling.'

12

'Customers are horribly rude to girls who serve in draper's shops,' Edward remarked. 'I've often noticed it.'

'Are they? I wonder why?' Emily said, perplexed. 'Well then, perhaps I could be a clerk or a typewriter. Lots of people use them nowadays.'

'Typewriters earn quite good wages, I hear,' Edward said mildly. Emily realised he was not taking her seriously, but Penny made up for it, putting a portion of pie down in front of her with unnecessary force.

'What on earth are you talking about, Emily?'

'Earning my living,' Emily said bravely. 'I have to do something.'

'No you do not,' Penny said, still too surprised to be angry. 'You're a lady! Whatever next?'

'Oh, but I wouldn't mind it,' Emily said eagerly. 'It would be fun! I've been thinking about it, Pen: I could live in London, in "diggings", and travel to the office on an omnibus, and go to a Picture Palace every Saturday – only think what bliss! I do so long to see a movie.'

'For shame, Emily!' said Penny. 'Movies, indeed!'

'Depravity on a grand scale,' Edward said, helping himself to potatoes. He thought it was all a joke, Emily could see. She would get no help from him.

'But movies are quite respectable,' she went on fighting the losing battle. 'The vicar's been to one, and he said it was topping, much better than magic lanterns, with a man playing the piano all through. If the vicar can go – '

'The vicar is not a lady,' Penny said unanswerably.

'All right, well I wouldn't go to movies,' she said desperately. 'I'd save up for a bicycle, and join a club, and go out for rides on Sundays. What could be more respectable than that?'

Penny was clearly annoyed. 'And eat in restaurants, I suppose?' she inquired ironically, as the most mentionable shocking thing she could think of. She firmly believed the dictate of her youth, that only loose women ate in restaurants.

Emily plunged on. 'No, honestly, I'd cook for myself in my own rooms – on a dear little gas ring.'

'And live off sardines and sausages,' Edward suggested, from the world of Big School and study teas. 'And bananas and crumpets and cocoa.' A vague look came over his face, and he began to drift away from the conversation.

13

'You'll do nothing of the sort,' Penny pronounced firmly. 'You'll stay at home with Papa like a good girl, until you marry.'

'But I don't see who'd marry me,' Emily said simply.

'You're the granddaughter of an earl,' Penny pointed out.

'Surely that isn't enough, not just that,' Emily said. Her father had gone far away, and she addressed herself to Penny. 'There are earl's *daughters* who don't get married. Surely I'd have to be pretty as well, or rich, or something?'

'That's not for you to worry about,' Penny said. 'Your aunt and your papa will find a suitable person for you when the time comes. You don't have to earn a living, don't you fret.'

'But Pen, I don't mind it. I'd *like* to be a New Woman. I'd wear a tailor-made to show I was serious, and have separate cuffs like a clerk – although I don't suppose typewriting is particularly dirty. But one can see it would be convenient from the laundry point of view. Oh, and think of shopping for myself, too! I'd buy my stockings from blissful Peter Robinson's! And I'd have proper drawers, with lace, no more horrid combinations – '

She realised just too late to stop herself that she'd allowed her enthusiasm to carry her too far.

'That's enough, Emily! You see where even talking about such an improper subject leads you. Let's have no more of it.'

'Sorry, Penny,' Emily said. In stony silence Penny handed the vegetable dish – new broad beans and young carrots from the Big House. They must have been sent before the news arrived that the family was coming tomorrow. Old Jowitt would never have parted with them otherwise.

The dish went to Edward, and he helped himself lavishly. 'Better to stay at home and be a poor relation, Emily,' he said, flourishing the spoon and revealing that he had been listening, even if he hadn't taken it seriously. 'Much more comfortable than sardines and gas rings.'

The following afternoon Emily walked across the park to the Big House for tea with her cousins.

She found them in the hall, as usual. The tea table stood before the huge open log fire which burned there winter and summer, since the warmth of the sun never penetrated to this vast Gothic chamber. The table was covered with a stiff, lace-edged cloth, and loaded with the familiar tea things: the willow-pattern china; tea-kettle

14

and chafing-dishes poised over exciting little blue flames; the silver pastry-forks, tiny silver butter-knives and filigree cake-baskets.

The table was presided over by Aunt Maud, very upright in the high-backed chair at one end of the table, and the latest Mamzelle, drooping meekly at the other. Governesses never lasted very long in the Tarrant household. Within a very short time of their arrival Aunt Maud invariably found them either ignorant, impertinent, or indecent – and on one sensational occasion, all three.

Between them in a row were Emily's cousins: Tom – Lord St Auben – the heir, who was eleven; Alexandra, nine; Victoria, eight; and Maudie, who was four. Their faces lit with flattering smiles as Emily appeared: four round, healthy Tarrant faces framed with curly black Tarrant hair, and with the round, bright-blue, dark-fringed eyes that could be seen staring out from ancestral portraits all over the house. All the Marquess's children looked exactly like him – just as though, Aunt Maud had once complained to her own mother, she had been nothing more than an incubator.

'Emily, dear, come and sit down,' Aunt Maud greeted her. Emily took the empty chair next to her aunt, pulled herself up to the table, and was immediately in trouble. 'No need to scrape the chair legs like that. A most disagreeable noise! You must consider other people in everything you do. And don't cross your feet – place them side by side on the floor and then draw them back slightly. Will you have a muffin?'

'Yes please, Aunt.' Bratton Park muffins were spoken of with tenderness in great houses throughout the land.

'I think you've grown again,' her aunt observed, examining her minutely. 'Yes, quite an inch, I should say. You had better leave off soon, or you'll find yourself embarrassed for partners. Men don't care to dance with females who tower over them – and if they don't dance, they don't offer, you may be sure of that.'

Alexandra and Victoria were giggling together helplessly but as yet silently at her discomfiture. Emily, to distract attention from them, said, 'I'm not sure I want them to offer, Aunt – at least, not for me.'

'Nonsense. All girls must marry,' said Aunt Maud. 'And it's particularly important for you to marry well. How else do you think you will secure an establishment?'

Emily took a deep breath. It hadn't gone down too well with Penny, but Aunt Maud had seen more of the world. Besides, it would

15

surely please her to know that Emily did not simply want to be a charge on her all her life.

'I thought perhaps I could go out to work. Lots of young women do. I could be a typewriter, or work in a telegraph exchange, or be someone's clerk – '

'Work?' said Aunt Maud horribly.

If Emily had wanted to make an impression, she would have succeeded. Apart from Maudie, who was engaged in spreading melted butter over as much of her surface area as possible, her cousins were staring at her wide-eyed as the novel idea took hold of their imaginations. Aunt Maud was as shocked as if someone had blasphemed. Even Mamzelle had looked up. Her pale, red-rimmed eyes, which always made her look as though she'd been crying, darted flinchingly between Emily and her aunt, waiting for the explosion.

It reminded Emily of a *Punch* cartoon: The Man Who Asked For Mustard With Mutton. She would have giggled if she had not been so much in awe of her aunt's disapproval.

'Girls of your degree do not go out to work,' Aunt Maud said finally.

'But Mama, Mr Cossins has a female clerk,' Tom pointed out with the freedom of the son-and-heir. 'So it must be a respectable thing to be, because he's a Member of Parliament.'

'Only for the Labour Party,' Aunt Maud said quellingly. 'Besides, his clerk is not a lady. Ladies do not take jobs. What can you be thinking about, Emily, to suggest it?'

Emily looked despondent. 'But then what am I to do, ma'am?' She hesitated, unable to express all her doubts about her future position, fearing to sound ungrateful, or as though she were begging.

Maud looked at her consideringly. Emily was not pretty in the way that her cousins were. All the same, with proper care she could be quite striking, with those tawny eyes, and the high cheekbones which gave them a somehow foreign look.

But far more of a disadvantage than her looks was her entire lack of dowry, and her eccentric upbringing. Maud might have done more for Emily – her own niece, after all – but she had held back at least partly out of delicacy, not wishing to hurt Edward's pride or to cause Emily to think less of her father.

Maud had offered The Lodge to begin with as an emergency measure, to get them both away from Paddington, which was damaging Emily's health and the family's reputation. She had assumed

Edward would pull himself together, once a suitable period of mourning had passed, and make a proper home for his daughter. But he seemed to have abdicated from real life, and the more he was helped, the less he would help himself.

Edward's income from his writing had not been enough to provide the elegancies of life – not even new clothes for Emily, far less a governess. Maud did not believe females should be educated, but she believed they ought to have the accomplishments and refinements that would fit them for the drawing-rooms of great houses. Emily's only accomplishment, Maud reflected, was fluent French, which was nowhere near as useful as being able to embroider or play the piano. As for refinements – with Mrs Pennistone her only guide and mentor, poor Emily was in danger of being mistaken for one of the Middle Classes.

Maud sighed at the end of this silent analysis, and Emily knew what that meant. She had been found wanting again, she thought, sighing in her turn. She knew she was a disappointment to her aunt.

'You are a Paget, Emily,' Maud said at last. 'It would reflect on the family in the most disgraceful way if it were supposed we could not provide for our female members without sending them out to work. It would reflect on *me* as your aunt,' she went on, working up a little annoyance, as was her way when faced with unwelcome thoughts. 'You had forgotten that, I suppose?'

'I'm sorry, Aunt,' Emily said.

'Yes, I should think you are sorry! You should try to think more of others, Emily, and less of yourself. I tell you this in your own interest, you know. Nobody likes a selfish person. And sit up straight, child, and try to look more agreeable.'

'Yes, Aunt,' Emily said. The argument, as so often with grown-ups, had soaked away in the sands of general disapproval. She was never left in any doubt about what she might not do; what she might do was another matter.

After tea Maudie was snatched away by the nursery maids to be unbuttered, and the other children went upstairs with Emily to the old night nursery in the west wing, which was their private place when they were at Bratton, their sitting-room and club, the place where grown-ups never came and secrets were exchanged.

'I think your idea's first rate,' Tom said judiciously when they had settled themselves in the deep window-seat with the old sofa pulled

17

up to it. 'I can see how you'd much prefer to earn your own living than stay at home doing nothing. But I can't see Mama allowing it.'

'I can't either. But why does everyone think it's so shocking?' Emily said.

'I shouldn't like to go out to work,' Victoria said. 'Nanny says either Lexy or I will probably marry Prince Edward, and he might not want a wife who'd done anything like that. He'll be King of England one day, and Nanny says you Can't Be Too Careful if you're going to be king.'

'I think I'd like to be an obelisk,' Alexandra said, bouncing on the sofa so that the springs twanged.

'An obelisk?' Tom frowned.

'It's probably the same as a menagerie,' Emily murmured, recovering her spirits a little. She found it impossible to be gloomy for long in the company of her cousins.

'Mamzelle had them in a book she was reading,' Lexy explained. 'They lie on sofas and have rose petals sewn all over them, and an Eastern prince comes and plucks a jewel out of your navel.'

'I bet you don't even know what a navel is,' Tom said with lofty good humour.

'I do!' Victoria broke in. 'They're the same as belly buttons.'

'Shut up, Vick. Don't be vulgar.'

'Well, that's what Nanny calls them. She says that's the mark the stork leaves with its beak when it delivers you.'

'That's not how babies come,' Lexy said scornfully.

'Oh, I suppose you know all about it?' Tom said. He had started at Eton that year, and the first action of the boys who had started the half before him had been to enlighten his ignorance on these vital matters.

'I've seen a hen lay an egg, and I bet it's about the same thing,' Lexy retorted smartly; but then her expression wavered. 'Only – well, think of babies, all arms and legs. Think of *Maudie*,' she added doubtfully. 'I don't really see how . . . '

There was a brief silence as Victoria also failed to see how. Maudie was an extremely square and solid child.

But Tom, the only one of the company who actually *knew* how, had grown impatient of the subject. 'Oh never mind about hens and babies and all that! I want The Story, even if you girls don't.'

'Of course we do,' Lexy said indignantly. 'Tell, please, Em.'

The Story was a tale Emily had been telling the cousins for years, about twins called John and Jessica, who had been orphaned at an

18

unspecified age and had brought themselves up alone, without the aid of adults. They lived in a cave halfway up a mountain with a dog called Bouncer, and indulged in hair-raising adventures that would have caused even Lionheart Lomas to blench. She made it up as she went along, but the cousins consumed every word avidly, and regarded her, on account of this talent, as the source of all wisdom.

'Where did I get up to?' she asked now. It was nearly three months since she had seen her cousins, but no matter how long it was between episodes, they never forgot what hideous peril she had left John and Jessica facing.

'There was a mountain lion that smelled their soup cooking and came down from the forest,' Victoria said promptly. 'It jumped on Bouncer and missed, and Bouncer fell down the cliff, but he got caught on a ledge.'

'Oh yes, I remember,' said Emily. 'Well . . . '

At that word the other three wriggled themselves into more comfortable positions, their round eyes fixed flatteringly on her face, ready to be transported out of this world and into another that she alone could make for them. Emily felt a brief but agreeable sense of power. Everyone wants to be loved, but with an unfatherly father and no mother but Penny, she had to take what she could get, and the adoration of her cousins was a fair substitute.

'Well,' she began, 'poor Bouncer was a stout little dog, and the ledge started to crumble . . . '

Chapter Two

Thomas Tarrant, Marquess of Westinghouse, was a genial, good-tempered man. He was indolent except in the pursuit of pleasure, and had a child's innocent self-centredness which allowed him to know nothing of other people's feelings and concerns. Almost everyone spoke well of him, largely because he was too much of a sybarite to make enemies.

He had inherited his father's title at an early age, and the vast estates came with a staff so well trained that he never had to think about the management of them. His mother had selected Lady Maud Paget as a suitable mate for him, and pointed him at her. Westinghouse, seeing nothing about her to dislike, offered for her within a month of their first meeting.

Maud had had no hesitation in accepting. Since her father's death her mother had spent more and more time with her relations in Russia, taking Maud's younger sister Eugenia with her. This had left Maud in the care and under the control of her brother John, whom she loathed. Westinghouse's offer, besides being one of staggering eligibility, offered her release from this bondage. She actually quite liked Westie, but she would not have refused him even if she had disliked him, or for any reason short of insanity, syphilis, or impotence.

When the wedding was over, the dowager marchioness had welcomed her daughter-in-law to Bratton, and then, with almost indecent haste, had taken her Pekineses, her Swiss maid, her valet and her cook and decamped for the South of France. There she lived in a tiny villa covered in bougainvillaea overlooking the sea, and shrugged off cares and years alike. She had inherited the mouldy Gothic barracks of Bratton from *her* mother-in-law, and had always hated it, while St Auben House in Piccadilly, she said, reminded her of a railway terminus.

Maud had metaphorically rolled up her sleeves, brought in an army of cleaners and painters, revolutionised the plumbing, ordered new mattresses for all the beds, had gas laid on in the kitchens, and enticed the eminent *chef de cuisine* away from one of London's leading hotels. She managed Westie's houses as efficiently as she managed Westie, and he was quite happy to leave all decisions to her, domestic and social.

When she had wanted to install her brother and his daughter in The Lodge, Westie had only been surprised that she'd thought it necessary to ask. He would have been quite willing to do more for Edward if asked – get him a Court position or a staff post somewhere, perhaps – but Maud had seemed to think The Lodge answered the case, so he had nodded, and instantly ceased to think of Edward as a problem.

He was glad, as the years passed, that he hadn't been asked to find Edward a comfortable billet elsewhere. One of the things he enjoyed about being at Bratton was being able to walk down to The Lodge to while away a couple of hours in his company. He also liked Edward's stories and read every one he could get his hands on. He thought him a dashed clever cove, and was not at all troubled by Maud's view that Edward could have been socially presentable if only he wrote proper books, instead of boys' adventures.

A couple of days after their arrival at Bratton, Westie tucked his precious Purdeys under his arms, whistled up a favourite bitch, and arrived at The Lodge while Edward and Emily were still at breakfast. Though mentally indolent, Westie enjoyed physical activities, and was always up early, no matter what time he had sought his bed the night before.

'I've come to chivvy you out of your burrow,' he greeted Edward. 'Take you out and give you a bit of a run.'

'You might have brought the paper with you, if you must appear so early,' Edward said across the eggs and bacon.

'Nothing in it but nonsense and row,' Westie said. 'Never is when the House is in recess.' At other times, two-thirds of *The Times* was taken up with the report and discussion of Parliamentary debates.

'Not *that* paper. I meant the *Housemaid's Joy*. There's a particularly gruesome murder I've been following. Limbs in a steamer trunk, head in a Gladstone bag: I want to know if they've discovered the torso yet.'

'You'll rot your brain reading that stuff. In fact, you read altogether too much. What you need is fresh air,' he added guilefully, looking towards the fragment of bright day visible beyond the narrow window. 'I thought we might go after some pigeons, get into practice for the twelfth, what do you say?'

21

Edward caught Emily looking at him. 'I don't know, Westie. Some of us have to work for a living, you know,' he said.

In fact, things were in desperate case. No work had come in by that morning's post, and he had finished all he had in hand. Nothing now stood between him and his novel. He had been writing it for the last five years and it bored him to death, but since no-one could read or criticise it while it remained on the stocks, he made sure he never finished it. Like HMS *Victory*, its component parts had been renewed so many times there was no splinter remaining of the original structure; but it was hard work. It took him all the writing he could do to stay in the same place.

'I suppose I could take an hour or two off,' he said at last, with deep reluctance. 'It might refresh me.'

'Good man,' Westie said enthusiastically.

'But for heaven's sake sit down and have something while I finish my breakfast. You'll give me indigestion, hovering like that.'

Westie sat obediently, and suddenly remembering his avuncular duty, looked at Emily and nodded by way of greeting. 'Going up to the house at all?'

'Yes, Uncle. I'm going riding with my cousins.'

'Ah! Your aunt would like a word.'

'My aunt?' Emily faltered.

'Drop in and see her, that's a good girl.' He turned away from her with relief: plain girls embarrassed him. 'She's had a letter from your mother,' he said to Edward.

'Oh, really?' Edward said with daunting lack of interest.

'This Russian imperial visit in August – thinks she might come along as well.'

'I didn't think the governments had agreed the date,' Edward said.

'Oh yes – first week in August – Cowes Week. They decided, you see, that it couldn't be London or Windsor, because of the security problems. Guarding a tsar's not like guarding the King and Queen. Besides, London's stuffed to the gills with Bolshevists and exiled revolutionaries.' He made a graceful throwing gesture with one hand. 'Boom! Don't bear thinking about. Assassination is always on the Imperial mind.'

'I should think it would be, when you remember he saw his own grandfather blown up.'

'Well, the idea is to confine the whole show to the Isle of Wight, and more or less seal it off. That way the Tsar and his family

22

can live on their yacht, and the navy can patrol the waters from Spithead.'

'The entire Royal Navy? They should be safe enough, then.'

'Only the Home Fleet,' Westie said seriously.

'I suppose the alternative would be to throw all the Bolshies out of London.'

'Can't do that,' Westie said. 'We have laws in this country. Anyway, how'd we ever identify them? We haven't got a secret police like HIM, damn him.'

'You sound regretful,' Edward remarked, helping himself to more bacon.

'Not at all,' Westie said. 'The best thing with revolutionaries is to leave 'em alone. They soon run out of steam. Make martyrs of 'em, and you've got a Cause on your hands.'

'Didn't the Tsar's assassinated grandfather try leaving them alone? Isn't that how he managed to get himself blown up?'

Westie looked uncomfortable. 'That was unfortunate, I agree. But he was going in the right direction. You can't resist change, you know. It's the tides of history. The way to stay on top is to recognise what's a tide and what's – '

'A backwater?' Edward was tormenting him, as was clear to Emily, if not to the victim.

'Politics is the art of the possible,' she said, and then blushed because she hadn't meant to say it out loud.

Uncle Westie looked at her in astonishment, as he might have done at his pointer if she had said the same thing. 'Art of the . . . Yes, by Jove! Jolly good! Well put indeed.'

'And what is the particular tide that's surging at the moment?' Edward asked.

'The popular vote. Been going on for generations,' Westie said. Coming from a long line of Ministers of the Crown, the constitution was in his blood, and he understood it as instinctively as he understood racehorses or gun dogs. 'Start off with all power vested in the king; but first the lords, then the gentry, then the lower orders, all want their say.' He put a hand up in the air and spiralled it downwards. 'Power slides downwards and spreads out, you see, like – '

'Like a fat woman taking off her corsets,' Edward suggested; then remembering Emily's presence said hastily, 'So how far are you prepared to go? The universal franchise? Give the vote to every man, regardless of his worth?'

Westie looked sorrowful. 'It's bound to happen, I'm afraid. The

23

time is coming when having the vote will be looked upon as a right instead of a privilege. The Labour members are already talking like that, damn them, and one or two Liberals as well – though that's for party reasons, of course, nothing to do with benevolence. But it looks inevitable to me. Tides of history, you see.'

'Sir,' Emily said breathlessly, 'what about women? Will they have the vote as well?'

Westie looked startled for a moment, and then both men laughed. 'Oh no, not women! There one does draw the line!'

'But, please sir, why?' Emily asked, hurt by their laughter.

'There are fundamental reasons why women can never vote,' Edward said. 'Natural reasons no-one can do anything about.'

'What reasons?'

Edward waved a hand at Westie. 'You tell her. You started all this.'

'Oh dear! Well, women are very different from men. They're emotional creatures, swayed by their feelings, bless 'em. They aren't rational, you see; you couldn't have a debate with 'em. Hard enough trying to have a drawing-room conversation, by George! But try to talk politics, and two minutes later they'd be drivelling about hats.'

Edward took up the lead. 'The female mind is completely taken up with trivia, Emily: servants, clothes, babies, who's been seen with whom. Women simply can't concentrate on purely intellectual matters.'

Emily frowned. Wasn't there a paradox here? How could he explain to her the intellectual concept of why a woman couldn't vote, if she had no intellect?

'But surely, Papa,' she began hesitantly, but he didn't wait for her. He had a mischievous look about him, though she didn't know which of them he was teasing.

'Wouldn't you also say that females are refined and delicate creatures, Westie, elevated above the coarseness and brutality of politics?'

'By George yes, of course!' Westie said, brightening at the sight of a bearer with fresh ammunition. 'One wouldn't like to see a lady exposed to the rough and tumble of politics. It wouldn't be at all proper. I'm sure your aunt would say so,' he added to Emily.

Emily had no doubt about that.

'The proof is in the Suffragettes,' Edward said. 'There's nothing at all feminine about them.'

'Oh Lord, don't mention them! Especially not in front of Maud,' Westie said.

'I must say they seem to give poor Asquith the most dreadful time, running him from pillar to post with their chants and placards.'

'God knows what will happen when we get in again, and they turn their attentions on Balfour,' Westie said gloomily. 'He's such a sensitive man.'

'What was that business at the Foreign Office, at the King's birthday reception in June?' Edward asked. 'Didn't one of them manage to get in? I read something in the paper about "a Suffragette disguised as a lady" – a very nice distinction, I thought.'

'Yes, that was quite a scandal. We still don't know how she got hold of the tickets – from some secret sympathiser on the invitation list, I suppose. No-one knew she was there until she suddenly jumped up onto the window-sill at the end of the room and started speechifying about women and votes.'

'How did she get past the detectives on the door?'

'Lord knows. One of them was Inspector Jarvis, the House of Commons detective, and he apparently knew the woman quite well from other disturbances, so I don't know why he didn't spot her. However, she went quietly enough as soon as he came up to fetch her.' Westie grinned suddenly at the memory. 'She walked down the room, bowing to left and right like royalty, and saying to each person, "You will see that we get votes for women, won't you?" I could hardly keep a straight face.'

Edward laughed. 'She sounds as though she had a sense of humour.'

'Oddly enough,' Westie said, 'I felt a sneaking admiration for her; so I slipped downstairs after them to make sure they weren't being too rough with her – you know how the police can be if they feel they've been made fools of. They were just charging her with disturbing the peace as I came up, and she turned to me as bold as brass and said, "But you know there was no disturbance of the peace, and if you insist on making the charge, I shall subpoena Lord Westinghouse." And then she reeled off a list of cabinet ministers who were present, and said she'd call 'em all up as witnesses too. You never saw detectives look so blue!'

'What happened to her, sir?' Emily asked, anxious for this stranger whose passion they took so lightly.

'Nothing. They kept hold of her until the important people had all left, and then let her go,' Westie said.

'The Government should be firmer with the Suffragettes,' Edward said. 'Asquith is a weakling.'

'No, no, they're nothing more than a nuisance,' Westinghouse said. 'It will all peter out in time, once they find something else to think about. I say, Ned, are you ever going to finish breakfast? It'll be noon before we get out after those birds.'

Left alone, Emily pondered on what it was about women that provoked such mirth in men. If it were men doing the same things as the Suffragettes, they would at least have the decency to be frightened of them, or angry with them. And *why* was it so impossible for women to vote? She knew that a great many gentlemen weren't particularly sensible. Why did simply being a man make you worthy to vote, regardless of how ignorant or foolish or even wicked you were?

It struck her, not for the first time, that it was a monstrous unfairness to be born a female. There was so little that you were allowed to do, and if you ever tried to change things the men just laughed at you. They didn't let you do anything, and then said that the fact that you didn't do it proved you couldn't. It was horribly frustrating – and worst of all, from her point of view, was that it seemed the only way she would ever be allowed to leave The Lodge was by marrying, which would probably make things worse. At least she knew Pa, and he didn't really take any interest in what she did. A husband would probably disapprove of all the same things as Aunt Maud, and end up being exactly like a gaoler.

On her arrival at the Big House Emily was met by Corde the butler, who told her that 'my lady wished to speak to her at once in the Peacock Room, miss'.

Corde had always terrified Emily. He was so unnatural, not like a real person at all, but some wonderfully brought-to-life old statue of a Family Retainer. His perfection as a butler was famous. Visitors to Bratton always said, 'Isn't Corde wonderful?' – usually in his hearing, as though he were a faithful old Labrador who wouldn't understand – and Corde would stand there not hearing them say it, being the Perfect Butler right down to his toes and not showing a spark of humanity. Emily sometimes got the feeling that if she walked round the back of him she'd discover that he was quite flat and painted on board.

'Thank you, Corde,' she said bravely. 'I can find my own way, thank you.'

'I will show you up, miss,' Corde said horribly, fixing her with his unwinking gaze. 'Her ladyship would expect it.'

Thus chastened, Emily followed the butler upstairs with her tail between her legs. It was an absurdity, she thought rebelliously, for him to show her to the Peacock Room, when she knew the way as well as he did, and to open the door and announce, 'Miss Emily, my lady,' just as if Aunt Maud might not recognise her.

But Aunt Maud, who was sitting at the writing-desk, turned her head and said, 'Thank you, Corde,' as if there was nothing strange about having her own niece introduced to her. Corde inclined his head a precise number of degrees from the vertical, stepped backwards through the door, and closed it soundlessly. If he had winked at Emily in passing, she would have died for him, but he remained the Wonderful Old Family Fraud to the end.

'Come in, Emily dear,' Aunt Maud said, surprisingly kindly. 'Sit down. I shan't be a moment. I must finish this letter.'

Emily sat on the sofa. The Peacock Room was Aunt Maud's private sitting-room, and Emily always felt it had been misnamed, for it conjured to her visions of blue and green, while this was very much a red room. It was called the Peacock Room because of the mouldings of the ceiling, which depicted peacocks in various poses of strutting and displaying amongst elaborate garlands of roses and vines.

Exquisite work it was, too, she saw that; but of course plaster is white. Everything else was red; crimson velvet curtains and upholstery, gold-flocked red wallpaper, crimson plush chimney cover with a bobble fringe; and the room could hardly fail to be dominated by the splendid red and gold cover of the grand piano, which fell to the ground in generous folds, concealing the instrument completely so that it looked like a Sultan's catafalque.

As her aunt wrote, Emily passed the time by gazing round at the objects which covered every surface in the room. Framed photographs, ornaments, vases, statuettes, dried-flower arrangements, pieces of china and silver crowded onto side-tables, occasional tables, shelves, piano top and chimney-piece; while the looking-glass was stuck all round with dance cards, invitations and programmes. The basic fabric of the room was seen only in glimpses between and around the vast assembly of keepsakes from a full and busy life. It would be impossible to move quickly in this room without damaging something.

Maud never did move quickly. She put down her pen at last, stood up, and came to take the chair facing Emily, surveying her grimly.

'Don't lounge, dear – sit up straight. A lady's back should never touch any part of the chair she's sitting in. And draw your feet back.'

Thus far all was as usual, and didn't seem to require any reply. Emily waited in silence.

Maud looked her over yet again. She was in riding clothes, of course, but then Emily almost always was. The habit itself was of good cloth – it was one of Maud's own, made over by Penny – but growing worn with continuous use, and the jacket was straining at the buttons. This was not, Maud acknowledged with an inner sigh, because Emily was fat, but because, though only fifteen, she was beginning quite definitely to have a figure.

It had been comfortable to think of Emily as a child, and therefore not requiring anything to be done about her just yet, but it was clear that Nature was now going to force the issue. Emily shifted a little in embarrassment under the thoughtful stare, and Maud brought herself to the point.

'I want to talk to you about your future. I had a letter this morning from your grandmother. I don't suppose you remember her, do you?' Maud asked. 'You could only have been four or five when she last saw you.'

'Was she – was she a lady all in black?' Emily asked hesitantly.

Maud nodded. 'Yes, she was in mourning for her brother at the time. Do you remember anything else?'

Emily searched her memory, and shook her head. 'Only that she smelled delicious.'

'Yes, Russians love perfume,' Maud said. 'It is something I remember about her from when I was a child,' she went on unexpectedly. 'She used to come and say goodnight to us children sometimes, dressed for a ball or a dinner. As she leaned over the bed, there would be a faint, lovely smell of flowers about her.'

Emily kept quite still, bemused by the unexpected confidence. Aunt Maud had never spoken of herself to Emily; indeed she hardly ever spoke to her at all, except to instruct or reprove. The sudden intimacy was like a physical warmth, as though the fire had just

28

been lit in a chilly room. A frail tendril of affection, always in Emily searching for something to wind round, reached out tentatively.

'Of course,' Maud frowned, 'she speaks of herself as Russian, and behaves like a Russian, but in fact she has hardly any Russian blood at all. Her mother was English and her father was half English. At any rate, she wants to see you.'

'Is my grandmother coming to England, ma'am?' Emily asked.

'Yes. She is coming in August, when the Tsar and Tsaritsa make their visit.' Aunt Maud tapped her finger briefly on the letter she held. 'She mentions you specifically, Emily, in her letter. She was in Paris earlier this year, and – for reasons we needn't speak of, I'm sure – it made her think of you, and planted a wish in her to see you.'

Emily heard the news with surprise and suspicion. The attention of adults was not something to be sought. It usually resulted in some disagreeable experience or other.

Her aunt seemed a little uneasy. 'Emily, I want to be quite frank with you. I know you're a sensible girl – on the whole – and really much older in some ways than your years. I'm sure I need not remind you of your situation, which, through no fault of your own – well, as I said, I need not remind you of what you already know. The important thing is that your grandmother expresses a strong desire to see you, and I have half a mind – in fact, I feel it my duty – in short, I believe I should make every effort to present you to her in the best possible light.'

Emily was now as bewildered as she was apprehensive. 'I don't think I understand, Aunt.'

'If your grandmother were to take to you,' Maud said briskly, 'she could do a great deal for you. She has a considerable fortune of her own, left to her by her mother, which includes extensive property in London whose value I can't begin to calculate. I believe she owns a large part of Kensington. Or is it Bayswater? At all events, her fortune is hers to leave wherever she wishes, and I see no reason why she shouldn't wish to settle something on you. If she likes you, Emily, and this is the crucial point, it could be something very handsome indeed.'

It was as bad as it could be, Emily thought. To be presented to her grandmother at all would have been an ordeal, but to be placed on approval, with such vast and important opportunities to disappoint, would be a nightmare. Besides, it seemed to her not quite right. To be living at The Lodge at her aunt's expense was one thing;

but to be making up to a complete stranger for the sake of her fortune struck Emily as almost dishonourable. She was sure Lionheart Lomas wouldn't approve.

'But how am I to meet her, ma'am?' she asked doubtfully. 'Is she coming to stay here?'

'No,' said Maud, 'and that is the tiresome part. She is coming only for the yacht-racing, and then intends going on to Marienbad to visit friends. Of course, she may change her mind, but one can't depend on it, which means that if I am to present you to her I must take you with me to Cowes.'

'I am to go to Cowes?' Emily stammered. 'To stay on the *Amoenus*?' Her aunt and uncle's yacht had lately been completely refitted with every possible luxury, and even her cousins had not been on it yet. Moreover, she knew that children were never taken to Cowes: it was purely a grown-ups' occasion.

Maud nodded, evidently not pleased about it. 'I see no help for it. It has its advantages, however: if she were to meet you in company with my children, she'd never notice you at all. And the Tsar and Tsaritsa will be bringing their children with them, so perhaps it won't look as odd as it might otherwise have done.'

Emily looked down. 'I'm afraid I haven't any clothes nice enough for Cowes,' she said. 'I shall let you down.'

Maud seemed irritated. 'You will do nothing of the sort. Of course I shall provide you with a suitable wardrobe. Your appearance I do not despair of, though it will take a little work. But there are many other things, Emily: your comportment, your manners, the way you conduct yourself in company. You have been very little in the world, and your upbringing has certainly been *odd*.'

'But, Aunt – '

'You must not, for instance, speak in that bold way I have heard you use with your father. As a girl not yet out, you must remain silent unless directly addressed. And when you are addressed, you must learn how to reply without offending by the freedom of your opinions.'

'Yes, Aunt. I mean, no, Aunt,' Emily said. 'Oh, but please, mayn't I say that it's much too kind of you – new clothes and – and everything – when you do so much for me already!' There were other considerations which she could not readily express: to be putting Emily above her own children, to be attempting to secure her mother's fortune for Emily rather than, say, Lexy, seemed altruism of no common order. Uncle Westie was extremely rich, but in the stories Emily had read, having one fortune never stopped anyone from wanting another.

'Nonsense!' said Aunt Maud, but she looked uncomfortable. The fact was that she could have done much more for her niece. She could have brought her up with her own children, let her share their governess and their lessons, for instance. Indeed, it had crossed her mind to suggest it some years ago, but there was always the problem that Emily was so much older than her girls, along with which went the irrational suspicion that Emily might influence them in some way – pollute them, perhaps.

Whenever she looked at Emily, she was reminded of the whole sordid and disgraceful business of Edward's marriage, and that made her dislike Emily. The fact that this was irrational and unjust, that Emily was a perfectly nice girl and deserving of a better fortune, only increased her irritation towards her hapless niece. I dislike you, she might have said, because it annoys me to feel guilty about disliking you.

'I am doing no more than my duty,' she said briskly. 'And, mark you, Emily, I promise nothing. I shall bring you to your grandmother's attention, that's all. The rest will be up to you.'

'Yes, ma'am,' said Emily.

It's just like a fairy story, she thought. The Transformation Scene, from rags to spangles, Cinderella goes to the ball after all – except that Cinderella hadn't seemed to have any doubt that she would be able to handle the protocol of a full-dress Court function.

The old earl, Emily's grandfather, John Paget, 3rd Earl of Oxhey, had been a man of upright character, whose formal, courtly manners concealed a deeply shy and reserved nature. He had spent a lifetime in the diplomatic service without his name ever having been linked with that of any woman. Then, in the autumn of his years, he astonished the world by marrying a beautiful seventeen-year-old Russan countess.

It was 1872, in Paris – a Paris just recovering from the shocking siege and the humiliating Treaty of Frankfurt which had ended the Franco-Prussian War. King William of Prussia had been crowned Emperor of Germany at Versailles in the Hall of Mirrors itself, and the wily Bismarck was busy reshaping Europe and politics in his own iron image. It was a tense time, the members of the diplomatic corps feeling their way delicately towards a new balance of power, and trying to avoid stepping on bruised toes.

Amongst the Russian Ambassador's suite was a Count Peter Kirov, accompanied by his wife and children. Countess Kirova had been a Miss Fleur Hamilton, an Englishwoman by birth, so it was natural for the Kirovs to seek the company of the British diplomatic group. Lord Oxhey became a particular friend, and was soon understood by everyone at the Palais to be desperately in love with the Kirovs' eldest daughter, Natasha.

Her loveliness, her charm, her high spirits dazzled him from their first meeting at the Opera. What was less to be expected was that she found herself strongly attracted to this grave, quiet, older man. It must have been because he was so different from anyone she had ever met before – which was not to say he was unlovable. His vulnerability touched her deeply, while his intelligence demanded her respect.

Oxhey, tongue-tied in his own language, could be fluent, witty and charming in several others, and Natasha was happy to be made love to in any or all of them. Oxhey had never before had the desire or the confidence to court a woman, but now he found both in such measure that within four months he had married his Natasha and carried her triumphantly back to England.

The marriage was successful, and produced five children in five years: John, Edward, Maud, Albert and Eugenia. The couple had nineteen happy years together before Oxhey went reluctantly to join his ancestors at the age of sixty-five.

While Natasha was still in deep mourning for the man who had been husband, lover and companion, an accident on the hunting-field robbed her of her third son, Albert, who was just sixteen. Rightly or wrongly, parents have favourites amongst their children, and this sensitive, thoughtful, handsome boy had been hers. He left behind him an emptiness the others could not fill.

Her second son, Edward, was quite different in character. Though good-looking and charming, he was careless and wild to a fault, always getting into trouble, and after his father's death he seemed to grow even more unrestrained. His father had been the only person who could tame Edward, and he had done so, miraculously, with nothing more than a quiet, steady look or a small shake of the head. His eldest brother, John, the new earl and head of the family, could only bully and bluster, which drove Edward to worse defiance.

In 1893, a year after his father's death, Edward was in his first year at Oxford, drinking, gambling, running up debts and threatening to be sent down for any combination of undergraduate sins. When during the summer recess he was invited to travel with a friend and his family to Paris, Edward's own family was only too glad to have him out of the way and in someone else's charge for a while. They looked forward to a summer of relative peace for a change; but in Paris, like his father before him, Edward fell in love.

For him, however, it was not the daughter of a Russian count, dowered, titled and wholly eligible to be fallen in love with, but a half-French, half-Hungarian ballet girl with no family or money at all. Ballet was not much regarded in Paris at that time – the rage was all for opera – and Isabelle was not even one of the great prima ballerinas of international fame. She was an ordinary, workaday *corps de ballet* girl, who was appearing in a balletic interlude inserted by force into *La Belle Hélène* to appease the gentlemen patrons who liked legs with their entertainment, and she had nothing to recommend her but her youth and blonde hair.

None of that mattered to Edward. He was young, inexperienced, reckless, hot-blooded, and had recently lost not only the father he respected, but a dearly loved younger brother as well. It would only have been surprising if he had *not* fallen in love with somebody unsuitable that summer. He telegraphed home ecstatically to say he had met the One and Only woman, and wished to marry her, and followed it with a letter describing her minutely over four pages of semi-coherent joy.

This was not well received by brother John. John was dull, painstaking, humourless, pompous and self-important – the very last person to sympathise with unregulated passion. He wrote back sternly forbidding Edward to marry a female who was obviously little more than a prostitute, and demanded his instant return home.

What could a young man of spirit do? Edward married Isabelle in Paris by special licence, and brought her home to a family row of epic proportions. John raged and lectured, accusing Edward of bringing disgrace on the family and – a barb that went home – of betraying his father's memory. Edward's duty was to have married a person of breeding and fortune who would enhance their standing in the world – like John himself, who had just become betrothed in grand style to the Lady Louisa Duckworth. Instead he had brought home a nameless, penniless trollop from the gutters of Paris, who – to judge from the seething interest she aroused in John's loins – was plainly no better than she should be.

33

John didn't mention this last, but, magnanimity itself, offered for the sake of the family name to try to untangle the mess Edward had made. He would arrange a divorce. Edward must return to Oxford alone, concentrate on his studies, and by exemplary behaviour try to live down this scandalous episode. The girl would be paid off and sent back to Paris. When Edward refused to be helped, John had no choice but to wash his hands of him, cut off his allowance, and let him sink into the gutter where he had proved he belonged.

The marriage was as short-lived as unfortunate. Less than a year later, in 1894, Emily was born, and Belle died of puerperal fever. John, in an access of generosity, offered to let bygones be bygones and receive Edward back into the family. Isabelle's death was a stroke of luck, he said. It was a pity about the child of course, otherwise the whole marriage episode might have been buried with her; but a widower, particularly a young one, attracted so much goodwill that the nature of the dead wife might be forgotten. With care and good dinners, John said, Edward's peccadillo might be erased from public memory.

John was deeply offended when Edward refused the olive branch. There was nothing for it, therefore, but to make sure Edward was cut out of the succession, and in pursuit of this end John fathered three sons on Lady Louisa in such a short space of time that she died shortly afterwards of surprise and exhaustion.

Left with her vast fortune and three heirs, a lesser man would have thought his purpose fulfilled. But John was not one to take unnecessary risks. In 1900 he married the Lady Mary Parker. She let him down badly with a female child in the year following their union, but made up for it in the following four years by producing three healthy male babies. By 1905, with six sons to follow him, John felt that, barring accidents, the title was safe from contamination by Edward, and he ceased to pad nightly along the corridor to Lady Mary's room. Whether she was glad or sorry about that does not come into this story.

Edward's impetuous marriage had many consequences, most of them unfortunate. The one lucky result, in Maud's view, was that when she answered Penny's plaintive appeal and brought Edward and his brat to live at Bratton, it so provoked John that he wrote her an eight-page letter of protest. He described all the evils that must result from such an act of misplaced forgiveness, and warned her that if she did not reverse her decision immediately, he would

regard her as contaminated by Edward's presence, and refuse thence-
forth ever to visit or receive her again.

The joy Maud felt while replying to that letter was probably the
only pleasure Edward brought anyone in his life, except through the
medium of his pen.

Chapter Three

Monday, August the 2nd, 1909, was a fine, warm day. There was a lot of hazy cloud, but high up, so that although there was little sunshine, the air remained very clear. It was clear enough for Emily, from the deck of the *Amoenus*, to see right across the Spithead strait to Southsea beach, where thousands of holidaymakers had gathered to watch for the arrival of the Russian flotilla. From this distance, their massed pink faces and the darker streak of their clothes looked like some kind of strange growth along the strand – the desert in bloom.

The Home Fleet was at anchor at Spithead, a magnificent sight, moored in three orderly lines, and each ship dressed overall, the gaily coloured pennants fluttering bravely in the stiffish breeze from the west. The bright water in between the great warships was crowded with vessels of all kinds, from private yachts like *Amoenus* to the little white pleasure-steamers which had brought sightseers from Cowes and Southsea for a Trip Round the Fleet at a shilling a head.

Away to Emily's left was the royal yacht *Victoria and Albert*. The pleasure-steamers made a respectful circuit of her, in the hope of providing the paying customers with a glimpse of the King and Queen. Sometimes they circled *Amoenus* too – so smart with her new paint and gleaming brass – and Emily found herself being stared at by sightseers wondering if she were someone important. Everyone seemed happy and good-natured, dressed in their holiday clothes, eating pies and drinking ale, and many of the boats had music playing, too. Once a woman lifted up her baby and made it wave its fat fist at her. Emily waved back, laughing. Like the famous Doge, she found the wonder of the sights and sounds and smells around her second only to the wonder of finding herself there.

Every moment of the trip so far had been sheer delight. To begin with, they had travelled by train to Weymouth, and she had never been on a train before – not to remember it. As she gazed out of the window at the countryside reeling past in its dark-green August splendour, she had a sense of confinement ending, as though she were an ex-caterpillar just emerging from the chrysalis. With every mile and every minute, she felt her damp, crumpled wings unfurling.

The *Amoenus* was waiting for them in the little cobblestoned harbour at Weymouth. Emily thought she must be the loveliest yacht in the world, with her graceful hull painted dark blue, and her superstructure of varnished wood shining like clear honey. Inside everything smelled deliciously of newness. Aunt Maud – who was not one of nature's sailors – might complain about cramped quarters, but no-one who had lived all their life at The Lodge could find *Amoenus* anything but luxurious. Emily especially loved her own little cabin, with its mahogany panelling, silver fitments and dark-blue carpet. The bathroom – which was all her own, not shared with anyone – she thought a tiny miracle of plumbing.

There followed a pleasant short trip up the coast to the Isle of Wight. Emily had never been on the sea before, and found it hard to take in so much beauty: the particular quality of the light filling the air and flashing on the water, the dazzle of white foam under the hull, the wonderful smell of salt on the wind. She loved the chuckling noise the waves made, and the sweet, harmonious movement of the yacht, as though sea and vessel enjoyed each other, and were not in conflict, as land traffic always was with the earth.

If they had turned back then and gone straight home, she would not have felt cheated, for in contrast with the rest of her life so far, they had been two days crammed with vivid new experiences. But of course it was only the beginning. They reached Cowes Roads, already stiff with the pleasure-boats of the wealthy, and found their moorings – elegantly close to the royal yacht's, for Uncle Westie was a lifelong friend of the King, and they had been meeting at Cowes every August for twenty years.

The first action of Aunt Maud on tying up was to go gratefully ashore. She took Emily for tea in the Royal Yacht Squadron gardens, which, Emily discovered, was where the *beau monde* gathered during race week. To the music of the Blue Hungarian Band, Emily sipped tea and ate shortcake and tried not to stare too obviously at the superbly dressed crowds strolling by. At this time of day they were mostly females, and since the favoured colours of the season were pale pinks, mauves, blues and creams, the effect, she decided, was rather like being dazzled to death by sweet peas.

Aunt Maud seemed to have a huge acquaintance: almost everyone nodded, smiled, greeted her with varying degrees of affection or insincerity. There were so many glittering names that Emily found each new one driving its predecessor out of her memory, though she realised despairingly that it was part of her education to recognise these people and that she was already letting Aunt Maud down. Her head began to reel, and she wondered if it were possible to get drunk on tea.

The one name which did stay with her was that of Countess Benckendorff, partly because she already knew the name of Benckendorff, the Russian Ambassador, and partly because the Countess stopped to talk to them with such genuine friendliness.

'Maud! How lovely to see you!' she said, as if it was, in fact, lovely. 'I hear that your mother is coming tomorrow on the *Polar Star*? I quite long to see her, but I suppose there will be official engagements every minute of this week, and I shan't have a moment's real conversation with her.'

'It will not be Mama's fault if you don't,' Aunt Maud said drily. 'Natalie, my dear, may I present my niece, Emily Paget?'

'But of course,' said the Countess, smiling and holding out her hand. She surveyed Emily's face. 'Yes, I can see you have Russian blood, Miss Paget! You have very much the look of the Kirovs about you! I know your grandmother very well, my dear. She and I are old friends. I hope we shall meet again.'

Emily could think of nothing to say to such kindness, but her shyness did her no disservice with her aunt. 'You did quite right,' Maud said afterwards when they were alone again. 'To have spoken would have been to put yourself forward unnecessarily. It was kind of Natalie to notice you,' she added musingly, as though it rather surprised her. 'A nod would have been enough.'

The next morning Emily was at breakfast on the afterdeck alone with her uncle: Maud slept badly on boats and was rarely seen before eleven. Westie, reading *The Times*, suddenly chuckled and passed the paper to Emily, folded open to the Cowes Week report.

'Results already. This'll please your aunt! What does it feel like to be famous, Emily?'

It was a report of the teatime crowds in the Royal Yacht Squadron gardens.

Among the many present were . . . she read, and then, at last, halfway down the column *. . . the Countess Benckendorff in a blue serge coat and skirt and a hat in a darker shade trimmed with white roses, and the Marchioness of Westinghouse in a costume of brown and white striped zephyr and a white straw hat, accompanied by her niece, Miss Emily Paget.*

Emily stared at it for a long time, entranced. Her first, and probably her last, brush with fame, for it was highly unlikely she would ever do anything else noteworthy in her life. But there she was in *The Times*, and she took up as much space in the column as the Russian Ambassador's wife's hat! What would they think about that when they read it at home? she wondered.

At noon the signal was given from the *Dreadnought* for the ships of the Fleet to change the British ensign at their mastheads for the Russian, and soon afterwards the approaching flotilla came into sight: three British battle-cruisers escorting the two imperial yachts, *Standart* and *Polar Star*, followed by two Russian cruisers and two destroyers.

The *Standart* came up alongside the *Victoria and Albert*, and her anchor-chain rattled out through the hawse-hole. A knot of smoke appeared suddenly above her, and immediately afterwards the bright air was shaken with the crash of guns as the first of the formal salutes was fired. The ceremonials were all very splendid, with the King and the Tsar inspecting the fleet together, passing through the lines in the royal yacht while the warships' crews manned the sides and cheered lustily.

The whole flotilla then steamed to Cowes Roads, and reached their moorings at about four o'clock. The *Victoria and Albert* and the *Standart* came up comfortably side by side for easy intercourse, with the other Russian ships nearby, and, dropping their anchors, made themselves bright with bunting.

The *Amoenus* got up to her moorings soon afterwards. Aunt Maud, with evident relief, ordered tea and then went below. Emily, almost bemused by all the excitement, stayed on the forward deck watching the comings and goings around the royal yacht, storing up every 'sighting' to tell Penny and the children when she got home – though home seemed an impossibly distant dream just then.

'I saw the King, Penny,' she heard herself saying, watching the tall, stout, jolly-looking man with the white beard who moved about the boat so nimbly, despite his age and size. 'And the Tsar – everyone said he was the image of the Prince of Wales, and they did look alike from a distance – but the Tsaritsa didn't come on deck. They say she walks with a stick, so perhaps it's difficult for her.'

Westie, staying on deck to smoke a cigar, obligingly named other visitors going up the side of the *Victoria and Albert* for her. It sounded like a recital of the *Almanach de Gotha*.

'That's the Crown Prince of Sweden in the white uniform . . .

There's Princess Beatrice and Princess Helena – what? Oh, they're the King's sisters, I thought you knew that . . . The Duchess of Argyll, another sister, of course . . . Oh, there's the Princess of Wales at last! You recognise her from her pictures, don't you? Pretty little thing, though your aunt don't admire her, says she's snub-nosed. She's been staying at Barton Cottage. Another one like your aunt, hates the sea . . . '

Later, the politicians arrived to pay their respects.

'All the handshakers going aboard now – pity the poor King! There's Mr Asquith, d'you see, Em? It's not fashionable to say so, but I have a lot of time for him – clever cove, y'know. And there's Sir Edward Grey, the Foreign Secretary. They'll want to talk about the Alliance, and good luck to 'em; I hear HIM is as stubborn as a donkey. That's Reggie McKenna, now. I wonder what the Tsar will make of him? He'll think we have some rum chaps in our Cabinet . . . '

Half an hour later, Maud came out on deck again.

'When are we going to meet your mother, my dear?' Westie asked her, throwing his cigar over the side in obedience to her glance. 'Has anything been arranged?'

'Not yet. But we're joining the King and Queen after dinner tonight on the royal yacht, so we're sure to see Mama there. We can make arrangements then.' She looked at Emily. 'I imagine she will want me to present you to her tomorrow morning.'

Maud and Westie walked away together, to take a stroll round the deck before tea. Not until tomorrow then, the ordeal, Emily thought. She wished it could have been sooner – not that she was so very anxious to meet her grandmother, but it was like having an appointment for the dentist hanging over you.

She had been idly watching a boat put off from the *Polar Star*, and listening to the sounds of preparation for tea on the afterdeck, when she suddenly realised that the boat, oared by six Russian sailors in their jolly blue and white uniforms, was heading straight for the *Amoenus*. A lone female figure was sitting in the stern sheets. Emily went cold as she understood the implication. The dreaded interview was not to be tomorrow after all: the mountain had decided to come to Mahomet.

The word 'grandmother' had irresistible echoes in Emily's mind. She had been expecting all along a Queen Victoria figure: a little, broad old person in bunchy black skirts, with a lace cap, a hatchet face, and stern, compelling eyes. But the figure which came up nimbly through the entry port was a revelation: neat and slender, quick-moving, jauntily dressed – surely too young to be anyone's grandmother?

But there was no doubt about it. Aunt Maud was calling her 'Mama', and Uncle Westie 'Natasha Petrovna', which Emily guessed was the correct Russian style: there was nothing Uncle Westie didn't know about protocol. There seemed to be a lot of kissing going on, and then they were coming along the deck towards her, with her grandmother talking rapidly all the while.

'You've had *Amoenus* painted. Much better! I like this blue. Yes, a delightful voyage, thank you – the sea was as calm as milk, and I have my old cabin on the *Polar Star*, so I am content. So here we are at Cowes – and have you noticed, there are no police? Dear England! Not a patrol boat in sight, no detectives, no secret service – just one large, fatherly policeman in uniform on the jetty! It couldn't happen in Petersburg. But my dear Maud – oh, that dreadful name of yours! How I wish I had overruled Vanya when he wanted to call you after his mother! I wanted to call you Elisavetta, much prettier, don't you think? And somehow "Maud" makes you seem older than your age. You are quite matronly already, and when I think of myself . . . ! Well, it is not your fault, my poor Mala – and I don't know how it is, but every year you gain you seem to take from me. In a year or two I shall be as light as a child, thanks to you!'

'Mama,' Aunt Maud interrupted with a hint of desperation, 'may I present to you your granddaughter Emily?'

A faint, beautiful fragrance, like the smell of lilacs, made Emily's nostrils twitch. Standing close to her, Emily could see that her grandmother was not young, but she stood and moved like a dancer, erect and graceful. All the impressions of elegance and beauty made Emily feel hopelessly plain and clumsy. She curtseyed, wishing there was anything she could do to please this lovely person.

She rose to the vertical again to find a bright gaze examining her face. Then Natasha's mouth trembled, and her hand came up to touch first her lips and then her throat in a disturbed, fluttering gesture.

'*Borzhe moi*, you have such a look of my father about you, it almost frightens me! Yes, you have your looks from my side; there is nothing of your mother in you. You are a Russian, little soul! Don't you feel it, Emilia? Don't you feel you have always been out of your place?'

There can be few girls who at some point in their childhood –
usually after a disagreement with Authority – have not felt that they
must have been a royal baby swapped in the cradle by gypsies. Emily
had read all the stories and made up a good few of her own, and
at fifteen ought to have been immune to that particular form of
romance; but all the same, she blushed now not with embarrassment
but with pleasure, and felt a rush of gratitude and affection towards
her grandmother.

She managed no more than a dumb nod of the head, but Natasha
seemed to understand.

'Yes, you have much to tell me,' she pronounced. 'Well, we shall
have long talks, my little Russian, and you shall tell me all your
secrets. But now,' she said gaily, turning from Emily, 'now I must
have tea, Mala, *tea*, even if it is an English pot. Don't tell me there
is not tea somewhere, at half-past four on an English yacht in Cowes
Week!'

Soon they were sitting under the awning on the afterdeck, little
wicker chairs grouped about a round table, a starched white cloth
and a steward placing the silver teapot in front of Aunt Maud.

Natasha continued to talk. Emily loved her voice: it was light and
pleasant, with a liquid, wren-like quality imparted by the Russian
'l's and the trilling 'r's. She spoke English with a slight and indefinable accent, but it was the emphasis she gave her words that made
her speech sound foreign. After the cool, level English voices she
had known all her life, Emily felt as though everything her grandmother said was underlined and dotted with exclamation marks.

'Only the English know how to serve afternoon tea properly,' she
pronounced now, looking with appreciation at the laden table. There
were fresh scones, shiny-topped and steaming in their napkin, and
muffins in a chafing-dish (kept warm with hot water – spiritlamps
were considered dangerous on deck), lemon cake, gingerbread, and
shortbread too.

'When one is invited to tea with the Empress . . . !' She lifted her
hands in horror. 'Every day it is the same: hot bread and butter,
and very dull biscuits which they *call* English. Can you imagine? I
asked her once why she did not order something different, and she
said, "Tea is always the same at Tsarskoye Selo. It doesn't matter
what you send for, when it arrives it will be hot bread and butter
and English biscuits." '

'Have a scone, Mama,' Maud said.

'Thank you. But is it not a disgrace to be dictated to by one's servants? I taught my children to command in their own house, did I not, Mala? You must always be firm with servants or they will take advantage.'

Maud smiled faintly. 'As I remember, Mama, the servants used to argue dreadfully with you.'

'Argued, perhaps,' Natasha replied unabashed, 'but they would not have dreamed of disobeying. Ah, but there is something depressingly middle-class about the Empress, I have often noticed it.'

'I can't think why,' Westie said, buttering a scone. 'She was Queen Victoria's favourite grandchild. I used to see her quite often around Windsor – pretty little thing, I thought, but rather shy. The old Queen wanted her to marry Prince Eddy back in 'eighty-nine, so she must have thought she was all right, because if Eddy had lived he'd have been Prince of Wales now.'

'I can't help it,' Natasha said, 'she is still a commonplace young woman.' Her eyes grew wide. 'Do you know how she has decorated the private quarters at Tsarskoye Selo? *Chintz!* English chintz, and furniture from Maples. *Quelle horreur!*'

Emily was so interested in all this that she had spoken before she could stop herself. 'I read somewhere that York Cottage, where the Prince and Princess of Wales live, is furnished from Maples too.'

Aunt Maud raised her eyebrows and gave her a frigid look, but Natasha nodded as though it were the most natural thing in the world for a fifteen-year-old girl to join in the conversation of her elders.

'I have read it too,' she said, with an emphatic nod. 'Ah, but what more need you say of an heir to the throne of England who chooses to live in a cottage *exactly* like a bank clerk's villa in Purley?'

'Natasha Petrovna, I don't believe you can possibly know what a bank clerk's villa looks like,' Westie interrupted, laughing. 'And when were you ever in the suburbs?'

'One passes them on the train,' Natasha said firmly. 'And besides, one of my English cousins, I'm sorry to say, lives in such a villa – of all places, in *Ealing*!'

'Give us this day our daily bread,' Westie murmured, 'but deliver us from Ealing!'

'One cannot entirely be blamed for one's relations, whom one does not at all choose,' Natasha said reasonably. 'But what kind of king will this Prince of Wales make, with his simple life and modest tastes? *Pah!* I tell you the age of great kings is over!'

'What about your Tsar Nicholas?'

Natasha looked at him a little suspiciously. 'Do you really want to know about him? He is kind, pleasant and simple, a loving husband, and a devoted father. He likes to take walks, and to read aloud to his wife in the evenings while she sews. He means well – and what can anyone say more damning than that?'

'But in government a man may be different from the way he is in private, with his family,' Westie suggested.

Natasha snorted at the idea. 'Does King Edward conduct his private life like a grocer? He is the last of the great kings! At all times he comports himself *en grand seigneur* – like the old Tsar, Alexander. But for the next generation we shall have grocers, and grocers' wives, and *chintz*. Well,' she gave a superb shrug, 'if the people rise up and slay them, it will be entirely their own fault. One may forgive wickedness, but *never* bad taste.'

'Do you dine with the imperial party tonight, Mama?' Maud asked.

'Unfortunately, yes. I know just what it will be like – the food will be cold, and the conversation tedious.'

'Conversation is always tiresome at a royal table,' Maud said. 'The old Queen was so particular it was impossible to say three words without offending her; and Queen Alexandra is as deaf as an adder and tries to hide it, so one ends up having two entirely different conversations at the same time. Quite exhausting!'

'It is the same in Russia,' Natasha nodded. 'The Empress is so cold and reserved she will say nothing but "Yes" and "No" at public functions, which makes them such a burden! It is one's duty to converse pleasantly at dinner, no matter what one's private feelings. Remember that, Emilia, when you come to attend great functions,' she added, startling Emily – who had not expected to be addressed directly – so much that she choked on a piece of shortbread and bit her tongue.

'Yes, ma'am,' she mumbled awkwardly, trying not to spray crumbs.

'I will say of the Tsar that he understands that much,' Natasha said, kindly removing her gaze from her discomfited granddaughter. 'He is always agreeable in public, and finds something to say to everyone.' She shook her head sadly. 'He is a very *nice* man, but the road to ruin was built by nice men with good intentions. Our troubles in Russia are not over. I have fears, Tomaso, I must tell you.'

'There are troubles everywhere,' Westie said gravely, and the tone of his voice caught Emily's attention. She looked at him quickly, and felt a cold breath of apprehension, like a shadow passing over the sun. 'Everything's changing so fast: ideas, traditions, loyalties.' He frowned in thought. 'Look back fifty years, and England's hardly different from today. But I have a feeling if we could look forward fifty years, we wouldn't recognise the world.'

Natasha spoke lightly into the small silence that followed. 'Well I shall not be here in fifty years, so I can say *après moi le déluge* with a light heart. And now', she drew up the little watch that hung from a fine gold chain at her waist, 'I must go back to the *Polar Star*, because the State dinner tonight will be very grand, and it will take me a long time to prepare for it. *Voyons, il faut être sérieux* about everything one does, even about dressing!'

Emily thought herself forgotten in the flurry of departure, but as Natasha Petrovna reached the entry port, she turned and smiled at her.

'I shall come and call on you tomorrow, and we shall have a long talk together, Emilia. I wish to get to know you, my little Russian!'

On Tuesday the sky was a perfect, cloudless arc, its colour reflected in the deep sparkling blue of the sea. A light, steady breeze kept the air fresh and made the bright sunshine pleasant, and Emily sat alone on the afterdeck, watching the myriad comings and goings amongst the yachts at their moorings, and feeling at peace with the world.

Her aunt and uncle had gone on board the *Victoria and Albert* last night to join the royal party and be presented to the Tsar and Tsaritsa, and evidently it had been quite a jolly gathering, because it had not been until the early hours of the morning that Emily had heard the boat bringing them back. After such a late night, her aunt would probably not emerge from her cabin much before noon. Her uncle had breakfasted in his own cabin and gone straight off to the Royal Yacht Squadron clubhouse to watch the race for the King's Cup in the company of various old friends such as Lord Ormonde, Lord Redesdale, and the Duke of Leeds.

She became aware that a boat was approaching from the *Polar Star*, and, squinting her eyes against the dazzle of the water, she saw that there was a female figure in the stern sheets. Her grandmother was an impressively early riser, she thought, and a mixture of pleasure and fear made her heart beat faster. She was looking forward to the 'long talk', which promised to be more interesting than anything else that had ever happened to her; but she did not wish to disappoint or to make a fool of herself, both of which seemed all too likely.

'Good mor-r-rning, Emilia!' came the trilling greeting as the boat hooked on to *Amoenus*'s chains. Natasha was up on deck in a moment, and Emily was engulfed in a faint but delicious cloud of bluebells as a cheerful embrace was bestowed on her. Russians did seem to kiss an awful lot, Emily thought with approval.

'We are going on shore for a walk, *mylenkaya*, because it is always easier to talk if one is moving. Run now and put on your hat and gloves, while I write a note to explain how I have taken you away.'

In a short time Emily found herself sitting beside her grandmother in the boat, while the Russian sailors pulled strongly towards the public jetty. She felt very shy and awkward. The idea that her grandmother had particularly wanted to see her, added to the responsibility of her aunt's wishes for her, her own reluctance to be a beggar, and the unnaturalness of being singled out for attention, made a burden as big as a boulder on her spirits. Her tongue felt leaden, her hands and feet felt huge. She was sure her face was scarlet, and had a morbid and unshakeable conviction that she was somehow a little grubby.

She heard her grandmother draw breath, and waited for the inquisition to begin – the stream of horribly penetrating questions that would expose her inadequacy and leave her with nothing to cover her shame.

But what Natasha said was, 'How pretty your hair is! It is the same colour as my father's, and the very same exactly as your uncle Albert's, who died before you were born. You have very much the look of him, you know. How old are you? Fifteen? Yes, he was just about that age when he died. I will tell you about him one day. Mothers are not supposed to have favourites, and I have wondered sometimes whether he was taken from me as a punishment, because I loved him best of all my children.'

'What did he die of?' Emily found courage to ask.

'He died of high spirits,' Natasha said promptly. 'And perhaps it is as well, for there are some people one could never bear to see grow old. Albert was like that – a golden youth. My brother Konstantin was another, though he was forty when he died fighting horse thieves in the Caucasus, but he was always a young man when he was on horseback. They both loved horses. You too? Yes, you are like my Albert. I see him looking from your eyes. Perhaps his

46

soul came back to earth in you, what do you think? Do you believe in reincarnation? I find it a most comforting idea.'

'I think you were in mourning for your brother the last time I saw you,' Emily said. 'I remember you were all in black.'

'Do you remember that? I am astonished! You were so very young then, four or five only. Jacob brought you up to the door on your pony, when I was visiting at Bratton Park. Dear old Jacob, he brooded over you like a cat with one kitten!'

'Did he?' Emily was intrigued. 'I never knew that.'

'He so much wanted to bring you to my attention, he did everything short of throwing you under my carriage wheels! But I have never been much interested in small children. It is a fault in me, I know, but they are too much like little animals; one cannot talk to them. There, now I have exposed myself, and you will despise me!'

Emily spoke, like a fool, before she could stop herself: 'Oh no, never!'

Natasha laughed. 'You *are* Bertie come back to me. He would have said just the same thing. God must have realised He made a mistake.'

Emily didn't remember afterwards where they walked, only that, with such skill the process seemed painless, her grandmother elicited the whole story of her life from her. She would not have thought there could be so very much to tell, but Natasha seemed to find the smallest detail interesting. Best of all, Emily sensed no disapproval or disappointment: her grandmother listened as avidly and uncritically as the cousins to another episode of The Story.

'There is a little of your father in you,' Natasha said at one point. 'You are a born storyteller. But of course he gets that from his Russian blood. You smile, little one? What are you thinking?'

'Only that you seem to think everything good comes from being Russian,' Emily said boldly.

Natasha smiled. 'It does! Everyone would be Russian, if they could.'

'Aunt Maud says you have more English blood than Russian.'

'The English are very like the Russians. It is the next best thing to be.'

'I'm only a little bit of either. My mother was half French and half Hungarian, so I'm an awful mongrel.'

Natasha looked at her sharply. 'It is the quality that counts, not the quantity, Emilusha. Tell me – '

She broke off, staring down the slope of East Cowes High Street towards a knot of people who seemed to be gathered outside a jeweller's shop.

'What is it, ma'am?' Emily asked, not seeing anything of particular interest in the crowd.

Natasha seized Emily's hand and started forward with rapid steps. 'Come, we must go to the rescue. What can have possessed them to allow them to walk alone in that way? There is no knowing what may happen!'

She seemed really agitated. Emily hurried along beside her, and said again, anxiously, 'What is it? Is something wrong?'

'I hope not. It is two of the Tsar's daughters – the elder two, Olga and Tatiana.'

Now Emily could see the two young girls, neatly dressed in grey costumes and white hats, their fair hair falling in long ringlets behind. The crowd, she could also see, was perfectly good-natured, and the pushing and shoving nothing but eagerness to get a better view. But then Emily remembered – as presumably her grandmother did – that tsars and their families had all too often in the past been a target for assassins.

Quite how Natasha did it, Emily could not tell, but the crowd seemed to part before them like butter under a hot knife. As they reached the beleaguered Grand Duchesses, the elder one, Olga, turned to Natasha with an expression of relief and entreaty.

'Oh, Natasha Petrovna, I'm glad you've come,' she said in French. 'We seem to have attracted a crowd, and I don't quite know what to do.'

Natasha took the situation in hand. Seeing the Chief Constable of the island and his deputy at a little distance, struggling to get through the crowds, she called out, 'You are too far off to be of any help there, Captain Connor. Come and hold the door. I will take their highnesses into the shop while you clear a space.'

She smiled round at the members of the public nearest her and said, 'Do have the goodness to stand back a little, good people! Princesses need to breathe, just as you do yourselves!'

Then, in French, 'Into the shop with you, Olga Nikolayevna – you too, Tatya. Emilia, go in, but remain near the door. I shall follow in a moment.'

Inside the shop, the proprietor and his assistant, thrilled by the

48

invasion, came forward with smiles of welcome, bowing themselves double. The two Grand Duchesses, despite their ruffling experiences, received them in a friendly and unassuming manner.

'What a lovely shop you have. May we look, please, at the brooches?' Olga said in perfect English.

'Certainly, your highness. Oh, most certainly, most certainly,' the proprietor cooed, backing towards the display counter and smiling so broadly his face seemed in danger of falling in half.

'I should like to look at some cigarette cases also, if you please,' said Tatiana, and let loose another flurry of acquiescence.

Understanding her grandmother's wishes, Emily stood just inside the doorway, so that anyone trying to enter the shop would have actually to shove her out of the way to pass, which she felt sure no English person would be rude enough to do. Behind her in the street the two policemen succeeded in clearing a space around the door, and the Grand Duchesses' attendants, who had got separated from them in the crush, were able to break through into it.

The crowd was growing all the time, but for the moment there seemed no likelihood that they would actually storm the shop. Emily could hear from the tone of the composite murmur that no-one meant any harm. Indeed, it seemed that at least half of them had no idea who the celebrities were who had gone to ground in the jeweller's shop. Some people even thought it was the Tsar and the Tsaritsa themselves shopping in the High Street.

Natasha came in at last and nodded approvingly at Emily. 'Well done, child, you did just right. And now, Olga Nikolayevna, what can you be thinking of, to be walking unprotected about the streets like this?'

The Grand Duchess turned with a friendly smile. 'Oh, don't scold, dear Natasha Petrovna! We did so long just to walk and look at the shops. This is England, after all!'

Tatiana joined her. 'When we came ashore this morning – all five of us – we meant to take a walk, but the policemen wouldn't let us. They made us go for a drive instead in a horrid carriage. So I said to Olga that if we were to come ashore this afternoon, just the two of us, without the little ones, they would probably let us – and they did,' she finished triumphantly.

'It was all right at first – no-one knew who we were, and we had such a nice time!' said Olga. 'We found a shop selling postcards, and there were pictures of Papa and Mama and King Edward and everybody. We've bought lots and lots, for everybody at home – look!'

'It was very foolish of the Chief Constable to allow it,' Natasha said. 'The High Street is so narrow, it was bound to cause jostling.'

'No, really, madame,' Tatiana said, 'it was all right until Basil Narishkin saw us and called out to us, and then suddenly people realised we were Russian, and guessed who we were.'

'I shall speak to Basil Narishkin when next I see him,' Natasha said grimly.

'We weren't really *frightened*,' Olga added judiciously. 'Only we did wonder how we were going to be able to get back.'

'Where did you come ashore?'

'At the Trinity wharf,' Olga said, 'and we came across the river on the floating bridge.'

'It was such fun!' Tatiana cried irrepressibly. 'We paid our ha'pennies, just like everyone else, and came across with all sorts of ordinary people, and no-one knew who we were at all!'

Natasha laughed. 'Well, if that is what you call fun, I dare say you will enjoy it all over again, for I can't see any other way back. Since we must all walk together, will you allow me to present to you my granddaughter, Emily Paget?'

The Grand Duchesses offered their hands in the most friendly manner. There was nothing about them, Emily thought, that would tell you they were the daughters of the most powerful autocrat in the world.

They completed their purchases, and the whole party moved out into the street and began to walk slowly down the hill, with the two policemen making a path through the crowds for them. Two other senior policemen came on the scene at last, and things became a little easier.

'Do you live on the island?' Olga asked Emily.

'No, on a country estate,' Emily said.

'Oh, just like us,' Tatiana said simply.

'Is it always like this, when you go out?' Emily asked, impressed with how calmly the Grand Duchesses treated the huge crowds that hemmed them in.

'We never do go out,' Tatiana said. 'Not walking, anyway, except in our own grounds. When we go outside, it's always in the carriage.'

'You're so lucky to be able to go wherever you want,' Olga said.

'Oh, but I can't! I'm not of royal blood, but I'm female, and we're always confined, aren't we?'

'Are people always telling you that such-and-such a thing isn't suitable for a young lady?' Tatiana asked.

'Always,' Emily said. 'I have an aunt – oh, she's very kind and good, but there's hardly anything I do or say that she approves of.'

Olga laughed. 'Aunts are always like that, aren't they?'

They walked on down the hill chatting pleasantly, exchanging stories and comparing experiences.

'You speak English so beautifully,' Emily said. 'Do you speak it at home?'

'With Mama we do,' Olga said. 'She speaks English better than Russian or even German, because she had an English governess, and she used to spend a lot of time in England with Great-grandmama – Queen Victoria, I mean.'

'But with Papa we speak Russian,' Tatiana said. 'He believes in everything Russian; and nearly everybody at Court speaks French, so we speak that too.'

'Where did you learn French?' Olga asked.

'My father taught me. My mother was half French, but she died when I was born.'

'Oh, how sad! I'm so sorry,' Olga said, offering instant, warm sympathy.

Emily didn't know quite what to do with it. It seemed fraudulent to accept it, and churlish to reject it, so she simply said, 'I think Russian sounds a beautiful language. I should love to learn it.'

'Perhaps you will come to Russia one day,' Olga said. 'If you do, I hope you will come and visit us. I'm sure it would be allowed, since you are Natasha Petrovna's granddaughter.'

'Thank you, I should like to very much,' Emily said, deeply touched. The first girl of her own age she had ever met seemed to have taken to her, she thought, and considering who that girl was, it was a double compliment. Then she said sadly, 'But I don't suppose I shall ever be able to. I don't suppose I shall ever see Russia.'

'That's what we thought about England,' Tatiana said positively. 'But here we are, you see.'

Chapter Four

'And what did you think of the Grand Duchesses?' Natasha asked Emily the next day. She had called for her granddaughter after luncheon and taken her on shore, where a hired carriage awaited them. The imperial family and the King and Queen had gone for the afternoon on a family visit to Osborne and Barton Cottage, and Natasha was entirely at liberty until the evening. She proposed driving across Wootton Common to Robin Hill, and back via Newport.

'I like them very much,' Emily answered. 'They seemed so *ordinary* – I mean, not grand like princesses.'

'They are very much confined,' Natasha said. 'It has never seemed to me a sensible system to bring them up like the daughters of a plain country gentleman, which they are not! A young woman should be prepared for the life she will lead. What good will it do them when they are queens of other countries, to have slept on a camp-bed all their childhood, and washed in cold water?'

'Do they really?' Emily asked, intrigued. 'They are worse off than me, then – we have a wonderful bathroom at The Lodge.'

'English plumbing is far superior to Russian,' Natasha said seriously. Emily looked at her doubtfully, and saw the gleam in her eyes.

'You're laughing at me,' she said.

'Yes, *durachka*, my little fool – do you mind?'

'Oh no!' Emily said. 'It's treating me like a real person. Grown-ups never do, do they?'

'And aren't I a grown-up?'

'You're very different, ma'am – is it all right to say that?'

'You can say anything to me, as long as it is the truth.'

'Then, you don't seem very much like a grandmother to me. More like – well – an older sister.'

Natasha laughed. 'I suppose I must take that as a compliment,' she said. 'So tell me, now, if I am your older sister, what is your father?'

'He isn't very much like a father,' Emily admitted.

'What do you think of him?' Emily looked at her doubtfully. 'Come,' she said encouragingly. 'We are in a carriage in the middle of the countryside. No-one can hear us. I wish to know the truth. Do you find my son Edward a wholly satisfactory person?'

This new way of talking seemed to Emily perilously exciting. Hearing her father referred to as 'my son Edward' made her see him suddenly as quite separate from her. It was stepping aside and looking at something unbearably familiar from a different angle – a hard trick to learn with people one was close to.

And suddenly she remembered all sorts of little fragments of things about him that she had absorbed over the years without really realising it: from Penny and her aunt and uncle, from tradespeople and people in the village. A satisfactory person? Was it possible that grown-ups could be measured in such a way, that they might have to fulfil expectations, in the same way that children were required to by them?

'I sometimes think,' she began hesitantly, and the sound of her own voice made her nervous about the enormity of what she was about to say. It would change her whole way of thinking about the world.

'Yes,' Natasha encouraged. 'Tell me what you think.'

She plunged. 'I sometimes think he doesn't try very hard. I mean, I know he has a Broken Heart because of Mama, and that he will Die With Her Name On His Lips; but I can't help feeling that if it were me, I wouldn't be quite so cast down by it all. It was a long time ago, after all. He never goes anywhere or does anything, just sits and writes his stories all day. It's as if . . . '

'Yes?'

'I think he escapes into them. He doesn't like living in the world at all. And if you're going to escape from the world, oh surely, *surely* you'd choose something a bit more important than Greyfriars School or Sinclair of the Scouts?'

She stopped, appalled by her own words. She fixed her eyes on the reeling road beside her, and waited for the storm to break over her head. There was a silence, and then a lavender-gloved hand was placed over hers, making her start. She looked up at Natasha Petrovna and saw no reproof.

'You are quite right,' Natasha said. 'All that you say is true – and what you have been too generous to say. He has not behaved well by you. To give up on his own behalf is one thing, but he had a responsibility to you, and you are right to be angry.'

'Oh no, ma'am!' Emily protested. *Angry* was too much.

'The truth between us, Emilia, always; I promise you I will never rebuke you for telling the truth. You have seen through the pretence, which is remarkable considering how few of the facts you have been allowed to know.'

'The facts?' Emily asked. The ground under her feet was shredding into a lacework of holes, and she had no idea what she was about to plummet into.

'Since your father refuses to be responsible for you, you must take responsibility for your own life. And you cannot do that unless you know the circumstances of your birth.'

'I don't –' she began, and stopped. She had been about to say that she didn't want to take responsibility, but realised that of course she did.

Natasha nodded. 'It may not be comfortable, but you will find – if you do not already believe, which I think perhaps you do – that it is always better to *know* than not to know. Ignorance is not bliss, child, it is helplessness.'

Really, Emily thought with one distant and bemused part of her mind, this is a most ungrandmotherlike conversation. She felt like Alice. It was like being mad, or being in a dream, where different rules applied; but like a dream, it seemed reasonable and real while you were in it.

And suddenly she remembered a fragment of conversation she had overheard accidentally between her aunt and uncle as she had been going towards the saloon last evening. The door was open, and their voices drifted down the corridor towards her.

'I had all sorts of advice to give her on how to behave,' her aunt was saying. 'But I see that whatever it is she's doing, Mama seems to have taken to her, so perhaps it's better to leave well alone.'

A pause, and a rustle of the newspaper, and her uncle's indolent voice: 'I shouldn't pin too much hope on it, my dear. You know your mother is most likely to leave everything to your sister's children. And after all, Emily's no trouble to us.'

'Not to you,' Maud said vigorously, 'but that's because you simply haven't thought what's to be *done* with her. She won't be off my hands until she's safely married, and how can I get her off creditably without any fortune at all?'

Had Uncle Westie yawned, or had she only imagined she'd heard it? 'I'm sure she's perfectly happy at The Lodge with her father, and pottering about the park. You don't have to do any more for her than you've done.'

What Aunt Maud might have replied to that, Emily hadn't waited to hear. She had run back to her cabin with her cheeks burning, and it had been some minutes before she was composed enough to return to the saloon.

At the time she had thought how hard it was to be considered a burden, when you were prevented from doing anything about it by the very people who wanted you off their hands. Now, in this strange and dreamlike episode of looking at things from outside them, she understood that her aunt and uncle didn't see her as a person at all. She was just a shape with a label on it that said 'Emily', a thing that had to be dealt with, like a hedge that needed cutting. When it had been cut, you didn't need to think about it any more, it was just there.

They had no right, she thought, to dispose of her like that – except, of course, that they had every right. She was helpless and dependent on them, a female without fortune, and, in a world where women bore the status and character of the man they belonged to, father or husband, with a father who would not exert himself for her.

Natasha watched her closely all through this long process of thought. When Emily came back to the present, to the carriage and the horses, the bright sunshine, the hedgerows of the English country lane rolling past, she found her grandmother waiting patiently for her conclusions.

'You don't tell children things,' she said slowly, 'in order to protect them. Knowing things is frightening.'

'Yes,' Natasha agreed. 'Life is a dangerous business. It is well to be prepared.'

'But I'm only fifteen!' Emily protested.

'It's old enough,' Natasha said. She held out her hands before her, turning the hands palm upwards as if they were to receive a gift. 'Ask me what you want to know.'

It took Emily a while to know where to begin. 'No-one ever speaks about my mother,' she said at last. 'I used to think it was because of Pa's broken heart, but lately I've begun to wonder if it weren't – '

'Yes?' Natasha prompted.

'Because Mama was a ballet girl.'

The bright gaze was steady. 'They have told you that is a disgraceful thing to be?'

'Not told, exactly, but one gets to know somehow.'

'It is a calling, like becoming a nun, and requires great dedication and much hard work. Though, of course,' she added fairly, 'in England it is not much regarded to be a nun, either. However, the ballet is perfectly respectable. In Russia all well-bred girls learn a little of it. It is essential in teaching one control and grace. Did you not notice how beautifully the grand duchesses move?'

'But it's different in England, isn't it? Or is it just different with my mother?'

'What do you know about her?' Natasha asked.

'Only that she was very beautiful, and my father was very much in love with her. My Uncle John didn't approve of her, that's why he won't have anything to do with us. But when she died Papa's heart broke and he retired from the world in grief.' She observed her grandmother's expression and said, 'Isn't that true?'

'Hmph! Not exactly. Your father married your mother out of defiance. And he retired from the world, as you put it so prettily, out of pique. His has been a grand sulk, Emilia, lasting sixteen years! But of course one can grow used to an attitude and not wish to give up the comfort of it, because it saves one from having to think.' She looked at her granddaughter keenly. 'Do I hurt you with the truth? Would you rather have the fairy story?'

Emily shook her head. 'I'd rather have the truth. At least, I think I would – I haven't had much experience of it.' She thought a moment. 'Was she very beautiful?'

'She was a pretty girl, but no great beauty.'

'But he was in love with her?'

'He wished to be in love with someone just then. She was not the woman he made of her in his mind – as he would have found out quite soon,' she added sternly, 'if his boy's fancy had not been turned into a crusade by opposition.'

'My Uncle John?'

'Edward would never have married her if John had not forbidden him to, and so I warned him – but John would never listen to me.'

'Were they happy together?' Emily asked tentatively.

'Eddy always kept a good shop front, as they say. But I think affection must have died very quickly. Consider, she had no education, no interests beyond the dance.' Natasha sighed. 'Your father was not made for poverty. Bertie would have made the best of

56

things, but Eddy was the last person in the world to bear muddle and discomfort, and Belle, poor creature, had no notion how to manage a household. She mourned for her lost career, grew peevish and sickly, and blamed Edward for everything. Which,' she added decidedly, 'she was quite right to do, for it was all his fault.'

'But if he didn't love her, why did he pretend to have a broken heart when she died?'

She shrugged. 'Pride. He had made a fool of himself, and wished only to hide it from the world. So everyone had to believe the fairy story.'

'You don't like him, do you?' Emily said in a small voice.

Natasha looked at her sharply. 'No, it isn't that! I loved his father so much, how could I dislike him? He was such a pretty child, but always defiant, hurting himself. He was the sort of child who would put his hand in the fire simply because you told him not to.' She tapped her temple. 'He did not think. He threw himself into things passionately, and then sulked when he got hurt.'

'My Uncle Albert was different, was he?'

'You remind me so much of him! He was thoughtful – not like the others, who never thought at all! Even when he was very small, he always knew if I was sad and came and cheered me up. He could always make people laugh – my little clown! But he was clever, too, and quick. I used to think what a great man he would make.' She stopped.

'How did he die?' Emily asked after a moment.

'A hunting accident. He and Eddy were out one day, competing with each other who would get the brush. They were great rivals. I think Eddy was jealous of Bertie.' She looked at a distant landscape. 'On this day they rode neck and neck at a hedge at full gallop. They took off together, but somehow the horses collided in the air and Bertie was thrown off.' She paused. 'I expect the horses tried to avoid him. They hate to step on a living creature. But Bertie was trampled to death. Edward came home without a scratch on him.'

'Do you blame Papa for that?'

'He had the one thing that Bertie was denied: life. And he wasted it. I suppose like you I find it hard to forgive him for giving up.'

There was a brief silence, and then Natasha looked around her with an air of waking. 'These lanes and hedges are very well, but we are not looking at them at all. Besides, I feel the need for tea coming over me, and when that happens, everything else is driven from my mind. Driver! Do you know a short cut to Newport?'

'Yes, my lady. If we turn off to the right about half a mile on and take the road to Staplers – '

'Very well, I do not wish a geography lesson. Newport, if you please.'

The driver took them to the Victoria Hotel, where tea was being served in the garden. As they followed the waitress out onto the lawn, a young man at a table nearby stood up with a gesture of recognition.

'Natasha Petrovna! *Comme c'est gentille de vous rencontrer ici*!'

Natasha looked stern. 'Oh, it's you, Basil Kirilovitch! How do you dare show your face after putting the Grand Duchesses in peril yesterday?'

The young man spread his hands. 'It was the most foolish mistake!' he said, changing to unaccented English without a blink. 'And I swear to you it was Basil Dolgorouky who did the harm, calling out to them like that in Russian! You know I wouldn't have dared to presume.'

'I know you are a wheedling rogue, and that your mother didn't beat you enough as a child. I shall tell her so when next I write to her.'

'Well, then, come and join me for tea, and you can rebuke me in comfort to your heart's content.'

'Very well, but I warn you I shall take my tea Russian style, and make figures of us all,' Natasha said, allowing him to draw out a chair for her. It was obvious that she could not be angry with him, and Emily, trying not to stare with her mouth open like a cod, wasn't in the least surprised. He was without exception the most beautiful human creature, male or female, she had ever seen: tall, golden and godlike, with a Greek profile and vivid blue eyes. As he stooped over Natasha's chair, Emily saw that his otherwise smooth hair had just two heartbreaking feathery curls nestling at the nape of his neck, and she was completely undone.

'Vasya dear,' Natasha said now, 'I must present you to my granddaughter, Emily Paget. Emily, this is Basil Narishkin.'

The glorious creature turned to her, and her heart tripped running. Now the blue eyes were resting on her face, her hand was in his.

'I am honoured, Miss Paget. Allow me . . . ' He pulled out a chair for her, and Emily sat, feeling weak inside from love and disappointment. He had smiled so charmingly, seated her so courteously, but his eyes had registered only that blankness with which grown-ups look at children – a look which says 'You have nothing to do with me'. She had felt very smart when she dressed that morning in the navy serge sailor dress piped in white, and the new straw boater with the striped ribbon. Now she was only horribly conscious of the shortness of her skirt, and that her hair was hanging loose behind in childish ringlets.

Perfectly unaware of the torment he had caused, Narishkin chatted lightly about the yacht-racing and who was at Cowes that week, until the waitress came back with tea and scones. Then he hefted the large china teapot and said, 'Now, Totya Natasha, will you tend the samovar, or shall I?'

'You pour,' Natasha said. 'And don't call me that foolish name. You know I am no relation to you really.'

He paused in mid-stream and opened his eyes wide. 'Spurned!' he cried dramatically. 'But you are my aunt by marriage, and in our Church that is as good as the real thing.'

'You talk such nonsense. The truth is you called me Totya when you were a little boy because your mother and I were such friends. How is she, by the way?'

'Just the same as always,' he said, 'but you shan't distract me from my argument. Miss Paget shall decide. Now Miss Paget, is Natasha Petrovna my aunt, or not? This is the case – '

'My brother Nikolai's boy Alexei married Basil's sister Anna,' Natasha interrupted firmly.

'Older sister,' Basil added conspiratorially, leaning his head towards Emily's. 'Very bossy.'

'Which means I am Alexei's aunt, Anna's aunt by marriage, and no relation to Basil at all,' Natasha finished.

'Isn't she cruel?' Basil asked Emily. 'Especially since if she *is* my aunt, that makes you a sort of cousin, doesn't it? What do you say – won't you side with me?'

Emily wanted nothing better, even though she knew it was nonsense, and not even nonsense designed for her amusement.

'I don't think one can ever have too many cousins,' she said.

Basil at once turned away from her, towards Natasha. 'There, you see! Cousin Emily sides with me, so that settles it. Here is your tea, Totya Natasha.'

Natasha shook her head and laughed, taking her teacup from him, and spooning in some of the raspberry jam which had come with the scones. She looked at Emily impishly over the rim. 'Maud hates me to do this, though when she was a little girl she wouldn't drink it any other way.'

'I can't imagine Aunt Maud as a little girl,' Emily said.

'She was hardly any different. Always well behaved, and quite unnaturally clean for a child,' Natasha sighed.

'Who can you mean? Not Lady Westinghouse?' Basil asked eagerly.

'Don't dare to repeat anything I say to Emily, bad boy!'

'As if I would,' he said with an unreliable look.

'In any case, it's all my fault. I neglected them dreadfully, my first three. I had five babies in five years, you see, so I never had much energy to spare for the older ones. And then John and Edward went away to school – such a dreadful custom, they were hardly more than babies!'

'My cousin Tom seems to like it at Eton,' Emily said doubtfully.

'I was at Eton too,' Basil said, 'and I hated every minute! It was all so barbarous – ferocious games in muddy fields, and only cold water to wash in afterwards.'

Emily bowed her head to hide her smile.

'I've often thought,' Natasha said, 'that the English do not really like children. They have them because they must, and have dogs for pleasure. And then, of course, they treat their children like dogs, and their dogs like children.'

'Don't Russian children go to school?' Emily asked.

'Not until they are older. When they are little we keep them about us. I wish I had loved your aunt more,' she sighed. 'Do you think she would have been different if I had?'

Emily shook her head. 'I don't know anything about love,' she said.

Natasha looked at her consideringly and then gave a strange little smile. 'That is not so. You know a great deal already, though where you learnt it is a puzzle.' And then she changed the subject, turning to Basil Narishkin and asking, 'Where are you staying this week, Vasya? On someone's yacht? Someone agreeable, I hope?'

In the carriage on the way back, Natasha suddenly asked, 'What do you wish, Emilia?'

Emily looked up, startled out of a reverie. 'I wish we didn't have to go back,' she said.

60

'How nice that is! But I did not mean now, this minute. Your long wishes – what are they?'

Emily frowned in thought. 'It's hard to wish anything, really, because I don't know what there is. I *think* I should like to go to London and be a typewriter or a clerk – something, at any rate, so that I could earn my living.'

'Why do you wish to earn your living?' Natasha looked perplexed.

'Because – because I don't want to live at The Lodge for ever with Papa, and I don't want to marry someone they find me just to be respectable, because that would probably work out to be the same thing.'

She didn't feel she was explaining things very well, but her grandmother seemed to understand.

'But this is such a very small wish, to go to London and work for your living. Can you not wish larger than that?'

Emily's brow cleared. 'Oh, as to sail-winged ships and white horses and jewels in the navel, I can do all that sort of thing – '

'In the navel?'

'My little cousin Alexandra wants to be an odalisque and wear a jewel in her navel.'

'Ah! And you?'

'I should like to travel and see the world and do something very wonderful and brave so that people will remember me when I'm dead. I should like to go to Russia,' she added, 'but I don't suppose I shall ever even go to London.'

'You are quite right, of course,' Natasha said thoughtfully, 'to look first to what is within reach.'

'But it isn't. Everyone says I mayn't go out to work. They say it's not proper. So you see, going to London is just as far off as the jewels and the prince on the white horse.'

'You will have them all,' Natasha said firmly. 'And you will see many countries. We Russians are great travellers – no, why do you smile?'

'It's the way you say "We Russians" with such a rolling of the "r"s,' Emily said. 'It sounds so grand.'

'It is grand, Russia is grand, everything Russian is grand,' Natasha said splendidly.

'Perhaps a fairy godmother will wave a magic wand and transport me there one day,' Emily said agreeably.

'*Chort*! I know both your godmothers, and they are not fairies, I assure you!'

61

'I don't believe in magic anyway.'

'Life is the great magic. You may believe in that. And in one other – look, *mylenkaya*.'

She drew up her watch, which hung on a chain at her waist, unclipped it and gave it to Emily. It had an ivory face delicately painted with tiny purple pansies; the case was of gold, and the back studded with pearls and amethysts.

'It's so pretty! I've never seen one like it,' Emily exclaimed.

'Vanya – my husband, John – ordered it for me from Monsieur Fabergé for my eighteenth birthday. It was his own design. There are words inside.'

Emily pressed the winding-knob and the back flew open. The engraved inscription was in Russian letters. 'What does it say?'

'In English it means something like "The heart does not know anything about Time",' Natasha said. 'He was much older than me, you see, so we always knew that time was not our friend. But with someone you truly love, and who loves you, the clocks do not run at the normal speed. That is the other real magic. Remember it.'

The following afternoon at about half-past three the Cowes guardship thundered out a salute as the *Standart* and the *Polar Star* slipped their moorings and manoeuvred slowly out from amongst the throng of yachts in Cowes Roads. Emily stood with her aunt and uncle on the forward deck of the *Amoenus* as the whole cortège moved out into the strait and sailed up Spithead towards the open sea, to a distant thunder of other salutes from the Home Fleet, and then from the shore fort at Ryde.

'Well, that all went off very well, didn't it?' Westie said. 'No unpleasant incidents – and perfect weather too. A good omen, for the Alliance – that's what the papers'll say.'

'Mother hasn't changed a bit,' Maud said. 'She still dresses and talks like a woman half her age. Still, I suppose it doesn't matter in Russia.'

'Damn shame about the boy being sickly – the Tsarevitch,' Westie said, turning away from the rail. 'Bad for the succession. I wonder what's wrong with him? He looked healthy enough, the few glimpses I caught of him.'

Maud followed him. 'Remind me when we go on shore to send a telegraph to Auchnachillan, to tell Mrs Mackie we shall be coming up a day early. Even in August that house is intolerable without fires.'

Emily heard them hardly more than the background nattering of the seagulls. She stood motionless by the rail, staring at the horizon where the ships had vanished, and struggling with the lump in her throat. There had been no more opportunities to talk with her grandmother after they had got back from Newport. She hadn't even been able to say goodbye to her today, and she knew that in all likelihood she would never see her again. The adventure was over. Tomorrow she would be taken back to The Lodge, probably for the rest of her life, and after this week it would be an irksome captivity. That, and missing her grandmother, made her want to howl.

Her aunt turned at the companion-way. 'Emily, dear, you had better go down to your cabin and rest for an hour. You know we're having guests here to dinner, and then there's the fireworks afterwards. It will be a tiring evening for you.'

'Yes, Aunt,' Emily said.

In her cabin she lay on her bed and stared at the ceiling, trying to recall everything her grandmother had said. She didn't want to forget any word of their conversations. What had happened to her this week had changed everything in her and nothing outside her; but if there was one person in the world who understood how she thought about things, and didn't condemn her for not being what Aunt Maud wanted, she felt she could bear whatever future was chosen for her.

After about ten minutes there was a knock on her cabin door. In the passage outside, one of the stewards – the young one, Billings – stood looking rather nervous.

'Oh, miss, I'm sorry to disturb you. I was asked to give you this.' He held out an envelope to her, and seeing her blank look, added, 'One of the stewards on the *Polar Star* gave it me. He said I was to give it to you when you were on your own.' The colour was rising from under his collar towards his ears now. 'I hope I did right, miss. I didn't know whether – '

'Yes! Oh, yes, it's quite all right. Thank you,' Emily said. A smile started to tug at her lips. Did he think it was from a man – that she had been having an assignation? Should she enlighten him? No, better not; he might keep the secret better this way. 'You won't tell anyone?'

'No, miss, of course not!'

When he had gone, Emily sat down on the edge of her bed and opened the envelope. Inside was a large white card with small, black, difficult writing on it.

'My dear Emilia Edvardovna,' it said, 'I want you to know that meeting you has been the greatest pleasure of this week. You have been such refreshment to me, and since no goodness ever goes unrewarded, I promise you that your fairy godmother *will* come with her wand. When she does you must work hard and prepare yourself for your place in the world. Meanwhile be patient, love well, and *never give up*. Your loving grandmother, N.P.'

Being back at Bratton was an agony. For the first time she really appreciated how empty and monotonous her life was. After the throngs of people there was just her, Papa and Penny. After the vivid, brain-stirring conversations there was silence interspersed with bare acknowledgement.

At first there were not even her cousins, for on their return from Cowes, her aunt and uncle took the children to Auchnachillan for the grouse-shooting, then straight to the South of France for a month, and then to London for new clothes. Emily spent the time tramping moodily about the park, or reading herself almost sick in the library.

It was obvious that Aunt Maud's plan hadn't worked, that however much her grandmother had liked her, she had not promised to leave her a fortune, and on the whole Emily was glad about that. But it left the problem of her future as unresolved as if she had never been to Cowes, and ten times as hard to bear.

When the family came down again for the hunting, things were better. It was possible while hunting four times a week to forget any trouble, however piercing; and there was an added attraction for Emily this winter. Perhaps driven to it by Jacob, her aunt summoned her to the Peacock Room to tell her that she couldn't bear any longer the sight of Emily on Sooty with her feet almost touching the ground. Emily was to be allowed to hunt Maud's second horse for the whole season.

Emily's gratitude was almost tearful. She had expected silent rebuke from her aunt for having let her down over the inheritance business; being allowed instead the privilege of riding King's Ransom was coals of fire.

But the hunting season does not last for ever. Spring came, the hunters were thorned for the last time and turned out, and Emily rediscovered the restlessness and worry which had been simmering gently in the back of her mind.

She was wandering rather idly about the vicinity of The Lodge one afternoon, with nothing in particular to do, when a carriage drew up outside the West Gate. Emily went towards it, ready to be helpful; it sometimes happened that lost travellers stopped at the gate to ask directions, and occasionally a new visitor to Bratton Park might arrive at the West Gate by mistake.

It was a handsome carriage, black and glossy, drawn by superb black horses, with a coachman on the box in a livery she didn't recognise. The sole occupant of the carriage was an elderly lady, dressed all in black as old ladies often were. That was the only usual thing about her, however. The person staring at Emily so imperiously was not draped in the dull and self-effacing weeds of the ordinary widow. On the contrary, she glittered with jet beads and sequins, her hat was decorated with black plumes that would not have disgraced a funeral horse, and she carried a black lacquered cane with a silver top.

With this cane she now leaned over and struck the gate ringingly. Emily was already on her way, but her progress was evidently too slow for the old lady, who poked the cane between two of the bars and rattled it briskly.

'Girl! Open this gate at once! At once, do you hear me?' Emily skipped, but the old lady rattled again anyway, like a butcher's boy on a railing.

Emily reached the scene, and felt it circumspect to curtsey. 'I beg your pardon, ma'am, but the gate doesn't open. If you were to – '

'Nonsense! What is a gate for, if not to open? Do you suppose it was put here for decoration?'

Emily took hold of one of the rusting bars, and put her other hand through to lift up and bring to the old lady's attention the enormous padlock, hanging on a chain massive enough to have anchored an ocean liner, that bound the two gates together. 'It's locked, ma'am, you see. It hasn't been used in years. No-one comes in this way.'

'Don't be pert with me, miss!' the old lady said, drawing her brows together. 'Do you think I don't know rust when I see it? Or bindweed, for that matter!' She pointed with her stick to the line of weeds along the bottom of the gate attesting to its unused state.

'You must have a key – fetch it!' And she whacked the gate with her stick so suddenly that Emily had to snatch her hand back.

'I'm not sure where it is. This isn't really a gatehouse, you see, ma'am. If you were to continue along this road, you'd come to the South Gate, which is the one in general use. It's really much more convenient for the house. I assume you are looking for Bratton Park?'

'I'm not looking for Bratton Park and I'm not looking for a gatehouse,' the visitor said with a childlike triumph. 'I've come to visit The Lodge, and if you don't stop bandying words with me and go and find the key to this gate, it will be very much the worse for you when I *do* get in. For I warn you, get in I shall, and I am quite famous for my ill temper and for never minding what I say to people. *Go and get the key!*'

It took Emily and Penny five minutes to find the right key, which turned up at last on the top shelf of the kitchen dresser, attached to a large luggage label on which the writing had faded almost to invisibility. The noise and activity attracted Edward from his study, which was fortunate in the end because it took the combined efforts of the coachman and Edward to force the gates open against the anchoring weeds and rust while Emily held the horses.

Eventually the coachman resumed his seat and drove the carriage through, halting it in front of The Lodge. A rap of her stick indicated to Edward that he should help the old lady down, and there she stood at last, five yards from where she had been sitting outside the gate. She could have walked through the wicket at the side of the carriage gates, and saved everyone an immense amount of trouble; but Emily noted in the old lady's demeanour a certain grim pleasure, and concluded that she actually enjoyed being a nuisance.

Even as she thought it, Emily found the bright old eyes had settled on her with a gleam of complicity. The fantastic hat nodded, and the old lady said, 'Yes, you see there are compensations for growing old! Very few, I admit, but that is all the more reason for enjoying every one of them.' She turned to Edward. 'You may close the gate now, and lock it. I shall be going up to the house afterwards.'

Emily could see that her father didn't like being given such uncompromising orders, but there was no-one else to close the gate, so he stumped off in silence to do it. The old lady now fixed Emily with a bright and birdlike gaze.

'You will take me to the drawing-room and I will have tea. Lend me your shoulder, child. I'm stiff with sitting.'

The hand she extended looked as frail as a bundle of twigs, but when it came down on Emily's shoulder, it gripped with surprising strength.

'Yes, I know,' she murmured in Emily's ear. 'It's disgraceful the way I bring people round my finger five minutes after meeting them. Why, you are my willing servant already, are you not, Emilia Edvardovna?'

Emily started. Really, she ought to have known from a number of small clues: the demanding behaviour, the breathtaking clothes, the faint trace of a foreign accent, the unconventional conversation. She stopped dead and looked at the visitor with wide eyes.

'You are the fairy godmother!' she exclaimed. 'My grandmother sent you to me!'

Chapter Five

The visitor raised an eyebrow. 'My dear child, do I look as if anyone sends me anywhere? But you are right in essence. I have come to The Lodge specifically to see you, and at the request of Natasha Petrovna.'

'Oh, ma'am, have you seen her? How is she?' Emily asked eagerly. 'Does she — '

The old lady held up her hand. 'Don't gush, please. We have very little time before we are disturbed, and we must plan our campaign logically. First, to the drawing-room!'

They were walking up the narrow path between the laurels and towards the front door, standing open after Edward's emergence. It reminded Emily that her father had been disturbed while he was writing — the most heinous domestic crime known at The Lodge. And this alarming old lady had just asked for the impossible.

'We haven't a drawing-room, ma'am,' Emily felt obliged to warn. 'Only a parlour, and it's rather small.'

'I'm not at all surprised,' she retorted. 'This is quite the most dismal, poky little house I have ever seen. What on earth are you doing, living here?'

Emily decided this was a rhetorical question. Crossing the narrow hall, she opened the parlour door, and stood back. The old lady looked in. 'Good God, do you really sit in here? No, no, it will not do. Now, *that* room', pointing with her cane at the study door, 'must be better. It is south-facing, if I don't mistake.'

'Oh, but ma'am, that's my father's room. We never sit in there. I mean, it's his private room. He's not to be disturbed.'

It was no use. The old lady stepped in through the open door, nodded with approval, and sat herself firmly down in one of the red plush chairs by the fireside.

'Much better. This must be the best room in the house. Your father's sanctum sanctorum, eh? How wise of him. Any fool can be uncomfortable, as the General used to say. And he's had the foresight to convince you that he mustn't be disturbed, so that he can make sure he keeps it to himself.'

68

Emily felt provoked to defend her father. 'It isn't that, ma'am. He works in here. He's a writer, you know, and his concentration mustn't be broken.'

'I have sharp eyes, my dear,' the old lady retorted. 'Sharper than yours, I dare say, where family loyalty blinds you. Your father was disturbed at his work when I arrived, was he? And what do you see on that desk?'

Emily looked in spite of herself. In the operative space, front centre of the desk, where her father worked, lay a few sheets of paper covered with her father's handwriting; but the breeze from the open window, compounded by the open front door, had blown them askew. Underneath, almost as if the papers had been drawn across to conceal them, was a half-eaten apple and an open book: H. G. Wells, *The War of the Worlds*.

Emily turned startled eyes on the visitor, and met a perfectly devilish look. Into Emily's mind had darted a dreadful vision, of her father sitting in this pleasant, sunny room reading a novel at his ease, knowing that he would not be disturbed. If anyone knocked on the door, he had only to slip the book into the drawer, pull a piece of paper towards him, and pretend to be writing. The noise of some crisis outside had brought him from his desk in haste, but he had pulled a sheaf of papers forward as he left to conceal his true activities.

Other thoughts clamoured thick and fast for notice on the heels of the vision. Why had Papa not made more money, like other popular writers? Why did writing those tales take him so long? Why had his novel never been finished? Could it be that he worked only a few hours each week, and not every day as they thought? Could it be that he was simply lazy?

Then she caught herself up. She should not allow this strange old person to put such ideas in her head. It made her remember her grandmother's disturbing question, 'Do you find him satisfactory?' She might have felt that Papa had given up too easily on the world, but to imagine that he cheated her and Penny in this way was too hateful.

'I would never touch anything on my father's desk,' she said stiffly. 'I know better than that, ma'am.'

The old lady didn't seem put out. 'He has you well trained, I can see! I begin to like him a little better. Selfish people are so much more interesting than unselfish ones. And much more reliable: you always know where you are with them. Don't you think so?'

'I don't think I know any of the other sort, ma'am,' Emily said, a little resentfully.

'Ha! Well said! Now, to business. Firstly you will want to know who I am: I am Lady Hamilton, widow of General Sir Richard Hamilton, Baronet. Natasha Petrovna is my niece; my husband's sister Fleur was her mother. Do you follow me so far?'

Emily said cautiously, 'Does that mean you are my great-aunt, ma'am?'

'Your arithmetic is a little faulty. I'm your great-great-aunt, but by marriage only.'

'Yes, ma'am. I see.'

'Your great-grandmother Fleur and I lived together in Russia when I was a girl. She married a Russian, and stayed in Russia. I married her English brother and came to England. Not that I've lived very much in England. I travelled with the General all over the world – India, Afghanistan, Egypt, Africa. Ours was a love-match, you see, so we would not be parted.'

She seemed to expect some reply to this, so Emily said, 'The travel sounds very exciting, ma'am.'

'Hm. Uncomfortable and dangerous, too – but an education in itself. I am walking history, child! I have dined with Lord Raglan, who was secretary to the Duke of Wellington at Waterloo, think of that! I nursed the survivors of the Charge of the Light Brigade, and advised Chinese Gordon on the medicine chest he took with him to Khartoum. A few hours' conversation with me is better than all the elementary education in the world! I confidently expect Mr Lloyd George to make me compulsory for all children under the age of fourteen, and to pay for me with another of his iniquitous taxes!'

Emily began to laugh. 'You are very like my grandmother, ma'am! I mean, in the way you talk.'

'Nonsense! She is like me. Think before you speak, please. She is like me because I did my best to make her so. It was a struggle, however. She takes too much after her mother, you know, and her mother was an Englishwoman of gentle birth, which condemned her to being Nice. Now I am not Nice at all. I never was, even when I was a girl. I did all the wicked things I could think of, and when I'd done them all, I invented a few more of my own.'

'I should like to hear about them,' Emily said.

'You shall, but not now. There's no time. I must explain to you why I'm here. I noticed the potential in Natasha Petrovna when she first came to England, and dedicated myself to making her as ungovernable as I was. She saw the same potential in you, and asked me to look you over. If I like what I see, she asks me to rescue you.'

'Rescue me?' Emily said with dawning hope.

'Unless, of course,' Lady Hamilton said sternly, 'you want to be nice. Speak up, miss: a life of respectability and self-sacrifice, prudence and caution? Is that your deepest desire?'

'Oh no, ma'am,' Emily said quickly. 'Please not!'

Lady Hamilton nodded. 'Very well,' she said. 'I shall proceed. But I must do it with tact, you understand, so say nothing until you hear from me.'

Edward came into the room at that moment, closely followed by Penny bearing a laden tea tray. Edward's appearance had undergone a hasty tidying and rust removal, but his expression was one of controlled resentment which in other circumstances – had it not been her own father, for instance – Emily might have found amusing.

'Well, ma'am, I hope Emily is taking care of you?' he said brightly, with the sort of smile that suggested he wished her at the devil. 'But why didn't you take our visitor into the parlour, Emily? This is my business-room, Lady Hamilton. We do not sit here.'

'I chose to sit here, sir, so you need not blame your daughter. I did not care to sit in the dark, and since I am a very old woman, older than you can imagine, there is no arguing with me and I must always be allowed to have my way. Ah, yes, my good woman, the tea! It looks excellent! Edward, find somewhere to put the tray. Emily, you shall pour me a cup, and bring me a piece of that fine-looking cake.'

By the time Edward had fetched a table from the parlour for Penny to put the tray on, and tea had been poured and the cake cut, the wind was out of Edward's sails, and the malicious gleam in Lady Hamilton's eyes had spread to her mouth.

'So, you know who I am,' she nodded to her discomfited host. 'I dare say you asked the coachman, for I'm sure you don't remember me, do you, Edward? No, why should you? You can't have seen me more than twice in your life. You were always away at school when I visited my niece.'

Edward made a noncommittal noise, the most he could manage without being actively rude, and sipped his tea.

'But you made good use of being at school, I understand,' Lady Hamilton went on with an admiring smile. 'My godsons all read the *Boy's Own Paper*, and eat up every word you write. You are quite their hero! It must be very pleasant to have such a talent.'

71

'Thank you, ma'am,' Edward said cautiously, fairly sure he was being roasted.

'You are wondering why I am here,' she went on. 'An aged relative descends upon you unannounced – relatives are the very devil, are they not? I have spent much of my life being intolerably rude to mine, simply to make sure they will never trouble me. But you can hardly be blamed for not having done the same, since I've never given you the opportunity. A person cannot be rude to someone they never meet, can they?'

Edward was growing tired of being baited. 'You cannot believe that I would ever have been rude to you, in any circumstances.'

'Oh, I can imagine the circumstances,' Lady Hamilton said airily, 'but I hope this is not one of them, for I've come to ask you a favour.'

'If I can serve you in any way, ma'am . . . '

'It is your permission only that I need. I want to borrow Emily.'

'I don't understand you.'

'No, why should you? But it is quite simple: I would like her to come to London for one or two days each week and stay with me, at my house. I'm an old woman, and I have a fancy for some young company.'

Emily directed a burning look at her great-aunt, and kept her mouth tightly shut. Edward looked taken aback. Whatever he might have expected, it had not been that, and he had no idea how to respond to it.

'I can't imagine it will be in her power, ma'am,' was what he managed to say at last.

'Not in her power? What can you mean? Do you say you will not allow it?'

'She is very young, ma'am, hardly more than a child – '

'Ah! You think I will not be a careful guardian, is that it? Or do you regard me as an unsuitable influence for a young woman?'

The sharp question threw Edward off balance still further. 'No, of course not. Not at all. It is simply that – '

A sweet smile. 'I understand. You are afraid you will miss her! But consider your work, my dear Edward – it will be much better for you not to be disturbed while you are *so* busy.'

And here she gave a fleeting but significant glance towards his desk. Edward glanced too. Emily could not know, of course, what he saw or what went through his mind, but she saw his nostrils flare and a spot of colour appear on each cheek.

'I couldn't make any decision about Emily's future without consulting her aunt,' he managed to say with an approximation of dignity. 'She has been like a mother to her – more than a mother. And she understands much better than I what is best for Emily.'

'Why, of course, *bien entendu*! I shall naturally take the matter up with Maud, but I could not do so in courtesy without making sure you had no objection to the plan. And so', she put her cup aside and put out an imperious hand to Emily to help her up, 'I shall go straight away. I like to have everything decided quickly, don't you? Emily, you may take me to my carriage.'

Emily had never been to a proper theatre, nor seen a proper play, but even she recognised a bravura performance when she saw one. It left Edward with nothing to say, and nothing to do but bow her farewell.

On the way to the carriage, the old lady squeezed Emily's shoulder and said, 'Did I not tell you there are advantages to being old? Oh, it is worth the stiffness and the wrinkles sometimes to be able to do that.' She glanced at Emily's face and said, 'Do you disapprove? Was I cruel?'

'Well, yes, ma'am, a little,' Emily said hesitantly. It was, after all, her father who had been the victim.

'Never mind. When it comes to getting my own way, I have no conscience, none at all!'

'But ma'am,' Emily said, 'I'm sure Papa is right, that Aunt Maud won't agree to it.'

Lady Hamilton chuckled. 'Don't worry, my dear, I know just how to handle it. Maud is no match for me! That's why Natasha chose me.'

And so, two days later, the summons to the Peacock Room; but this time with something other than the anticipation of embarrassment. This time, a secret hope lay warm and close under Emily's ribs.

Aund Maud, Emily thought, seemed puzzled. She had the air of someone who has agreed to something only because she could not identify the pitfall she was sure was there.

'Lady Hamilton spoke to you, I believe, before she came to me. Did she explain her proposal to you?'

'No, Aunt,' Emily was glad to be able to say with truth.

Maud frowned. 'She used to visit us sometimes when I was a child, but I've hardly seen her since Mama went to live in Russia.

Her late husband, the General, you must have heard of. The Hero of Pretoria they used to call him.'

'I think I've seen his picture in the *Strand Magazine*, Aunt,' Emily offered.

'Yes, you may have,' Maud said. 'He was a very great soldier, and undoubtedly devoted to Lady Hamilton.' She stopped again.

It seemed to Emily that Aunt Maud was trying to convince herself of something. 'Has he been dead for many years, Aunt?' she asked, to help things along.

'Three or four years, I believe. Of course, it may well be that Lady Hamilton feels lonely.' She made up her mind to proceed. 'Well, Emily, it seems that your grandmother wishes to interest herself in your education. Lady Hamilton brought me a letter from her. Mama wants you to take lessons in certain subjects in London, and since you live at such a distance, the proposal is that you spend two or three days there at a time. Lady Hamilton has offered to have you to stay, and to chaperone you, or provide you with a chaperone, which is very kind of her – I'm sure you agree.'

'Oh yes, Aunt!'

'Your grandmother will pay all your expenses, of course, but still it is a very generous offer on her part.'

Obviously the generosity puzzled Maud. 'What would the lessons be in, ma'am?' Emily asked.

'Dancing, music, French conversation, and Russian.' Maud looked at her sharply. 'Do you understand the implications of this?'

Emily shook her head cautiously.

'It must mean that your grandmama is preparing you for some position in society, which in turn must mean that she intends to settle something on you. It's what I hoped for you when I introduced you to her last year.'

Emily bowed her head.

'I could wish she had gone about it in some other way, but it seems that this is how it must be. Well, Emily, what are your thoughts on the matter? I would not like to make any arrangement that would be wholly repugnant to you.' There was hope in Aunt Maud's voice.

'I should like to go, please, Aunt.'

'To stay with a lady of advanced years and uncertain temper, with whom you have not the slightest connection? It will not be difficult for me to refuse on your behalf, if you feel you would be uncomfortable with the arrangement.'

'Oh no, Aunt. I liked Lady Hamilton very much. I would very much like to go – if you don't mind.'

'Very well,' Maud said with deepening gloom. 'I shall speak to your father again, and if he is fully in accordance, I will undertake the arrangements. It will take some weeks to settle everything, so don't expect to be off tomorrow. There will be plenty of time for you to tell me if you change your mind.'

Maud probably delayed matters as long as she could, but she was dealing with an *intriguante* of far greater skill and experience than herself. So it was no later than the second week of April 1910 that Emily made her first trip to London.

She travelled alone on the train, a privilege for which she guessed she had Lady Hamilton to thank, for Penny sulked dreadfully about it, and insisted on taking her to the station at any rate, to make sure she got on the right train.

'It's not right, a young lady travelling alone!'

'I'll be perfectly all right,' Emily protested. 'I've only got to sit still until the train gets to Paddington. I can't even miss my stop, now can I?'

'Suppose there's no-one there to meet you?'

'There will be. Lady Hamilton's sending a footman.'

'She might forget.'

'She won't. Don't fuss, Penny. I'll be back on Wednesday with nothing but interesting stories to tell you.'

The journey was perfectly uneventful. Emily was a little frightened at Paddington: there were so many people, so much noise, so much steam and smoke and rushing about that she felt bewildered after the long silence and emptiness of the countryside. But it was only a matter of adjusting, she told herself firmly. She picked up her portmanteau and followed the direction of the crowd down to the barrier.

As soon as she stepped through, a man came up to her and said, 'Miss Emily Paget? From Lady Hamilton, miss, to take you home.'

Emily smiled at him. He was a little, thin man with amazingly bent legs, like a lifelong horseman, and a friendly, bright, perky face on which bits of whiskers seemed to be growing almost at random.

He took her portmanteau from her hand and said, 'This way, miss, if you please.'

Emily fell in beside him. 'How did you know it was me?' she asked.

'You got the family looks, miss.'

'Have I?' Emily was pleased.

'Lord, yes, miss. Hamilton writ all over you.'

'But my grandmother says I look like the Kirov side of the family.'

The little man didn't seem put out. 'All faces is a mixture of both sides. Like all horses is a mixture of their dam and their sire.'

He must be a groom, then. 'What's your name?' she asked.

'Lovibond, miss.' A smile lit up his features. 'Silly name, isn't it?'

'It must be nice to have an unusual name. Mine is so very ordinary.'

'It's what you make of it that counts,' Lovibond said comfortably. 'Here we are, miss – her ladyship's Benz.'

Gleaming, dark blue and silver, polished to perilous brightness; luxurious leather upholstery and finest coach-cloth hood; as big as a ship, and as grand and stately: her ladyship's Benz stood waiting for them by the kerb and looked as though it might sing operatic arias if requested.

'A motor car!' Emily breathed. Her aunt and uncle kept only horses. 'I've never been in a motor car.'

Perched high on the fragrant leather seat, Emily felt like a coachman up on a box, but with the long, gleaming bonnet ahead of her instead of the shiny rumps of horses.

'It does feel strange!' she said. 'It's rather like a ship, isn't it – a steamer gliding along?' She glanced at her companion. 'But didn't you used to be a groom? I'm sure you must have worked with horses.'

'That's right, miss.' He seemed pleased. 'I was her ladyship's head man for years and years, and before that I was the General's servant, in the cavalry, miss. That was when I was a young man, o' course. You wouldn't hardly believe how old I am now.'

It didn't seem polite to ask, so Emily left it. 'And then they made you chauffeur?'

He nodded. 'Her ladyship don't keep no horses in Town. Just the Benz, and the Electric Victoria for the Park, and the small Renault. We don't use that much. Her ladyship was meaning to learn to drive it herself. A very sparky lady, her ladyship. But I didn't encourage it, not at her age.'

'Don't you miss the horses? Wouldn't you sooner drive a carriage than a motor car?'

76

'Well, some ways yes, and some ways no. As her ladyship's always saying, you've got to be modern, and go with the times. And at least you don't have the worry of the horses catching cold, waiting about outside opera-houses and balls and such until all hours of the night, which was a cruel thing in the winter.'

'Yes, I do see that,' Emily said. 'But I don't think I'd like to give up horses.'

'The thing is, miss,' Lovibond said sadly, 'that these is cheaper than horses all round. Take a country doctor, miss: he can get a little motor car now that will do about twenty miles an hour quite steady, which he can run for fourpence a mile. Now even a pony and trap will cost him more than that, with the groom and the stabling and everything. Then he's got the problem of tying up every time he gets out to make a call. Can't just leave a horse to stand like you can a motor car. And you know horses, miss – always something ailing 'em. A sprain here, a big hock there, and everything taking time to mend.'

'Yes, I see.'

'Now I don't like it any more than you, but horses is going out, and that's a fact. Look over there, miss – d'you see that? They've even started bringing on motor buses! In a few years' time, you won't see a horse in the streets of London, not if you was to travel from Stepney to Hammersmith and back.'

'Perhaps it's better for the poor horses,' Emily said. 'It can't be very nice for them in London.'

'They're going out everywhere,' Lovibond returned smartly. 'Horses is finished. It'll be all motor cars, wherever you go. I don't mind for myself – I'm an old man, and I've spent my life with horses, and never regretted a day of it. But what about the younger men, men in the prime of life, who don't know nothing but horses? What's to become of them?'

While Emily was grappling with the question they arrived and pulled up at the kerb. 'Here we are, miss, home at last,' he said cheerfully. 'In you go! Don't worry about your bag – I'll have it sent up.'

Lady Hamilton was alone in her sitting-room when Emily was shown in.

'My dear child, I'm so glad you've come.'

Lady Hamilton looked just the same, except that she was in purple instead of black, glittering with spars and beads of crystal, and with ropes of creamy pearls about her neck. Without a hat, she revealed a rigid and old-fashioned coiffure of iron-grey pleats and curls. Her manner, however, was distinctly more affable.

'Was it a pleasant journey?'

'Yes, thank you, ma'am. I love trains,' she added impulsively.

'So do I! Ring the bell, and sit down. We shall have coffee and cake, and talk a little.' Emily sat, and the old lady surveyed her with satisfaction. 'I must tell you I almost despaired at times of getting you here. Your aunt is a bonny fighter. She inspected my house and interviewed my servants. I think she may even have enquired into my past life – which would have given her little satisfaction!'

'Why didn't she want me to come, do you think?' Emily felt emboldened to ask.

'She wants to mould you in her own image – but your grandmother wants you moulded in hers. Yes, come in, Katya! Whereas I, of course, simply wish to be entertained.'

An elderly servant had come in with a tray, which she placed on a small table between them.

'Emily, this is Katya, who is my faithful right hand. You will be seeing a lot of each other. Katya, this is our Miss Emily, as promised.'

Katya surveyed Emily closely, and then smiled. 'She's very like the General,' she pronounced firmly. 'I see him in her eyes.'

'Nonsense,' Lady Hamilton said at once. 'She is all Kirov. She's Count Peter all over again. You're getting old, you don't remember. Go away now.'

Katya smiled and obeyed, dropping a friendly wink on Emily as she passed her. Emily wondered if all Lady Hamilton's servants would be as friendly as the two she had met. It was very different from Bratton, where they were either frosty, like Corde, or grumbled at her, like Jacob.

'You may pour,' Lady Hamilton said to Emily. 'What are you looking at?'

'Oh – the piano. I was thinking how nice it looks uncovered, like a horse when you take off its tack and turn it loose in a field. I've never seen one before. Aunt Maud's has a heavy red and gold cloth over it.'

'I'm afraid poor Maud has absorbed too many English notions. Nakedness, even of a piano, shocks her.' She sipped her coffee, and cocking her head said, 'Do you know what your aunt's piano cover is?'

Emily shook her head. 'I thought it was just a piano cover.'

'Few things are what they seem. In fact, it was the train of her Court dress, from when she was presented. There were strict rules about trains – they had to be a certain length, and very elaborate – and there was always a lot of grumbling about the expense. You only wore them once, and what could you do afterwards with ten feet of embroidered velvet? Maud's, as I remember, was particularly elaborate – sewn all over with pearls and rubies.'

'It must have looked splendid,' Emily said.

'Damned silly, but that's Court rules for you. But then Maud got betrothed just a few weeks after being presented, and proudly announced she was going to make hers into a piano cover for her new husband's drawing-room.' She sighed. 'I don't know where she got such ideas from. I told her that if God had wanted pianos to have covers, he'd have made trees with upholstery.' Emily smiled. 'You haven't been presented, of course?'

'No, ma'am. But I saw the King and Queen at Cowes,' Emily said. 'King Edward looked very kind and jolly. Grandmama said he is the last of the great kings.'

'She's right, for once. Kings used to be grand and mad. My first husband used to say that's what they were for, to take every human attribute to extremes, just to see what happens. But they're getting more ordinary all the time.'

'Is that bad?'

'Only that the time will come when they're so ordinary we'll ask ourselves what they're for. A king should be a monster of virtue or a demigod of depravity. The French had one who rode a bicycle once. They deposed him: even the French couldn't put up with that. But now, my dear, we must discuss your visits to me, and how we are to spend our time.'

'I thought I was to take lessons, ma'am,' Emily said.

'Oh yes, there are to be lessons. I expect you will enjoy them, too. Gravitsky is to teach you singing and musical appreciation. You ought to play the piano, but you're too old now. It's appalling that you have been brought up without music. It would not happen in Russia.'

'I did take piano lessons for a little while at the vicarage, when I was small, but we don't have a piano at The Lodge.'

'You should have had a piano,' Lady Hamilton pronounced, and seemed to feel that was all that needed to be said. 'Then you will go to Maklarova for the dance. She will teach you to walk, sit and

79

curtsey, and give you exercises to make you graceful. You will learn Russian from Princess Volkinsky, and since she does not speak English, that will give you French conversation as well. And finally – though I do not at all understand it, but it is your grandmother's wish – you will learn typewriting.'

Emily heard this with interest and pleasure; it was her grandmother's special gift to her, she thought. Aunt Maud had said nothing about typewriting. Perhaps it was to be kept secret from her. 'One must be modern, ma'am,' she said.

Lady Hamilton shook her head. 'One may go too far. But I suppose she has her reasons. But now, to the rest of our activities.'

'Won't the lessons take up all my time, then?'

'Not a bit. Your lessons will take up the whole morning, and since I am old and need to rest, I am never up in the mornings, which will suit us both. The afternoons and evenings are what matters. The lessons were just an excuse to keep your relatives happy. Your grandmother's real purpose in having you sent to me was to educate you, Emilia, to feed your young mind and expand your untried soul. Conversation and experiences, that's what you shall have. Exhibitions, art galleries, theatres, concerts – all the treasure of civilised society.'

'I am to go to the theatre?' Emily asked, her eyes shining.

'I must warn you, before your excitement overtakes you, that I am not always as you see me now. I suffer from pains in the joints, which come and go. At the moment they are quiet, and I am good-humoured; when the pain is bad, I am ferociously bad-tempered, and I do not care whom I bite. So if I am sometimes cross and cruel to you, you must not mind it. Do you think you can face me in a rage? I should not wish to find you dislike me.'

'I could never think of you with anything but gratitude, ma'am,' Emily said, almost indignantly. 'When you've shown me such kindness, and generosity – '

Emily was interrupted, just before Lady Hamilton would have stopped her anyway, by the door opening. The butler announced visitors, who bounced into the room so closely upon his words that they almost knocked him over.

'Look, look what we've got on! Don't you think it's just extraordinary?' said the tall young woman.

'Hobble skirts! Absolutely the latest go!' said the short young woman. 'What do you think, Lady H?'

'Absolutely hideous,' Lady Hamilton pronounced promptly.

'That's what I've been telling them,' said the godlike young man, 'but they wouldn't listen to me.'

'Oh, we never listen to Basil. He's such an old fogy, isn't he, Syl?'

'You're a fossil person, Basil darling, you know you are.'

'Children,' Lady Hamilton reproved them, 'you are forgetting why I asked you here. You must allow me to present my great-grand-niece – what a dreadful expression that is! Miss Emily Paget: Lady Frances Hope, Miss Sylvia Partridge.'

Lady Frances was the tall one. She shook hands and said, 'How do you do?'

Miss Partridge grinned and said, 'I hope you're undyingly attached to the Cause, Miss Paget, or you'll never survive an hour in this house!'

'And this is my godson, Prince Basil Narishkin,' Lady Hamilton completed the introductions.

Basil had been smiling with delighted recognition for some moments now. When he smiled, Emily noticed with what wits were left her, his eyes, blue as gentian, narrowed into slits in the most endearing way.

'Miss Paget and I have already met,' he said. 'How do you do, Cousin Emily?'

'Cousin? What's this, Basil?' Lady Frances exclaimed. 'Are you and Miss Paget related?'

'Her grandmother is aunt by marriage to my sister Anna,' Basil said. 'So I reckoned that made us cousins of a sort, and Miss Paget was kind enough to allow it.'

'You don't know what you're taking on!' Lady Frances said. 'He's frightfully troublesome even as a friend. As a relative he'll be impossible!'

'Is your father Lord Oxhey, Miss Paget?' Miss Partridge asked, and then frowned, realising that didn't fit. 'No, wait a minute – '

'My father is his brother, Edward Paget,' Emily said. She waited for some adverse reaction: she had no idea how widely her father's ostracism from the family was known.

Basil's eyes widened. 'Good Lord, not Edward Paget the writer?' Emily nodded. 'I had no idea! How absolutely splendid! I've read all his yarns. I practically modelled myself on Lionheart Lomas, you know. And do you have ambitions in that direction yourself?'

Emily, pink with relief and pleasure, had no chance to answer, for Miss Partridge seized on the name.

'Oh, Lionheart Lomas, don't tell me! I was absolutely in love with

81

him when I was fourteen! I used to steal Perry's *BOP* before he had a chance to open it and hide with it in the linen cupboard! And your papa actually writes the stories? What a thrill!'

'Miss Paget means to be a writer herself,' Narishkin said with blithe assumption. 'Isn't that right, Cousin Emily? Don't tell me you haven't got a pet character already seething in your mind!'

Emily smiled as a wicked thought came into her head. 'Well,' she said, as if reluctantly, 'I have started a story about a young woman brought up in retirement in the country, who comes up to London to make her fortune.'

'No! Don't tell me! It sounds riveting!' said Miss Partridge helpfully.

'And on her very first day in London she meets three fascinating people – two ladies and a gentleman – '

'She's roasting you, Syl,' Lady Frances said drily. 'And quite right too, Miss Paget. They've been bouncing all over you. You have to think of them as large puppies,' she explained kindly. 'They mean no harm, but they're full of unrestrained enthusiasm.'

Emily was slightly breathless at her own daring, but it seemed to have done her no harm; and indeed, the Prince was looking at her with keener attention, as though noticing something about her for the first time.

'It's a good thing for the Cause that we are,' Miss Partridge was saying, 'because we've a long way to go yet.'

'We came to tell you, Lady Hamilton,' said Lady Frances, 'that we have some hope the Conciliation Bill will be read towards the end of this month, or early in May, as soon as they've got through the first reading of the Parliament Bill.'

'You have Asquith's promise of a reading?' Lady Hamilton asked, surprised.

'Oh – well, no – not a promise. But Harry said Lytton thought it was likely.'

'Hmph! I shouldn't pin too much faith on that. Lytton's hopes are bound to outrun his judgement in this case.'

'I think we're bewildering Miss Paget,' Narishkin said. 'I'm sure she doesn't understand a word we're saying.'

'I know what the Parliament Bill is, because I've heard my uncle talk about it,' Emily said, glad not to be revealed as entirely ignorant. 'It's to limit the power of the House of Lords to veto bills. He's furious about it.'

'Yes, I suppose he would be,' Narishkin said.

'But I don't know what the Conciliation Bill is. Or the Cause.'

'The Cause is female suffrage – votes for women,' Miss Partridge said promptly. 'Hadn't you twigged?'

Emily was surprised. After all her aunt, uncle and father had said on the subject, she would have expected Suffragettes to be very rough and vulgar people; but these two ladies seemed like normal gentlewomen, and – apart from a certain vigour of conversation, which Emily liked – would have fitted perfectly well into Aunt Maud's drawing-room.

'No, I didn't guess,' she said.

Lady Hamilton looked at her cannily. 'Only one head apiece, and no horns or tails?' she suggested.

'My uncle says women can't have the vote because they think about hats and babies all the time,' Emily began.

'Oh, they always say that. It's such utter rot!' Miss Partridge cried.

'Well, I do know some women who think about clothes all the time,' Emily said reasonably, 'but then I know men who think about nothing but guns and dogs, and no-one says they shouldn't vote.'

'Bravo! I see you are one of us,' said Lady Frances.

'And will this bill you mentioned give the vote to women?' she asked, pleased.

'Not entirely,' Lady Hamilton said. 'The Conciliation Bill is meant to do just that, to conciliate by giving the vote to the women who are causing all the fuss: well-to-do, single women. If it went through, it would enfranchise only those women who occupy premises for which they are responsible – about one million in all.'

'There was a division of opinion about whether we should go ahead with it or not,' Lady Frances explained. 'Some of us thought that it would weaken our cause, and that we should go for full enfranchisement or nothing. And others thought – '

'That anything was better than nothing,' Miss Partridge interrupted. 'And that we could get to our goal just as well by degrees.'

'It doesn't matter,' Lady Hamilton said impatiently. 'It won't go through anyway.'

'Oh, but Lady Hamilton!'

'Asquith and McKenna are violently against the Cause. Churchill loathes women. Grey is politely against it, and Lloyd George only pretends to be for it. He'll vote against this bill, you'll see, and find a reasonable-sounding excuse for doing so.'

'Why are they all so against it?' Emily asked. 'What harm would it do for women to have the vote?'

'I sometimes think men hate us,' Miss Partridge said sadly.

Lady Hamilton shrugged. 'The lower classes don't want it because they think women will take their jobs. The middle classes don't want it because they think women will enforce teetotalism. And the upper classes don't want it because they've arranged life cosily to suit themselves, and they don't want to be disturbed.'

'Oh come, that's too sweeping,' Narishkin protested. 'Surely – '

Lady Hamilton interrupted. 'Talk of something else now, or I shall grow bored. What are these ludicrous gowns you are wearing, girls? You can hardly walk in them.'

'Oh, but that's the idea!' Miss Partridge exclaimed. 'And, I must tell you, there's a perfectly divine sort of fetter made of braid that you can buy to wear round your knees, to stop you taking big steps! You'd simply die!'

'Very likely I would,' said Lady Hamilton grimly. 'But it's not the first ridiculous fashion I've seen, and it won't be the last. I remember when hoops first came in . . . ' The conversation went off in other directions.

As she lay in bed that night, Emily's mind was seething with new thoughts and impressions. She liked Lady Frances and Miss Partridge, and was glad to learn from Lady Hamilton that she would be seeing a lot of them, that they had been invited to take part in the scheme of educating Emily. She had enjoyed every moment of the lively conversation that had gone on while they were there, and had even had a share in it. It was a wonderful experience to be able to join in without being frowned at, or snubbed, or withered.

Best of all was meeting Basil again. Lady Hamilton had not explained his presence, but as he was her godson, it was perhaps not surprising he had come calling. From the way they all spoke to each other, it was plain that he spent a lot of time in the company of the two young ladies, so perhaps, she thought with cautious hope, that meant she would see a lot of him, too.

She wriggled a little lower in bed, and brought his image before her mind. He was just as beautiful as she remembered him; and although he still obviously thought of her as a child, he had spoken quite a lot to her. He must *like* her, she concluded after careful consideration, or he wouldn't have bothered. Of course, it could never come to anything more than that, she didn't mean to fool herself; but she felt sure he liked her, and that was something. That was a lot!

Chapter Six

On the morning of her sixteenth birthday, Emily was up early, and ready to go half an hour before the time for the arrival of the brake which now took her to the station.

'I should have thought you'd stay home on your birthday,' Penny said, dusting the hall table with offended vigour. 'We see little enough of you. First it was two days a week, now three – '

'But Pen, I mustn't miss my lessons. And Lady Hamilton's giving a dinner especially for me, and afterwards, though it won't be a regular ball, there'll be dancing with a proper orchestra.'

'What's that?' Edward asked, coming downstairs. 'Who's dancing?'

'We are, at Lady Hamilton's, Papa. It's my birthday.'

'That's not until May, surely?'

'It is May. It's May the 7th today,' Emily said patiently.

'Good Lord, how time flies! Is my breakfast ready, Penny?'

'Yes, sir. I'll fetch in the toast.'

Edward moved towards the dining-room, and paused only to look back and say, 'Oh, many happy returns, by the way.'

'Thank you,' Emily said, to his retreating back.

She refused to feel cast down. When had her father ever remembered her birthday? And look what she had to look forward to today: Katya was going to put her hair up, and she would sit down to dinner – not only a proper grown-up dinner, but one at which she would be guest of honour. Basil would be there, and afterwards when the dancing started, she couldn't believe he wouldn't ask her to dance at least once, seeing it was her birthday. To dance with Basil Narishkin! It would be utter, utter heaven!

The time came and went, and there was no sign of her transport. Emily went to the front door and stared anxiously up the track.

'Don't stand there gawping like a kitchen maid,' Penny said, crossing the hall with the coffee-pot. 'It won't come faster for you watching.'

'I shall miss the train,' Emily complained.

'Then you'll miss it,' Penny said unhelpfully.

'But I'll be late for my lessons. I think I'd better start walking.'

'You'll do nothing of the sort! What kind of a state do you think you'd arrive in? Your aunt will send the brake when it suits her. And if she doesn't, you must learn to accept disappointments like a lady.'

Emily didn't argue. She knew why Penny was so scratchy. Not only was she peeved that Emily would not be there for her usual birthday tea, but she didn't approve of Lady Hamilton. Emily had found out from her cousins, who had wheedled it out of Nanny, that Aunt Maud had said that Lady Hamilton was an adulteress: she had run away from her first husband to marry the General. Since Penny and Nanny were great friends, the judgement was bound to have been passed on.

'Oh, here it is at last!' Emily's voice lifted with joy and relief at the sight of a carriage coming from the house. Penny came out from the kitchen to join her.

'That isn't the brake.'

'No. How odd! They've sent the barouche for me.'

A few more moments, and the carriage was close enough to see that it was not empty. 'It's my aunt and uncle!' Emily exclaimed.

What on earth could be bringing them to The Lodge? They would never come there to visit. If they wanted to see Edward or Emily, they would send for them to the house.

'What've you been up to?' Penny asked in an awful voice.

'Nothing,' Emily said at once, but her cheeks coloured with automatic guilt. Such a State call could hardly presage anything pleasant. The carriage pulled up in front of them, and Penny sank in a reverential curtsey.

Aunt Maud leaned out just enough to be able to fix Emily with a gimlet eye. 'I have come to tell you, Emily, that you will not be going to London today.'

Emily's stomach fell away from her in disappointment and apprehension. She had been discovered in some sin, then.

'Mrs Pennistone, go and get the key to the gate, if you please. It will save time if we go out this way,' Aunt Maud continued. Penny bobbed and scuttled off.

'Has – has something happened, Aunt?' Emily asked.

The grave eyes looked through and past her. Now Emily saw that her aunt was upset, shocked perhaps, but it was sorrow rather than anger. 'We have had a telephone call from Lord Knollys. The King died just before midnight last night.'

Emily could think of nothing to say. King Edward had been such a giant figure, it was impossible to think of his not being there. It was like being told that the sun wasn't going to come up tomorrow.

'Your uncle and I must go up to Town at once. You, of course, will stay quietly here during the period of deep mourning.'

Emily wanted to ask how long that was, but Lord Westinghouse looked across his wife at her, and seeing his face, Emily remembered that he had been a personal friend of His Majesty. The question didn't seem very tactful.

'Better tell your father, Emily,' he said.

Deep mourning, it seemed, lasted only for a month, but the period of Court mourning was a whole year, during which all Court functions and many social events would be cancelled or severely curtailed. When mourning ended there would be the coronation of the new king, George V, which would probably take place in June or July of 1911. Emily had no idea how long she would be kept at home. She tormented herself with the worst possible scenario: that Aunt Maud, who disapproved of the whole London scheme, would use the excuse to keep Emily at home until the autumn after next.

The month without her trips to London halted by. Emily's only contact with her lost and longed-for world lay in reading the newspapers, which she devoured from cover to cover every day, reading even the advertisements with painful delight.

There was a great deal in them about the late King's lying-in-state, the curious coincidence that Halley's Comet had passed over on the day after his death, and what it might mean for the world at large. There were pages about the funeral, its pomp and splendour, its expense: the bill for the funeral banquet alone came to £4,644. Eight kings and two emperors attended the obsequies. King Edward's pet terrier, Caesar, was given a place in the procession, and the Emperor of Germany said afterwards that he had done many things in his life, but had never before been obliged to yield precedence to a dog.

There were pages, too, about the new King and Princess May – who was to be called Queen Mary – praising his seriousness and goodness and their simple way of life. There was quite a lot, particularly in the *Servant's Delight*, about the royal children – Edward, Albert, Mary, Henry, George and John – and how handsome, good and clever they were, and how simply they had been brought up,

87

just like anyone else's children. Emily thought this was a strange thing for the paper to be pleased about.

It seemed, however, that King Edward's death might bring some benefit to the Cause. From genuine national feeling, the two sides of the House agreed to drop any contentious matters for the time being, and to hold a conference during the summer to try to settle their differences over the Parliament Bill. As this bill had been occupying their whole time since the session began, it meant that there was now plenty of parliamentary time for other matters, and the Conciliation Bill was at last put down for its first reading on the 14th of June.

Emily hoped she might be in London by then, to hear about it at first hand; but fate decreed otherwise. At the beginning of June there was an outbreak of measles in Tom's house at school and he was sent home. He appeared to be quite healthy, but the disease was merely incubating in him, and he passed it meanwhile to his sisters. All four children went down with it simultaneously, and the whole top floor of the Big House was turned over to suffering, spots, flannel jackets, friar's balsam, Lysol, and barley water.

Emily could not distance herself from it all, though she knew that any contact with the sufferers would place her in quarantine and delay her return to London. Still, Nanny, Mamzelle and the maids had enough to do with the nursing, feeding and washing of the patients, without trying to entertain them out of their misery. Emily knew where her duty lay. For two weeks she read aloud, told stories, set puzzles, and simply chatted with the hot, miserable, itching children.

Tom and Victoria quickly fought their way back to health, and Lexy, who was less robust, fortunately had only a light attack. It was otherwise with little Maudie. She was very sick indeed, and needed careful nursing. For a time there was talk of serious after-effects: deafness, and possibly damage to the heart. Emily wasn't even allowed to see her – she had to be kept completely quiet.

At last she began to recover; but on the day that Tom was first allowed out of bed, she suffered a relapse so serious that a telephone call was put through to St Auben House. His lordship could not be contacted, but Maud set forth within a few hours. Before she reached the bedside, Maudie was dead.

*

Emily had known great generosity from her aunt, and had been grateful, but she had never been able to feel affection for her, nor supposed it would have been welcomed. But seeing the depths of Maud's grief over her youngest child's death, Emily longed for some way to offer love or comfort. It was impossible, of course: Maud stricken was even more inaccessible than Maud in normal spirits. She withdrew into herself, and only her silence and her haunted eyes told what she was suffering.

When the funeral was over Lord Westinghouse went immediately back to Town, but Maud remained at Bratton, shutting herself up alone in the Peacock Room day after day, seeing no-one, and hardly ever stirring out of the house. It was a trying time for everyone, particularly for the cousins, pulled down by their recent sickness and bewildered over the death of Maudie. Over them their mother's grief hung like a brooding presence, making even the most innocent laughter seem an outrage. Emily devoted her time to entertaining and comforting them, for which she got nods of praise from Nanny and grateful looks from Mamzelle. For her part, she was glad to feel that the time of her exile was not wasted, for there was no hint from the Big House as to when she might be allowed to go back to London.

Then, one day in July, she was summoned quite unexpectedly to the Peacock Room. It smelled of gloom and dust and stale grief, and was almost dark, for the black mourning drapes – put up for the King and left up for Maudie – were pulled almost closed against the sunlight. The pictures and looking-glasses were covered with gauze, the chimney cloth and piano cover had been changed for black velvet, and there were black feathers instead of flowers in the vases.

On a table in the corner a photograph of Maudie in a silver frame was bound with black satin ribbon, with a rosette at each corner. Almost invisible inside this drab decoration, the cheerful, chubby face beamed out of a lost and sunnier past which seemed emphatically to have nothing to do with this theatrical display of mourning.

Aunt Maud was sitting in her accustomed chair, as rigidly straight-backed as always: grief could not override deportment. She was all in black – the drab black of deep mourning, unornamented, with a black lace cap over her hair. Emily felt – though uneasy with herself for thinking it – that all this was out of proportion to what she could believe Maud had ever felt for a child whom she had hardly ever seen. Her aunt's face was thinner than when she had last seen her six weeks ago at Maudie's funeral, but when she glanced into it cautiously, it seemed to Emily that there was almost more anger than unhappiness. It was as if Maud were grieving wilfully, to spite herself.

Having presented herself, Emily waited in vain to be noticed. Eventually she said gently, 'You sent for me, ma'am?'

'Yes,' Maud said at once, impatiently, as though Emily were being importunate. There was another long silence, and then she said abruptly, 'Do you wish to resume your visits to London?'

Emily wasn't sure how to respond. It seemed callous, in these surroundings, to say yes. 'Well, Aunt, if I can be useful here in any way, of course I shouldn't want to go. My cousins – '

'Don't concern yourself on their behalf. I employ staff to look after my children. Do you imagine they can't manage without you?'

'Oh! No – I – '

'I am here, now, to supervise their regime. St Auben will be going back to school, of course, and as to the girls – I have plans for them. They will have little leisure for playing with you in future, so you may dismiss them from your mind.'

Emily was used enough to the light by now to be able to discern that her aunt was looking at her with something close to dislike.

'Have I offended you, Aunt?' she asked anxiously.

'How could *you* offend *me*?' Maud said witheringly. 'The best thing you can do is to resume your lessons, and do what you can to overcome the disadvantages of your birth by learning how to behave in polite society and making as many of the right sort of friends as possible. It's a pity your grandmother chose Lady Hamilton for your chaperone: you cannot be too careful with whom you associate, considering who and what your mother was.'

Emily felt as though her face had been slapped. Her aunt had never spoken to her like this before, so angrily and contemptuously, about something for which Emily could hardly be blamed. Tears and resentment fought for control of her voice. 'Lady Hamilton has been very kind to me, ma'am,' she managed to say.

Maud cut her off with a sharp sound almost like a laugh. 'Kind? You simpleton, she's been paid very well by your grandmother for having you in her house. That's why she's so anxious to have you back, of course. Did I mention that she has written to me to ask when you'll be returning?' Emily shook her head in dumb misery. 'Yes, a very impertinent letter, I would call it, pressing me to let you resume your lessons. She even suggests I allow you to remain the whole week with her, and come home only for Saturday-to-Mondays.'

90

Emily felt cornered and baited. She searched for something safe to say. 'I don't want to do anything you don't approve of, ma'am. I never meant to upset you.'

She saw her aunt take a breath to reply, and then let it out. The muscles of her face seemed to tremble, and she lifted her hands a little from her lap, as though some movement just then were essential. Then she said in a different voice, not so much more gentle as less harsh, 'It will be better for you to go.'

She said nothing more, and after a moment there seemed nothing for Emily to do but to curtsey and leave. A year ago – before Cowes and her grandmother and London – the interview would have reduced her to uncomprehending tears; but she was not the same Emily now, and what she felt most of all was a terrible pity for the stricken woman, and a longing to communicate in some way. At the door she hesitated, but she could think of nothing to say except, 'I'm sorry.'

There was no movement in the gloom, and she was almost out of the door when she heard her aunt say very quietly, 'It isn't your fault.'

Lady Frances Hope, Miss Partridge, and Miss Paget stood in the corner of a flat field in Buckinghamshire watching Lady Hamilton's Benz bump slowly round the perimeter. Lovibond sat very upright in the front nearside seat, his right hand hovering near the brake lever. In the driver's seat, holding on for dear life to the steering-wheel over which she was only just able to see, was the diminutive figure of Miss Chitterley.

Miss Chitterley was a new member of their circle, the daughter of a retired colonel of the Lancers who was one of Lady Hamilton's numerous army acquaintances. She was also a member of the middle classes which Aunt Maud so anathematised, and it was a sign of Emily's depravity that she had actually been to tea with the Chitterleys in their house in Kensington, and had witnessed nothing to offend her sensibilities.

'She's doing awfully well,' Miss Partridge said wistfully. 'Much better than I did first go.'

'It's very hard to concentrate on your hands and your feet at the same time, until you get used to it,' Emily said.

'Oh, but you were terrific, Emily!' Lady Frances said. 'You took to it like a duck to water. Not like me, driving into the hedge all the time. Poor old Lovibond kept asking me if I thought I was a sparrow.'

'I must say, it's frightfully sporting of Lady Hamilton to let us learn in her car,' said Sylvia.

'The real hero is Lovibond,' Frances said. 'He's the one who has to clean the mud off when we've finished.'

'I wonder if I could get a job as a chauffeur,' Emily said. A Miss Aileen Preston had recently become the first woman to qualify for the Automobile Association's Certificate in Driving, and had been taken on as chauffeur by Mrs Pankhurst.

'It'd be more fun than being a typewriter,' Sylvia said. They all knew – and approved – of Emily's ultimate ambition to earn her own living.

'Aunt Maud would have forty thousand fits. She'd have half of them if she even knew I'd been learning to drive a car. Besides, who'd employ me? There aren't any more like Mrs P!'

'An American,' Frances said promptly. 'They're terribly modern about women.'

'Mrs P says they think it's shocking the way we're treated over here,' Emily said. 'In America they take women seriously.'

'While over here they just laugh at us.'

'Not all of them,' said Sylvia. Last November her fiancé had asked to be released from their engagement following the Suffragette demonstration which had ended in such terrible violence that it had been dubbed 'Black Friday'. He claimed the newspaper publicity was harming his career – despite the fact that the violence had all been directed towards the women, who had simply been marching peaceably; and the even more pertinent fact that Sylvia had not been present.

'Darling Syl, don't be sad about David,' Frances said. 'If he could be so arbitrary and unjust he wasn't the man for you anyway. You're better off without him.'

'I know, but it's hateful to be rejected,' Sylvia said. 'Mostly I'd like to wring his neck.'

'It's been a horrid winter all round, what with all the strikes and the riots in South Wales and everything,' Emily said.

'And with the never-ending trouble over the Parliament Bill, it doesn't look as though the Conciliation Bill will ever get a reading,' Sylvia added.

'In fact, if we didn't have the Coronation to look forward to, we might as well all cut our throats,' Frances finished for them, to make them laugh.

The Benz was coming towards them, and Sylvia said, 'I say, do look at Angela – just like Papa's retriever on a hot day! I hope she doesn't go over a bump, or she'll bite that tongue off!'

The car came to a rather uncertain halt a little way off, and they walked up to congratulate the driver, who was panting from having held her breath most of the way round the field.

'Jolly good, Angela!'

'You did better than me the first time!'

'It isn't as difficult as I thought it would be.' Angela's fair face was pink as a marshmallow, and wisps of her ash-blonde hair stuck to her damp forehead.

'Don't you think she was wonderful?' Sylvia prompted Lovibond. Angela was their 'baby', and they all conspired to bolster her confidence.

'Very fair indeed, miss,' Lovibond said generously, 'to say this is a big, heavy motor car, not really a lady's vehicle at all.'

'Why didn't you teach us in the Renault, then?' Emily asked.

'Ah, I've got a reason for that, Miss Emily,' Lovibond said cunningly. 'If you can drive a motor car like this Benz, you'll be able to drive anything; but say I'd started you on the Renault, you'd have never made the change upwards, see what I mean?'

'You're wonderfully illogical! You teach us to drive a motor car you think is too heavy for a woman, but you won't teach us to change the wheel!'

'That's different,' said Lovibond with obvious sincerity. 'Changing wheels is not for ladies. You'd get yourselves all mucky.'

'Heaven help us if we ever drive ourselves out and have a puncture miles from anywhere!' Frances said.

'You'd have to wait for a gentleman to come along,' Lovibond said inexorably. 'Or better still, take one with you. Is it back to London now, m'lady?'

'No, we're going to have tea with my mother first, at Greenlands,' Lady Frances said.

'The big question, Mummy, is what's going to happen to Emily this year,' said Lady Frances, handing her mother's cup.

Lady Ongar reclined on a day-bed, with a pretty Persian silk shawl over her legs. A bad fall while out hunting ten years previously had

93

put an end for ever to both riding and walking, and she now lived permanently on the ground floor of the small, pleasant country villa at Chalfont which her lord had originally bought for spending Saturday-to-Mondays while the House was in session.

Frances visited her often, and brought as many of her friends as she could to enliven her mother's tedium. Since Lady Ongar's views grew more liberal the longer she was confined to the sofa, it was not difficult to persuade the friends to come.

'Because you see, she's seventeen in May,' Frances went on, 'and she ought to be coming out, but who's to bring her?'

'If she's not out by June, she won't be able to go to all the marvellous balls and parties there are bound to be for the Coronation,' Sylvia added pertinently.

'Are there no plans to bring you out, then, Emily?' Lady Ongar asked. 'I know there won't be any presentations this Season, but that isn't essential.'

'No-one's said anything, and there isn't anyone I can ask,' Emily said. 'Papa would simply say it was Aunt Maud's business, and I never see Aunt Maud now.'

'But surely you could make an appointment to see her, Emily dear?' Lady Ongar said.

'If it were business or something serious, it would be different; but when someone's grieving over a lost child, how can you disturb them about something like this?' said Emily helplessly.

'My dear, are you sure she's so very grief-stricken?' Lady Ongar asked carefully. 'Could there not be some other reason for her withdrawal from society?'

'I can't think what else it could be,' Emily said. 'It only started when Maudie died.'

'Something else may have happened at about the same time,' Lady Ongar suggested.

'I suppose it might,' Emily said doubtfully. 'I can't think of anything. And what else could account for the way she's changed towards my cousins?'

Since last September, Aunt Maud had instituted a rigorous time-table of lessons for Lexy and Victoria which no-one was allowed to interrupt. Emily could see her cousins only by arrangement and outside their hours of schooling, which meant in practice once a week on Saturday afternoons, when they usually went riding together. As a result, Emily hardly ever entered the Big House at all.

'It's awful now,' Lexy had complained to Emily recently. 'Tom spends all his holidays with schoolfriends, and Vick and I are treated like heathen slaves, practically locked up and starved.'

'Oh come,' Emily protested. 'It can't be that bad.'

'You don't know, Em,' Victoria said earnestly. 'We used to feel sorry for you, but look how things have turned around. You're gadding about in London every week, and we're shut up on the top floor like Rapunzel and never seeing anyone.'

'Your lessons must be interesting, though?'

Lexy made a face. 'We don't want to be educated. I don't know what's come over Mama. She used to hate blue-stockings worse than mice. And fancy sending away Mamzelle! It isn't fair. She let us do just as we pleased, and now we've got Macbeth's three witches going on at us all day, with history and geography and I don't know what else!'

'What a gang of plug-uglies!' Lexy said. 'You'd think she deliberately chose the oldest, plainest governesses she could find. At least Mamzelle was nice to look at.'

'Does it matter what they look like, if they're well educated?'

'If Mama wants us to be educated,' Victoria said resentfully, 'she might at least send us away to school.'

'Yes, we long for Cheltenham,' Lexy agreed. 'At least there we'd have other girls to talk to. And dormitory feasts and house matches and merry japes, whatever they are. Such bliss – just like your pa's stories!'

'You know your mama thinks boarding schools are for middle-class girls,' Emily said.

'She used to think education was only for middle-class girls,' Lexy pointed out. 'It's my belief she's gone mad, you know. And I suppose the next thing you'll get married and go away, and then we'll never see another human soul for the rest of our lives.'

'We'll never even be missed, up in the attics where no-one ever comes. Our skeletons will be found here in hundreds of years' time, huddled together in a dusty corner,' Victoria added with gloomy relish.

The children's nonsense might make her smile, but Emily was afraid they might be right about Aunt Maud. It did seem as though she must be deranged with grief, for why else should she give up London and smart society, and shut herself up at Bratton, dedicating herself to her daughters in what she would previously have considered a vulgar and unnecessary way? But if it was madness, it made it doubly impossible for Emily to importune her for her own selfish purposes.

'Couldn't someone else bring Emily out, Lady Ongar?' Angela asked in her breathless, eager way. 'Does it have to be her aunt?'

'I say, what about Lady Hamilton?' Sylvia said. 'I'm sure she wouldn't mind.'

'My dear child, I don't think Lady Hamilton would be up to it,' Lady Ongar said. 'However lively her mind is, she must be over seventy, and sponsoring a young girl through a whole Season is enormously tiring. Besides, who is to pay for it?'

Sylvia looked crestfallen. 'Oh, is it very expensive, then? I thought if there were no presentation − ?'

'Even without the expense of a Court dress, there'd have to be *some* new clothes, and at least one ball. You can't go to everyone else's without having one yourself.'

'I suppose so,' Sylvia said. 'I hadn't thought of that.'

'Wouldn't it be possible for someone to approach Lady Westinghouse on Emily's behalf, Mummy?' Frances asked hopefully. 'Someone of her own generation?'

Lady Ongar smiled. 'If you're thinking of me, my darling, I can only tell you that much as I would like to help Emily, it would be a piece of impertinence on my part which Lady Westinghouse would have every right to take exception to.'

'Oh, no, please,' Emily said, hastily, 'I wouldn't dream of it. Anyway, I don't care about the *coming* out, I just want to *be* out.'

'The proper approach, I think,' Lady Ongar went on, 'would be for Emily to consult Lady Hamilton − since she is standing more or less *in loco parentis*, Emily dear, while you're in London − and for Lady Hamilton to decide whether to approach your father or your aunt.'

Emily looked doubtful. 'Wouldn't it seem − well, very *coming* of me, ma'am?'

Lady Ongar smiled. 'I think Lady Hamilton is quite capable of telling you if she thinks your request is unreasonable.'

'Oh Mummy,' Frances laughed, 'if that's supposed to be a comforting thought − !'

Emily did not raise the matter with Lady Hamilton. On the one hand, despite Lady Ongar's comment, she did not like to put Lady Hamilton in a position where she might feel obliged to do something she didn't want to; and on the other, she still felt tender about intruding on Aunt Maud's grief, even through the medium of another.

Life was exciting enough as it was. Her music lessons had been discontinued, to the common relief of both her and Gravitsky, who had given lessons to Chaliapin and Larinkov and had only been persuaded to take on Emily through his old friendship with her grandmother.

But she still had two dance lessons every week with Madame, which Angela Chitterley now also attended. Emily liked Angela, and was grateful to her for being eight months younger, three years less sophisticated and five years shyer. Since Angela had joined her dancing class, Emily felt much more graceful and accomplished. Despite being as small and slight as Madame herself, Angela had surprisingly little control over her body. Madame had always made Emily, who at five feet four was five inches taller than her teacher, feel like a rogue elephant; but next to Angela she moved like a feather drifting in the breeze.

The Russian and French lessons with Princess Volkinsky also continued, though they had become more like social occasions. Emily went twice a week to the Princess's tiny apartment in Covent Garden, and one of the delights was that she was allowed to walk there, instead of being driven in the motor car. Katya accompanied her, for Lady Hamilton would not have permitted Emily to go anywhere alone, but Emily enjoyed talking to Katya, who had an independent mind and a novel way of looking at most things.

At the apartment, the Princess would begin formally enough by looking over Emily's exercises from the previous lesson, or testing her on new vocabulary, while Katya sat in a corner sewing and pretending to be the perfect servant. But no Russian could go very long without tea, and as soon as the samovar was wheeled out the atmosphere changed, for with tea there must be conversation. Before long the three of them would be deep in animated chat in a mixture of Russian, English and French, usually ending up with an argument between Katya and the Princess about someone of whom Emily had never heard.

But her lessons were no more than the surface excuse for her presence in London. The rest of the time she was meeting people and having fun. With Lady Hamilton, or more often a group of friends, with perhaps a young married woman as a chaperone, she went to exhibitions, talks, art galleries and museums; to the zoo, to

Kew Gardens, to the Crystal Palace; to tea at each other's houses, or at the Ritz or Fortnum's.

In the evenings she was taken to theatres, concerts, operas and ballets, or she stayed at home with Lady Hamilton and people came to visit them. Lady Hamilton had acquaintances from many different interests within Society, and the conversation was always absorbing, if it was sometimes difficult to follow.

In fact, Emily told herself, there was little that being 'out' would add to her life. She could not go to balls, or dine out formally, or go to receptions or evening parties at other people's houses, that was all. If it weren't for Basil Narishkin, she wouldn't even want to do those things; but in any case, Basil had been in Russia all winter, and who knew when he would be returning?

And if he did return, she went on being stern with herself, what difference could that make to her? It was common knowledge, wasn't it, that he and Frances Hope were all but engaged? To allow herself to harbour any wishes in that direction, simply because Basil and Frances treated each other in public with the calm, detached friendliness of distant cousins, was not only foolish, it was probably wicked.

Emily had thus talked herself back into a state of contentment when Lady Hamilton, coming down to luncheon one day in April 1911, said, 'I have been in communication with your grandmother, Emily, about your coming out. She believes there is no benefit in waiting another year, and I must say I agree with her.'

'My – but – am I to come out, then, ma'am?' Emily said stupidly.

'Of course you are. How else do you propose to take your place in Society?'

Emily tried to assemble her words. 'As I hadn't heard anything from Aunt Maud, ma'am, I thought – that is, I didn't think – '

Lady Hamilton nodded briskly. 'Your grandmother understands the situation. She has asked me to sponsor you on her behalf. I shall write to your aunt and offer to undertake it. Of course, if she does not agree, that will be an end to it, but I can't imagine she'll object. Your grandmother's wishes have carried before.'

'It's most awfully good of you,' Emily said, remembering the conversation with Lady Ongar.

Lady Hamilton cocked her head to the tone of voice. 'Well? What is your difficulty?'

Emily swallowed. 'The trouble to you, ma'am. And – and the expense!'

'My dear child, it won't be the slightest expense to me. Surely you know your grandmother pays for everything?'

'Well, Aunt Maud did say – ' Emily began, blushing to remember her aunt's suggestion that Lady Hamilton made a profit out of her.

'I'm sure she did,' Lady Hamilton said cynically. 'As to the trouble, I assure you I'm far too selfish to put myself out. I shall give a ball for you for your birthday, and take you to one or two important functions. For the rest, there are plenty of respectable young matrons who will be happy to escort you on my behalf. Now, have you any more objections?'

'No, ma'am. I'm very grateful – '

'No need for that,' Lady Hamilton said briskly. 'I shall write to Lady Westinghouse today – and to your father, of course. I suppose I shall have to ask him to be present, but with any luck at all he'll refuse.'

Emily would have liked an explanation of this last, intriguing comment, but on second thoughts, remembering how little respect Lady Hamilton had for Edward, decided she might not like the answer.

Emily's ball took place on the last day of May. The scale and extent of the preparations necessary astonished Emily, who had foolishly thought that you just sent out invitations and hired a band. As the days passed and the whole household – it sometimes seemed the whole world – was sucked into the maelstrom, she began to feel quite sick at the thought of causing everyone so much trouble.

She didn't see Aunt Maud's reply to Lady Hamilton, but 'She says you may go to the devil as far as she's concerned', was Lady Hamilton's précis.

Emily took this to be a fairly free translation, especially when it emerged that Aunt Maud had said the ball should take place at St Auben House (Lady Hamilton had no ballroom, and the alternative was a hired house) and that the staff there would be placed fully at their disposal.

It seemed to Emily a kind gesture, and a sign that Aunt Maud, though indisposed by grief to take an active part, was nevertheless lending her countenance to the occasion. She couldn't understand why Lady Hamilton viewed St Auben House as a liability rather than a benefit.

It seemed to involve a great deal of work to make the house

presentable by Lady Hamilton's standards. A small army of extra servants was hired to clean it to within an inch of its life. A special man came in to spend a whole day in the ballroom, mysteriously bouncing on the tips of his toes at various points all over the floor, before the French-chalkers could begin. The orchestra was booked, a carpenter came in to build a larger dais for them, and a man came to tune the drops on the five great chandeliers so that they shouldn't ring when the music played.

Flowers had to be bought and a small Kew Gardens of shrubs hired. The red carpet and striped awning for the front were got out of store, sighed over and steam-cleaned. Lady Hamilton summoned a very senior policeman to discuss traffic and the management of crowds, and the editors of several newspapers were sent guest lists. The supper was ordered from Gunter's, but a note came from Lord Westinghouse to say that he was providing the champagne.

'Guilty conscience,' Lady Hamilton said curtly and inexplicably when she read it.

And all the time invitations were going out and replies coming in, and Lady Hamilton was spending hours on the telephone talking to potential guests. This last disturbed Emily, who got the notion that her sponsor was having to persuade people to come because she, Emily, was a nobody.

But when she mentioned it tentatively to Frances, Frances said, 'It's a popular date. There are three other big things going on on the same night that I know about, so I suppose she's making sure everyone comes to your ball rather than any of the others.'

All other considerations, however, were secondary to The Dress. It began with an impromptu consultation between Lady Hamilton, Emily, and Princess Volkinsky.

'White, of course, is the colour for debutantes,' the Princess said. 'White or pink – young innocence! One likes to see it, though it does not last long.'

'Not white,' Lady Hamilton said firmly. 'Not yet. In two years, perhaps three, she will look breathtaking in white. We must save the effect.'

'With her colouring – tawny hair and eyes – she should wear yellow,' the Princess said thoughtfully, 'but for a *début*? I don't know.'

Lady Hamilton lifted a hand. 'No, I have it! I see it! Look at her, Sonya, what do you see? An English maiden reared in a gloomy English mansion? Not a bit! Look at those eyes, those cheekbones

– there's hardly a drop of English blood in her! We'll give 'em the East, with a vengeance! Not yellow, my dear friend: she shall be dressed in *gold*!'

Princess Volkinsky clapped her hands in delight, spilling tea on her lap and making all her bracelets ring. 'Milochka, you are a genius! Yes! Present her in gold, and let them say what they like!'

Let them say what they like. It was by gathering hints like that, overhearing the tail-ends of servants' conversations which stopped when she entered the room, and the odd word or two Lady Hamilton let drop when she was out of temper, that Emily finally worked out why St Auben House was a liability, and why Lady Hamilton had to bolster her invitations with personal calls.

Emily was the granddaughter of an earl, and her connections were impeccable, but she was the daughter of a *mésalliance*. In English the expression 'ballet girl' was almost a euphemism for prostitute, and she guessed that in asking Lady Hamilton to sponsor her, her grandmother had been trying to focus attention as far away from Emily's parentage as possible.

Aunt Maud had torpedoed the plan by insisting on St Auben House, and then not being there herself. It made the debut look like a patched-up business. The Westinghouses couldn't quite bring themselves to disown the girl, people would say, but on the other hand they wouldn't present her themselves.

Defiance, Emily thought, was the order of the day. She believed the idea of dressing her in gold had something to do with defiance, but as the gown was created around her by two strange little Russian ladies – who made for Lady Hamilton and whom she treated with almost unique deference – it became its own justification.

The gown was of plain gold-coloured satin, with a low neckline, and straight sleeves to the elbow, ending in a gold silk fringe. Over this was a loose overskirt of almost transparent gold net, with a scalloped border of beading to give it weight and movement; the bodice was draped with soft folds of chiffon like a luminous cloud.

The effect was dramatic, and yet feminine. Looking at herself in the mirror, Emily thought how unlike her plain English name she looked. *Transformation scene*, she thought. It was not Cinderella who would go to the ball, but Princess Aurora.

Her hair was dressed in the style of that season, with a broad headband covering the front of the head, and the hair drawn into a soft chignon behind. Emily's band was of beaded gold cloth, which completed the effect by looking a little like a crown.

'And now', Lady Hamilton said, when they were about to go down and receive their guests, 'there is nothing English about you at all. No-one will make any connections. Are you nervous?'

Emily nodded. She was so nervous she was feeling sick, and was afraid to open her mouth to say so in case she was.

Lady Hamilton nodded briskly as though she understood all that. 'It does no harm. You have a very handsome pallor. And I assure you you will not actually *be* sick – one never is.'

Emily managed a flicker of a smile.

When they went downstairs, it seemed as though someone had arrived before time, for a footman met them looking baffled and embarrassed. 'I beg your pardon, my lady . . . '

Following him, correctly dressed in evening clothes, was Emily's father.

'This fellow didn't want to let me in because I didn't have an invitation,' he said as soon as he saw Lady Hamilton, frozen on the stairs with annoyance. Then he looked properly at Emily, realised who she was, and stared as though he'd been hit on the head.

'Emily,' he said. 'Emily. You look – you look – ' And he lifted his hands, palm upwards, as if to show her they were empty of vocabulary.

Emily tried to smile, aware of a bristling current of indignation and dislike coming off Lady Hamilton in waves. 'Papa. It's nice of you to come.'

'I know I wasn't going to, but at the last moment I thought I really ought to,' he said slowly. 'I'm glad now that I did.'

Lady Hamilton sighed like an exasperated steam engine. 'Damn you, Edward. Why can't you make up your mind to be thoroughly worthless, so that everyone knows where they stand? Well, since you are here, I shall have to make the best of it. But for God's sake be careful what you say. In fact, it's safer if you say nothing. Just nod and smile and try to look like an imbecile. Remember, if you can, that this is Emily's evening. Don't spoil it for her.'

Edward looked again at his transformed daughter, and smiled in a way that Emily had never seen before, a smile without shadows or sub-plot or reservations. 'I wouldn't do that,' he said.

Chapter Seven

It was a hot summer, dominated by the constitutional struggle between the Liberals and the Lords embodied in the Parliament Bill. Even Emily, absorbed in the excitements and the demanding schedule of a debutante, could not help being aware of the momentousness of what was going on, especially as so many of her daily companions were the children or grandchildren of peers.

'I don't understand what it's all about,' Angela Chitterley confessed to Emily one day as they were dressing for a ball together. Since Kensington was so very far from the centre of the universe, she was sometimes asked to spend the day with Emily when they were invited to the same evening function. 'I suppose it's because Daddy isn't a lord or anything, otherwise I expect Mummy would have explained it to me. Everybody seems to think it's frightfully important.'

Emily remembered what Uncle Westie had said about the flow of history. 'It's an inevitable step on the road to democracy,' she said, inspecting her silk stockings. Dancing was very hard on the heels of them, and Emily was a vigorous dancer. 'I could explain it to you, if you like.'

'Oh, yes please,' Angela said humbly. 'You're so much cleverer than I am.'

Emily grinned. 'When you say things like that, I can feel myself swelling like a toad.'

'Oh, but I mean it!'

'I know, that's what's so nice about you! Well now, you know that we have two political parties, the Liberals and the Unionists?'

'Um – what about the Labour Party?'

'Oh, they don't really count. They've only got a few seats. Well, the thing is that the peers in the House of Lords are almost all Unionist, as you'd expect, and since the Lords can veto any bill they like, it means that if the Government is Unionist it can be sure of getting its legislation through, but if it's Liberal it can't.'

'Yes, I see. But why is that a bad thing?'

'Oh Angela! It's not democratic, that's all.'

'I suppose not,' Angela said doubtfully. 'But . . . '

'What's your trouble? If people vote for a Government, that Government ought to be able to get its bills through, don't you think?'

'Oh yes! Except that when so few people vote for the Government in the first place, it isn't really democracy anyway, is it?' Emily stared, and Angela began her usual reddening process, but for once stuck to her guns. 'Lots of men still don't have the vote, and none of the women. I've heard Mrs Pankhurst say that less than a third of all adults are voters. So it doesn't really matter if their bills get through or not, does it? It's still a wicked cheat.'

'Goodness, what a fire-breather you are!' Emily said. 'I didn't know you cared so much about the franchise.'

'I care about the Cause more than anything,' Angela said in a low but passionate voice. 'I would die for it.'

Emily was quite taken aback. 'I don't think that would help.'

'We have to *force* them!' Angela said fiercely. 'They won't give it to us. They'll *never* give it to us.'

Emily remembered her father and her uncle laughing; her uncle telling her that the tide of history wouldn't rise quite *that* far. She said, 'No, I don't suppose they will.'

'Sometimes I think I hate them,' Angela said quietly.

'But Angela, why do you care so much about it? I mean, you don't understand politics. You didn't even know what the Parliament Bill was.'

'No, I don't understand politics, but I know that we have to have the vote if we're ever to be free. As long as we don't have it, they'll never listen to us.'

Emily could hardly have been more surprised if her hairbrush had wriggled round in her hand and bitten her. She had always thought of Angela as such a milky little lamb, the image of her milky little mother. But then she remembered that Angela's mother, like Lady Hamilton, had travelled all over the world with her soldier husband, and faced many hardships and probably dangers, so there must be steel in her, however little it showed on the outside.

For the last two weeks of June, in honour of the Coronation itself, the consitutional battle was set aside, and the nation gave itself over to pleasure. At the same time, Emily's own personal barometer rose rapidly, for Basil Narishkin came back from Russia.

'I'm so sorry I missed your coming-out ball,' he said to Emily when they met at Grosvenor House – their first meeting since his return. 'Everything took longer than I expected.' He smiled engagingly. 'But tell me about your ball. Was it very splendid? Everyone says you looked quite extraordinary – like a Tartar princess.'

'I hope they meant it in a nice way,' Emily said.

'Fanny Hope did.' Emily's heart sank a little. Of course, he would have hurried round to see her the moment his train came into the station. 'She said you were all in gold. I'd have given anything to see that! Not that you don't look very pretty tonight,' he added with just perceptible surprise.

He had noticed for the first time that the child was growing up, Emily thought painfully.

'What do you call that colour?' he asked, touching the edge of her sleeve. He was so close to her it was making her tremble.

'Old rose.' She reached desperately for a neutral subject. 'Tell me about your business. Did it go well?'

'Oh, it was much ado about nothing,' he said lightly. 'A trouble-maker amongst the workers – the usual thing really. They start agitating about reform and the next thing you know you've got a strike, riots, lost orders and everything. The factory manager didn't know his job – all it needed was a firm hand. The last thing you want to do is give in to them – like that damned Stolypin with his land settlements and his free peasants. Such a lot of nonsense! It just encourages them to be lazy and contentious, and God knows Russian peasants don't need more encouragement in *that* line.'

There was a frown between his fair brows; just for a moment he had evidently forgotten who he was talking to. Something important must have happened to him in Russia, and everything that happened to him was important to Emily.

'Who's Stolypin?' she asked eagerly. 'What are the land settlements?'

He looked at her blankly for an instant, and then the frown disappeared. 'Prime Minister,' he said. 'Trying to change the way the peasants farm, to make them more efficient. He thought if they actually owned the land, they'd take more interest in modern farming methods, but of course they hate change of any sort, even when it's to their benefit. What puzzles me is how he ever got the Emperor to agree – '

He stopped himself abruptly in the middle of the most intensely felt thing he had ever said to Emily, and smiled charmingly. 'But I mustn't bore you with that sort of thing, when you're standing there

105

looking as pretty as a picture and probably longing to dance. Have you a space left on your card for me, Cousin Emily?'

'Yes – yes of course,' she said, disappointed.

'You're too kind to me, considering I was infamous enough to miss your come-out! I shall try to make it up to you. Did you know that the *Ballets Russes* are coming to London on the twenty-first? You've heard of the amazing Diaghilev and his wonderful company?'

'Yes, of course! Madame Maklarova saw them in Paris last year, and she said they were superb.'

'He has all the best dancers from the Imperial Ballet, so they should be. Karsavina, Nijinsky, Pavlova . . . '

'Madame says Fokine's choreography is inspired, and that Cecchetti is the best dancing-master in the world! The Italian style is much more rigorous than the French, which means – '

Basil laughed. 'I can see you know more about it than I do! And there was I, trying to impress you! Well, I've taken a box for Mama for the whole season, including the Royal Coronation Gala, and we intend to make up some very jolly parties, so I hope I can at least invite you to watch them dance with me, even if I can't tell you anything about them.'

Emily couldn't resist. 'I should love to. And I'm sure Lady Hamilton will be inviting you to her reception for the company next week, before their opening night. She's one of the patronesses, you know.'

His heavenly blue eyes opened wide. 'You're making fun of me!'

'Just a little.'

For a fraction of time he seemed put out. Then his smile reassembled itself. 'You know, there's a streak of wickedness in you, Miss Emily Paget, that wants kissing out of you, and if we weren't in the middle of a public ball – '

A knot of warm excitement formed in the pit of Emily's stomach. She felt suddenly that she could say and do anything. She felt as though she could fly. 'You think you are the man who can tame me, do you, Basil Kirilovitch?'

He had been smiling as a man does when teasing a much younger relative, but now he looked at her quite differently. 'How bright your eyes are,' he said. 'Like a cat's.' Emily felt her excitement tinged with a delicious fear, as if she had woken an animal that might turn out to be dangerous. The moment extended itself perilously, and then with piercing disappointment she saw him withdraw from it. His eyes became opaque and his smile polite and playful as it had always been before.

'You mustn't tease me,' he said. 'We elderly people need our dignity.' And then he lightly changed the subject. Emily reminded herself that he was as good as engaged to Lady Frances, and rebuked herself for flirting. But for that one moment, an exultant inner voice whispered, for that one moment he had not been thinking about Lady Frances at all . . .

The reception for the *Ballets Russes* company promised to be different from any other party Emily had attended. Lady Hamilton seemed to blossom for it. She was never a dull dresser, though she normally kept to blacks and lilacs, but for this party she emerged in purple and gold splendour: a swirling-patterned, orientally draped gown, a turban with plumes, and ropes and ropes of pearls. Emily had never seen so many pearls on one person before, and an eye that was beginning to be discerning could tell they were superb ones.

She displayed herself to Emily almost girlishly. 'Well?' she demanded. 'How do I look?'

'Sumptuous!' Emily said. 'Like – like a great empress. Like Catherine the Great.'

'Foolish child,' Lady Hamilton said, pleased. 'Almost all our guests will be Russians – my friends. Tonight I can be Lyudmilla Ivanovna again, and pretend I am back in Petersburg. Tonight I can do and say anything I like, and it won't count tomorrow. Do you understand?'

'Yes, I understand,' Emily said, and she held up the crossed fingers of childhood games. 'It's fen larks!'

Lady Hamilton smiled one of her rare smiles. 'I like you, Emily. You are turning out well,' she said enigmatically.

When the guests began to arrive, Emily was astonished to discover how many Russians there were living in London. Some she already knew about, of course – Monsieur Gravitsky, Madame, Princess Volkinsky, Basil and his mother; the Benckendorffs and others from the Russian Embassy whom she had met at public places. But they were only the tip of the iceberg, and when the members of the ballet company arrived as well, the rooms were filled to bursting-point with vividly dressed, smiling, talking, kissing, arm-waving Russians, and the air rang with cries of Mischa! and Grishka! and Tatya! and how long it had been! and what a joy it was to meet again!

There was so much noise and laughter and colour and movement that Emily's senses were dazzled, and she began to feel quite drunk with it. She imagined a bee in a rose garden in full bloom might feel something of her delicious confusion. A sense of unreality overtook her, in which it did not seem at all strange that she should be presented by Madame to Mischa Fokine as 'my little pupil', and that the great man should question her about her dancing abilities, as though that were the most interesting thing about her.

When they learnt – again from Madame – that Emily's mother had been a ballet girl, the dancers crowded round her and pelted her with questions she couldn't possibly answer, which didn't matter because they answered them for themselves. It was finally decided that Grigoriev remembered Isabelle – or the Little Kertesz as he called her – and that one of the wardrobe mistresses had actually danced in the same company with her once. This meant that Emilia Edvardovna was absolutely one of them, and could have her health drunk with fervour and many times over in Lady Hamilton's excellent champagne.

They mourned for her that she had not begun her lessons earlier, and that she had grown so tall: Tamara Karsavina, the prima ballerina, was tiny – less than five feet – and delicately built, too. But then after all, they said, Vaslav could lift anyone, for though he was short, he was very strong. The dancer Nijinsky certainly looked strong, Emily thought through a haze of champagne and foreign languages: bull-necked and muscular, with a puggy, coarse, broadnosed face and terrible teeth. A moment later she found herself soaring through the air towards the chandelier with the gappy grin surprisingly below her, as Vaslav proved to everyone's satisfaction that he could indeed lift anyone, even a well-fed English girl of his own height. Beyond their immediate group, no-one even turned a head.

After that Emily felt the evening couldn't possibly get any more strange, not even when Giorgi Rosay, the character dancer, lined up three ladder-back chairs from the dining-room and vividly portrayed Diaghilev being seasick on the Channel crossing; or impish little Lydia Lopokova acquired a pack of cards and set up in a corner to tell fortunes.

Everyone was having a wonderful time, except, Emily noted with a corner of her attention, Basil and Lady Frances. They appeared to be trying to have a serious conversation, which at that particular time and place seemed definitely eccentric. Finally Frances got up and left the room, leaving Basil looking very moody. Freeing herself gently from the group she was with, Emily made her way round the edge of the room to Basil's side.

She found from the direction of his gaze that he was watching his mother, the old Princess, being charmed by Diaghilev, who was an extraordinary-looking man with a pure white streak down the centre of his glossy black head of hair, and a way of holding his head up like a horse, so that although he was short he managed to look down at everyone.

'He's after her money, of course,' Basil said as she reached him. 'Look at him! He could get blood out of a stone, the old snake!'

Emily realised with a start that Basil was drunk. He didn't show it much. His eye was moist and his cheek bright, both of which rather became him; but he was obviously not minding his tongue as he would if he were sober.

'I suppose it must cost a lot of money to run a ballet company,' she said soothingly.

'He charms it out of rich old ladies,' Basil said disagreeably. 'All the same, these pansies – too much charm.'

Diaghilev didn't look at all like a pansy, Emily considered. If you were to think of him as a flower at all, it would have to be something much more striking and exotic, certainly not anything as English and cottage garden as a pansy. 'He looks more like a lily to me,' she said. 'Or an orchid.'

Basil stared at her, perplexed. 'You shouldn't have let that peasant touch you,' he said at last, 'the vulgar little brute.'

'What peasant?'

'The dancer. D'you know the only reason he's here is that he was dismissed from the Imperial Ballet for coarse behaviour?'

'What did he do?' Emily asked, enjoying herself. This was much better than being treated as the simple little country cousin.

'He went on stage in front of the Dowager Empress without his trunks. No trunks, just tights! She didn't know where to look.'

'Basil Kirilovitch, I haven't the least idea what you're talking about,' Emily said. 'But I expect it's just as well. Have you and Fan been quarrelling?'

In normal circumstances she wouldn't have dared to ask, but she felt, like Lady Hamilton, that tonight was 'fen larks', especially when Basil was plainly squiffy.

Basil sighed. 'Not quarrelling, just arguing. I was trying to get her to set the date, but she won't even discuss it.'

'Surely not the best place to try to talk about something like that?'

'I know, but Mother's getting impatient. She says she wants Fanny and me to get married before she dies. Not that she's about to – it's just her way of hurrying me. I keep telling her, it isn't me that's dragging feet, it's Fanny, but she doesn't believe me.' He hauled his eyes away from his mother and looked down at Emily. 'I say, you might go and see if she's all right, would you? She was a bit upset.'

Emily nodded and turned away, thinking that Frances was more likely annoyed than upset at having a proposal of marriage made to her in this parrot garden of noise and colour. It was ironic, she thought as she slipped from the room, that she of all people should be chosen as a go-between. But on the other hand, it had its virtues: she would sooner know what was going on between them than not know.

Lady Frances was in one of the ladies' rooms, trying to tuck up a tendril of hair that had come loose. Her face was rather flushed – which was no surprise in that heat – but she did not seem otherwise disturbed. She smiled at Emily in the mirror.

'Quite a party!' she said. 'You seem to be popular with the dancers.'

'Madame keeps telling everyone I'm a pupil of hers, so they think I'm a dancer too. I keep trying to explain she only teaches me to curtsey, but they don't listen. Shall I do that for you?'

'Would you? I keep pulling it out again. Maddening.'

Emily went up behind her and took the hairpin she offered over her shoulder. 'Someone was worried about you – thought you might be upset.'

'Basil? No, not upset, but he keeps asking me to marry him, and I get tired of it. He won't take no for an answer. I suppose I should be flattered.'

'I thought it was understood,' Emily said with distant shock. 'I thought you were more or less engaged.'

Frances made an exasperated noise. 'Yes, Mummy and the Princess make sure everyone does think that, and Basil goes along with it. He's such a jellyfish.'

Emily felt stunned at hearing that godlike creature, her hero, described in such impatient terms. 'I thought you were in love with each other.'

'Do we behave as if we're in love with each other?' Frances said wearily. 'It's a plot hatched up between our mothers. I'm very fond of Basil, but I don't want to marry him – only he's so Gothic he thinks he has to do what his mother tells him.'

Emily was reeling. 'Oh no, Fan. I'm sure he loves you. Really!'

Annoyance bubbled up in Lady Frances like a fresh spring. 'Not

110

you as well, Emily! Let me tell you – Basil loves only Basil. He thinks he ought to get married for the sake of the family fortune – sons and heirs, you know – and he'd just as soon marry me because he's known me all his life, and he's too lazy to go through the business of courting someone new, whom he might have to try and please.' She stopped abruptly, biting her lip.

Emily said nothing. She couldn't believe that anyone lucky enough to be the object of Basil's affections could be so indifferent to him. They had quarrelled, she reminded herself, and Frances was angry with him. She didn't mean these things.

'Besides,' Frances said in her usual, cool tones, 'I couldn't possibly leave Mummy all alone, with no companion. And if we do ever get the Conciliation Bill through, only single women will get the vote, so I'd be a fool to marry, wouldn't I?'

Emily laughed. 'Oh Fanny, as if that would stop anyone!'

Lady Frances shook her head sadly. 'You're only a Suffragette from the neck upwards, that's your trouble.'

It was one of the hottest summers ever recorded, and the temperature in August reached such heights that even Lady Hamilton, who hated everywhere except London, Paris and St Petersburg, was forced to leave town for a few weeks. She accepted an invitation from Princess Narishkina to go and stay with her in her house in the Cotswolds, and sent Emily home to Bratton.

Her cousins greeted her rapturously.

'You've got to rescue us!' Victoria said. 'Can't you come and visit us wearing several sets of clothes, like that Jacobite lord's wife, what's-her-name, and smuggle us out?'

'Is it really that bad?'

'You don't know!' said Lexy. 'Tom came back for two days, and went straight off to stay with Arlington in Devon for the whole summer, that's how bad it is.'

'I call it mean,' Victoria added indignantly, 'leaving us to hold the bridge alone.'

'Well, you seem to have learned quite a lot of history, at any rate,' Emily noted.

'Actually,' Lexy said fairly, 'some of the lessons aren't half bad, once you get the hang of it. But it's the atmosphere in the house, Em. Talk about your rumbling volcanoes!'

'We've learned some geography, too,' Victoria put in sassily.

'There is definitely something very odd going on,' Lexy said gravely, 'but we can't find out what.'

'Is your mama still very unhappy?'

'If that's what it is,' Lexy said. 'She comes in looking like an iceberg – smooth, you know, nothing to get a grip on – hears a bit of our lesson, and asks us a few questions to see how we're getting on.'

'And sometimes she says we must work hard, because an education is a valuable thing,' Victoria added solemnly. 'I mean *Mama*, you know, and *education*!'

'And why doesn't Papa come home? We haven't seen him since Christmas. Do you ever see him in London, Em?'

'Well, no, but that's not surprising. We don't exactly haunt the same places, you know. As to why he doesn't come home – that's easy. Haven't you heard there's a constitutional crisis? It must be the one time in history that the House of Lords is absolutely full.'

'Papa never bothered about politics before,' Lexy said.

'He never had to before.'

'Oh well, never mind. Now you're here, you can take us out riding – unless you think you're too grown up for us now,' Lexy added anxiously. 'I must say you look quite different with your hair up like that. And your face has got different, hasn't it, Vick?'

'It's my belief someone's been making love to her,' Victoria said gloomily. 'She's going to get married, and then we'll lose our only ally.'

'Wrong on both counts,' Emily laughed. 'Stop talking nonsense, and we'll go and have that ride. And to show you I'm not too grown up, I'll tell you a bit of The Story when we get back.'

'Thanks,' Lexy said, exchanging a glance with her sister, 'but I think we're too old and sad for that. It wouldn't be the same without Tom and Maudie here. You can tell us about London instead, and being a debutante.'

Nothing at The Lodge had changed, except that the rooms seemed smaller and darker than she remembered. Penny greeted her in her usual unemotional way, remarking that she had grown taller, and then, disapprovingly, that she had grown thinner.

'I can see it in your face. I suppose you've been gadding too much and wearing yourself out. I hope you haven't got faddy about food, like some girls? I noticed you picking at things at luncheon, and you were never a picker. You always had a healthy appetite from a child.'

Edward was even more the same than when she had left, Emily thought; in fact the only odd thing he had done in years was to come to her ball. Even that he had managed to do in recognisably his own way – arriving unannounced, staying to shake hands and eat a large, silent dinner, and disappearing as soon as the dancing started. He had been gone again when Emily woke the following morning, and Katya had told her that he had spent the evening in Lord Westinghouse's library, and had caught a very early train back to Wiltshire, leaving no message, not even of farewell.

Now when she encountered him at home for the first time in months he smiled at her in a pleased sort of way, and asked if she'd heard anything fresh about the Parliament Bill.

After the political cease-fire for the Coronation the battle had been resumed in July with a bang, with Asquith revealing to the Commons that as long ago as the previous November, the King had promised, if necessary, to create up to three hundred new peers to swamp the Unionist Lords and vote the Parliament Bill through the Upper House.

When the news became public, it rocked London. Even those fashionable ladies who normally passed into a deep and peaceful sleep at the very mention of the word 'politics', were able to grasp that this was a perilous crisis, a shocking scandal, and unprecedented enough to be worthy of top billing in their drawing-rooms.

How it had been possible to keep the King's promise secret for so many months exercised many minds. There was a saying about the Cabinet that if you told them anything, however sensitive, they all told their wives, except Asquith, who told other people's wives. Yet no breath of this had become public. Opinion was severely divided about the King as to whether he was good but weak, and had been bullied into it by Asquith; or whether he was a monster devoid of conscience and had not needed bullying.

Some – particularly the wives and sons of peers – averred that it would never happen, that it was an empty bluff on Asquith's part. Others assured them earnestly that Asquith had actually submitted two hundred and fifty names to the King, which the King had already approved – *and that they had actually seen the list!*

The contents of that list was a subject of such intense speculation that at times the crisis itself seemed in danger of being forgotten. Some names were easily guessable – men of substance, knights and

113

baronets, privy counsellors, senior soldiers. Others were tossed in the air like so many glittering and insubstantial balls to catch the conversational spotlight: this composer, that financier, such another solicitor.

The pollution of their ranks by such a *canaille* was so abhorrent to the Lords that they could not bring themselves to believe the King would do it, and despatched Lord Crewe to ask him. The King responded with a formal statement to be read out in the Upper House, which left their lordships in no doubt.

The final debate on the Parliament Bill took place on the 9th of August, a day so hot that an unprecedented 100° Fahrenheit was recorded at Greenwich Observatory. The Unionist peers were divided into those who felt it prudent to hedge their bets by abstaining and waiting to see what happened, and the furious die-hards, who saw their ancient rights under threat and were determined to die at the last ditch rather than submit. *The Times* thus christened them Hedgers and Ditchers.

Since the Hedgers numbered about three hundred, the Ditchers about a hundred, and the existing Liberal peers only about eighty, it looked as though the Parliament Bill might yet be scuppered, and the mass creation of peers would bring shame and ridicule on the sovereign, the House, and the nation.

The debate dragged on in furious heat, and it was not until after eleven o'clock the following night that the result of the vote came in. The next morning *The Times* carried the news that the Bill had passed with a majority of just seventeen. Lord Curzon, Lord Rosebery, and the Archbishop of Canterbury had persuaded twenty Ditchers and twelve of the bishops to change sides. Democracy had made a great stride forward, *The Times* applauded. The Lords could no longer veto, but only delay a bill for two years. The Commons was supreme: the People's will would prevail.

What people, though? Emily thought, remembering Angela's passionate outburst about democracy. Still, it must have been good for the Cause in one respect: they now had to persuade only the Commons that women should have the vote, rather than both Houses; and the Upper House had always looked the harder of the two to sway.

Lady Hamilton went back to London in September, and immediately requested Emily's return.

114

'I must have you here, to bring young people to me,' she said in defence of her peremptory command. 'Did you have an agreeable time in the country?'

'Yes, thank you, except that I'm worried about my little cousins. I think the regime is too harsh for them. They ought at least to have the chance to meet and play with other children.'

Lady Hamilton eyed her curiously. 'You did not. And they at least have each other.'

Emily frowned. 'Yes, but it was different for me. I'm not sure why – I just know I don't feel easy about them.'

'Did you see your aunt?'

'Yes, once. Papa and I were invited up to dinner when Uncle Westie came down for a few days.'

'You sound as though you didn't find her well.'

'She seemed cheerful, which wasn't like her. She talked much more than I ever remember, and laughed, and asked me about London parties and things,' Emily said in a puzzled voice. 'I couldn't understand it at all. She's *never* been like that.'

'How did your uncle respond?'

'He didn't say much, really, just sat there eating, you know, and watching. She asked him things once or twice, and he seemed to be saying as little as possible – just "Yes" and "No" and "Not really". I think he thought she must be ill, too, because he must know that isn't like her. I've wondered sometimes – well, if perhaps she's – '

'Mad?' Lady Hamilton said brutally. Her eyes looked sly and bright, as if she were enjoying Emily's confusion. 'No, I don't think so. I must tell you, child, that what goes on between married people is rarely comprehensible to the outsider, particularly to a young relative.'

Emily sighed. 'I suppose you must be right. In any case, Uncle Westie didn't stay long, and if he'd been worried about Aunt Maud, he wouldn't have gone away so soon, would he?'

'As you say,' Lady Hamilton said. 'And where has he gone?'

'Papa said to Marienbad. Before Maudie died, they all used to go to the seaside at this time of year – the whole family. And then I believe he's going to Scotland, but not to Auchnachillan. I suppose he wouldn't want to go there without Aunt Maud. He's going to stay with some American people who've bought an estate somewhere near Balmoral – within boasting distance, Papa said,' she added with a smile.

'There do seem to be a great many Americans around these days,'

115

Lady Hamilton acknowledged. 'It's becoming quite the thing for our best people to marry them. Of course, the ones we see over here are all very wealthy, but I can see no call to be going to those lengths.'

'I've never met an American lady, but I hear that they're very lively,' Emily said. 'Perhaps that's the attraction.'

Emily settled down to enjoy the second half of her year. Some things seemed different since the August break. The political temperature had dropped considerably now that the constitutional crisis was resolved, and things looked better for the Cause. The Conciliation Bill was revived, and there was more public sympathy than heretofore: the *Standard* had taken up the Cause and was even devoting a whole page in every edition – entitled 'A Woman's Platform' – to articles and letters in support of the enfranchisement of women.

In October Mrs Pankhurst left for a lecture tour of America, and Angela and Sylvia were amongst those who went to see her off. They came back to Lady Hamilton's afterwards for tea, where Lady Frances was already sitting with Emily.

'It was splendid! You should have been there!' Sylvia exclaimed as she came through the door. Angela, very pink under a large blue hat, was close behind her. 'There was such a crowd, and everyone in such good spirits. Someone stuck up a flag in the WSPU colours on the front of the engine.'

'Lots of people were wearing favours in the colours, too. I wish I had,' Angela said wistfully, 'only I know Daddy wouldn't approve.'

'Everyone's going to America these days,' Emily said. 'You'd think it was the Promised Land.'

'It is for some people,' Frances said. 'Certainly society is much more free over there.'

'Lax, you mean,' Lady Hamilton said with spare humour. 'I understand divorced people are received even in the most exclusive circles.'

Angela evidently felt the main point was in danger of being lost. 'Mrs Pankhurst made a tremendous speech,' she said. 'She said things had never looked brighter, and that we mean to have the vote next session.'

'Yes, and that Mr Asquith had definitely promised to give facilities to the Bill,' Sylvia joined in. 'So perhaps it really will happen this time.'

'The Lords can't stop it now, at any rate,' Emily said.

'Time for all us unmarried ladies to persuade our fathers to buy us houses, then,' Frances said wryly.

116

But November brought a great setback: when Parliament resumed on the 7th, Prime Minister Asquith announced that the Government would be introducing a Manhood Suffrage Bill, to give the vote to all men.

'It means that the Conciliation Bill will have to be dropped in its present form, because it's based on existing franchise laws,' Frances said.

'And if they get the Manhood Suffrage through, which they probably will,' Sylvia added, 'we'll be back where we started.'

'No, we'll be worse off,' said Frances bitterly.

'Why worse off?' Angela asked.

'Because it will make the division between men and women absolute. As long as some men didn't have the vote, it was possible to pin the difference on something else – property, rank, status. But if all men have the vote, regardless of who or what they are, it will become enshrined in law that women are barred from voting by reason of their sex.'

Angela looked bewildered, like someone newly bereaved. 'You mean – that we'll never get it? That they'll say we can never have it?'

'It will make their position impregnable,' Frances said.

'Perhaps they'll include something for women in the Manhood Bill,' Sylvia said, ever the optimist. 'We still have sympathisers amongst the Liberals.'

Frances shrugged. 'If they don't, it will set the Cause back fifty years. Worse, it will establish men as a ruling caste, with women in complete subjugation to them.'

It was soon learned that the Manhood Suffrage Bill was to contain no provision for enfranchising women: it aimed to give the vote to all men over the age of twenty-one, subject only to a six-month residential qualification.

Furthermore, the news soon circulated amongst interested groups that Asquith had assured those most hostile to the women's cause that he believed it would be a disastrous mistake ever to grant women the vote.

There was to be a meeting of the Women's Social and Political Union at Caxton Hall on the evening of the 21st of November to decide what to do about the 'torpedoing' of the Conciliation Bill.

During the day Angela Chitterley came to Lady Hamilton's house,

117

and finding Sylvia and Emily there, burst into pink and breathless exhortation.

'The meeting tonight – I met Mrs Pethick Lawrence – she asked me to come – to bring all my friends – '

'You're not a member of the WSPU,' Sylvia objected.

'She says it doesn't matter. It's to be our reply to the Manhood Suffrage Bill. She says it's an outrage to the honour of women. They want everyone they can get to march on Westminster – a really massive protest! She says they're hoping for a thousand women this time!'

'It won't do any good,' Emily said. 'They'll never let the women reach the House. There'll be squadrons of policemen to turn them back.'

'Oh we know! I mean, she knows,' Angela cried excitedly. 'But if we are turned back, there's to be an organised stone-throwing. All the windows in Whitehall are to be broken – every single one if possible! We're all to carry a muff, and hide the stones inside, and that way no-one will suspect – '

'Angela, you aren't going,' Sylvia broke in, with something that was half question, half statement.

Angela grew pinker still. 'Yes I am,' she said proudly. 'Mrs Pethick Lawrence herself asked me, and I've come to ask you both to come as well.'

'Us? Impossible,' Emily said, as startled as Sylvia.

'It's important,' Angela said. 'We can't let them destroy our chance of freedom without lifting a finger to protest. We've got to *show* them!'

Sylvia shook her head. 'Breaking windows won't do any good. It only annoys them. They just call for the glazier, and say that women are irrational and hysterical.'

'I don't care,' Angela said fiercely. 'At least it will make them notice us! Make them see we mean it!'

'But you can't go, anyway,' Emily said.

'Emily's right,' Sylvia agreed. 'Your mother and father would never let you.'

'I won't tell them, then.'

'Angela, you can't have thought,' Emily said, dismayed. 'You'd be arrested and put in prison, and you can't imagine how awful that would be! The dirt and smells and squalor, being degraded and insulted – '

'I've read all those reports,' Angela said quietly. 'I don't care what

118

it takes, we have to make them see that we won't give up. Will you come with me? Will you help the Cause?'

'No,' said Emily distractedly.

'No, of course not,' Sylvia said. 'And you're not to either. You're too young.'

Angela gave them one last burning look, and went away.

'She won't, will she?' Emily asked anxiously. 'The thought of her being manhandled by policemen is too horrible!'

'Mrs Lawrence should never have suggested it. I don't know what she was thinking of,' Sylvia said. 'But in any case, it won't happen. Mrs Chitterley would never allow her out alone at night.'

'Oh, yes, of course, you're right,' Emily said, relieved. 'I hadn't thought of that.'

Lady Frances rushed in just as Emily was about to go up and dress for the evening.

'Emily, what's this about Angela? I've just met Con Lytton, and she says that Angela's pledged herself to some kind of protest action with the WSPU tonight. Is it true?'

Emily faltered. 'She did say she meant to, but I can't believe she'd really do it. I know she's very keen on the Cause, but – '

'It's madness. She must be stopped. Did she go home, do you know?'

'She didn't say where she was going, but I think she must have. She was only wearing a day dress, and she could hardly – '

'I'll go straight there, then, and speak to her mother. She mustn't be allowed to leave the house tonight. If necessary, they'll have to lock her in her bedroom.'

'Oh, surely it won't – ' Emily began, but Frances had gone.

Half an hour later Emily was called to the telephone. 'Emily, it's Fanny.'

'Oh, did you see her? What did she say?'

'I telephoned to tell you it's all right. She's promised me she won't join in the stone-throwing tonight. She took a bit of persuading, but when I said if she didn't give me her word I'd have to tell her mother to lock her up, she gave in.'

'Thank God! Was she very upset?'

'She cried a bit. However, better that than the alternative. I thought you'd want to know.'

'Yes, thank you, Fanny. I was very worried about her.'

'All right. Perhaps we can take her out somewhere tomorrow to make it up to her. I feel rather Judas-like.'

'It was for her own good. You had to do it,' said Emily.

Emily went to the theatre with Lady Hamilton that evening with an easy mind. When they came out, they could hear the noise of unusual activity in the streets, and Lovibond, waiting with the Benz, told them glumly that the Suffragettes had done a fine job.

'At the Government offices in Whitehall, my lady – not a pane of glass between 'em. And when the police managed to surround 'em there, blow me if they didn't start up again in the Strand! We'd best go back a different way, my lady. There's terrible crowds down there.'

'Nonsense! I want to see what they've done. It's all quite futile, of course, but it's good to know some women have the spirit to protest.'

It was hard to get the motor car along, for the road was not only choked with traffic, but with the unusual crowds spilling off the pavements. There were policemen everywhere, some trying to hold the crowds back, some with flares trying to direct the traffic, and others dragging the offenders off to Bow Street. The worst blockage of all was where a motor car had apparently gone out of control, crossed the pavement and crashed through the window of the Civil Service Stores, creating considerable damage.

Lovibond managed to get them through at last, and they completed the journey in silence. Emily was shocked at the extent of the damage. It was one thing to talk about it, but quite another actually to see it, and she was more glad than ever that Frances had persuaded Angela to have nothing to do with it.

The appalling news did not reach them until the following morning, when it arrived simultaneously by telephone, by word of mouth, and in the newspapers. Angela had kept her promise to have nothing to do with the stone-throwing. Instead, she had slipped out of the house disguised in a man's coat and cap which she had bought from a second-hand shop nearby, stolen their next-door neighbour's motor car, and deliberately driven it through the window of the Civil Service Stores.

As a means to attract attention it had succeeded far beyond her intentions, for the violence of the crash had thrown her against the metal frame of the windscreen and broken her neck.

Chapter Eight

Sylvia, Frances and Emily had been roller-skating at the Aldwych skating-rink.

'I think it's more difficult than ice-skating,' Emily said as they emerged into the early evening.

'Can you ice-skate?' Sylvia asked, impressed.

'We were all taught from an early age, on the small lake at Bratton,' Emily said. 'I suppose it must be the Russian influence.'

'This must have seemed tame to you, then.'

'Oh no,' Emily said. 'I like the music and the lights and the crowds. And I love being allowed to go without a chaperone – just the three of us together. It's the sort of thing I thought I'd never be allowed to do.'

'But it seems strange without Angela,' Frances said. 'Wrong, somehow, to be enjoying ourselves, when she – ' They were walking up Drury Lane, only just around the corner from where she had met her death two months earlier. 'I feel so guilty whenever I think of her.'

'But you mustn't,' Sylvia said quickly. 'It wasn't your fault. You did everything you could to stop her.'

'I should have told her mother,' Frances said bleakly.

'Angela gave you her word not to go stone-throwing,' Sylvia said. 'You couldn't know she'd do – that other thing instead.'

'Poor Angela, the Cause's first martyr,' Frances said. 'Who'd have thought she cared that much about it?'

Emily remembered Angela saying she would die for the Cause. She couldn't have known, of course, that her action would result in her death, but Emily felt that if she had known she would still have done it.

'It's Lovibond I feel sorry for,' she said. 'He blames himself for teaching her to drive in the first place.'

'That's silly too,' Sylvia said almost crossly. 'If it's anyone's fault, it's Mr Asquith's, for not giving us the vote.'

'The Cause has come of age,' Frances said. 'It makes a principle respectable to have someone die for it.'

121

'Oh Fanny,' Emily protested, and then stopped. On the corner of Russell Street there was a restaurant, one of those very private little places with curtained windows where it was possible to imagine the most fascinating intrigues going on. As they drew opposite it, but on the other side of the road, the door opened and a woman came out – a smartly dressed woman in a draped velvet opera-cloak, an enviable hat, and one of the huge fur muffs that were the fashion that winter.

Emily had only glanced at her idly because she happened to be looking in that direction, but a motor car coming up Russell Street at the same time illuminated her with its headlights. She was young and attractive, laughing vivaciously, and diamonds flashed at her ears and throat as she turned her head towards her companion. The companion was also spotlighted: a tall, distinguished gentleman in evening dress, a cigar between the fingers of one hand, the other hand cupped tenderly beneath the lady's elbow as she paused at the kerb to let the motor car go by. He was looking very pleased with himself. He was also unmistakably Uncle Westie.

'What is it, Emily?' Frances asked, breaking into her silence.

All the implications burst like white fire into Emily's mind, blanking out the capacity for thought. She reacted instinctively, turning her head so that her companions should not know where she had been looking, walking on quickly so that her uncle should not see her.

She said the first thing she could think of. 'I thought I saw Basil, but it turned out to be nothing like him.'

'Oh, can't we have one evening without the subject of Basil cropping up?' Frances sighed.

Sylvia grinned. 'You're going to have to say yes to him sooner or later, Fan! He's a most determined lover.'

'I've told you a thousand times there is nothing between me and him.'

Sylvia was undaunted. 'Perhaps, but there's definitely something between him and you.'

'I mean to be an old maid. In fact, at twenty-six anyone but you would think I already was one.'

'Your parents will never let you be an old maid. Anyway, you'd hate it. Better marry anyone than be an object of ridicule.'

'Nonsense! I shall be free, don't you see? In four years' time, Papa will accept that I'm never going to marry, and he'll give me an allowance and let me live on my own.'

122

'He won't,' Sylvia said with conviction. Emily could see that whatever she might say, Frances was not sure of it either. 'Anyway, I'm sure you must love Basil really.'

Frances made a wry face. 'Oh yes, he's so very lovable, isn't he?' Emily had the curious feeling that Frances didn't mean it. Now, if he were to ask *me* to marry him, she thought . . .

As a counter-irritant the topic was well chosen: Frances was soon obliged to change the subject and keep the conversation elsewhere until they parted at Lady Hamilton's. So it was not until Emily retired to her room for the night that she had the time and privacy to let her thoughts loose on the shocking discovery she had made in Drury Lane.

Now she knew, she realised that there had been many clues along the way which she could have picked up, if she had been half as sophisticated as she imagined herself. Poor Aunt Maud, never going to London any more, shutting herself up alone at Bratton with her grief – how unhappy she must have been! And it had not been mourning for Maudie, or at least, not all of it; the rest must have been the anguish of a wronged wife.

Emily remembered the dinner at Bratton last August, and how Aunt Maud had chattered brightly – so unlike herself! Even at the time, Emily had thought it odd. She had been trying to pretend everything was all right; sparkling at her husband vivaciously across the table as though they were the best of friends – trying to win him back, perhaps?

Emily remembered too, with a slow brewing of resentment, how Uncle Westie had carried on eating, not responding, not helping her; not caring, it seemed, whether she succeeded in protecting him or not. Unkind! But this was Uncle Westie she was thinking about; Uncle Westie whom everyone liked, because he was so genial, so easy to get on with. How could he be so wicked and cruel?

She paused there. She had read and heard enough to know that gentlemen sometimes took mistresses (*ballet girls*!) and that wives were supposed to turn a blind eye to it. And then again, Aunt Maud had always held that it was vulgar to let anyone know what you were feeling. If this had been going on for so long, and Aunt Maud minded it enough to allow it to show, must that not mean that it was not the sort of mild peccadillo the world winked at, but something more serious?

She thought of the woman she had seen in the street: a young woman, attractive and vivacious, but definitely not a tart; expens-

123

ively dressed, but not vulgar. She had looked like a lady; and now she thought of it, there had been an air between her and Uncle Westie of – what was it exactly? – of *belonging*.

He never went down to Bratton any more. He spent his Saturday-to-Mondays with 'friends' – those friends, presumably, who would not object to his bringing The Lady. Last summer he had gone to Marienbad – which the former Prince of Wales, that marital intriguer, had made popular with a fast, international set – instead of to St Malo with his wife and children. Had he gone with Her? And afterwards he had gone to shoot grouse not at Auchnachillan, his own estate, but with 'some Americans' – friends of The Lady perhaps.

Or relatives? Was she an American? Emily remembered some pointed-sounding remarks Lady Hamilton had made. (Lady Hamilton must know; Lady Hamilton always knew everything.) She had said that everyone was marrying Americans these days, and that Americans were lax about divorce. Emily's palms were damp. My God, could it be? Was Uncle Westie actually thinking about *divorce*?

It would account for Aunt Maud's sudden interest in the cousins' education. Had she decided, her own marriage proving hollow and painful, that they should have an alternative, the possibility of living their lives without the protection of men? Had she even considered that it might become necessary?

And Tom avoiding Bratton now, spending all his holidays with schoolfriends. Did Tom know? Had some worldly-wise older boy enlightened him? Boys could be very cruel. Poor little Tom!

Another thought: was that why Lady Hamilton had been so annoyed when Aunt Maud offered St Auben House for Emily's ball, and why she had had to telephone people to persuade them to come? And was it why Papa had suddenly decided to attend and lend her his countenance, so people shouldn't notice so much that the Westinghouses were absent?

Then Emily remembered Lady Ongar suggesting that Aunt Maud might not be grieving for Maudie, that 'something else' might have happened at the same time. But it must have had something to do with Maudie. Aunt Maud had been in London with Uncle Westie right up until Maudie's relapse; and it was only after the period of mourning that Aunt Maud had refused to go back to London. There must be a connection.

Emily knew only one person to ask. It was late, but sleep was very far from her, and she knew Lady Hamilton liked to read in bed before going to sleep. With the weariness of reluctance, Emily got up and went quietly along the passage to Lady Hamilton's room. There was still a rind of light along the bottom of the door, so she knocked.

She had to knock a second time before Lady Hamilton called out, 'Come in! Don't stand there tapping away like a woodpecker.' Emily entered and saw the old lady in a lilac froth of bed-wrapper and a frilled cap, propped up against her pillows with – thank heaven! – a book in her hand.

'Oh, it's you. I thought it must be Katya with another toothache. She's such a coward about pain. What is it, child?'

'I – I hope I'm not disturbing you – '

'What a stupid question! Of course you are. But that is not to say I mind being disturbed.' The keen old eyes surveyed her. 'You haven't been to bed: something must be worrying you. Are you in trouble?' She laid her book aside. 'Come and sit here. I promise you I am all attention.'

Emily sat on the edge of the bed as directed, and folded her hands in her lap, looking down at them because it was easier than meeting even sympathetic eyes. How to begin? It occurred to her suddenly that if Lady Hamilton *didn't* know, any question she put would betray the situation.

'Well, out with it,' Lady Hamilton said at last. 'You aren't in love – it isn't *that* sort of unhappiness, I can see.'

Emily looked up. Lady Hamilton's face seemed suddenly the least threatening thing in the universe. 'I saw my Uncle Westie this evening,' she said, trying for a casual note, in case she had to cover her tracks.

It was not necessary, however. Lady Hamilton scanned Emily's face keenly and her mouth turned down. 'Ah! I wondered how long it would be before you found out about that! Well, at least you saw for yourself. I dreaded that some officious person would feel it their duty to tell you.'

'Why didn't *you* tell me?'

'It wasn't necessary for you to know. You might never have found out, after all.'

'Who is she?'

'She's a Miss Pamela Montgomery. Her father is Fife Montgomery, an American. Have you heard of him?' Emily shook her head. 'He is what they call a self-made man. He has made millions

125

out of minerals – cobalt and bauxite and so on. Don't ask me what they do with them, but they seem to be much in demand.'

Emily was silent. All possibility that she had misjudged was wiped out. It was fact after all – and the fact was taking time to assimilate. Uncle Westie and a Miss Pamela Montgomery. The idea, white and painful, shifted about in her mind, trying to find a space to fit into.

'So is it – does everyone know? I mean, is it a regular thing?'

Lady Hamilton considered before answering. 'It's hard to say. Naturally no mere acquaintance would be impertinent enough to mention it to me. All I can say is that I have known about it for months, and since they do not seem particularly to embrace discretion, I imagine a great many people know.' She paused, and added, 'It has been going on for some time. I rather fear it may be serious.'

Emily felt the falling-away sensation of apprehension in her stomach. *Serious.* 'Do you mean – ?' She couldn't ask, but Lady Hamilton seemed to know what the question was.

'There is no sense in hiding the facts from you, Emily. You are not a child any more, though you may feel like one at the moment. The fact is that a man of substance may take a mistress without shocking anyone, without even attracting the disapproval of more than a handful of people. But he cannot divorce his wife to marry another woman without initiating the very worst kind of scandal.'

'But – does he – is he – ?'

'The Americans are a curious people,' Lady Hamilton went on. 'They do not regard divorce as a disgrace as we do here. On the other hand, they have a curiously naïve disapproval of *affaires*. Miss Montgomery's people would be outraged if she were to be known as Westinghouse's mistress, however generously she were treated and however widely accepted in society; but as his second wife she would be fêted as though your aunt had never existed. And it has to be faced that he is a marquess, and Americans love titles. I should be surprised if her father did not make a push to see his daughter a marchioness.'

Emily could only nod miserably.

'It would be useless to pretend to you', Lady Hamilton went on, 'that if there is a scandal, it won't affect you. But you will weather it; and the behaviour of those who matter will not alter towards you.'

But Emily could not yet consider that aspect of it. Her mind was still on her aunt and her cousins; and there was something else she had to ask, however little she wanted to possess the information.

'Ma'am, the night my cousin Maudie died, my aunt didn't set off immediately, even though she was at St Auben House when the telephone call went through. She arrived too late to see Maudie, and my uncle didn't come down until the following day.'

'I understand she tried to locate him, and in the end could only leave messages in various places. I dare say she blames him for the delay.'

'He was with Her?'

It was not really a question, and Lady Hamilton's slow nod was more acknowledgement than answer.

Deaths, they say, always come in threes. For Emily there was Angela's death, the death of her innocence, and, on the following morning, when she rose heavy-eyed from an unsatisfying sleep, the news sent from Lady Ongar to Lady Hamilton that Princess Narishkina had suffered a heart attack the previous evening at her house in Richmond, and was not expected to live out the day.

It gave her at least something else to think about, between sympathy for Basil's bereavement, and wondering what effect it would have on his courting of Frances. It was two weeks before she saw him; then he called at Lady Hamilton's house one morning, looking more beautiful than ever in the stark black of mourning clothes.

'I hoped Fanny might be here,' he said when they had exchanged courtesies. 'Her aunt said she was coming to call on you.'

'She hasn't called yet this morning,' Emily said, realising sadly it had not been for her sake that he had come to the house. 'Do wait for her, if you'd care to.'

Basil sat down rather absently, and was silent, staring in deep thought at the carpet. After a while, Emily said, 'You must have had a great deal to do in Richmond. Did you have anyone to help you?'

He looked up at her blankly, evidently not having heard a word; and before she could repeat it he seemed to make up his mind to something, and said, 'Cousin Emily, can I confide in you?'

'Of course,' she said simply.

'The thing is, I proposed to Fanny again last night, and she refused me. I'm afraid I got rather upset, and said some things – well, I felt I must see her again today anyway. She doesn't mean what she says, I know she doesn't, but I have to have an answer. I can't wait for ever. Now Mama's gone, I have to arrange my business affairs, and

127

Anna thinks I ought to go back to Russia because things are so unsettled there. So I told Fanny this was the last time I would ask her, and that I must have my answer by today, one way or the other.'

'You're going back to Russia?' Emily picked out the thing that mattered most to her.

'It depends on Fanny. If she refuses me, I shall go. Of course, if she accepts, I wouldn't expect her to leave her homeland. If she marries me, we'll live here.'

Ironic, Emily thought, that I can only hope to see him again as someone else's husband. If she refuses him, he's lost to me entirely. 'I don't see how she could refuse you,' she said sadly.

Basil looked worried. 'She said she didn't need until today to decide. But she only says those things to tease – don't you think so?'

'Is that what you wanted to ask me?' Emily said.

'Yes, I suppose so. I mean, Fanny and I have known each other all our lives, and we've always known we were to get married one day. Why does she keep refusing me now? It can't be my position or my fortune. My family's old and noble enough, and though mine is only a junior branch of it, I'm very wealthy.'

'Are you?'

'Oh yes. My father was a Railway King, and my grandfather was a Textiles King. He owned quite a bit of Australia. Fanny can't be in any doubt about that.'

'I'm sure she's never even thought about it,' Emily said. 'She doesn't care for money, except just to be comfortable.'

'Well of course,' Basil said, a little impatiently, 'that's all anyone cares.' Which was true, Emily thought; except that one man's comfort was another man's luxury. 'So why does she refuse me? I thought perhaps she didn't care for the idea of living with my mother. Do you think that was it? If so, she must change her mind now – '

The door opened, and Lady Hamilton's butler announced Lady Frances Hope. Basil brightened as he sprang to his feet, but Emily's heart sank at the thought of what she might be about to witness.

'Emily, I – oh, hello Basil. You here!' She didn't sound entirely pleased about it.

'Mrs Partridge said you would be calling here, and Emily said I might wait for you.'

'How kind of her,' Frances said, throwing an indecipherable look at Emily. 'You don't mean to bring up the topic of last night again, I hope?'

Basil looked astonished. 'But you said you would give me your answer this morning!'

'No, Basil, *you* said that. I gave you my answer last night.'

'You didn't mean it,' Basil said. 'You were upset.'

Frances made a movement of exasperation, looked from him to Emily and back again, then said, 'You never believe anything I say, unless it's what you want to hear! I'm sorry, Emily, but perhaps if he hears it in front of a witness he'll do me the courtesy of accepting my answer. For the last time, Basil, I won't marry you. I'm fond of you, but I don't love you in that way, and I don't believe you love me either. No! Let me finish! I must tell you that I don't mean to get married at all, not ever. I have better things to do with my life.'

Basil was perplexed. 'What things? What could you possibly do if you don't get married?'

'I mean to dedicate myself to the Cause. Because of what's happened recently, we have it all to do again from the beginning. The Cause needs dedicated women, even those like me who have no particular skills.'

'The *Cause*?' Basil said between astonishment and contempt. 'The votes for women nonsense? You can't mean it!'

Frances bristled. 'You have been interested in it yourself, may I remind you!'

'Only out of politeness,' Basil retorted. 'It's merely good manners to pretend to take an interest in what ladies talk about.'

'Basil, no, you don't mean that,' Emily said quickly. His pride was hurt, she thought, and he was hitting out at Fanny.

'Yes he does,' Frances snapped. 'Like all men, he thinks nothing in the world can be so interesting as himself.'

'I should be a sorry creature if I weren't more interesting than your stupid Suffragette nonsense!'

'Only a fool would think it stupid.'

'So I'm a fool now, am I? Then I'm one of a very large majority.'

'I agree. Most men are fools. But let me remind you that Angela died for the Cause, and I won't let her death be in vain!'

'Much comfort that will be to you, when you are old and poor and everyone laughs at you!'

'Oh, stop it!' Emily cried. 'Both of you! You don't mean these things. You're just trying to hurt each other.'

There was a brief silence. Basil looked shamefaced. 'Sorry! Bad form. I beg your pardon, Emily.'

But Frances looked sad and tired. 'I'm sorry too, Emily, but you're wrong. We do mean these things. The only reason we've never quarrelled like this before is that neither of us cared enough to bother. So you have your answer now, Basil. Find yourself a nice pretty girl who thinks you're wonderful, and be happy with her.' She seemed about to add something else, but changed her mind, nodded briefly to Emily, and left.

'Well,' said Basil at last, stranded on the sandbank of embarrassment.

'I'm so sorry, Basil,' Emily said helplessly. 'I hope you won't mind it too much.'

'It's damnable,' he said gloomily. 'Sorry, Emily! But after all these years! Oh well, I'm glad there was no-one but you to hear the things she said to me. I should have been mortified if anyone else had been here.'

There was a way to look at that, Emily was sure, which would make it into a compliment. It only needed thinking about.

The storm, when it broke, broke suddenly. One morning in February Emily was about to leave the house to visit Princess Volkinsky when her father arrived, looking pale and rather hectic.

'Papa! What's the matter? Is somebody ill?' Emily asked quickly.

Edward cast a quick, warning glance at the butler as he turned her around and propelled her towards the morning-room. 'No, of course not,' he said, trying for a little composure. 'Can't a father come to visit his own daughter once in a while?'

Once inside the room he closed the door firmly behind him and said, 'Sorry, Emily, but I've got something to tell you that must be kept absolutely secret. We don't want anyone, especially servants, to have anything to gossip about.'

Emily surveyed his face anxiously. The usual veiled, other-worldly look had gone, and the tiredness and shadows in his face made her realise, by contrast, how unmarked he had always been before by the passage of life.

'What's happened?' she asked.

He hesitated. 'It's rather delicate. I don't quite know how to tell you. It concerns your Uncle Westie . . . '

The hollow feeling again. 'And Miss Montgomery?'

His eyebrows went up. 'You know about it? Good God!'

'I saw them together a few weeks ago, and made Lady Hamilton tell me the truth.'

'Oh yes, I'm sure Lady Hamilton knows all about it,' Edward said bitterly. 'I don't know why we bother to try and keep it secret!'

'She would never tell anyone. She didn't even tell me. She's the last person in the world to gossip – or to listen to gossip,' Emily said firmly. Edward didn't look convinced, and Emily went on, 'But why are you here, Papa? Has something new happened?'

Edward sighed, gathering himself. 'Westie has bolted.'

'Bolted?'

'He's gone off to America with the Montgomerys. He left a letter behind for Sir Archibald Craig, his solicitor, and Craig came straight down to Bratton last night, as soon as he'd made sure it was too late to stop them, to break the news. As you can probably imagine, all hell was let loose.'

'Oh poor Aunt Maud! But she knew, Papa, I'm sure of it! When I think back, we all ought to have guessed long ago that there was something wrong.'

Edward looked blank. 'I don't know what you mean. But whatever she knew or didn't know, she could hardly have expected this latest development. Westie must be out of his senses. His letter to Craig says – ' He hesitated, and then resumed. 'You have to know the truth, Emily, but you must prepare yourself for a shock. Your uncle wants to divorce your aunt to marry this Montgomery woman and live with her in New York.'

It *was* a shock, even though she had been expecting it. 'What would happen to my aunt, in that case? And my cousins?' she asked at last.

'It won't happen. It can't happen. It's unthinkable. He's got to be brought to his senses. And most of all we must keep the whole thing secret; there must be no scandal. That's why I've come to fetch you home. There are bound to be one or two people who suspect, and they'll come buzzing round like flies and wheedle the story out of you.'

'I wouldn't tell anyone anything,' Emily said indignantly.

'My dear child, you're too young and innocent to be able to stand out against the kind of people I'm talking about. They'd get the truth out of you one way or another, so I'm taking you out of harm's way, back home to Bratton, until it's all been sorted out.'

'But – '

131

'There's no time to argue. Go to your room now and pack your things, while I have a word with Lady Hamilton. I presume she's in? I called early to make sure I'd catch you both.'

'She's still in her room,' Emily said. 'She doesn't come downstairs until luncheon. But Papa – '

'I'll have to send up word that I want to talk to her, then,' Edward said, looking round for the bell. 'I shall tell her that your aunt is unwell and asking to see you. That will be your story, if there should be any necessity to tell anyone why you're leaving Town in a hurry.'

'There's no point in lying to her, Papa,' Emily said firmly. 'She'll know. She knows everything. And besides, after all she's done for me, it would be very rude not to tell her the truth.'

'Go and pack,' Edward said, ringing vigorously. 'Leave me to deal with this in my own way.'

It was a dismal way to be going home, and the weather was in sympathy with the occasion, raining in dreary swathes from a low, blank sky as if it never meant to stop. The windows of the railway carriage soon fogged over, and Edward buried himself in the paper, plainly disinclined for conversation, so that there was nothing for Emily to do but sit and think. There were two bright spots in her memory to comfort her. One was that she had insisted on going in to say goodbye to Lady Hamilton, and the old lady had, for the first time, taken her hands and kissed her fondly.

'I shall miss you, but your father is quite right. It would be very unpleasant for you in London if the scandal does break. You will come back when it's over.'

'I hope so. Yes, please,' Emily said, not knowing if it were a statement or a question.

Lady Hamilton nodded and released her. 'Remember, nothing is ever as good as you think it's going to be, and nothing is ever as bad.'

And when Lovibond helped her down from the car at the station, he took the opportunity to press her arm slightly and whisper, 'Don't worry, miss. Everything'll turn out all right. You'll see.'

Two moments of warmth and kindness to remember. But there had been no opportunity to say goodbye to other friends; and she hadn't seen Basil for over a week, since he had called to tell her and Lady Hamilton that he was definitely going back to live in Russia. No comfort anywhere there: Frances had broken his heart, and he was going to Russia, and she would never see him again. If this dreadful business of Uncle Westie's was not cleared up quickly, Basil might leave without her even having the chance to say goodbye to him.

She looked at the raindrops chasing down the carriage window, and then had only to think of Angela to be in floods of tears.

The family closed ranks. By the time Emily got back to Bratton, Tom had also been brought home, and during the evening her Uncle John – Lord Oxhey – arrived, bringing with him his wife, his four younger children, a complement of servants, and the Oxhey family solicitor, Sir Barratt Hanwell.

'What a caravan! You should have seen it,' Tom said to Emily when she met him in the park the next day. His voice had broken since she had last seen him, and for the first few minutes it made him seem like a stranger. 'There was an absolute mountain of luggage, too,' he went on. 'It looks as though he's come for a long stay.'

'But isn't Sir Archibald Craig still here? Why did he need to bring another solicitor?' Emily asked.

Tom made a face. 'Archie Craig is Papa's man of business, so Uncle John thinks he can't be trusted to look after Mama and the girls. You should have heard him last night when he arrived: "You're a Paget," he said to Mama. "The Pagets always look after their own." Pompous old ass! He practically had Mama in tears, and you know how hard that is to do.'

'Has she sent Sir Archibald away?'

'No, of course not. That's just Uncle John's nonsense. Archie Craig and Hanwell are completely in agreement that this divorce business simply isn't on, and that Papa must be persuaded to come back. And anyway, Mama trusts Craig. It was she who chose him, when Grandpa's man of business died.' He sighed. 'I wish we could do without Uncle John, but we might need his influence. Lord knows what it will take to persuade Papa to do the right thing. And of course we need his money.'

Emily looked her surprise. 'But surely – '

'You don't understand,' Tom interrupted, and she saw the resentment and anger he was trying to conceal. 'Craig can't authorise any unusual payments from the estate – not even his own fees – without Papa's say-so. This is likely to be an expensive business, according

133

to what Craig and Hanwell were saying, and Mama's allowance won't be enough to cover it.'

They reached the house, and Tom left her to seek the solace of the stables while Emily paid her obligatory respects to her uncle. He was a tall, beak-nosed man, with an almost lipless mouth which didn't move when he spoke. He was thin except for a considerable paunch, which made him look as though he were wearing it for a friend – an effect increased by the forward stoop of his shoulders.

Emily didn't remember ever seeing him before. He had refused to acknowledge her existence, because of her mother's lowly status, and that he did so now was proof of the strength of his family feelings at this moment of crisis.

'At a time like this, much can be overlooked,' he told her generously. 'We must all pull together. Blood is thicker than water, after all, and you have some Paget blood in you. We must hope for your sake as much as ours that it is strong enough to overcome the other influences.'

His countess was remarkable only for her complete lack of chin: her face merged into her neck without let or hindrance. She did not speak when Emily said how do you do to her, only blinked rapidly a few times, so that Emily did not know whether she was deaf, proud, shy, or absent-minded.

Aunt Maud was there, looking exhausted, but oddly more human and approachable because of it. She greeted Emily with more kindness than before, and almost apologised for interrupting her pleasures.

'You understand that we could not risk your remaining in London. This must not become public, whatever happens.'

'I understand, Aunt,' Emily said, trying to infuse the words with sympathy. She wanted to say how sorry she was, but didn't dare.

'Very well. You may go upstairs and see your cousins now. You will not, of course, discuss this matter with them. They have no idea of the truth, and it would not be proper for them to know the facts, at their age. I would have kept it from you,' she added, with a bitter look, 'but your father persuaded me you must be told.'

Some finer instinct prevented Emily from blurting out that she had known for weeks. For Aunt Maud, she reflected as she went upstairs, the humiliation must be the worst of the hurt.

Upstairs, Lexy and Victoria were in a state of ferment nearing overboil, made worse by the restraining presence of Aunt Mary's four children. They had also had the misfortune to inherit their father's nose and their mother's lack of chin.

'Poor things, they have trouble just standing upright,' Lexy said unkindly to Emily at the nursery door.

'Lexy! They'll hear you!' Emily whispered.

'No they won't. Anyway, too bad if they do. Why should we be lumbered with them? Simply too stupid!'

Victoria joined them. 'And what about this business of Pa and his Trollop? No wonder Mama got rid of Mamzelle!'

'Young, pretty and blonde, just like the Trollop,' Lexy said. 'Gall and wormwood to Mama. The only wonder is she didn't strangle her and bury her in the kitchen garden.'

'You aren't supposed to know about it,' Emily said.

'Tom told us. Well, why shouldn't we? It's our father, after all. I just don't see why Uncle John had to come and drop his horrible offspring on us. They don't know about the Trollop, which means we can't talk in front of them.'

'You must stop calling her that,' Emily said. 'It isn't proper – and besides, she isn't one.'

Four round eyes grew rounder. 'Have you seen her? Oh prime! Now you can tell us all about her!'

'Tom only knows what Fellowes at school told him, and that wasn't much. Is she really pretty?'

'Why has Pa gone dotty over her? It can't be her money, because he's got oodles of his own.'

'Not now,' Emily said firmly. 'It's too rude to ignore your cousins, poor things. And besides, I don't like to hear you talking about it so lightly. It's very serious, you know.'

'You don't need to tell us that,' Lexy said.

'It's just our way of coping,' said Victoria. 'Every time I think about Mama, I want to howl like a dog. What's to become of us, Em?'

'Everything will be sorted out,' Emily said, trying for a confident tone. 'Nothing is ever as bad as you think it's going to be.'

'Sometimes it's worse,' Lexy said. 'We never expected little Maudie to die, for instance. And nothing seems to have gone right since then.'

After long discussion, it was decided that Edward and Sir Barratt Hanwell should go to New York. Originally John had wanted to go, but Maud had persuaded him that Westie would be more likely to listen to Edward, because he liked him and thought him clever. She managed somehow to hint, without actually saying it, that he would regard Edward as a companion in sin, who thus knew whereof he talked. This was at least more tactful than telling John that he inevitably set people's backs up as soon as he opened his mouth.

Edward was willing to go, but had wanted Craig with him. John insisted on Hanwell.

'This is a Paget matter,' John pronounced, 'and there is no-one better able to put across what incurring the weight of Paget disapproval will mean than Hanwell. Besides, Craig's position is too delicate.'

'But Craig agrees that it's in Westie's best interests to come back,' Edward said. 'There's no conflict there. And Westie trusts him.'

'Professional ethics,' John insisted. 'He can't take my money when he's already retained by Westinghouse.'

So it was settled. Edward and Hanwell set off, and the rest of the family could only wait for news, and hope. It was a miserable time. The weather was cold, wet and blustery, and after so long away, The Lodge seemed cramped and dark to Emily. The chimneys wouldn't draw properly, so the inadequate fires smoked and sulked in the chilly rooms. Penny crept about like one bereaved, alternately sunk in silent grief over Aunt Maud's betrayal, or prognosticating worse to come in the form of divorce, disgrace, and probably death as well.

Emily did her best to entertain her cousins and keep their minds off things, but otherwise she had nothing to do and too much that was unpleasant to think about. Her own future was bound up with that of her aunt and cousins. She had always thought of herself as under her aunt's patronage, but Bratton was her uncle's property. If Aunt Maud was forced to leave, Edward and Emily would be homeless too.

She had one letter from Lady Hamilton saying that the scandal had not broken openly. So far there was nothing more than speculation, some people connecting the Montgomery absence with Westie's, others maintaining that he had gone to New York for business purposes. This, on the whole, good news was counterbalanced by the bad news that Basil had finished winding up his mother's affairs and would be leaving for St Petersburg at the end of the month. Emily hoped against hope that she might have a chance to see him once more before he left, or even that he might write to her to say goodbye, but March went out and April came in, and she knew he had gone without anything to mark the transition.

Then a cable came from Edward in New York. 'Have succeeded. Hanwell returning immediately to explain plan.'

'What can it mean?' Emily puzzled when Tom rode over to The Lodge to tell her about it. 'If Papa's succeeded, why isn't he bringing my uncle back? Why does he need a plan?'

Tom shook his head. 'I don't know any more than you do, but it might have something to do with this.' He handed her that morning's newspaper, folded open at the social column. Emily read it, and felt rather sick.

'It's only speculation. You see they don't know for sure.'

'They just write it that way to protect themselves,' he said. 'The fact is that it's got as far as the newspapers. Their names have been connected publicly. Nothing can stop the scandal now.'

'But this is an English paper. Papa wouldn't have known about it yesterday, would he?'

'Mama says this newspaper probably got the story from an American one. They send each other stories if they think they're interesting. She says Uncle Ned probably read something like this in New York several days ago.'

'How is my aunt taking it?' Emily asked.

Tom was grave, looking older than his fourteen years. He had grown up so much in the past few weeks.

'She's very calm, but I know how much it hurts her. I'll never forgive Papa for this, never!' he added fiercely. 'I wish to God there was something I could do about it! I wish to God I was grown up, then I'd show him!'

The plan, it turned out, had been thought up by Sir Barratt Hanwell to deal with the growing body of gossip in America. It was as Tom guessed. Westinghouse's name had been firmly linked with that of Miss Montgomery, and a fine scandal was ripening fast in New York.

Edward had managed to persuade Westie that he must return to his wife and family only with great difficulty. Some time afterwards, when he too returned to England, he told Emily, 'He was quite out of his mind about the girl. I told him that John would sue him penniless, and he said it didn't matter because the Montgomerys had plenty of money. I told him he'd never see his children again, and

137

he said he didn't care because he'd be starting a new family with Pamela.'

'Oh Papa, no!'

'I've never told anyone else all this. This is between you and me, you understand.'

'Yes, of course. But how did you persuade him in the end?'

'I told him that Maud would never agree to a divorce. He could live with Pamela, but he couldn't marry her and make her his marchioness. He didn't care about that either, at first, until it dawned on him that Pamela wouldn't want him on those terms.'

'She doesn't really love him, then?'

Edward shrugged. 'She loves the Marquess of Westinghouse,' he said succinctly. 'Then I told him how unhappy Maud was without him, and he ended up in tears.'

The plan, then, as Sir Barratt explained it, was for Lady Westinghouse and the children to join his lordship in New York for a holiday.

'We can then let it be known that his lordship simply went on ahead to conduct some business. It will be seen that it was always intended for you to join him, and when you all travel home together, the gossip will be completely quashed.'

Maud didn't think much of the idea, and said so forcibly. 'Stuff and nonsense. Let him come back here as quickly as possible. That's the way to kill gossip.'

But Sir Archibald was in agreement with his colleague. 'I really think, ma'am, that if you can bring yourself to do it, it will be best for you to be seen in New York with your husband. Otherwise, it leaves that field entirely clear for the Montgomerys to say what they like by way of face-saving. And what is known there on Monday is known in London by Friday. If you are seen in New York *en famille* – and a happy and loving family to boot – there will be nothing that can be said against Lord Westinghouse.'

'How long must I spend there?' Maud asked, scowling furiously.

'Oh, a month, I think, ma'am, would be enough.'

'A month!' And another thought occurred to her. 'And then there's the crossing. I hate boats, as you very well know.'

'It's only a week, ma'am. These modern ocean-racers are very fast, and fitted out with every luxury.'

Maud didn't care about the luxury. 'A week on a boat, without setting foot on shore? Out of the question!'

She left for Southampton two days later, accompanied by Lexy and Victoria, who were beside themselves with excitement.

'Only think, New York! What bliss! I'm almost ready to forgive Pa now!'

'Don't you envy us, poor stuck-in-England Emily? What tales we shall have to tell you when we get back!'

Tom refused absolutely to go. To his mother he said, 'It's better that I go back to school and scotch the rumours there. And after all, it wouldn't be natural for you to take me out of school just to go on holiday.'

But to Emily he said, 'I want nothing to do with it. I won't pretend to be a loving son just to save Papa's hide. I hope I never see him again, actually, and if I can arrange to spend all the vacations with friends from now on, I may just manage it.'

'Oh, Tom!'

'No, Em, I don't care. What he did was wicked and wrong, and he broke Mama's heart. I'll never forgive him.'

BOOK TWO

GROWING

Chapter Nine

For Emily, the moment when she first saw St Petersburg from the deck of the SS *Verschagin* was like waking from a long, bad dream. The journey had not been a pleasant one. As soon as they rounded the North Foreland out of Tilbury they had encountered the North Sea and its humours, and it was not until the ship entered the still waters of the Kiel Canal that any of the passengers had felt like eating. Then, once they were into the Baltic, it was all freezing fog and ice-floes, and the mournful hooting of the foghorn as they crept slowly northwards.

Emily was the only Englishwoman on board. Most of the passengers were German and spoke only their own language. She did once strike up a conversation with a Finnish deck-hand who spoke Russian, but since what she could understand of his strangely accented speech seemed to concern ghost ships, sea monsters and evil spirits that lurked in the Baltic fog and lured mariners to their doom on sharp rocks, she didn't repeat the experiment.

Simply being on a ship brought back to her every day the horror of the deaths of Aunt Maud, Lexy and Victoria. She did not know exactly how they had died when their ship struck an iceberg in mid-Atlantic and sank, only that they had not been among the survivors. But her imagination offered her images all too readily: of darkness and icy water pouring in; of terror and choking screams; of lonely, struggling death in a small, confined space.

It was an extraordinary, freak accident, everyone agreed. People travelled all over the world every day in ships large and small and arrived safely. That particular vessel was new and of the most advanced design; the weather had been good and the sea calm. The chances of such a thing happening were not one in ten million. Still, Emily was glad of every day her father put off his return, and when he did finally embark in New York, she almost held her breath until he arrived, weary and haggard, at Bratton.

Once he was back inside the haven of The Lodge, he seemed to want most of all to forget all that had happened, and sink back into his private world of school-days, jolly japes and adventures that

143

always worked out well. Emily could only extract information from him piecemeal, over a period of some days. It made no more pleasant hearing than telling; and the end of the story was that her uncle was going to marry Miss Montgomery as soon as the mourning period was over.

Emily tried to think logically about it, to tell herself that it could make no difference to Aunt Maud now. It would be absurd for him not to do what he had been going to do anyway, now that he could do it in all propriety. But it didn't help; she still felt that it would be a callous and heartless thing to install her rival in Aunt Maud's place.

Penny went further. 'He murdered her,' she said. 'A great lady he wasn't fit to kiss the feet of! She wouldn't have been on that boat if it wasn't for him running off with That Woman. He murdered her just the same as if he plunged a knife into her.'

Emily's intellect might protest, but Penny's words pretty well summed up her feelings. And what was to happen to them now?

'Westie says we can stay here,' Edward told her. 'The Lodge is ours for as long as we want it, on the same terms as before. Nothing has changed.'

'Everything has changed,' Emily said. 'How can you say that? I don't see how we can go on living here if he brings Miss Montgomery to Bratton.'

'I don't see how we can do anything else,' Edward said.

'But Papa, Aunt Maud was your own sister, and this woman is nothing but a – '

'Don't rant at me, Emily. I've had enough of that in my lifetime,' Edward snapped, the cracks showing for once in his façade of indifference. Emily remembered belatedly that her own mother had been *nothing but a* in the eyes of the family, and was ashamed.

'It isn't our business who he marries,' Edward went on after a moment. 'And he'll be marrying her perfectly legally – in Westminster Abbey, if the lady has her way. Besides,' he added wearily, 'where could we go? I can't provide a home for us on the little I earn.'

Emily saw the blessed chance of escape fading before her eyes. 'But other writers manage it,' she said urgently. 'Frank Richards must earn enough to – '

'I'm not Frank Richards. And I'm not going to live like a pauper in a flat in Paddington. It suits me here. It's quiet. No,' he stemmed her protest. 'I can't go amongst people again, Emily; I'm not used to it. New York', he added feelingly, 'was hell.'

144

She saw again how haggard he looked, and let the argument drop. But every day the feeling was stronger in her that she couldn't go on living at Bratton, mouldering her life away, particularly as a dependant of Miss Montgomery. In that, at least, Penny concurred with her.

'I'm not having my wages paid by a murderess,' she said shortly, once she understood that Edward really meant to stay put. 'I shall find another position.'

Emily protested, although not very hard, not believing right up to the last moment that Penny would actually go. But she announced at breakfast one morning that she had secured a position as housekeeper to a vicar in Yeovil, and would leave as soon as Emily had found a replacement for her.

Edward made no objection, seeming almost determinedly not to notice anything that happened outside his study. Emily felt hurt to be so easily abandoned, and at such a time, though she reasoned with herself that she would have left Bratton if she could, leaving Penny behind. Still, on the day Penny walked away towards the station in her black coat and hat, carrying her battered suitcase – pathetically small to contain a whole lifetime's possessions – Emily half expected to hear the rumble of The Lodge collapsing into its component bricks in protest.

But no cataclysm marked the parting. Emily promised, tearfully, to write to her, and made Penny promise to write back, and that was that. The woman who had been all the mother she had ever known walked out of her life with nothing more than a cool, 'Goodbye, then, Emily'; and if she shed a tear, it was not until she was out of Emily's sight.

The replacement Penny had helped her to find was a small, meek, mousy woman called, appropriately enough, Mrs Vicar. Unlike Penny, she was a genuine 'Mrs', the widow of a baker. She rarely spoke above a whisper, and looked too frail to do all the work even of such a small house. But she proved perfectly adequate to the task, and cooked as well as Penny ever had. Most of all, which had been Penny's main concern, she was never likely to 'presume'. She kept rigidly to her own quarters, did not speak unless spoken to, and called Emily 'miss'.

Emily wondered how Mrs Vicar would cope with the isolation at The Lodge, but the few times she put her head round the kitchen door of an evening, Mrs Vicar seemed perfectly happy sitting by the fire, knitting little garments for a seemingly endless succession of

145

newborn relatives, or reading the Good Book, following the words with moving forefinger and lips. She had no further hopes of this world, she told Emily on the one occasion she unbent about herself. Mr Vicar having gone above, she was simply waiting to join him, and wished only to keep herself free from sin so as to be sure of getting to the Right Place when the time came.

With this jolly addition to their household, Penny gone, her father more reclusive than ever, and Bratton deserted, there was nothing to distract Emily from the mixture of grief, anxiety and frustration that gnawed at her. The summer passed in its usual beauty, but seen by Emily as though through glass, at one remove from her. The Lodge seemed to grow smaller around her every day, as though the walls were drawing together. She had terrible dreams at night of being trapped in a tiny windowless room, and of water bursting in and choking her as she beat frantically against the shrinking, strait-jacket walls.

There must be some way to escape. Now that Aunt Maud was dead, surely there would be no-one to object if she worked for a living? Whom could it now disgrace? In fluttering hope she wrote to Lady Hamilton, asking if she would help her find employment.

Lady Hamilton telegraphed back curtly, saying, 'Wait. Matters are in hand.'

And a month later came a letter from Emily's grandmother, inviting her to come and live with her in Russia.

'It was always what I intended, my Emilia, but you were too young before, and I was too busy. Now I think you are ready, and it is time to take up your new life. You are a Russian at heart, little one, and you will be happy here – happier than you can think possible.'

To travel! To see Russia! To see her grandmother again, and resume those wonderful conversations that started nowhere and led anywhere. 'Take up your new life' – what singing, magical words! The cage door had swung open, and a fresher breeze blew in to her than she had dreamed of. She took the letter to her father, and waited in breathless silence while he read it.

At last he looked up. 'So, you want to go away and leave me here all alone, do you?'

Emily quivered. 'Oh, Papa!'

Edward almost smiled. 'No, no, I'm only teasing you. Of course you must go. God knows, there's nothing for you here. I can't

146

provide for you, and who knows how far Westie's new wife's philanthropy will stretch.'

'I won't go if you don't want me to,' Emily said simply.

Edward met her eyes. For once he was really there, close to the surface, so that she could see him clearly. She carried with her, as children do, an image of him which bore little relationship to his reality – a situation his determined detachment had prolonged beyond the usual age of undeception. Now, for the first time, Emily saw how the real Edward looked strangely shrunken and unsubstantial beside the shape in her mind labelled *Papa*. She was reminded of the wasps' nest old Jacob had shown her once, after it had been fumigated and removed from under the stable roof. She had been surprised to find it so light, papery, hollow; so little of a threat, now the wasps were gone.

She and Penny had erected a monument called Papa's Work; they had made a creative genius out of him, and tended their creation like two vestal virgins. But the truth was that Edward was incomplete, part of a man masquerading as a whole one, incapable of surviving away from the sustaining world-within-a-world he had chosen for himself with such an uncanny instinct for the trivial. Emily had also now to acknowledge to herself that she was no part of his comfort. It would make no difference to him whether she were there or not. He didn't love her; and though he had probably sometimes been quite sorry about that, it would never change.

Still, she made the offer; and it was to do with her duty to herself rather than anything to do with him.

Edward said, 'It would be a waste of your life, and I'm not worth that. You should go to Russia. You don't really belong here.'

She reached for him in this moment of realism. 'I'll come back one day.'

But he was going from her, swimming back down into the depths where she could see him only as an indistinct, moving shape. 'When you've made your fortune,' he said lightly. 'You'll come back covered in jewels and forgive everyone who was unkind to you, and set your cruel stepsisters to tend the palace pigsties.'

Emily let him go. 'Hard luck on the pigs, I should think,' she said, 'if they really were cruel.'

*

147

That left only Tom, and she did feel bad about him. She wrote to him of her plans: as his father was still in America, he was spending the summer with the family of a schoolfriend.

'It's not bad here,' Tom wrote back, 'except that Arlington's got a ghastly sister who simpers at me across the table and puts me off my grub. Arlington mater is all right, and pater takes us out fishing in his own boat. I caught four mackerel on Saturday, but we put one back because it was too small. Arlington pater says I can stay here as long as I like, which is prime, because otherwise it would be Uncle John's, which I couldn't stand at any price.

'I'm glad you're going to Russia. I really envy you. But don't worry about me. I shall never go back to Bratton if I can help it, once Pa's set up his floozie there. I'll spend all the vacations with Arlington or Deeping or someone and as soon as I finish school I'll be off. I mean to be an explorer or something – anyway, to travel the world – so perhaps I'll come and visit you in Russia one day.'

The sad summer wore away. In October, when his period of mourning ended, Lord Westinghouse married Miss Montgomery and brought her home to Bratton, and on the same day Emily said goodbye to her father and took the train to London. She was to stay a few days with Lady Hamilton, to say goodbye to friends and do some shopping.

'Grandmama says not to bring much with me. She says most of my clothes will be unsuitable.'

'So they will,' Lady Hamilton said. 'It's colder outside and warmer inside than you can have any idea of. Quite the opposite of England.'

She bought Emily a fur hat in the Army & Navy Stores. 'This is one thing you will certainly need.'

Emily tried it on, and found, as with her gold ball-dress, that it made her look instantly more foreign. I have hardly any English blood, after all, she thought. 'You've been so kind to me, ma'am,' she said to Lady Hamilton. 'I shall miss you very much.'

The old lady chuckled. 'Bless you, child, you won't miss me at all! You'll find hundreds of me in Russia.'

Frances visited briefly to say goodbye. She was tremendously busy with the Cause, having lately joined Mrs Pankhurst's militant group. Various supporters within Parliament were trying to get an amendment on the women's vote into the Manhood Suffrage Bill, but without success; and public opinion seemed not nearly so sympathetic as last year.

'Are you sure breaking windows and chaining yourselves to railings is doing any good?' Emily asked. 'I'm worried you might be arrested.' There had been stories of dreadful brutality towards the Suffragettes in prison. Some of them had gone on hunger strike, in protest at being treated as common felons instead of political criminals, and had been subjected to the unspeakable process of forcible feeding. The idea of Frances undergoing anything like that made Emily turn cold.

'It's the best we can do,' Frances said. 'We're women: we can't hurt and kill men to get our own way, we can only attack their property. When it comes to it, you see, we can't *force* them to give us the vote. All we can do is to go on annoying them until they give in for the sake of a quiet life. Pitiful, isn't it? But that's how it is for the oppressed, for people without power.'

'Well – you will be careful, though, won't you?' Emily asked, but Frances only smiled.

'That isn't what I'm for,' she said.

Sylvia paid a longer visit. 'Don't forget to write and tell me absolutely everything!' she said, a little wistfully. Frances's deeper involvement with the Cause had left her a little lonely. 'I'll try to keep an eye on her,' she said when they discussed Fanny's activities, 'but she's so pigheaded. And she still blames herself for Angela's death. She doesn't talk about it, but I'm sure that's what all this militant business is about.'

On the day of Emily's departure Lady Hamilton's rheumatism was going through a bad phase, so she said goodbye at the house. Lovibond drove Emily down to Tilbury Docks. As the ship went down the Thames on a chilly November afternoon, and she watched through tears the grey, familiar shape of London disappear into the mist, she thought it was somehow appropriate that his had been the last friendly face she saw.

The slow, difficult passage seemed still a part of the strange and uncomfortable dream of the past year. It was not until the *Verschagin* nosed carefully past Kronstadt, where some little vessels were already frozen in and were waiting for the ice-cutter to come and free them, and Emily saw the skyline of St Petersburg for the first time, that she really felt her new life was beginning.

Then, like a good omen, the sun broke through the fog and caught dazzlingly on a hundred golden spires. *I'm going to be happy here*, Emily thought. The exotic and beautiful city lay welcomingly before her, marvellously new, and yet oddly familiar, as though she had known it in another time, a waking time before the dream which the whole of her life so far had been.

She was taken first to her grandmother's house at Tsarskoye Selo – the Tsar's Village. Here, fifteen miles from St Petersburg, a succession of Russian emperors had created for themselves an enchanted place whose beauty and order was untouched by the outside world. Within a landscaped park, complete with artificial lake and numerous monuments and follies, lay two palaces, exquisite as jewels, where the imperial family lived at the centre of a complex web of protocol and protection. Liveried servants performed daily tasks hallowed by ancient ritual, mounted Cossacks in scarlet tunics and black fur caps patrolled the boundaries night and day, and sad policemen with umbrellas and gumboots lurked amongst the shrubs and flitted over the lawns, looking for terrorists.

Between the iron gates of the imperial park and the railway station was a wide, tree-lined boulevard along which stood the houses of the aristocracy; and to either side were lesser streets, a whole town of fine houses, shops, even a theatre – everything one could need for an elegant life.

Natasha Petrovna's house was small in Tsarskoye Selo terms, having only ten bedrooms, but it was very comfortable and well placed, just off the main street, with gardens that ran down to the canal.

'Empress Elizabeth began the canal so that she could travel to Petersburg by water; but it was never finished, and now we have the railway, it never will be. Still, it's pleasant for bathing,' Natasha explained to Emily. 'Your great-grandfather – my father – built this house as a summer retreat for my mother, to replace Schwartzenturm. That's our dacha, about twenty-five miles out of Petersburg, near Kirishi. Neither of them cared much for it. I think it had unhappy memories for them.'

'What happened to it?'

'When Papa died it went to my brother Nikolai, and when he died to his son Alexei. It's a strange house, but I always liked being there when I was a child. I dare say you will see it some time.'

For the moment, Emily had enough to cope with in getting used to Natasha's house in Tsarskoye Selo.

'We live in a small way here,' Natasha said. Emily calculated bemusedly one evening that thirty-two people would be sleeping

150

under the roof that night. After years of living at The Lodge – even after Lady Hamilton's house, with its small, well-trained and almost invisible staff – it was hard to get used to such a multitude, especially when they were all so exuberant. Self-effacement was evidently not a part of the Russian servant's creed. They did their work, and as well or badly as did English servants, but they talked about it, and themselves, and each other, all the time; and what happened to any member of the household was of passionate interest to them all.

Natasha did not live here alone. Emily was greeted on her arrival by the aunt she had never yet seen: her Aunt Eugenia, or Yenya, as she was known. Emily found her uncannily, poignantly like Aunt Maud in looks, and as unlike her as she could be in every other way. The stern, unbending, order-creating aunt of the Peacock Room had been softened and diffused into a smiling, loving, woolly-minded creature who welcomed Emily with a motherly embrace and tear-filled eyes and couldn't remember which room she'd had prepared for her.

'Never mind, we'll find it. The important thing is that you're here, dearest Emilia. We've all been so longing for you to come! Oh, and now I remember, I put you in the Pink Room, because I've just got my bee orchids to bloom, and I wanted you to have the pleasure of them.'

From her great-grandfather, Yenya had inherited a passion for growing flowers, and rare and exotic plants were coaxed into life and flourished under her care. Every window-sill in the house bore its row of pots, and even in the dead of winter all sorts of things bloomed against the background of the still white snowscape outside.

Inside, Emily discovered, it was as warm as a greenhouse. Each room had its huge wood-burning stove, decorated with silver scrolls and coloured porcelain tiles, which perfumed the air with the scent of birch and pine. The windows were covered by glazed second frames which shut out the fierce cold and all sound from outside, so that the air inside was quite still and warm. Draughts, the plague of every English house in winter, were unknown here.

In one corner of each room stood a little table bearing a pierced-work lamp, which threw a flickering lacework of light over the sad golden face of the saint in the icon on the wall above it. In the evenings, when the short winter day had drawn to a close and the lamps were lit, when the samovar was singing softly in the back-ground, and everyone drew together to work or talk, there was an

151

atmosphere of quiet intimacy and warmth which was balm to Emily's soul.

By contrast, the days were all sound and movement. This was partly due to Yenya's children, who were hardly ever still or quiet. Anatoli – Tolya – was fifteen, and had reached the agonising point of manhood where his voice was beginning to break and his moustache to grow and he didn't know whether to be embarrassed or thrilled about it. Trapped between adulthood and childhood, he veered between a scorching dignity tinged with true Russian melancholy, and wild frolickings with his little brother that usually ended with him lying on the floor, helpless with giggles.

He was painfully shy with Emily for the first week; and then, with the suddenness of water breaking a dam, he decided she was a soulmate, and sought her out for long, serious discussions about the Condition of Man. He had always been mad to be a soldier, and was intended for the Cadet School next year, but of late he had started having doubts as to whether it was right to kill one's fellow man after all. Emily talked to him as she would have to Tom, listened to his troubles and did her best to lighten his burden of responsibility for all mankind. In return he treated her as a fount of wisdom and threatened her self-control by gravely repeating her opinions to his elders: 'Yes, sir, but you see *Emilia* says . . . '

She was in no danger of becoming a saint to Evgeny, universally known as Yenchik. He had an overdeveloped sense of humour, and an abominable love of the practical joke, and if he had not also been blessed with more than his fair share of charm, he wouldn't have survived to the age of twelve. Some of his teases were puzzlingly obscure. For several days, for instance, Emily was haunted everywhere she went by a clothes-peg. She would find it pinned to the hem of her dress, or attached to her sleeve; it lurked in her purse, or between the pages of the book she was reading; it was rolled inside her napkin at dinner, and nestled on her pillow when she went to bed.

She had no idea what it was all about. The whole thing seemed perfectly pointless, but Yenchik went about with an expression of intense saintliness, which meant he was laughing like a fiend inside. Yet when Emily had been the butt of one of his jokes and tackled him with it, he would fling his arms around her and smile seraphically. 'It's only love, you know, Emilusha!' he would say. 'Love with a crooked tail.'

Roxane, aged five, whose pet names were legion, had probably never gone more than ten minutes in her whole life without being hugged by somebody. Aunt Yenya said, with devastating frankness, that she had come as a great surprise to everyone; but all Russians love children, and there was never any danger that the unexpected arrival would be other than welcomed. She was a bottomless well of good humour, and never seemed to mind how often she was interrupted in her plays to be picked up or kissed – which was just as well.

She soon had Emily marked out as a tireless storytelling machine, and displayed quite a firm will in taking Emily by the hand, obliging her to sit down, and then climbing onto her lap for yet another exposition of 'The Three Bears' or 'The Tinder Box'. She liked stories to have three of something in them, would listen almost holding her breath through numbers one and two, and join in with a triumphant shout when it got to number three.

If Tolya was Tom to Emily, then Yenchik was Lexy and Victoria, and Zansha was little Maudie. Emily's love found new channels of expression, and her grief began to be exorcised in those first, settling-in weeks.

Yenya's husband, the other member of the household, was Count Valentin Surinov – Uncle Valya to Emily. She didn't see very much of him, for he seemed to work very long hours and was frequently away in Petersburg, where he had something to do with the Ministry of the Interior. Quite what he did Emily was never able to find out. Yenya was hopelessly vague and said he was some kind of government official, and when Emily once dared to ask Valya himself, he only laughed and said that in Russia everyone was some kind of government official.

Emily gained the impression that Valya was not a contented man, and that some of his absences from home were out of choice. Of course, she was not in a position to know what troubled him, but it was possible, she decided at last, that he had not realised when he married her how woolly-witted Aunt Yenya really was. Old Mamka, Natasha's former wet-nurse and Yenya's nanny – an ancient and brooding presence who ruled the house as a bear in a cave rules a mountain – said of Yenya, 'If her hair was on fire she'd still ask you for a candle.'

More seriously, Yenya had been bitten by the craze for spiritualism which was rife amongst society ladies in Petersburg. Valya strongly disapproved of it, Mamka went further and declared that it was the

Devil's work, and that Yenya would burn for ever if she didn't give it up.

Emily wondered whether Valya disliked living in his mother-in-law's house and wished he could have a home of his own. She was surprised to discover, when she had been there for some weeks, that in fact they did have several houses: one in Petersburg, one in the Crimea, and a dacha in the country.

'We're only *visiting* Mamochka,' Yenya made all clear at last: they had come for Christmas in 1905 and had simply not got round to going away again. This was apparently not unusual in Russia. 'I don't much like any of our houses,' she went on. 'It's much nicer here.'

'Why don't you sell them, then?' Emily asked.

Yenya looked blank. 'But then where would we live?' she asked simply.

As December advanced, Emily couldn't help noticing that the word *Rozhdestvo* – Christmas – was creeping into the conversation more and more often. The degree of excitement she could feel building up was something of a puzzle.

'But surely you celebrated Christmas in England?' Aunt Yenya asked.

'We had special church services, of course,' Emily said. 'And if Aunt Maud and Uncle Westie were at home, we were invited up to the Big House for dinner on Christmas Day, but it was always rather stiff and formal, not very enjoyable. The Boxing Day meet was the part I liked best – and tea afterwards with my cousins in the nursery.'

'Was that all?' Yenya asked. 'Didn't all your friends and relatives come and visit you?'

'We didn't have any friends,' Emily said, feeling rather ashamed to admit it. 'Sometimes the Big House family would go and stay with Uncle John, but Papa and I weren't invited, of course. Uncle John didn't acknowledge us.'

Yenya's eyes filled with tears. 'Poor Mala! What a terrible thing it must be, to marry an Englishman! Christmases were never like that when we were children, though they weren't as much fun as here.'

'Will you have lots of visitors?' Emily asked.

'We haven't much family left now, with Maud and Bertie dead, and Eddie and John in England. My uncles are dead, and my Aunt

Tatiana lives in Constantinople. She married a Frenchman in the *corps diplomatique* and he's stationed there, and they only come every fourth year. But my cousins always come to stay – Alexei and his family, and his brother, Adishka – and visitors drop in, and we have celebrations and presents for everyone and a grand dinner.'

Christmas presents meant trips to Petersburg by train. Emily went in with Natasha – the first time she had left Tsarskoye Selo since her arrival – and saw for the first time the wonderful shops in the Nevsky Prospekt, all lit up and decorated for Christmas like magic caves full of treasure. She had no experience of buying presents, and was surprised to find how seriously her grandmother approached the business. Every present had to be exactly right for the individual, and no-one was forgotten, down to the least servant.

'At Bratton, Aunt and Uncle gave the servants presents on Boxing Day,' Emily mentioned, 'but it was always the same for everyone – scented soap for all the maids, for instance, and handkerchiefs for all the men.'

Natasha reacted in the same way as Yenya. 'Poor Mala,' she sighed. 'She was not at all like a Russian. It was the fault of her upbringing. Things were always too formal at Tolpits, though I tried to change them. But servants are the most conservative creatures in the world, and as stubborn as donkeys, and the governess was such a monument! I suppose I might have got rid of her, but I dare say anyone else would have been just as bad, and Mala was fond of her.'

Natasha had arranged for Emily to be paid an allowance, and she now had the pleasure, for the first time in her life, of spending it on presents for other people. Her first thought was of Tom, and the result of a consultation with Natasha was that a parcel was made up for him containing presents from everyone, together with homemade sweets, biscuits, and traditional Christmas spice cakes called *kazulies* in fancy boxes. Emily asked Tolya's advice about her own present for Tom, and acting on his considered reply, purchased the best penknife she could find, with six blades, a marlin-spike, and a device for getting stones out of horses' hooves.

One place they visited on the Nevsky Prospekt was the English Shop, which was full of things like Pears' soap, Twining's tea, woollen comforters, and a fair sprinkling of English governesses and clerks doing their shopping. Emily had a moment or two of intense nostalgia as she wandered about while Natasha chose a leather notecase for Uncle Valya. At one counter was a display of English

155

books and periodicals, and when Natasha came to find her, Emily was gazing in a stricken way at a copy of the *Boy's Own Paper*, whose cover bore an illustration of a story about Richard 'Lionheart' Lomas, fresh from the pen of Edward Paget.

Natasha dealt with this outbreak of homesickness in a practical way: she bought the copy of the *BOP*, and whisked Emily off to a nearby restaurant for coffee and cakes.

'It was just a momentary lapse,' Emily explained a little later. 'I suddenly saw him at his desk in his study, and the red plush chairs and the faded carpet and all the familiar things, and I missed him.'

'Very natural and proper,' Natasha said. 'I should be sorry if you didn't. As long as you know that you can go home any time you want to – '

'Oh no! I'm very happy here. I don't want to go back. And it doesn't really seem like home any longer.' The end of the sentence came out rather more wistfully than she had meant it to, and she changed the subject hastily, turning it to a discussion of what present one could get for Yenchik that would not prove a danger to the rest of the household.

One evening, after Yenchik and Zansha were in bed, Mamka brought a basket of walnuts and a bowl of milk into the drawing-room and put them down on the table.

'These are the best, *barina*,' she said to Natasha. 'I've sorted them out myself. All the shells are nice and clean and smooth.'

'Ah, good. Stay and help us, Mamka – you have the best touch. Yenya, Emilia, come and sit at the table.'

Yenya brought a lighted candle, a stick of sealing-wax, and some green wool cut into lengths, and Natasha fetched from her bureau some little paper booklets about two inches square.

'What's going on?' Emily asked, taking her place beside Tolya.

'We're going to gild the nuts,' he answered, surprised. 'Haven't you ever done it before? I'll show you, then.'

Each booklet contained twenty thin leaves of pure gold with cigarette paper between them, each leaf so delicate it made the cigarette paper look thick and coarse by comparison.

'To get it out you have to blow on it, like this. Look,' Tolya said. He blew gently, and the almost weightless leaf lifted free of the paper with a faint rustling sound. 'Your hands have to be clean and dry, or the gold comes off on your fingers.'

'Like the bloom on a butterfly's wings,' Emily said, trying it for herself.

Each nut had to be dipped in the milk, then carefully wrapped in the gold leaf. When they were dry, the two ends of a strand of wool were placed on the top of the nut and sealed down with a drop of molten wax to make a loop.

'They're so beautiful!' Emily said. Gold paint would have been nothing to it, a dull and meagre imitation. These nuts shone with all the lustre of pure gold, like little suns, like tiny church cupolas. 'What are they for?'

'For hanging on the Christmas tree,' Tolya said, all amazement at her ignorance. 'You must have seen a Christmas tree before.'

'We don't really have them in England, though I think Queen Victoria used to have one at Windsor, because of Prince Albert.'

'But didn't your aunt have one at Bratton?' Natasha asked.

Emily shook her head. 'Everything at Bratton was done the English way.'

Natasha and Yenya exchanged a glance of complicity. 'We must all make an extra effort this year,' Natasha said. 'This will be your Christmas, Emilusha, one you will never forget.'

'It was always bound to be that,' Emily pointed out.

The guests arrived on Christmas Eve, in the early afternoon, before the short winter day closed in darkness. Natasha's coachman, Seva, had taken the horse-drawn sleigh down to the station to meet the train, and as it pulled onto the sweep in front of the house, everyone was at the windows to see the arrival.

'Oh, but Alyosha isn't there!' Yenya exclaimed. 'Now what's happened? I suppose he's been called away again. It's too bad!'

'Affairs of State show scant respect for family celebrations,' Valya said gravely.

Yenya knew she was being teased. 'Well I don't see how there can be a crisis at Christmas,' she objected.

Into the vestibule they went, to meet the fur-wrapped, bright-cheeked guests, to strip off their outer wrappings and hug and kiss the beings thus revealed. Yenya drew Emily forward.

'This is Emilia, Edward's daughter. Emilusha, this is Vladimir Nikolayevitch.'

A bright, catlike stare – much like Natasha's, except that the eyes were dark – and a thin, rather pinched face under a fair beard.

157

Emily felt instinctively in that first brief glimpse that there was something not quite right about him. He was a young man, in his mid-twenties she would have guessed, but there was an indefinable look of age in his face, a worn look about the eyes, like that of a sickly child.

But he smiled as he took her hand. 'Your cousin Adishka,' he said. 'Yes, I see you are a Kirov all right. Don't you think she has a look of our grandfather, Yenya? That portrait over the stairs at Schwartzenturm.' He bent his head – not very far, for he was hardly taller than Emily – and kissed her on either cheek. 'Welcome to Russia,' he said. 'I hope we shall see a great deal of you.'

And then, releasing her, he moved away to greet the children, who were hopping up and down with impatience to be noticed. Emily had not seen him descend from the sleigh. Now her questions about him were answered as she saw him move: his right leg was twisted and he dragged it as he walked, the effect, she supposed, of a childhood disease – tuberculosis, perhaps, or infantile paralysis.

She had no time to explore her thoughts further, for she was being presented to 'Anna Kirilovna, your cousin Alexei's wife,' and she found herself looking into a ravishingly pretty face which was oddly familiar.

'How do you do?' said Anna. 'I believe you are a friend of my brother Vasska?'

More fallings-into-place. Of course, this was Basil's sister Anna, on whose remote account he had presumed to call her Cousin Emily! The adjustment took place instantly, and Emily replied without a hesitation. 'Yes, I did meet him in England. Of course, he's in Russia now, isn't he? He's well, I hope?'

'Oh yes. He's . . . ' Anna's rather blank, blue gaze shifted slightly away and then back. 'He's very well,' she finished, as though that had not been what she first meant to say.

The rest of the party was made up by Anna's children, Modeste, a solemn, blond little boy of three, and Tatiana, who was a little more than a year old, and their nursemaids. The servants brought in the luggage, and then the winter afternoon was shut out, and Christmas began.

Christmas dinner began at six that evening with the *zakuski*. The butler and the footman brought into the drawing-room a wheeled table on which were laid out salted cucumbers, stuffed mushrooms, green and black olives, marinaded tomatoes, stuffed eggs in their shells, two kinds of caviare – red and black – and open tartlets filled with creamy concoctions of smoked fish and spiced chicken. Flasks of vodka sat in ice buckets, and as soon as the plates were filled, the glasses were charged and Natasha proposed the first toast – to Yenya and Yenchik, whose name-day it was.

Everyone drained their glasses in unison, and then tasted the *zakuski* while the servants went round refilling for the next toast. Emily had been in Russia almost six weeks now, and knew the procedure. She had found the vodka rather startling at first, but there was no doubt that it warmed up the atmosphere of any gathering very quickly, as toast after toast was drunk, and the delicious *hors-d'oeuvres* were consumed.

It was seven o'clock before they moved into the dining-room, where the servants brought in the soup and the hot *pirozhkis* – small pasties filled variously with minced meat, onions and cabbage, and mushrooms – which went with it. The vodka was exchanged for wine now, but the toasts went on, and the laughter and conversation rose a notch. Emily's whole body seemed to be filled with a warm astonishment: it was different as it could be from those stiff Christmas dinners at Bratton. She was seated between Adishka and Tolya, and the former kept her entertained with stories about Petersburg society, while she had never seen the latter so animated and unselfconscious.

After the soup there was *kulebiaka*, a noble pie made in *millefeuille* layers of crisp pastry filled with salmon, sturgeon, mushrooms, chopped eggs, and rice flavoured with onions and dill. Then, for the main course, there was the Christmas goose stuffed with cinnamon apples, and partridges cooked in sour cream. When it came to the dessert, the cook, Borya – a large Georgian with huge moustaches of which he was intensely proud – brought it up from the kitchen himself, and marched in bearing it proudly before him on an enormous silver platter: a traditional English plum pudding, flickering bravely with blue flames of ignited brandy and crowned with a sprig of holly.

There was great applause and laughter, and Borya, beaming delightedly, swept it under Emily's nose, almost singeing her front hair, and proclaimed, 'For you, *barishnya*, especially in your honour!' and then added the only words he knew in English: 'Thank you very much! God save the Queen!'

Emily, laughing with the rest, responded in form. 'Thank *you*, Borya – and God save the Tsar!'

159

Out of the corner of her eye she was aware that the footman had approached Natasha with a murmured message and was receiving orders, which he acknowledged with a deep bow; but she was fairly light-headed now, and made nothing of it. The clock on the overmantel, she saw to her surprise, said five to ten. No wonder Yenchik was bright-eyed with exhaustion.

When the pudding was put aside, Natasha nodded to Anatoli. 'Very well, Tolya. You know what to do.' Tolya nodded, slipped from his seat, and went through into the next room. It was, as Emily knew, a large chamber meant as an extension to the dining-room for banquets, but hardly ever used. She had only been into it once, when being shown over the house in her first week.

Now Natasha said, 'We must have one last toast before we go next door. Emilia, my dear, we want you to know how glad we are to have you here, and how much we hope you will be happy. As I told you, this is to be your Christmas, and we have a surprise for you in the next room. But before we take you through, let us all charge our glasses and drink to the long life, health and happiness of Emilia Edvardovna – *our Emily.*'

'*Nasha Emilia,*' everyone cried, and drank. There was the tinkling of a small bell from within the next room, and Natasha stood up and held out her hand to Emily.

'It is time. Come.' Bemused, almost tearful, Emily rose from her seat and walked towards her grandmother. As she reached her the lights went out, plunging them into darkness, and then the double doors to the next room were opened wide.

Before her was the first Christmas tree she had ever seen, stretching right up to the ceiling, ablaze with light, a beautiful, glorious thing against the darkness of the room. It was decorated with the gilded nuts she had helped to make, which shone with the soft brilliance of true gold; with small, polished bell-shaped Christmas apples; with little nets of sweets wrapped in shining foil; with crystal icicles and snowflakes, and silver bells. On the top was a fairy dressed in silver tinsel with a diamond crown; and everything seemed to shimmer in the light from the candles which trembled on the ends of the branches, making a cascade of light, layer upon layer of quivering flames, each surrounded with its own golden halo.

Everyone crowded round her as she gazed, bemused, and kisses and hugs and good wishes were rained on her. She felt herself smiling, smiling until her cheeks ached, felt the warmth and innocence of their love for her wrapping itself around her. She felt as though all her life she had been outside looking in, pressing her face to the window like the Little Match Girl, and now suddenly the door had been opened and she had been beckoned inside. There is still magic, she thought confusedly, but not in England any more – only in Russia.

Someone turned the lights up again, and she saw that the dining-table had been pushed to one side of the room, and that on it were heaps of presents, a separate heap for each member of the family, and another heap at the end for the servants. They were now coming into the dining-room behind Emily to join the celebration – she heard their pleased chatter and soft oohs and aahs of pleasure at the sight of the tree.

But the surprises were not over yet. Tolya was standing to one side with the pleased look of the successful stage-manager on his face. He, of course, had opened one side of the double doors; but who had opened the other side? He stepped forward now, holding out his hands, smiling at Emily in a way that made her heart stand still, and the babble of explanation of his late and secret arrival faded into the background like the unimportant murmur of water over stones.

'Now we meet at last in Russia, and I can call you Emilia Edvardovna, as I always wanted to in England,' he said.

Her hands were in his, and his hands were warm and dry; and now he was bending over her to kiss her, and she could smell the sandalwood toilet water he always wore. His lips imprinted golden stars on her cheeks, and flickering flames encircled her head like a crown. *Did I think that?* she thought. *I really must be drunk after all.*

'Basil Kirilovitch,' she heard herself say. *Enough wit left for that, at any rate.*

'Happy Christmas, Emilusha,' said Natasha.

Chapter Ten

'I never noticed it in England, but snow has a special smell, hasn't it?' Emily said.

She and Yenya had driven in to St Petersburg, a journey that would have been tedious, if not unendurable, at any other time of year, but which in winter took only a little more than an hour. The morning was bright as silver, the air crystal, the snow fresh and perfect under an arc of sky the colour of chicory flowers. The velvet-padded sledge was harnessed to the troika – the three-horse rig in which only the centre horse ran between shafts, while the outer horses ran free, harnessed by a strap, and driven with a single rein. It was spectacularly fast.

Petersburg looked at its best on such a day. The sun poured down over the dazzling snowscape and the silver thread of the frozen Neva. It illuminated the huge façades in surprising, pastel colours, glinted on a thousand gold crosses and cupolas against the enamelled sky, and painted long blue shadows down the edges of wide streets and vast public squares.

'How beautiful everything is!' Emily said. 'Do you remember when you first saw it, Aunt?'

'Not the very first time – I was only a child then. But when I came here to be married, I was about the same age as you are now. It's a good age for seeing the magic in things – especially when one is in love.'

Emily had nothing to say to that. After a moment, Yenya went on.

'I wonder who Anna will have to meet us? She said there would be a special guest at luncheon. And then there's the ballet this evening, and supper afterwards at Cubat's. How nice it is to be able to eat at restaurants! Do you know, when I was your age no lady could ever be seen in one. They were for gentlemen only, and – well, professional women,' she added with a significant nod.

Emily quickly rejected the image of female doctors and lawyers her mind had offered her as her wits caught up with the conversation.

162

'Everything seems much easier and freer for women here than in England,' she said.

'We can thank Catherine the Great for that. She made sure women had equal status with men,' Yenya said. 'I wonder Queen Victoria didn't do the same for women in England.'

'A matter of personalities, I suppose,' said Emily. 'When you have absolute power as the Tsar does, personality must matter very much.'

Yenya was struck by the thought. 'Did you think of that yourself? How very clever! Oh, here we are in Fourstatskaya Street. I do wonder that Alexei should choose to live in such a dull place. Most of the big buildings around here are barracks, you know, and just down there is the Tauride Palace, where the Duma sits – our version of Parliament. Not a theatre or a shop to be seen.'

Seva slowed the troika before a pair of high, wrought-iron gates, even now being dragged open by the *dvornik*, an old man in a brown coat and sheepskin hat. Beyond the gates was a wide gravel courtyard and a square, three-storey house in the neoclassical style, complete with pediment and four fake Doric columns set into the façade. Everything about it was massive: even the doors were twelve feet high.

They passed through them into the vestibule, were relieved of their outer garments, and then trod up the crimson-carpeted steps to the inner, double doors, which opened onto the hall. It was huge: black and white marble squares, massive red marble pillars, chandeliers, and a magnificent curving marble staircase with elaborately wrought bannisters and a handrail embellished with monster acorns. Emily was beginning to feel oppressed by the size of everything as the butler led them towards the stairs; but then Anna came running down.

'My dears, how lovely to see you. Welcome to our house, Emilia. I thought I'd come down and meet you in case you were overcome by everything.'

Emily was about to respond to this kind thought, but Anna went on at once and spoiled it.

'You mustn't mind if you feel a little awkward at first: we shall quite understand. You must behave just as you did at home. I don't suppose you've ever been in a house like this before. It probably seems huge to you.' She surveyed Emily's expression with her blue, blank look. 'Of course, it seems poky and dark to me, and all this marble – so gloomy, like a mausoleum. I feel mad every time I pass that beautiful, beautiful Kirov Palace on the English Quay! Alyosha's beast of a grandpa sold it to the government back in the eighties and it's a museum now – such a waste! I had to give up so much when I married – born a princess, you know, and now only a countess, and this horrid ugly house to live in. Well, never mind, I've made some of the first-floor rooms tolerable. My private suite is charming. I've modelled my boudoir on the dear Empress's at the Alexander Palace, everything in mauve, you know. Have you met the Empress yet, Emilia? No? Of course the *entrée* to the palace is jealously guarded, for obvious reasons. One couldn't have just *anyone* trotting in and out. Still, you never know, Natasha Petrovna might be able to arrange it for you. Such a charming woman, the Empress – so sensitive. She suffers dreadfully from her nerves. Well, women do, who are married to men less sensitive than themselves.'

Emily listened in surprise as she trod up the endless stairs behind her. Yenya didn't seem to notice anything amiss, but this was a very different Anna from the one she had met at Christmas. Then she had thought Basil's sister quiet and innocuous, with nothing to say for herself beyond the commonplace, but on the whole pleasant and friendly.

Now, in her own house, she had exposed herself in the first few moments as vain, snobbish and spiteful. What had caused her to change? Ah, wait though – *in her own house*. Perhaps while under Natasha's roof she was obliged to bite her tongue, particularly if she valued Natasha's acquaintance – and since Natasha had the fabled *entrée* to the imperial court, she might well do so. Well, Emily had learned to bite her own tongue in a good school, and this was Basil's sister, after all. But how different from Basil! Thank God he had somehow come under gentler influences. She followed in silence, and tried hard not to be completely overcome by the grandeur of Anna's house.

Upstairs, the floors were of polished parquet, and the ceilings a little lower, perhaps only fifteen feet above Emily's head; but there were false Corinthian columns of red and black marble set into the walls at intervals, niches containing huge malachite and basalt vases, and a vast *trompe-l'oeil* mural along the walls of the staircase as it continued upwards.

The room into which Anna conducted them, however, had been decorated in the modern style. The walls were papered with a floral pattern, and the floor was almost completely covered by a thick carpet. The chairs and tables were of light wood; there were modern paintings on the walls, and a number of large, comfortable sofas and armchairs covered in chintz were arranged around the room. The company disposed about them was entirely female: fashionable matrons, mostly young, and all, to judge by their clothes and jewels, very wealthy.

Yenya and Emily were absorbed into the group, introductions were performed, enquiries made and answered about common acquaintances. After a few minutes of this kind of exchange, Anna was called away by her butler. She returned shortly and announced in a voice brimming with pride and excitement, 'Ladies, our guest has arrived!'

Emily looked up and saw a man in peasant garb of white tunic, baggy black cloth trousers, and leather boots. He wore a gold chain around his neck with a heavy gold cross dangling against his chest. His face was unrefined: a bulbous nose, loose mouth, and coarse-pored skin which seemed none too clean. His hair was untidy and greasy, and he wore a long straggly beard.

Even Emily could see he was not what you would expect to find in a Society lady's drawing-room. One would have dismissed him as merely a dirty peasant had it not been that under his shaggy eyebrows was a pair of unpleasantly piercing eyes, which seemed to be scanning the room like an eagle looking for rabbits.

Yenya obviously knew who he was. Her hand fastened itself round Emily's wrist in alarm.

'Rasputin!' she whispered urgently. 'My God, if Mamochka finds out about this, she'll murder me! Promise you won't tell, Emilusha! I didn't know, truly!'

In England Emily had just heard of Rasputin: that he was a monk who was supposed to be the Tsaritsa's confessor, though the more scandalously minded whispered he was her lover. The word *monk* had made her think of a sort of other-worldly recluse, mild of expression and gentle of language. The last thing she would have expected was this coarse, dirty man with bolting eyes who was striding across the carpet with such insolent confidence.

The rest of the company, however, was stirring not with indignation, but with pleased anticipation. Glancing quickly around, Emily saw fluttering looks, simpering smiles, rapt and almost ecstatic gazes from these flushed and plushy matrons. They might almost have been welcoming a lover, she thought with surprise.

'Well now,' Anna was saying, 'you all know our distinguished guest, Father Grigori – all except you, I think, Emilia. Father Grigori is our most famous *starets*. He's a healer and a medium, a man

165

chosen by God to exercise remarkable gifts. Father, this is my husband's cousin from England, Emilia Edvardovna Paget.'

Emily would have been reluctant to take his hand, but she wasn't given the choice – he took hers. His hand seemed burning hot, and he gripped hers lightly, but with a grasp she could not easily have broken. He dipped his head towards her, and his disturbing eyes seemed to bore into hers, as if he were looking straight through into her mind – or perhaps even deeper, into her soul. She shivered with distaste.

'Are you married, or unmarried?' he asked her abruptly.

'Unmarried,' Emily replied faintly.

'Bad! I like married women best. I like all women, they are like beautiful, silken horses, but married women are best, when they have been broken in, and respond to the rider's hands and legs.'

Emily hardly heard him. She felt icy cold, and her head was swimming. She struggled against the probing stare. It seemed an unclean thing to her, as though those dirty fingers were exploring her body, uncovering her, exposing her. Yet it was hard to struggle, harder with each passing second. The room was fading away. His eyes seemed to be all there was in the world . . . growing bigger . . . she was falling . . .

The voice became caressive. 'That's right, you must not resist me. You must let God speak to you, possess you, through me.'

He's trying to hypnotise me, said a faraway voice in her brain. The vicar at Bratton had once told her about a hypnotist he had seen at a music-hall show, who had made a man roll up his trouser legs, take off his shoes and socks and paddle across the stage, believing himself to be at the seaside. The vicar's homely face and no-nonsense voice, robustly amused, pierced the clouds in Emily's brain. With a determined effort she wrenched her hand away from Rasputin's and broke their locked gaze. For an instant she felt sick, as though with violent vertigo; and then the room reassembled itself around her, and she heard the *starets* laugh uproariously.

'From England, eh? Have they heard of me even in England? But I am a man sent by God, He speaks through me, and His power comes down through me. You need not be afraid, little sister. I will not harm you.'

He turned away abruptly, and went to greet the other women. His loud voice and boisterous laughter filled the room and made the drops in the chandeliers tinkle in protest. The other ladies were eager to be noticed by him, and didn't seem to mind what he said to them, though most of it seemed verging on the indecent.

'Now then, mother, you're getting fat as a pig! It's love turned sour in you that makes you eat all those sweetmeats. You should have brought your husband here today, so that I could see how things are between you. And you, little mother, what have you got round your neck? Do you know you could feed a peasant family for a year with what you hang on your body? I'll have it off you, that's what I'll do! Yes, I'll have everything off you! You must humble yourself to come before God.'

There was a glass of Madeira in his hand, which was constantly refilled. 'Russian Madeira,' he exclaimed. 'How I love it! It doesn't look like much, but it could fell a horse! Don't worry, little mother, it isn't a sin to drink. The Devil doesn't drink or smoke, but he's still the Devil!'

Yes, Emily thought, looking round at the flushed faces and heaving bosoms, they like being outraged. The risqué talk, mixed with religion, was a heady brew to these silly women, probably so bored with life they simply longed for any novelty. No wonder her grandmother disapproved of him. She glanced towards Aunt Yenya and saw her almost open-mouthed, looking very much like Zansha discovering a spider under the sofa – fascinating, but definitely not to be picked up.

They went in to luncheon at last, but there was no relief from the coarseness of the *starets*.

'We are having a very simple luncheon,' Anna announced proudly as they took their places. 'Father Grigori prefers plain food, and eats no meat. It is the way of holiness.'

'Plain food?' Yenya whispered indignantly to Emily. 'It's peasant food! Anna Kirova invites us to luncheon, and then serves us peasant food!'

The bill of fare was fish soup and black bread, grilled fish, hard-boiled eggs, salted cucumbers, and a dessert of sweet cakes and fruit. Emily, seated halfway down the table, tried to keep her eyes away from the bearded figure at the head, but it was hard to do, though what she saw often made her feel either sick or indignant. He ignored the cutlery provided, fishing the solid pieces out of his soup with his fingers, and sopping up the liquid part with bread. His beard glistened with spillings, and now and then he wiped his fingers on the loose end of it, as though it were a napkin.

He ate everything with his fingers, pulling the bones out of the fish and sucking them noisily, cracking his eggs on the edge of the table and dropping the shell just anywhere. As he sank glass after glass of wine he grew more outrageous, reaching across the table and taking pieces of food from other people's plates, and, to Emily's disgust, taking bites out of his own cucumber or hard-boiled egg and then passing it to one of the ladies to finish.

'Eat!' he cried. 'You must learn humility, little mother!'

When the meal was finished at last, they returned to the drawing-room for tea. Anna presided over the samovar, and glasses of tea were distributed, along with saucers of lemon, pieces of sugar, and bowls of jam. Rasputin took his tea with jam, but ignoring the silver spoon provided, he scooped jam into his glass with his fingers. Emily watched from across the room with the fascination of distaste. The *starets* had been talking and laughing to the woman next to him, but suddenly his jam-smeared fingers seemed to catch his attention. His voice became slurred, his words muddled, and he stared at his fingers with wide, staring eyes.

'Full of pride, full of guile,' he said. He muttered something inaudible, and then, 'Through humility is salvation! I am a sinner, but God loves me, he loves all sinners, and we must love each other, and bow ourselves before him.'

He turned to the woman next to him, his eyes burning like phosphorus light, and thrust his hand at her face, his fingers splayed and rigid. 'Lick them!' he commanded. The woman seemed both fascinated and repelled, like a rabbit staring at a snake. 'Humble yourself!' Rasputin cried. 'Lick them clean!'

And to Emily's horror, the woman reached out and took hold of his wrist, closed her eyes, and slowly inserted his soiled fingers into her mouth.

A moment later Emily almost jumped out of her skin as Yenya seized her arm so hard it hurt her, and pulled her to her feet.

'I'm so sorry, Annushka, but we really must go now,' she said in what was for her an astonishingly strong voice.

Anna, who like everyone else had been watching the scene across the room, jerked her head round, looked shocked and then angry, and said, 'Oh, really Yenya, not now!'

But Yenya was already heading for the door, covering their retreat with light chatter. 'I'm sorry, dear, we really must,' she said. 'It's been delightful, but there are things we have to do in Petersburg this afternoon . . . '

Out in the passage, Anna closed the door sharply behind them.

168

'Why do you have to leave now? Father Grigori's going to do some healing and special readings of our problems.'

'I'm sorry, Anna dear, I should have mentioned it when we arrived, but we have an appointment at Dr Flemmer's. Poor Emilia has chipped a tooth and the rough edge is making her tongue sore. She's going to have it filed down, and I promised to go with her and hold her hand.'

Emily, stunned by such richness of invention, tried to look like someone with a sore tongue.

'But we will be back, of course, in plenty of time for dinner. So good of you to arrange such entertainment for us. I'm so sorry we have to run now, but it can't be helped . . . '

Once they were safely in the sleigh and heading towards the centre of the city, Emily said, 'What an accomplished liar you are, Aunt!'

'Oh dear! I don't mean to be, but I had to get us away. It was all quite shocking. Such an unsavoury man – *pungent* is the word Mamochka uses. You know the way she talks! She'd be so shocked if she knew I'd let you meet him. You won't tell, will you, Emilusha?'

'Of course not. It wasn't your fault. But if he is so disagreeable, how is it that he's accepted by the imperial family?'

'Mama says that of course he behaves himself quite differently with them – very reverent and respectful. The Empress thinks the world of him, and relies on his spiritual advice. And he truly is a healer. Even his worst enemies admit that he has a great gift.'

'Who does he heal at the palace?'

'I don't know, dear. The Empress, I suppose. She's been suffering for some years now from an enlarged heart, and – '

'What on earth is that?'

'I don't really know, but it gives her headaches and fainting fits and so on. And she has sciatica too, such an unpleasant complaint, and I think rheumatism – something that makes her walk with a stick, at any rate. But she doesn't know anything about the side of Rasputin that we've just seen. She thinks he's a real holy man, sent from God, and she trusts everything he says, which is very bad because of course *she* has great influence with the Emperor, which means that the discontented people – the socialists and so on – say Rasputin rules Russia, which they don't at all like, and who can blame them?'

'Why doesn't someone tell the Tsar and Tsaritsa what he's really like?'

'Oh dear! Because they wouldn't believe it, of course. They only see him on his best behaviour, and if anyone speaks against him, they think it's just envy and malice. The last person who tried was banished to Siberia for their pains, so of course no-one's going to take the risk. It's all very difficult. But I'm shocked that Anna should be so taken in. He's very popular amongst a certain set, and,' her voice became wistful, 'he really is a tremendously good medium, much better than my Madame Beloffsky. He gets wonderful contacts with the Other Side, so I hear.'

They idled the afternoon away amongst the shops and cafés in the city centre – no great hardship to Emily – and at her request drove back via the English Quay so that she could see for herself the old Kirov Palace which Anna had mentioned so feelingly.

'Here it is now,' Yenya said.

'Where?'

'Here. This is it.' Yenya gestured to the endless pale-blue façade of porticoed windows they were passing. Emily had taken it to be a government building of some sort. 'The blue building.'

Emily was almost lost for words. 'Your family owned all that?'

Yenya nodded unemphatically. 'The Kirovs were very powerful back in the time of Catherine the Great. Rastrelli designed this palace for us, at the same time as the Catherine Palace at Tsarskoye Selo. You can see it looks a bit like it, although Valya says the great hall and public salons are better. It doesn't have much of a garden, though – none of the houses along this side have. Still, it's a pity it should be a museum, though I can't imagine what Anna would want all those rooms for. Alyosha doesn't care for large parties.'

It was all said so naturally that it completely disarmed Emily. Such fabulous riches as this monstrous palace represented held neither fears nor attractions for her aunt. But the Kirovs who had built and owned and lived in it were her ancestors too. She had had no idea her forebears had been so powerful and important.

Emily came down before the dinner bell, and found Basil sitting alone in the drawing-room, reading the newspaper. He flung it aside when she came in and jumped up.

'Emilia! There you are! And looking so pretty. I like the way you've done your hair.'

Emily's hands were taken, her cheeks kissed. The warmth of his greeting made her glow, and when he didn't release her hands, but

170

stood looking down at her and smiling, she was tongue-tied with pleasure.

'When I think of the way you looked when I first met you – hardly more than a schoolgirl – I can't believe this is the same little Emily! Though you're still just as shy with me, I see.'

'Oh no, not shy, only . . . ' Emily lifted her eyes to the godlike face and felt the blood rushing to her cheeks. That was a sentence she could hardly finish with any honesty.

Basil smiled as though he knew that. '*Only?* If I were an unkind person, I'd make you finish what you've begun; but I'll spare your blushes, for now. Come and sit down. We've a good ten minutes before anyone else will be joining us. What it is women take so long to do in their rooms is a mystery.'

She allowed herself to be drawn to a sofa and sat beside him. He leaned back in the corner and crossed his legs, surveying her face in a rather sultan-like manner which she did not find unattractive.

'And what have you been doing to annoy my sister Anna?' he asked after a moment. Emily hardly knew what to say, but Basil filled in the silence for her. 'Rushing out of one of her *salons* in order to visit the dentist? Rather a lame excuse, wasn't it?'

'I had to – that is, Aunt Yenya seemed to think – '

'Oh, it's all right, I perfectly understand! While you live in Natasha Petrovna's house you have to abide by her rules, and she's frightfully stuffy about some things.'

'You don't think there's any harm in Rasputin?' Emily asked, interest overcoming her embarrassment.

'Lord, no, he's just another of these mystics that turn up from time to time. The women go crazy about them for a few weeks, and then some newer fad comes along and they're forgotten. It keeps them amused. But you've certainly put Anna's nose out of joint by cutting off like that.'

'Oh dear! Is she very upset?'

'Practically foaming at the mouth, but don't let it bother you. She's always been bossy and impossible; it does her good to be crossed now and then. But you should have heard her!' he chuckled. 'Calling you a little provincial nobody, and I don't know what besides!'

Emily didn't find it amusing. 'I didn't mean to be rude, especially when she'd gone to so much trouble to invite us and arrange all this entertainment for us.'

'Don't worry about it. If Alyosha had been home, he'd have put

171

a stop to it anyway. And as to inviting you, it was I who put her up to it.'

'You?'

'How else could I get to see you? If I called on you at your grandmother's house, she'd be watching us like a hawk all the time.'

Emily hardly dared to believe what she wanted to believe, but there was no mistaking his interest in her. Her heart was beating so hard it made her feel slightly sick. Being in love seemed to be attended by such very physical sensations that she wondered the poets had never thought to mention it.

Basil, still watching her, didn't seem to need any more encouragement than her confused blushes. 'I was just thinking the other day of all those jolly times we had at good old Lady Hamilton's. Do you remember that party she gave for Diaghilev's ballet company? You were the centre of attention that evening, as I recall – and rightly so. You were as pretty as a picture!'

Emily's strong vein of honesty protested at this, pleasant nonsense though it might be. As she recalled, Basil had been too drunk, and too involved with his own troubles, even to notice her.

'I'm sure you didn't look twice at me that evening,' she said. 'You were watching Fanny the whole time.'

'I assure you I wasn't! Poor Fanny, what a strange life she's chosen for herself! I'm afraid she'll never marry now. Have you heard from her at all?'

Was his indifference a studied pose? Emily supposed it must be. 'Not *from* her since before Christmas; but Sylvia wrote to me about her. It wasn't good news, I'm afraid.'

'I hope Lady Ongar's health isn't failing?'

'Oh no, she's as well as ever – but Fanny's been in trouble. The WSPU mounted a campaign in November of attacking pillar-boxes, and Fanny was arrested for setting fire to one. I'm afraid she was sent to prison.'

'Good God! Fanny Hope in prison?'

'Yes, I know, it's horrible to think of. And what's worse, she went on hunger strike, and they – they force-fed her. With a nasal tube.' Emily shuddered. 'It doesn't bear thinking about. Poor Fanny was so ill they had to release her early. Sylvia says when she went to meet her at Holloway she hardly recognised her, she was so pale and sick, and her face so swollen.'

Basil's perfect features registered disgust. 'How utterly revolting!' he exclaimed.

Emily suppressed a pang. Of course, he must still care about Fanny; those feelings wouldn't die away in such a short time. 'Yes, it's dreadful. She went back to Greenlands to rest and get her strength back, but Sylvia says that even on the journey down there she was talking about writing an article on her experience for one of the radical papers. Her courage is amazing.'

'Pity it's so misplaced!'

'Oh, Basil,' Emily said reproachfully, 'you believe in the Cause!'

'Of course I do,' he said hastily, 'but it should be left to men to argue it out in Parliament.'

'Then nothing would ever happen. They've been talking about it for fifty years already!'

'You can't rush important matters,' Basil said, and then seeming to realise this was not an entirely satisfactory argument, forestalled her quickly by saying, 'Anyway, that sort of thing isn't your worry any more. You're in Russia now, Emilia Edvardovna. You must interest yourself in Russian things.'

She felt it wouldn't be polite to argue further. 'Oh, I do! I mean, I am. Everything about Russia fascinates me.'

Basil's smile became very particular. '*Everything*? But any one thing more than another?'

Emily's confusion had to be his answer.

Natasha came into the morning-room, and found Emily standing by the window, staring out into the frozen garden. She was obviously too deep in thought to have heard her grandmother's footfall. Natasha stood for a moment looking at the slender back and the fawn hair piled in that newly grown-up style above the fragile neck, and saw her granddaughter draw a deep sigh.

She stepped forward in quick concern. 'What is it, Emilusha? Are you unhappy?' Emily turned, and Natasha blinked at the radiant face. 'No, not unhappy, I see!' She smiled, holding out her hand. 'You had better come and tell me about it.'

Emily sat down at the table with her, rested her elbows on the surface and her shining face in her hands. She was perfectly willing to talk, but didn't seem to have the words.

Natasha started her off. 'Is it Basil Narishkin?'

Emily hesitated a moment, and then nodded. 'I suppose it must seem foolish to you, when he's the most beautiful man in the world, and I'm sure he doesn't care the slightest bit about me – '

173

'Not foolish at all. I saw the first time you met him, in the Isle of Wight, that you liked him, and no wonder. And I'm quite sure you're wrong, and that he likes you very much too.'

'Oh, no,' Emily denied automatically, rather like crossing fingers to avert bad luck. 'He's been in love with Fanny Hope for years and years.'

'That was a perfectly foolish engagement, all his mother's idea, and now she's dead there'll be nothing more said about it. Fanny's much too old for him. It would never have worked, and I'm sure Basil knows it. Tell me how you got on with him in Petersburg.'

'Oh, very well! He was so kind to me, and attentive. He sat beside me at the ballet, and in the interval he asked me to walk along the loggia with him, and told me all sorts of interesting things about the dancers and the people in the other boxes. And then at the restaurant – '

'Yes? What then?'

'Oh, it wasn't anything really. Not worth mentioning.'

'Tell me!'

'Well, when the attendant came to help me take off my coat, Basil waved her away and helped me off with it himself. And when we went through to the table, he pulled out my chair for me, and took the seat next to me, even though Adishka was about to sit there.'

Natasha nodded. 'Just as I thought. He's courting you.'

'Oh no! Surely not!'

'You sound as though it were a tragedy!' Natasha laughed.

'It's just that – well, I don't want to presume that – to start hoping and then – '

But Natasha patted her hand, her eyes bright and her mouth full of secret pleasure. 'Don't be afraid. It's all as I hoped and planned for you, Emilusha, from the first day I saw you together; and a little more work will bring it off.' She gave a strange little nod, as though to herself.

'What do you mean, Grandmama?' Emily asked, half excited, half afraid. One part of her knew that Basil could never care for her in *that* way, and dreaded to be made a fool of; another part purred with excitement and a sense of inner power, an entirely unreasonable conviction that the man who chose her to be in love with would never regret it.

Natasha was following her own train of thought. 'We'll have to work quickly, though. If we don't fix it by *Maslenitsa*, we shall have Lent upon us, and that will never do.'

'Grandmama!'

'Don't worry, Emilusha. Leave everything to me. I know just what to do.'

'But I don't think Basil thinks about me like that. I'm just a child to him – his "little cousin".'

Natasha gave her a shrewd look. 'Tell me, how does Anna behave towards you.'

Emily hesitated. 'Well, it's hard to say. At Christmas, when she was here, she seemed very nice and friendly; but at her house, she seemed sometimes – as though she didn't like me very much.'

'There's your proof, then. You see, Emilia, if Basil doesn't marry, all his share of the Narishkin fortune will go to Anna and her children. Did you ever wonder why she was so eager to have him come back to Russia when the old Princess died? She couldn't keep an eye on him while he was in England. She likes to have him close at hand, so that she can spike the guns of any hopeful young woman, and keep him single.'

'But Grandmama – '

'No, no! Don't you see, if Anna has taken to being rude to you, it means she thinks she has something to fear; and who would know better than a sister with a keen personal interest?'

Looking back afterwards, Emily saw those early months of 1913 as a strange and exotic dream through which she moved, as one does in a dream, without volition, having things happen to her. She was between identities: her Emily-self was finished, a story that had concluded when she left England, a closed book in which nothing more would ever be written. What she was to be had not yet taken shape: her Emilia-self, begun during that journey in the freezing fogs of the Baltic, but not yet ready to take action alone.

So she drifted in a daze of delight, surprise and pleasure through the dazzling, rainbow-coloured experience that was Petersburg in the Season of 1913. It was a city filled with the new, the exciting, the *avant-garde*; a showcase of the arts, of innovation, of experimentation. Every aspect of society was touched with a restless brilliance; old ideas, old values were tested, and discarded for the new.

The names of that Season were the names of the revolutionaries of style: Kandinsky, Bakst, Malevich, Cocteau, Chagall; Chekov, Gorky, Bely; Rubenstein and Stravinsky; Diaghilev and Stanislavsky. At the opera, the giant body of Chaliapin produced a voice almost

175

too beautiful to be human; at the ballet, Karsavina and Pavlova danced as though they were disembodied spirits never touching the earth. New restaurants sprang up overnight; night-clubs flourished; the city never seemed to sleep.

To Emily, Petersburg was like a Fabergé egg, an exquisite, jewel-bright thing, which opened to reveal ever more treasures within. And the personification of its beauty was Basil Narishkin, exquisite, delightful creature, who escorted her through the dazzling pleasures and was unconsumed by them, like a salamander moving in its element of flame. He was always on hand to hold her coat, to pull out her chair, to retrieve her napkin, to open her programme. He moved through her dream in a nimbus of light, the prince in her own personal fairy tale; and to fill out the cast there was Natasha, the fairy godmother, and Anna, the wicked witch, locked in battle for the outcome of the story.

The Petersburg Season ended with *Maslenitsa*, the week of Carnival before the beginning of Lent, when the whirligig excitements reached a frantic climax of balls, parties and galas which might have left a detached onlooker – if such a creature could exist – with the impression that the world was about to end and the participants were grasping at the last pleasures they would ever know.

Emily, with Natasha, Yenya and Valya, had been invited to the ball at the Surinov Palace. Anna Kirova was there, still escorted by her brother-in-law, Adishka: her husband's absence had been extended a third time, which perhaps accounted for her being out of temper. She greeted Natasha and the Surinovs with a grim and rather glittering smile, acknowledged Emily only by a nod, and delivered herself of the triumphant message that Basil would not be there that night because he had gone to the Razumovskys' ball instead.

It was a severe disappointment to Emily. She had expected to see him there, had looked forward to dancing with him, especially as it was the penultimate night of *Maslenitsa*. There would be only one more ball, and then all public pleasures would stop for six weeks: Russians took Lent very seriously. However, she would not expose herself before her family, and especially not before Anna Kirova, so she did her best to hide her disappointment. By now she had acquired a circle of acquaintances in Petersburg, so she was not entirely lacking for partners; and Uncle Valya kindly stepped in during a fallow spell to take her out onto the floor.

It was while she was circling in his calm and avuncular arms that

Basil arrived, looking a little flustered, and asked permission to cut in. Valya yielded gratefully, and headed for the smoking-room and his own friends.

'I thought you weren't coming,' Emily said as Basil steered her away, rather jerkily for him, into the glittering crowd. 'Your sister said – '

'Yes, I know what she said,' he snapped, his noble brow furrowed with what, in an ordinary mortal, might have looked like ill temper. 'Damn it, she's gone too far this time! When I get hold of her – !'

'But what is it? What has she done?' Emily asked, but she already had an idea.

'She told me that you'd left a message saying you were all going to the Razumovskys instead. I suppose she thought once I got there I wouldn't bother to come back. There were a lot of my friends there, and – oh, I don't know what she thought! It really is ridiculous!' he finished in a burst of irritation.

'Perhaps she made a genuine mistake,' Emily said, doubting it entirely. 'At any rate, it doesn't matter – you're here now.'

'I suppose you're right,' Basil said, subsiding a little. 'It's just that she takes too much on herself. It's not as if – that is – oh well, never mind. I just don't like being made a fool of.'

'I don't think you could ever look foolish,' Emily said. Basil shot her a suspicious look for an instant, and then his face cleared and a smile worked its way slowly to the surface.

'You're very sweet,' he said. 'And very pretty. You're looking lovely tonight, little cousin. I wouldn't mind anything, if I hadn't missed so many dances with you! I suppose all the other men were fighting for your hand?'

'Not fighting exactly, but I only had to sit out one, and then Uncle Valya rescued me.'

Basil smiled a little more. 'It's damned hot in here, isn't it? Come out into the orangery for a moment, and let's get away from the crowd.'

Emily would have gone anywhere with him for the sake of that smile, despite a notion somewhere in the back of her mind that Aunt Maud would not have liked to hear of unmarried girls going into orangeries without chaperones. What fate she might have embraced there she was never to know, for at the door of the ballroom Anna confronted them, shot a venomous look at Emily, and said sharply, 'I want a word with you, Vasska. In private.'

'Yes, and I want a word with you,' Basil retorted. He stepped away from Emily without apology, and she was left stranded while brother and sister moved across the vestibule, then turned on each other and proceeded to quarrel in a fierce undertone that spared Emily nothing but the actual words.

Finally Basil broke away, came walking rapidly back towards Emily, and seizing her hand, almost dragged her off into the orangery, his cheeks pink and his eyes bright with indignation. They were not the only couple seeking seclusion, and it took Basil a few moments to discover an unfrequented corner of the vegetation. When he did, he turned Emily almost roughly to face him, took hold of her other hand, and looked down at her, breathing fast. It was odd, Emily thought with the one unoccupied corner of her mind, that in this moment he looked unusually like his sister: anger had given his eyes that blank, blue opacity of Anna's.

After a moment, he seemed to grow calmer. 'I suppose you know why I've brought you here,' he said.

Emily's heart was knocking against her ribs in a most unregulated way. 'No, not really. I mean – '

'Oh, don't be too coy,' Basil said with a faint renewal of irritation. 'Even my *sister* is in no doubt about my feelings towards you. I should have thought I'd made it obvious enough.'

Emily faltered. 'I didn't like to presume – '

The answer seemed to please him. 'Didn't you? That's my modest little cousin – though I must really stop calling you that now. Fortunately, we aren't really cousins at all.'

'Fortunately?'

'In our Church it's forbidden for first cousins to marry. And since I mean to marry you, my dear Emilia Edvardovna, it's a good thing we aren't related.' He surveyed her face. 'Well? What have you got to say?'

Emily sought for words to respond to what seemed even more of a dream than the dream she already moved in. 'Isn't it customary to ask first?' she heard herself say.

'Oh certainly,' Basil said obligingly. 'On my knees, if you like.' He dropped gracefully to one knee and clasped both hands about one of hers. 'Will you marry me?'

'Yes,' said Emily. 'Yes please.'

It was odd in that moment of perfect fulfilment that she should have the nagging sense that something was missing, that some important element of the ceremony had been omitted; though she could not for the life of her think what it could be.

178

Chapter Eleven

Emily was married just after Easter, 1913. The seven weeks between Basil's proposal and the ceremony passed in a blur of preparations, during which she never seemed to be still for long enough to appreciate her happiness.

The first shock occurred almost immediately, when Uncle Valya announced that he had been transferred to Archangel, and that the whole family must move there at once.

'It's been in the offing for some time, but I hoped it might be put off for a while yet. However, there's no help for it. We shall come to the wedding, of course. Archangel's only two days away by train.'

But Aunt Yenya mourned. 'I shall miss all the fun of the shopping and the presents and the clothes and everything, and I was so looking forward to it. In some ways it's the best part of a wedding.'

For a week Natasha's house was a turmoil of packing, and then with hugs and kisses and tears they were all gone – Yenya, Valya, the children, the nurses, their personal servants – leaving a silence like a vacuum behind them. Emily did not have to endure it for long, however. The following week she and Natasha left as well, to go to Natasha's house in Petersburg, on the corner of the Kronversky Prospekt, overlooking the Troitsky Bridge. It was from here that Emily would be married after Easter, and it was more convenient to be there during the preparations.

The second surprise was the attitude of Anna Kirova. Emily had been braced for hostility, but when she and Basil made their first formal visit to the Kirovs' house after the engagement had been announced, Anna received her perfectly pleasantly. She made no reference to previous unpleasantnesses, smiled, kissed Emily's cheeks, and admired her ring.

'It's beautiful! Vasska always had such perfect taste. Well, you will be a lucky young woman indeed, to be marrying my brother, as I'm sure you already know. I can't tell you how many female hearts will be breaking in Petersburg – ladies of wealth and position too – but never mind about that now! Where do you mean to live afterwards, have you decided?'

179

'We'll go into the country for a while, for our honeymoon,' Basil answered for her, 'and then I suppose we'll have to build a house in Petersburg, since our old palace was sold when Papa died.'

'Even if it hadn't been, you wouldn't have wanted to live there,' Anna pronounced. 'Quite the wrong part of town.'

'Natasha Petrovna says we can live in her house for as long as we like, until we have somewhere of our own,' Emily said.

Anna beamed. 'She is a wonderful woman! So generous! You are lucky to have such a grandmother, Emilia. Well, I have some good news of my own: Alyosha writes to say he's coming home after Easter. Perhaps he may even be back in time for your wedding, if we're lucky.'

Emily thought perhaps that accounted for Anna's change of heart, and was glad to set it down as evidence of her future sister-in-law's love for her husband.

She was immensely busy, not only in having fittings for the extra-ordinary quantity of clothes Natasha seemed to think necessary, but in writing dozens of letters. To begin with, she had to get her father's permission to marry, since she was still under twenty-one. She had not expected him to refuse permission, but she was disappointed that he declined to make the journey to Petersburg for her wedding.

'I can't see the point in travelling all that way just for a ceremony. You have my blessing, Emily. I believe this is something you've been wanting for a long time, so I'm sure you'll be happy. You can write afterwards and tell me how it all went off.'

She shed a few tears over that letter, but was comforted by the warm and loving replies she received from Sylvia, Frances and Penny. Lady Hamilton, to her surprise, seemed less enthusiastic.

'It seems that everything is settled between you, so I shall say only that I hope you will be happy. Remember, whatever happens, that you have no more genuine well-wisher than me.'

The 'whatever happens' might be rather unnerving, but the letter was accompanied by a parcel containing the most beautiful pair of Georgian silver candlesticks, and Emily put the words down to being just Lady Hamilton's way.

Wedding gifts had now begun arriving at Kronversky Prospekt every day.

'I don't know any of these people,' she said to Natasha, looking at the card which had come with a pair of spectacularly ugly *famille noire* vases. 'Why would they send me presents?'

'It's a Society wedding, *mylenkaya*. When you become Princess

180

Narishkina you marry the whole of Petersburg Society. Besides, I expect many of these are distant relatives of Basil's. Let me see . . . Oh yes, old Princess Galinovska was one of his godmothers. A foolish choice I always thought – she was far too old. She must be over ninety now; and those vases have stood in her hall for the last fifty years. I remember her telling me she always hated them. Ah well, I expect they're very valuable, even if they are hideous.'

A special trip had to be made to the bank to view the family jewels, which came to Emily on her wedding. For once she really did feel oppressed as in a darkened room she sat at a baize-covered table under a low, overhead light while piece after piece was laid out before her. She had never owned any jewellery before her engagement ring, and though that was quite plain – a single ruby set in a wreath of gold leaves – she had still had to come to terms with the idea that it was probably fabulously valuable. Now she was shown necklaces, rings, bracelets, brooches, tiaras, parures, ropes of pearls – a glittering king's ransom which seemed to prove conclusively that she was dreaming and would soon wake in her bedroom at The Lodge.

But Basil leaned across her shoulder and handled the pieces casually, like a stableman picking through a litter for the best puppy. 'This was one of mother's favourite sets – hideous, isn't it? Those diamonds are horribly yellow . . . This is nice. I think you should wear rubies, the colour suits you . . . I remember Mama wearing this necklace to a ball at the Winter Palace. The stones are good, but the setting's old-fashioned. We could have it made over, perhaps . . . You must have lots of pearls for everyday wear. Mama had a good eye for pearls . . . '

'I can't wear all these things,' Emily said at last, near to despair.

Basil didn't seem to understand the thrust of her complaint. 'Well, no, some of them are just too ugly and old-fashioned; but we can always have them broken up and reset. You can leave anything you really dislike here for the moment. We'll take the rest home, though. And look, you must wear this right away. It's only a trifle, but it goes rather nicely with your dress.'

The trifle was a necklace of gold flowers with rose diamond centres, which he picked up and slipped about her neck. 'There, what do you think?' He picked up a hand-mirror and held it up for her, and she saw her face looking rather pale and startled against the dark background; her white neck ending suddenly at the collar of her brown dress, as though she had been decapitated. She felt

181

suddenly ill at ease and superstitious: she didn't want any of these jewels. They would bring her bad luck.

Now I'm really starting to think like a Russian, she chided herself; but the feeling of unease persisted. Then Basil's face appeared behind her as he stooped to look over her shoulder, and her fears fled. She was marrying her fairy prince – a dream come true. What had she to fear? She angled the mirror to reflect only his face, and he smiled.

'We're rather a handsome couple, aren't we? Do you know, Emilia, I think once you're dressed up, you're going to look really quite passable.'

The legal settlements had to be gone into. Emily never fully understood them, for by the time the formal exposition took place at the lawyer's office, she was beginning to feel very tired and confused, and some of the Russian professional terms were unfamiliar to her. She gathered that her grandmother was paying a dowry, Basil was making a settlement, and there were various provisions for his death and her death, for the children who were expected to make their appearance sooner or later, for *their* marriages, and so on and so on.

The immediate and practical aspect of it was that after the marriage she would have a monthly income all her own to spend as she pleased, and when she finally grasped what the figure was, she was sure that some noughts must have been transposed, or added in error.

'How would I ever be able to spend half that much?' she asked Natasha afterwards as they drove back home. It was snowing again, and the large, soft flakes brushed her cheeks like furry moths. Under the low grey sky, pregnant with snow, the golden domes of the churches gleamed with a surreal brightness.

Natasha smiled. 'You don't have to spend it all. But you'll probably find you do. Don't worry about it, *durachka*! Better to have too much than not enough.'

It will be different when I'm married, Emily told herself, as the horses jogged along the broad street, and umbrellas sprang open like mushrooms along the pavements before the illuminated shops. This dreamlike feeling will stop. I'll emerge from the chrysalis and live in the world again, and the new me will know how to cope with all these strange sensations. Everything will be all right when I'm married.

But there was one small corner of her mind that remained unconvinced. Little Emily Paget from The Lodge, the poor relation, the wearer of cast-off clothes, was going to become a princess? It was too hard to believe. Emily wondered if perhaps Cinderella hadn't been secretly rather relieved at the stroke of midnight when her rags reappeared, and she faced the long walk home from the palace to her lonely but familiar kitchen.

The preparations for Emily's wedding were not the only things going on in Petersburg. Nineteen thirteen was the tercentenary of the Romanov dynasty, and the celebrations began with a *Te Deum* in Our Lady of Kazan Cathedral. Emily did not attend – the cathedral was not large enough to hold everyone who wanted to go – but she heard about the unfortunate incident that occurred at it.

Most of the congregation was standing, as was normal for an Orthodox service, but at the front there were a few rows of seats reserved for the imperial family, foreign diplomats, Government ministers, and members of the Duma. Shortly before the Tsar and Tsaritsa were due to arrive, the President of the Duma made his way forward to take his seat, only to find Rasputin sitting in it.

The President, furious at such insolence from a peasant, ordered him out, but Rasputin refused. There followed an unseemly brawl in which the President, who was bigger and stronger than the *starets*, yelled, kicked, and finally ejected the interloper physically. It was not a propitious beginning to the celebrations, particularly in view of the general opinion of Rasputin in Petersburg.

But the rest of the celebrations went off without a hitch. The imperial family came from Tsarskoye Selo to take up residence in the Winter Palace for the duration, and everywhere they appeared in public they were cheered hoarse by subjects of every degree in a remarkable display of unity and affection. There were receptions for foreign representatives, presentations, and investitures; gala performances at the opera and the ballet; and, finally, a grand ball given jointly by the nobility of Petersburg for the Romanov family.

It was at a ball that Emily saw the Tsar and Tsaritsa for the first time at close quarters. The Tsar disappointed her to begin with, for remembering King Edward, she thought him a little, undersized fellow, not nearly big or impressive enough to be emperor of half the world. However, he smiled pleasantly behind his beard, and seemed to have a kind word for everyone.

The Tsaritsa was taller than him, thin, standing very upright and rather stiffly. Her face was pale, the features fine but severe, as

183

though sculpted in marble, and she never smiled. She was all in white, hung with diamonds, emeralds and ropes and ropes of pearls, and with a diamond tiara on her crown of hair, which had faded from red-gold to sand.

Close to, Emily was struck most of all by the expression of sadness in her face. Her eyes seemed to be fixed always on some remote prospect of tragedy that had nothing to do with her immediate surroundings. Emily could see why people wouldn't like her at the first meeting: next to the smiling, pleasant Tsar she seemed cold and proud, as though above being pleased.

The four Grand Duchesses were also there, all in white taffeta and wearing the diamond-embellished ribbon of some order across their breasts. Olga and Tatiana greeted Emily with the warmth of old friendship, and she was touched that they remembered her.

'We hear you're going to marry Basil Narishkin,' Tatiana said. 'How lovely for you! Are you very excited?'

'Yes, your imperial highness. I have to keep pinching myself to see if I'm dreaming.'

'I think I would too,' Tatiana laughed. 'He is so very handsome!'

'We do hope you will be very happy,' Olga broke in more seriously.

'Of course she will,' Tatiana said firmly. 'How could she not be?'

'And may we send you a wedding present?' Olga went on. 'From all of us,' indicating her younger sisters, who were standing beside her.

'We like to send presents jointly,' the youngest, Anastasia, said, 'because we can afford nicer things that way. I know we haven't been introduced, but Olga and Tatya told us about meeting you in Cowes, so we feel we know you.'

'We'd like it very much if you'd come and visit us at the palace when you get back from your honeymoon,' Marie said, a little wistfully. 'If you could spare the time. We see so few people.'

'I'd like to very much, your imperial highness,' Emily said.

Tatiana leaned forward conspiratorially. 'Only, when we are alone, you won't keep calling us that, will you? It's so very embarrassing.'

Except for the one or two formal functions they attended, Emily did not seem to see much of Basil as the days of their betrothal ran out and the wedding day approached. When she did see him, he was charming, attentive, and seemed very pleased with life; but what he did all day long and in the evenings when she didn't see him was as completely unknown to her as it had been when they were in London.

But she didn't worry about it. She had no experience whatever of how married people conducted their lives, and was therefore free to suppose what she wished, which was that they would spend a great deal of their time together. In a very short time now Basil would be hers absolutely and for ever, and she would grow old looking at his beautiful face across the dining-room table and sleeping on the pillow next to hers in bed.

In stories, the wedding day was the end, beyond which came only the words 'they lived happily ever after'. Girls were brought up to see the ceremony as the goal, and what came afterwards was never discussed; but Emily's life had been so empty of incident or direction that she was sure it must rather be the start of the real story. She endured the preparations and looked forward to the day only as things to be got over before real happiness would begin.

And now it was all over. The day had been long, a kaleidoscope of colour and glitter and fragmented images which seemed to have no connection with Emily. But of course, she was forgetting: Emily was no more. It was Emilia Edvardovna Narishkina who now sat in the troika beside her new-wedded lord, being rushed off down the frozen road towards Kirishi; Princess Narishkina, wrapped up warmly in her gloriously glossy sables – a wedding present from the bridegroom – with a broad wedding ring of heavy red Russian gold on her hand inside the huge muff.

What a strange ceremony it had been! Crowned like a queen with a circlet of diamonds, she had gone to the cathedral in a carriage drawn by white horses. Russian brides carried no flowers, for as they stood before the altar the bride and groom held lighted candles entwined with orange blossom. The cathedral under its high golden dome seemed filled with a million tiny points of light, like a fallen firmament of stars; from deep within rolling lilac clouds of incense issued the mysterious, sweet singing of a choir of male voices.

The priests chanted, the boys shook the censers, the unseen choir sang. Far, far away at the other end of the universe Basil placed a ring on her finger and she placed one on his, and they walked solemnly round the lectern, led by the priest and followed by the groomsmen holding the marriage crowns above their heads.

When the ceremony was over, and the bells began to ring – a delightful cacophony, not like English change-ringing, but an exultant, undisciplined tumble of chimes – she and Basil rode back side by side in the carriage to Fourstatskaya Street, where the wedding feast was to be held, Natasha's house being too small for the occasion. The state dining-room had been prepared for a hundred and fifty guests, and the white-clothed table seemed to stretch away for ever like a frozen and snow-covered river whose banks were crowded with smiling, well-wishing strangers.

An army of liveried servants in white gloves served the army of guests. Champagne flowed, and there were endless toasts accompanying the endless procession of courses. The new princess ate little, drank probably too much, and smiled and smiled until her cheeks ached.

Every now and then a guest would exclaim, 'This champagne is bitter!'

'Definitely bitter!' someone else would agree, and then one by one they would all take up the chant, '*Gorko, Gorko . . .* !' The only way to sweeten such bitterness was for the true lovers to kiss. Seated side by side at the top of the table, Emily and Basil turned and kissed each other, and satisfied cries and laughter rewarded them. It was a custom the guests seemed to like to have repeated at frequent intervals; the bride and groom had no objection.

Eventually it was time for them to change into their travelling clothes, and then they were thoroughly kissed and hugged and waved off into the winter afternoon, while the guests went back inside to continue to celebrate. It seemed a little odd to Emily that they should be the first to leave their own wedding feast, but they had a two-hour journey ahead of them, and it must be completed before darkness closed in.

'Do you suppose they are still celebrating back there?' she asked at last. Her voice, breaking a long silence, shocked her a little.

'I don't doubt it. Youna and Dima will keep going till dawn if they have the chance.' Basil's voice came back to her, it seemed, from a long way away. 'Trust them to make the most of a wedding.'

Youna and Dima were the groomsmen, bosom friends of Basil's from his school-days; pleasant young men, as easy to like as spring sunshine.

'I wish they were coming to Schwartzenturm with us,' Emily said.

186

A snort of laughter from Basil. 'Fool! Here, have some of this to keep out the cold.' He put a small flask into her hand, and she tasted obediently, expecting vodka; but it was brandy.

'*Gorko*,' she murmured bemusedly, handing it back.

'Are you afraid?' he asked abruptly, turning to look at her.

'Afraid?'

'Of being alone with me?'

'No,' she said at once, and then, after a pause. 'But I wasn't sure just then if I would recognise your voice. I don't seem to recognise my own. Things that ought to be fixed and immutable seem to be rather flowing about at the moment.' He didn't respond to that and fearing she had offended, she added, 'I'm sure I'll get used to it very soon.'

'You'll like Schwartzenturm,' he said, as though that were what she had been talking about. 'It's a strange house, but very English in some ways.'

'Yes,' she said; hesitated, and then decided to leave it. Probably this was not the ideal time to try to start a profound conversation. They had both drunk a great deal of champagne.

It had been Anna's idea that they should have their honeymoon at Schwartzenturm.

'No sense in wasting good money hiring a dacha when it's standing there doing nothing. Stay there as long as you like. The servants need something to do.'

Emily thought it was very kind of her. She had long wanted to see the place – one of the places – where Natasha had spent her childhood, and it seemed more pleasant to be spending their first days together in a private home rather than an impersonal hotel. Basil had seemed less sure about it, until Anna had added, 'And it's nice and handy for Petersburg, in case you get bored.' Then he had smiled and thanked her.

'I expect we'll come down and join you for a day or two, once Alyosha gets home,' Anna had said. 'But you'll want to be on your own at first, of course.'

'Nearly there, now,' Basil said suddenly. Emily realised it was getting dark. It was dusk inside the carriage, and outside the snow had taken on the strange luminosity of twilight, which made it look unreal, like a stage set. With the loss of the sun, the temperature was dropping quickly, and even the air inside the carriage was stony.

'You'll see the gate arch any moment,' Basil took another gulp from the flask. 'Are you cold?'

'No. Well, a little perhaps.'

'I'll warm you up later,' he promised mysteriously.

And so to the last act in the play. After bathing, changing, and taking a pleasant, informal supper – Emily found herself ravenously hungry at last, and ate everything that was offered with good appetite – it was time for bed. Emily went up first while Basil had a last glass of brandy before the fire. She was glad of a moment or two alone to compose herself. It seemed a solemn thing, to be approached with an undivided concentration.

The bedchamber which had been prepared was a state room, large and imposing, but very beautiful, the walls hung with gold-coloured watered silk, the thick carpet in shades of green and blue, the bedcover and hanging of sea-green and gold. The furniture was mostly French, Louis XIV – 'Wrong Louis,' Basil had said dismissingly. 'No-one collects it nowadays!' – together with some charming, light English pieces, Sheraton perhaps, or Hepplewhite.

In this room, in this bed, she waited, her hair loosened and hanging round her shoulders, her lips lightly parted, her eyes bright with anticipation. I am to lose my virginity, she thought, and it seemed odd to describe in terms of loss something in which she must be immeasurably the gainer.

At last her prince came to her. 'You look almost beautiful,' he told her as he stood beside the bed. 'I knew you'd come up nicely, with a little trouble. Well, Princess Narishkina? Shall I put out the light?'

'Oh – is it necessary?' she asked, disappointed. She wanted to look at him a little longer, her beautiful fairy-tale prince.

He grinned. 'Well, no, not if you don't want. You aren't afraid?'

'Of you? No! How could I be?'

'Very well. With the light on it shall be, then.'

Afterwards, he fell asleep. Emilia Edvardovna Narishkina, the marriage consummated and therefore real at last, lay awake, gazing up at the golden ribs of the canopy over her head. She was blissfully happy. So this was love! This was two people made one, uniting their bodies as they had united their souls. It was a moment of profound and holy joy. I shall never be alone again, she thought, hugging herself.

The candlelight flickered and the icon lamp glowed steadily in the 'beautiful corner'. She thought of all the mystery that was made of it, this loving act; she remembered conversations with Lexy and Victoria, things read and things told and things wildly guessed from secret hints. But why did it all have to be such a mystery? Her poor cousins had gone to their watery grave never knowing the answer to the riddle. She felt a huge, warm pity for all the men and women who were alone, who had not experienced this simple and beautiful and important thing, or who had known and lost it.

What a pity he was asleep. She wished they could do it all again. Perhaps he would wake up soon, she thought hopefully, turning towards him. He was lying on his front, his hair sticking up wildly where she had ruffled it in her passion, his flushed and handsome face half buried in the pillows. She smiled and reached over to stroke his head, thinking how lovely it was to be licensed to do so, just like that, whenever she wanted.

But he didn't wake, and she settled herself on her side so that she could continue to look at him, and in a little while fell asleep.

Morning light woke her. A servant had been in to draw the curtain and make up the stove, and she opened her eyes with that delicious internal sensation of something delightful having happened which she had temporarily forgotten.

Then he stirred, and she remembered. I'm married! I'm Basil's wife, and I know about love now, she thought. She turned eagerly towards him, and found him looking at her, his blue eyes blank, a slight frown between his fair brows.

Then the frown cleared. 'I'd forgotten where I was for the moment,' he said. 'Good morning, Princess Narishkina!'

'Good morning, my prince,' she smiled.

'Well,' he said. 'Well.' He seemed to be a little at a loss for words. 'I've never been married before,' he offered, as though it were an explanation.

'Nor have I,' she said. 'I've never even shared a bedroom before, let alone a bed. Isn't it wonderful to wake up beside the person you love best in the world?'

'Do you love me best in the world?' he asked her, beginning to smile.

'But of course I do!'

189

'Hmm.' He seemed pleased, and she dared to reach out and put her arm around him.

'Basil, last night . . . ' she began shyly.

'Yes? It went rather well, I thought,' he said.

It seemed such a funny thing to say that she laughed. 'It was wonderful!' she said. 'I understand now why so much has been written about love. But how strange that they don't describe it better, all the poets and writers.'

'That wouldn't be proper.' The idea seemed to strike him as alarming. 'You're not supposed to talk about it,' he said; and since she seemed inclined to, he stopped her mouth with a kiss. Her response was so immediate and so passionate that he was aroused, and after a moment he slid over on top of her again, and felt her flattering eagerness for him, which was really quite exciting.

'What would you like to do today?' he asked at last, when it was over. She felt she would simply like to stay in bed all day doing what they had been doing, but didn't like to suggest it unless he did first. He didn't. 'Would you like to go out riding?'

'Yes, that would be lovely,' she said. 'Are there horses here?'

'Not very exciting ones,' Basil said. 'Just common hacks, but they'll do for now. Later, when we have our own place, I'll buy you a good horse, a Karabakh or an Arabian.' A thought struck him. 'You do *ride*, I suppose?'

'Yes,' she said. 'Since I was three.'

'Thank God for that! I suddenly thought – but of course, you were brought up at Bratton. Anna exaggerates sometimes,' he said puzzlingly. 'Very well, we'll go riding this morning, and this afternoon I'll show you something of the house, if you like.'

He got out of bed and reached for his dressing-gown. 'Order what you like for breakfast – I should have it here on a tray if I were you – and I'll meet you downstairs at, say, eleven.' He went round the foot of the bed, heading for the door.

'But where are you going?' she asked in dismay.

'To my room. Where did you think?'

'I thought this was your room.'

He came back to the beside to kiss her in a brotherly fashion on the forehead. 'Foolish one! Married people of our rank don't share bedrooms. You didn't really think so, did you?'

*

190

After a huge breakfast – love had made her unaccountably hungry – she had a bath. There were no bathrooms at Schwartzenturm, she discovered, which seemed in an odd way both primitive and luxurious, since it resulted in a movable bath being brought to her in her bedroom. It was delightful, filled from cans brought up by servants and mixed until she declared the temperature to be exactly right. It would be most inconvenient, she saw, if one didn't have a large number of servants, since getting in and out inevitably involved a certain amount of spillage; but after her faux pas over the bedrooms she felt she ought to start behaving like a Russian princess, and forced herself not to apologise.

Then Masha, the girl who had been assigned as temporary lady's maid to her, helped her dress. It was a strange experience even having her garments laid out and handed to her; but when Masha crouched down and proposed putting on her stockings for her, Emily rebelled.

'Just hand me the things. I'll put them on myself.'

'Yes, *barina*,' Masha said, without inflection; and Emily saw that it wouldn't matter to the servants what she did, as long as she did it with conviction. Probably they had to get used to more eccentricity in their employers than she could think up in a lifetime.

When it came to her hair, however, she was glad enough to allow Masha to do it, and had to admit the result was better than anything she could have achieved.

'That's very nice. Thank you,' she said. Masha looked startled, and then smiled faintly. 'You do it very well.'

'Thank you, *barina*.'

It was Masha's surprise at being thanked that warned Emily not to say any more. Aunt Maud, she supposed, would have known better than to chat to the servants, and would have deplored her niece's inclination to do so as the result of her middle-class upbringing at the hands of Mrs Pennistone.

Outside, a bright, hard day had crisped the latest fall of snow and made the sky as deep blue as Kiev enamel. In the front yard – a vast area dominated by a gigantic fountain of mermen wrestling with sea snakes and cavorting dolphins – a friendly bay hack was waiting for her. Her husband (the thrill of using that word!) was dressed in a magnificent greatcoat with a collar of some blue-grey fur which seemed somehow to show up the colour of his heavenly blue eyes, and had a shotgun slung over his shoulder.

'I thought we'd head towards the woods, and take a shot at a few pigeons. Or rabbits, if we see any. But let me know as soon as you get tired or cold.'

'I'm sure I won't be either,' she said. 'I feel so full of energy, I could race this nice horse on my own two legs!'

Basil only gave her a slightly startled smile, and turned away to allow the groom to leg him up.

It was a wonderful day. They rode out over the vast white plain, pausing at the top of a long, shallow slope to look back at the house.

'Dreadful, isn't it, with that mixture of styles?' Basil said.

'Not dreadful – funny!'

'It looks as though it were designed by a madman.'

'Several madmen – but nice ones. I like it.'

'Do you? Well, I do too, in a strange sort of way, though it isn't what one ought to admire. The Black Tower is supposed to be haunted, you know.'

'By whom?'

'Oh, some woman who was locked up in it to die. She lures people up onto the leads and makes them throw themselves off, according to the legend. The servants believe it, anyway. We have to keep it locked, or they'd be flinging themselves off like lemmings.'

'Are they so unhappy?' Emily was startled.

'Oh, I don't suppose so. But suicide is part of the Russian tradition, you know. There's a deep vein of melancholy in the Russian character.'

They rode to the woods, and Basil took a shot at a few rabbits, without hitting anything. Emily was glad he missed: the rabbits had been enjoying the sunshine, and she was so happy she didn't want anyone, even a rabbit, to be less so on this glorious day of days. To prevent his shooting any more, she asked if he would teach her, and he seemed glad to. He taught her how to hold the gun and fire it, and then let her take aim at a tree.

'You're really not bad at all,' he said approvingly, finding she hit the trunk every time. 'You've got quite an eye.'

'My cousin Tom taught me to use a catapult. I think a gun's easier, as far as aiming goes anyway.'

'If you like, we might get you a gun of your own, once we have our own place.'

'Are women allowed to shoot in Russia?'

'A princess – particularly a Narishkin – may do exactly as she pleases in Russia,' said Basil.

When they returned from the ride, they changed and had luncheon, and then Basil showed her through the main state rooms of the house.

'The paintings aren't much to look at,' he said. 'You can see they're mostly family portraits, and by the look of them I'd say they were done by an estate painter.'

'What's that?'

'Oh, a talented serf kept for the purpose – though not too talented in this case.'

'Do you know who they are, the people in the pictures?'

'No, you'd want Anna for that. She learned them all off by heart when she married Kirov, though she's probably forgotten them again by now. They don't come here much.'

Emily thought it a pity. She was hungry for family, and would have liked to know who was who among these ancestors of hers. At either end of the drawing-room was a pair of pictures obviously done at the same time. The woman was dressed in the style of the 1860s, and from working back the dates, she thought they might be her great-grandfather and great-grandmother, Natasha's father and mother. If so, he would be the Count Kirov she was supposed to resemble, but of course one could never tell from a painting. There was nothing much to hang a resemblance on, except that he had tawny eyes like hers.

Basil was obviously tiring of the tour when the butler came to announce that tea was ready; and after taking a cup and a desultory piece of bread and butter, he excused himself to her and said he would see her at dinner. Emily felt a piercing disappointment at the thought of three and a half hours without him; but against that she had the delicious thought of the coming night to dwell on and treasure. She felt she would like to be with him for every instant of the day, and was faintly surprised and hurt that he didn't feel the same; but she told herself that men were different from women, and that she mustn't take it personally. He wouldn't have married her if he didn't love her as much as she loved him. It was just that it took him differently.

She thought she would read a book until it was time to dress, but in the end she just sat and stared into space, indulging in the sort

193

of day-dreams she would never have expected to come out of her sensible head. When the dressing-bell went, she went up to the sea-green bedroom, and found Masha waiting for her with hot water and a request to know which evening gown to lay out.

She and Basil were dining alone, but Masha seemed to expect a level of formality, so in the end she chose a low-cut, short-sleeved gown of garnet-coloured silk. She was going to put on the gold necklace Basil had chosen for her on the day they looked at the family jewels, but Masha, opening the casket, silently proposed a ruby and diamond set of necklace and earrings, which, though it looked excellently with the dress, seemed over-sumptuous for a private dinner.

'Isn't it too much?' she asked nervously, looking at her reflection. It seemed to her that the jewels changed her: she looked older, more like a real grown-up, unfamiliar.

'Oh no, *barina*. And if you'll allow, something for the hair is needed. This, perhaps?'

Well, it wasn't quite a tiara, at least: a half-hoop of platinum which fitted down into the piled sides of the hair, bearing at the centre front a scrolled embellishment set with diamonds. Perhaps if I am a princess I must always wear a crown, she thought as Masha settled it and teased the hair out around it.

When she arrived in the drawing-room she saw that Masha had been right. Basil, in full evening dress, stood as she came into the room, and looked at her with an appreciation that made her feel warm and rather liquid inside.

'I'm glad you dressed,' he said. 'I meant to mention it before, but I see I didn't need to. You look – superb!' He came to her, and lifted her hand – the one weighted with her glowing ruby and her wedding ring – and kissed it.

'I knew rubies would suit you,' he said, looking into her eyes in a way that made her feel almost faint. 'I'm glad I married you, Emilusha.'

She had nothing, absolutely nothing to say, but a man must have been a block not to have seen it all in her face. What she was thinking was that she wished they could forget about dinner and go to bed right then; and perhaps at that moment her thoughts and Basil's weren't so very far apart.

*

194

On the third day, the thaw began. In the dream-drowsy moment of waking, Emily thought she was in a boat drifting down a stream; then, as she came to the surface, she realised it was the sound, missing from the world ever since she had come to Russia, of running water. For a while she lay contentedly, listening to the gurgle and watching, beyond the window, the fascinating sight of a steady grey drip-drip-drip from a gutter somewhere above the window.

Then Basil woke and said, 'Damn.'

She turned to him. 'What's the matter.'

'The thaw's come. That's the end of our riding.'

'Is it?'

'Of course it is. Don't be a fool! There are tons and tons of snow out there to melt and run away before the ground will be firm enough to ride on. We'll be confined to the house for at least a week, damn it.'

The idea of the thaw seemed to be making him strangely cross. Being indoors together couldn't be such a hardship, could it?

'Never mind,' she said, turning towards him and slipping her arm round him, ready for their usual morning love. Even three days of marriage can hallow customs. 'If we can't ride, we can stay a little longer in bed.'

Basil kissed her, but rather perfunctorily, and after a moment he pushed her away quite firmly and started to get up. He didn't seem to want love this morning, and Emily watched him with a sinking feeling of disappointment. She never seemed to be able to have enough of it, and here he was already cutting her ration in half!

'Must you go?' she asked. He was putting on his dressing-gown.

'Grusha will be waiting for me,' he said.

This seemed a new departure, to be worrying about the servants. 'Surely he won't complain,' Emily said, but Basil was going – going – and gone. She sat up and stared at the closed door, perplexed. What strange, cross things men could be, put out by the smallest thing. It seemed quite an exciting idea to her, the vast blanket of snow that covered the earth all melting away at once, and the green and brown coming through again after so many months of white.

When she went downstairs after breakfast, there was no sign of Basil. Eventually she asked the butler, and was told that he was spending the morning in the shooting-gallery. Emily felt completely at a loss. She would have quite liked to go too, and practise her shooting, but since he had gone without her, she had to presume he didn't want her company. She wandered disconsolately about the

195

drawing-room and the Octagon Room for a while, and then caught herself up sharply, gave herself a talking-to, and dedicated the morning to writing the promised letter to Sylvia describing the wedding.

Basil reappeared at luncheon, still a little uncommunicative; but after most of a bottle of claret he unbent and offered to teach her billiards, and they spent the afternoon knocking the balls about, which cheered him up since she was so unconditionally hopeless at it.

'I'll learn,' she protested when he laughed at her. 'I'll get better with practice.'

'I don't want you to get better at it,' he said, grinning at her. 'I like you just the way you are.'

Dinner began well, then seemed to deteriorate. Basil drank rather a lot of vodka and told her amusing stories about jolly times he had had with Youna and Dima and other bosom friends; but the stories grew longer and less amusing as Basil's eyes grew more fixed. Emily began to have difficulty in laughing at the conclusion of each, and was rather relieved when it was time to leave the table.

In the drawing-room it was better, for she asked Basil to play the piano for her, which he seemed pleased to do. But he tired of it after a while, and came back to the fire and began drinking brandy, which seemed to make him silent. She tried conversing, but as he answered her in monosyllables and would not initiate a subject himself, it was impossible to get on.

Finally she left her chair and went to lean over him from behind, slipping her arms round his neck and kissing his ear. He grunted, which she took for encouragement, so she kissed him again and rested her cheek lovingly on his head.

'Don't fuss me,' he said, reaching up to unloose her hands. 'You're always touching me and fussing me,' he said peevishly.

She straightened up and rested her hands on the chairback, more surprised than hurt, since it obviously wasn't true. She didn't yet dare to touch him very often, except when they were in bed together.

He must have interpreted her silence as hurt, however, for he half turned his head and said, 'I'm sorry, Emilia, but I don't like being fussed all the time.'

She came round to stand beside him, and he looked up at her. It was odd, she thought with one distant part of her mind, how with the light at this particular angle, his eyes looked quite inanimate, like the glass eyes of a stuffed toy.

He smiled at her uncertainly. 'Sorry,' he said again. 'Didn't mean to hurt your feelings.'

It was enough for her. She smiled too. 'I wasn't offended,' she said quickly. 'I'm sorry if I annoyed you. It's just that I love you so much, it seems natural to touch you.'

He grunted in response, and his eyes slid away from hers. Perhaps he too was shy, she thought, with a sense of revelation. She had simply assumed from the beginning that he was fully in control of the situation, but perhaps he was as shy as she was, only better at hiding it.

Perhaps, too, it was better now to avoid any more talking. There would be fewer misunderstandings if they relied on their bodies to communicate.

'It's getting late. Shall we go to bed?' she said as beguilingly as she could.

He looked up, but his eyes missed hers by an important fraction. 'You go on up, if you like, I'll come in a minute or two.'

She hesitated. 'You won't be long?'

'No, no,' he said, with the faintest return of irritation. 'I'll just finish this glass.'

She would have liked to kiss him, tempt him to leave the damned brandy, but in the prevailing atmosphere she didn't quite dare. In the sea-green bedchamber she undressed herself, turned the lamps low, and got into bed to wait for him, eager not only for love, but to wash away with the act of it the slight taste of misunderstanding. But he didn't come, and after some time she fell asleep, and woke in the morning alone in the bed.

Chapter Twelve

Emily had always preferred the outdoor life, but she acknowledged that if one had to be confined indoors, Schwartzenturm was not a bad place to be. Apart from the sheer size of the place, which made it possible to get quite a lot of exercise just walking from room to room, there was a well-stocked library, and the billiard room and shooting-gallery for amusement. The succession-houses contained a miniature Kew Gardens for refreshment, and just across the yard was the bathhouse, where one could happily while away a whole morning basking in the steam and being massaged in a variety of pleasant ways by the attendant.

Besides, if one was on one's honeymoon, what could be better than being alone with one's beloved? But that, she discovered sadly, was not Basil's view. It wasn't his fault, she saw that; it was just that he grew bored horribly easily. After that first unhappy day of the thaw, Emily took care to keep him amused, rather as though he were a child in her charge. She made sure the time between the various meals was broken up into sections, with an activity planned for each, and it worked excellently. Basil regained his equilibrium. He seemed happy, and was charming and affectionate towards her, which was her reward – that, and their nights together.

Lovemaking was a fresh delight to her each time, and she only wished there could be more of it; but once when she tried to embrace him in the billiard room before the dressing-bell he shook her off quite crossly and said, 'Not here! Not now!' So she accepted that it must only be in bed, after they had retired for the night. Well, after all, he knew the rules as she did not.

Outside, the thaw continued in drips and drizzle and raw white fog, and as the snow disappeared the earth became a brown morass, cutting them off from the outside world. A thick layer of straw was spread in the stable-yard and the grooms led the horses round and round it for hours each day, to keep them exercised. Once, when Basil had taken himself off alone to the bathhouse, Emily put on her outdoor things and went to watch, thinking she might offer to help simply for something to do. But her appearance amongst them

198

perplexed and embarrassed the servants so much that she didn't make the offer, and soon took pity on them and went away.

At last, one afternoon, the sun finally sucked up the fog, and the world was revealed steaming gently in the sudden warmth. After tea she and Basil went out onto the terrace to walk up and down and look at the view. The snow was almost gone, lingering only in a few pockets here and there. There was still a snowy freshness to the air, but the sunshine was warm on Emily's head, and she could hear birds larking about in the shrubs below the terrace wall.

'A few days of this'll dry up the ground,' Basil said cheerfully. 'You'll see the difference once the grass starts sprouting and the leaves begin to come through.'

'Will we be able to go riding again?'

'Not for a day or two. The ground will still be too heavy. It'll take time for the surface to dry out.'

Emily accepted his judgement without question; so the next day when she came downstairs she was surprised to find him in the hall dressed for riding and about to be helped into his greatcoat. The day had dawned sunny again, and the slight early mist had dispersed to reveal a clear sky of tender spring blue. She had been indoors for a week, and was longing for some vigorous exercise.

'Are you going out?' she asked eagerly. 'Oh good! I thought you said the ground would be too heavy.'

Basil held his head up very high, so that he was looking at her from under his eyelids. 'Too heavy for you,' he said. 'The roads are still vile. I'm going across country to Grubetskaya – our nearest neighbours, the Kovanins. They usually come down before Easter, so they'll probably still be holed up there with the thaw.'

'Oh, but – but can't I come too?'

Basil's head went even higher. 'I've just told you, the ground will be too heavy for you. It's over twenty versts away. It's going to take me a couple, maybe three hours, and I shall be plastered with mud by the time I get there.'

Emily smiled. 'I don't mind. Anyone's who's ever been hunting in England is used to being plastered in mud.'

He sighed, took hold of her arm and walked her a step or two away from the butler. There was the hint of a pinch in his grip.

'Please don't make a spectacle of us both,' he said quietly. 'If I'd meant you to come I'd have asked you.'

'You don't want me to?' she said, still more surprised than hurt.

He sighed again. 'I can't spend every moment of every day with you. Married people don't live in each other's pockets. You must try not to be such a provincial, Emilia.'

Now it hurt. She bit her lip and said nothing.

'If the Kovanins are there, I probably shan't come back tonight,' he said with the air of a stern but kind father administering a needed lesson. She could imagine him saying, 'This will hurt me more than it hurts you.'

'I see,' she managed to say. She thought she had done rather well in saying it neutrally, but Basil frowned.

'And please don't sulk,' he said. 'Remember you are Princess Narishkina now. The last person to bear that title was my mother. You must try to live up to her memory.'

Aunt Maud had said things like that to her since she was old enough to stand up without swaying, but this was different – this was Basil! Tears rushed upwards, not so much at the words but at the fact that he was rebuking her. She shut her teeth firmly to stop them escaping. Now was not the time to cry or protest.

Satisfied, apparently, by her silence, Basil released her arm and turned back to the butler to be helped on with his greatcoat. Then he put on his hat, received his gloves, and turned back to Emily with a smile.

'Goodbye, my dear,' he said kindly.

The slight flush of anger in his cheeks made him look more divinely handsome than ever.

'Goodbye, Basil,' she said, and felt herself smiling back, though what sort of a smile it could be she wasn't sure. It seemed enough for him, however. He gave a little satisfied nod, and clattered away down the stairs to the lower hall.

It seemed absurd to eat a ceremonious luncheon all by herself, so she rang for a servant and cancelled it, took a couple of apples from the exquisite arrangement in the Octagon Room, and decided to go and explore the Black Tower. Basil had shown her the door at the far end of the picture-gallery which gave access to the tower, but when she reached it she had to ring again for a servant, because it was locked. There followed a lengthy delay, at the end of which Adamo, the butler, appeared, followed by Masha clutching a thick shawl. Emily stood meekly by as Adamo unlocked the door, but when she discovered that he meant to conduct her, she demurred.

'Oh no, really, there's no need to take you from your work. I can go by myself.'

'My work is to serve you, madame,' Adamo said unanswerably.

'I'm quite used to exploring by myself,' Emily protested.

Adamo considered. 'You would prefer to be accompanied only by Masha?' he tried.

'No, I want to go on my own. Please.'

The *please* seemed to take him aback. He bowed very low and stepped aside.

Masha took her cue. 'You'll need this, *barina*,' she said, stepping forward with the shawl. 'It's very cold in the Black Tower.'

Emily didn't like the look of the shawl, and it smelled rather musty, but to avoid further argument she accepted it, meaning to shrug it off as soon as she was out of their sight. She hadn't reckoned on the dank and chilly atmosphere inside the tower, however. Its windows were unglazed arrow slits, and there was no form of heating; the air felt as though it came straight from a mediaeval dungeon. Musty or not, she was glad of the shawl.

The body of the tower contained only the spiral stone staircase: the rooms were at the top. When she stepped in off the staircase she found it was much warmer, for there were glazed windows, and the sun was shining through them, illuminating the dust she had disturbed for the first time, she supposed, in years. Apart from the dust, and the skeleton of a small bat lying in the middle of the floor, there was nothing to see. The rooms were completely empty: they could not have been used for decades.

Pulling the shawl closer around her, she climbed the stairs up onto the leads. Up here the air was exhilaratingly fresh, and the sun felt quite hot on the top of her head, though wherever a shadow fell, the dark strip was like icy water. But it was worth the climb after all: the view was magnificent. Emily walked slowly round the perimeter, pausing every few steps to gaze out over the parapet at the plain which stretched away in each direction, seemingly for ever.

Finally her steps slowed and stopped. She stood with the sun behind her and simply stared. Never before had she experienced such a sense of space all around her. It had a strangely calming effect: her own concerns, her recent disappointment and hurt, seemed tiny and unimportant in the face of these distances. She gazed towards the horizon, the misty rim of the world, and thought, at last I have found it. This is Russia: this quiet space, this still vastness.

It is a permanence, she thought – an enduring. There has always

201

been this, and whatever restless, impermanent people come and go over its surface, it will remain for ever. It is in my blood, too, this Russia. It is part of me, and I am part of it. I feel it as a weight inside me, binding me to the earth; and as a spirit, buoying me up like the wind under a raven's wings, setting me free. Yes, she thought, drawing in the vastness with each breath, Russia is in me; and wherever I go after this, anywhere in the world, I shall never leave it.

She was still standing like that, her hands resting lightly on the parapet, her face turned towards eternity, when she heard footfalls in the room below. A little cold breeze trickled over her temples and then was still, leaving the sudden heat of the sun, and the sound of a pair of crows calling harshly from the top of the nearest tree. The footsteps started up the stairs, an ominous sound, the sound of approaching fate: the prisoner in his cell, the child afraid of the dark, listen for it. But I'm not afraid, Emily thought firmly, turning slowly towards it. What harm can come to me here?

A complete stranger came up into the sunlight, ducking his head out under the doorway. He turned to look at her, but the sun was shining into his eyes. He put up a hand in an uncompleted gesture as though to fend it off, and then moved round to the side of her out of its glare.

'I'm sorry,' he said. 'Did I startle you?'

'I thought it might be Basil,' she replied.

They were staring at each other in a way that would not have been considered polite had they been in company. He was ten years or so older than her; a man of medium height, strongly built, and with a way of carrying himself – very upright without being stiff – that made him seem somehow impressive. There was a quietness in his face, and a self-possession, as though he had spent a great deal of time waiting and watching for danger. A sailor, or a soldier, or a game-hunter might look so; a man who, when danger came, had only himself to rely on.

She saw these things before she registered the more immediate facts about him: that his hair was brown with barley-coloured lights in it, bleached to gold on the temples and the forelock; that his mouth was a strange and subtle thing, the upper lip and the lower lip seeming so little a pair they must surely have some other more important function than to lie against each other; that his eyes were light brown, tawny brown, with gold flecks, beautiful, watchful, full of light.

'I think you'll know me again,' he said at last. Ah, that's what the lips were for, then, she discovered, as he smiled at her.

'You're the most real person I think I've ever seen,' she said. Now what on earth possessed me to say that? she thought in surprise.

'Then you won't forget me. That's useful. The world is very large and so full of people, it's a wonder we can ever find anyone when we want them. And it's always the people one likes most whom one seems to mislay.'

Emily felt a sharp concern at the word. She didn't want to be mislaid.

'No, it's all right,' he went on immediately, as if she had spoken. 'And yes, I did know what you were thinking. You haven't yet learnt the knack of hiding inside your face, which is delightful for me, though you will find it an inconvenience in polite society.'

It occurred to her then that of course he knew who she was, which put her at a disadvantage; and yet she didn't at all mind standing here having him say such things to her. She was alone at the top of a tower with him, and he might be anyone, but she smelled only trust coming from this man, and liking. The sun, moving round, touched her eyelids. She half closed her eyes and smiled, holding out her hands a little from her sides in the gesture of a child offering itself for inspection. *Here I am*, the gesture said; *tell me about myself*.

'Did you know I'd be up here?' she said.

He came the last step towards her, and they both turned and stood side by side, looking out. His hands resting on the parapet were broad, strong, quiet – a horseman's hands. The fingernails were nicely shaped and well cared for, the sides of the forefingers calloused from handling reins. The middle finger of his right hand was crooked, as though it had been broken at some time and had set wrongly. That must have been awkward for him, she thought: she felt he was a man who used his hands a great deal.

'I knew Princess Narishkina was up here. Adamo told me, so I came up to pay my respects, even if it is an odd place for you to receive callers. But I didn't know, of course, that it would be *you*.'

She understood exactly, but wished she might be dishonest enough to ask him what he meant, just for the pleasure of having him talk about her.

'Did you come to see Basil?' she asked instead.

'Yes and no.'

'What is the "No" part?' she asked curiously.

'I came to see both of you; and I certainly didn't come all the way up the tower to see him. Are you warm enough? You must keep your throat covered. You lose a great deal of heat from around the throat and neck. Remember that if you are ever lost in the snow. The throat and the head must remain covered.'

He reached out to pull the fold of the shawl more closely together at her neck. She watched his hands approaching, and was suddenly seized with a fierce desire to be touched by him. She looked up at him in surprise at her own feelings. His hands completed their small task, and then he touched her head with the tips of his fingers, as though that were all he dared allow himself.

He drew in a long breath and rested his hands lightly on her shoulders. Everything seemed to slow: the world stopped turning, and the tug of time against the braked wheel of this moment of contact made her feel vertiginous and weak. She thought she had put her own hands up to touch him, thought she was reaching up on tiptoe towards him, though in fact she hadn't moved.

'Christ alive,' he muttered, 'this wasn't supposed to happen.'

She wanted to say 'What?' but her mouth was dry, and she was rather afraid of what might leap out if she opened it. All they were doing was looking at each other. All? The bones seemed to have been taken out of her legs, and all sorts of bits of her were whimpering like puppies to be picked up and held tightly, tightly by him.

'I'm going to let you go now,' he said. Well, perhaps he didn't actually say it. Perhaps he only looked a warning before he removed his hands very slowly and carefully from her shoulders and put them down by his sides.

Then he drew a deep breath and said, 'Look at the nice view, there's a good girl. If you keep looking at me like that I shall get confused.'

She supposed she must have obeyed him, for she became aware that they were again side by side and staring out at the crows'-nest tree. The crows were still there, settling their wings pleasurably in the sunshine: it had all taken no time at all. Perhaps it had been a fit of vertigo; or the sun on her head making her faint? Perhaps she had simply imagined it all? No, something had happened, though she had no idea what it was. There was this unaccountable hollowness inside her, for one thing; and such a feeling of attachment and belonging to this man. It was a very completing feeling; she was not afraid. At all events, she must be safe with him.

'What was it for, this tower?' she asked at last.

There seemed a long pause before he spoke, but when his voice came, it sounded normal, comfortable. 'The story is that an old princess who was a recluse built it and locked herself up until she died to get away from the world.'

'Is that why it's supposed to be haunted?'

'No, I don't think so. It's the peasants who say it's haunted, not the servants, but peasants are always seeing ghosts and visions and fairies. Their lives are so monotonous and hard they like to enrich them with fantasies: saints and virgins and bleeding wounds, spirits sent from beyond the grave with dire warnings for the living, portents and omens and two-headed calves. You have to remember that half the time they're drunk with weariness from their labours, and the other half drunk with vodka from the *kabak*. And then there's famine: hunger is a great producer of visions. That's why all the old religions advocate fasting, of course.'

'Our Lord going out into the desert?'

'Quite. Alone in the vastness – the night sky over the desert is a breathtaking thing – and with nothing to eat or drink, who wouldn't see visions?'

'They weren't real visions, then?'

'Of course they were real. *Que voulez vous?* You can trust the evidence of your senses, can't you? Of all your senses.'

There seemed to be some kind of message in the last part and she glanced at him for enlightenment, but he was looking out at the view, a small smile curling up the corners of his mouth.

'I used to come up here a lot when I was a child,' he said after a while, in a different voice. 'It was my special place, my hiding-place, where I came to be happy or sad.'

'I had a tree like that, when I was very little,' she said. 'Later on, though, it was books.'

'Yes, books make good hiding-places,' he nodded. 'What did you need to hide from?'

She thought for a moment. 'Not belonging, mostly. What about you?'

'I suppose it comes down to the same thing. I didn't get on with my father; and I didn't approve of my mother. She did things – oh well, they were hers to do, but I minded. Children make little hells for themselves; there's no way to stop it.'

She nodded doubtfully. She had been too recently a child and at the mercy of adults entirely to agree with him.

He looked at her. 'Adults too,' he said, as though answering her.

'My God, I of all people know that! And you, I suspect, are about to find it out. You are getting cold, though. I can see you shivering.'

She turned to look at him, hoping he might put his arm round her to warm her, and he grinned and shook his head.

'Now you stop that! Whatever you're shivering for, that is not the answer! Come, we'll go down, and have our talk in more comfort. You haven't offered me refreshments yet – falling down in your duties as chatelaine, you know. Have you had luncheon?'

'No. I wasn't hungry.'

'You can offer me a glass of wine and a biscuit, at least, to keep my strength up until teatime. There is always an excellent afternoon tea in the English style at Schwartzenturm.'

He started towards the stairs to go down before her, and she followed a step, and then said, 'Wait!' He turned. 'Who are you?'

'You know who I am,' he said. His intense eyes were burning into hers again, and she was aware that more things were being said than voiced. 'You have all the information you need.'

'You are . . . ' she began slowly, thinking it out. Yes, of course she knew it really. 'You are my Cousin Alexei.'

'Alexei Nikolayevitch Kirov.'

'Anna's husband.'

That seemed to have been the wrong thing to say.

'Of course, Anna's husband,' he agreed quite genially, but the pleasure had faded out of his face, like the colour leaving the sky after the sun has gone down.

In the Octagon Room Adamo brought them wine and biscuits.

'And now you can tell me what on earth you're doing here,' Alexei said when they were alone.

Emily fought down the disloyal desire to spill out her resentment.

'Basil said the going would be far too heavy for me. The house he's visiting – I've forgotten the name – is over twenty versts away.'

'Grubetskaya, I suppose. That's the nearest house to here, unless you go into Kirishi. But that's not what I meant. I meant, why are the two of you here at all?'

'It's our honeymoon,' Emily said doubtfully. Surely he must know that, even if he had missed the wedding?

'Nonsense! Nobody goes into the country at this time of year, and particularly not for a honeymoon. Honeymoons are spent in the Crimea, or the South of France, or Paris, or even Rome if you have a fancy for cities. Whose idea was it to come to Schwartzenturm just before the thaw? You might just as well have stayed in Petersburg – at least there you'd have had some company. No wonder Basil got bored and dashed off to see the Kovanins. Or rather, laboured off! If he gets there in under four hours, it'll be a miracle. And if the flood-water has washed out the bridge at Birchwood Ravine, he'll never get there at all.'

She looked at him askance. 'I don't see why you're so angry about it. It's his business – and mine – and I don't believe it can be that difficult or dangerous, or he'd never have gone.'

Some of the tension went out of his face. 'You're quite right, of course. I have no *right* to be angry.' It seemed a curious emphasis to her, but he went on quickly, 'Just tell me whose idea it was for you to come here.'

Emily belatedly saw the open trap. 'Oh – well – it was – I think it was Anna who first suggested it. But Basil agreed to it,' she added quickly as he groaned. 'And I'm sure she meant it kindly.'

'My dear child, you had better learn as quickly as you can that Anna means nothing kindly. Everything she does is done either to promote her own comfort, or to annoy.'

Emily felt shocked, but not as shocked as she felt she ought to be, which was more shocking still. 'Why did you marry her, then?' she asked him in retaliation.

He didn't seem to mind the question. 'Ten years ago I was young, too – not much older than you are now, I imagine. Did you think we were born masters of the universe, we men, just because we rule you? Yes, I see that you do think it! Well, I don't want to spoil your illusions too soon. To give you another reason, they say all men marry their mothers, just as all women marry their fathers – the first time round, at least.' He looked into her face as she thought furiously. 'Am I right?'

'No! Basil's nothing like my father at all,' she said quickly.

'Ah. Then you've nothing to worry about, have you?'

'This really is a very odd conversation,' she said aloud. 'Do you always talk to people like this?'

'*Au contraire*, hardly ever. There really are so few people in the world worth talking to. Do you like the wine?'

'I should be asking you that, shouldn't I? As your hostess.'

He smiled in the way she had first noticed, which seemed to give an entirely different meaning to everything, and to use all the separate pieces of his face so that they took on a new relationship to each other – like shuffling tarot cards and laying them out in a new pattern. She felt he could almost have talked with his face, without ever using words.

'Yes, of course you are. But then you see, it's *my* wine.'

'Oh Lord, so it is! I'd forgotten this is your house. What a strange situation!'

'Playing house together. Well, I don't know that it's so strange. Shall we pretend we've known each other for years and years, and that we're old friends, and can say anything we like to each other?'

She looked at him, struck with the realisation that that was how she already did feel. Why should she need to pretend it? 'Playing games?' she asked doubtfully.

'Why not?' he said, and the smile rearranged itself slightly, this time to reveal a distant sadness. 'It's what most people do most of the time. At least you and I will be doing it in full consciousness. And I assure you,' he added, as though to himself, 'the alternative would be disastrous.'

'What alternative?' she asked.

'I'll tell you one day. Not now.'

'Why?'

'One day, perhaps, it won't be disastrous.'

Through the rest of that long, strange day they talked. For Emily it had the quality of being perfectly natural and utterly dreamlike at the same time. The conversation flowed easily and constantly like a deep river, and there were times when she hardly knew which of them had said what. He was like another self, but a wiser, more experienced, more knowledgeable self who could answer her questions and satisfy her curiosity.

Her usual sense of inequality was missing. He was a man, a grown-up, one of the masters of the universe, as he had put it, but though she was aware of her inexperience, she did not feel humble or impotent with him.

He said to her at one point, 'I love your mind! It's like the very best sort of curio shop, full of fascinating things collected together for no better reason than that they once interested the proprietor.'

'Magpie's nest?' she suggested.

'Not much more methodical, I grant you; but with the difference that all your curios have an intrinsic worth. Your taste is very sound.'

'Because it's like yours?' she suggested.

'What other way is there to judge?' he said seriously.

She told him about her childhood, her father, Bratton, the Tarrants, and her education in London. Only when she came to the last few months in Russia did her narrative falter, and she was at a loss to understand why. Her letters home to England had been full of Basil, his courtship and the wedding plans, but she didn't seem to want to talk about Basil to Alexei. When she tried to, she found it difficult to meet his eyes, and their bright, golden gaze seemed hard and watchful, like a hunting cat's.

He said, 'You were in rather a hurry, weren't you? Not here five months yet, and you've married the first man you met in Russia.'

'I didn't meet Basil here. I knew him in England. I've known him for years.'

'Ah, have you,' was all he said, but she felt stung into wanting to defend her choice. 'You don't know him at all.' No, he hadn't said it, but he might as well have done, because she saw it in his face.

After tea they walked on the terrace and watched the sun go down, and he told her about his childhood and his parents.

'My father married for love the first time, and was very happy, so I understand. My old *mamka*, Marfa, told me that he used to sing around the house – a hard thing to imagine for anyone who knew him only in later life. He used to bring my mother things he found on his walks – just like a cat, Marfa said. A pretty leaf or an interesting stone, a hatful of wild strawberries. And at night, after dinner, if they were alone, he used to dance with her on the terrace, and sing the tunes in her ear.'

'How nice! She must have been very happy, too. What was she like, your mother?'

'I don't know. She died when I was only two.'

'Oh, I'm sorry.'

'It's all right. I don't remember her at all. But her death changed my father's nature. He became something of a recluse – and there could hardly be a better house to be a recluse in than this one. I suppose he might even have been contented, living all alone with his books and his greenhouses and waiting to die so that he could rejoin my mother. But my Uncle Kostya died unmarried, and according to Marfa's story Papa felt one puny male child was not enough to carry the family name. So he married again, this time not for love.'

'What for, then?'

209

'She was pretty, she came from healthy stock – a well-to-do family, though not of the nobility. She probably seemed charming, suitable to him to breed from, and to be a mother to me. I expect she pretended to be attached to me during the weeks of courtship – '

'Only pretended?'

'She never liked small children,' he said neutrally. 'I was five years old then. I don't remember much about her in those early days, except that she seemed always to be dressed up and on her way to a party. Then Adishka was born, when I was seven. She was made very ill by it, and swore never to have another, but by then I think Papa had lost interest in her anyway, so she wasn't required to. They went their separate ways – he to his books, she to her parties. Adishka and I were brought up by Marfa, then by tutors, and saw our parents for five minutes about once a week. Unusual in Russia, though perfectly normal in England, as I understand it.'

'So Adishka is your half-brother. Did you and he get on together?'

'Oh yes. There was never any rivalry between us in those days. But then the poor little beast contracted infantile paralysis when he was eight, and we were separated for a couple of years. He was sent to clinics all over Europe to try to straighten him out. He was finally brought back when my father died in 1900. The estate was left to Mother in trust until I reached my majority and she didn't want any more money wasted on expensive treatments, which she was convinced wouldn't work. By the time I gained control of things, it was too late to help Adishka.'

'Is that why you don't like her?'

'One of the reasons.'

'What else? You said you disapproved of her.'

'She had affairs – blatant ones. Children can be very censorious.' He was frowning with thought. 'I suppose there were excuses for her. Papa kept her short of money, and she'd been brought up accustomed to every luxury. Her only recourse, I suppose, was to keep company with rich lovers until Papa died. Then she had three years of freedom, and as soon as I reached my majority, she whisked herself out of my clutches by marrying a fabulously wealthy Jewish textiles merchant. So now she's Madame Baline, the best-dressed woman in Moscow, a leader of Society. Adishka goes to see her sometimes. She has a very gay time, I believe, amongst the fast set there.'

'You hate her, don't you?' Emily hazarded.

He gave a crooked smile. 'No, not really. She isn't worth hating, poor, silly woman. What I deplore is the waste, and my own stupidity. It was in reaction against her, you see, that I married Anna the very moment I had control of my father's estate.'

'Oh!'

He smiled at her, his eyes half closed against the long red-gold light of the sunset. 'Yes, *oh!*, as you so precisely put it. You have an extraordinarily expressive face you know, little one: you'll never be able to dissemble to me.'

'Shall I want to?' she dared.

'Perhaps, at times. One can't depend on life, you know, to deal the right cards; and to play out a bad hand takes courage. Not the quick, hot-blooded kind that comes when you're faced with sudden danger, but the slow, grinding sort that goes on and on enduring. Have you that kind of courage?'

'I don't know. Have you?'

For once he evaded the question. 'Why should you think I need it?' he asked with a teasing smile. 'Adishka has it. I suppose anyone who goes through continuous pain has to develop it. I remind myself of that when he does anything particularly annoying or stupid.'

It began to grow dark, and they went inside when the servants brought the lamps – there was no gas at Schwartzenturm.

'Basil won't be coming back today, then,' she said.

'Did you think he would?'

'Well, I thought he might. No, I suppose I didn't. He wanted to – '

'Yes?'

She hesitated for a moment, thinking it would be disloyal; but really, it didn't seem to matter what she said to Alexei, and after all he was her cousin, and she knew she could trust his discretion. 'He wanted to punish me for being a provincial,' she said. She tried a smile, but it wobbled rather. 'It was like that with Aunt Maud; she was always afraid I would turn out to be middle-class.'

He hadn't smiled. 'As we shall be alone for dinner, shall we dispense with formality? Not bother to dress, just have a quiet, comfortable, informal dinner together?'

'It would be nice, but wouldn't Adamo disapprove?'

He studied her face. 'You've never had servants before, have you?'

'No,' she said. 'Only a housekeeper, who was more like a sort of mother. I mean, she kept me in order, not vice versa.'

'And the few months at Natasha Petrovna's house?'

'I was still a child then,' she said, thinking it out as she spoke, 'so

211

I had to do what my grandmother said, and she commanded the servants.'

'Yes, I understand exactly. But now, of course, you are not a child any more. Will you allow me to advise you a little?'

'About servants? Yes, please. Tell me how to manage them.'

'You must remember they do not think of you as a human being. They regard you rather as a savage views his native gods: the inexplicable source of commands, wages, praise and censure; to be obeyed and placated when necessary, but not understood. You may be as eccentric, demanding, even unreasonable, as you like, and they will not be in the least surprised; but you must never explain or apologise.'

'But surely – '

'No, I'm serious. Listen to me. If you want your servants to serve you well, and be happy, you will be considerate of their persons and their feelings; pay them well, look after them when they're sick; but when you give them an order, make sure it's an order, not a request. Deliver it pleasantly by all means, but make them know you expect it to be obeyed.'

'Oh dear,' Emily said, 'I think Aunt Maud was right to be worried. I must be middle-class after all. I really can't bring myself to believe I'm a princess.'

He smiled. 'You must pretend you're in a play. Haven't you ever taken part in amateur dramatics? I understood the English were very keen on them.'

'Oh yes, we had them at Bratton. I used to act with my cousins.' She sighed. 'Just at the moment, though, I get the feeling that I'm in the wrong play.'

'I'm quite sure you are,' he said. 'But that will change. For the moment, you must throw yourself into the part as it is.'

When Adamo came discreetly in to see why they hadn't gone up to change, Alexei, acting out of old habit, glanced up at his butler and told him to bring them champagne.

'Always champagne for new brides,' he said to Emily. She saw how Adamo accepted the command and the altered circumstances without so much as a flicker of an eyebrow, and, smiling inwardly, compared his indifference with the silent but icy criticism of Corde. Perhaps, she thought, it was the well-trained English servant who was the true guardian of middle-class mores.

Unchanged, she and Alexei sat side by side before the fire, drinking Russian champagne out of tall glasses and talking, and when dinner was announced they walked through into the dining-room without breaking conversational stride. Dinner was both magnificent and exquisite, and the perfumed wines rose like golden mist inside her head, lifting her a finger's breadth above the earth as they talked and laughed.

But in Russia it seemed sadness was never far beneath the surface of laughter, even as laughter was never far away in times of sorrow. She knew, even as she knew that what had happened here tonight was for ever, that the happiness would soon be over; but she turned her face away from the knowledge, and let herself slip unresisting into the golden stream.

When dinner was over, they returned to the Octagon Room. She did not remember who first suggested it, but he sat down at the piano and played to her, while she stood watching him, resting one hand lightly on the polished surface of the lid. He looked at her as he played, an unwavering, bright gaze that seemed to go with the music.

'It's beautiful. What is it?'

'Chopin. *Berceuse* in D flat, Opus 57. Simple and sweet and tender and a little sad. Appropriate for this evening.'

He came to the end and stopped.

'Yes, why does happiness make one feel sad?' she asked.

'A pleasant sadness, though, don't you think?'

'Oh yes.' She studied his face, astonished that it could be true that she had never seen it before this day. 'You seem so familiar to me, as if I've always known you. Your face seems to be one I've always known. Do you think we look alike? Is that it? After all, we are cousins.'

'I don't know. But I know I have to look at you all the time tonight, to make sure I remember exactly what you look like, every separate hair of your brows, every eyelash, every movement of your mouth. I don't want to forget anything. No-one has ever called you beautiful, have they?'

'No,' she said. 'I'm not beautiful.'

'If anyone but me ever says you are, you will know they are lying,' he said.

She looked quizzical. 'I'll tell them so.'

'You can pretend to believe them if you want. After all, if you're acting in someone else's play, it's only courtesy to learn the lines.'

213

'Am I in your play now?' she asked. She felt the question was dangerous, but was light-headed enough to dare.

His smile was almost grim. 'Do you really think I have that much control over things? I must have been behaving far too well.' He stood up abruptly. 'Now we must go out on the terrace for a moment. Will you be cold?'

She shook her head. He went to pull back the curtains and open the double doors. The terrace beyond was flooded with a theatrical blue light that fell almost vertically, so that there was no shadow.

'What a moon!' she said, following him out. The air was briskly cold, but very still. 'You'd almost think it could burn you, it's so bright.'

They walked forward to stand by the terrace rail. Above, the sky seemed polished and pale like a curved metal shell around the white-hot disc of the moon. 'It's perfect, isn't it? Completely full?'

'Yes,' he said. 'That's why we had to come out and look. You must make a wish on it.'

She stared up into its burning face, and wished that she would never be less happy than tonight.

'You too,' she said when she had finished.

'Yes,' he said. 'I've already done it.'

She looked at him, wanting to know what he had wished, and then not wanting to. 'Will they come true?'

It was a childish question, and he hesitated a moment, as though wondering whether to tell her the truth or humour her. But then his strange, mismatched lips curved into a smile of truth, and he said, 'Yes.'

She sighed, and looked out across the landscaped park, very English except for its scale, and in the flooding blue moonlight a simplified thing of shapes and shadows. In a moment she would begin to shiver, and they would have to go in, and she knew instinctively that that would be the end of the evening. But there were a few moments left to savour this extraordinary feeling of wholeness, of being a part of something great and continuous and undamageable.

She knew he was looking at her, but she couldn't take her eyes from the wide view.

'What are you feeling?' he asked out of the flowing river of the moment.

She knew that he wanted a substantial answer, and she waited an instant for the right words to come.

'Alive,' she said.

The next day she hurried downstairs after breakfast, eager to talk to him again, but Adamo told her that the master was occupied about estate business and would not be free until luncheon. Emily hid her disappointment, but the two hours left of the morning stretched before her like a desert. She fetched her writing-case, determined to keep herself occupied and still having letters home about the wedding to finish; but once she had written the address and date at the top of the first sheet, no further words came. The ink dried on her nib and she stared at nothing, between thought and daydream.

Just after eleven she was disturbed from her reverie by the distant sound of voices, and a moment later she distinguished Basil's amongst them. She jumped up and rushed out into the hall just as he came up into it from the lower hall, at the head of a party of young people.

'Emilusha!' His face lit flatteringly as he saw her; he held out his hands to her; her heart bounded, and she ran to him and was caught up and soundly embraced.

'Basil! I'm so glad you're back!' His lips touched her upturned face tenderly. The fur of his collar brushed her cheek with a silken touch. His firm young skin was cool from the open air and smelled faintly of sandalwood. She forgot each time she was away from him how astonishingly handsome he was. And he was hers, her husband, her own love!

'I've missed you, darling,' he said warmly. 'And look, I've brought you company! Youna and Dima you know, of course, but here are some new faces for you. Everyone,' he said proudly, 'I want you to meet my wife, Emilia Edvardovna, the new Princess Narishkina!'

They came crowding forward to meet her, handsome young people, smartly dressed, smiling, laughing, filling the hall with life and movement: the Kovanin brothers, Andrei and Ivan, Andrei's wife Nina, and Ivan's fiancée, Leone Duvitska. Youna and Dima claimed her as an old friend and kissed her exuberantly; Andrei looked at her with the frank and permitted admiration of a married man and said, 'How ever did you get her to say yes, Vasska? I can see at a glance she's much too pretty and clever for you!'

215

'Yes, I know,' Basil said, putting his arm round Emily's waist. She looked up at him, surprised, and saw that he was quite sincere. 'I'm a very lucky man,' he said, smiling down at her.

'I hope you will do a great deal of entertaining when you get settled in Petersburg, Princess,' Leone said, shaking her hand firmly. 'We desperately need some new life. We're all so bored with each other's conversation!'

'Of course we will,' Basil said. 'This Princess Narishkina is going to be one of the great hostesses of our time! Didn't I tell you?'

'You did,' Ivan agreed. 'He did, you know,' he added to Emily. 'He's been talking about you non-stop ever since he arrived yesterday.'

'Really?' Emily looked from him to Basil, who gave a pleased smirk.

'Yes, really. And nothing would do but that he must bring us all back to pay you homage.'

'Oh, please don't do that,' Emily laughed. 'I should find it most embarrassing. Let me offer you hospitality instead – ' At the words, she remembered the events of yesterday, the meeting at the top of the tower, and turned to Basil to tell him that his brother-in-law had arrived.

Before she could speak, however, he was amongst them, coming as though she had called him. He stepped lightly across the marble spaces of the hall, alert and quiet, like a hunter in open, hostile country.

'Well, Basil, there you are! Andrei, Nina – everybody. How nice of you all to come. You are going to stay now you're here, I hope? No rushing off after five minutes.'

'Alyosha! We had no idea you'd be here,' Nina Kovanina exclaimed with obvious pleasure. 'Is Anna here too?'

'I hope she and the children will be down in a few days' time, when the roads are better,' he answered smoothly.

'When did you get here?' Basil asked, with the slightest edge of coolness to his voice. Emily glanced up at him. No, it was not dislike, she saw, just reserve – uneasiness, perhaps. In a flash of understanding she saw that a simple, straightforward person like Basil might find Alexei unnerving, with his shining, mocking eyes and his air of always meaning more than he said.

'Yesterday. I came on horseback as soon as I thought I could get through, not realising that you'd have exactly the same idea. It was brave of you to dash off like that and risk your life fighting your way through to Grubetskaya to bring back company for your lovely bride.'

'Oh, it wasn't as difficult as that,' Basil said modestly.

Emily looked up at Basil in surprise, having heard as clearly as if he had voiced it Alexei's question: why did you need anyone else, when you were here on your honeymoon? She thought Basil's answer a piece of tight irony, but he was only smiling, evidently pleased at the praise from so unexpected a source. No, it's just me, she thought hastily, reading in lines that aren't in the play. I must curb this writer's desire to create sub-plots all the time. But whose play are we in now?

Basil, his arm still round her waist, went on speaking. 'So, you've been here since yesterday? I quite envy you, being able to spend the evening with my Emilia. I hope you took good care of her.'

'We took care of each other,' Alexei said.

Emily looked at him, but his eyes were veiled, his smile as impenetrable as a cat's. He looked at her, but did he see her?

Basil squeezed Emily's waist, looking exuberantly at his friends. 'Didn't I tell you she was beautiful?' he said.

Chapter Thirteen

Emily saw a familiar figure in a brown suit stumping along the unshaded side of the road, and told her coachman to stop.

'Adishka! What are you doing, you madman? You'll give yourself heat-stroke!'

He paused, glared towards hers, and then seeing who it was, began to smile, and limped across the road.

'I might have known it was you, Emilia Edvardovna. No-one else drives in an open carriage in St Petersburg these days.'

'I'm English, and we're all mad, didn't you know? Where are you going? Let me drop you somewhere.'

He hesitated a moment, and then said, 'Oh, all right. Very kind of you. But I don't want to go home yet. Take me to your house and give me tea.'

He threw his bag up and climbed in after it. He settled himself on the seat opposite her and carefully stretched out his bad leg.

'Is it troubling you?' she asked with quick sympathy, but his lined face gave away nothing.

'Not at all,' he said. He would never admit to pain. 'It's just that I've been sitting too long. That's why I was walking from the station instead of taking a cab.'

'Yes, but why were you walking in the full sunlight?' Emily pressed him. 'Seva says that in England they drive on the left, in France they drive on the right, and in Russia they drive – and walk – in the shade.' She studied his face a moment. 'You were angry about something, and taking it out on yourself.'

He laughed uneasily. 'You begin to know me too well, sister-in-law! Yes, all right, I was trying to walk it out of my system. I'm just this minute back from Moscow, which is enough to make a man mad. Moscow is the true heart of Russia; this place is a sham, a hollow sham.'

'Oh dear, didn't things go well? You've been to see your mother, haven't you? I hope she's well.'

'Of course she's well. Mama was never ill in her life, except when she gave birth to me,' he said darkly. 'And this year she has been

218

having the time of her life, with the tercentenary celebrations and the Tsar himself arriving in Moscow. She made me go out on the street with her that day to watch him go past. What a sight! The peasants were flinging themselves down as he passed just to kiss his shadow!'

He said it in tones of violent disgust, but Emily's enquiring mind had already pictured and rejected the scene.

'I don't see how that can be true,' she said. 'In June, in the middle of the day, the shadows would be at their shortest. Allowing for the width of the road and the soldiers guarding the route, his shadow couldn't possibly have reached as far as the crowd.'

Adishka glared for a moment, then dissolved into laughter. 'Oh Emilia, how you do spoil a good story! Well, all right then, but there was an hysteria of adulation at any rate, which was sickening to see. He's not a god you know.'

'He is to them,' she said. 'I don't see that it does any harm. Poor people like to have a symbol to look up to; and a procession brings a little colour and excitement into their lives.'

'It's no fun arguing with you. You're altogether too reasonable. Tell me how you are instead. Are you settling in nicely in Natasha Petrovna's house?'

'Very nicely. She's been so kind. She's virtually given it to us, you know. She even moved all the furniture out and put it into store, except for the pieces we said we'd like to stay, so that we can furnish it as we like. Actually,' she admitted, 'I wouldn't have minded keeping her furniture, but of course Basil wanted us to have our own things, and his taste and Grandmama's don't run exactly together.'

'It does sound funny to hear you call him Basil. It makes him sound like an English gentleman.'

She grinned. 'Tell him so. It's what he most aspires to be. He's ordered all our bedroom furniture from Maples.'

'Like brother, like sister,' Adishka commented not quite charitably. 'And how are you getting on with Anna these days?'

'Very well,' Emily said. She caught Adishka's eye, and laughed. 'No, really, I mean it. She couldn't be more polite and friendly. Indeed, she invites me far more often than I can accept – '

'Particularly when she has her little *séances*, eh? Oh, don't worry, I'm not one to stir up trouble. Besides, I imagine she must know by now how you feel about that sort of thing.'

'It's the way I was brought up,' Emily said carefully, because in spite of his words she was quite sure her brother-in-law *was* one to

219

stir up trouble. 'The Church of England abhors any kind of meddling with spiritualism. It's absolutely forbidden.'

'But you're Russian now, Princess Narishkina. And when in Russia – '

'Drive in the shade,' she finished for him quickly, wanting the subject changed.

Adishka looked at her slyly. 'And my revered brother? Have you been seeing much of him?'

'Not lately, but then we haven't been round to dinner for a couple of weeks,' she said. 'Of course I never see him when I go there during the day. But now that you're back,' she turned it on him, 'we must have you all over for dinner. We haven't had a proper dinner party yet, because the table we ordered has only just been delivered. You will come, won't you, Adishka? It'll be a feather in my cap as a hostess if I can get you up to my table and keep you there.'

He burst out laughing. 'She-devil! I'll show you! I'll come to dinner and behave more like a perfect English gentleman even than Vasska!'

'I'll hold you to that. Ah, here we are at home! I'm beginning to think of it as home now, especially since I've started doing things to the garden. You must let me show you my pleached walk – or what will be a pleached walk one day. It's more a row of sticks at the moment, but one must have vision.'

The tea table was set up just inside the open French windows of the drawing-room, which gave onto a small balcony overlooking the garden. There was thin bread and butter to go with the tea, strawberry tarts, and a chafing-dish of which Adishka lifted the lid as he sat down.

'English muffins!' he gloated.

'It took some doing to get the cook to make them. He seemed to take it as a grave insult when I gave him a recipe.'

'I should think so. How did you persuade him?'

'Told him I'd buy them from Filippov's, and tell everyone I'd done so. He produced a perfect batch the same day. Have some tea.'

Emily now handled the samovar like an expert. She would have preferred her tea in a cup from a pot, but when she had company she always did it the Russian way. She filled Adishka's glass and handed it to him, then watched with private amusement as he sprinkled sugar on his bread and butter and spooned jam into his tea.

'So tell me,' she said when he had sipped a little, 'what you really

220

went to Moscow for, and what really made you angry enough to walk from the station.'

'You don't think the tercentenary is enough?' Adishka asked through a mouthful. 'Three hundred years of Romanovs! Three hundred years of oppression and tyranny!'

'Don't rant, Adishka! Look at yourself – you're hardly oppressed and tyrannised, are you?'

Adishka licked butter off his fingers. 'But what power do I have? What power have any of us got?'

'What power do you want?' Emily asked, refilling the pot.

'Political power, of course! I'm surprised you should ask that. Vasska told me you were a Suffragette. Didn't you want the vote?'

'As a means to an end, that's all. In England, women are still prevented from doing most things – working, owning property, living alone, being properly educated – if not by law, then because of attitudes. If we had the vote, we'd be better able to demand other freedoms. But you – ' She waved a hand over him. 'You seem to me to have all the freedom you need.'

Adishka rolled up his eyes. 'God save us from women's logic!'

'Well, what can't you do that you want to do? You can have any job you like, go where you want, do what you want – '

'That's all you know! We – people like me – have wealth but no voice. The Duma has a voice, but no responsibility. Ministers have responsibility but no power. Everything is vested in the person of the Tsar, Nicholas the autocrat, who answers to no-one.'

'That's very good,' Emily said admiringly. 'I didn't know you were such a speech-maker.'

'Oh – well – it wasn't me, actually. It was Kerensky said that.'

'Ah, lawyer Kerensky, as Basil calls him. We seem to be hearing a lot about him these days. He always seems to be haranguing the Duma about something or other. Is he the coming man?'

'He's wonderful. You should meet him, Emilia! When he speaks, there's real power and passion in every line of his body! He isn't one of your clockwork, contrived orators – he speaks from the heart. He's the real reason I went to Moscow. He was to speak at the All-Russia Conference of the shop assistants' union there; but when it came to it, he was elected chairman of the whole conference. It was a tremendous step forward, because it meant he was an accredited leader of a working-class organisation at last.'

'Why does that matter? What has he to do with the working classes?'

'Because that's where true power lies – with the peasants and the factory workers!'

Emily took back his glass and refilled it. 'Isn't it strange how there is always a "true" version of everything which has exactly the opposite qualities to what everyone always thought; like poverty being "true" wealth and imprisonment being "true" freedom? Only moments ago you were telling me that the Tsar had all the power; now you tell me that the working classes have the "true" power. I wonder what sort it is the poor Tsar has been left with?'

'*Poor* Tsar? There's nothing poor about him! Do you know what he did? As soon as he realised the conference was attracting attention, he ordered it to be closed down. There's no free speech in this country, I can tell you! They all hate Kerensky – all the people in power – because he speaks out about Government corruption, and tries to improve the lot of the workers!'

'Are these the workers with the true power, or some other ones you haven't told me about?'

'Oh, there's no point in talking to you,' Adishka said in exasperation. 'You should have more sympathy, after your experiences in England. You know what it's like to have your aspirations mocked.'

'Yes,' she said, looking contrite. She remembered Uncle Westie and her father laughing at the idea of women having the vote. 'I'm not mocking you really. What is it that you hope to set up, in place of the present system?'

He looked at her suspiciously, but couldn't resist the opportunity. 'A proper parliamentary democracy, like the English one, with the Tsar at the head, but answerable to Parliament, like your king.'

'You don't want to topple the Tsar and establish a republic, then?'

'Lord, no! That's the Bolsheviks – they're all mad. Not that they don't have some good ideas – getting the working classes on their side, for instance. But they keep dividing the party with their extreme ideas, and Sasha says we'll never get anywhere unless we unite behind the single idea of democracy.'

'Sasha?'

'Kerensky,' Adishka said. 'He and I are quite friendly, you know.' Emily smiled into her tea-glass, and Adishka said, 'Why don't you come along to a meeting one day and see? I think you'd find it interesting, I mean, you are quite interested in politics and so on, aren't you?'

'Yes, I suppose so. But wouldn't they mind a woman being there?'

'Good lord, no! This isn't England, you know. We don't have any artificial barriers between the sexes.'

Emily curbed the urge to ask what sort of barriers they did have. The desire to play with words was always strong in her when faced with people taking themselves too seriously, but she knew it was a reprehensible trait. 'Perhaps I will then, one day. What else do you want, besides a constitutional monarchy?'

'All the things that go with true democracy – I mean, with democracy,' he corrected himself hastily. 'We want freedom of speech and association, no arbitrary arrests, no secret police, fair trials, no more government corruption and an end to unfair privileges.'

'That all seems very reasonable,' Emily nodded. 'The difficulty will come, I suppose, in persuading the people who have the privileges to give them up. It won't seem reasonable to them.'

'If they won't see reason, we'll have to make them,' Adishka said firmly.

'Yes,' said Emily doubtfully. 'But then it ceases to be reason, doesn't it?'

The long-promised call on the Grand Duchesses took place at last, and was followed by a visit by them to Natasha Petrovna's house in Tsarskoye Selo for tea. Emily enjoyed both occasions, though they also made her sad. The princesses were growing up – Tatiana was sixteen, and Olga would be eighteen in November – but their lives were hardly any less restricted than when they were children, and Emily felt she had left them far behind in the four years since they had first met.

They listened round-eyed to everything Emily could tell them about life outside their walls, and plied her with questions about the most ordinary things, which were extraordinary to them.

'You are so lucky!' was their perpetual sigh; but in spite of the dullness and monotony of their lives, they remained cheerful, modest, optimistic girls, simple in their affections and their ambitions. Their greatest hope was that they might be allowed to go to one or two balls in Petersburg next winter; their worst fear that fair, blue-eyed, painfully shy Olga might be made to marry the Prince of Wales.

'I know Grandmama would like it of anything,' Olga sighed. 'Mama would too – she'd love me to be Queen of England, because she grew up there, and was happy.'

'Wouldn't you like to be Queen of England?' Emily asked.

'I'd sooner stay home with Mama and Papa,' said Olga. 'I don't mind if I never marry.'

'We dread the idea of being split up,' Tatiana explained. 'There's always been just us, you see, and we can't imagine not being together. I suppose we'll have to part eventually, but we don't want it to be yet.'

The great affection between the five children was perhaps not surprising, given their isolation from the rest of the world. It was the one thing Emily envied them. She would not have changed places with the princesses for any consideration, but she often wished she had siblings to love and be loved by in that way – someone really close, to talk with, who knew everything about one.

'But you have Basil now,' Olga pointed out when Emily mentioned something of this.

'Yes, of course,' Emily said.

When the Grand Duchesses had gone and the tea things had been cleared, Natasha took Emily for a walk in her garden to refresh themselves. Admiring her grandmother's bowered walk, Emily remembered Adishka's visit, and told her about it.

'Politics!' Natasha sighed. 'Of course, it's just boredom. These young people with no proper occupation always have to have something to fix on. Adishka should have been a lawyer or a surgeon, but his illness prevented that, of course – and his father dying when he did. Still, Alyosha could have done more for him, I think. Even at fourteen it wouldn't have been too late for Adishka to have studied for university. He was always a bright boy.'

'You don't mean Cousin Alexei prevented him from going to university?' Emily asked. The notion was very disturbing, though she couldn't have told why.

'No, not that. But he was always too soft with Adishka, because of his leg. Indulged him too much, didn't drive him, shake him out of his indolence. I suppose he felt guilty, though really what happened wasn't his fault in any way.'

'No,' Emily agreed, 'but one can feel guilty about things that aren't one's fault. I felt guilty for a long time that my cousins were dead and I was alive.'

Natasha reached out quickly and pressed her arm. 'My poor little one! You must miss them, I know. But you're happy, aren't you?

Now you're here in Russia, with a family who love you, and a husband of your own?'

'Oh yes, very happy! But that's part of the guilt, of course. And I expect it was the same with Cousin Alexei.'

'Perhaps. At all events, it's left Adishka as just another rich and idle young man to join in with the latest craze for passing the time. Ten years ago it was sex, and a very unpleasant time that was, with dreadful books full of perversions and titillation being circulated, and a lot of loose talk about free love – as though love were ever free! Then it was modernism: cubism and discordant music and poems that made no sense. Next, of course, we had the craze for spiritualism and table-turning and mysticism – and very glad I am that your aunt's been taken away from those influences, before they addled what little brain she has. And now it's all nihilism, talking about the world coming to an end and nothing mattering any more, which seems to be nothing more than an excuse for excesses of pleasure: orgies and drunkenness and opium and suicide.'

'Is suicide a pleasure?'

'Oh yes, to those twisted minds. Exciting, dangerous, mystical. Sexual, too, in a horrid way. Well, I suppose at least politics may keep Adishka from worse things, though if he meddles with any of those revolutionary parties, it will be just another form of suicide. It's a great pity he never married. That might have kept him occupied. His mother ought to have found him someone; that's what mothers are for.'

'He doesn't speak about her with great respect,' Emily said. 'Probably he would have refused to be matched.'

Natasha shook her head. 'You have it wrong: he adores her. That's why he's always dashing off to Moscow. He's only afraid she doesn't love him.'

'She must have some influence over him,' Emily smiled. 'She managed to make him watch the Tsar's procession into the Kremlin.' A thought struck her mind, and she turned to her grandmother as they reached the end of the walk.

'There's something I've been meaning to ask you, Grandmama, for some time, but I keep forgetting. Adishka said that the Tsarevitch should have walked behind his father in the procession, but that he had to be carried instead. Is he really so sickly? I must say that the few times I've seen him – though it was only at a distance – he's looked quite rosy and strong.'

225

'He had a very bad illness last year at Spala – their Polish estate – and he hasn't fully recovered yet,' Natasha said cautiously.

'But the Grand Duchesses talked about him a lot, and they never mentioned any illness. What can it be, that makes him not able to walk?'

Natasha looked at Emily thoughtfully for a moment, then sat down on a stone bench and patted the seat beside her. 'Come, you'd better sit down. I'll tell you about it, but you must promise never to breathe a word to a soul.'

'Why? Is it a secret? I don't quite see how it can be, if everyone knows he's sickly.'

'You must promise,' Natasha insisted, 'or I can't tell you.'

'Very well, I promise.'

'You won't tell anyone? And by that I mean not anyone at all, not even Basil.'

Emily nodded, mystified. 'I promise.'

Natasha assembled her thoughts and began. 'The Tsarevitch looks healthy enough because in the general way he is. In fact, I don't think he's ever ailed a thing in the normal sense. But he was born with an hereditary affliction called haemophilia.'

Emily frowned. 'I've heard the word, but I don't really know what it means.'

'It means that his blood doesn't clot properly. If he cuts himself, even slightly, his blood goes on flowing. It might flow for hours, even days.'

'How dreadful! The poor little boy!'

'That's not the worst of it. A cut isn't so serious. As long as it's bandaged tightly, the bleeding will stop eventually. But if he falls, or bumps himself, or gets a blow, he may start bleeding inside, and there's no way to bandage that. The blood just goes on seeping invisibly. First there's a bruise, then a swelling, which gets larger and larger until the internal pressure finally stops the bleeding. The blood is gradually absorbed and the swelling goes down, but all the time the sufferer is in agony.'

'Oh God, how awful!'

'Worst of all is when a limb is involved. The blood flows into the joint cavity, and the pain is agonising; then the blood attacks the joint and starts to eat it away.'

'Don't. No more,' Emily said, feeling sick. 'What a hideous thing! And he's suffered like that from birth?'

Natasha nodded grimly. 'You see now why the Empress is so

withdrawn and never smiles. I think it's the uncertainty that's probably the worst: a bad fall might mean nothing, or the lightest bump might start the bleeding. Sometimes it doesn't begin at once. That's what happened at Spala, I believe. He'd had a fall earlier and escaped with a small bruise; but then a drive over a bumpy road started the bleeding in earnest. He lay for a week in the most appalling agony. The doctors could do nothing. They thought he was going to die. He recovered, but it's left his leg twisted and shortened.'

'But – but why is it kept a secret? Surely to have to pretend nothing is happening, when all the time – '

'He is the heir to the throne, the only son. They believe it would harm the dynasty if it were known. And, although he's unlikely to live to a great age, he may perhaps survive long enough to beget an heir.'

'And pass on the disease? Didn't you say it was hereditary?'

'It only passes through the female. The Tsarevitch got it from his mother. Females never suffer from it, but they carry it and pass it to their sons.' She met Emily's eyes. 'You see the irony?'

'Yes. I see. At last after four daughters – and then this. What a terrible burden for the Empress to bear, knowing that it was she – '

'Quite. And there's nothing she can do about it. No human agency can help, and prayer hasn't answered. It isn't surprising that she turns to mysticism, especially since she's a woman of weak intellect.'

Emily stared, thinking hard. 'You mean – is this something to do with Rasputin?' She remembered something Aunt Yenya had said. 'They say he's a healer.'

'Yes. Well, unfortunately it seems that when the Tsarevitch is suffering, the only person who can help is Rasputin. He seems to be able to stop the bleeding, and the pain. At Spala, when they thought the boy was dying, the Empress telegraphed him. Rasputin telegraphed back: "God has heard your prayers. The little one will not die". And from that moment the boy started to recover.'

Emily was silent. It was against all her English Protestant common sense to believe in something like that; but this was not England. There is magic left in the world, her Russian blood whispered to her. The mind does not believe, but the heart *knows*.

Natasha shook her head. 'I don't understand it, but it seems to be undeniable. He does have the power of healing. And it's no surprise, therefore, that the Empress has gone from gratitude to reliance, and from admiration to worship. To her Rasputin is God in human guise, and of course he never reveals to her the side that's seen outside the palace. He behaves with absolute propriety and respect when he's with the imperial family.'

'What a dreadful situation,' Emily said.

'It is very, very unfortunate. Since the people at large know nothing of the Tsarevitch's affliction, and see only the worst side of Rasputin, they conclude that he's the Devil, and that the Empress has some vile purpose in keeping him near her. Neither side understands the other. Look – look at this.' She reached into her pocket and brought out a coin, which she handed to Emily.

'It's the commemorative rouble that was struck for the tercentenary,' Emily said.

'With Nicholas in the foreground, and behind him, in profile, the likeness of Michael Romanov, the founder of the dynasty. A shadowy, bearded figure looming behind the throne. You can see why the peasantry think it's Rasputin.'

Emily stared at it thoughtfully. 'Can't anyone tell her what the people believe? Make her understand, so that she can make him behave better?'

Natasha sighed. 'The Empress is obsessed with her son's illness, with religion, with mysticism, and with the Tsar – all mixed up together in an emotional pot-pourri, one sniff of which would keep a more level-headed woman perpetually drunk. You can't reason with her.'

'The Tsar, then?'

'He's just as impossible, in a different way. He believes in his autocracy, which must be maintained at any cost, and the immutability of fate, which means he can't alter anything and therefore needn't try. I wouldn't even consider trying to enlighten them.'

'Perhaps if the Tsarevitch's illness were more widely known – '

'You gave your promise,' Natasha said sharply. 'You tell no-one.'

'But I can't see why they want to keep it secret.'

Natasha was not without fatalism herself. 'It's their secret to keep, if that's what they want. It's not for us to choose.'

Basil was home when Emily arrived back at the Kronversky Prospekt.

'Did you have a nice time? Did you see the Grand Duchesses?'

'Yes. They had tea and stayed quite a long time. I wish you had come too, Basil. They asked after you most particularly. They were very disappointed you weren't there.'

228

He laughed. 'It would have caused dreadful problems of protocol if I had been. You can't imagine the sort of chaperonage it would have involved.'

'But you're a married man,' Emily said in surprise.

'Am I such an old and unattractive one?'

'Not at all,' Emily smiled, and slipped her arms round his waist. 'Quite the reverse. Every time I see you I'm amazed at my good fortune.'

'There you are, then,' Basil said, reaching round to detach her hands and give them back to her. He stepped away from her. 'What are we doing tonight? Is it the opera?'

Emily tried not to feel rejected. She found it difficult to get used to the notion that love could be turned on and off. 'The ballet, at the Maryinsky. *Scheherazade*, don't you remember?'

'Oh yes, good! I like that one. And it means you can dress up in oriental style. You always look so good in those rich colours,' Basil said with enthusiasm. 'What will you wear? Your gold and green gown with the tassels?'

'Yes, if you like,' Emily said, half piqued, half amused that he could be so interested in dressing her up when he was not interested in her person.

'And you must wear the Narishkin emeralds – perfect! And yes, I have it: the Roman tiara, because it's shaped like a *kokoshnik*. You'll look like an oriental priestess! Where do we dine afterwards?'

'Cubat's, I imagine. We usually do, don't we? Haven't you booked the table?'

'No matter, they'll keep a table for us,' he said airily. 'When they see you, they'll probably offer us the whole restaurant!'

'Oh Basil, you are absurd!' she gave in at last, and laughed.

'Absurd? Because I'm proud of my beautiful, exotic wife?'

'Are you proud of me, Basil?' she asked shyly.

'You know I am,' he said briskly. 'Now, let's go up and look at your gown. I have an idea about your hair, but I'm not sure if that maid of yours will be able to do it. You ought to have a proper lady's maid with experience, not a skinny little housemaid promoted before her time.'

'Perhaps I ought to have a dresser from the Imperial Theatre.' Emily laughed, following him to the door.

'That's not a bad idea, you know,' Basil said seriously.

*

Emily loved the ballet. She loved the other world created for her there on the stage, within the blue and gold proscenium: brilliantly lit, vividly coloured, full of movement and passion and drama. For that little time she could enter another reality, live someone else's life, escape the confines of personality. It happened for her also when she read books, but with the ballet there was the added dimension of the music and the dance – which, after all, were in her blood.

When the lights went up and the applause began, she sank into herself again with a sigh that was part satisfaction and part disappointment it was all over. But there was Basil beside her, looking exquisite in the black and white of evening dress, with the splash of colour at his throat of one of his hereditary orders, his hair like yellow silk, and his profile like a Greek marble. Between applauding the dancers coming out through the folds of the curtain, he was glancing round at Emily and bestowing on her the benison of his smile.

Afterwards they went to Cubat's, where Basil stage-managed her entrance, making her pause in the doorway long enough for everyone to look round and see her dressed *à l'Orient*, crowned with the *kokoshnik*-shaped tiara, her high-cheekboned face emphasised by the collar of gold around her throat, the fabulous Narishkin emeralds glowing like dragon-fire against her pale skin.

'Perfect, perfect,' Basil breathed. 'You're a triumph, my darling!' She felt the breath of a kiss against the back of her neck, but before she could turn to him he gave her a little shove forward, and they went to join one of the groups of acquaintances who were waving to them from the tables.

The food was delicious, the champagne flowed, the talk was lively and punctuated by laughter. It was pleasant to be with these good-looking young people who, if they had nothing very important to say, at least said it with style and enthusiasm. It was pleasant to see how Basil was liked and admired, and how the other females in the group looked at her with respect as the woman who had captured him. It was pleasant, when she ventured on a small joke, to have it appreciated; to be asked how something-or-other was done in England, and have her answer listened to attentively.

It was pleasant, above all, to have Basil smile at her, admire her publicly, show her off to his friends; even, once, lean across the table to pick up her hand and kiss it in a sort of homage that was only half pretence. All these things were delightful, and Emily had every reason to be happy. If she felt again that strange sensation of

230

being separated from what was going on by a thin sheet of glass, it must, she reasoned, be because of the champagne. The happy group around the candlelit table in this fashionable restaurant at the heart of the most exciting city in the world was real life; it was wrong that it should seem to her like an unconvincing scene in a play acted out amid flat stage scenery.

Basil had gone from champagne to brandy, and seemed to be very happy indeed, his cheeks flushed becomingly, his blue eyes as bright as polished glass, his smile making the females in the group flutter and compete for his attention. Varvara Sabinina was emitting so many sparks in his direction, she was in danger of setting light to her hair.

Perhaps, Emily thought on the tail of this caustic observation, the problem was that she hadn't had *enough* champagne. She turned to her neighbour – Sasha Suslov, Dima's younger brother, who was on the verge of being too young to be in their company – and asked him to refill her glass. He was evidently delighted to be asked by her, and complied with such enthusiasm that the eager *mousse* overflowed onto her hand.

'I've always wondered what it would be like to bathe in champagne,' she said, mostly so that he would not feel embarrassed by his clumsiness. Sasha laughed adoringly, as though she were the wittiest creature in Petersburg. Hanging on my lips, she thought, and almost literally, since in the babble of conversation he had to lean towards her and watch them in order to catch her words.

She smiled her thanks, drank deeply, allowed the eager Sasha to fill her glass again, and drank some more. Ah yes, that was better. She felt the watchful, separate part of her which kept her behind the glass screen drift off to sleep. It was as though an eye somewhere in the back of her mind had closed, and she was now free to be as frivolous as the rest of them. Obviously the answer was more champagne, not less – she must remember that in future.

Eventually the party broke up and they were whisked to the Kronverksy Prospekt in Basil's motor car – he hadn't Emily's devotion to the other sort of horsepower. Basil seemed very pleased with himself. He leaned back against the fragrant leather and sang a little song in his small, tuneful tenor – a foolish song that was popular at the moment, about a crocodile walking along the Nevsky Prospekt. Emily felt a warm affection for him surging about her blood with the bubbles of the champagne. Home and to bed with her lover, she thought gladly; how *convenient* marriage could be sometimes!

'What a lovely evening,' she said. 'The ballet was magnificent, and your friends are so pleasant.'

'Our friends, darling,' Basil said. 'Did you see how they all stared at you? You looked every inch a princess tonight. I was so proud of you.'

'Thank you,' Emily said, slipping her hand into his and turning her face to him so that he could kiss her, if he liked. He lifted her hand and kissed that instead, then put it back in her lap.

'We must have Bakst to dinner,' he said. 'We might persuade him to design some really spectacular clothes for you.'

When they walked into the house, Basil said, 'I'm going to have a last brandy and smoke a cigar. You go on up, darling. I'll be up in a little while.'

Emily obeyed. The pleasant golden haze had thinned a little, but was not completely dissipated. She felt happy, confident and unafraid, tingling a little from the evening's pleasures and the anticipation of pleasure to come. Tanya, her maid, was waiting, eyes almost glued together with tiredness, and Emily only let her help remove her jewellery and put it away before dismissing her to her bed.

When Basil finally came upstairs, Emily was in her nightdress, her hair loose down her back, sitting at the dressing-table and smiling at her reflection.

'Who would have thought it?' she said as Basil came in.

'Thought what?'

She swivelled round on the stool to face him, and held out her hands. 'Thought that we'd be married. That I'd be your wife. When you think back to when we first met.'

Basil had come near, but ignored the invitation of her hands. He cocked his head at her. 'I think my wife must be a little drunk.'

'Oh, not drunk – at least not with wine! I'm happy, dearest Basil! I'm so glad you married me!' She jumped up and went to put her arms round him.

'Well, so am I, of course,' he said warily. He held her briefly. 'I think it's worked out very well.'

She felt that he was about to let her go, so she held him more tightly and put her face up to be kissed. He put his lips on hers, and at their touch passion bloomed in her, and she kissed him with all her love and desire, pressing her body against him avidly.

But after a moment he withdrew his mouth, and then put her gently but quite firmly away. She remembered his strictures about

232

time and place and backed towards the bed, catching his hand smilingly to draw him with her. He pulled himself free, frowning.

'What is it?' she asked in consternation. 'What's the matter?'

'Nothing, nothing at all,' he said lightly. 'You must be tired, darling. I'll leave you now to get to sleep.'

'I'm not in the least tired,' she said. The golden mist was dispersing fast. 'Don't go away, Basil. Come to bed.'

'No, I'll sleep in my own room, if you don't mind.'

Everything in her cringed from the confrontation, but she had reached a point of desperation. Her body ached with restlessness, with physical desire; she was hollow with longing to be held and touched and possessed.

'Please don't. I mean yes, I do mind. I want you to sleep with me,' she said, feeling herself tremble at the directness of the words. 'Please come to bed. I want you to – to make love to me.'

The faintest expression of distaste came over his handsome features, and for Emily it was like being struck, not hard, but shockingly. 'My dear, you really mustn't say things like that,' he said.

She stood her ground, though the air seemed to be full of the sound of shattering glass. 'But you're my husband,' she stammered. 'Why can't I say what I feel for you?'

He hesitated, looking at her with opaque eyes. She thought he wasn't going to answer, that he would simply leave her without speaking, and she lifted her hands slightly and said, 'Please, Basil – '

His mouth turned down. '*That's* what I mean. I'm sorry, Emilia, but it's quite horrible to hear a woman of your rank *asking* for physical relations. It simply isn't nice. It makes you sound like – well, I'm sorry – but like a whore!'

Emily looked at him with stricken eyes. 'What are you talking about?'

He seemed to take courage from her distress. 'I don't like to have to speak to you in this way, but you force me to. God knows, I've given you enough hints. I hoped you would model your behaviour on mine. But I can't seem to get through to you that it's very off-putting for a man to have his wife thrust herself on him like this. It's not what one expects from a decent female. The sort of – *unrestrained exhibition* that you treat me to when we're alone together is quite out of place between us. It belongs in a brothel, not a marriage bed.'

Emily stared at him, distress and shock and anger churning her

233

brains so that she wanted to scream. Let me go mad, she whispered inside herself. Or let me die.

'God,' she said faintly, between clenched teeth. 'God.'

Basil lifted his head, looking at her from under his eyelids in that way she now knew from other occasions. It was his way of detaching himself from unpleasantness. 'I couldn't expect you to know about these things before you were married, but I'm telling you now. A man likes to make up his own mind about when and how relations take place with his own wife. Just take your cue from me in future, and we'll get on very well. I'm sure we won't have to talk about this again.'

He turned away and went to the door. It was almost over, she told her trembling body. Only a few seconds more to endure.

At the door he turned and said kindly, 'I think you should try to keep your mind off – well, that sort of thing. Women can become unbalanced if they dwell on it, you know. Perhaps you should take up a hobby of some sort – something ladylike. Needlework, or something. Give your mind a more wholesome direction.'

Chapter Fourteen

Humiliation and helplessness together make a formidable wad to swallow. Left alone with rage and pain, Emily wanted to weep and howl, to slash and tear, to bring the house down in ruins about her, to curl up very, very small and quietly die. Of course, she did none of those things. She went to bed, pulled up the covers, and grieved in silence.

To offer love and be rejected was hard enough; but to have the love condemned as unwholesome, to be regarded as somehow mentally unbalanced for feeling it in the first place, was wounding. How could she live, knowing that's what he thought of her? How could she ever again express a feeling for him, smile spontaneously at him? How could she face him in the morning when he thought her a whore?

She would have liked to weep, but the shock was too deep for tears. She drew her knees up against her as a child in pain does, thought she would never be able to sleep, and slept quite soon and dreamlessly.

In the morning, with the sunlight slanting into the room, and the birds making their cheerful morning racket in the garden below her window, things seemed one degree less desperate. She still had a clawed feeling inside from the anguish of last night, but the situation did not seem hopeless. Basil after all *was* her husband, and nothing could change that. They must find a way to be reconciled, since they must live together for the rest of their lives.

Hurt pride had no place in her thinking in the new light of morning. She longed to be taken back into favour. The need to love and be loved was strong in her, and if she must change herself, modify her behaviour, so be it. After all, he was older than she, more experienced, and a man. If he said that was the way of things, she must accept it. Her knowledge of life came only from literature: Basil must know better.

So she went downstairs chastened, wistful, hopeful. The first meeting, she thought, was bound to be embarrassing, both of them being conscious of the enormity of what had passed between them last

235

night. But embarrassment did not kill; it had only to be endured for a while, until it faded. She had chosen her prettiest day dress, a lavender-blue crêpe with a huge artificial rose on the bosom, and wore in her hair the Fabergé enamel butterfly clips he had given her for her birthday. She thought she looked the model of propriety, and would make sure she behaved that way.

They were supposed to be going to a military review that morning, and then joining a late luncheon party at the Kovanin Palace on the English Quay, but she was prepared to find the arrangement cancelled. Some unpleasantness, she reasoned, would have to be lived through; but he must surely take her back into favour eventually.

He was in the morning-room reading the newspaper. He looked up as she came in and smiled. 'Ah, there you are! You look very pretty. Yes, I like those clips with that dress. But you should have more pearls. Don't be afraid to put on several strings: you can never wear too many pearls.'

Emily felt as though she had gone up a stair that wasn't there. She surveyed his face carefully, but it revealed nothing but normal good humour and natural spirits. She had prepared herself carefully to face any sort of aftermath of their confrontation last night – anything, but that there should be none. No embarrassment, no recriminations, no coolness, no stern sorrow. In the face of these absences, she stood silent, at a loss to know how to respond.

'What's the matter, Emilusha?' he asked at last with mild concern. 'You look rather odd. Aren't you feeling well?'

'No, it's all right,' she said. 'I'm perfectly well. I was just wondering what pearls to put on.'

'Mother's three-strand collar, and two long strings,' he answered, examining her judiciously. 'And the bracelets with the amber clasps, I think.'

He didn't know. He wasn't pretending composure in the face of deep embarrassment: he simply wasn't embarrassed. The knowledge, with the concomitant realisation of all it implied, sank in only slowly. As she sat to breakfast, listening to his small talk and answering automatically, she felt it trickling through her thoughts and feelings like cold, black liquid.

To him last night had not been a confrontation, a scalding emotional experience, as it had been to her. What, then? She saw that it had not disturbed him, and that he had not expected it to. For him it had obviously been no more personally wounding then rebuking a servant.

And how could that be? How could he so little know how much he had hurt her? The watchful part of her mind stepped away from the tangle of pain and shock and looked coolly at the man she had loved and married. Fanny's words came back to her: *Basil loves only Basil.* She had been warned long before there was any prospect of its mattering to her. But what woman in love ever listens to warnings?

All that day, at the review, at luncheon, in the car coming home, in her bath, resting on her bed before dressing, she thought it out as objectively as she could. Fanny had been only partly right, she decided; love was too strong a word for what Basil felt about anything. He was interested only in himself, but even that fascinating subject could not arouse anything as demanding as passion in him. He did not know how much he had wounded Emily, because he did not know such feelings could exist.

The mistake had been hers, the wilful self-delusion. He had not changed: he was what he had always been, and she ought to have had the intelligence to see it. She had not seen it, because she hadn't wanted to. The desire to love, to be loved, to *belong*, had overpowered her natural sense, and she had made him into the creature of her fancy, not Basil at all.

The adjustment in understanding that had taken place as yet affected only the intellect. Her feelings would take much longer to come to terms with it, and as she lay staring at the ceiling above her bed, her throat was tight and her chest aching with unhappiness. He was her prince, her love, her dream – her husband. She had loved him for four years, and it would take time, time and suffering, to stop.

The trouble with disillusionment, her watchful mind observed, was that by its very nature it always came too late.

They dined that evening amongst a large group of friends at the Sapetskys. Adishka arrived late in company with Borya Duvitsky, Leone's brother, a rather strange-looking young man with bulging eyes and a head that seemed too big for his body. They were seated at the opposite end of the table from Emily during dinner, but when everyone migrated to the saloon afterwards, Adishka brought Borya over to meet her.

To get near her he was forced almost to climb over Sasha Suslov, who since that precious moment in Cubat's restaurant had decided that he was in love with Emily, and was hovering over her so attentively he was almost sitting in her lap. Basil was at the other end of the room, being heaved at by Varvara Sabinina's bosom; Adishka came as a welcome relief to Sasha's silent worship.

'Emilia, you must meet Boris Efimovitch – Leone's brother. He's a leading light of our little organisation. I told him you were interested in our ideas. Borya, my cousin Emilia Edvardovna Narishkina.'

'How do you do?' Emily said, holding out her hand. Borya did not smile, and only just touched her fingers, bowing his head slightly to her without taking his eyes from her face. He had an air of melancholy preoccupation, as though the social amenities were something that used up valuable mental energy urgently needed elsewhere.

'Adishka says you want to come along to our meetings, he said. His voice was deep and slow, suited to his lugubrious looks. 'The Constitutional Socialist Party always welcomes new members.'

'I thought you were the Socialist Revolutionary Party?' Sasha interrupted, looking at Adishka. 'Didn't you tell Dima – '

Adishka looked put out. 'No, no, the SRs are the party Kerensky belongs to. We're a sort of affiliated movement. Some of our aims are slightly different, but we don't have anyone in the Duma, so we get together with them from time to time.'

'I thought Kerensky's party was the Constitutional Democrats,' Emily said.

'You're confused. That's the Kadets, who have the majority in the Duma. They're very pro-Tsarist,' Borya explained kindly. 'Then there are the Popular Socialists, who are very revolutionary, and the Socialist Democrats, who are divided into the Bolsheviks and the Mensheviks. The Mensheviks tend to be conciliatory, while the Bolsheviks vote against everything and everybody. The Socialist Revolutionaries are sort of halfway between them; the Constitutional Socialists – that's us – are halfway between the SRs and the Mensheviks, and the Kadets are the most conciliatory of all.'

Emily listened to all this gravely, and then said, 'I'm sorry, I lost the thread somewhere.'

'It's quite simple,' Borya said, and with the patience of a humourless man prepared to say it all again.

'No, it's all right,' Emily said hastily, 'I'm sure I'll get the hang of it in time. But don't you think,' she offered hesitantly, 'that it

238

might be better if you all worked together, instead of having so many different parties?'

'Well, that's what Kerensky says, of course,' Adishka said eagerly; 'that we should agree on a central core of ideals.'

'That's all very well,' Borya said with some insight, 'when you're talking about other people giving up some of their ideals, but when it comes to giving up some of your own, it's a different matter.'

Adishka sighed agreement. 'I wouldn't mind working with the SRs, but there's no dealing with the Bolsheviks, and the Kadets aren't going to compromise with anyone as long as they've got the majority.'

'When it comes down to it,' Borya said seriously, 'we're right and they're wrong, and you can't compromise about that.'

'So what do you think, Emilia?' Adishka asked. 'Would you like to come along and hear what we have to say? There's a lot of good work to be done. We get up parties to visit comrades in prisons and hospitals, and raise money for deserving cases, as well as for our political activities.'

Emily looked past him at the crowd of smart young people laughing and chatting. There was quite a group around Basil now. Varvara Sabinina was smoking a cigarette in a long amber holder, blowing the smoke into his face with a fascinating smile, and Basil didn't seem to be objecting. Well, he had told her to get herself a hobby, something other than lovemaking to occupy her mind. Nothing could be further from sensuality than the concerns of these earnest young men, she thought wryly. And at least they believed in something. It was possible that there was useful work to be done, and that this might lead her to it. She had a need to be useful.

'Yes, I'd like to come,' she said. 'When will the next meeting be?'

Adishka looked pleased and plunged into an exposition of their timetable. By the time the shifting tides of conversation broke up their grouping, it was all arranged. Somehow or other, Sasha Suslov had got himself included as well, but there didn't seem to be anything one could do about that.

As soon as the SS *Princess Victoria* docked, Emily hurried on board, collared a steward, and made him show her to Lady Frances Hope's cabin. Fanny was there, sitting patiently on a hard chair with her luggage beside her, her hands folded in her lap. She was much thinner than Emily remembered — her brown coat and skirt were too big for her, though Emily could see they were well cut and of fine material – and her face was gaunt. Her eyes had a dull look, and there were brown shadows around them. Most noticeably of all, she looked older: youth seemed to have gone from her.

But when she saw Emily, a slow pleasure suffused her face, and she rose to her feet and held out her arms to embrace her old friend.

'Emily, my dear Emily, how good to see you again!'

'Oh Fanny!'

Released, Fanny pulled out her handkerchief. 'Stupid of me, but I seem to cry terribly easily now. Not over sad things, but over happy ones. Dear Emily! You're so fine I hardly recognised you. Let me look at you properly.'

Emily felt almost ashamed of her opulence against Fanny's plainness. Her long coat of Siberian sable, with the matching hat and diamond brooch, hung open to reveal her dress and jacket of dusky pink silk and the eight rows of pearls she was wearing that day. She was blooming with health, and her cheeks were bright from the frosty air outside.

'Yes,' said Fanny, with a little nod, 'you look every inch the princess. I make a sad contrast.'

'Poor Fanny, you've had such a terrible time of it. We'll feed you up and make you well again. Oh, I'm so glad to see you!'

'It was good of you to invite me.'

'No, it was good of you to come. I didn't think you would.'

'I didn't think so either,' Fanny said with a thin smile. 'But Mama insisted so hard. Not that I didn't want to see you, you understand – '

'Yes, I know. Come, I have the sleigh outside. It's a good job you didn't come a week earlier – the weather's been foul, sleet and slush and raw fog. But now you'll see Peter at its best.'

'Peter?'

'That's what the natives call St Petersburg,' Emily said.

'And you're a native now?'

'Yes, I feel like one at last. Come, are you ready?'

Emily got Fanny through the customs shed with only a little delay.

'How confident you are,' Fanny said admiringly. 'Russia has been good for you. When I remember the shy, silent little girl I first met at Lady Hamilton's – !'

'How is Lady Hamilton? Have you seen her recently?'

'I've got a letter for you from her in my bag. She's as well as can be expected, considering her age. The cold, wet autumn hasn't been good for her. Is that your sledge? Who's that standing beside it?'

'That's Seva, my driver. He used to be my grandmother's, but she gave him to me on a long loan when I got married.'

'No, not that one – the little fellow all muffled up. Or isn't he anything to do with you?'

'Oh! Yes, that's Sasha Suslov. He's a sort of – friend, I suppose. I'm so used to his being around I hardly notice him now. I'll tell you about him later.'

Fanny stopped and caught Emily's arm.

'Emily, will Basil be there, when we get to your house? I'd just like to be prepared.'

'No, he's out all day today with Youna Volkov, a friend of his. I don't suppose he'll be back until after we've gone to bed, so you won't have to meet him until tomorrow.'

'Ah. Good.'

'But I don't think you need worry, Fan. He won't say anything embarrassing. He's a very different person now.'

Fanny glanced at Emily curiously, but said no more, and walked on towards the sleigh. The muffled figure in the astrakhan hat came forward eagerly and revealed himself to be no more than a boy, and one with a violent crush on Emily. There were obviously many things to learn about her friend's new life in Russia that she had not written in her letters.

In the wonderfully warm house, furnished with its uneasy mix of the ancient and the modern, to the gentle background singing of the samovar, Fanny and Emily went cautiously about rediscovering each other. Each found many changes. Emily seemed to Fanny to have grown up, to have gained a surprising degree of confidence and command in only one year. She dressed like a princess, moved more gracefully, and spoke in a firm and unhesitant voice. She dealt with the languishing boy, too, with surprising skill, treating him kindly but checking his excesses and eventually sending him away without upsetting him. But then, Fanny remembered, she had always been good with children.

The change in Fanny that Emily detected was not just in her altered appearance. There was a stillness about her – not the restful stillness that came from inner peace, but the stillness of one who had become accustomed to restriction of movement. When she sat,

241

she sat absolutely motionless; when she moved, it was slowly and cautiously, as though sudden or voluntary movement might invoke punishment. Her voice at first was flat and uninflected, though after some hours of conversation it became more animated. And there was an air of resignation about her, a fatalism, as though she had lost the joy of self-determination.

These things were all understandable, given what she had been suffering over the past months. It was not until they had been talking for some hours that Fanny described what it was like to be forcibly fed, and Emily was glad she had been fortified by a large English tea before hearing it.

'It's a doctor who actually does the thing, but they have three or four wardresses to hold you down. They have to have them, because however much you mean not to, you can't help struggling, even though you know struggling makes it worse. But there are some things you just can't submit to . . .

'They throw you down on a bed or a bench, and the doctor pushes the rubber tube into your nostril. They're supposed to lubricate it with Vaseline, but they don't usually bother until the nasal passage becomes so inflamed it simply won't go in. Then it goes down the back of your throat. It makes you retch, you can't help it, but retching hurts. The edge of the tube catches you inside, you see.

'Then, when it's in your stomach, they fix a funnel on the other end and pour the warm fluid in. It makes you feel so sick, Emily. I just can't describe what a horrible feeling it is when that liquid hits your stomach. And then, when that's over, they pull the tube out, and you start retching . . . '

Emily found that her hand was being gripped tightly by Fanny's, so tightly it was hurting her, but she didn't complain. She put her other hand over Fanny's, and stroked it, unable to think of anything to say in the face of such a story.

'They just leave the equipment lying around, you know. They don't sterilise it. When they took me down to the sickbay one time, I saw a tube just lying there in a basin, with dregs of the liquid food and flies landing on it.'

'Oh Fanny!'

'And they take any excuse to abuse you. One of our girls stumbled a little as she was being dragged along, and they pretended she was resisting, and held her by the hair and hit her face.'

'But Fanny *why*? Why would they do such horrible things?'

'Because they hate us,' Fanny said simply. 'They hate what they do to us, because it degrades them as well. So they hate us for making them do it. It gets worse all the time. All of them – not just the doctors and the wardresses, but the politicians too – they know that what they do is vile and unjust, that they are behaving worse than beasts; and the more horrible things they do, the more they hate us for it.'

'This Cat and Mouse Act we've heard about – ?'

'It's a thing of desperation. Those of us who were hunger-striking were becoming so ill that either they had to let us go, or let us die in prison. So they passed this act to say that when we grew so ill we were likely to die, we would be released, but not pardoned. As soon as we've recovered enough, we can be rearrested to finish the sentence. And re-released, and rearrested as often as they like.'

'It's a wicked piece of legislation,' Emily said indignantly. 'I'm sure it's unconstitutional.'

'It's cruel. You never know, you see, when they'll come for you. How long you've got. It's always hanging over you, the knowledge that you've got to go back in and go through it all again.'

'But Fanny, why do you do it? Why do you go on? It isn't doing any good, only making you ill.'

Frances sighed, looking down at their linked hands. 'We've come too far to let it end.'

Emily frowned. 'Is it because of Angela? You don't still blame yourself for her death?'

Frances looked up. 'It isn't a question of blame.' She paused as if not sure she could make Emily understand. She went on slowly. 'Angela died to make a point. No, wait. Her death was part of a whole process, a whole train of actions dedicated to achieving an end, and if I don't go on doing my part, it means her death was wasted – her death, and Emily Davison's; and my sufferings, and the sufferings of all our sisters.'

'But where will it end? If they never give you the vote – '

'There comes a point when you can't stop, short of your own death, because to do so would be to waste everything that's gone before.' Her eyes slowly focused on Emily's anxious face, and she gave a ghostly smile. 'It isn't as bad as you think. Once we manage to convince *them* that we'll never stop, they'll have to give in. They don't really want to kill us, you see.'

'Oh Fanny!'

'That's what any war really consists of, you know – finding out

243

which side really is the most determined. Such a pity it can't all be done verbally, without actually having to demonstrate it.'

Later, over dinner, Frances asked, 'What about your new interest? The Social Democrats, or whatever they're called?'

'Constitutional Socialists,' Emily corrected, with an amused look. She gave Fanny a brief outline of the main parties at present claiming to be socialists of one sort or another. 'The Social Democrats are the oldest party – they're the ones who split into the Bolsheviks and Mensheviks.'

'Yes, of course, I remember. The Bolshies had their headquarters in London – a flat above a pub in Islington or somewhere, didn't they? I remember Papa fulminating about them, saying they should be rounded up and sent back to Russia where they belonged.'

'My uncle used to say it was better to let them rant rather than build up a head of steam.'

'I suppose that might be true. But tell me about your particular drawing-room revolutionaries. Are they nice? Are they clever?'

'They're terribly serious, bless them,' Emily smiled. 'I'm afraid they think I'm rather frivolous, and get upset when I make little jokes. I don't think they understand you can make a joke about something you take seriously.'

'Ah, not clever then?'

'I don't really know. They certainly use a lot of long and difficult words, and quite a few of them can speak German, which strikes me as very clever indeed.'

'But you speak Russian – that's clever.'

'Russian's easy,' Emily said. 'It flows off the tongue so nicely, it makes you believe you've known it in another life.'

'You probably have. But what do you do with your socialists? Is it all meetings?'

'Yes, with my lot it is. They do sometimes go and visit "comrades" who are in prison for political crimes and take them comfort parcels, but I don't go with them. Basil wouldn't like it. Adishka did introduce me to Kerensky, though, who's a member of the Duma and quite an important figure in the democracy movement, and when I told him I could typewrite, he asked me if I would help out at the legal advice centre. His wife used to do it, but she has too many babies now to spare the time.'

'What's the legal advice centre?'

'What it says. It does a lot of good work, giving advice to people who can't afford to pay for lawyers. I'm learning quite a lot about the law in the process – though really in Russia it could almost be whittled down to one rule: don't annoy the man immediately above you.'

'You're becoming cynical, Em! It rather suits you.'

'I sometimes think how horrified poor Aunt Maud would be if she saw the kind of people I mix with there, all as middle-class as can be! But I bless her every time I put my hands on the keys – if it weren't for her, I'd never have learned to typewrite. I always knew it would be useful one day.'

'What do your people think about it? Do they mind what you're doing?' Frances asked curiously.

'Not nearly as much as Aunt Maud would. You can do pretty much what you like in Petersburg, and there are few differences for a woman, especially amongst the socialists. They even think it's a noble thing for a woman to leave her husband and children for the good of the cause – though they're noticeably less keen when it's their own wife who wants to do it. But that's human nature for you.'

'But what about Basil? Doesn't he mind?'

'He does and he doesn't. I think he's quite glad that I have something to occupy my time, but he'd sooner I mixed with important people. None of the CSPs are important, you see. And he complains about them being ugly.' She sighed. 'There do seem to be rather more than the average of odd-looking people amongst them, poor things, but I'm sure it can't be catching. Basil seems to think mixing with them will ruin my looks. He thinks politics the most awful lot of nonsense.'

'It doesn't sound as though it's much fun. Why do you do it?'

Emily looked at her sidelong. 'That, from you?'

Fanny smiled faintly. 'Do you think they're achieving anything?'

'I don't know. Probably not. But at least it gives me the illusion of being useful.'

She said it lightly, but Fanny heard the undertone and looked at her friend sharply. There were things to be told, that was obvious; but it didn't seem that this was the right moment to probe further. There was plenty of time for more discussion, and sooner or later, she thought, Emily would tell her. Better that it should be in her own time.

*

245

The first meeting with Basil did not take place until the next morning, for he had not come home by the time they went to bed. Emily and Fanny were breakfasting together in the morning-room when Basil walked in, surprising Emily: after a late night he did not normally get up until luncheon.

He surprised Fanny by showing no self-consciousness at all. When she thought how vehemently he had pursued her, and in how much pique he had left England after her last refusal, she would have expected a little stiffness or embarrassment. But he breezed in, smiling broadly, and said, 'Well now, Fanny, here you are at last! Let me kiss you. It's quite proper in Russia, you know – and I'm an old married man now!'

He took her hands and bent over her to give her the three kisses of the Russian greeting on alternate cheeks.

'You're looking very well, Basil,' she said mildly. 'Marriage must suit you.'

He straightened up and looked at her keenly for an instant. 'Yes, it does,' he said. He turned to Emily and smiled. 'How could it not, when I'm married to the best little woman in the world? Good morning, Emilusha, my darling! You're looking radiant this morning!' And he bent to kiss her lovingly, and to lay the back of his hand a moment against her cheek in a gesture of tenderness that made her knees feel momentarily weak. 'Did you sleep well, my love?'

'Yes, thank you,' Emily said, blinking in this sudden sunshine. 'Did you have a good evening with Youna?'

'Wonderful! We dined at his mess, and then half a dozen officers from the Semyonovsky came in, so we had rather a party of it. I didn't get home until five o'clock.'

'I'm surprised you're up so early, then,' Emily said. 'You must be tired.'

Basil moved round behind her so that he could look at Fanny over her head. He put his hands on her shoulders and said, 'You see how she worries about me, Fanny? A man couldn't want a better wife.' He kissed the top of Emily's head and then sat down beside her. 'I didn't want to miss seeing our guest on her first morning. Pour me some coffee, will you, darling? I'm sorry I wasn't here to greet you yesterday, Fanny, but I expect you two girls had a lot to talk about. I would probably only have been in the way.'

'You're fishing for compliments, Basil,' Fanny said drily. 'I can tell you that you wouldn't have been in the way, but since that means we weren't discussing you, I don't know if it will please you or not.'

'You haven't lost your sharp tongue, I see,' Basil said, not at all put out. 'Well, you may not have been talking about me, but I was talking about Emilia – but then, I usually am. We toasted you half a dozen times in the mess, darling. Youna must get tired of the sound of your name sometimes!'

The look on Emily's face – a mixture of surprise and pleasure – was not lost on Fanny.

'What have you got planned for Fanny today?' Basil asked next, sipping coffee.

'I hadn't really planned anything. I thought she might prefer to stay quietly at home – ' Emily began.

Basil broke in energetically. 'Oh, but that won't do! We mustn't waste a moment of your stay, Fanny, with the whole of Petersburg dying to see you. Now, I propose to take you to see the paintings at the Tretyakov – there's a new Malevich and a new Goncharova that you simply must see, and the best cubist collection outside Paris – and then we'll go to luncheon at Anna's.'

'Basil, Fanny must be tired after her journey,' Emily said gently, 'and Anna won't be expecting us.'

'You're not tired, are you?' Basil asked Fanny, and without waiting for her to answer he said, 'There you are, you see, darling! As for Anna, I shall go and telephone her at once. Once she knows you're here, Fanny, she'll be mortified if she doesn't have you to lunch the first day, before all the other hostesses get hold of you.'

He thrust back his chair and got to his feet. 'We must give a dinner for Fanny very soon, darling. Everyone will be at the exhibition today – we can sound people out about dates.'

Left alone, the women looked at each other. 'Is he always like this?' Fanny asked with a wry smile. 'It must be exhausting.'

'No, not at all. I don't know what's come over him. I'm sorry, Fanny. If you are tired, you must say so, and I'll go after him and make him stop.'

'It's all right. I shall enjoy the stimulation. My life has been rather lacking colour lately,' Fanny said. 'And I'm sure we'll have lots of time for quiet conversation.'

'It's very odd, all the same,' Emily said, creasing her brow.

'Not at all. He wants to show you off to me, and why not? What could be more natural?'

Emily's cheeks were pink. 'I thought he wanted to show *you* off.'

'Nonsense. He doesn't care a jot about me,' Fanny said firmly. She wished she could have been sure that he cared a jot about Emily. But despite the kisses and extravagant words, she grew more convinced as the day went on that her first instinct had been right, and that the whole charade had been mounted to impress on Fanny what she had missed by turning him down.

Emily and Fanny had been window-shopping in the Nevsky Prospekt. There had been a heavy fall of snow the night before, and the traffic was fast and quiet on the new crust; but it was very cold, and the sky was yellow-grey with the threat of more snow. They were ready now for the comfort of coffee and cakes at Gerstein's.

'I love it when it really snows heavily,' Emily said. 'No more motor cars, with their noise and stink. It's like stepping back in history when there's nothing but the sleighs. Think how peaceful the world must have been before machines were invented!'

'It seems very peaceful now that Basil has dropped his frenetic programme of amusements for me,' Fanny said. 'It didn't last long, but it was exhausting while it lasted.'

'Oh poor Fanny! You should have said.'

'No, no, I enjoyed it, though I'm glad to ease the pace a little now. Petersburg is a wonderful city. I can see that a person would never want to leave once they had settled here.'

'Do you think so? I love Peter – and you haven't seen it in the summer yet, Fan, when the nights never get properly dark, and you can see the sun move around the horizon. The light is a wonderful silvery lilac, and the city is like a magic place.'

'I think you're in love,' Fanny smiled.

They entered the café and shed their outer garments, and in the steady warmth that was still a surprise to Fanny, used to English chills and draughts, they were shown to a table.

'Wouldn't you like to come and live here too?' Emily asked when they were settled. 'I wish you would! I'm sure you'd be happier than in London. Women have so much more freedom here. You can be what you like, without shocking people.'

Fanny looked at her with wry amusement, as if she had been expecting it for some time. 'I have work to do in England. You know that.'

'Oh. But if you didn't go back, it wouldn't matter that you wouldn't have the vote there, would it?'

'Of course it would! What a terrible thing to say,' Fanny said. 'I've explained it to you before, love – it's my task. I have to finish it.'

'I see.' Emily didn't press the point, only looked disappointed as she poured coffee in silence.

'Aren't you happy here, Emily?' Fanny asked after a moment.

'Oh – yes. Of course. But I thought how nice it would be to have a friend here, a proper friend I could talk to.'

'What about your sister-in-law? She seems very pleasant.'

'Anna?' She made a face. 'It's funny about her. Before we were married she was quite different, really horrible to me. Now she behaves as though she likes me.'

'You don't think it's genuine?'

'Would you? But anyway, I don't like her. I suppose I ought to try, but you can't, can you, if you just don't.'

'Well, there must be lots of other young women.'

'There are, of course, but I don't seem to get to meet the right ones. The females in Basil's circle are all so empty-headed – they flirt and gossip and chatter about clothes all the time. And the ones I meet at the socialist meetings are all so earnest and severe they won't talk about anything but politics and the cause.' She smiled ruefully at Fanny. 'At least the Suffragettes we used to meet were happy some of the time, and laughed and talked about normal things too.'

'Poor Emily! You must widen your circle. There must be lots of normal, well-educated women in your Peter that you could make friends with.'

'I suppose so. I just don't know where to find them.' She hesitated, and looking up, met her friend's waiting eyes. The moment had come, she felt, to 'tell', as Lexy and Vick used to say about deep confessions. 'I thought, before I married, that one's husband would be one's best friend. I suppose that was foolish of me?'

There was only the faintest of question marks on the end of the sentence. After all, Fanny was a spinster; but her patient eyes seemed to promise understanding.

'If that was what you hoped for,' she said gently, 'you should perhaps not have married Basil.'

Emily sighed, and let go of restraint. 'No. Of course, you know him very well – probably better than I do. When I first met him, he was so keen on the Cause, I thought he saw women as equals – as people, you know.'

249

'Basil? Never! He's your true Victorian. Women are precious, fragile, exquisite things, to be owned and displayed and admired like a piece of porcelain, but never to be taken seriously.'

'But, the Cause – ?'

'It was what he considered appropriate behaviour for courting me. If I'd been mad about hunting or tennis or music, he'd have gone along with that. He wouldn't have expected to have to mean it.' She studied Emily's averted face. 'He seems very attentive to you, from what I've seen.'

'Oh yes, in public,' Emily said. 'He's kind and courteous and makes everyone believe he loves me. But in private – ' She broke off, remembering Fanny's virgin status. 'Marriage isn't a bit like what I expected,' she went on, looking at her friend. 'I thought we'd spend all our time together, and be like – I don't know – '

'Two doves in a nest?' Fanny asked wryly.

Emily laughed, a little spurt of escaping tension. 'I suppose so,' she admitted. 'But in reality I don't see him any more often than before. We have engagements that we go to together, but otherwise he's off on his own all day, goes out with his own friends half of the evenings, has his own quarters at home. We don't share the same bedroom even. He says that's normal practice. I don't know. But we don't – he doesn't – '

Her cheeks were pink, but Fanny's were not.

'In private,' she went on bravely, 'he seems quite indifferent to me. I don't know why he married me.'

'Go on,' Fanny encouraged.

Emily shrugged. 'I've tried to be like the others, like the other married women. They get together for luncheons and teas and shopping expeditions – the same group endlessly permutating, the same conversations endlessly recycling. I tried to be absorbed by the house and garden, ordering meals and training the servants, buying clothes, having my hair done. I've tried to be a "model wife", and it was all right while I had Basil to love. But if he doesn't love me, there's no point to it, is there? That's why I've tried to get interested in Adishka's political movement. But it isn't what I wanted, not what I expected at all.' Tears were close to overspilling now. 'Fanny, you know Basil. Why did he marry me, if he doesn't love me?'

Fanny reached across the table and touched her hand. 'You don't know that he doesn't love you.'

'It's not what you read about in novels and plays and poetry. Think of Antony and Cleopatra, or Cathy and Heathcliff – all right,' she added when Fanny made a protesting sound, 'think of Emma Woodhouse and Mr Knightley, if you like. No-one, however clever, could write a novel about Basil and me.'

'Poor Basil,' Fanny said. 'It's not his fault he's not a story-book hero. He's just not made that way. He's a plain, simple Victorian gentleman. You must frighten him to death sometimes with your expectations.'

Emily smiled faintly. 'You don't know the half of it, Fan! But *why* did he marry me? My cousin Alexei says men always marry their mothers, and I can't believe I'm anything like the old Princess.'

'Emily, I can't tell you what was in Basil's mind.'

'Please!'

Fanny sighed. 'You remember a long time ago when we talked about him wanting to marry me? I told you it was simply because he knew me from childhood, and didn't want the bother of courting a stranger?'

'Yes, but – '

'Hasn't it occurred to you that he was a stranger himself when he came back to Russia after all those years? And when you turned up, you were then someone he'd known for years, an old friend, someone he didn't have to try hard with. As head of his branch of the family, he'd be expected to marry for the sake of the name, and he'd rather marry you than a complete stranger.' She surveyed Emily's expression, and added gently, 'I expect he does love you, as much as he's able to. But he isn't very bright, you know. You mustn't expect too much of him.'

Emily nodded – a gesture only of acknowledgement, for she was pursuing thoughts. After a moment she said, 'Alexei said that women always marry their fathers, too. I didn't understand what he meant at first. But I see it now. Papa was always remote to me, a sort of hero to be admired at a distance, someone too far above me to be understood, only to be served, and placated if possible. But my grandmother made me see that he is really quite selfish, and interested in no-one but himself. All that remoteness – it isn't deep, splendid thought, the preoccupation of genius – '

'Oh Emily! You couldn't have thought Basil a genius!' Fanny protested.

An unwilling smile tugged Emily's mouth. 'There's simply no knowing what I thought! A woman in love isn't rational. Oh Fan, I can't tell you what a relief it is to be able to say all this, and know you understand, and don't condemn me!'

251

'Condemn you? You haven't done anything wrong.'

'It was wrong to marry Basil. I'm not the right wife for him. And silly.'

'It's a mistake I might just as easily have made myself,' Fanny said.

'You? Oh no. You were too strong.'

'There was many a time I was on the verge of giving in. You don't know, Em. After all these years of being a Suffragette and wanting to be taken seriously, I begin to feel that there is a sort of natural weakness in women, that makes them want to be loved and taken care of, at any cost.'

'I don't think it's a weakness,' Emily said stoutly. 'And if it is, I'm sure men must feel it too. Some of them, anyway.'

Adishka came with Emily to see Fanny off on her journey home to England. He had taken a great shine to her, which seemed to amuse Fanny.

'Why shouldn't he admire you? Nothing could be more natural,' Emily defended her firmly.

'Tailless foxes,' Fanny said, laughing, and wouldn't explain further.

Adishka monopolised Fanny's conversation all the way to the docks, but then kindly declared his intention to wait in the motor car so that Emily could have a private farewell with her friend on board the ship.

'You will write, won't you?' he said, pressing Fanny's hand. 'Tell me everything that happens. And you won't forget that book?'

'Bagehot's *English Constitution*? No, I won't forget,' Fanny said.

'And whatever you do,' Adishka said earnestly, 'Never give up.'

'Nor you,' she replied in the same tone.

Alone with her, walking to the cabin, Emily said, 'I don't know that I'd say the same as Adishka. I wish you would give up, Fanny. You've done your part. Let someone else take up the fight.'

'Sometimes I wish I could,' Fanny said. 'Sometimes I feel very tired of it all. But then I wake up in the morning, and there's the work to be done, so I take it up.'

She spoke lightly, but Emily was not eased. 'It's not too late to change your mind,' she urged. 'Come back with me. Stay here in Russia. I do wish you would, Fanny. I need a friend.'

'And what would I do in Russia? I have to be useful, Em.

"Fashioned for labour, not for love", like Jane Eyre. No, don't protest. I have to go back. I'm sorry.'

Emily sighed. 'I didn't think you'd stay. But I wish I knew what to do – about anything.'

'You'll find the way. Just rely on your own judgement, not other people's. Other people aren't bound to be right, you know.'

In the cabin they faced eath other. Fanny looked less thin and worn and tired than when she had arrived, and that had to be Emily's reward; but other things had not altered. That stillness, and that dreadful patience, were unchanged. Emily felt tearful, and full of a numb dread that she would never see Fanny again.

'You'll write?'

'Of course.'

'And you'll come again one day?'

'Perhaps. It will be easier for you to visit London, though. You're immensely rich.'

'Basil is.'

'It's the same thing.' She touched Emily's hand lightly. 'Don't wait. Goodbyes are dreadful things.'

Emily nodded, unable to speak without crying. She hugged Fanny quickly, and went away.

The afternoon traffic was heavy coming back from the docks. Everyone seemed to have taken advantage of the brief thaw to get out and about and there was a hold-up at every bridge. Emily blessed Adishka's tact in not talking about Fanny, though she wished he would talk about something, rather than leave her alone with her thoughts. But he seemed deep in thoughts of his own.

Emily looked out of the windows as the sunset flamed the sky and everywhere the lights began to come on in the gathering gloom. She thought about London, imagined the narrow streets and the fog and the policemen in tall helmets. How far away it all seemed now! Could she go back for a visit? Would Basil agree to it? Perhaps he might like it – somewhere else to show off, somewhere where he could shine even more brightly than in Petersburg. Perhaps she would suggest it to him, very tentatively, and see how he reacted. It would be nice to see Lady Hamilton again. They could stay at the Savoy, and be handy for the theatres . . .

They were passing a large house which was unusual in having blinds rather than curtains at the windows; the blinds were drawn down, but there was a light in every room. She thought idly that they must be having a party, for even the top-floor windows were illuminated; though the front door was closed, and there was only the most discreet of lamps to illuminate the steps up to it.

Then the door opened, and in the brief escape of light from within a man came out, still settling his hat on his head, and trotted quickly down the steps as an unseen hand closed the coor behind him. She saw him only for an instant before he hurried round a corner; but a woman who has been in love knows every shape and movement of the beloved. She knew that gesture of Basil's of settling his hat as she knew her own face in the looking-glass.

'What's that place?' she asked Adishka.

'Eh? What? What place?' He came back with a jerk from his own thoughts.

'There – the house we're just passing, with the blinds. It looks as if they're having a party, with all the lights burning.'

Adishka laughed. 'There's always a party going on there, of a sort.'

'Well, who lives there?'

'No-one lives there,' he said. 'No-one you're likely to know, at any rate. It's Madame Clavin's. Surely you've heard of it?'

'No,' Emily said, puzzled. She thought she knew all of Basil's friends, by name at least. 'Who's Madame Clavin?'

'She isn't anyone. At least, I suppose there might have been a Madame Clavin once, for all I know.' He looked impatient at her continued puzzlement. 'It's a brothel, foolish! The most celebrated one in Petersburg. I thought everyone had heard of it.'

'No,' Emily said, hearing her own voice quite calm and steady from a long way away. 'Not everyone. Have you ever been there?'

'I couldn't afford those prices,' he said shortly.

Chapter Fifteen

All the shops were jewelled caves, decorated for Christmas and pouring over with fabulous merchandise; but Maendel's, the toy-shop, was the most magical of all. Emily was quite sorry to leave it, though she and Natasha had been in there over an hour already. There had been so many children, of various ages, faces turned upwards to wonder, holding tightly to the hands of mamas or governesses or tutors as though they feared rapture might snatch them away. The atmosphere had been one of tense longing and held breath.

Natasha seemed impervious to it. Coming out into the wintry street, she thrust her hands deep into her muff and said, 'Well, that's the most difficult part finished. Now you can take me home, Emilusha, and give me tea. I must have tea! Shopping always makes me thirsty.'

'Of course, Grandmama. There's Seva, over there.' They walked down towards him. The pavement had been cleared of snow, and the bank of it along the roadside was growing so high that only the horses' heads were visible. 'I do wonder, though, whether the chemistry set for Yenchik is a good idea.'

'It's what he wants,' Natasha said simply. 'He's been talking about it for weeks.'

'But you know what a devil he is. He may blow up the house.'

'Well, what of it? Valya can afford the repairs. It might do him good to be blown up from time to time – he's such a stick!'

'Oh Grandmama! Don't you think a book might be – '

'Would you rather have had a book when you were thirteen?'

'No, I don't suppose so,' Emily admitted with a grin.

'The boy has an enquiring mind,' Natasha said, climbing into the carriage, 'and it's my purpose in life to feed enquiring minds where I find them. As I did yours.'

Emily sat beside her and Seva shut them in. 'Yes, and I'm grateful to you every moment of every day for rescuing me as you did. When I think what my life would have been like – '

'I don't need gratitude, little one.' Natasha smiled. 'You are all

255

the thanks I need. When I look at you, how beautiful you've become and how Russian, every inch a princess! It was for that I had you taken to London and educated, you know – so that you would know how to conduct yourself as Vasya's wife.'

Emily stared. 'But – you can't mean – '

'Didn't you guess?' Natasha chuckled. 'The first time I saw you together, the whole plan fell into my mind like a ripe apple. I could see how you had fallen in love with him, and what a perfect couple you would make. Mala would have married you off to someone dull and unsuitable, and probably poor into the bargain, whereas you were made for wealth. Oh, money isn't eveything, I grant you. It is possible to be rich and miserable; but since there are such things as silk and jewels and furs in the world, they may as well be worn by someone who will do them justice, don't you think?'

Emily was bemused. 'But how could you know Basil would marry me?'

'I didn't, of course, but I had a fair idea he'd come round to it. I've known him since he was a little boy, remember. And when the time came, he didn't need more than the very lightest of pushes.'

'I don't understand. Pushes?'

'Never mind! You're married, and you're happy. I wanted that for you. I know you had an absurd idea of working for your living, but you weren't designed for such a cold, bare life – a spinster's life it would have been, too. There's a passion in you, Emilusha, and I wanted to see it fulfilled.' She patted Emily's hand. 'I married for love, you see, and I wanted nothing less for you.'

Emily's mind was racing. *Could* her marriage have been arranged? But what inducement could have been offered to Basil to marry her? Oh, this was worse than ever! Bad enough, if Fanny were right, that he might have married her not from love but from laziness; but if he had been persuaded, *bribed* even . . .

Natasha was still talking. 'Whenever I see you together, I see how right it is. Your happiness is my reward – and you are happy, aren't you, my dear child?'

'Oh – yes! Yes, very.' Emily did her best, but even Natasha in her rose-coloured cloud of vicarious pleasure noticed that the reply was less than rapturous.

'Is something troubling you, little one?' she asked with quick concern. When Emily didn't immediately answer she said carefully, 'Marriage requires a great deal of adjustment, in so many ways, particularly when one has led a sheltered life. If there is something you wish to ask me, child – ? Remember, you can say anything to me.'

Could she? Emily hesitated, tempted to allow all the hurt and worry to spill over, longing for advice as to what to do about it all. But could she so disillusion her grandmother, who had been so kind, and wanted nothing but her happiness?

'Grandmama, can you tell me – ' she began cautiously.

'Yes?' Natasha encouraged. 'Anything, anything at all.'

'Have you – have you ever heard of a place called Madame Clavin's?'

Natasha's face sharpened. 'Yes, of course. One knows about it, though it isn't discussed, not in front of women at any rate. But you don't mean to tell me that Basil – '

No, she couldn't do it. Her happiness was what Grandmama wanted, and she should have it, whatever it cost Emily. 'Oh no, of course not!' she said, and the consciousness of the lie made her blush, which in this case helped to make the lie convincing. 'Adishka told me what it was, when we drove past it on the way back from taking Fanny to her ship.'

'Yes, Adishka would,' Natasha growled.

'It's just that – I thought I saw someone I knew coming out from it. The – the husband of someone I know.'

Natasha looked at her searchingly for some time before answering, and Emily kept her countenance as well as she could, staring before her to avoid the bright eyes, keeping her lips pressed together firmly.

'Well,' Natasha said at last. 'Well.' She thought for a little, and then said, 'I think I understand what you are worrying about. You are afraid that if Basil's friends do it, so might Basil. You are wondering if all men go to such places?'

Emily nodded, grateful to have the questions supplied as well as the answers.

'No, I don't think all men do. Many, perhaps most at some time in their lives . . . '

'My grandfather?'

'Vanya? No! No, never. When a man marries for love, and the love is returned, there is no need for him to seek elsewhere.'

'But it's not love, is it, at Madame Clavin's?'

Natasha frowned. 'I don't know. I'm not a man. I suppose it may be love, of a sort – the act is the same even if the intentions are different. But then, who can be sure always what the intentions are?' She seemed almost to be talking to herself. Emily kept still, waiting for the worst. 'Men have – certain urges; I'm sure you've heard that said. Some men more than others. Some men seem to need – more. Or sometimes different. Never mind that!' She changed her mind and waved her hand quickly to erase the last words. 'At all events, it is not a thing to concern yourself about. If it were to happen – and there's no reason to suppose it will – there would be no need for you even to notice it, certainly not to be upset about it. It doesn't mean anything, you know.'

Emily turned at that. 'How can you say that, when you remember how Aunt Maud grieved?'

Natasha looked startled. 'That was quite different!' she said hastily, and then more calmly, 'It was different, Emilusha. Tomaso was consorting with a respectable lady, one of their own class – well, more or less. If he had merely *discreetly* visited an establishment like Madame Clavin's – and indeed I believe he did quite often – it wouldn't have mattered in the least, and Mala would not have taken the least notice of it. No, if Vasya were to have an affair – an open affair – with a woman of substance, that would be something to upset you. But he won't, of course. You are worrying yourself unnecessarily.'

Emily thought of Varvara Sabinina, imagined Basil making love to her, and compared the feeling it gave her with the feeling she had had ever since she saw him coming out of the brothel. No, she thought, it wasn't different. It was the same feeling, the same burning, resentful pain. He would not make love with her, called her a whore for wanting him to, but gave himself freely to other women. And she was supposed to accept it as nothing important? No, never!

Natasha had been watching her, and now closed her hand around Emily's and pressed it steadily. 'You're teasing at yourself, *durachka!* Trying to find something to worry about. I've seen it before. When people are happy, they sometimes get such a mad desire to destroy everything. Don't do it! You love Vasya and he loves you. You're both as happy as larks, and when the babies begin to come along, you'll be even happier. You have nothing in the world to worry about. Now isn't that true?'

Emily returned the squeeze and smiled. *Someone else's play*, she thought. *One must have the courtesy to learn the lines.*

'Yes, Grandmama. You're right. I was just being silly. Everything's all right.'

Natasha's face cleared. She released Emily's hand, and sat straight, looking ahead of her with a small, pleased smile as she pursued some thought of her own. After a moment she said lightly, 'And who knows? Christmas is a very good time to get pregnant. I've known it happen again and again. And babies conceived at Christmas are always good-tempered – I've often noticed it.'

Because of engagements, Basil and Emily did not go to Anna's house until Christmas Eve, by which time Natasha and the party from Archangel were already installed there. When they arrived it was the children who reached them first, running out into the vestibule while they were still being divested of their outer garments by the servants. Yenchik and Roshka came running, dragging between them their cousin Modeste, who in the last year had suddenly grown and lost his baby chubbiness, making him look like a geranium kept too far from the light. Tolya followed with more dignity, holding the hand of little Tatya, who was walking now, and pulling down his mouth in a self-conscious smirk of pleasure.

They all exploded into talk at once. Roxane had lost a tooth and produced it proudly from her pocket to show it to Emily in all its archaeological horror. She seemed to find it fascinating. If she left it under her pillow the fairies would exchange it for a present, she explained, but she would rather keep the tooth. Did Emily know any stories about teeth?

Yenchik, having walked round Emily inspecting her with an air of solemn satisfaction, reverted abruptly to his own age and began expounding the glories of the chemistry set and the experiments he hoped to perform with it. Tolya, now sixteen, his voice settled at last into a manly baritone, was eager to engage Emily on the topic of Humanism, which he had decided might be the answer to his philosophical troubles.

Modeste fixed his eyes silently and appealingly on Emily's face until she took the hint and lifted him up into her arms, tall boy that he was, growing too fast for his soul. Only Tatya, obviously destined to be a vamp, noticed Basil, smiled ravishingly and held up her arms to him.

So it was with an appearance of harmony that they entered the hall, the older children bobbing about them like tugs, Basil carrying Tatya and Emily Modeste; side by side, Prince and Princess Narishkin, the fairy-tale couple, Prince Florizel and his Cinderella. The irony, Emily thought, was that Basil probably wasn't aware there was anything wrong. Life was being lived according to his plan: he

259

was flatteringly attentive and loving to her in public, and saw very little of her in private, which was how it had always been.

Emily was complaisant when they were in company together, acting the part she had been cast for in Basil's play, his protégée and his prize. But he had not come to her bed since Fanny had gone home, and she had no idea how she would react when that finally happened. She needed love, ached for physical contact, remembered their former lovemaking with wistful longing; but the thought of taking him into her arms without a hint of what she knew, with no word of reproach, no demand for explanation or apology, seemed unlikely. She didn't think she could do it. Her resentment and hurt were too great.

And if she confronted him with it, what then? He would be angry, that was certain. She guessed he would tell her it was not her business. Probably he would walk out and leave her loveless – cut her off completely, perhaps, and then what would she do? She didn't want the confrontation, and yet to live with the secret, to let him go on smiling and thinking himself safe, seemed intolerable.

And here was Christmas to be got through, a whole houseful of people to deceive, day after day, into thinking that nothing was wrong. Anna had planned great things. They were to stay for a week at least. How was she to survive?

As soon as she was through the door, she was enveloped, Modeste and all, in Aunt Yenya's embrace.

'Oh, dear Emilia! How long it's been! I wish you'd come to Archangel with us. The children have missed you so. You're looking splendid – but thinner. Don't you think she's thinner, Valya?'

Emily had had to put Modeste down to cope with the greetings, but his cold little hand stayed slotted firmly into hers. Valya stepped forward, removing his pipe to say calmly, 'Yes, a little, but it suits her. I'm glad to see you, Emilia. Vasska, how are you?'

Adishka greeted her casually, as befitted someone who saw her almost every day, and Emily, nodding to him, found herself automatically looking round for Sasha Suslov. She missed the lad like a chafing collar.

'We've a grand dinner and a masked ball planned for Tuesday,' Anna was saying, kissing her briskly, 'so I hope you've brought something suitable to wear. If you haven't, no matter – it's no trouble to send a servant back to your house. All the Sapetskys are coming to stay for it, and Princess Galinovska; and Grand Duke Vladimir's promised to look in – he's Vasska's godfather – so it

260

should be a great occasion. Don't let these children bother you. I should have them sent to the nurseries anyway.'

'They don't bother me,' Emily said quickly. 'Please let them stay.'

Basil had been greeted by Natasha with warmth and kisses on both sides, and their initial conversation had already drifted, via Princess Galinovska, to a subject of perennial interest to them both: royal families and who was related to whom.

'No, no, that was the elder daughter,' Emily heard Basil saying. 'It was Adelaide who had the pet bear and married the youngest Hesse-Cassel boy.'

'Oh yes, of course, I remember now.'

'And *his* mother was a Saxe-Saafeld, which meant they were third cousins anyway.'

'That's probably why their children were all so bloodless and chinless. I remember Bismarck saying to my husband once that they reminded him of tapeworms.'

'Really, Natasha Petrovna, I don't believe Bismarck ever said any such thing!'

'Oh well, perhaps it wasn't him then. Perhaps it was Granville . . . '

With all the conversation and the clamour of the children, it was some time before Alexei managed to reach Emily to shake hands and exchange a threefold kiss with her. When he straightened up he didn't let go of her hand, looking down searchingly at her in a way that made her feel, strangely, both exposed and comforted.

'Something's happened,' he said at last. 'Something's wrong, isn't it?'

Denial flew automatically to her lips, but he didn't let her voice it. 'It's all right, I know, not here and now,' he said. 'There'll be plenty of time to talk. I have to go away soon for a while, but I'll be here for at least two weeks yet – perhaps even three. I'll arrange it so that we can talk properly and privately.' He smiled, and she felt light-headed, though that might have been from craning her head back to look up at him. 'Don't worry, everything will be all right.'

His words might mean anything or nothing; logically, she thought, they must mean nothing. But she felt soothed, calmed by them. The days ahead no longer reared up like an impossible cliff to be scaled. Everything would be all right, he had said, and so it would be. She smiled as he let her go, his attention required by Tolya, and turned her head to see Basil and her grandmother both smiling at her.

261

'Isn't she lovely?' Basil demanded rhetorically. 'Well, darling, our first Christmas together as man and wife! I don't think I could possibly be happier.'

Emily was saved from answering by Anna.

'Shall we go up, everybody? I can't think why we're all standing here. Vasska, why don't you lead the way with your princess? It's almost time for luncheon, and we must have a glass of champagne to toast your first Christmas as a married man.'

Basil's sleeve was presented to Emily, and his handsome, smiling face beamed upon her, his blue eyes crinkling in that way she had loved so long and surely must love still. She placed her hand on his arm and he bent his head to kiss it to a small murmur of approving laughter from the company, or the female part of it, at least.

Looking down at his bent head, Emily noticed again the two heartbreaking little curls at the base of his neck, and felt a pang of tender sadness, such as one might feel, she supposed, when looking at the photograph of someone loved and long lost.

After luncheon everyone went out into the garden to begin the construction of a gigantic snow hill for tobogganing. Outdoor games were a traditional part of Christmas, and useful for working off the large amounts of extra food consumed. Everyone joined in, wielding spades, working up a glow. There was a lot of laughter and horse-play, some snowballing and an inevitable soaking or two. Spirits rose so high that even Anna smiled, if rather stiffly, when Yenchik got her in the back of the neck with a wet handful.

Emily worked with a will, enjoying the physical exercise and the simple pleasure of the children. But it was not only that. Whenever she looked up, her eye would find Alexei somewhere near, usually helping Modeste or defending him against Zansha's exuberance. And always, at the same instant that she looked at him, he looked round at her, so that the simple contact of eyes became something significant, like a deliberate touch of a hand, something that could not have happened by accident.

The great scarlet sun wobbled down behind the bare trees; the robin who had been watching them from his various vantage points around the garden suddenly flicked and was gone; and from afternoon it became dusk. The air was suddenly noticeably colder, and everyone's thoughts turned naturally towards tea, hot buttered muffins and spiced *kazulies*. Tatya, a tiny bulky bear in her minuscule fur coat and hat, beamed rosy as a Crimean apple from the haven of one pair of male arms or another, but pale Modeste was looking distinctly chilled.

'Alyosha, that child is practically grey with cold,' Anna called. 'You shouldn't have let him stay out so long.'

Modeste raised burning eyes to his father: he hated to be made to feel small and weak, especially in front of his boisterous cousins.

'He's all right, my dear. We're all going in now, anyway. Emilia, take a hand, and we'll give him a Blériot ride – shall we, Modeste? Come on, everyone.'

Emily caught Modeste's hand, and between them she and Alexei 'flew' him through the air, saving him face and the extra effort of struggling through the snow to the house. After tea the nursery staff swept the little ones upstairs, and in the drawing-room there was a hiatus – an hour or so to fill before it would be time to go up and dress for dinner.

Valya had already settled himself with his pipe and a book. Anna and Yenya were carrying on an absorbing conversation in low voices not meant to be overheard. Basil and Natasha, more audibly, had got on to the Coburgs and Hamburgs; Adishka good-naturedly offered Tolya a game of chess. Emily felt Alexei's presence behind her like a flame, and turned to meet his eyes.

'Well, as there's time now, I'll show you the family portraits you wanted to see,' he said. His voice sounded as natural as could be, but she was afraid she must be looking horribly like a conspirator. 'Does anyone else want to come?' he asked the room in general. No-one even looked up, absorbed in their own interests. A small, wicked smile, it seemed to Emily, curled like smoke about his lips. 'Anna? What about you?'

She looked up now. 'What? Of course not. We've all seen them. Don't be tedious, Alyosha. Don't let him bore you, Emilia.'

'No – I'd like to see them. Really,' she said.

'Come, then,' said Alexei, and she followed him gratefully out of the room. As she paused outside while he reached in to close the door, she saw Valya watching them, expressionless as a cat on a wall. Yes, she thought uncomfortably, nothing would ever escape him.

She followed Alexei without a word, up stairs, along corridors. Here was a gallery full of paintings.

'This is the hall of ancestors. I'll show you them one day. Some of them are quite interesting. This one, for instance, is Count Peter, Natasha's father. If you work our family tree backwards, he is our first common ancestor – yours and mine, I mean.'

'Oh, he's the one I'm supposed to resemble! And is that his – '

'Not now. Another time. For the moment I simply want you to know where they are so that you shan't be caught out by a casual question.' He smiled crookedly. 'Don't look at me like that! You didn't really want a tour of them now, did you?'

'Then where are we going?'

'To my study. The best room in the house. The only tolerable room in it, in my view. It has served in many capacities in its time. Today you may look upon it as a sickbay.'

The room into which he led her at last was small by Russian standards, though easily three times the size of papa's study back at The Lodge. It was furnished like an English country-house library, with three walls covered with bookshelves right up to the ceiling. The fourth wall contained three tall windows – velvet-curtained now against the dark – between which hung a large number of paintings, mostly landscapes, but one or two sailing ships and spaniels holding dead pheasants in their mouths: paintings that were never meant to arouse emotions, all very soothing and masculine.

At one end of the room was a huge leather-topped desk with a brass lamp and standish and an antique wooden globe amongst the scattering of papers. There were comfortable leather chairs and sofas, and a dark-red Turkey carpet. At the other end of the room from the desk a bright log fire burned within a large marble fireplace, a densely shaggy rug lying invitingly before it.

'Oh!' Emily breathed in delight. 'How lovely! I hadn't realised until this moment how much I miss open fires!'

'Our stoves are much more efficient,' Alexei said, watching her face with pleasure. 'An even temperature, no draughts – '

'But it isn't the same! You can't curl up in front of a stove and gaze into the flames and see pictures!'

'Well, you could if you wanted to,' he smiled, 'but I'm playing devil's advocate. I love an open fire myself – that's why I had this fireplace imported all the way from England, and had it installed here in the face of considerable resistance. Anna thought I was mad, and the servants were convinced it would burn the house down. Go and curl up in front of it, then, while I pour a glass of wine for us both.'

'Would you mind if I sat on the rug?'

He laughed. 'Not at all. That's what it's there for.'

He brought two glasses of wine, and having handed Emily hers, sat in the most shapeless of the armchairs at the fireside where he could see her face. She sat hugging her knees, looking into the fire, and the gold-rose light moved shapes and shadows about her face and hair. She looked contented for the moment and he was sorry to disturb her, but he knew their time was limited.

'Well?' he said at last.

She moved her head a little towards him in acknowledgement, but did not take her eyes from the flickering flames. 'This is so nice!' she said softly. 'This is the first time I've felt completely real since I left England. No, before that, really – since I found out about Uncle Westie.'

He picked his way economically through the words. 'You haven't felt real in Russia?'

'Oh – it's hard to put into words, really. It's as though there's a sheet of glass between me and the real world. I can see it, and it can see me, but I'm apart from it – outside looking in. Like being in a dream. I thought I'd wake up from it when I came to Russia. Then I thought I'd wake up when I got married. But it didn't happen. Maybe I'll never wake.'

'There are those who think that all of life is a dream, and that everything in it is just a faint, imperfect image of the real world beyond.'

'Yes, I know. I think I believe that too. But it isn't what I mean just now.'

He felt horribly conscious of time pressing against the door, scratching to get in. He wanted to walk softly through her thoughts and go unnoticed, but there was no time, no time. 'You had better tell me what has happened since I met you at Schwarzenturm.'

'But I've seen you since then – many times,' she said into the fire, puzzled.

'Emilusha, don't play the idiot with me,' he said, surprising her into looking at him. 'That's better. You know perfectly well why we're here. Didn't I tell you this was the sickbay? Tell me about you and Basil. You came in through the door like the casualty of a battle, shocked and grieving. What has he done to you?'

She didn't answer, though he could tell from her eyes that it was not unwillingness, only not quite seeing how to begin.

'Or not done to you,' he added, even more gently.

265

Then it all came. She put down the glass on the hearthstone without noticing she had ever held it and told him everything.

'It was so wonderful at first – loving someone, and being able to show it in such a positive way! I thought it was the most marvellous thing. I couldn't understand why they'd always made such a mystery of it, why we hadn't been told about it as children, as something to look forward to – like birthdays and the seaside all rolled together!'

He laughed at her delight. 'Yes, with the right person, it's all those things. But a grave responsibility as well – not to be taken lightly.'

'Oh no! I mean, I do see that. It was wonderful and delightful, but solemn too. Because of being in love.'

He closed his eyes for an instant, as if against a twinge of pain.

'I thought Basil felt it too,' she went on, puzzled, 'but it was only at first. Then it seemed he didn't like it as much as me – or at least not as often as me. Then it seemed he actually disliked it. It . . . ' Her lips quivered with the shameful memory. 'It disgusted him.'

'Ah, no,' he said softly, in protest. He slid from his chair onto the rug to be nearer her. She sat up on her knees, hugging herself with her arms, and began to rock back and forth a little as she told him.

'He didn't like me to touch him in public. Well, I accepted that – I supposed it was etiquette, you see. But then when we were alone together, he was always moving away from me, keeping his distance, avoiding being touched. And then, one night – ' Her cheeks and eyes were bright from more than the firelight. 'One night I *asked* him – you know, to come to bed with me – and he said – he said it was disgusting.'

He couldn't help himself: he had to touch her. He reached out and unfolded her arms to take hold of her hands. She let him, stopped rocking, knelt straight before him with her hands in his as though she were about to make a vow. It didn't occur to her for a moment that it was strange to be telling him these things. He didn't seem particularly separate from her just then. She felt almost as if she were telling him things he already knew, simply to clarify them for herself.

'He said that no decent woman would ever ask. He said a man likes to choose for himself when, and how often. He said no decent woman would be eager for it, as I was. He said my wanting it was *unwholesome*.'

He felt her pain. 'Oh *doushka!*'

'Well, I didn't know. How could I? I thought he must know better than me. I thought perhaps nobody did it very often, and that maybe

266

I was ill in my mind, or something. But then, then I found out – '
Her expression hardened, and her hands tightened in his. 'He goes
with prostitutes. I saw him coming out of Madame Clavin's. He
gives *them* what he won't give me, and calls *me* unwholesome.'

That seemed to be all. After a moment, when he saw she had
finished, he said, '*Doushka*, you know it isn't you, don't you? Inside
yourself, where you always tell yourself the truth, you know that
there's nothing wrong with you, don't you?'

She frowned in thought. 'But then it would have to be Basil, and
I don't want it to be him. I love him so. I don't want to think
he's – '

'He's what?'

'I don't know.' She looked suddenly blank. 'What does that make
of him? I don't understand. I can't believe he said it only to torment
me – it didn't seem like that. I think he really meant it; but then
what about – what about the brothel?' She sighed in perplexity.
'Can you explain it to me?'

'I think I can, a little,' he said gently. 'It isn't a thing unique to
him. I have met a number of men who don't really enjoy having
physical relations with what they think of as decent women. Some
of them can't do it at all. Some of them simply avoid it except as a
duty.'

'But why?'

'It's usually because they had a mother they loved very much and
were very close to who was very strict with them. Sometimes it was
an older sister. In Basil's case, I think, both.'

'The old Princess . . . ' Emily said thoughtfully.

'And Anna. When he was a small boy, they both doted on him,
petted him, babied him. His father died when he was very young,
so he had no male influence over him. Anna told me she used to
dress him up and carry him about like a doll, even when he was old
enough to walk and talk by himself. And he never played with other
little boys.'

She was following everything with her eyes, but now she asked,
'But why would that make him not want to . . . ?'

Alexei shrugged. 'I don't know all the medical words for it. There's
a Viennese doctor who's worked out a whole science about such
things. But there are men who regard all decent women as in some
way being like their mothers and sisters, and therefore untouchable.
The only females they feel able to enjoy physical relations with are
fallen women, whores – or servants, sometimes. Does Basil . . . ?'

'No!' she said violently. Then, tilting her head a little, screwing up her eyes in a mixture of pain and puzzlement: 'It all seems so horrible and silly. You're not making it up, are you?'

He looked down at her hands and chafed the back of them gently with his thumbs. 'Do you really believe I would do such a thing?'

'No,' she sighed after a long pause. 'No, I suppose not.' She drew her hands from his, and sat down facing the flames, taking up her glass again and sipping. He moved to sit beside her – cautiously, afraid she had withdrawn from him. But after a while she said in a normal voice, almost as a friendly question: 'Why do you suppose he married me?'

'Is that a philosophical or a practical question?'

She looked at him and smiled, and relief sang in his heart. 'I don't know. Both I suppose. I don't know what you mean, really.'

'Are you asking why did he marry, or why you?'

'I suppose he married because of the name and so on. For an heir.'

'Yes, partly. I imagine also he just felt it was the thing to do. Most people want to get married, in a vague sort of way, even before they've met anyone to love. You do it because it's the next thing to do.'

'Is that why you married?'

'Yes, but we're not discussing me yet.'

'Yet?' she said, interested.

'As to why he married *you* – '

'What did my grandmother have to do with it?' she interrupted bluntly.

'She provided the money, of course.' He looked at her quizzically. 'She paid Basil a large dowry on your behalf, and altered her will in your favour. When she dies, everything of hers – apart from one or two small bequests – goes to you for your lifetime, and to any children you have by Basil thereafter.'

She stared in astonishment. 'How do you know that?'

'It's common knowledge.' He frowned. 'It's not a secret, Emilusha. It was all in the marriage settlement. How come you didn't know? They must have read it to you.'

'I – I expect I wasn't listening. So much was happening so quickly. I was tired, and thinking of other things – '

She broke off, and he saw the tears close to the surface. Now was the moment, he thought; there might not be another. He removed her glass from her fingers, and took her into his arms.

'*Doushka, doushka*, what is it?'

She leaned against him, trembling lightly, gulping at the tears. 'She bought him for me! I was afraid of it, after what she said in the carriage that time, but I couldn't believe – ' Her body heaved as she forced down the tears. 'He never loved me at all, did he?'

He pressed his lips to her hair, fighting desperately for control. 'Do you really want me to answer that?'

'Yes,' she said defiantly, like a child.

'He never loved you. He isn't capable of it. Not love as you feel it. Not as you want to be loved.'

'How do you know? How can you know that?'

'I know what you are capable of. But you never really loved him, you know.'

'I did! I do!'

'No. It was make-believe. A fairy story. Emilia? Wasn't it?'

'No!'

'Yes. You were looking for someone, and you mistook Basil for him. He was not who you thought he was. That's why you've felt you were in a dream. You've been in the wrong play all this time.'

She heaved once more in resistance, and was still. He held her quietly for a while, feeling her relax against him. After pain came sleep, he knew that, and he didn't want her to sleep in his arms – not here, not yet – so in a little while he sat her up straight again, turning her to look at him. She met his eyes solemnly, like a bereaved child.

'You said all women marry their fathers.'

'Yes.'

'I didn't think Basil was anything like my father, but I see now that he is, in a way. Papa didn't love me either, though I think sometimes he must have thought he did.'

'That's not your fault, you know. It's they who have failed, not you.'

She was searching his face. 'You knew, didn't you, when you first met me. But how? You hadn't even seen Basil and me together.'

'I already knew he had gone off and left you alone on your honeymoon.'

'So you did. But it might have been my fault. You didn't know me.'

'I've always known you,' he said.

She felt a peculiar sort of thump inside her at the words, though they had been spoken without emphasis – as if she had suddenly

269

noticed and recognised something that had been right beside her all the time. She looked at him with wide eyes, and saw how piercingly familiar his stranger's face was to her; its every shape and contour somehow personal to her, as if she was looking at her own face in the looking-glass. But how could that be? She remembered the dizzy moment on the top of the Black Tower, when she had felt the wheel of time brake and eternity flood in. Yes, it had been a moment of recognition. She had known then, and knew now, that she could trust this man absolutely, not just with her life but with more than her life, with what was more precious – her *self*.

'Yes,' she said, 'I feel as though I've always known you, too.'

Then he put his hands to either side of her face, holding it very gently, and kissed her. She felt herself trembling lightly, and the sensation of his unpaired lips against hers seemed more than simply a touch of flesh against flesh, but something almost unbearably significant; as if she were being asked a question too difficult for her, upon whose answer the whole of her life depended.

Then he let her go, and smiled at her, and it seemed as though she had answered it without knowing. His expression was faintly rueful, but full of kindness and affection.

'Not yet,' he said.

'I don't understand,' she said.

'It's all right,' he said reassuringly. 'Well, Emilusha, has the sick-bay done you good? Removing a splinter can be painful, but you're better off with it out. Now the healing can begin.'

'You can't call Basil a splinter! And he isn't out, is he? I still don't know in the least what to do about him, or anything.'

'Him and anything are the same thing.'

'I see that, but what am I to do?'

'You know, really.'

'Do I?'

'Deep down inside yourself.'

'Where I always tell myself the truth?'

'Yes. You know all the answers.'

She hesitated, not wanting to disappoint him. 'Truly, I don't think I do.'

'What do you feel?'

She thought about it. 'The pain has gone. I feel – empty, and tired, and puzzled.'

He nodded. 'It's all right. The answers are there. You'll find them in time. Only – '

270

'Yes?'

'Try not to be too long, will you?'

That same faintly rueful look, and again the words seemed unbearably significant, but she didn't know why. She had no chance to ask, however, for he seemed suddenly to change his mind about something, stood up, and held his hands out to her. 'Come, we must go back. The dressing-bell will ring in a minute, and I'd sooner it rang when we were downstairs with the others.'

She let him pull her to her feet and, while he still had hold of her hands, she said seriously, 'Thank you for letting me talk to you. For helping me.'

'Has it helped?'

It seemed an odd question coming from him. 'You know it has. I do feel much better now – stronger. I just wish I knew what to do. But I will – I'm sure I will,' she added hastily, so transparently eager to please him that he laughed.

'For the moment, I suggest that we behave as though this conversation hadn't taken place. Unless, of course, you want to precipitate a conclusion?'

'Oh no, not now. I mean, it's Christmas, and everyone's together, and the children are – '

'Quite. Then we must go down and behave towards our respective spouses as though nothing had changed. Can you cope with that?'

'Of course,' she said. 'I'm in someone else's play. But I don't mind, now I don't feel alone any more.' She looked up at him frankly. 'I always wanted a friend. You are my friend, aren't you?'

That seemed to amuse him. 'At the very least,' he said.

Chapter Sixteen

It was easier in some ways, and it was harder. The feeling that Alexei was there behind her, understanding and supporting, her friend, gave her a warmth and strength inside, as though she had partaken of a good hot meal before venturing out into the snow.

Yet having forced her to come to some conclusions about Basil, he had left her with the problem of what to do about it all. And it wasn't so simple, she often thought with faint resentment. The structure of loving Basil that she had erected so carefully was not easy to take down, and she wasn't even sure she wanted to, for where would it leave her? If she didn't love him – and she was not yet entirely certain she did not, for when he smiled at her, or paid her a compliment, or pulled out her chair for her at dinner, she still felt a rush of tenderness and longing for him, and if that wasn't love, what was it? But even if she didn't love him, she was still married to him, and they had to live together one way or another.

Actually, she thought, plodding round the garden dragging a toboggan on which small Tatya sat being the Snow Queen driving her milk-white reindeer, while Zansha pranced along beside being a hunting-dog – actually, the living together wouldn't be so very difficult. Basil had already arranged things for convenience, so that although officially they were married, they were more like lodgers under the same roof. He was handsome, good-tempered, and well mannered, and it was really no trial to share a house with him, especially such a large house.

But if she removed the loving-Basil structure from her life, she could see that there would be an enormous space to fill. What would her life be for, without that? She supposed she might find a Cause to dedicate herself to. It didn't have to be Adishka's. She was sure there must be lots of worthwhile things she might do, and as a married woman, and a rich one, she had the freedom both to seek one out and to be truly useful to it.

But when she contemplated that scenario, it looked hollow, false, cold, like a stage set viewed in the undeceiving light of day. Was that really all her life could be for? And where, *where* was love to come from? She must love someone: she needed human warmth.

'Faster, Milya, faster!' Zansha shouted. 'Make her gallop, Tatya! Crack your whip. Look, I'll show you – like this!'

Children, Emily thought. Perhaps that would be the answer – perhaps she and Basil would have children, and she could dedicate herself to them. She felt that she would like children; she loved other people's, after all, and how much more would she love her own, particularly if they inherited Basil's good looks?

But that brought her straight back to one problem she hadn't yet faced up to. To have babies, she first had to have Basil in her bed, and how was she going to feel about that?

Was it possible, was it even *likely*, that Alexei was right about him? That business of not being able to do it with decent women? It seemed so strange and inexplicable. And yet the other side of it – as she understood it – seemed unpleasantly possible, in the abstract at least, if not necessarily applied to Basil. For a man to be able to perform the act only with fallen women – with women he could regard as somehow 'dirty' – yes, that made a sort of grubby sense. Little children – little boys especially – loved to play in the dirt, to dabble their fingers in mud. Little boys were notoriously fascinated by things horrid, messy, loathsome. The unemotional, objective part of her mind, she found, was quite able to accept as a thesis that a man might find a perverse pleasure in sleeping with a prostitute *because* she was a prostitute.

But it was all so horrid! She shook her head violently to shake the thought away. Not Basil, who was so elegant, neat, nice in all his ways. And if it were true, how could she bear to let him touch her? She cursed Alexei for putting such ideas into her head. What business had he polluting her thoughts like that? Decent men didn't talk about such things to innocent girls! She directed a brief, violent hate towards him. Why did he do it? She had been all right before he had interfered!

She hauled round the corner of the garden, and her eye jumped to his figure at the top of the toboggan slope, carefully preparing Modeste to launch himself down it. Even from here she knew every line of his body. Even from here she could see the tenderness in his handling of his son. The hate dissipated like a pricked soap bubble. Hate him indeed! How could she possibly do anything but love him?

'Milya, why have you stopped?' Roshka came prancing towards

her and jumped up and down, tugging at her coat. 'Don't stop, keep pulling! Milya!'

She heard the voice, felt the tugging as though at the other end of the universe. All her attention was directed towards that distant figure in the blue-grey greatcoat, upright now against the snow-heavy sky as he watched Modeste go down the slope. The whole scene before her, the whole garden, seemed to be drawn with unnatural clarity, and every detail was minutely, crystally sharp, like the view from a mountain on a perfectly clear, still day.

She looked at him standing there on the top of the mound, quite still, and knew the exact moment when he looked away from Modeste and towards her. She couldn't possibly have seen his eyes from that distance, but their eyes met all the same. She felt his hand on the back of her neck, and shuddered.

'You must have thought me a complete idiot,' she said aloud.

'What? What, Milya?'

Fortunately she had spoken in English. She put her hand on Zansha's head in acknowledgement while her thoughts tumbled on. A complete blind fool! He had given her all the information she needed, but she had gone on looking everywhere except at what he held up before her eyes. *You were looking for someone, and mistook Basil for him.* She laughed, looking down into Zansha's surprised, chubby face.

'No I didn't!' she said, seeing the child beam in automatic reflection of her expression. 'Not really! I knew all the time. What an idiot! I knew all the time, Roshka!'

'What do you mean? Milya, who are you talking to?'

'Never mind. Would you like to go on the toboggan slope?'

'Yes!' A bellow of delight. 'Only Totya Anna says I'm too little.'

'Never mind – Uncle Alexei's there. He can say if it's all right. Come on, let's run! Hold tight, Tatya!'

There were steps cut into the snow on the climbing side of the mound. Alexei saw her coming, burdened with Tatya in her arms and pulling the toboggan behind, bumping up each step. He reached down and took his daughter from her arms, hitching her over onto one side so that he could offer the other hand to Emily. She took it, and even through two thick, fur-lined mittens it felt like no other hand on no other occasion. At the top she stood before him and they looked at each other, smiling. She saw that she didn't need to tell him. He knew. He had heard her, across the frozen garden.

'Hello,' he said.

274

'Hello.'

It was all that was needed, for now.

All the rest of the day, she felt as though she were floating just an inch or so above the ground. She felt powerful, invulnerable. She didn't care what happened now. She loved Alexei, and he loved her, and she felt about it none of the glittery surprise, fear, gratitude, that she had felt about Basil. It seemed as natural and right as breathing – although breathing didn't seem to be a thing she needed to do a lot of. She seemed for the moment to have become independent of all the laws of physics.

There was no opportunity for private talk, but it didn't seem to matter just then. Only one brief exchange in the doorway, when everyone was going up to dress for the ball. He stood back for her, and she passed close to him, looking up for a moment into his gold-tawny eyes.

'You made up the ground more quickly than I expected,' he murmured.

'Is it terribly obvious? I feel as though I'm wearing a nimbus.'

'Only to me.'

Basil came in as she sat at the dressing-table, taking the pins out of her hair. Anna had provided them with a pair of rooms, joined by a communal dressing-room, but so far they hadn't met in either. He had stayed up later than her every evening, drinking and talking with Alexei. Emily wondered suddenly whether Alexei had deliberately kept him from bothering her, and a small smile of amusement curled her lips.

'You seem very gay,' he said, and stooped to kiss her nape. It was a gesture of unaccustomed affection, since they were alone except for Tanya and there was no-one to impress, but for the first time it left her completely unmoved. He might as well have pressed a piece of cold cooked sausage to the back of her neck for all the emotion it stirred.

'Yes,' she said, smiling at his reflection. 'I'm looking forward to the ball.'

'Are you? I'm glad. I had the feeling since we got here that you weren't quite enjoying yourself.'

'I'm having a very pleasant time. Would you mind if I weren't?' she added curiously.

He looked quizzical. 'Of course I would. What an odd thing to say. You're my wife – I want you to be happy.'

It was an important point to remember, she thought, that nothing had changed for him. The Great Revelation in the Garden had happened to her alone. Basil, poor Basil, wasn't able to love much, but such as he was capable of, he had chosen to bestow on her. His name, his protection, his public affection: what more could any woman ask? That his idea of marriage – not being bothered by someone – was not hers was her secret alone.

'Yes, of course you do,' she said. 'Well I am happy, so you needn't worry.'

In reflection he saw Tanya backing out of the wardrobe with her gown. His face lit. 'Is that what you're wearing? Oh good! I hoped you'd choose something very splendid. That's what I came in to say. You needn't be modest and retiring tonight – that's the whole point of a masked ball.'

The gown was anything but retiring – purple, green and gold, in a swirling Bakst pattern, very flowing, with oriental sleeves.

'I shall be Scheherazade tonight,' she said, with private significance.

He laughed simply. 'Why not? And what jewels will you wear? The Razumovsky emeralds?'

'Yes, I thought so.'

'The whole set?'

'Except for the tiara. I thought the Potemkin tiara would be better.'

It was one of the grandest – emeralds and diamonds in starry rays.

'Perfect,' Basil said, putting his hands on her shoulders. 'You'll outshine them all!'

She was his doll for dressing up and showing off in public. Well, I can still do that for you, at least, she thought, meeting his eyes and smiling.

His own smile grew tender. 'I'm very proud of you, darling, you know that,' he said softly. She sensed danger. It had been an unusually long time since he had bothered her, and it would be like him to come to her tonight, of all times. She mustn't encourage him too much.

'Thank you, Basil,' she said, trying to be brisk, 'but you'd better let me get on with dressing, or I'll never be ready in time. Off you go and get changed.'

'Yes, of course,' he said, removing his hands. But still he smiled at her in the glass. 'I'll see you later,' he said, and she thought she detected an unwelcome significance in the words.

It was some time before she managed to get away and stand by herself in a corner of the ballroom, half concealed by the potted palms. Alexei appeared behind her at once, like sorcery.

'What a burlesque!' he said into her ear. 'Anna loves all this. She sees herself as queen of a mediaeval court. She was born out of her age, poor soul; and she lowered herself so much by marrying me, a mere count.'

'That was almost the first thing she told me,' Emily said. 'But how did you know this was me? It could be anyone under this mask.'

'Don't be silly,' he said. 'And what on earth are you wearing?'

'I'm Scheherazade,' she said simply, and he caught the reference at once.

'Very good!' he laughed. 'I hope you can keep it up.'

'Keep him up, you mean. And on that subject, have you been – '

'Doing my bit? Yes. I didn't think you'd noticed.'

'I didn't, until today. I was just grateful for the respite. Now I can be grateful to you.'

'No need. I acted from purely selfish motives, though even then I wasn't sure I'd been completely successful. He has remarkable powers of recovery, damn him.'

She looked up, hardly seeing the mask he was wearing. Merely looking at his mouth made her shiver with desire.

'You were successful,' she said.

'Good.' There was a breathless pause, and then he said in a different voice, 'Damn, we're about to be disturbed. We'd better go and dance, or we'll be separated.'

They drifted out onto the floor, where he was licensed to put his arm round her publicly. She thought they were probably well camouflaged out there. Wearing masks seemed to change people quite a lot: all around them there were couples at various stages of kicking over the traces. They danced for some time in silence. Emily felt completely content just to be there, close to him.

After a while he said, 'It isn't what I planned. The first time you danced with me ought to have been a very special occasion.'

'It is,' she said.

His smile was ironic. 'In this bear garden? You don't need to humour me, you know.'

'I wasn't,' she protested. 'It is. I'm just glad to be – home.'

His arm tightened around her in reply, and they were silent a while. Then he said, 'Listen to me, *doushka*. I may not be able to talk privately to you again. Like it or not, I am host tonight, and I shall have to behave like one.'

'It's all right. I understand.'

'Don't be so hasty! I haven't got to the point yet.'

'Sorry,' she said meekly.

'Minx! The point is, this will probably go on until the small hours, but there's no need for either of us to stay to the end. The very young people will go on flirting and dancing until five o'clock, and the married men will retire to drink and smoke in the ante-room until they fall unconscious.'

'The married women?'

'They'll go to bed. I want you to find some way of letting me know when you go. Then I'll deal with Basil.'

She put her hand against his chest, and looked up. 'I think he means to – to visit me tonight.'

'Damn his impudence! I'll deal with him, I tell you.'

They were interrupted.

'Will you dance with me, Emilia Edvardovna? May I cut in, sir?'

A slight, male figure she would not have recognised, but the voice was Sasha Suslov's. She met Alexei's eyes and the same startled thought occurred to both of them. They both laughed.

'The eyes of love,' Alexei said. 'Take her, then, Sasha, but don't make a nuisance of yourself.'

She danced a great deal, with Sasha, with Adishka, with Andrei Kovanin, with Dima Suslov, who apologised profusely for his younger brother's importunity, and several times with Basil. He was merry, and grew merrier as the evening progressed. Emily wondered guiltily whether Alexei was already trying to get him drunk, but whenever she looked round, Alexei was prominently playing the host, dancing with self-important dowagers and shy wallflowers, standing at the side of the floor and talking gravely with substantial gentlemen.

At about half-past twelve she felt she had had enough: her feet were very hot, her legs and head ached. She excused herself to her latest partner, looked around, couldn't see Basil; but Alexei was near, and turned his head towards her as she looked. A slight nod was all that was needed, and then she slipped away.

In her bedchamber Tanya was curled up asleep in the armchair. Emily roused her and let her undress her and take down her hair. When she was in her nightgown she said, 'All right, Tanya, off you go to bed. I'll manage on my own.'

When the maid had gone, Emily put on her dressing-gown and sat down on her bed to finish brushing out her hair. She didn't feel at all sleepy now, only terribly hungry and thirsty – supper seemed a long time ago. She wondered if Alexei would be successful in keeping Basil away. Alexei! She'd hardly had time to think about him, and yet she had thought about no-one else. She felt that she was waiting, held in a pause between two acts of a play – the musical interlude, while behind the curtain fundamental changes of scene were taking place. When the curtain went up something new would happen – new and surprising, she felt. She hummed a tune under her breath, content to wait, brushing her hair in long, even strokes.

She picked up a strand of it and curled it round her fingers. His was a shade darker, barley-coloured, toffee-coloured, but fair where the sun had bleached it. And his eyes, golden like a wild cat's, full of changing thoughts. And his mouth, so alive, made for things other than eating and speaking. She shivered with premonition; and the door opened softly.

He stood there, clothed except for his coat. 'Success,' he said. She stopped in mid-stroke, brush suspended, waiting for what would come next. 'How beautiful you are,' he said.

'Where is he?' she asked. She didn't feel safe yet.

'Gone,' he said, and smiled. 'God bless Youna Volkov for ever and ever, amen! A suggestion dropped like a stone in the untroubled pool of his mind sent out ripples, and ten minutes later he was wheedling Basil away to the mess for a night of drinking and cards. They, the Suslovs, and Vanya Kovanin are gone, gone, gone.'

She smiled too. 'I'm saved, then.'

He cocked his head. 'There is a little supper laid out for me in my study. Would you care to share it with me, Princess?'

She felt the thump of recognition deep inside her, and this time she knew exactly what it was. 'I was just thinking how hungry I am,' she managed to say.

279

'I know,' he said. 'Go along – can you find the way? I'll join you in five minutes.'

The leaping firelight – someone must have been in to make up the fire quite recently – and a lamp turned low. On a small table near the sagging armchair a tray with a decanter of wine, a plate of sandwiches wrapped in a napkin, and a bowl of fruit: Crimean apples and pears, grown specially for the Christmas market, and hothouse grapes, red and white. She sat down on the rug, drawing her robe around her, feeling rather like a child allowed to sit up late. On the chimney-piece a French ormolu clock ticked lightly and unimportantly; the logs in the fireplace made the comfortable small sounds she had grown up with in England. *Not all Russian*, she thought, *not every bit of me*.

The door opened soundlessly and he came in, wearing a silk dressing-gown now. The sight of it made her suddenly nervous, and he must have seen it because he said, 'All serene. Don't be afraid.'

'What about . . . ?' She didn't really like to ask, but he knew what she meant.

'Anna? She's still enjoying the ball. I told her I'd had enough.'

'But won't she wonder where you are?'

'We have separate bedrooms. I often come in here to read when I can't sleep. And she never comes in here. Anything else?'

'Don't laugh at me.'

'All right. Have some supper. We'll have to share a glass. I ordered it before the ball, but I didn't quite like to ask for two glasses. It seemed like tempting fate.'

He came to sit on the rug with her, cross-legged. She had never seen a grown-up man do that, and it charmed her. His feet were bare, she noted, and that made her feel rather strange. They were very white, the toes long and knobbly: she had a sudden and foolish desire to hold and protect them, as though they were unfortunate plain children.

'What it is?' He paused in handing her the glass. Really, he was absurdly sensitive to her thoughts.

'I've never seen your feet before,' she said.

'I should hope not,' he laughed. 'Is that all? My dear lovely candle-flame, don't make me completely helpless before we've had some supper.'

'Russian endearments are so nice,' she said, taking the wine.

280

'Candle-flame, little soul, little star – romantic. English ones sound embarrassed. Englishmen only call their wives "my dear" – short and gruff, you know, like clearing one's throat.'

'I imagine you know as little about what English husbands do and say as I do. Have a sandwich.'

'What are they?'

'Pâté de foie gras, of course.'

She laughed. 'How traditional!' They chatted softly in the firelight as they ate and shared the wine. He took the bowl of grapes into his lap and fed them both alternately, putting them into her mouth carefully, as though feeding a bird.

'What are you thinking?' he asked.

'Oh, how easy and comfortable this is.'

'Shouldn't it be?'

'Yes, yes it should, but I didn't think it ever would be with a man. It's just as if we aren't different sexes at all.'

He put the bowl away from him. 'Well,' he said, his eyes very still, though his voice was a little unsteady, 'you seem to have brought us most succinctly to the point. Come here.'

She obeyed at once, though she was trembling with anticipation. She moved across the rug to sit beside him. He put his hand to the back of her neck, pushed his fingers up through her hair so that she felt them against her scalp. His face was close; he looked at her with grave attention.

'Was it only a few days ago that I kissed you here? It seems like a thousand years.'

'I'm sorry I kept you waiting,' she said. 'I was very stupid.'

'Is this the right time to say it? Yes, I think so. So that there should be no doubt: I love you, Emilia Edvardovna. I am your love.'

Then he drew her head towards him; his eyes fluttered closed, and he laid his lips against hers, very quietly, as though it were a ceremony and a pledge. She breathed his breath, her eyes closed so that they shared the same darkness. She felt his presence close and warm in the darkness, passing through her and wrapping her round, as if it inhabited some other dimension than space, as if it came to her through time – something she knew and would know and had always known.

She brought up her own hands to his head, and at the rough-silk feeling of his hair and the heat of his skin everything inside her seemed to loosen and unravel. She felt also the yielding in him, and then they were kissing and holding on to each other as though

281

battered by a flood they feared would sweep them apart. She clung to him, his arms around her now, her self stripped naked, delusions ended, knowing that this, *this* was what she had been born for, what she must have.

They broke apart only to breathe. She stroked his head, marvelling at the feeling of it; looked into his face, felt hollow and helpless, hungry and desperate and light-headed, impermanent as a sand pattern before the advancing sea. She felt as though she might disintegrate and stream off into the aether. He cupped her face, and seemed to hold her soul in his hands: if she slipped she might be lost for ever.

'Alexei!'

'I'm here. *Doushenka.*'

She took hold of his shoulders to keep herself near him. Under his dressing-gown he was naked. She pushed the neck of it aside, wonderingly touched the fine, smooth skin over his collar-bone, and found herself gulping for air as though she were drowning. She met his eyes wildly, going down for the third time. 'Oh, what is it?'

'It's only love,' he said tenderly. 'Love, that's all.'

Ah, was that all? He took off her robe and laid it aside, every movement unhurried; took off her nightgown, and she was naked in the firelight, shivering violently, though he seemed to know it was not with cold. He took off his own robe, and there he was, close and real, hers to touch, no barriers between them any more. His body was smooth and golden, flat and spare where hers was rounded, with long bones and firm muscles, every line of it taut with desire.

'Alexei,' she said. She was desperate for him, but she wanted to say to him don't hurry, take for ever. She held his eyes pleadingly: don't be swayed by my fever, take until the end of time.

'Yes,' he said. 'Yes, it's all right.'

And he didn't hurry; or perhaps it was just that the wheel stopped again and let infinity in. He laid her down on the rug and arched himself across her, covered her nakedness, kissed her forehead and nose and lips, kissed her neck and breasts, all unhurriedly, while she ached for him, burned up like paper with wanting him.

'I love you,' he said finally. 'I've always loved you. Since the world began. Until it ends.'

'Yes,' she said. 'Alexei – I know now.'

'Emilia, my soul,' he said; and then he came into her.

Love, she thought through all her senses. Only love. Only that. And then there was no room for thought, only sense; only being.

'Now it begins,' he said. He was sitting up, leaning against the chair. She leaned against him, his arms around her, hers holding his against her. He kissed the top of her head, rested his cheek against her hair. She could feel his contentment, and it seemed a glorious thing to be part of. 'Just beginning, Emilusha, think of that. Everything still to come.'

'I was so stupid,' she said, but without heat. She watched a flame flicker along the top of a log. It was the bluest thing she had ever seen, bluer than sapphire, than gentian. She thought she had never seen anything so exquisite. 'You knew all the time, didn't you?'

'From the first moment I saw you.'

'Why didn't I know? Why was I so stupid and blind and – '

'Don't curse yourself.'

'But all the time I've wasted – !'

'Anticipation can be sweet.' Then he laughed. 'Well, to be truthful, it's been hard to hold off all this while. Many's the time – but I knew you must do it on your own, or it wouldn't work. You had to come to me.'

'Oh, Alexei . . . '

His arms tightened. 'The way you say my name,' he said. 'Oh my soul, we are going to have such a love!'

She smiled into the flames. 'Antony and Cleopatra?'

'Better than that!'

'And will it go on for ever?'

'Longer.'

She turned her head to kiss his arm, the only part of him she could reach. 'Absurd!'

'I love you,' he said, as he had said already many times. He seemed to like to say it very often. It reminded her of something, and he felt the thought, and said, 'What is it?'

'How do you always know when I think of something?'

'I know you. I know everything about you. What did you think?'

'I just realised what it was that was missing when Basil proposed to me. He never said he loved me. Now I think of it, he never has.'

'Ah yes, Basil!'

'Oh dear, shouldn't I have mentioned him?' She wriggled round

283

to face him, and he looked down at her pointed breasts brushing his chest.

'If you do things like that, it won't matter what you say,' he said. 'Conversation will be out of the question.'

She smiled, running her hand over his skin. The side nearest the fire was as hot as sand, the other side cold as water. 'I don't mind. I want to do it with you for ever. I see now with Basil it was the thing itself that I liked, nothing to do with him.'

'If you talk about doing it with Basil again I shall probably have to strangle you.'

'No, but listen, don't you see? It's a pleasant, good thing just in itself – '

'Shameless woman!'

'But with you it becomes more than that – it's life and death and earth and God and heaven and forgiveness!'

He laughed shakily. 'All that?'

'More! Everything! Oh Alexei, I love you! I want to make love with you all the time, for ever!'

'My love.' He folded her against him, unable to find any more words just then. He held her close like a child, almost afraid of the simplicity of her passion. It made her so vulnerable; he was terrified she would be hurt. 'I would ask nothing better,' he began, but she anticipated him, pulled herself enough free to look up at him.

'*Would* ask? Isn't it that simple?' she asked. Apprehension. 'What's the matter? What are you going to say to me?'

'*Doushka*, don't be afraid. Nothing bad, I promise you. Yes, it is that simple – simple, but not easy. Our affairs are a little complicated, you must see that. There are a great many things to be done.'

'But we will do them?'

'Yes, of course, but not now, this minute. Don't look at me like that! Do you really want to rush out of this room now and wake everyone up and tell them about us?'

'Yes!' she said. And then, as he continued to look at her steadily, a reluctant smile tugged at her lips. 'Well, no, then. Not this very instant. Not with Christmas and a house full of people and everything. Is that cowardly of me?'

He laughed. 'No, eminently sensible! Now listen to me. I have to go away soon. I wish to God I didn't, but it's the Tsar's business, and I have no choice.'

'Go away?'

She sounded as if it were a sentence of death. Well, he didn't want to leave her either. 'To Germany and France. I shall be gone about six weeks, I expect. I hope not more.'

'When do you go?'

'In a week's time. You see why we can't trumpet our love from the rooftops? I'd have to go off and leave you with the row.'

'Yes, I do see, Alexei. It's just that I – I didn't – '

'Want any subterfuge to cast a shadow over our love?'

She bit her lip. 'You're laughing at me.'

'No, *doushka*. It's very hard to speak of love without sounding like a three-volume novel. They took all the words, damn them.'

She ran a hand over his flank. 'Bodies say things better,' she agreed.

'Again?' he asked, raising an eyebrow, and more.

'If you're going away, we mustn't waste any time.'

He returned her caresses, but still held off a moment.

'Will you be all right while I'm gone? You won't start to doubt, or think you must have imagined it all?'

'No, I'll be all right,' she said serious. 'I'll just wait. I'm good at waiting.'

'You trust me?'

'Yes.'

'Will you be able to cope with Basil?'

'I'll think of something. Now make love to me again, please, Alexei. I want as much as possible to remember you by.'

They had to part before the servants got up, and she felt that it must surely be the hardest parting of their lives, however many more there might be. In her mind she knew that it was all right, that it would be all right, but her senses seemed to feel they were being torn from him for ever.

'It's like leaving your dog behind, and not being able to explain you're coming back,' she said.

'You do say the most extraordinary things.'

'Well, so do you.'

'We'd be wasted on anyone else.'

At the door. 'Say goodbye here. We must creep through the passages. Kiss me, love. I'll try to find a way for us to be together again before I go, but in case we can't – '

Some time later. 'I heard someone moving upstairs. We must go. I'll see you at breakfast.'

'Breakfast!' she waid wonderingly. 'What a strange word, when you come to consider it. So the ordinary world still exists after all?'

'All too solidly,' he said, turning the doorknob.

'Alexei, how will we manage?' she said suddenly. 'With the others, I mean. Won't they notice?'

'Just act naturally. You'd be surprised how little most people see. Besides, neither of us is as interesting to any of them as we are to each other.'

'I shall cling to that thought,' she said gravely.

Valya came into the morning-room where Emily was sitting on the floor playing picture-cards with Roxane and trying to keep Tatya from eating them.

'Have you been left with those children again? It's shameful the way you're exploited,' he said in his mild way.

'I'm not exploited. I like it,' Emily said, looking up and smiling.

He paused on his way to his chair to look down at her, and consider her radiant face. 'I don't think Anna would like to see Princess Narishkina sitting on the floor like that.'

'This isn't Princess Narishkina,' she laughed. 'It's only Emily Paget.'

'Yes,' he said thoughtfully, almost to himself, 'I was rather afraid of that.'

She didn't hear him over Zansha's voice. He sat down on a hard chair nearby and watched her for a few minutes as she advanced the game against fearful odds. When a pause came, he said carefully, 'My dear, I know it isn't really any of my business – '

She looked up in quick apprehension, confirming his suspicions.

'I beg your pardon, sir?'

'I think you may be heading for disaster,' he said quietly. 'Most people go about with their heads under their arms, but everything gets noticed sooner or later.'

She was scarlet with embarrassment, but still did not speak.

'Must you do it?' he asked at length.

'Yes,' she breathed; then, 'It isn't what you think!'

He stood up. 'Really, I don't think anything.' He began to turn away.

'Uncle Valya,' she said impulsively.

He turned back, but she seemed not to be able to finish what she had begun.

286

'I shouldn't like you to be hurt,' he said at last. 'I think I'm rather fond of you.'

'So is he,' she said, almost too quietly to be heard.

'Yes,' he said, studying her face, his own quite expressionless. 'Yes, that is apparent. The looks you give each other I could light my pipe with. Well, as I said, it's not my business. And he at least is old enough to know what he's about.'

Oh, he was going, and the pain was so bad she didn't know how to hide it. How calm everyone else was, conditioned by his frequent absences. 'How long this time, Alyosha? If you see any more of that special schnapps on your travels, you might bring some back.'

Anna was cross. 'I don't know why the Emperor can't send someone else once in a while. There's the Razumovskys' ball coming up, and I suppose you won't be back in time for it!'

'No. I'm sorry. But Adishka will take you.'

'Oh, Adishka! It's always Adishka! I don't know why I didn't marry him in the first place!'

'Because I didn't ask you,' Adishka retorted, stung.

'I'll bring you some dress silk from Paris.' Placatingly. To Adishka: 'And a new hat for you.'

'Just come back safely. I don't want your wife on my hands permanently.'

Really going now. In the hall, the last farewells. Kissing Tatya, too young to fear partings. Lifting up Modeste. 'What shall I bring you back, my son?'

My son! Emily ached: the children of him that should have been mine!

Modeste looking solemnly into his father's face. 'A pony,' he said at last, judiciously.

'Shall I pack it in my valise, or in my trunk?'

Modeste didn't understand. 'Will you finish the story tonight?'

'Not tonight. I shan't be here tonight. I explained to you, I'm going away for lots of nights.'

'How many? This many?' A starfish hand spread before his father's face.

'Lots more. Mama will explain it to you.'

Emily's turn now, almost the last. His hand holding hers, everything of them streaming through that one point of contact: they ought to light up like electric globes! She lifted her eyes to his face, and felt numb and dumb, not to be able to tell him everything she meant. *I love you! Oh come back soon! Be safe! Think about me all the time!*

He smiled – surely he never smiled like that at anyone else. 'Goodbye, Emilia. Keep out of trouble, won't you? Don't go changing the world until I get back.'

'I'll wait,' she said.

And then he was gone. When the door was finally closed she turned back with the others into the house, and felt utterly lost. She hadn't an idea how to pass even the next five minutes. What would she do with six whole weeks?

Chapter Seventeen

Going back to her own house was better, for there weren't things to remind her of him in every room. To occupy her mind she flung herself into a violent redecoration of rooms that really hardly needed it. Not that it mattered: there was no shortage of money, and Basil approved. He liked new things. Given the choice, he would always be changing and redesigning.

Emily wished it had been summer, so that she could have worked on her garden. She thought plants would have been more soothing than furniture. Aunt Yenya had given her some indoor plants, and she did her best with them, repotting and taking slips. Beyond the double windows the silent snow fell thick and soft as feathers on a silent world, muffling, disguising, smoothing out. Sleep, world, until he comes back. Nothing important can happen until then.

Adishka came to see her, trailing Sasha like a loose cotton on his coat that he hardly noticed any more.

'What did Alyosha mean about keeping out of trouble? Was that a dig at me?'

'It was only a joke, I'm sure. You know he's very fond of you.'

'I wonder sometimes.' Adishka's joints ached in the winter, and his mood was often low. 'I must be a drain on him – living in his house, eating his food, taking up his time – '

'For goodness' sake!' Emily said briskly. 'You can't think he cares about that.'

'I don't know. No, I suppose he doesn't. He's the most generous man in the world – that's what makes it worse. You like him, don't you?'

'Of course.'

'You see – he has everything. Handsome, rich, highly placed with the Emperor, and likeable into the bargain. If only one could dislike him, it would be easier.'

'Adishka, don't be absurd!'

'Being highly placed with the Tsar isn't much of a privilege,' Sasha said. 'When the new order sweeps Bloody Nicholas away – '

'Sasha, you mustn't talk like that in my house,' Emily said firmly. 'Anyway, you don't mean it. You're not a revolutionary.'

'Yes I am!' Sasha said stoutly. 'I've been reading some of Ulyanov's writings over Christmas – '

'Who?'

'Ulyanov, the leader of the Bolsheviks. He's in exile in Switzerland. Anyway, he says we can't change the old order; it has to be swept away completely.'

'I don't care what he says, you're not to say it in my house. And if you go on talking like that I shan't speak to you any more.'

Sasha went red, part embarrassment, part frustration.

'Just ignore him,' Adishka said contemptuously. 'He doesn't know what he's talking about. Emilia, you will come to the meeting on Tuesday? We're going to make a resolution calling for the annulment of the emergency laws, and I'm sure you must know more about the law than most of us, with working at the legal advice centre.'

'Gross flattery,' Emily said. 'You just want me to take you in the motor car.'

But she would go. She must have something to fill the time until Alexei came back and life began again.

Natasha had gone back with Yenya and Valya to Archangel for a long visit. Emily missed her company, the tea visits and shopping trips they usually made together. She didn't blame her grandmother for advancing the match with Basil. After all, it had been what she herself had wanted, and Natasha was not to know how Emily had mistaken her own wishes.

She saw, now the pink clouds of delusion had been blown away, that she had overestimated her grandmother's powers of intellect and penetration. Natasha was a kind, warm-hearted, lively, amusing, affectionate woman; but she was of her generation, her education was no more than moderate, and she had never either desired or been obliged to stretch her mind. Emily saw clearly what her own mistake had been – the same mistake over and over again. As a child she had looked up to adults as creatures with greater power and greater knowledge than herself, and she had simply not got out of the habit. She had gone on assuming anyone older than her must know better, not understanding that there were those who stopped learning quite early in their lives, and that it was possible for her to be better equipped mentally than some of them.

Still, she missed her grandmother's company. Anna was no substitute.

'I wish you would come to luncheon tomorrow, and stay for the afternoon. You seem to have made a great hit with Modeste. He keeps talking about you and asking when you're coming again.'

'I'll come tomorrow afternoon with pleasure – '

Anna interrupted her.

'Oh, but come to luncheon too. I know you're on your own tomorrow – I checked with Basil.' Her eyes met Emily's and then slid away. 'It's all right, it will be quite respectable.'

'I didn't suppose – ' Emily began in surprise.

'I've given up spiritualism and all that sort of thing,' Anna said, addressing the wall behind Emily's shoulder. 'I started to think that perhaps it wasn't quite nice. Leone Duvitska says quite a few people are beginning to be disgusted with Father Grigori. Oh, he's a great healer, I'm sure of it, but he – well, he does horrid things with some of his female supporters. And after all, he is a peasant. It isn't right. So – no more *séances*.'

'I'm glad,' Emily said. 'But I should still have to check with Basil about luncheon.'

Anna opened her eyes wide. 'But I told you, you'll be on your own. Basil is lunching with the Kovanins and Leone. Didn't he tell you?'

Emily looked puzzled. 'No, he didn't.'

'Oh well, you can't expect to know where he is every moment of the day. You can't expect husbands to be accountable. I'm sure I hardly ever know where Alyosha is when he isn't at home.'

'But I don't understand. Surely they must have invited me as well?'

'Well, hardly! Varvara Sabinina's going to be there.' Anna surveyed Emily's face. 'Don't tell me you don't know about Basil and Varsha? Good Lord, that's been going on for years! Everybody knows.'

Emily felt cold. 'I don't know. What about Basil and Varsha? You'd better tell me.'

To her credit, Anne looked uncomfortable. 'Oh well, it isn't anything really – just a flirtation. Varsha was mad as fire when Basil married you – you must have noticed *that*. She always thought he'd come back for her, though really she'd be as comfortable to marry as a cactus, so she's only herself to blame. And she carries on with so many different men she's got no reputation left. But she takes Basil back into favour every now and then, and he doesn't like to waste the opportunity. He's got a soft spot for her, after all. They used to play together as children.'

Emily felt as though the ground had heaved under her feet. 'Let me get this straight. You're telling me that Basil is having an affair with Varvara Sabinina?'

Anna looked shocked. 'Oh, nothing like that! Good God, Basil would never actually – well, not now he's married. I suppose *before* he might have. Leone hints as much, but she doesn't know everything. I told you, it's only a flirtation – nothing to it at all. They meet now and then, dine together and so on. It doesn't mean anything serious.' She made an impatient sound. 'Everyone knows about it. You mustn't be so stuffy, Emily. Petersburg isn't the provinces. You're not some factory owner's daughter from Tula, you know.'

Emily hardly heard her. Well, she was thinking, what price Alexei's theory now? Unless, of course, Varvara counts as a fallen woman, because of her reputation. Or could Anna possibly be right that Basil doesn't actually *do* anything? It might account for Varvara's irritation. On the other hand, the reverse might account for the fact that he hasn't visited me for so long. Or perhaps he merely flirts with Varsha, and takes his exercise at Madame Clavin's.

At all events, I'm hardly in a position to object to anything Basil does; and anything that keeps him away from me is fortunate. She felt a smile working its way upwards and struggled to push it back down. Anna might think laughter at such a moment inappropriate.

Anna was still talking, advancing Emily's education in the ways of the fashionable world. 'It's quite accepted you know, as long as it's discreet. No-one thinks anything of it.'

Emily's logic reared its head. 'But if everyone knows about it, it can't be called discreet.'

Anna looked cross. 'You're just trying to be difficult. You know exactly what I mean. Anyway, your precious Natasha Petrovna's been having affairs for years! Why do you think she's gone to Archangel now?'

'To be with her family, of course.'

'Nonsense. Much you know! She's been having a passionate affair with Count Obrovitch for four years, and he's just been sent to Archangel to join the Governor's staff, so I suppose she'll be visiting Yenya pretty often over the next couple of years. And before Obrovitch it was Naumoff, and before him – '

No wonder she didn't bring me to Russia before, Emily thought with amusement. Well, she was a widow; what she did was her own affair. 'I seem to have been living in a different world from everyone else,' she said aloud.

Anna softened. 'You mustn't mind it. I tell you, it doesn't mean anything. Basil's really devoted to you. He just amuses himself with Varsha.'

'And does everyone in Petersburg amuse themselves? Or are there exceptions?'

'Oh, lots of them. Well, everyone knows the Tsar and the Empress are devoted, for a start.'

A devil tweaked at Emily. 'What about you and Alexei?'

Anna's nose went up. 'A woman in my position could hardly amuse herself in that way. And as for Alyosha – '

'Quite. Well, you've opened my eyes, Anna. I'm very grateful to you.'

'You'll come to luncheon, then?' Anna asked, sticking tenaciously to the point. 'It will just be you and me and Masha Sapetska. I know you like her.'

'Yes, I do, very much. Very well, I will come. Thank you.'

Emily sat alone in her private sitting-room, nominally writing a letter to Sylvia but not getting very far with it. There had suddenly become too many things she couldn't write about. She let the pen dry in her hand, and stared unseeingly at the flickering light of the icon lamp as her thoughts roved.

Human beings were strange, inconsistent creatures, she thought. Here was she, having – not to be euphemistic about it – having committed adultery, and evidently meaning to do so again, and yet she still felt pique and hurt and even jealousy at the thought of Basil's frolicking with Varsha Sabinina.

But that was different, said one part of her mind, and she hauled it out by the scruff of its neck and made it justify its statement. Different? Because she loved Alexei but Basil didn't love Varsha, was that it? Yes, perhaps, but not entirely. Because Basil's actions were light, thoughtless, and hers were of grave intention? Better, but not there yet. Because Basil had done it before, while Emily was still his faithful loving wife? Ah, yes, that was it! Absurd, illogical, self-centred, but that was it after all.

So recently had she loved him that the habit of it had not entirely faded yet. She ought to be grateful for his infidelities, such as they were, because they freed her from the need to feel guilty. But then, of course, it is never to other people that we answer, but to ourselves – which is why, she proposed, the same action may be a sin in some people and not in others. Heretical thought! But sin and crime are not the same, after all. Crime is our actions as they affect other people, sin our actions as they affect ourselves.

So loving Alexei is not a sin? she questioned herself sternly. A crime against Basil, against Anna, but not a sin? Convenient reasoning! It was all a matter of chronology, she thought, making fun of herself. She and Alexei ought to have met first. They had always belonged to each other; they just happened to miss each other the first time round, that was all.

But Varvara Sabinina, of all people! Her basic femininity reared its head at that point. That obvious woman, with her décolletage and her amber cigarette-holder and her silly airs – Basil preferred her to Emily! Preferred, growled her pique, anyone to Emily! Well, she need feel no guilt on his behalf, after all. And when Alexei came back . . .

She drifted off into a dream about Alexei as the sky darkened and more snow fell. Winter lay across the land like a frozen realisation of time, separating past and future with an immutable present. In the midst of changelessness, it was logically impossible to believe that anything would ever change.

She had flattered herself that Varvara and Madame Clavin together would secure her safety, but trouble hadn't gone away, only taken its eye off her for the moment. Basil came into her bedroom one night while she was sitting up in bed, reading. He looked rather flushed and strangely ruffled for him.

'Hello! This is early for you, isn't it?' Emily said, unsuspecting. 'Usually when you go to the mess you're not back until the small hours.'

'Didn't go to the mess,' Basil said. 'Dined at Felicien's with Vanya and Leone and – and some others.'

'It's still early,' Emily said. 'Wasn't the food good?'

'Oh, I had a quarrel. Well, a disagreement, anyway.' He approached and sat down on the edge of her bed, and she smelled cigar smoke on him, and brandy, and a rather heavy scent, a woman's – gardenia, she thought. Leone's, possibly – or possibly not.

'With Vanya?' Emily asked sweetly. 'What about?'

'Not with Vanya. Oh, it doesn't matter anyway,' he said hastily. He was looking at her rather owlishly. 'I thought you might like some company.'

'I was just about to go to sleep,' Emily said cautiously.

'All right,' Basil said, evidently taking it for an invitation. He pulled at his tie, and then, without standing up, began to shrug himself out of his coat. This, thought Emily, was growing perilous. His movements wafted the heavy perfume towards her, and she felt a rising irritation. Some silly lover's tiff with Varsha had spoiled his evening, and he was coming to her for comfort?

'So who else was there, at your dinner at Felicien's, to which I wasn't invited?' she asked tartly.

'I didn't think you'd want to come,' he said feebly, his coat off, pulling again at his tie. 'I know you're not fond of Leone.'

'I like her better than some of her friends,' Emily said. The tie came off, and he began fumbling with his shirt buttons. 'Varsha Sabinina, for instance. I suppose she was there.'

His fingers faltered. He looked towards her cautiously. 'Why should you think that?'

'Because you reek of that awful scent she wears – the one you can smell right across the room.'

He looked at her for a moment in surprise and confusion, and then tried for dignity. 'That's a very unladylike remark. I think you ought to remember who you are.'

'And you should remember who you are!'

'Who am I, then?' he retorted childishly.

Emily caught herself up, about to say *my husband*. Dear me, this business is full of pitfalls. She threw her largest brick. 'I should have thought Prince Basil Narishkin would have been above carrying on an affair with someone like Varvara Sabinina!'

It fell disastrously short. Basil chuckled in a pleased sort of way, his fingers continuing with the buttons. 'Why, Princess Narishkina, you're jealous! My dear little Emilusha, how very nice and flattering! But there's no need.'

'I think there's every need,' Emily said desperately, as he bent down to pull off one boot. 'It's not very flattering to me, is it, when my husband consorts openly – '

'It's only a flirtation, darling, nothing to upset yourself about.' The other boot came off and he straightened up. 'I assure you, I keep myself wholly for you. All for you, my darling wife. But I've

295

been neglecting you recently, I admit. I'm sorry. Let me make it up to you.'

Emily cowered back on the pillows as he leaned towards her, his shirt gaping, but held at the neck by his collar-stud and the ribbon of his order, which he had forgotten to take off.

'No, Basil. I don't want you. Go away!'

He grinned. 'Well, this is a change of heart, I must say. What ever happened to my eager little wife, who used to pester me in such an indecent way?'

'She learned better. Go away, I tell you! How dare you come to me stinking of that woman's scent?'

That seemed to annoy him. 'I'll come to you any way I please. You are my wife, remember. I have some rights in this house.' He pressed her down against the pillows, crushing her hands under him, and tried to kiss her. She twisted her head back and forth on the pillow to avoid him.

'Basil stop it!' She wasn't really in any danger. He was still fully trousered, and with the bedclothes between them as well he couldn't possibly get at her. 'Get up! You're making a fool of yourself!'

That penetrated the brandy fumes – that and perhaps the indignity of getting a mouthful of her hair by mistake. He hauled himself slowly off her and sat up, trying to look unembarrassed.

'I don't know what's got into you,' he said, and there was a quaver of righteous complaint in his voice that made her, even in this distressing moment, want to laugh. 'There's nothing really between Varsha and me. Nothing to be jealous of, anyway. It's just a little harmless fun. You should have more pride.'

'I'm not jealous of Varsha,' she snapped incautiously.

'Well, what then? I thought you loved me?' He grew peevish. 'You have a duty to me, you know. You're supposed to provide me with a son.'

She was stung to retaliation. 'If you want a son, you can father one on one of your whores at Madame Clavin's!'

He looked utterly amazed. 'What?'

'I saw you coming out of there. You can't deny it.'

'I wouldn't dream of denying it. You must be mad to speak of such a thing to me! Quite mad! No decent woman would think of mentioning such a place.' He seemed genuinely indignant. 'I think you must be unbalanced – I've thought so before. You've let yourself dwell on unwholesome ideas, and it's turned your mind.'

Emily suddenly felt exhausted with the whole mad, futile

argument. 'Oh go away, Basil. You're giving me a headache.' He opened his mouth to speak, and she said desperately, *'Please!'*

To her surprise, he stood up, picked up his discarded clothes and went, and she was able to collapse on the pillows and reflect on how badly she had handled things. She was trembling with distress. She had never quarrelled with anyone in her life, and now to quarrel with Basil, of all people – to have deliberately picked a quarrel with him! She felt guilty and confused and uncomfortable. What a dreadful situation it was. She longed desperately to run away, and for a heady, foolish moment or two visualised herself doing it, packing a bag and slipping out of the house.

But there was nowhere for her to go. She had no friends who were not Basil's first, and her grandmother was far away. Oh Alexei, she thought, why aren't you here, protecting me? She didn't even know where he was at this moment. She had said she would be all right while he was away, that she would cope. Arrogant words! She had made a mess of the very first encounter. She rolled miserably onto her front and buried her face in her arms for comfort.

She must have fallen asleep, for she woke suddenly with a prickling sensation at the back of her neck, a premonition of danger. She snapped her head up, rolled over in a quick defensive movement, and saw Basil coming towards her across the room. The sound of the door opening and closing must have woken her. He was dressed in his nightshirt now, with a dressing-gown hanging loose over his shoulders, and had obviously sluiced water over his face, for his front hair stood up in damp spikes.

A quick glance at the clock across the room told her that she must have been asleep for about half an hour. Basil seemed to have sobered up, from the steadiness of his gait, but he hadn't recovered his good humour. His face was set in rather ugly lines, and his eyes, slightly pink around the blue, looked hard and shiny, like a stuffed animal's.

'Basil? What are you doing here? I thought you'd gone to bed,' she said nervously. He didn't answer, didn't speak at all as he walked across to the bed, shrugged off his dressing-gown, trod out of his slippers, and took hold of the bedclothes. 'What are you doing?' she said, trying to hold them down.

He whipped them back with a sharp movement of his arm, and climbed in beside her. The look on his face made the flesh shrink on her bones.

'What are you doing?' she said again, her voice and hope fading.

He pulled the covers over them both, and began to pull up her nightgown. 'I thought it was about time we both did our duty,' he said.

'No!' She pulled at his hands, but he was stronger than her. She began to struggle.

'Stop it,' he said with horrible calm. 'You'll only hurt yourself.'

'I won't let you,' she said with growing panic. 'Go back to your whores! I won't let you after you've been with them.'

He didn't answer. Her nightgown was up around her waist now, and he began to climb on top of her. She pushed at him futilely with both hands, her breath sobbing with the effort, and with fear.

'No! No! Don't you dare!' But he caught one hand and twisted it out of the way, holding it to the pillow with his, holding the other hand down with his elbow. His knees were between hers. She finally understood that he really was going to do it, that she couldn't stop him. Horror and helplessness flooded her. 'I'll scream. Basil, I warn you!'

He was unperturbed, going about his purpose with an indifference that was the worst thing of all. 'Scream away,' he invited. 'Who do you think will come running? You're my wife.'

She didn't scream. She felt him against her, and then inside her, and gave only a small, despairing cry. The thing was done in silence except for her sobbing breaths, and then he was finished. She stopped struggling. They were both still for a moment, and then he withdrew, pulled himself off her, sat up with hunched back towards her. She lay absolutely still, afraid to move, as though she were broken and only held together by immobility.

After a while he swung his legs out of bed, picked up his dressing-gown, and slid his feet slowly and clumsily into his slippers. Finally he looked at her, lying as he had left her, her arms flung back, head turned to the side, like a dead bird broken in flight. He felt a piercing shame. He no longer remembered what their quarrel had been. He felt as he had felt as a small boy, when once in defiance he had deliberately smashed his mother's spectacles because she had berated him for something he had done. She had hurt his feelings, so he had smashed the nearest thing to her he could find, something that was almost a part of her; but as he had looked at the twisted gold frames and the shattered glass lying on the floor, he had felt as though it was her body lying there, crushed under his feet.

'Emilia?' he said tentatively. 'Emilia, look at me.'

She didn't move, only closed her eyes, and a tear seeped out from under her eyelashes. He felt utterly bereft, rebuked, driven out. He was alone in a large and confusing universe, and his mother had turned away from him.

'I'm sorry,' he said in a small voice. 'Oh forgive me!'

Still she did not move. After a moment he turned and crept out, grieving, back to his own room, to crawl into bed and pull the covers over his head.

The thaw came early, bringing the usual inconveniences of mud and flood and raw fogs that tore at the throat, colds and coughs and fevers, and swollen, chilblained feet. It was a time to reflect that only a visionary who was also a madman would have built this great city here, in a swamp at the northern end of the Baltic.

Ice floes jostled their way along the Neva, bumping and grinding along the quaysides, and a cousin of Masha Sapetska's – a handsome young Guards' officer noted for his singing-voice – was crushed and drowned in the course of trying to win a bet that he could not cross the river by jumping from iceberg to iceberg.

The people who came into the law centre – shapeless, androgynous bundles of coats, shawls, scarves, even sacks – coughed and dripped through their stumbling requests. Because the door opened and closed so often, it was impossible to keep the office properly warm. Peter the Great had a lot to answer for, Emily thought, stamping her feet under her desk to keep the blood moving.

But soon it was over, the fog cleared, the spring bulbs were thrusting through the brown-earth, and the pussy willows were furring the branches. The cold wind still blew, but at least it was a drying wind, and when it dropped for a moment or two, there was real warmth at last in the sunshine. Emily walked in her garden again, suddenly revealed like a room when the dust covers are whipped off, and marvelled at the tender mist of green spreading through the bare black trees, at the sturdiness of the first fragile flowers, at the astonishing power of the wren's song.

The trees of her pleached walk were about to break any moment. She paused to look along it, imagining it as it would be. Three years, she thought, would see it grown into shape. In the summer of 1917 I shall walk under its perfectly knitted shade, and then I shan't be able to remember what it looked like now.

Well, no, she thought, with a mixture of satisfaction and wistfulness, of course I shan't be here in the summer of 1917. By then

299

Alexei and I shall be together (oh God, I hope and trust!) and we'll be – wherever it is we go. She tried and failed to imagine what was going to happen. The future had never looked more impenetrable to her, not even when she was fifteen and fretting to escape from the prison of Bratton. Well, the world held more prisons than she as a child had guessed. This house – her own house – even this garden: a prison was wherever you didn't want to be.

She walked to the end and turned, and there was Alexei, standing by the door from the garden-room, a familiar figure in his blue-grey greatcoat, his hat in his hand and his light hair stirred by the cold young breeze. A moment of disbelief, and then not so much rapturous joy as huge relief. She thought she would have run to him with outstretched arms, but she stood still, rigid with pleasure, and he came at last to her.

He halted a few paces off and they looked at each other seriously.

'You've got thinner,' he said finally.

'So have you.'

He was studying her face. 'I didn't realise you would be so unhappy. I'm sorry.'

'You've been gone so long. Twelve weeks, not six.'

'Twelve weeks and three days and six hours since I last saw you. You see, I've missed you too.'

'Oh Alexei!'

He crossed the space between them and both her hands were in his, drawing life into herself. She could feel him trembling.

'I want to kiss you, but I can't, not here. Are you really all right? You said you would be.'

'It's all right now, but it has been – very bad. I'll tell you, but not now. How long have you been back?'

'Since last night.'

'So long?'

'Couldn't you feel it? You ought to have known I was near.'

'Couldn't you have come before now? Sixteen, eighteen hours – '

'You must know that the first thing I wanted to do was to rush round here to you, but I couldn't. We must do things properly. *Doushka*, I've got to see you; I've got to talk to you.'

'Yes! Yes, but where? When?'

'When do you go to the law centre?'

'Tomorrow morning. I work there from eight to twelve.'

'I'll pick you up at twelve.'

'Where will we go?'

'Don't ask questions now. I'm going to kiss you – can you bear it? And then I have to go. I'm on my way to the Ministry.' He bowed his head and laid his lips against hers softly, and she tasted his breath and the scent of his skin, and her sleeping self stirred towards him. She felt him begin to respond, and then withdraw.

'Not now,' he said, blinking like someone coming out of a dark house into sunlight. He let go of one of her hands, lifted the other to his lips, and gave it back to her. 'Tomorrow. I have an interview in the morning. If I'm a little late, don't worry. Wait for me.'

'I'll wait.'

'God bless you,' he said hurriedly, and went quickly away.

'What is this place?' It was a part of Petersburg she didn't know, quiet, clean, respectable – eminently middle-class. Nursemaids in blue uniforms and white veils pushed perambulators or held the hands of little boys in sailor suits. Women in replicas of the Empress's clothes stepped out of taxi-cabs laden with shopping. The block after block of apartment buildings were alike, anonymous and self-effacing, and every window had lace curtains or lowered blinds, the better to maintain privacy.

'It's an apartment belonging to Blavatsky at the Ministry. His mother used to live in it. She's dead now, but he hasn't got round to letting it again.' He saw her expression out of the corner of his eye. 'She didn't die of anything infectious,' he protested.

'It's not that. It just seems – '

He understood her reservations. 'Better this than a hotel,' he pointed out. 'I'll arrange things better another time, but it was the best I could do at short notice. I had to see you.'

'Yes. I'm sorry. I shouldn't be so nice.'

'You should be. And you shall be as nice as you like when things are sorted out.'

There was a frown between his brows, though, and she reflected that, innocent as she was, she couldn't begin to guess how difficult things might be to *sort out*. She remembered all the fuss and lawyers when Uncle Westie had wanted to divorce Aunt Maud – this casting-the-first-stone business again! Well, but that was England, and Uncle Westie was a marquess and Aunt Maud an earl's daughter. Things, as far as she could gather, were easier in Russia, and she at least was a nobody, even if he was Count Kirov and head of the family.

301

And then, of course, he hadn't yet said that divorce was what he meant; but she didn't want to think about that.

The apartment was dark, because the shutters were closed, and cold, and it had a smell about it like dead chrysanthemums. Alexei went in ahead to let in the light, and Emily lingered in the hallway, glimpsing through open doors the ghostly shapes of furniture under holland covers and bagged chandeliers. *Not here*, said her Russian soul, *not amongst these shrouds. It's unlucky.*

The light flooded the room directly ahead of her. 'Emilia, come in here,' he called. She followed his voice reluctantly.

'It's not bad, is it?' he said, tugging covers off furniture and raising surprisingly little dust. The windows had double frames fitted, keeping out both noise and dirt, and everything had been left clean. The smell, she decided, must be the residue of lavender furniture wax.

'No, not bad.' The furniture was heavy and solid, typically nineteenth century: velvet-upholstered chairs, overstuffed sofas, elaborately legged occasional tables, bamboo plant stands in the windows, knick-knack shelves; an upright piano with a walnut case, ruched red silk under fretwork at the front, and curly brass candle-holders. Her mental eye supplied with ease the forest of framed photographs and ornaments that ought to be colonising the bare surfaces, and the jungle of palms and ferns and aspidistras in the window. The personality of the previous tenant had been conveniently removed, and what was left reminded her, comfortingly, of Aunt Maud. 'Not bad.'

He eyed her carefully. 'Come here,' he instructed.

She walked into his arms, was gathered in, enfolded at last, pressed as closely to him as she could be without actually standing inside his clothes. She felt everything in her sigh with relief.

'It's been so awful,' she said into his chest.

'Yes, I know,' he replied into her hair. After a moment she felt him lift his head. 'You know, we might make this our base for the time being. Blavatsky would be glad enough to get it off his hands.'

She freed herself to look up at him. Here? This? What was going on? 'Surely it wouldn't be worth it, for so little time,' she said cautiously.

He eyed her with what might almost have been apology. 'It may take a while to work things out. Come and look at the other rooms.'

'A guided tour? I don't like it that much,' she objected.

He smiled in a particular way, and desire arrived at last with a

302

thud in the pit of her stomach. '*Doushka*, I need very badly to make love to you, and none of these sofas is suitable.'

So she put her hand in his and went with him. He opened the door into the master bedroom. A huge bed with a walnut bedhead and a stiff white cotton counterpane; a massive walnut wardrobe, double-fronted, with mirrors; walnut tallboy; mahogany washstand with basin and ewer; icon of Our Lady of Kazan and silver lamp. The white bed gleamed in the dimness, reflected in the looking-glass. The smell of dead flowers was stronger in here – not the smell of furniture wax at all, Emily realised, but of an old lady's lavender sachet. Her eyes widened. Blavatsky's mother hadn't gone from this room. Emily was seized with a sudden unreasonable conviction that the wardrobe door would begin to swing open, and that inside all the old lady's clothes would still be hanging, rack upon rack of legless, headless ghosts, smelling of her – faintly, corpsily, of lavender sachet.

'Not in here,' she whispered, her hand cold in Alexei's. 'I can't in here.'

He looked at her once, and stepped back into the hall, closing the door of the bedroom behind him, shutting the ghost in. 'Perhaps not,' he agreed. He opened another door. Spare bedroom. Emily's hair lowered itself onto her scalp with relief. Nothing had ever happened in here. There was no trace of humanity, no old lady, no smell, just the dustless odour of infinity.

'All right?' Alexei asked.

'All right.'

The counterpane was clean and white and unmarked. They didn't bother to open the blinds. In the half-light of the shuttered room they took off their clothes and lay down on top of the bed. Emily thought there might be some difficulty after so long, some shyness, but his body seemed dear and familiar to her, and as he stretched out beside her she felt only a hunger and a haste to be part of him again. His mood seemed in tune with hers. He waited only to kiss her thoroughly before moving over her, and she turned willingly under him and welcomed him in.

Afterwards he held her tightly in his arms, and drew the other half of the counterpane over them, for their flesh was chilled by the unheated air.

'That's better! Oh God, how I've missed you,' he said. 'I was so afraid that I'd lose you, that I'd come back and find you gone away, or different – changed your mind about it all.'

'That couldn't happen,' she said. 'It was real.'

'Yes. But you are different. Not towards me, but something's happened, hasn't it? You seem so much older.'

'Sometimes lately I've felt as old as there is,' she said; and pressed closely in his arms, she told him what had happened between her and Basil.

He listened in silence so absolute that she was sure he was holding his breath. When she came to the end of the first part and paused, he said, 'I should never have left you with him. I should have taken you away, installed you somewhere, to wait for me.'

'You couldn't do that,' she said. 'That would have made me – I don't know – your property. It would have been wrong.'

'Better than to leave you at his mercy. I should have guessed.'

'No, listen – you said before that I had to come to you in my own time, and you were right then. I can't be less than you, or what is there to love? We are equal, or we are nothing. That's what I've been thinking while you've been away. We're different from other people, and that means we can't do things the same way. Sometimes it will make it easier, but sometimes harder.'

'You're right, of course.' He smiled against her hair. 'You *are* older. About ten years older than when I went away, I think. I suppose coping with Basil did that. You know, don't you, that I want to kill him?'

'Oh no, poor Basil! It wasn't so bad, Alexei, really. It was horrible at the time, but afterwards – he was so sorry, and so unhappy. Since then he's been like a remorseful child; and so kind to me, and polite, and thoughtful. We've lived very peacefully together since then. And it had one good result, that he hasn't troubled me any more. I don't think he will. I don't think he'll ever be able to approach me in bed again. We're like brother and sister now – a much older sister. I'm really – quite fond of him.'

He was silent a while, and she could feel him thinking. They were not all good thoughts, she knew that. In the end she pushed herself back from him, and lay on her side so that she could look at him. Their legs were interlocked, their hands clasped, their faces half a pillow apart.

'So, then,' she said, 'what is to happen to us?'

He didn't answer for a while. Then he sighed and said, 'Do you know where I've been?'

'To Germany and France, wasn't it?'

'Yes. Ostensibly to look at machinery and methods for improving agriculture. In reality, to make an assessment of the number and capacity of their munitions factories.'

'Munitions?'

'Implements of war.'

'Yes, I know what they are. But why? Was it just a routine tour?'

'You haven't heard any talk of war, then?' Emily shook her head. 'You will. It's already being discussed at ministerial level. It won't take long to filter through to the drawing-rooms.'

She was puzzled. 'But when? Against whom?'

'Neither of those things really matters,' he began.

'Oh, come,' she protested. 'You can't have a war against nobody. You can't have a war without a reason.'

'All wars are without reason,' he said, and at her sound of protest, he smiled crookedly. 'All right, it was a tempting piece of rhetoric, I grant you. But the fact is that at the moment every government in the world knows that a war is possible, even likely, and it won't be long before it tips over from being likely into being inevitable. They all think it's worth the risk, that they'll come out of it with advantages. When the time comes, an excuse will be found to start it. The bonfire has been assembled; any match will do to light it.'

'But wars don't happen like that, surely? A war between *whom* anyway?' she insisted.

'I don't know yet. Listen, *doushka*. England, Germany and Russia have all been industrialising themselves at a tremendous rate. England had a head start, of course, but in the last eight years Russia has increased her production so fast she stands third in the world only to those two countries, and if things go on at the same rate, she'll overtake them in three or four years' time. Hundreds of thousands of peasants are leaving the land and going into factories. Thousands of miles of railroads have been laid. And then there's Austria, France, Italy – they're all scrambling into a new, industrial world. All over Europe, goods are being made, wealth created, and wealth is power, in states as in individuals.'

'I see that, but – '

'England is an old empire, powerful, but being challenged on all sides for markets and trade routes. She has social unrest, clamour for political change – you know that! – a desperate situation in Ireland. War is always good for a government, to take the people's minds off its shortcomings. And the rewards of war may be new markets for old goods.'

'England would never go to war except for a good cause,' Emily said. She felt his words were nonsense, but they frightened her.

'Look at Germany, then – a new nation, only forty-odd years old; vigorous, ready for expansion, longing for an empire; and ruled by a man who adores wearing military uniforms and holding reviews, who has his personal deformities to avenge on all of mankind. Look at France – torn with internal tensions, notoriously unstable, longing for a chance to avenge its defeat by Prussia forty years ago. Look at Austria, an ancient empire falling to pieces, desperately trying to contain a population of Catholics, Orthodox Slavs and Turkish Muslims, all seething with mutual hatred.'

'And what about Russia?'

'Ah, what indeed? Well, *doushka*, Russia is the Tsar even more than Germany is the Kaiser; and Nicholas is a weak man full of high moral sentiment and mystical ideals. If he gets it into his mind that it is his righteous duty before God to go to war, nothing will stop him.'

'But Alexei, none of these things really means there has to be a war.'

He seemed suddenly exhausted by the effort of explaining. 'It doesn't make any sense, I know, at the level on which people like us argue. But the sum of things is usually greater than the individual parts. I can only ask you to believe that I know what I'm talking about. I don't know when, maybe this year, maybe next, but there will be a war. Such advances have been made in the science of warfare that it's now possible to kill people in greater numbers than has ever been imagined.' He freed one hand to pass across his face, as though he wanted to wipe off a memory. From behind it he said, 'I've seen the rate at which these countries are increasing their armies and building up their stocks of weapons, and when a state has such a power, sooner or later it will use it. If you really want a reason,' he lowered his hand and looked seriously into her eyes, 'Europe will go to war because it *can*.'

She returned his gaze steadily. 'Maybe this year, maybe next?' He nodded. 'Then,' she said carefully, 'we must make sure not to waste any time.'

'We must be together,' he said. He sounded dazed. 'That's the one thing that matters. But I wish to God it weren't so complicated. There's so much to sort out. There will have to be a divorce – two divorces – before we can marry.'

She could have cried out with relief that he didn't just want an irregular liaison, that he wanted what she wanted. She shouldn't have doubted it, perhaps, but she had been without him for so much longer than she had been with him. But she only tightened her hand in his, and said, 'Yes.'

'You won't mind?' he asked. 'You won't feel – sullied by it?'

'I was never really married to Basil. And if I can marry you, I won't care for anything else. No, I won't mind. As you say, the only important thing is to be together.'

'*Doushka*, it's going to take a long time. Basil alone might let you go, for your own happiness, but I have a feeling that Basil and Anna together are going to resist. The settlements will be difficult to negotiate. And then there are my children to consider.'

'Yes,' she said in a small voice. It was hard that anyone else should be involved in their fate. It should be for them alone to decide.

'And there's one thing more.' She saw from his expression that he had come to something he was reluctant to voice; something he knew was going to hurt her. 'You said if there is war coming, we must waste no time. I wish it could be that way. But I can't begin proceedings yet, not for some months.'

'Why not?' she asked, and seeing his face, her anxiety sharpened. 'Alexei, what's happened?'

He sighed, seeing no way to soften it. 'Anna's pregnant.'

She could not have been more surprised if he had slapped her face. For a moment she couldn't speak.

'*How?*' she said at last.

He looked a protest. 'You know *how*. Don't make me tell you.'

She was bewildered. 'But – when?' And then, reproachfully, 'How could you?'

'Don't,' he said quietly. 'My darling heart, these things happen. It was just before Christmas. You were still in love with Basil, and I was in despair of ever making you notice me. I saw you with him at the Maryinsky, in your box – you looking so lovely, and him fawning over you, licensed to touch you and kiss you and talk to you and sleep with you. I was mad with jealousy. I don't think you can imagine how bad it was for me, not knowing if you would ever just turn your head and see me.'

'I think so,' she said. 'I'm sorry. But – '

'Don't,' he said again. 'It was a kind of madness, I suppose. I meant to be careful. I didn't intend *this* to happen.'

'Oh Alexei! Oh God, Alexei!'

'I know. I know. It's the last thing – I love Modeste and Tatya, but I didn't, I don't want another child of Anna.'

'I want your children!' the cry broke from her. 'It should be mine, not hers! Mine!'

He gathered her against him. 'I know. Don't you think I know? It's my punishment, but it shouldn't be yours – or hers, poor creature. She doesn't deserve to suffer for it.'

'What will you do?' she asked, her head buried in his shoulder. Her voice sounded despairing. She knew what he was going to say.

'Wait,' he said. 'I must wait until after the child is born. I couldn't spring this on her while she's pregnant. It wouldn't be fair.'

'Fair!' she moaned into his neck.

'It might be dangerous. When it's over, when the child is born, I will arrange things. I promise you.'

But, she thought, when the child is born, how will that be any more fair or more easy? Will Anna, babe in arms, be less vulnerable than Anna, babe in womb? A new child would be a new tie to fetter him to his old life, the life she had no part in.

'Is she happy about it?' she asked. He didn't answer. She lifted her face and looked at him fiercely. 'Tell me! Is she glad?'

He looked back at her steadily, facing the situation, not flinching, and in his courage she saw the foreshadowing of defeat. 'She seems so.'

She rolled over on her back, away from him, feeling bereft. All a matter of chronology, she thought bitterly; how right I was. Not fair, not fair! I didn't come first, that's all; and when my chance came, I was too slow, too stupid, too blind. If he had come home that first Christmas, when I met Basil again. If I had found out about Madame Clavin's a few weeks earlier. If Fanny had married Basil when he asked. If Anna had married Sapetsky when he asked. Only a matter of timing. Not fair! Oh, not fair!

He hung over her, wiped a tear from her cheek with a careful finger. 'My star, my soul, don't, please don't. It will be all right. Everything will be all right.'

She looked up at him, wet-eyed. 'You should have done it, that time at Schwarzenturm. You shouldn't have waited. You should have made me your lover then.'

'We were lovers,' he said tenderly. 'Then and always. Nothing changes it. We have this.' He kissed her lips, stroked her body and felt it arch under his hand. 'All this. I love you.'

'I love you too.'

'Emilusha, don't be afraid. I will never be apart from you.'

He stretched across her, and she put her arms round him, and they made love, slowly and tenderly, as if each were soothing the other of an intolerable ache. The hurt of one was the hurt of the other. She possessed and was possessed by him, pressed her mouth to his face and tasted his tears; and ceased to know where she ended, and he began.

Chapter Eighteen

He took the apartment from Blavatsky, and Emily, accepting what she could not change, made it comfortable. Alexei brought his old *mamka*, Marfa, out of retirement and installed her there as house-keeper. Emily didn't like the idea at first, fearing cold looks or silent criticism, as might be expected from an old and privileged retainer. But Marfa adored Alexei, whom she called *Al'sha*, and cared for nothing but that he should be happy. When she was first presented to Emily, she smiled shyly, peeping at her from under her brows, and curtseyed with as much respect as if she were meeting her nursling's wife for the first time.

Since they continued to use the spare bedroom, Alexei insisted that Marfa make use of the master bedroom. 'She's going to be here all the time. She might as well be comfortable.'

'But won't she mind the ghost?' Emily protested.

Alexei laughed. 'Peasants live with ghosts all the time! I'm sure Marfa knows more dead people than live ones. Ask her!'

And sure enough, Marfa only smiled when Emily tentatively broached the subject of old Madame Blavatsky's putative presence in the bedroom.

'Oh yes, *barina*, she's there all right. She and I have had quite a few talks. A very fine lady, most generous. I apologised for sleeping in her bed, and she said we were both mothers, and that's what mattered.'

Emily was intrigued. 'What do you talk about?'

'What mothers everywhere talk about, *barina* – their children, and the price of things.' Marfa hesitated. 'There was one thing, *barina*.'

'Yes?'

'Madame Blavatsky was worried that you might move her piano. She says it mustn't be put where the sunlight will strike it, or it will fade.'

Emily felt a chill finger on the back of her neck. She had actually been thinking that the piano was rather awkwardly placed, and would be better on the other side of the room.

'I wondered why it was placed where it is,' she managed to say lightly. 'You may tell her that of course I won't move it, if she doesn't like.'

'Thank you, *barina*,' Marfa said serenely. 'That will ease her mind. Quite agitated about it, she was.'

One of the first things Marfa did was to set up a beautiful corner in the spare bedroom. 'It isn't fitting you should sleep here without a blessed saint to watch over you, *barina*,' she said. Soon there was a small, cheap icon above the lamp, of a rather comfortable-looking saint holding in one hand against his chest what appeared to be three daffodil bulbs.

'I brought it from home, *barina*,' Marfa said. 'I thought it would be nice for you.'

'Which saint is it?' Emily asked.

'It's our St Nicholas, to be sure,' Marfa said. 'Don't you see his little money bags?'

'Oh, is that what they are?' It seemed rather an odd symbol for a saint. Weren't they supposed to be unworldly?

'Don't you know the story, *barina*? Well now, in the town where the blessed saint lived, there was a poor man with three daughters. He couldn't afford dowries for them, to get them wed, so he was going to make them into prostitutes. When our St Nicholas heard about it, he went past the house and threw three bags of gold in through the window, and all the girls were able to be happily married.' The dark eyes were unfathomable as she looked up at Emily. 'So he is the patron of unmarried girls, along with all the other people he looks after. If they pray to him, they get to marry the man of their choice.'

The apartment became a small world apart within Emily's world. She felt safe there. No-one in her other life would ever visit that part of Petersburg: the chances of being seen there were remote. It had its own little routines and customs, its own characters: the concierge, who lived like a crab in a dark, tea- and sausage-scented cave by the front door, and scuttled out to sweep the entrance obsessively every time anyone passed the threshold; the blind match-seller who was always on the corner, who Alexei said, only half jokingly, was probably a police spy and not blind at all; the gap-toothed girl who brought the milk every morning, in buckets with gauze covers weighted with blue beads; the pieman who came past

311

every afternoon, towing a brazier on wheels to keep hot a supply of *pirozhkis* and tea in which he did a brisk trade amongst taxi-cab drivers.

One day a sharp spell caused a pipe to freeze up, and Marfa brought in her son to unfreeze and repair it. Mischa was a pleasant-looking man with quick, brown eyes that spoke intelligence, and an educated way of speech. Alexei arrived while he was still there and greeted him with a hug.

'Mischa! It's good to see you! How's Fima? And the children? Is Kolya's leg healed up now?'

They chatted about Mischa's family, and it was obvious that Alexei had a close and detailed knowledge of them all, and that there was a great deal of affection between the two men.

'Mischa's my milk-brother, you see,' he explained to Emily. 'Such relationships are very important in Russia. We used to play together when we were boys, and Papa paid for Mischa to go to school. He's done very well for himself, haven't you, Mischa?'

'Yes, I'm an engineer in a clothing factory – not far from the advice centre where you work, *barina*,' Mischa said to Emily. 'I've seen you there many a time. You do a great deal of good there, if you'll forgive me. I've sent people along to you more than once, from the factory, and from our neighbourhood.'

Emily raised an eyebrow. 'I only type the letters,' she said. 'It's the lawyers and clerks who really have the knowledge to help.'

'But you make people feel welcome, and that means everything,' Mischa said. 'I don't expect you know how frightened they are when they go through that door, but you smile and take the terror out of it.'

'God will bless you, *barina*,' Marfa said, nodding. 'He misses nothing that goes on. And I pray for you every night to Our Blessed Lady.'

Undeserved praise, Emily thought, could be as hard to accept as undeserved rebuke.

She and Alexei met at the apartment as often as they could, and for all its drawbacks it was a haven, where they could be alone and behave naturally. Inevitably, much of the time they were together was in the presence of other people, most often Basil, Anna and Adishka, and it was hard, especially for Emily, to dissemble. Many a slip was made, many a time she betrayed a knowledge of something she shouldn't have known, or spoke with more warmth and ease then she should to her brother-in-law. Fortunately, neither Basil nor

Anna was particularly noticing, and Adishka usually had weighty matters of politics on his mind. Still, it made her nervous and ill at ease.

The news of Anna's pregnancy was formally announced at a family dinner party. Basil was rapturous on Anna's behalf.

'Oh Annushka, how wonderful! I'm so happy for you!'

Anna, looking pleased and almost shy, seemed younger and prettier than Emily had ever seen her. She had to force herself to smile, to go up in her turn to kiss Anna and congratulate her. 'You must be very happy.'

'Yes, I am.' Anna glanced, smiling, towards her husband. 'Alyosha and I have been wanting another boy, but he's been away so much, there's never seemed to be time to do anything about it until now.'

Emily's hand felt icy as she placed it in Alexei's. His face seemed to waver in a mist of anguish as she raised hers to kiss him formally, sisterly. Her teeth were ground so hard together that she couldn't have got a single word out, certainly not one as long as *congratulations*.

He covered for her. 'I think you know what I must be feeling,' he said as his lips touched her cheek. They felt cold, too.

'What if it's a girl?' Adishka said out of the dense, clammy fog that filled the room.

Alexei's hand was holding hers so tightly she could feel the bones grind together. 'Girl or boy,' he said above her head, 'if Anna's happy, that's all that matters.'

Well, something had to be said. Emily smiled, ate, drank the toasts, nodded, smiled. Her jaws ached from smiling, her throat from not crying. You're too old to cry in public, she told herself. Her twentieth birthday was a month away, but tonight she felt a thousand years old.

Somehow the evening was got through. In the motor car going home, she sat silent, trying not to think, trying not to feel. She had entirely forgotten Basil, sitting beside her, until he said suddenly, 'I know you're upset, Emilusha. Do you want to talk about it?'

Emily came back from her different world and looked towards him cautiously. The fat yellow of the street lights waxed and waned as they passed them, lighting his fair, handsome face and then losing it in the shadows of his corner, so that he seemed to loom and fade like an uncertain apparition.

She smelled cigar, sandalwood, leather – brandy when he spoke; expensive, evocative, but unthreatening smells. Well-bred, wealthy

313

men everywhere must smell much the same, she thought. Uncle Westie, King Edward, Uncle Valya, Andrei Kovanin, Basil – all indistinguishable from one another, just members of the vast society of male adulthood. Only one man in the world was different, stood out from the multitude by virtue of being *hers*, loved by her, her lover. If she were blind, deaf and dumb, she would still have known Alexei apart in any company; and because of that, she couldn't feel that Basil any longer had anything to do with her. He was her husband, but what was that? Just a title.

But he must be answered. 'Upset? No, not at all. I was just thinking.'

'Yes, I know. About Anna's baby.'

'Yes. It's – it's wonderful for her, isn't it?'

'You are upset, I can tell,' Basil said. 'Emilia, we haven't really talked since – since that bit of trouble we had.'

She didn't want to talk about that. 'Please, let's just forget it.'

'I've said I'm sorry – over and over. I know it was a terrible thing to do. Can't you forgive me?'

'I do forgive you.'

'But you can't forget it,' he said, not bitterly, but sadly, which made her feel uncomfortable. 'And now Anna's having another baby, and you haven't any.'

'That's not what I've been thinking about,' Emily said hastily, and he interpreted her haste his own way.

'It's all right, I'm not going to force myself on you,' he said, and the faint hurt in his voice tweaked at her guilt. 'I know it will be some time before you feel you can really forgive me. But I wanted to say to you that when you are ready – well, don't let pride stand in your way. I know you'd like to have children, and I'd like that too.'

For a brief moment she thought what it would be like to have Basil's child, and the idea was horrible from beginning to end; like a kind of incest, she decided, not to be contemplated. Yet he didn't feel like that, it was obvious. What feelings he had ever had towards her, he had still; and in any case, having a child was for him a matter of sentimental intent. It would not be his body that was colonised, used up, made over for the purpose. He could have a baby with little more trouble or personal involvement than if he walked into a shop in the Nevsky Prospekt and picked one out from a shelf.

'Just let me know when you want me to come to you,' he went

314

on, speaking gently, being everything that was considerate. 'It can be – just as you like.'

Anger spurted in her. She compared this humble, gentle Basil with the arrogant, thoughtless husband who had rejected her advances, who had ridden off and left her alone at Schwartzenturm on their honeymoon, who had flirted publicly with Varsha Sabinina, who had visited whores and told her to mind her own business when she objected. He was sorry now, but she had been an ardent, untried girl when he first trampled on her feelings.

'It can never be as I like!' she retorted. 'You've seen to that.'

'Not now, perhaps, but one day – '

'Oh, just leave me alone! Go to bed with anyone you like, just as long as it isn't me!'

'Very well, if that's how you feel.'

He subsided, hurt, into his own corner. She wished it unsaid the moment it was out, but words, like blows, can't be reversed. Better for them not be reconciled, given that she meant to leave him; but whatever he had done, hitting out at him made her feel wretched and bad. It was like kicking a puppy – impossible to justify.

'I went to the legal advice centre yesterday to see you,' Adishka said, 'but you weren't there. I thought Tuesday was your regular day?'

'Only Tuesday morning. Eight until twelve.'

'So they told me. I had an idea you'd been doing the whole day lately.'

Emily continued making the tea and didn't answer.

'Sasha Suslov was hanging around there,' Adishka went on. 'He said you told him you did the whole day on Tuesday.'

'What is this?' Emily said, trying for humour. 'Have you been recruited into the Okhrana?'

'I just wondered why you told him that,' Adishka persevered.

'To buy myself a little peace and quiet. You know how he hangs around me all the time.'

'So where were you, then?'

Emily handed his cup. 'Drink your tea and stop asking impertinent questions,' she said firmly. 'I'm not accountable to you or Sasha.'

'I'm sorry,' Adishka said, though he didn't look abashed. He took his cup and sipped thoughtfully.

'What was it you wanted me for?' Emily asked after a moment, not feeling the peril was past.

'Hmm?'

'Yesterday. Why did you come looking for me?'

'Oh, nothing. Nothing really. I just wanted to chat.'

They were interrupted by the arrival of Alexei. Emily's heart leapt with a mixture of joy and disappointment, which she saw mirrored exactly in Alexei's eyes and his rueful smile as he saw she was not alone.

'Ah, good,' he said cheerfully, all in the same instant. 'I hoped I'd be in time for tea. You always have the best tea table in Peter, Emilia; I suppose it's being English. But I see my brother has discovered the fact before me.'

'Hello, Alyosha,' Adishka said, not entirely welcomingly.

'Am I disturbing you? Would you like me to go away?'

'Don't be silly. That's not for me to say,' Adishka said gracelessly. 'Just as long as you don't start making fun of me.'

Alexei took the seat Emily had silently offered, and looked at his brother with raised eyebrows. 'When do I ever?'

'All the time, about my politics,' Adishka muttered. He had counted on having Emily to himself, and did not take disappointment well.

Alexei stretched out his legs with an air of ease. 'If you espouse silly ideas, you must expect to be made fun of,' he said casually.

'You may think they're silly. A lot of people take them very seriously.'

'I'm not responsible for the number of fools in the world.'

'Alexei, don't,' Emily said, passing his cup.

'I'm sorry. I shouldn't, at your tea table.'

'You shouldn't anyway. Have a teacake. Adishka is perfectly serious in his views.'

'That only makes it worse that they are so wrong.'

'You see how it is, Emilia,' Adishka said angrily. 'No-one else but him is entitled to an opinion.'

Alexei smiled infuriatingly. 'You are entitled to your opinions, of course. They just happen to be foolish.'

'All right, if you're so confounded clever, you tell me where I'm wrong!' Adishka said hotly.

'How long have you got? You are wrong about everything, from the bottom upwards. Wrong about the poor, about the factory workers, about the peasants – especially about the peasants – '

'Oh, you've just got a bee in your bonnet about the peasants!'

'I think I may claim to know a little more about agriculture than you, little brother. And the worst thing that you and your Social Democrat friends propose in your brave, new world is the continuance of the commune system.'

Adishka's eyes were bright with conviction. 'The commune system is part of our tradition. It goes back in history – '

'So did serfdom. I take it you'd like to see that restored?' Alexei by contrast was cool and nerveless, like an experienced dueller – and therefore deadly.

'Don't be ridiculous! Not all traditions are good, I grant you. But the commune system is what the peasants themselves want. It's the way they like things. You ask them – they'll tell you the same thing!'

'Yes, I know. And ask an opium addict if he'd like another pipe. It doesn't make it the right thing for him.'

'Precious few of them took up the offer of owning their land outside the commune when it was offered,' Adishka sneered. 'They didn't think so much of your precious Stolypin and his reforms – '

'I've heard that name,' Emily said to Adishka, hoping to defuse the situation. 'Basil mentioned it to me years ago, when I was still in England. Who was he?'

But Alexei answered first. 'Peter Arkadyevitch was our prime minister for five years, until he was murdered in 1911. There had been one or two attempts against him – '

'Because of his brutal suppression of every dissenting voice raised against him and his ideas,' Adishka said.

'I think rather,' Alexei said calmly, 'because he was achieving something that would make the peasantry contented and prosperous. There is an element amongst the revolutionaries – Adishka knows who I mean – that believes it is better to let the people starve than to improve their lot, because that might reconcile them with the present order.'

'Basil didn't seem to think Stolypin's ideas were very good,' Emily said tentatively. 'What's wrong with the communes, after all, if it's what the peasants want?'

Alexei smiled. 'Because it's a wasteful and inefficient way of farming – which England abandoned two hundred years ago, one might mention. All the land belongs to the commune as a whole. It's divided into strips, and the members are allotted strips by the central committee, scattered about the holding, often a long walk from each other. The committee also decides what crop each member may grow on his various strips. There's no incentive to improve the land, because the member is allotted new strips every year. They're too small to make machinery worthwhile. The peasant who uses his efforts or ingenuity to farm more efficiently gets no benefit from it, while his neighbours' bad methods spill over onto his strip. The committee decides everything – tenure, crop, method, market. The individual can't benefit.'

'So what did Stolypin propose?'

'That any peasant who wished should be allowed to leave the commune, and take his holding in one consolidated piece of land which would be his property, to do with as he liked. He wanted to create a class of prosperous, independent peasants who would have a stake in the land they farmed, and who would therefore wish first to become educated, and then to have a say in the government.'

'You pretend that's what he wanted, do you?' Adishka said. 'The way I've heard it, he wanted to break up the communes so that the peasants would be isolated from each other, working against each other instead of together, weakening their power – '

Alexei grew heated for the first time. 'Power? What power do they have, in thrall to the dictatorship of the commune? At the mercy of every petty, arbitary whim of their own ignorant elder?'

'Just because they aren't educated doesn't mean to say they're ignorant! You may despise the peasantry, Alyosha, but they have the wisdom of tradition and of the land – '

'Sentimental bunkum! You and your revolutionary friends are content to allow the peasants to go on starving, as long as they do it tidily and romantically in their picturesque villages, as far away as possible from your comfortable drawing-rooms! The peasants who left the communes did very well, but that doesn't fit in with your nursery picture-book ideas of the way the world should be, does it?'

'The peasants themselves chose not to leave, so you can – '

'They wanted to leave all right, but the commune elders wouldn't let them go – in defiance of the law, I may add. Told them that if they left they'd forfeit half their holding, or offered them only the worst, unfarmable corner as their portion.'

'Oh rubbish! That's not true!'

'Yes it is, Adishka,' Alexei said, growing cool again. 'That's a fact I'm telling you. Remember, I've been intimately involved with the negotiations, and the assessments. I know whereof I'm speaking.'

Adishka looked uncomfortable. 'All the same, it was a bad idea philosophically,' he said, changing foot. 'You'd like to make the

318

peasants all as selfish and self-seeking as the upper classes, instead of working together for the common good as they do – '

'Sentiment again,' Alexei said shortly. 'Why is it you drawing-room revolutionaries talk such whimsical rot, instead of facing facts? Do you think the peasant in his *izba* has different basic desires from you and me? Do you think he doesn't want enough to eat, a sound roof over his head, clothes and shoes and firewood, a pretty wife and healthy children? Do you think he doesn't want life to be better for his sons than it is for him?'

'But people also have generous, unselfish impulses, don't they?' Emily suggested.

'Certainly. Whoever said they didn't? But there's no essential reason why a man's improving his own lot should be at other people's expense – and that was the whole point of Stolypin's reforms. He wanted to make it possible for the peasant to do what was best for himself and benefit the state at the same time.'

'Enlightened self-interest,' Emily said, her face lighting. 'Jeremy Bentham!'

'Precisely,' Alexei said, his smile reflecting hers. 'Now we're getting somewhere!'

Adishka had not heard of Bentham. 'Well, when the revolution comes, it's going to be the peasants' revolution, that's all! All men will march side by side, hand in hand, to secure the interests of the working – '

'Oh Adishka, don't spout your slogans at me!' Alexei said, still smiling. 'Tell me, when this revolution is over, who is going to be in charge?'

'Well, we are, of course.' Adishka stepped uncertainly, knowing he was going to have the rug pulled out from under him.

'We. That means you and your friends? Not the peasants?'

'Well, obviously at first they won't have the education, or the political awareness. We will have to actually run things, on their behalf. Of course, in time it's hoped that the best of them – '

'Quite.' The word was deadly. 'You know how, and you know best. No, I'm not making fun of you. I'm just pointing out that, as history will tell you, all revolutions are middle-class. The peasants, or the poor, or the working classes, whatever you like to call them, are just the blunt instrument, the club with which to beat the rulers of the day.'

'We have their best interests at heart,' Adishka began hotly.

'And do you think the Tsar believes any differently? Yes, don't

319

sneer! Whatever you may think of his methods, he sincerely believes that what he decides is what is best for his subjects. He doesn't sit in his palace deliberately plotting to make people miserable. The trouble is, I think – '

Emily could see that he had stopped talking to Adishka, and was musing aloud for his own sake, though she could also see that Adishka hadn't noticed the change. But then Adishka wasn't in love with him.

'The trouble is that Russia is too big to be ruled as a whole without a single, unifying personality at the head. Otherwise, there'd be nothing to stop it splitting off into small regional kingdoms – which is almost the way it is now, except that they're satrapies, with the satraps paying tax and homage to the centre. In that sense – the unifying sense – there are no good tsars or bad tsars, only weak ones and strong ones. Above all, you can't have a constitutional one,' he added, looking at Emily, not his brother, 'much as we may all wish it. Real democrats, you see, are not ruthless enough to force their ideas through, because ruthlessness is not a democratic trait.'

'I see that,' Emily began, but Adishka interrupted.

'It works in England,' he said, 'and I don't see that mere size makes it any different here.'

'Size makes all the difference,' Alexei said, 'when it takes weeks to communicate with the outlying parts. Supposing it took a week for your head to send a message to your feet? Your feet might well decide that they were damned if they were going to go on doing all the walking, and simply refuse to take any more orders, hoping that you'd eventually give up the idea and stay in bed. Only by instilling them with a sense of your personality – either through love or through fear – could you ensure they went on obeying your orders and walking away down there without close supervision.'

'What are you talking about, you madman?' Adishka laughed unwillingly. 'Head, feet, whatever next?'

'But there's another point to consider, brother mine. Democracy works in England because it evolved slowly, from the bottom upwards. We have a population largely made up of ignorant, illiterate, superstitious paupers who haven't yet entered the nineteenth century, let alone the twentieth. That's why Stolypin's way was right – to create a class of independent peasants first, and then give them self-determination. You can't do it the other way.'

'You can't do it your way,' Adishka said, suddenly serious. 'Do you think if Stolypin had lived, and done what he wanted, the

320

Emperor would have said, "Well done, Peter Arkadyevitch! Now let's give them the vote"? You know as well as I do that Nicholas wants his power intact to hand on to his son. Until he goes, there can never be democracy. He won't allow it.'

Emily could see that Alexei agreed with him, though he didn't like it.

'I thought you told me you didn't want to be rid of the Emperor,' she said to Adishka, suddenly nervous.

'We want to keep the office,' Adishka said. 'But I can't see Iron Nicholas agreeing to be a constitutional tsar. It may be that he will have to abdicate in favour of his son.'

'But – ' Just in time, Emily remembered that she was sworn to secrecy about the Tsarevitch's illness. She bit her lip. 'What if he won't agree to abdicate?'

'Ah, there's the rub, eh, Adishka?' Alexei said lightly. 'I tell you one thing – you won't have any difficulty finding volunteers for the post. I never met a revolutionary yet who didn't secretly want to be tsar himself. And if one of your fanatical chums ever does succeed to the purple, whatever his title may be – tsar or president or chief co-ordinator of the people's revolution – you can bet your last rouble that he will out-caesar Caesar in the most spectacular way.'

'Oh, rubbish!' Adishka said uncertainly.

'It'll be a poor lookout for you and me then, brother. We kindly liberals will be the first to be strung up from the lampposts.'

'At least it would be good for the peasants,' Adishka countered feebly.

'You think so? You have greater faith in human nature than I have, then. But the peasants at least would survive – that's what they're best at. They endure, like the earth. When the wind of change blows a hurricane, they just crouch down and wait for it to blow over.' He looked at Emily. 'If you want an image for Life itself, think of an old woman in a headscarf, plodding along a country road, with a bundle on her back and a lifetime of endurance in her eyes.'

'Too gloomy,' she said. 'It may be true, but even for her that isn't all life is. She had her moments of poetry too – on her wedding day, perhaps, and when she held her first child in her arms. Even for a peasant,' she added severely, 'the sunrise isn't merely a matter of physics, you know.'

Alexei laughed. 'Well said, *doushka*! That was my Russian melancholy coming to the fore!'

'I don't know what you're talking about, either of you,' Adishka said. They had briefly forgotten him. Emily blushed, realising Alexei had called her *doushka*. Adishka looked at her curiously. 'You always seem to be able to keep up with him, though. I suppose I must just be stupid.'

'I'm sorry, Adishka,' she said quickly. 'It was rude of me. Will you have a piece of cake?'

'Thank you,' he said, wheels still visibly turning behind his pale, pinched face. 'It's clear you think alike about a lot of things. I must say it's nice to see you getting on so well together.'

'Emilia's court is large enough to embrace many disparate characters,' Alexei said serenely. 'You, me, Basil, Sasha Suslov – the four points of the compass there, I'd say.' He stood up. 'Well, I must be off, I'm afraid. I only called in in the hope of a cup of tea – for which I thank you kindly, Emilia – but the conversation was so thrilling I forgot the time. Don't ring, I'll see myself out. Will you be at the Razumovskys' soirée tomorrow? Then I shall see you there.'

When he had gone, Emily poured Adishka some more tea.

'How do you know Mischa Ivanov?' he asked casually, watching her hand for steadiness.

'I don't think I do,' she said after a moment. The amber stream arched steadily from pot to cup: no drop was spilled.

'Alyosha's milk-brother. Sasha says he saw you talking to him in the street last week.'

'Oh yes. I didn't know his surname.' Emily looked up. 'What a busy little soul Sasha has been lately.'

Adishka reddened. 'I just wondered how you knew Mischa, that's all, him coming from such a different background from you. Princess Narishkina and the factory worker – not exactly hand and glove, are they?'

'That's the joy of the centre – one meets all sorts there,' Emily said lightly. 'He came in to ask for information on behalf of one of his men, and knowing who I was, he asked if he might introduce himself to me. Now, is there anything else you'd like to know? What I had for breakfast this morning? Who I met for lunch yesterday?'

Adishka would dearly have liked to know that, but she had effectively prevented him from asking, even in a roundabout way.

*

The Razumovskys were having one of their musical soirées. It involved two separate recital rooms, a card room, a roulette room, a supper-room, and a great many walking-about- and sitting-and-chatting-rooms in between. It was ideal for getting separated from the people one arrived with, which was probably why they were so popular with all the bored sets of Petersburg society.

Alyosha's diplomatic and ministerial circle hardly ever overlapped with Basil's largely military and Anna's chic-artistic ones, but the Razumovskys knew and catered for everyone. Schubert was being played in one music room, and Stravinsky in the other; there was gambling, gossip, scandal, food and drink, whist, high politics, and for those who wandered far enough away in the rambling Razumovsky palace, opium and a little discreet sexual licence.

Alexei found Emily sitting quietly at the back of the Stravinsky recital, and beckoned her out. Basil had gone with Youna and Dima and some other Guards friends to the roulette room to try to lose a fortune; Anna was in the supper-room eating for two and helping Leone Duvitska dismember a few reputations.

'What made you choose that room?' Alexei asked as soon as they were outside. 'You don't like that stuff, do you? It's the sheerest racket.'

'It's a piano version of *The Rite of Spring*,' she corrected. 'I thought it was a racket when I first heard it, but I'm not so sure now. It grows on you, you know.'

'Good God! Tell me, do you like avant-garde paintings too?'

'I'm not sure. I think I do some of them, if they're not too strange. Basil knows all about them – he tries to educate me.'

'Well come and look at Lydia's collection. She has everything from Picasso to Malevich – and also some rather fine Monets, which I *can* see the point of.' He took her arm and escorted her down a corridor towards the stairs. 'We can also be sure of finding no-one else up there.'

'I wouldn't have thought, in such mixed company, you could be sure of anything of the sort. There may well be modern-art lovers here.'

'Well, in that case, we can claim to be amongst them, and have the perfect excuse for our presence.'

She laughed. 'Unscrupulous!'

'What was Adishka about yesterday? Did he ask you troublesome questions after I left?'

'Not really – only how I knew Mischa, which was easy to parry. I said he came to the centre, which is true enough.'

'How did he know you know Mischa?'

'Sasha Suslov saw me talking to him.'

'That boy needs strangling. Why do you encourage him to hang on your skirt?'

'He doesn't need encouraging. He thinks he's in love with me.'

Alexei looked down at her. 'I suppose I have to sympathise with that. I'm sorry I forgot myself and called you *doushka*.'

'I'm not.'

'Don't look at me like that, or I shall forget myself again.'

'It wasn't such a bad slip. I wasn't too pleased with you for rushing off, though, and leaving me with him.'

'I thought I'd better go before I made things worse. I wish you didn't spend so much time with my fool of a brother.'

'I know perfectly well you're very fond of him.'

'It doesn't make him less of a fool.' Alexei sighed. 'And that's largely my fault. I should have seen to it that he was properly educated and put in the way of doing something useful.' She pressed his arm comfortingly, and he glanced down at her. 'Why do you waste your time with his movement and his silly friends?'

'I must do something. And at least they try to help.'

'Help?'

'The poor people,' she explained kindly.

He laughed. 'Oh my dear, I don't suppose any of them has ever seen how the poor people live.'

'Have you?' she asked, stung by his tone.

'Oh yes,' he said gently. 'If you want, I could show you – though they are not a circus sideshow, to be stared at. But Mischa will tell you all you need to know, without risking your sensitivities.'

'Don't talk nonsense to me about sensitivities. Remember I was born plain Emily Paget, not Princess anything. And I used to help the vicar at home, visiting the sick and the poor.'

He shook his head. 'I hope and pray you have never seen anything like the conditions the factory workers live in. The factory owners put up barracks to house them – often just rackety slums slung together out of wood and plaster, but in some cases quite decent buildings – but they were never meant to house the numbers packed into them. Men, women, children, crowded together without privacy, living twenty to a room in the most hideous degradation. No furniture, nothing but a few piles of rags to lie down on; no water to wash in; no facilities for sanitation. Women trying to cook over a handful of wood chippings in a tin tray. Children picking the lice out of each other's hair for want of any other amusement. Old and young lying down together, to sleep, to copulate, to die within sight and sound of each other. And the stench – it sinks into your clothes, your very skin, so that you smell it for days, no matter how much you wash.'

Emily listened. She had seen nothing of this in her eighteen months in Petersburg. Oh yes, she had seen poverty, ragged children begging in the street, homeless families sitting on the steps of the churches or crowding round the stoves kept alight for them in the vestibule; she had seen drunkards slumped in doorways or sitting hopelessly at roadsides waiting for death or a policeman to move them on. She had seen glimpses of the decent poor, coming and going from the darker, narrower streets that existed in between and alongside the beautiful sunlit Peter that she inhabited. All of those things she knew about, and she had seen them in England, too. Urban and rural poverty had always existed and always would. She knew of dank, slimy cottages in the village at Bratton where people lived teetering on either side of the line that divided poverty from starvation. She had seen emaciated old folk, tubercular adults, rickety children.

But her vivid imagination showed her what Alexei had seen, and it appalled her. There was nothing as bad as that in England, she thought. Not in the twentieth century. Nor should there be anywhere.

'Why?' she asked. 'Why do the factory owners do it? Why don't you – people like you – do something about it?'

'I don't think you realise the scale of the problem. I wonder if anyone does,' he added thoughtfully. 'The peasants have poured off the land into the cities. Our industrial output has doubled since the beginning of the century, and it's accelerating all the time. No-one ever really had time to think about what it would mean in social terms.'

'But now – you could do something now.'

'What would you propose?' he said with a faint smile. 'Give them money?'

'It would be a start,' she said indignantly.

'Even if I gave away all I owned, I could only help a handful amongst so many. Who would I choose? On what basis would I select those to be helped and those to be abandoned? And there are more coming along behind them all the time.' His hand sketched a gesture of marching multitudes. 'More, always more. No, charity is not the answer.'

'Well, what is, then?'

He held up his hands in a gesture of surrender. 'Politics isn't the answer either,' he said, anticipating her thoughts. 'Not Adishka's brand. The revolutionaries all want power for its own sake, you know. They only use the poor as their excuse for taking what someone else has. They say, "If only we were the ones with the power, we could make everything all right", but you try asking them how they plan to do it! They haven't an idea, any of them. They're so interested in the process of taking power, they haven't begun to think what they'd do with it.'

'And you have, I suppose?'

'My love, why are you attacking me? I'm not trying to take power. Are you so dedicated to Adishka's party you feel you have to defend it against me?'

'No, of course not. I'm sorry. But it seems too easy to say they have the wrong answer, when you haven't an alternative to offer.'

'But I have,' he smiled quizzically. 'I've already told you what it is. Not charity, not politics – economics.'

'What, you mean Stolypin's reforms?'

'Yes, amongst others. It begins with seeing people as they really are – '

'Benthamism?'

'Yes, that; but also realising that however you mete out the corn amongst the people, some will always end up with the lion's share, while the rest divide the scraps between them. That's simply human nature.'

'So?'

'So we must eliminate waste and corruption and increase production so that even the mouse's share will still be enough. That's the only solution that will work. None of your "isms" can do it, because they all rely on changing the basic nature of mankind, and even God never managed to do that. The trouble is, it's a very long-term plan, and starvation is a short-term problem.'

'Yes, I see that,' she said. 'It must be hard for ardent young men like Adishka to see anything that would take generations to work as a solution.'

He smiled at the description of Adishka. 'Quite. And of course they have a grave problem to overcome: this love of the romantic, the noble savage, the purity of the commune. Our home-grown revolutionaries want to slaughter the rich and condemn the peasant to the commune because they're basically sentimental.'

'They sound brutal to me.'

'Sentimentality is brutal. It doesn't see people as people, only as cogs in a machine, or brush-strokes in a painting.'

'Oh dear,' Emily said, remembering where they had begun, 'but it's still all just words. What's really going to happen?'

He looked lost for a moment. 'I don't know. I hope that basic common sense will get us by; but then there's the war to take into account.' He grimaced. 'Kokovtsev – the Prime Minister – told the Tsar back in January that war was inevitable. That's why I was sent on my tour. But nothing has come of it. Kokovtsev has been dismissed for his pains, and the Tsar simply stares into space when you try to talk to him about it, and says "All is in the will of God". But if we fight a war, I'm afraid it will let loose not only the Four Horses, but revolution as well.'

She found her hands being gripped by his. 'What will we do then?'

'*Doushka*, how can I tell? It depends what sort of revolution, how and who and where and when. It depends on so many things.'

'And Anna. And Basil,' she added.

He tightened his grip. 'We will be together. Do you want me to swear it?'

She didn't answer that. Instead she said after a moment, 'Did I tell you I had a letter this morning from Lady Hamilton?'

'No, you didn't. How is she?'

'Not well. She says she is going to die soon. I think she may.'

He took her in his arms. 'I'm sorry. I know how fond of her you are.'

She rested against him lightly, thinking. 'I don't think she minds the idea of dying. She hasn't enjoyed life very much over the last year, in pain all the time and unable to get out of the house. She hates being confined.'

'She may rally, now the better weather is coming. Old people are often low in winter.'

She accepted the comfort, but her mind was elsewhere. 'In her letter she said that since she knew she hadn't long left to live, she had made certain changes to her will that she wanted me to know about. She's very rich, you know.'

'Is she? No, I didn't know.'

'Most of her estate will be divided between her godsons and their families; but she says that she's leaving me her house in London, together with a small amount of money to cover its running expenses.' She lifted her face from his chest, where it had been resting, and looked at him seriously. 'In case I need it, she says.'

'Does she anticipate a revolution, too?' he asked, half amused, half perplexed.

'No. But she was never pleased about my marrying Basil. She thinks he won't do. She thinks the time may come when I want to run away from him, so she's making sure I have somewhere to run to. She doesn't know about you, of course.'

'No,' he agreed. He surveyed her face, and read in it more than one sort of anxiety. 'My soul, do you really believe I am making false promises to you?'

She drew a short sigh, which he felt rather than heard. 'No. I believe that you mean it. But I don't know – neither of us knows – how things are going to turn out. Things may happen that we can't control. If I have to run, and I can't run to you, I just wanted you to know that I have somewhere to go.'

'If you had to go without me, I would follow you,' he said.

'That's where I'd be, then, waiting for you,' she said bleakly.

It was absurd and unfair of her, but she wished he had pooh-poohed the whole thing, assured her that there'd be no need of it. It was ridiculously feminine, but she wished he had said he'd die rather than let her go anywhere without him.

328

Chapter Nineteen

The early summer of 1914 was marked by weather of particular clarity and beauty. The sun shone from skies of cloudless purity, which made it impossible to believe that anything dark or bad could ever happen. In Petersburg the White Nights had come, and through the long, luminous dusk that replaced the night-time, the magical city lay softly gleaming in mysterious shades of lavender and dove, and nobody ever seemed to go to bed.

The beginning of June took Alexei from Petersburg again on the Tsar's business, to Tula and then Kiev, and Adishka took the opportunity of travelling with him as far as Moscow, to pay a visit to his mother. Natasha was still in Archangel, so Emily was left with only Basil and Anna for company.

Anna, in her sixth month, was growing large and disinclined for much company. She still liked to go to the theatre and the ballet, where she could sit in the dark in her private box and not be seen, but otherwise she was much confined to the house and garden, and spent many a hot day sitting in the shade fanning herself peevishly and wishing the summer over.

Basil was in good spirits, having settled down to a more or less bachelor life that seemed to suit him. Anna, preoccupied with her insides, was now a less bossy older sister, pleasant to sit and chat to. Emily he treated like a favourite younger sister. He squired her proudly, enjoyed having her glitteringly dressed upon his arm in public places, and adopted an almost avuncular attitude to other women of his class, from whom he now plainly felt he had immunity. Emily was torn between sadness and amusement to see him being ponderously flirtatious towards some unmarried female only a few years younger than himself, secure in the knowledge that he would never be suspected of wanting to marry her.

Varsha Sabinina had transferred her affections to a colonel in an infantry regiment, which everybody considered very bad form. He was of low origins, like most of the infantry officers, and without personal fortune to supplement his poor salary, which meant Varsha had to pay for everything. It was acknowledged, however, that his moustaches were magnificent, and that he had the trick of managing Varsha, who became almost meek in his company.

Basil took her defection very well. He had begun to grow bored with her – Varsha was a woman he found he liked in fairly small doses – and he had in any case been smitten by the burgeoning attractions of a very young *corps de ballet* girl from the Imperial School. Lately he had set her up in her own house, conveniently close to Kronversky. Nina Antonova came from a respectable lower-middle-class family, and her father had had to be persuaded that Basil had her best interests at heart before he would allow her to leave home. As a consequence, Basil had not only to guarantee that Nina would be allowed to continue with her career, but had also had to lodge a fair sum of money with a lawyer against the loss of his favour, and to pay for her brother Senka to go to cadet school.

Leone Duvitska had annoyed Anna by describing the negotiations to her with great amusement, saying that Basil was being led by the nose by the most calculating rogue of a papa who had ever played the pander.

'Poor Vasska won't be able to call his soul his own after this. They'll be coming to him every week with their sly little demands: a new dress for Mama, a silk hat for Papa – and don't forget Babushka needs a new set of teeth! Talk of your *nostalgie de la boue*! I must say I hadn't expected him to go through this phase quite yet. It's a very middle-aged thing, for a man to be falling in love with vulgar chits of seventeen!'

'Vasska is not in love,' Anna had said coldly. 'He is arranging things in a comfortable, civilised manner, that's all. And if you mock my brother, you mock me, Leone Ivanovna. You are no longer my friend.'

Emily knew about Nina. Not only had she no right to object, but she was glad to see Basil happy and occupied. When Nina had no class or performance, Basil took her out driving or shopping; he went to watch her on stage whenever she danced; and she took care of his sexual demands so adequately that he no longer visited Madame Clavin's, about which Emily was vaguely glad. She supposed Nina must fall into a sufficiently ambiguous category in Basil's mind not to come under the ban which had prevented his taking pleasure of Emily's flesh.

When not occupied with Nina, Basil spent most of his time with his friends in the Semyonovsky Guards, and Emily only saw him when, by agreement, they attended an evening function together. As far as Basil was concerned, it seemed to be an ideal arrangement, and Emily thought with wry amusement how Fanny might have predicted it all. It would make it easier for her to leave him, she thought, when the time came – if the time ever came, her doubts whispered. Being with Anna so much only seemed to remind her of the difficulties that lay in their way.

One hot, clear day in June, another in the seemingly endless succession that summer, found Emily at her grandmother's house in Tsarskoye Selo, gazing with bemused affection at a suntanned young man in the uniform of a midshipman of the British Royal Navy, who was smirking in exactly the self-conscious way she recognised from Tolya.

'Oh Tom!' she said. 'Is it really you? I can hardly believe it! You've grown so tall.'

'Gunroom food,' he said. 'They feed us up like fatstock, and keep us below the water-line for ballast. I say, Em, you look so very fine!' He waved a hand to encompass her dusky pink silk crêpe suit, cream lace jabot, diamond brooch, and the prince's ransom of pearls around her neck. 'Who'd have thought you'd turn out so pretty? I like your hair done that way, too. It makes you look taller.'

'I am taller, stoopid!'

'Well, you look grown up, anyway. Every inch a princess.'

'Thank you. You look grown up in that uniform, and every inch a middy.'

Tom laughed, a nice, open, frank sort of laugh that tugged at Emily's heart. 'That's no compliment!' he said. 'Middies are the lowest form of life. I can't wait to get my commission! Still, at least in the navy one knows that everyone's been through it, right up to Admiral Beatty himself.'

Tom's presence in Russia was due to the increasing pace of diplomatic manoeuvring which was taking place all over Europe as the powers felt their way towards alliance. State visits were the order of the day: King George of England to Paris, the Kaiser to Austria, President Poincaré of France to Petersburg; and in response to the rapid expansion of the German High Seas Fleet, four battleships of the Royal Navy under Admiral Sir David Beatty had yesterday sailed up the Baltic on a diplomatic mission, and were at this moment swinging idly at anchor on the smooth, enamelled waters at Kronstadt.

The imperial family had watched the ships arrive from the deck of the *Standart*, and had then gone on board the flagship *Lion* for luncheon. Afterwards, while discussions went on between the Emperor, the Admiral, the Foreign Minister and the British Ambassador, a group of midshipmen were told off to give the Grand Duchesses a tour of the ship. Today Beatty and his staff were visiting Tsarskoye Selo for a return of hospitality.

It had taken some delicate negotiation on Natasha Petrovna's part to persuade the Empress to ask the Tsar to ask the Admiral for permission for her grandson to visit her on shore. As Tom put it, 'Admirals aren't a whale on giving special privileges to mids.' But at length it was agreed, and here he was in his best uniform and on his best behaviour, ready to admire his grandmother's house and garden, and to put away, with complimentary gusto and frightening appetite, the large luncheon she had provided.

Now Natasha had tactfully left Tom and Emily alone together as she went upstairs, ostensibly to look out some old photographs in which she thought Tom might be interested.

Talk was on neutral subjects at first, as they felt their way back towards their old intimacy. 'I say, Em, I liked your Grand Duchesses very much: such jolly, unaffected girls! Pretty and nice, you know, like somebody's sisters.'

'They are somebody's sisters,' Emily pointed out, amused.

'Yes, the Tsarevitch, of course. I wonder why he didn't come with them on the tour of the ship? You'd have thought a lad of his age would have sooner done that than sit and jaw with ambassadors and such.'

'He is the heir to the throne,' Emily said.

'I suppose so. Only the girls enjoyed the tour so much! Somers had them in fits describing how to sling a hammock – he's very fat, you know, and to see him roll into it! The youngest one – Anastasia is it? – was a real sport. Dashwood showed her how to coil down a fall, and she asked to have a go, and got it off first time.' He eyed Emily thoughtfully. 'The tall one – Tatiana? – spoke warmly of you when she discovered we were cousins. She said very nice things about you and your husband. He's not here, I take it?'

'No, he was otherwise engaged today,' Emily said lightly.

'Pity. I'd have liked to meet him – see if he's good enough for you,' he added, with a ponderous attempt at humour.

'I'm sorry. This was all arranged rather at the last moment.'

'Of course.' He struggled with a sixteen-year-old's reticence. 'I say, Em, you are happy, aren't you?'

'Yes, of course I am. Need you ask?'

'Only you seem – so different.'

Emily looked at him for a moment, thinking of all that had happened since the days when she sat in the window-seat of the old nursery and made up stories for Tom, Lexy, Victoria and Maudie. It seemed a lifetime away; and she was not the same Emily.

'It's been so long,' she said. 'I'm bound to seem different.'

'I was sorry to hear about old Lady Hamilton. I know you were fond of her. She left you her house, didn't she?'

'Yes, and Lovibond and Katya are to be paid wages to go on living there and take care of it for me. I'm glad they can stay on – it's their home, after all.'

'Well, you'll have somewhere to come home to, then, if you ever want to go back to England. You won't have to go to Bratton.' His expression revealed what he thought about that as a fate.

'How are things at Bratton, Tom?' Emily asked. 'How is it with you?'

He made a face. 'It's been awful since you went. I only go home when I have to. You wouldn't know the old place – *she's* done it up to the nines. Everything redecorated. New furniture, new plumbing, electric light – '

'Not really!'

'Everything has to be done the Yankee way,' Tom said gloomily. 'There's even central heating: a boiler down in the cellars the size of the one that drives the old *Lion*, and miles and miles of iron pipes full of hot water. Corde hates it. He says it's making the panelling warp, and destroying the paintings.'

'And is it?'

'I dunno. Never claimed to know anything about pictures. But what gets to me most', he burst out, coming to the heart of it, 'is that she's changed the Peacock Room. For the first year it was just the way Mama left it, and I thought the Guv'nor must have told her he wanted it kept that way. But she was just biding her time. The next time I came home it was gone.'

'Gone?'

'Oh, the four walls are still there,' he said impatiently, 'but everything else is different. New wallpaper, new carpet, all Mama's little bits and pieces and whim-whams packed up and sent off to an attic. Her piano's in the long gallery now, and there are concerts once a month. Soloists come down from London, and the place is full of frightful coves in cravats and females smoking Turkish cigarettes, all being brainy about music while she queens it over 'em.'

'Oh poor Tom! I hoped you'd learn to like her in time.'

'Not in these trousers! Anyway, why should I?'

'Oh, because it would be better, that's all. Always better to get on with people, if you can.'

'Well, I've no intention of getting on with *her*. And there's no need. I told you I'd get away as soon as I could, d'you remember?' Emily nodded. 'Well, I was such a bum at school that there was no expecting me to stay on and go to Oxford. I told the Guv'nor I wanted to go to sea, and after a bit of um-ing and ah-ing he went for it.'

'I'd have thought he'd be rather reluctant to let you go,' Emily said thoughtfully.

'Why?'

'Well, I don't know what you've heard, but a lot of people here are pretty sure there's going to be a war sometime soon.'

'Lord, yes! Everyone knows that. That's the whole point. One wants to be where the fun is, don't you see?'

'Oh Tom, fun!'

'Come on, Em, don't be stuffy,' Tom said, looking uncomfortable. 'Someone's got to defend the old country. Even the Guv'nor saw that in the end.'

'I'd have thought he'd be reluctant to risk you, though, considering you're the heir.'

Tom's face hardened. 'Oh, as to that, that don't matter any more. *She's* going to have another baby. The first was a girl, but they're positive this is going to be a boy. So you see, I'm expendable.'

'Oh Tom!'

'I don't care, I tell you,' he said fiercely. 'I don't want it anyway. Bratton! All that's bosh, the title and the estate and everything. Let her have it, and her brats. It's just a tie. I mean to step out and see the world, just as you did. You don't mean to tell me,' he said with harsh sarcasm, 'that you'd want to go back, now, after all this?'

She didn't answer. He was only sixteen, she reminded herself, and he had lost mother and sisters and, in his own mind, father and home as well. Bratton modernised? she thought wonderingly. Aunt Maud would have had a fit. And then, she thought, perhaps not. Her aunt had never been devoted to any particular style; and after Maudie died, she had lost interest in the place as a possession.

'How's my father?' she asked abruptly.

Tom's scowl relaxed. 'Oh, he's having a whale of a time. Gets on with *her* like a house afire. When she'd finished with our house, she descended on The Lodge, though there wasn't all that much she could do with it, seeing it's so small. But she put in the telephone and electric light, and bought Uncle Ned a typewriting machine.'

Emily laughed aloud. 'No! Whatever did Pa make of that?'

'He was thrilled. No, really! The thing is, they all think the world of Uncle Ned over in the States – he has a huge following, and she looks on him as a sort of Charles Dickens and William Shakespeare rolled into one. Nothing's too good for him. So when she found he couldn't use the machine, she hired a secretary for him – female called Foston, who comes in from Shepton Mallet every day, Monday to Friday. He dictates to her, and she types it all down.'

'But – does it work?'

'He loves it. He writes all his stories that way, and he's started on a history of the family now in between. It must be quicker for him, because he's writing so much more.'

'He never told me any of this in his letters,' Emily marvelled.

'P'raps he was embarrassed, liking *her*. He dines up at the house whenever she's there, and they talk endlessly, about every subject under the sun. He says she has intellectual curiosity, whatever that means.' He shrugged. 'He impresses her friends, too – mostly Americans. Whenever she's got company, he's invited. I tell you, it's a different world there now.'

'So it seems,' Emily said, bemused. This image of a Bratton thoroughly modern and seething with vivacious company was hard to grasp. 'Well, at all events, he's happy I suppose?'

'Oh yes,' said Tom flatly. 'But you see why I couldn't stay there. So that's that. I really hope there is a war, Em,' he added passionately. 'Things need shaking up. We need a fresh start at things.'

Emily shook her head. 'It's what everyone always longs for, Tommy, but as long as you take your self along, it never happens. You're always you, you see. One day you'll have to go back and face up to it.'

He sighed. 'I suppose you're right. But at least one might have some fun in the meantime.'

Natasha came back in, carrying a large cardboard box. 'I've brought all the loose ones down, my dear, and we can look through them together. I have some in here somewhere of your poor mother which I think you'd like to see.' She glanced from him to Emily. 'Have you had a nice chat?'

'Oh yes, ma'am, thank you,' Tom said. He smiled shyly. 'I wish my stay could be longer. Emily's a gem, isn't she – and she's turned out so pretty!'

'More than pretty – I think she's quite a beauty,' Natasha said judiciously.

'When you've quite finished talking about me!' Emily protested. 'Tom, what about old Jacob? Is he still at Bratton? And my dear old pony? Don't stop talking while you look at the photographs. I want to hear everything about home. Papa never tells me anything.'

Tom's visit was rather unsettling, leaving Emily feeling homesick and lonely; but she had only a few more days to wait. At the end of the month Alexei arrived home. He came to her first at her house, and was grateful to find her alone.

'I can't stay – I haven't been home yet. I just called on my way from the station to make sure you're all right.'

'I am now,' she said. 'But it's been a long month.'

'For me too!' He picked up her hands and kissed them, one and then the other. 'Oh, this is a hellish situation! Would to God it were all over!'

'It will be. Only a few months more,' she said. Quite a reversal, she thought wryly, for her to be comforting him!

He seemed to think so too, for a faint smile touched his lips. 'So I keep telling you. Listen, *doushka*, can you get away tomorrow? I think I can get to the apartment in the afternoon, after I've seen the Minister.'

'Yes, I'll manage somehow.'

'Good. Because I need very badly to hold you in my arms. I must go now.' He kissed her hands again. 'Until tomorrow!' Then he was gone.

He was later than she expected, and for a while she thought he wasn't coming. Then the doorbell rang, and Emily ran, easily beating Marfa down the short hallway.

He came in looking agitated, and her heart misgave. 'What is it? Something's happened!'

'There's been an assassination attempt,' he said, and paused to

336

slide his arm round her waist and kiss her. 'That's better,' he said when he finally released her.

'You brute! *Who* has been killed? What a place to stop!'

He grinned. 'Would I have stopped if it had been bad news? No, my star, it's that vulture Rasputin. Not dead yet, but there's little chance of his recovery, so I understand.'

Marfa, in the background, crossed herself, and Alexei looked at her ruefully. 'Yes, indeed, you remind me most timely. We are all God's creatures, even the wolves and scorpions of this world, and I suppose He must have put Rasputin amongst us for a purpose. But it will be the best thing for Russia, Marfa, if he does not recover, so don't pray too hard for him.'

'He is a *starets*,' Marfa said simply, 'so one may not curse him. But I see no harm in asking God if He wouldn't care to have him back now.'

Alexei laughed. 'Yes, well put.' As the old woman turned away, he twisted his arm round Emily's waist, walked with her quickly into their bedroom and shut the door. 'Now I must make love to you before something else happens. I'm developing a morbid fear of delays. There was such a fuss at the Ministry about Rasputin I thought I'd never get away.'

'You'd better tell me about it first,' Emily said, 'or I shan't be able to concentrate on you.'

'You'll concentrate,' he said, drawing her face up and kissing her slowly, like a man long thirsty who has finally found clean, cold water.

Emily's hands came up to hold on to him, and when he lifted his mouth from hers, she said only, 'Don't stop now.'

'What about the story?'

'Later!'

It was quite a long time later that they finally got back to the subject of the assassination. They were lying on the bed, arms and legs intertwined, rather sweaty but much more at peace.

'It happened in Pokrovskoye, Rasputin's birth village in Siberia,' Alexei said in answer to her, by now, rather languid question. 'He'd been sent there by the Emperor more or less in disgrace because he behaved himself so badly in the Crimea when he followed the imperial family down in the spring. I don't need to go into details, do I? You know what he's like. Well, Rasputin was walking down the village street when a woman in a shawl came up to him begging

337

for money. As he put his hand into his pocket, she whipped out a knife and stabbed him in the stomach.'

'Oh! How awful!'

'Yes, I suppose so. Poor devil, it must be an agonising way to go. It was apparently a very bad wound – she drove the knife upwards right to the ribs, and the intestines were exposed. The local doctor patched him up and transported him to the nearest hospital at Tyumen, but the chances of survival are poor, as you can imagine. Even if the shock and loss of blood don't kill him, he's almost certain to get an infection and die of peritonitis.'

'But who was she?'

'They don't know yet. She tried to kill herself, but they caught her, and they're holding her now. He has plenty of enemies, of course; or she may just be a madwoman. Apparently she's badly disfigured by syphilis, so the latter is quite possible.'

'The Empress must be very upset,' Emily said thoughtfully.

'She doesn't know yet. The family's on board the *Standart*, of course, for their summer cruise. They're going to telegraph the news to the ship, but they're all arguing about the wording of the message.' He grimaced. 'She'll be the only person on board, I imagine, who'll want him to recover.'

'Will it really make so much difference if he dies?'

'I don't know. Most people think so. The trouble is not so much his influence with the Empress, but hers with the Tsar. And not even so much that his actions reflect badly on the imperial family, but that through the Empress he influences the appointment of ministers and advisors. She goes to the Tsar and says "Our friend doesn't like so-and-so. He says he is not to be trusted." And out goes he. It makes it impossible to get policies through unless Rasputin approves of them.' He sighed. 'Advising Nicholas is a difficult task anyway; Rasputin makes it harder.'

'Yes, I see.' She stretched against him, stroking the silky skin of his shoulder. It was white, and dusted with tiny freckles. She loved him very much.

'There's only one way in which he could conceivably be good for Russia: he's very much against our going to war, and I suppose if anyone could influence Nicholas to stay out, if it does start, it would be him.'

'Why doesn't he want us to fight?'

'He thinks it would be disastrous. Well, so does anyone who

338

knows anything about it. When it comes, if it comes, this will be a twentieth-century war; all Russia has is a nineteenth-century army.'

'It's a very large army, isn't it?'

'It's a mess,' he said bluntly. 'The rank and file are peasant conscripts, badly equipped, badly trained and badly paid. The junior officers in all but the cavalry and the Guards regiments are of humble origin, and are so badly paid they have to rely on corruption to cover their expenses. The rest of the officers are nobles, who despise everyone else and obstruct any change that might make them less comfortable. The generals are appointed by the Tsar, who chooses them for their loyalty to him and for having foreign names, because generals in the Russian Army have always been foreigners and the Tsar loves tradition.'

'Oh Alexei!'

'It's true. And to round it all off, the grand dukes – uncles and cousins of the Tsar – are automatically made inspectors-general of the armed forces, and allowed to interfere in any way they please, just as the whim takes them. Thank God the Minister of War, Sukhomlinov, knows what he's doing – he's the only man who does. He's managed to bring about some improvements; but I've seen something of the German Army, and Russia's isn't in the same class. We haven't enough arms or ammunition, and we haven't the factories capable of making them. We haven't the agricultural capacity to feed an army, and we haven't the transport system to distribute the supplies effectively.'

'But if Sukhomlinov knows all this, as you say, why doesn't he tell the Tsar?'

Alexei laughed. 'Sometimes I don't think you listen to a word I tell you!' He rolled her onto her back and leaned over her, kissing her brow and nose and lips. 'The Tsar has mystical reasons for everything he does. Mere human logic doesn't come into it. I've told you before, if he decides we go to war, we go, and that's that.'

She looked up at him gravely. 'I wish you wouldn't talk like that. I don't want there to be a war. My cousin Tom was here, and he seems to think it would all be an adventure.' She told him about Tom's visit.

'The lines are being drawn up,' he said when she had finished. 'Next month President Poincaré comes here for a State visit. Russia, England and France; Germany and Austria. Everything in readiness: all that's needed is the match. There's nothing you and I can do about it, *doushka*, except enjoy each other while we can.' He stroked her, and felt her stirring towards him, and wanted her again. 'At least we'll have the summer,' he murmured through kisses. 'No war in history was ever started before the harvest was got in.'

It was late when Emily went home, and she only just arrived before Basil. They were to go to Anna's that evening, a welcome-home dinner for Alexei. She had just got to her room and was hastily undressing to take her bath when Basil came in, looking excited and ruffled.

'Basil? Has something happened?'

'Yes, something rather horrid. I dropped into Cubat's for a glass of schnapps on the way back from the theatre, and Felix Sapetsky told me. There's been an assassination.'

Emily just managed not to say *yes I know*. Making love with Alexei all afternoon had addled her wits. She tried to look surprised and concerned. 'How dreadful! Who is it?'

'It's the heir to the throne of Austria – the Emperor's nephew, Franz Ferdinand. He was on a State visit to Bosnia, and some madman shot him at point-blank. Shot his wife, too, the swine.' He shook his fair head in mingled pity and outrage. 'I know Austria's our old enemy, but one can't help feeling sorry for the Emperor. He's well over eighty, and his nephew was his only heir. And there's something cowardly and unsporting about assassination, like shooting at a sitting duck, you know. But I suppose I spent a long time in England. You can't expect people like the Slavs to understand the notion of fair play.'

The talk of the assassination in Sarajevo dominated the evening. It wasn't so much that the shooting itself was surprising – in the Balkans, murder, conspiracy and revolution were everyday events, and nothing much to write home about. But it was generally agreed that the Emperor Franz Joseph was to be pitied. He had come to the throne in 1848 – an incredible, prehistoric date, it seemed to Emily – and had outlived all his heirs and most of his contemporaries.

His brother had been assassinated in Mexico, and his wife in Vienna, while his only son had committed suicide in a tragic pact with his mistress. Even Franz Ferdinand, his nephew, had caused him grief by defying him in order to marry a commoner for love, which meant that their three children – orphans now – were barred from the succession.

'What do you suppose was behind it all?' Emily asked when they sat down to dinner. It was moments like this that were especially hard for her, sitting at the dining-table cater-corner to Alexei at the head, close enough to reach out and touch him at a stretch, but having to maintain the fiction that they were merely cousins and friends, trying to speak to him neutrally.

'Slav independence,' Alexei answered. 'The Austrian Empire – or Austro-Hungary if you like – is a sprawling mass of provinces, with a population of about forty million. Three-fifths of those people are Slavs, but the rulers are the Austrians and the Magyars. Naturally, I suppose, the Slavs don't like it.'

'So they look to Serbia,' Basil said. 'Was it a Serbian fired the shots, do we know?'

'I think so. I haven't heard all the details yet.'

'Why Serbia?' Emily asked.

'Serbia is an independent kingdom,' Alexei said. 'A Slav kingdom. It's small and weak, but it has ambitions to weld the Slav provinces together with it into one Balkan state. It's been known for a long time that there are secret organisations within Serbia – '

'The Black Hand,' Basil interrupted with relish. 'Ruthless terrorists!'

'Dedicated to striking at Austria whenever they can, hoping to weaken it enough for a Slavic revolution to succeed.'

'It looks as though they've struck a pretty devastating blow this time,' Basil said.

'I don't know why you're so sympathetic towards Austria,' Anna said. 'They've always been our enemies; and the Tsar is the traditional protector of the Slavs.'

A thought struck Emily. 'Alexei, is this it, do you think? Could this be the match?'

'Match? What match?' Basil said.

Alexei said, 'No, I don't think so. It's a matter for police action on Austria's part, that's all. I can't see why anyone else should become involved. Besides,' he smiled at her, 'didn't I tell you we have to wait for the harvest?'

'I do think it's rude of you two to have private conversations at my table,' Anna complained. 'Now Alyosha, pay attention to me for a change. After all, I haven't seen you for a month, and I've been feeling dreadfully ill these last couple of weeks.'

'I think Anna ought to get out into the country,' Basil took up on her behalf. 'The heat is getting too much for her. What do you say, Alyosha? What about the seaside? Livadia's nice at this time of year.'

'Not the Crimea.' Alexei shook his head. 'I can't be so far away, not at the moment. But we could go down to Schwartzenturm if you like, Anna?'

'Oh, I hate that ugly old house,' Anna said peevishly, 'but I suppose if that's the best you can offer . . . '

'The children like it there,' he said soothingly. 'I think you ought to consider staying there until the baby's born. Peter won't be habitable again until October anyway; and if you're at Schwartzenturm I can spend more time with you than if you were further away.'

'Oh, all right,' Anna said with pretended reluctance. She had long ago made up her mind that that was where she would be going. 'As long as I can have lots of people to stay.'

'As many as you like,' Alexei said genially. 'In fact, I think I'll ask Yenya to come and bring the children – they'll be company for Modeste and Tatya. And you'll come and stay, won't you, Vasska?'

'Oh yes – for a while, anyway,' Basil said. 'Won't we, Emilusha? You know, Anna, I have to go back to Petersburg now and then. I can't stay with you all the time. But Emilia will keep you company.'

'I'm counting on that,' Anna said.

July turned close and sultry. They did well to get out of Petersburg, for it was ringed with peatbogs which had caught fire in the burning heat of June and smouldered throughout the summer, sending acrid clouds of smoke over the city. In the sweltering weather, tempers grew short, and strikes and minor riots broke out. There was window-smashing and some demonstrations, though things were got back in order before the visit of the French President, Monsieur Poincaré.

Even at Schwartzenturm it was oppressively hot, and the horizon was ringed with storms, rumbling distantly like gunfire, and occasionally spitting lightning against the plum-coloured clouds. Alexei, Anna, Valya and Emily were sitting on the terrace in the shade of a striped awning. Anna, in a wide silk kaftan to hide her shape, rocked slowly on the swing-seat, looking a little like an awning herself; weary with heat.

Valya had lit his pipe as a defence against the swarms of little black thunder-flies. He removed it from his mouth now to say, 'You

342

can see that the Austrians timed their ultimatum to Serbia so that it would arrive after Poincaré had left Petersburg. They didn't want us to be able to discuss our response.'

'There can only be one response,' Alexei said. 'Sazonov summed it up: *"C'est la guerre européenne"*, he said when he read it. It was deliberately provocative. The Serbians couldn't possibly agree to terms like that. No self-respecting state could.'

'If Austria really does attack Serbia, we will have to go in on their side, I see that,' Valya said thoughtfully. 'The Tsar made personal guarantees about protecting Serbian independence back in '09, and he won't go back on his word. But it needn't come to war.'

'Oh come!' Alexei protested.

'Yes, yes, obviously the whole ultimatum business is really just the same old Austrian challenge to Russia, but if Russia faces it out boldly, I believe the Austrians will back down. Their Emperor is an old man; he wants to live out the last few years of his life in peace. We must just play for time and let tempers cool.'

'That's what the Tsar's told Sazonov to do. At least we've managed to convince him at last that we're not in a fit state to fight a war. He's asking Sir Edward Grey to act as mediator between Austria and Serbia.'

'Grey's a sound man,' Valya said, blowing a calming cloud over the seething host of insects above him. 'And as for Serbia not being able to accept Austrian terms, we only have to ask them whether they prefer annihilation to humiliation. I suggest they're not in a position to be proud – not if the Tsar instructs them otherwise.'

'But if you're right,' Emily said, 'and the Austrians were being deliberately provocative, they won't accept a soft answer, will they?'

The two men looked at her in surprise.

'Uncomfortably penetrating reply,' Valya said. 'But Austria won't go to war with Russia without Germany on her side, and I don't believe the Kaiser wants war. He has too many other irons in the fire to want to be distracted; and he won't care to have his hand forced by Austria.'

'Besides,' Anna said, 'the Tsar and the Kaiser are friends as well as cousins. They'd never declare war on each other.'

'Certainly the Tsar doesn't want to fight Germany,' Alexei said with grim humour. 'But I wouldn't wager a cracked egg on being able to predict the Kaiser's moods or intentions.'

Yenchik came running up, with Tolya and Modeste behind him.

343

'Milya, will you come and teach us cricket now? You said you would, and it's a lot cooler now, really it is.'

'Not if you don't like to, of course,' Tolya added wistfully.

'Ridiculous child! Expecting Emilia to run about in this heat!' Anna exclaimed.

Emily looked rueful. 'I suppose I did promise,' she said. 'The trouble is, though, that we really need more than three.'

'How many?' Tolya asked.

'In England it's played with two teams of eleven,' Alexei said mischievously. 'Isn't that right, Emilusha?'

'Twenty-two people?' Yenchik cried despairingly.

'And two umpires,' Alexei added.

'Perhaps we could get some of the servants to join in,' Tolya said hesitantly, after a pause.

'You could not!' Anna said indignantly, while Valya and Alexei roared with laughter. 'And Modeste is not to run about in the sun, either. In fact, you all ought to be sitting down.'

Alexei stood up and stretched himself. 'I think the time has come for a little exercise of fatherhood. Come on, Valya, show your worth! We can't play a proper game,' he said to Yenchik, 'but we can knock the ball about a bit, if Emily will oblige by telling us the rules.'

'You know them perfectly well,' Emily laughed, standing up.

'Don't worry,' Alexei added to his wife, 'we'll play very gently, over in the shade of the horse chestnuts. I won't let them get overheated, I promise. Coming, Valya?'

'I suppose so. I'm being eaten alive here, anyway. With your forgiveness, Anna?'

'That's right – and keep that vile pipe of yours going. I'll find you a nice stationary role to play. If Vasska and Adishka come back, Anna dear, you can send them over to join the fun.'

'Fun!' Anna said. 'Your idea of fun seems to be courting heatstroke.' But she seemed obscurely pleased, Emily thought. The next sentence revealed why. 'I suppose it's as well for you to get into practice, though. I'm sure this one', patting her front, 'is going to be a boy.'

Emily had turned away from Anna, and her expression was hidden from her; but Valya saw her face, and he looked grave as he slipped his pipe from his mouth and knocked it out against a flower urn.

*

Serbia, persuaded of the unwisdom of war, returned an answer to the Austrian ultimatum so humble as to be positively obsequious; but the Austrians, evidently determined on wiping out the Serbian blot once and for all, ignored it, declared war, and on the 14th of July began a bombardment of Belgrade, despite the white flags fluttering from its rooftops.

The next day Alexei was called urgently to Tsarskoye Selo, and was away for several days. Basil had been in Petersburg seeing Nina, and he came back on the afternoon of that day with the news that the Tsar had ordered a partial mobilisation of Russian forces, along the Austrian frontier only.

'It was inevitable. He couldn't let the Austrians attack poor little Serbia when she'd done everything she was asked,' he said. He seemed oddly cheerful, Emily thought, as if he'd dined very well amongst friends. 'But they're saying he still hopes to avoid a wider conflict. He's telegraphed the Kaiser personally to explain and ask him to help keep the general peace, and promised that our forces along the border will only act defensively, and not fire the first shot.' He chuckled. 'It's made the Guards' officers mad as fire! I was at the mess with Youna and Dima, and they're all frothing, desperate to get out there and smash the Teutons!'

'Did you see anything of Alexei?' Emily asked. 'He was called in to see the Tsar.'

'No. I expect he's still at Tsarskoye Selo. There are tremendous comings and goings there, by all accounts. Ministers, ambassadors, generals. Lights burning at all hours. I don't suppose he'll be getting any sleep for a day or two.'

Later, when Emily was in bed, Basil came in to see her. He walked about the room restlessly for a while, talking disjointedly about what he had seen and heard in Petersburg, as if there were something on his mind he could not quite bring out. Emily watched him patiently. At last he came to the point quite abruptly, sitting down on the bed and looking at her with an air of suppressed excitement.

'Emilusha, if it is war, I'm going to go.'

'Go?' The word puzzled her.

'Join the Guards, go with them,' he said impatiently. 'You know I'm a reserve officer? Well, you must know that I was a cadet with Youna and Dima when we were all young. Of course, I left when Mama took me to England, but I've always kept my links with them.'

'But surely they wouldn't expect it of you?' Emily asked. 'After such a long time?'

'No, you don't understand! I want to go!' He jumped up and began walking about again, nervous with excitement. 'God, what an adventure! It's the most exciting thing that's happened in my lifetime, you must see that. You can't expect me to miss it!'

'Exciting,' she said flatly.

'Everyone will be going, you'll see! No man of spirit could resist this call. And the Germans have been asking for it for years. If we don't smash them now, they'll take over the whole of Europe! They've got to be put in their place once and for all.' He looked at her expression. 'Oh, you're a woman. You don't understand.'

'No, I don't,' she said, and smiled faintly. 'But it doesn't matter, does it? If you've made up your mind, you'll go, whether I want you to or not.'

He paused in his pacing, and his expression was odd. 'Don't you want me to go?'

'You must do as you wish. It's nothing to do with me.'

'Well, you are my wife – '

'Oh, you remember that, do you?' But she said it without rancour, almost teasingly.

He didn't smile in return. Instead he came back and sat down again, looking grave and rather embarrassed.

'Emilia, there's something I've got to ask you. Well, tell you first. It's a little awkward: not something one naturally talks to one's wife about.'

'I'm intrigued. Go on.'

He was actually blushing. 'I don't know whether – well, perhaps you do know, though naturally you couldn't say anything, or admit – ' He coughed. 'It's a delicate subject. I have to tell you, my dear, that I have formed a liaison with a girl – a young woman. Not a person of rank, of course,' he added hastily. 'She's – '

'It's all right, Basil.' Emily took pity on him. 'I know about Nina Antonova, if that's what you're trying to tell me.'

'How do you know?'

'Leone Duvitska told me.'

He seemed deeply embarrassed. 'You shouldn't know. It's something which no – Emilia, I'm sorry if it upsets you. I know we had that trouble some time ago, and coming from a different background you don't really understand how it is – '

346

'I don't mind about her,' Emily said gently. 'Really, I'm glad for you. I'm very fond of you, Basil, and I want you to be happy.'

He seemed taken aback by that. He looked at her for a long time, puzzled and ill at ease, and she could almost see the questions forming and dissolving as he tried to calculate her feelings about their marriage. At last he simply blurted it out.

'Nina's pregnant.'

Emily didn't move or speak. She stared at him, feeling numb. How far from her Basil had gone! How alone she was. Everyone else seemed attached to life and the renewal of life except her. She alone was condemned to this frozen in-between state, endlessly waiting for life to begin.

At last Basil spoke again. 'Emilia, I hate to have to ask you this, but if it's true that you don't mind – and I've felt lately that we are friends, after all – I don't know anyone I'd sooner turn to than you.'

'Yes, Basil?' she said at last, but she knew what he was going to say.

'If it is war, and I do have to go away, would you – would you keep an eye on Nina? I've made provision for her anyway, but you know how women can be when they're with child.'

Emily wanted to laugh at that, but suppressed it, knowing it was inappropriate. 'Surely she has a family?'

'Yes, but she may not feel like going to them. Her life is different now – you understand. I don't think she feels she has much in common with them.' He bit his lip. 'And of course she'll have to give up dancing. I wouldn't ask you, but – just a distant eye, to make sure she's all right. Would you? Could I tell her that she could come to you, in case of need?'

It was surely the strangest request that would ever be made of her, she thought. But Basil was right – she was much more his friend than his wife.

'Yes, all right,' she said. 'If it comes to it – all right.'

Two more days passed in strange silence, without news. Emily occupied herself by playing with the children, starting to teach Tatya to ride – three, she told Anna firmly, was considered quite old enough in England – and when it grew too hot for physical activity, gathering them in the shade and telling them stories. For Yenchik's sake she revived her endless tale of the twins, updated a little and transposed into a Russian context: they lived in a cave in the Caucasus now,

347

and regularly thwarted bands of wild mountain bandits and rescued kidnapped Tartar princesses. Roshka listened agog, though she would really have preferred triplets to twins. Tolya felt himself too old for stories, but he listened too, glad to have anything to take his mind off the tension of the unendurable wait.

Emily was woken from a deep sleep in the early hours of the morning of the 20th. She thought at first in her half-waking state it was Basil coming to seek comfort; but as soon as he touched her, she realised it was Alexei.

She was wide awake at once. 'What is it?'

'Sshh! Don't make a noise. No-one knows I'm here yet.'

'What time is it?'

'Just after four o'clock. It'll be light soon. I've just come from Peterhof, from the Tsar. I had to come to you first.' He stroked her night-tumbled hair back from her face tenderly.

'You look exhausted.'

'It was a long meeting: Sazonov, Sukhomlinov — most of the ministers — the ambassadors Buchanan and Paleologue. I sat outside on a chair for hours on end. They called me in from time to time. Sazonov would have had me in the whole time, but the Tsar sets store by protocol.' He smiled faintly. 'Old Fredericks brought me some supper on a tray, otherwise I'd have been forgotten.'

'Is there news?' she asked.

'Hold me, *doushka*,' he said. She sat up and put her arms around him, and he held her close. She could feel him trembling with weariness — at least, she assumed it was that. He smelled of night and long travelling and long meetings. She ached to take him into her bed and hold him properly, but she didn't suppose he would risk that, not here, not now, after such a long time of being careful.

After a while, he spoke, his voice muffled by her hair. 'I suppose you've guessed — it's war. Germany declared war on Russia last night.'

'Alexei!'

'The Kaiser demanded the Tsar cancel the mobilisation. The Tsar refused. Pourtales handed Sazonov a note from Berlin at seven o'clock yesterday evening. It must all have been decided days ago.'

'What does it mean?' she asked after a moment, holding him, not sure if it was for his comfort or hers.

'France is sworn to come in with us,' he said. 'Britain is bound to come in as soon as Germany moves — she can't stay neutral in the face of German aggression, not with that huge German fleet

348

hovering at the mouth of the Channel. It's as Sazonov said days ago: *la guerre européenne.*'

'European war,' Emily repeated. 'So it's here at last.'

'Yes,' said Alexei.

They remained as they were, arms around each other, silent; each wondering what it would mean for them even more than what it would mean for the world.

BOOK THREE

SURVIVING

Chapter Twenty

It was as though the whole of Petersburg had decided simultaneously to give a party. Where people had found bunting and banners to decorate their houses at such short notice puzzled Emily; or had they bought them in advance against just such an occasion? It was a baking-hot day, the skies brazen with a vast stillness which seemed to look down, remote and pitiless, on human aspiration – fear and festival alike. Flags hung limp as dead hares from the flagpoles of government buildings; in the square before the Winter Palace, the crowd waiting for the Tsar was packed to immobility, sweating with heat and excitement, the paint of the cheap icons they clutched staining their damp fingers deep blue and crimson.

Elsewhere, along the streets and the quaysides, the crowds moved and jigged, milled and cheered, drank from up-ended bottles and embraced each other, singing. Any man in military uniform was seized upon with an exuberance of joy as likely to kill as congratulate, thumped on the back until his teeth loosened, kissed to swooning by rapturous girls, drowned in kindly vodka and deafened with loyal toasts. The bridges were jammed solid with celebration, every lamppost hung with cheering boys. Nervous horses evacuated copiously as their cursing, smiling drivers tried to force a way through. The river teemed with boats of every size and description, decked with flags and crowded with spectators, so many that the surface of the water couldn't be seen. It was hardly possible that day, even if dead drunk, to fall overboard.

The moment all were waiting for arrived: the Tsar, coming from Peterhof by boat, landed at the Winter Palace quay. As he stepped ashore, dressed in plain khaki uniform like a mere infantryman, the cheeis began: '*Batushka, Batushka, Batushka, Bat*USHKA . . . ', the sound swelling into a relentless rhythm as voice after voice took it up. He passed through the multitude, the little, plain, pleasant-faced man, faintly smiling behind the camouflage of his beard: Tsar of All the Russias, the Little Father of the People, greeted now with a pure and religious fervour as the saviour of the country.

The Tsaritsa, with pale, set face, was beside him, her hat brim turned back to show her face; the four Grand Duchesses walked behind, two by two, as they did everything – the Big Pair and the Little Pair as the family called them – dressed all in white, solemn in the face of such emotion. Into the Winter Palace, up the Grand Staircase towards the Salle de Nicholas, where the *Te Deum* was to be said. Five or six thousand were crammed together there under the glittering chandeliers: a more genteel crush, this one – a perfumed stickiness, a well-bred rolling murmur instead of hoarse-throated cheers.

'No Tsarevitch,' Emily whispered to Basil as the party went past them towards the altar hastily set up in the centre of the vast marble hall. 'I wonder why, on such a day?' Was he ill again? she wondered. Bad for them all if he was. This was not a time for the Tsar to be distracted. Was that why the Tsaritsa was so pale? Or was it the thought of being at war with the country of her birth?

Prayers, singing, blessings, hands all around making the sign of the cross over and over, like willow branches blowing about in a breeze. An icon on the altar, and a confused explanation from Basil: very sacred, very traditional, miraculous powers. The Tsar taking an oath, speaking well, his pleasant voice ringing and firm at such a moment: 'I solemnly swear that I will never make peace while a single enemy remains on Russian soil.' Heady stuff, this, throat-tightening words: peace, enemy, soil. The good earth of our own, our motherland; and peace, the springing corn untrampled, the rosy children undefiled.

There was a moment of tremulous solemnity, of palpitating silence. And then, to cheers, the Tsar's party left the Salle, and there was a scramble for windows. Everyone wanted to witness the next act: the imperial family was to appear on the small, red-draped balcony in the exact centre of the vast façade overlooking the square; appear to the people down below, for the Tsar to address them and make the same pledge he had made in his oath before his nobles.

The tiny figures stepped out, and a vast, composite sound like a moan of accomplished love went up from the crowd as it sank by the thousand to its knees. The Tsar raised his hand; a small, lapping silence like a lakeside wave rippled outwards from the front of the crowd, but lost momentum, meeting the wall of noise from the back. Overcome with emotion, the Emperor bowed his head, and seeing it, the crowd roared its love and approval.

A few voices, lost at first, began to sing 'God Save the Tsar', and gradually more and more took it up as the impetus was passed back

354

from mouth to mouth. The fervent song rang round the huge arena, begun at different times, and sung at different speeds, and over and over again, so that the familiar tune boomed and swelled like ocean waves in a cavern: the unstoppable and beautiful and frightening sound of human co-operation.

Emily was exhilarated and astonished by this seemingly universal mood of patriotism and fervour. The newspapers were full of it, and even allowing for exaggeration, her own observations allowed her to believe that the scenes in the streets of Petersburg had truly been repeated all over the empire. The party of that first day went on all night, the streets seething with cheering, drinking, singing, kissing men and women; and on subsequent days the enthusiasm did not wane, only spread further.

The surprising thing to her was the deeply religious element to the fervour. The church bells rang almost incessantly, and there was a constant stream of communicants going to the special services of dedication. Banners displayed and slogans shouted all invoked the holiness of Russia and the cause; where crowds gathered, half the waving hands clutched an icon or a crucifix.

Brought up in the cool, polite, understated religion of the English, Emily had not, even in the two years of her Russian residence, understood the depth and simplicity of belief amongst even sophisticated Russians. God, Christ, the Virgin, the Blessed Saints were real people here, known intimately, loved passionately; vital and close as if they were standing, flesh and substance and glowing presence, in the very next room.

War fervour pervaded all classes. Basil came in one day to tell Emily that the striking factory workers had all voluntarily gone back to work.

'I came across a crowd of them taking down one of their barricades. They were even trying to right a streetcar they'd overturned. I couldn't get by at first – they were filling the road. Then one of them spotted me and called out to ask if I was a military man.'

'Oh dear. I hope they didn't get rough with you?'

'No, they were as good as gold. I told them I was a reservist and going out as soon as I could, and they became very friendly and called me "Captain". So I took a chance on asking them how come they'd given up their strike. "Oh," says they, "this is our war, Captain, not just yours. The whole of Russia is involved now. We want to do our bit to make sure the Germans are beaten!" And then someone pipes up with "God Save the Tsar", and off they all went, singing like bulls. I had to stand to attention and take off my hat, or I think they'd have lynched me!'

Emily laughed. 'I had Masha Sapetska here this morning, assuring me that this isn't a politicians' war, it's a fight to the death between our sacred traditions and the Teutonic yoke of despotism. I have the feeling those weren't her own words.'

'The newspapers are full of that sort of stuff,' Basil grinned. 'Tremendous, isn't it?'

'She also said two of her footmen and her second cook have asked permission to enlist straight away. She was very annoyed, but what could she say? They'd probably have been called up anyway – they're the right age.'

'I suppose they're afraid of missing out. I must say, I sympathise with them – this war is going to be over so quickly, those who don't get in at the beginning won't see any of the fun.'

'Oh, I'm sure there'll be plenty for all,' Emily said, half amused, half alarmed.

'Well, I don't want to take any chances. I'm going to see the Colonel this afternoon, and if he agrees, I shall be in uniform by the end of the week.'

'If you can find a tailor to make it that quickly.'

On the 23rd of July the German Army invaded Belgium, and Britain declared war on Germany. The war fervour rose another pitch. Crowds swarmed about the French and British Embassies, singing the national anthems and waving anything they could find that was red, white or blue. At an open-air concert in the park, the orchestra struck up before the overture with the anthems of all three allies, and the audience stood with tears of pride and excitement in its eyes.

'Thank God we're on the same side, at least,' Emily said to Alexei during a snatched meeting at the apartment. He was perpetually tracking between Ministry and palace, hardly having time to eat or sleep, and they had spent very little time together of late.

'It makes our chances for victory so much better,' Alexei said. 'I can't believe that Germany can win against the might of Britain. As long as she keeps fighting, we've a chance.'

'Britain won't give up,' Emily said certainly. 'Not now she's begun.'

He was silent a moment. Then, 'It's astonishing how unpopular the Germans have suddenly become. You'd think the Kaiser was the Devil himself. Did you know a mob broke into the German Embassy today and smashed everything in it? Furniture, paintings, tapestries – everything. They even pulled down the bronze horses on top of the portico. A terrible act of vandalism, that. They were beautiful, those horses.'

'Perhaps people need something to hate,' Emily said. 'We're so civilised these days. We never talk about the Devil, and we all have to live together in close proximity without fighting. It's not natural. Hating some mythical enemy is a sort of catharsis.'

'There's nothing mythical about the Germans.'

'There is to most people. The ordinary people in the street have never met a German; and the ones they hate aren't real Germans, anyway. They're the embodiment of evil and fear. Hobgoblins. Seva was telling me today exactly what Germans do to captured nations. The most Gothic stuff you ever heard! I can't imagine where he got it from, but he was enjoying every bit.'

'I think you may have something there,' Alexei nodded seriously. 'Shall we call it Paget's Special Theory of Warfare?'

She laughed. 'You've never called me Paget before.'

'I don't care for the alternative. Are you and Basil going down to Schwartzenturm at the weekend?'

'If Basil hasn't marched away by then. I want to see Aunt Yenya and the children before she takes them back to Archangel.'

'I'll try to come down. I want to have a few moments of peace with you before I plunge back into these mad meetings. The Tsar hates confrontation. He smiles and nods to everything, and then sends out letters afterwards saying the exact opposite of what you think you've agreed. It's all so exhausting.'

They were all together one last time at Schwartzenturm before the party broke up. Basil was elated, having secured a commission in the Preobrajensky Guard.

'It took some negotiation, too, I can tell you. Even getting past the adjutant was a major task, with everyone trying to get in to see the Colonel. And now that crook Narbov wants to charge me practically double to make the uniforms in time.'

'Why did you go to the Preobrajensky? I thought you'd have wanted to be with your friends,' Emily said.

'Yes, with Youna and Dima,' Anna put in anxiously. 'You won't know anyone, Vasska. You'll be lonely.'

'Oh, don't be silly, I know people in all the regiments,' Basil said. 'And this way, I'll be at the front first. We'll be off on Monday, and get a head start on the rest of them.'

'Besides which,' Alexei said drily, 'if you'd joined Youna and Dima you'd have been junior to them.'

Basil was so high-spirited he didn't even take offence. 'There is that, of course,' he said cheerfully. 'I couldn't fancy calling Youna "Sir" after all these years.'

'Sasha Suslov called on me yesterday', Emily said, 'to tell me that he's enlisting in an infantry regiment, of all things! He said his whole class at the university voted to go down to the centre together and sign up.'

'Yes, it's become quite the fashion for students,' Valya said. 'It's supposed to be more patriotic to fight alongside the peasants, God knows why.'

'The Kobin boy who was at the Conservatoire has joined the artillery,' Anna said. 'There's a waste of a good pianist! I never knew an artilleryman without at least one mangled finger. His mother must be heartbroken.'

'I should think she'd rather be proud of him for volunteering,' said Basil.

Tolya turned a face of flame to his parents. 'Oh, then you must let me go, Papa, Mamochka!' It was the renewal of an argument that had been going on for days. 'You see everyone is going!'

'Not everyone,' Yenya said flatly. 'You're too young.'

'I'm seventeen – '

'Just!'

'They're taking men of seventeen. Papa!' He flung the appeal away from the distaff side, his voice quavering a little on the word *men*. If anyone should laugh at him now, his heart would break. But no-one laughed.

'You have to finish your studies, Tolya,' he said, with an eye to his wife's feelings. 'In another year perhaps; when you're eighteen – '

'But it'll be *over* by then!' he almost wailed. 'Six months, that's what everybody says is the most it can last. Isn't that right, sir?' He

358

turned to appeal to Basil. 'I've heard the Guards officers saying they'll be riding into Berlin by Christmas.'

'Well,' Basil hesitated. He had no wish to upset Yenya either.

Tolya felt himself on firm ground. 'Isn't it true, Uncle,' he appealed to Alexei, 'that the Government's preparing for a short war? And the British and the French – they all believe it will be over in six months.'

'Yes. That's true,' Alexei said, but he went on: 'That doesn't mean they're right, though.'

That seemed like heresy to Tolya. 'But sir, the Germans can't fight, everyone knows that. They're just a race of swaggering sausage-eaters.'

'What have sausages to do with it?' Yenya asked, mystified.

'Nothing, Mama. Just that we're bound to win.'

'You think we're invincible, do you?' Alexei asked in amusement.

'We have the largest army in the world,' the boy said seriously.

'That's right. And we have the capacity to put an endless supply of men into combat,' Valya said, forgetting himself in the interests of the argument. 'For sheer numbers, the Germans can't beat us.'

'I've heard it said', Basil agreed, 'that with our population regenerating itself normally, we can keep five million men in the field for ever.'

Alexei shook his head. 'You haven't taken into account those not liable for military service – the Muslims, the Jews, the Finns – and the boys under twenty-one.'

'Oh, but – ' Tolya and Valya objected at the same moment, though for different reasons.

'Our last census showed that half our male population is aged twenty or under,' Alexei went on relentlessly.

'They'll volunteer,' Valya said.

'Perhaps they may; but they'll be untrained, raw recruits against professional soldiers.'

'The Russian soldier is the best in the world,' Basil said with some indignation. 'Everyone know that. For courage and endurance, he hasn't his equal. He's unstoppable.'

'It's not enough to kill a Russian soldier,' Vanya smiled, quoting an old saw, 'you still have to push him over.'

'He has endurance, I grant you, and he's stoical in the face of death. His life on the commune teaches him to obey orders without question, as long as they're backed up by fear of punishment. But you can't drill him into a killing-machine, like a German, or an active patriot like a Briton. He's essentially lazy, good-natured and parochial. Let discipline waver for an instant – let his officers be killed, for example – and he'll drop his weapon and head off home to his village as fast as his legs will carry him. If he has a weapon, that is. If he has legs.'

Emily could see that his words convinced no-one.

'Well, all I can say is that you're in a minority of one, Alyosha,' Basil said easily. 'Everyone *I've* spoken to says we'll beat them within six months without the slightest trouble.'

'And that means it'll be over before I'm eighteen,' Tolya said, sticking to his own point. 'If you make me wait, I'll have missed it.' He looked urgently at his mother, sensing a weakening of resistance. 'I'd have thought you'd want me to do my duty to Russia, the Tsar and the Faith.'

'Of course I do,' Yenya said. 'It's just that you're so young.'

'Does one have to be over twenty-one to be patriotic?' he asked guilefully. 'You wouldn't want people thinking I was a coward, would you?'

Valya took his pipe from his mouth. 'Yenya? We've always talked about the importance of duty. Maybe it's our duty to let him go.'

She turned her face away. 'You can't expect a mother to think that way.'

'Please, Mamochka,' Tolya said. 'I'll be all right, truly I will. I'll come back safely. And I'll bring you the finest hat in Berlin for your Christmas present.'

Yenya gathered him briefly against her, and then set him back to tweak his collar straight in an automatic gesture, loving him, letting him go. 'A cavalry regiment, though. I'm not having my son in the infantry.'

Tolya bore with it, quivering with the effort of staying still. 'Thank you, Mamochka. Can I go and find Yenchik, and tell him?'

'Yes, go then.'

He was gone like a sprinting greyhound, and as soon as he was round the corner of the terrace they heard him bellowing for his brother, his voice slipping for once into a very unmanly shriek in his excitement. 'Yenchik! *Yenchik*! They said yes! I'm going to go!'

Basil was gone, just one small figure in the seemingly endless procession of cavalry and artillery divisions which clogged the roads out of Petersburg every day. The air was full of white dust, the sound of rumbling wheels and horses' hooves, the smell of sweat and manure. Cavalrymen, field guns, ammunition carts, waggons piled high with officers' baggage, field kitchens, ambulances, farriers' carts, strings of remounts: all thronged in confusion, in no particular order, in a bedlam of lost articles and lost men and shouted orders, mounted messengers cantering up and down the lines looking for Authority. Once out of the city, the columns spread out over the fields like a clogged stream overflowing its banks. The men smiled as they headed south, sometimes singing, sometimes breaking into chants: 'Faith, Tsar and Country!'; 'Down with the Prussians!'; 'No more Germany! No more Kaiser!'

Basil had gone in a state of elation, looking, with his cheeks flushed and his eyes bright, hardly older than Tolya. He had parted from Emily affectionately, confidently; his only worry that his dress uniform, which he would need for the victory parade in Berlin, had not been finished in time.

'I'll send it on to you,' Emily promised.

'Make sure Narbov finishes it this week as he promised. You'll probably have to bully him – everyone else will be. And make sure he packs it carefully. I don't want the lace crushed.'

'I will. Don't worry.' Emily said. 'You'll have it in plenty of time.' She felt a surge of affection for him: her husband, after all, though today seeming more like her son. Perhaps every woman is a mother, when she sees a man off to war. 'You'll take care of yourself?'

'Of course.' He smiled rather kindly. 'I'll be back before you know it. And you'll take care of things, won't you? I know I can trust you. Look after Anna.'

'I will.'

He hesitated. 'If by any chance I'm not back before Nina – before the baby's born – ' It was a delicate matter for a gentleman to broach with his wife.

'Yes?' Emily encouraged.

'If it's a boy, I'd like it to be named after my father.'

'I'll see it's done.'

He kissed her on both cheeks, and then lightly, shyly, on the lips. 'Goodbye, Emilusha. Thank you for everything.'

'God bless you, Basil,' she said.

Tolya left a few days later, by train from the Warsaw Station. Emily went with Yenya and Valya to see him off.

361

The station was swarming. Response to the first call for volunteers had surpassed all expectation, and men had been streaming into the recruitment centres and marching into Petersburg at a phenomenal rate. Now they were being shipped off to the front by every train, volunteers and regulars together. Such was the response that there were only enough rifles for two out of every three men.

The train was in, the huge black engine steaming and hissing like a friendly dragon, hitched to a long snake of waggons: carriages for the officers, cattle trucks for the men, horseboxes behind, and then luggage vans. The soldiers were packed tightly into the trucks, khaki uniforms already white with dust from their long march. Under the caps the faces were smiling, bewildered, resigned, elated, one or two red with secret drink, one or two slobbered with tears. They leaned out wherever they could to take a last farewell of those thronging the platform: parents, wives, sisters. Here a man kissed a cross held up by a bearded priest, there a baby held up by a weeping girl in a kerchief.

Tolya looked very young with his clean-shaven face, though there were others as young around him. He had found a place in one of the carriages with some other subaltern volunteers, and stepped back down onto the platform to say goodbye.

'You see they're all nice fellows, Mamochka. I shall have good company.'

'You'll write, won't you?'

'Of course, as soon as we get there. I say, we'll be the first at the front, nearly the very first!' He glanced around at the beards and moustaches of the regular soldiers. 'I'm glad you let me have your old valise, Papa,' he confided. 'The other lads have new ones, and it makes a man look such a raw!'

Emily said goodbye. 'You aren't troubled any more by the idea of killing your fellow man?' she asked curiously.

'No,' he said seriously. 'I see now I was mistaken. When a fellow threatens your own land and your own people, you just have to get on with it, don't you? It's a sacred duty.'

'Go on thinking that way.' She kissed him.

Kisses, hugs, words of advice, tears from Yenya; and then it was time to go. The whistle was blown, doors slammed, the engine groaned and shuddered as it took up the strain and jerked, jerked at the overloaded train. Finally, slowly, it chugged forward and away, out of the lamplit station and into the darkness. The men leaned out, cheering, waving, last messages shouted, three or four

362

different songs taken up in the cheerful roar that passes at such times for singing. The crowd on the platform waved and waved until the last glimpse of the red tail-light wagged out of sight, and the singing faded to nothing; and then a silence fell. It was an odd moment. Everyone just stood, staring at where the train had been, reluctant to move, as though there were still something left to do, something left unsaid which must be remembered before they could go.

Then at last someone sighed, someone moved, and the moment was over.

'Shall we go, my dears,' said Valya. 'We have our packing to do, if we're to be off tomorrow.'

'Yes, I suppose so,' said Yenya.

'He'll be all right. You can't keep the boy wrapped in cotton wool for ever. The experience will make a man of him.' And then he added kindly, 'I gave him my medal of St Seraphim to wear. It kept me safe all the way to the Yellow Sea and back.'

Yenya smiled. 'Oh well, that's all right, then,' she said.

Emily sat at the table in the small day nursery, helping Modeste and Tatya make up farewell parcels for the soldiers going to the front. Into each went a pair of woollen socks, a piece of soap, a square block of *makhorka* – soldier's tobacco, cheap and rank and highly prized – and a small icon card printed with a saint's likeness and a short prayer. To add improvement to charity, Emily was persuading Modeste, whose writing left a lot to be desired, to include a note with each parcel he finished, wishing the recipient good luck and a safe return.

Anna had come back to Fourstatskaya Street when Yenya and Valya went home, and Emily could hardly blame her for not wanting to remain at Schwartzenturm with all the excitements going on in Petersburg. Ah, no, she must remember to call it Petrograd now. By order of the Tsar, the name had been changed to make it sound Slavic rather than Germanic. All things German were now suspect, even to the extent that Modeste's tutor, who had left Prussia over twenty years ago, had been taken away under armed guard to be deported. The governess, who was French, had also left to go home: she had parents and siblings in France with whom she wished to share the danger. Anna had asked Emily, with the supreme confi-

363

dence of one whose requests were never denied, to help with the children until a new governess could be found.

'You're so good with children. And you can improve their English and French while you play with them.'

The danger to France was apparently very great: the Germans were advancing with astonishing speed. Since the moment Russia entered the war, France had been sending frantic requests for her to mount an offensive which would draw German troops away from the Western Front and give the French Army some relief. In response, Russia had sent the first fruits of the mobilisation helter-skelter for the frontier with Eastern Prussia, and a second force to the Galician border, where the Austrian troops were massing.

Although Sukhomlinov, as Minister for War, had the automatic right to become commander-in-chief of the armed forces, he had declined the post with, according to Alexei, muted horror at the very thought of living in a railway carriage in a forest somewhere in Poland.

'He likes his comfort,' said Alexei.

'A massive understatement, if half what one hears about him is true,' Emily said with a smile.

'Very well, he is a devoted sybarite, a *bon viveur* with a voluptuous young wife and expensive tastes. But one can't help liking him; and he knows how to get things done, which is always important in Russia, with a bureaucratic system dedicated to obstruction and inactivity.'

The Tsar's uncle, Grand Duke Nikolas Nikolayevitch, known to his family as Nikolasha, had been given supreme command, and had gone off to set up Stavka – headquarters – at Baranovichi.

Emily looked it up on a map. 'It seems to be a long way from anywhere,' she said doubtfully.

Alexei shrugged. 'It's halfway between the two fronts. And it's nearer than Petersburg. It doesn't really matter, anyway. The commanders at the fronts will make their own decisions. Stavka only has to dictate overall policy, and everyone knows what that is by now – even the Germans.'

Emily was startled. 'What can you mean?'

He gave her a grim smile. 'Our gallant troops in Lithuania have moved so fast in their eagerness to get into battle, they've outrun their logistical support – including their field telephones. They've been sending back status reports by wireless, and in clear – '

'In what?'

'Not in code. So anyone with a wireless receiver, including the Germans, can hear and understand.'

'Oh Alexei!'

'It probably doesn't matter,' he reassured her. 'They were bound to know we were there sooner or later, and as for numbers, they knew long ago that we would outnumber them. If we crush them quickly, it won't have made any difference.'

'Do you think it will be a quick war too, then?'

He hesitated. 'I hope so.' He seemed about to say more, and then changed his mind. 'I hope so.'

'So do I,' she said, though for largely different reasons.

Those reasons were becoming more uncomfortable all the time, Emily thought now, as she supervised the children's war efforts. Anna, as she grew bigger and less inclined for company or exertion, relied more and more on Emily, and seemed to expect her to be at her command at all times. Emily felt she was being drawn into a relationship which would ultimately place her in an ignoble position. Every advance in intimacy deepened her hypocrisy, and would make the final betrayal worse. She dreaded what she was going to feel when –

The door opened and Natasha came in. Emily looked up quickly.

'Yes, it has definitely started,' Natasha said briskly. 'The silly girl must have got her dates wrong.'

Emily found her mouth dry. 'How – how long will it be?'

A faint frown pulled down Natasha's fine brows. 'It ought to be quick enough, being the third, but I'm not sure. There's something about the way she's started . . . However, we won't be alarmed until we have to. Do you want to go and see her?'

'Does she want me to?' Emily asked reluctantly.

'She didn't ask for you. She has the midwife with her, and old Mamka. And Dr Kovnodsev is coming soon. I suppose we had better send a message to Alyosha.'

Modeste looked up at the sound of his father's name. 'Have you been with Mama? Is she ill?'

'No, *mylenkaya*,' Natasha said, 'but she's very busy, so you can't see her for a while.'

'What's she doing?'

'Something secret.'

'A nice secret? Like a present?'

'You'll see. Emilusha?' Emily came back from a deep and not very happy thought. 'Do you know where Alyosha is?'

'He went to the Ministry. They'd know there, I expect,' she said. Upstairs another woman was in labour with the child of the man she loved. She wished herself anywhere but here.

It was a difficult labour. Emily, keeping the children amused in a part of the house out of earshot, supplied the cries and moans for herself in full and generous measure. She lived every moment of the agony, helped on by Natasha's unnecessarily frequent bulletins, delivered over the children's heads in a mixture of rapid French and significant nods and gestures – at any rate, Emily thought confusedly, not in clear.

It was a breech birth, it transpired, no happy matter for any mother, and exacerbated by the fact that Anna, though she had grown very fat in pregnancy, was comparatively small-boned.

'If only she hadn't eaten so much,' Natasha complained at one point, coming down from the torture chamber to recruit her strength on tea well laced with raspberry jam. 'The *enfant* is as fat as a porpoise, which doesn't help at all, and not nearly such a helpful shape. All that picking at sweet stuff for nine months! But she always was greedy – she and Vasya both, though it doesn't show in him yet, lucky boy. Still no word from Alyosha?'

'No. They said they'd pass on the message, but he's gone up to the palace, so he's probably in a meeting he can't leave.'

'Ah well, he'd only be in the way. Men tend to panic at such times, especially if there's any little complication.'

Later she was not so sanguine about the 'little complication'. 'He ought to be here.'

The children had gone to bed now, and there was no more need for code.

'Is she in danger?'

'She's getting very tired.' Natasha hesitated. 'I don't *think* we'll lose her, but Alyosha ought to be here, in case.'

Emily felt cold with misgiving. If Anna died, she was so afraid that she might catch herself feeling glad. No, not that, God, please! She had enough on her conscience already. Sometimes she dreamed of Aunt Maud, pale and reproachful, staring in at her through a streaming window from a wet, dark night, and she would wake in a guilty sweat.

Natasha saw Emily's expression, and patted her hand comfortingly. 'Try not to worry. Mamka's been praying non-stop to Our Lady and St Anne, and the power of prayer can move mountains. Kovnodsev is gloomy, but I've never met a doctor who wasn't. Anyway, he comes from Pskov, and that's enough to make anyone want to slit his throat.'

It was after midnight when Alexei came home at last. He found Emily waiting up for him, sitting at the table in the drawing-room. She had rested her head on her folded arms, and the yellow light from the table lamp gilded the curling hairs at the nape of her neck, which were always too fine and short to catch up with the rest. The attitude was one of sleep, but even before he spoke he could see by the gleam under the lashes that her eyes were open.

'Is it over?' he asked.

She raised her head, sat up, looked at him wearily. 'Yes. You got the messages, then?'

It sounded reproachful. 'I couldn't come,' he said. 'I was with the Tsar or the Cabinet the whole time. Sometimes both. Is she all right?'

She seemed to have difficulty in answering. He went closer, but something about the brittle angle of her body made him feel he might not touch her.

'She had a bad time of it. It was a breech birth.' She looked at him, absurdly, to see if he knew what that meant. 'Kovnodsev says she'll be all right, but she'll be weak and tired for some time.'

'Understandable,' he said carefully. 'And the baby?'

'It's all right.' She stood up, and he could see that the movement was involuntary, the physical residue of a mental desire to escape. 'It's a boy. Quite a big one, too. That's what made it so hard for her. A boy, perfectly healthy.' She wrapped her arms round herself as though she were cold, her eyes anywhere but with him. 'Anna's seen him. She held him for a while, and then Kovnodsev gave her something to make her sleep.'

'Emilusha,' he said gently, 'look at me.'

She did, still hugging herself. Her eyes looked wide and frightened. 'So, you're a father again. Congratulations! You must be very happy.'

He shook his head slowly. 'Come here,' he said. She didn't move, so he went to her and took her in his arms. She felt cold and rigid, resisting him. '*Doushka*,' he said. 'You've known for so long this had to happen. Nothing has changed.'

'Everything has changed!' She began to cry. 'You don't know, do you? You don't know what it's been like, what I've been feeling. All through today, knowing she was up there, suffering – and now the baby. Yours, but not mine! What does that make me?' He held her tighter, and she struggled angrily. 'It's no good! I see it now. You said we must wait until the baby was born, but how can you leave now? It's here – *he's* here! He's real, a real person. I've seen him. And when you've seen him, how will you be able to leave him? We're worse off than we were before.'

'*Doushka*, don't. Don't tear at me. It will be all right, I promise you. Listen – '

'No!' She wrenched herself away from him, stood back, trembling with the effort, her fists clenched, her eyes and nose red with crying. She looked like a frightened child. He reminded himself that she was not twenty-one yet; but that made him feel old.

'I want it to end now,' she said. She swallowed as though her throat hurt. 'I can't go on with it. It's got to stop before it gets worse.'

'I can't stop,' he said quietly. 'Don't do this, Emilia. I can't live without you.'

Her mouth bowed with pain. 'But you *do*!' she cried; and suddenly she broke and ran.

'Emilusha, wait!' She was at the door, fumbling with the doorknob two-handed, clumsily, because she couldn't see. 'Wait, I have to tell you something.'

She stopped and turned her head. He could see the tears rushing down her face, and pain and pity made it hard to speak. 'I have to tell you,' he said helplessly. 'There's news from the front.'

She took an uneven breath. 'A battle?'

'Not – quite.' He made a useless gesture with his hands. He wanted so badly to touch her that he didn't know what to do with them. He let them fall to his side. 'General Rennenkampf – commanding the First Army at the East Prussian border – '

'Yes,' she acknowledged.

'Mindful of his orders to hurry and relieve the French, he attacked the German border troops as soon as he got there, with whatever he had. His cavalry had outridden his infantry and artillery, of course; but Rennenkampf is a cavalry officer anyway. The sabre charge is everything to men like him.' She nodded. 'The Germans had field guns. He ordered our cavalry to charge them.'

She looked at him now, apprehension stopping her tears at source. He could read everything she wondered, and it was not as she thought. 'It must have been like the British cavalry at Balaclava – brave and dashing and mad. They attacked so fiercely they actually drove the Germans back; but the cost was appalling.'

'Who is dead?' she asked. She sounded quite calm.

'Tolya,' he said. He knew she had prepared herself for it to be Basil, but there wasn't anything he could have done about that. She took a moment to understand him.

'Tolya? Not Tolya. Please, Alexei – '

'He was shot from the saddle in his first charge. His regiment lost more than a third of its officers. They led their men from the front, of course.'

He stopped speaking, and to Emily his face seemed to crumple. She acted without thought, crossing the space between in a few steps and putting her arms around him. They held each other tightly. She remembered Tolya's flamelike face as he pleaded to be allowed to go, for the glory of being first at the front.

'First blood,' she said aloud. He had promised to be home before Christmas, she thought mechanically. Well, so he would. So he would.

Alexei pressed her tighter against him, as if it might be the last time, and rested his face against her hair. 'Poor little boy,' he said. 'The war was only five weeks old. He lasted only five weeks.'

Chapter Twenty-One

It would have been impossible for Natasha not to be aware of Emily's misery, but she had no difficulty in supplying a reason for it. In the first five months of Emily's life in Russia, she had been a daily witness to the special affection between her and Tolya. It was to be expected that Emily would grieve for him, and draw no comfort from the thought that he had given his life for his country.

She felt it was unwise, however, for Emily to shut herself up all alone in the Kronversky house, seeing no-one.

'Don't stay here,' she said persuasively one afternoon. 'It's bad for you to be alone. Why don't you move in with Anna for a while, just until the war's over? You'll be company for each other.' She remembered there was another reason for Emily's unhappiness. 'She worries about Vasya too, you know,' she said gently.

Emily shivered. 'I don't want to live there. I can't live there.'

'Yes you can! Now that's just silly. Besides, think of poor Anna. It really is too bad of you to desert her like that, as soon as her baby's born. She feels very low and weak, and she needs someone there all the time. I'd do it, but you know she's never cared for me – nor I for her. But she likes you – and the children miss you, too.'

Emily gave her a helpless, trapped look. 'Please, Grandmama, I just want to be left alone.'

'That's the worst thing for you. It's unhealthy. You need people around you.'

'I want to live here – '

'That's another thing! I would really like you to move out of here because I want to turn it into a hospital for wounded men from the front. They'll start arriving soon, and I'm positive there hasn't been enough provision made for them. Besides, Princess Razumovska is sponsoring a whole hospital train, and one can't allow oneself to be upstaged by her. Now, what I'd like is for you and me to finance it jointly. What do you think about that? If you like, we could call it the Anatoli Hospital, in memory of our poor little boy.'

'Oh Grandmama!' Emily was half touched, half appalled.

'It's going to be very much needed, I assure you. Everyone always underestimates the casualties in a war. And it will only be for a few months, after all. Can that hurt you?'

'I haven't very much money, only my allowance, but you're welcome to that – '

'*Durachka*! Vasya left you full power of attorney, surely he told you that? You have the spending of his entire fortune, and he would certainly approve of this, being a soldier himself. So if you move in with Anna, we can put your furniture in store, and then have a wonderful time ordering beds and linen and all the equipment. I promise you, it will take you out of yourself! You'll be so busy thinking of others you'll have no time to think of yourself.'

Emily bowed her head, unable to think of any way out of the trap. It had taken all her strength to walk away from Alexei; now she was to be forced to walk back. The only consolation, if it could be called that, was that he was likely to be very little at home. But still she would be living under his roof, with his wife and children, seeing daily how hopeless the situation was.

'Yes, Grandmama,' she said resignedly. She had no more will to fight. She would do whatever she was told.

Natasha, hearing the weariness in her voice, went to sit beside her and put an arm around her. 'Did you hear that Tolya's going to be awarded the Cross of St George, for courage on the field of battle?' she said gently. 'He'd have liked that, don't you think?'

Emily didn't answer. If he had lived, if he had come back, he'd have received it with enormous and embarrassed pride, his lips pulling into that self-conscious smirk she remembered best of all his expressions. Instead, awarded posthumously, would it give Yenya any pleasure? She doubted it.

The news from the fronts was all wonderfully cheering. In Galicia the Russians had inflicted decisive defeat on the ramshackle Austrian Army. Two hundred thousand Austrian soldiers had been taken prisoner. Lemberg, the capital of Galicia, had fallen, and the Russian Army was pressing slowly forward towards Vienna.

In East Prussia, Rennenkampf's force had been attacked by nine divisions of the German Eighth Army, and had driven them off. They were calling it the Battle of Gumbinnen. The Second Army under Samsonov was even now struggling through the wastes of northern Poland to join up with Rennenkampf, and when they met the Germans would be caught in a pincer and completely destroyed. Then the Russian Army would march unopposed on Berlin.

Berlin by Christmas! Everyone said it now, from the pie-sellers and tram-drivers in the streets to the wealthy revellers drinking champagne in the Astoria Hotel. It would all be over in no time. Meanwhile, war fever did not abate. Soldiers going off to the front were handed little packages, flowers and religious cards, were preceded to the station by bands playing stirring songs, were cheered on their way by excited crowds. The Tsar's picture was everywhere, in every window, schoolroom, bank, hotel. Never since the first days of his accession had he been so popular. Everyone remembered now how he had always spoken Russian and preferred the Russian style of clothing. He was truly the Little Father: he would lead them to splendid victory.

Emily's concerns were a little closer to hand. Anna had been delighted to have her come to live with her, and Emily had moved back into the room she had occupied with Basil when they had stayed there together. Anna's baby (she hoped by thinking of it as Anna's rather than *his* to take the sting away) was thriving at the breast of a plump girl named Epifania. By Alexei's wish he was to be called Piotr, after his great-grandfather, which rather puzzled Anna.

'I expected him to want to call him Nikolai, after his father – Alyosha's father, I mean. After all, it is rather traditional, and he didn't name Modeste for the family. However, Piotr Alexeyevitch has a nice ring to it. I suppose he has some reason for favouring his grandfather over his father.'

Emily didn't comment on it. She couldn't help remembering the time Alexei had shown her the portrait of Peter Kirov: 'Our common ancestor'. Had he chosen the name Piotr to make her feel somehow attached to the new baby? To remind her that they were bound together by blood?

She hadn't spoken to Alexei privately since she had moved back into Anna's house – indeed, she had hardly seen him. But she felt him all the time, a constant presence, like a thorn grown deep in the flesh that one was always, simply, aware of. Every room in the house held echoes of him, whether he was there or not. She knew the moment he came home, even if she heard no sounds of arrival. Often it was late, after she had gone to bed, and in her imagination she would follow him from room to room, feel him going to his study to sit brooding there, thinking about her, perhaps, waiting for her.

It would have been so easy to get up and go to him. It would have been such relief to have his arms around her again, to lie with him and be consumed and caressed and comforted. She wanted it so badly that sometimes she found she had half risen without realising it. But she wouldn't go. It was a subtle poison, sweet on the tongue, corroding afterwards. It would ultimately make her more miserable, that was sure, because there was no possibility of his leaving Anna, now that Piotr was here. If he could not leave her pregnant, how much less could he leave her weak, bedridden, and newly a mother?

In such a short time Petrograd descended from euphoria into despair. The news came in of a terrible defeat; and then another; two battles lost, casualties beyond number. The Second Army was no more; the First Army was in retreat back across the East Prussian border. There was no more cheering in the streets. Crowds gathered in bewildered silence outside official buildings, waiting for news, for the casualty lists; and after the silence of shock came the mutterings of discontent. Why had this happened? Who was to blame? Somebody must be punished!

Alexei came in late and weary night after night to the same questions. Anna wanted only to know whether Basil was safe. When she had been told that there was no news of him yet, she retired to her room to brood: she was not yet leaving her bed for more than a few hours each day. On the occasions he was in time for supper, Alexei took it alone, or with Emily, and it was to her that he told the details of the disaster.

The Germans were calling the first battle, against the Russian Second Army, the Battle of Tannenberg, in revenge for a defeat of the Teutonic Knights by the Slavs on the same site five hundred years earlier.

'It wasn't really Samsonov's fault,' Alexei explained wearily. 'His orders were to join forces with Rennenkampf as quickly as possible, but I don't think Stavka knew what the terrain was like that he'd have to march over. I've been there: it's a wasteland, pine and birch forest, marsh and river. No towns or even farms, nothing for the army to live off, and forced marching meant they outstripped their supply train. When they came on the Germans they were exhausted and half starved, short of rifles and short of ammunition. They fought astonishingly well – managed to hold the Germans off for almost four days virtually with bayonets alone – but ultimately they had no chance.'

'What were the losses?'

'They're saying a hundred and seventy thousand captured, dead or wounded,' Alexei said bleakly.

The numbers were almost incomprehensible. Emily could only stare.

'There is no more Second Army,' Alexei went on. 'After they surrendered, Samsonov walked off into the forest and shot himself. At least that will give us a scapegoat.'

'What happened to the First Army? Weren't they supposed to join up?'

'Rennenkampf lost the Germans after Gumbinnen amongst the Masurian Lakes. Well, it's a hellish place to track down an enemy; and when the enemy knows exactly where you are because he's intercepting your wireless messages, it's easy enough for him to avoid you. When the Germans had destroyed the Second Army, they turned north and caught the First Army by surprise. We lost another sixty thousand men.'

Emily was silent a moment. 'But in Galicia – we're doing well in Galicia?'

'We were. We were across the Carpathians. I think there was every chance of reaching Vienna within the month. But France is under severe pressure on the Western Front, and Paleologue had a message from Paris begging us to continue the attacks on East Prussia, to keep the Germans occupied. So the Tsar has ordered us back over the Carpathians, and two of the four armies there are to be moved north to attack the Silesian border.' He sighed. 'We must keep faith with our allies, I see that, but it's hard when we were within an ace of eliminating the Austrians altogether. And now there's talk that Turkey might come in against us. That will give us another frontier to protect.'

'So it won't be a short war after all?' Emily asked after a moment.

'No, I don't think so.' He looked at her across the table on which the supper had been laid, and lay still untouched. 'In East Prussia alone we've lost a quarter of a million men, five hundred of our best field pieces, God knows how many horses. We were short of rifles in the beginning; now we're short of ammunition as well, especially

374

artillery shells. It will take time to make up those losses. No, I don't think it will be a short war. A year at least. Perhaps even more.'

Emily's last hope died. 'I see,' she said.

'Emilia, *doushka*,' he began urgently, but she stood up, cutting him short.

'Don't. Please don't.'

'But we must talk about it at least.'

'I can't. You must understand – '

He was suddenly angry. 'I don't understand! What do you want of me? What do you want me to do? Have I had a moment to myself that I haven't given to you? Since the war began – '

'The war doesn't make any difference. The situation would still be the same.'

'It makes all the difference. If we weren't at war, a few more months would have seen everything resolved. But I have duties, responsibilities – '

'To your wife.'

'That too. But I would have dealt with it – *will* deal with it, in time.' The disbelief in her eyes rankled him. 'You think there's nothing to it, that one can just walk away. But you haven't got children. For all we know, you haven't even got a husband now – '

'Ah, no,' she said, very quietly.

He stopped. Why in hell had he said anything so crassly stupid? 'I'm sorry,' he said.

'It's all right,' she said. Her face was as closed to him as an alabaster mask. 'I know you didn't mean it.' She turned away.

He lifted his hands. 'Emilia, *please*. This is killing me.'

'Perhaps I should go and live with Grandmama at Tsarskoye Selo,' she said with her back still turned.

'No, don't do that,' he said, and he sounded defeated. 'I won't press you any more, but don't leave. I won't even speak to you if you don't want me to.'

'Don't be silly,' she said, and left the room. He had to accept that it was the best he could do for now.

The wounded began to pour into the city. Every train was loaded with its freight of misery, and the public hospitals were soon full. The equipping of the Anatoli Memorial Hospital was hastily completed, and it opened its door to the wounded.

From what Anna and Natasha had said, Emily had thought that

her part in running the hospital would be confined to paying some of the bills, and to occasionally helping out with bandage-rolling or chatting to the convalescents to keep them amused. But when she saw the numbers of the wounded and the extent of their suffering; when she saw how patiently they bore it, how humble they were, how grateful for any attention however slight, she knew she must help in some more positive way.

'I'm going to study for the Red Cross certificate,' she told Anna one evening. 'I've made enquiries, and there's a four-week training course in war nursing one can take at the Giorgievsky Hospital. Then I'll really be able to help.'

Anna was against it. 'You can't want to do anything so unpleasant – dirt and smells and people dying! And I'm sure it can't really be necessary. There are plenty of women of lowly origins who can do that sort of work. You must remember you're a princess now. What would Vasska say?'

They had lately had news that Basil was not amongst the casualties. A brief letter had come from Kovno, where his division had camped after retreating from the Masurian Lakes, saying very little except that he was not wounded, but was desperately short of shirts and socks, having had to abandon much of his luggage in the retreat.

'He of all people would approve,' Emily said firmly. 'He must have witnessed the suffering of the wounded. He'd want me to do everything I could to relieve it.'

'He'd want nothing of the sort,' Anna said with certainty. 'He'd want you to stay at home and keep me company and supervise the children. If you want to help the wounded, you can always knit socks like other ladies, or help get up a concert for the widows and orphans.'

'You do the knitting,' Emily said. 'Basil needs socks, after all.'

'Don't be silly! You know perfectly well he only wears silk ones,' Anna said crossly. 'However, I can see you've made up your mind, so I'll say no more. I only hope you don't regret it.'

Anna's feelings were somewhat soothed by the news that the Empress and her two eldest daughters had also enrolled in nursing schools, and that the Catherine Palace at Tsarskoye Selo was being converted into a military hospital. If the work was not considered to be too gross for the Grand Duchesses, then presumably it would not demean a princess.

'I just hope you don't bring back some horrible disease, and make the children ill,' she grumbled on a descending scale.

'I'll be sure to change and bathe before I come home,' Emily promised.

The work at first was exhausting both to the body and the spirit. The men arrived by the Red Cross trains every morning, filthy, verminous, bloodstained, exhausted and grey with pain. Many were feverish, moaned and gabbled and clutched at anyone who came near them; others were silent, withdrawn into the loneliness of dying. Their courage and patience brought Emily almost to tears a dozen times a day. 'How are you?' she would ask each newcomer she approached. 'It's nothing, little sister,' they would answer. 'Just a scratch. Nothing at all.'

Under the supervision of the trained nurses and the doctor, Emily and her fellow students worked at cutting away the filthy clothing, washing the men, lifting off the maggoty field dressings, bandaging the less serious wounds. At first Emily found the smells hard to bear: the halitus of blood, the cloying smell of pus and gangrene, the sweet stink of lice. But nothing was spared them.

'If you're going to be useful,' the nursing sister said briskly when one of their number turned pale green at the sight of a mangled leg, 'you'll have to get used to these things. If you can't, you must go away. All I ask is that if you're going to faint or be sick, you go outside and do it, where you won't be in anyone's way.'

Some of them left the first day, one or two on subsequent days, a slow bleeding away of numbers. Then it stopped. Amongst those who stayed a strong bond grew up, which Emily imagined must be something like the bond that exists between soldiers. When you have faced unpleasant things together, and know you can trust each other, there develops a closeness not found in everyday life. Together they progressed from the reception stage to more serious nursing; changed from a rather frightened and helpless group of women with tears of pity in their eyes and mouths clamped shut against disgust, to being of real use.

The work went on being horrible, but it was no longer so frightening. The sight of a wound did not fill them with hopeless panic; they knew they could at least do something to help. They removed field bandages, cleaned wounds, prepared patients for operations. By the beginning of October, Emily was working in the operating room, and after the first shock of the sight of the operations, she found it slightly less harrowing than ward nursing. At least in the operating room the victims were made unconscious, and temporarily relieved of their suffering. Emily held the ether mask, handed instruments, held bowls; quietly took amputated limbs from the hands of the surgeon and put them in the bins that went every day to the incinerators.

Amputations were not the worst thing, though they were the most frequently performed operations. The extremities of human bodies seemed the most vulnerable parts, she thought at first; later she added the realisation that those wounded in other places often did not survive long enough to be brought to the hospital.

The belly wounds were the worst of all to bear. Emily worked most often with a fellow student named Galina Strakova, a pretty young woman with fair hair and blue eyes who reminded her a little of Angela, except that she was taller and much less shy. But the first time they were presented with an abdominal wound to dress, Galina almost came to the end of her tether. The soldier was a beardless young man, probably no more than twenty-two or twenty-three, and he had been torn across the belly and groin by flying shrapnel. When Galina removed the field dressing, the blue-white coils of his intestines surged through the gaping lips of the wound, and Emily had to make a lunge to keep them from spilling over. Galina, the dressing in her hand, turned white, unable, while Emily struggled to hold the sides of the wound together, to keep her eyes from the rest of the damage. The boy was scarcely a man any more, and what little was left was already black with mortification.

'Galya, for God's sake!' Emily hissed, terrified her companion would faint or run away, leaving her clutching this poor creature's belly and unable to let go. 'Give me a dressing pad!'

The soldier opened his eyes at that point, and looked past Emily at Galina. 'Is it bad?' he whispered.

Galina's eyes were taking up most of her face, and Emily could see that she simply couldn't speak: everything in her had gone rigid.

'No, not so bad,' Emily answered for her, trying to sound cheerful, though to her, her voice sounded strained and unnatural. 'The surgeons here are very good. They'll patch you up all right.'

The boy tried to lift his head to look at his wound, but fortunately hadn't the strength. 'Will I still be able to get married? I've a girl at home, in my village,' he said. The stark fear in his voice brought the blood rushing back to Galina's head. She put the soiled dressing aside and reached for a clean one, the largest size. She smiled, and Emily was astonished at how sweet and natural it looked.

'Of course you will,' she said, and if her voice shook, it was remarkably little. 'She's a lucky girl, whoever she is, to have a soldier hero for a fiancé. What's her name?'

And she kept the boy talking about his girl and his village while between them they dressed his wound so that he could wait his turn for the surgeon. Afterwards, when they went to the sluice room to wash their hands, it was Emily who collapsed, trembling, against the sink.

'Oh, dear God,' she said. 'Dear God.'

'You were wonderful, Milya,' Galina said. 'I'm sorry I let you down. It was just that – '

'I know. But it was you who made the difference, talking to him like that. You sounded so calm.'

'He'll die, won't he?' Galya said. 'That's what I kept telling myself. He can't live, with such a wound.'

Emily looked down at her bloody hands, seeing again unwillingly the ripped flesh they had held together. 'I don't know. Yes, I think he will die.'

'Better that he should,' Galina said starkly. 'What kind of life would it be for him?'

In the middle of October Emily finished her course, and along with her companions was presented with her diploma and medal as a certificated war nurse. It was one of the proudest moments of her life. For the first time she had achieved something entirely at her own instigation and through her own efforts. The next day she dressed herself in her grey nursing dress, put on the white cap and apron, pinned her medal proudly to her bib, and went to work in the Anatoli Hospital.

The wounds were no less horrible, the smells and sights no less sickening, the work no less exhausting and harrowing; but she felt for the first time in her life that she was doing something useful, that her presence on earth made a difference to someone for the better. She went home at the end of each day too tired to do more than bathe, eat supper, and fall into bed. She was certainly too tired to think about her situation or worry about the future, and that was all to the good.

At the end of October, Turkey declared war on Russia, and a new front opened up. Basil came back to Petrograd on his way to the Caucasus, where his regiment had been transferred.

Emily felt rather shy of him: glad that he was still in one piece, but unable to get near to him spiritually. He seemed like a stranger to her. He had lost a lot of flesh, but though leaner he was also fitter. His more angular face made him look older, and he seemed strangely distracted – or perhaps it was not so strange, given what he had seen and done since he went away. He asked Emily what she had been doing, but expressed only the faintest surprise to learn that their house had been turned into a hospital; and none at all that Emily had become a nurse.

'Splendid,' he said vaguely. 'I'm sure you must be very good at it.'

'I hope you don't mind it,' Emily began, and he smiled and shook his head.

'It does the men a great deal of good to know that if they should be unlucky, they'll have the best of care back home.'

He asked Emily a question or two about it, but seemed unable to grasp what she was telling him, as though the effort of being interested was too great for him. His mind was heavily preoccupied with his own world, which was plainly much more real to him than the surroundings he now found himself in. Whatever they began to speak about, he would revert after a few words to his own experiences, his men, his campaign, their sufferings and their losses. After one or two attempts Emily stopped trying to converse, and let him talk uninterrupted.

'It struck me more than once that they really didn't know what to do with us down there – the cavalry, I mean. The terrain was dreadful, too – marsh and wood, the ground cut up with little streams. Nothing for us to do really, except scouting duties, and the Cossacks are much more suited to that than us . . . Well, it's the Caucasus for us now! Much more our kind of terrain. It'll be a proper horse-soldier's war down there, real cavalry actions, sabre charges, neck-or-nothing stuff . . . Some of the fellows are put out, think we're being pushed down a backwater. The only real war is the war against the Germans, that's what they think. I've heard them say they might as well chuck it in if they can't have a crack at the Prussians. I told them that was nonsense . . . '

Eventually he ran himself down. Only then did he start to worry about his appearance. He certainly had an unkempt look about him, though that was hardly surprising. His hair looked as though it had been trimmed with a scythe. 'I think I'll go and have a bath,' he said. 'What happened to my clothes that I left behind at home? You didn't put those into store, did you?'

'No, they're in your dressing-room – the one you always use when you stay here.'

'Oh, good. I'll have something decent to change into, then. Just ring for Grusha for me, will you?' At the door he paused and looked back at her vaguely, as though she were another guest in the house whom he had only just met and would probably never meet again. 'I suppose I'll see you later,' he said. 'Do you dine in tonight?'

He found, to his mixed chagrin and amusement, that his old clothes didn't fit him properly: his trousers were too large in the waist, his coats too tight over the shoulder. 'Damned if I know how a man can change shape in such a short time,' he said, pleased.

When he was shaved and dressed, with his hair decently trimmed by his servant, he emerged looking very little more like his old self, and plainly still not at ease with the world he had left behind. After fidgeting around the rooms for half an hour, he said, 'I think I'll just go out for a while. Go down to the mess, perhaps, see if I can find any of my old friends.'

'Yes, do,' Emily said cordially, relieved at the thought of getting him out of the house. 'And you ought to look in on Nina,' she reminded him.

For a moment he looked blank, and if she had been in love with him, it would have been a moment of triumph. 'Good Lord, yes! Has there been any news?'

'I would have told you if there had. But she must be near her time now.'

'Yes, I suppose so. Of course she must.' He pulled himself together. 'I'll call in on her on the way back. Yes, must do that. It's only right.' He didn't look as though the visit would give him much pleasure.

Emily didn't see him again that night, and learned the next morning from Anna, who was peeved about it, that he had found no-one he knew at the mess, but had gone on to the Astoria and there found two 'splendid fellows' on convalescent leave and spoiling for a chinwag. They had spent the whole evening and much of the night drinking and talking, and Nina Antonova had had to go without her visit.

He put things right by calling on her during the day, while Emily was at the hospital. Basil had to leave again that evening, and Anna had planned an early family dinner in his honour, so Emily left the hospital and came home in time to bathe and put on something a little more festive than the plain skirts and blouses she wore these days whenever she was not in uniform.

The dinner was quite a success, thanks largely to Alexei, who kept things going, carried them over many a sticky conversational patch, and encouraged Basil to talk about the more interesting aspects of his experiences. As the time drew near for Basil to leave, however, the talk grew more serious, and turned on the Russian losses in the first three months of war.

'I don't know the exact figures,' Basil said, 'but even from my own experience I can tell they're pretty high. What would you say, Alyosha – a million or so?'

'Oh, surely it can't be that bad,' Anna said. 'I've heard some stories, but – '

'It must be going that way. There was a new draft this month of three-quarters of a million men,' Alexei said, 'and they must be urgently needed, because they've only been given four weeks' training. Worse than that, we only have rifles for one in two of them. The rest will have to wait until someone gets killed.'

'I'd like to know why we haven't any rifles,' Adishka complained. 'We had enough warning that this was coming.'

'Oh come, you don't need me to explain it to you,' Alexei said. 'Don't forget the Tsar believed until the last moment that Germany wouldn't come in against us. If we'd only had the Austrians to fight, it would have been all over by now.'

'Well, why aren't we making them now?' Adishka asked, changing foot. 'Good God, we've been at war three months!'

'Because arms and ammunition can only be made in State-owned factories, you know that! They've been working flat out, but they can't cope with the demand. Until we can change the law so that other factories can be put on to the work, we'll have a shortage.'

'It's not the only shortage,' Basil said sharply. 'I tell you, I'm half glad to be going to the Caucasus. At least there one will have decent food, and fodder for the horses; live like a gentleman again. Some of those little towns – Pyatigorsk and Vladikavkaz – one can have quite a decent time in when one's not up at the line.'

Soon it was time to go. With needless tact, Anna made sure Emily and Basil were left alone for a few minutes to say their farewells. Emily could think of nothing she wished to say to him, beyond what she would say to any departing soldier.

'Goodbye, then. You'll take care of yourself?'

'Of course. Don't worry about me. I dare say we'll thrash the Turks in a month or two, and I'll be back home by midsummer.' He cleared his throat. 'Emilia, about Nina – you know I saw her today?' Emily nodded. 'She's very close to her time. It could be any day now. I've told her to keep you informed – '

'I'll write to you and let you know if it's a boy or a girl,' Emily promised.

'Ah, yes! Thank you. And I've told her to come to you if she needs anything. She's very young, you know, and not very worldly-wise.'

'Yes,' said Emily shortly. 'I understand.'

He stood for a moment in awkward silence, as though wondering what more was required of the ceremony; and then he bent his head and kissed her cheek. She felt as though she were being kissed by a stranger. His lips felt harder, his skin rougher; he didn't even smell the same. She shrank from touching him; and she thought that he was not much more eager to embrace her.

He seemed aware that this was not as it should be. 'Afterwards,' he said hesitantly, 'after the war, we'll have to get to know each other again. I know things haven't always been quite as they should between us. But when all this is over, we'll sort everything out, won't we? Get back to normal.'

'Yes,' she said hopelessly. Normal? They were not the same two people; and surely the world would not be the same world.

'Yes,' he said, equally at a loss. Then he said, 'I'm very proud of you, Emilia – of what you're doing. Nursing and everything. I want you to know that.'

'Thank you, Basil,' she said gravely. 'I'm proud of you, too.'

When he had gone, Anna retired to her room to weep a little. Alexei had gone with Basil to the station, Adishka to meet Borya Duvitsky. Emily, left alone, sat in the drawing-room for a while, trying to read, and then gave it up and went upstairs, planning to go to bed early. She would be back on duty at the hospital in the morning – that was reality. As for what would happen after the war, there was no sense in thinking about it now.

She was sitting at the dressing-table, slowly rubbing lanolin cream into her hands – they suffered from being so often in water – when there was a soft tapping at her door. She knew from the way the hair rose on the back of her neck that it was Alexei, even before he opened the door.

'Will you come and take a little supper with me?' he asked.

He said it in a perfectly neutral tone, but she looked at him warily. 'In your private study?' She had a brief, glorious vision of a past occasion, and knew she could not trust herself. 'No. I can't.'

'I have something to tell you.'

'Tell me here.'

'I want to talk to you properly.' His mouth made an uncertain smile which tugged painfully at her. 'I can't stand on one foot in your doorway. Please, Emilia, have a little respect for my dignity.'

'Oh don't,' she said softly. 'Don't make me laugh. It isn't fair.'

'Come,' he said, and grew grave. 'I have to go away soon; and every condemned man is allowed to speak.'

'Go away?' He would not say any more, only stood waiting for her to be generous, and so at last she sighed and stood up, and walked before him out of the room.

His study was like a haven, the fire glowing under the chimney, the clock ticking softly, a tray of supper and a decanter of wine set ready on the table.

'Sit down. Let me pour you some wine. You won't refuse to drink with me? It may be our last chance for some time.'

'Where are you going?'

'At first to Stavka. After that, to the front – Galicia or Silesia, I don't know yet. That will depend on General Nikolasha.'

'You're going to the war?'

'Don't say it like that, my soul, or I shall lose what little control I have left.'

'But why? Why you?'

'Oh, it isn't only me, of course. Listen, love. You know what terrible losses we have suffered amongst the men. Perhaps you don't know that amongst the officers our losses have been proportionately far worse. Basil's regiment, for instance, has already lost fifty out of its seventy officers. The division Tolya served in has lost three hundred and fifty officers out of three hundred and eighty.'

'But why?'

'Partly because they're dashing, hot-blooded young men; but also it's a matter of fashion, or pride, or what you will. It's considered cowardly for an officer to be careful of his life. He must lead his men from the front, and expose himself to the heaviest fire. In the face of enemy bullets, he may tell his men to crawl on their bellies for safety, but he himself must walk upright.' He shrugged. 'So they're hit first. It's utter folly, but it's what happens when gentlemen command rather than professional soldiers.'

'You couldn't wish them not to be gentlemen?'

He looked restless. 'I begin to wonder. How can we prosecute a war in a gentlemanly manner, when the enemy does not? We don't question our prisoners if they are officers, because one couldn't ask a gentleman to betray his fellows. But isn't an honourable war in itself an absurdity, a contradiction in terms?'

'I don't know.' She didn't want to stray down this path at this moment. 'But why are you going? Have they called you up?'

'No, not exactly. But there's a desperate shortage, especially of experienced officers. Sazonov has ordered three thousand cadets to be given their commissions immediately and sent to the front, even though they haven't finished their courses yet, and another fifteen thousand students from the universities are starting a four-week training as subalterns. But none of them will have had any experience in action. The Tsar is reluctant to call on older reserve officers yet; but he's given a strong hint to any who aren't doing essential work that they should volunteer.'

'Your work is essential, isn't it?' she said quickly.

He smiled wryly. 'I haven't been given a hint. I've been given a direct request, and from the Emperor, which is the same as an order. I'm to take a message to Uncle Nikolasha at Stavka, and then I'm to place myself at his disposal.'

'It may be a staff job, then – not the front?'

He didn't think it worthwhile pursuing that. 'The point is that I have to leave here very soon, and I don't know when I may be able to return. It is even possible I may be away until the war ends. That's what I want to talk to you about.'

She gave him a lost look, holding the glass of wine he had given her in both hands in her lap, unaware it was there; her hair, loosened for the night, falling over one shoulder in a long, loose curl the colour of hay. She looked so young and helpless, and yet he knew her strength. Once before he had told her that she must come to him willingly, and that at least had not changed. She must understand completely, or whatever happened, he would lose the best part of her.

'We've had some rotten luck, haven't we?' he said gently.

'Luck, you call it? All a matter of timing, I suppose,' she said bitterly.

'Emilia, I don't want to go away with this unresolved between us. If I leave with things as they are now, what will there be for me to come back for?'

'What will there be anyway? You have a wife and children,' she said. 'I can't forget that, if you can.'

He shook his head, holding out his hand to her. 'Come here, my star, and let me talk to you. Come – what harm can it do to listen to me?' She gave her hands reluctantly, knowing that if he touched her she would be lost. As he took them, she felt as though a current of power were running through them from him into her. He drew her down onto the hearthrug in the firelight, and sat beside her, very close. For a moment they were quiet, breathing very carefully, as though not to disturb something sleeping nearby. Then he began.

'I've told you from the beginning that the new baby made no difference, and it's true. Yes, it is! Of course I love little Piotr. I love all my children; and I'm fond of Anna, in a way. But those things are like a candle to the sun compared with my love for you. You are everything to me. Without you, my life is joyless. I will live it miserable, if I have to; but I beg you not to make me.'

'How can you ask me that?' she said. 'It's not up to me. It never has been.'

'I'm not asking you to settle for second best. I wouldn't do that to you,' he said, understanding her. 'Anna is my problem alone – '

'That's not true!'

She spoke so passionately that he was forced to pause and think. 'Very well, I agree. She is our problem. But the solution is mine. If the war hadn't come, then in a very little time – another month or two – I would have made my dispositions. I would have brought everything out into the open, made the arrangements, and claimed you properly, publicly.'

'You'd have left her with the new baby?'

'*Yes*! How often do I have to tell you, simpleton? It's not what I'd have wished in an ideal world, but I won't run away from a fact just because it's unpleasant. I'd have provided for them the best way I could, that's all.'

She was silent a moment. 'But now the war's come, and everything's different.'

'Different and the same. It means that I can't make the arrangements yet. I have to wait until the war is over.' He saw her expression, and grew angry. He gripped her hands tighter and shook her a little. 'Why do you doubt it? Am I a liar? When did I ever try to deceive you? You see that I have other things I have to do, matters of urgency, of duty, that can't be put off. Surely to God even you must allow that!'

'You're hurting me,' she said sullenly. He eased his grip, but his face was still hard with anger and frustration.

'All I'm asking is that you be patient and trust me. If you love me, why is that so hard?'

She looked at him a moment longer in defiance, and then her resistance crumpled. 'Because I'm *jealous*!' she cried, and with the admission of the horrible truth, she began to weep.

'Jealous?' he said faintly. 'Dear God! Jealous?' He drew her against him, and this time she came, folding into the planes of his body like water flowing into a cup. He felt her cheek against his neck, and the slipperiness of the tears; he pressed his mouth against her hair, and felt the childlike fragility of her skull close under the tawny silk. 'Emilusha, my poor, lovely, idiotic one, how could you be jealous? Don't you know I love you with all my soul? That I'm miserable without you? That I want no-one but you, ever, ever!'

He began to kiss her, her hair and the tip of her ear at first, all he could reach; and then, as she began to turn her face towards him, her wet cheek, her nose, her mouth. Her hands came up and held his face, and they caught fire from each other, consumed with a passion long unslaked. There was only one will between them, to discard their clothing and couple in fierce need, there in the firelight, at once, without delay; to lie together in joy and tenderness, and relief that loneliness was at an end.

'Don't,' he said, kissing her as he lay above her, 'don't ever leave me again. Don't.'

Afterwards she lay in his arms, contented, at peace.

'When do you go?' she said after a long silence.

'In a day or two. We have a little while still. Tomorrow, will you take time from the hospital and be with me?'

'Yes,' she said. She wanted nothing more than to be with him, all the time and for ever. Would it ever happen? Could human beings be so blessed? 'You will come back?'

'Yes,' he said.

'Promise me,' she said. 'You won't get killed?'

'I promise you I will come back,' he said solemnly. 'We'll have the rest of our lives together. We'll grow old together. I promise you.'

What power had promises over shell and bullet? But she accepted it, and was comfortable. 'Make love to me again,' she said, turning against him, and feeling his ready response.

387

A day, two more days, how much longer? In need and in love he lay with her, and filled her with himself against the empty days to come.

Chapter Twenty-Two

When they came off duty, Emily and Galina changed into street clothes and walked up to the Astoria Hotel with the intention of taking tea in the lounge by way of relaxation. In the interests of health and sanity they had two short days each week when they finished early, and three whole days off every fortnight. They liked to spend their off-duty time together whenever possible, now that Galina was working at the Anatoli as well. Emily found that she felt ill at ease nowadays with people like Nina Kovanina and Masha Sapetska, to whom the war was a distant thing played out on a table with brightly coloured lead soldiers. However much they might care about the war and the casualties, they didn't *know*, and it made it difficult to talk to them.

At the Astoria they were greeted by an extra low bow from the doorman, and the manager himself, who happened to be in the vestibule, came across to greet them. 'Tea, your highness? Certainly, certainly. We have a delightful table for you and mademoiselle opposite the door, just where you like it. This way, your highness. If you please, mademoiselle.'

Emily exchanged an amused glance with Galya as they followed the smiling, bowing man. There was no doubt that in certain circles being known to be active in nursing had its advantages.

They were just seating themselves when Galina said, 'Isn't that your cousin, Milya? Just going past the door – '

Emily started and half rose to her feet before she saw, through the open glass doors that led back into the vestibule, the figure of Adishka limping by. Of course it wasn't Alexei, she told herself sternly. He'd have told her if he'd been coming home.

Adishka was the next best thing, however. The manager hurried out to pursue Adishka and bring him to their table.

'I was just going to see if there was anyone in the saloon, but tea with you will be even better,' he said, smiling down at them. 'May I join you?'

'Of course – sit down. You know my friend Galina Strakova, don't you?'

'We did meet, just once,' Adishka said. 'On the Troitsky Bridge last January. You were wearing a blue *shooba* and a chinchilla hat.'

Galina's cheeks were slightly pink. 'What a wonderful memory you have,' she said. 'I couldn't have said what I had on.'

'Ah, but you didn't have the pleasure of looking at you, as I did,' Adishka said gallantly.

Emily looked at him in amusement and affection. The war had turned out to be a good thing for Adishka. At the beginning, when the volunteers were going off to the front and everyone was making a fuss of soldiers, he had been very quiet and withdrawn, keeping himself in the background. His physical shortcomings meant that he could not serve, and the awareness was bitter to him. His patriotism was denied an outlet; he would never be a hero.

Even his revolutionary activities were curtailed, for the whole group had spontaneously agreed, like the members of the Duma, that every other consideration must be put aside for the winning of the war. 'No politics until victory' was the slogan taken up by everyone from the Cabinet downwards, and solidarity with the ruling order left Adishka's group without present purpose. In any case, more than half the members had themselves volunteered, soon to be numbered among the million and more dead of the first months of the war.

Sasha Suslov had fallen in February of this year, 1915, at Przasnysz, where for lack of rifles the Russians had stormed the German position armed with nothing but bayonet knives. It had been a remarkable victory, but the cost, especially in junior officers, had been high. Emily, faced daily with the results of such heroic charges, tried not to think of how Sasha might have died. She had been glad when he went to war, for the relief of not having him hanging at her elbow; now she would have been glad of the annoyance.

But things had taken a turn for the better for Adishka. From the beginning the Duma had declared itself solidly behind the Government's war effort, all except for a handful of Bolshevik members. Their exiled leader, Vladimir Ulyanov, continually urged singularity of purpose on them, and saw the war as an ideal opportunity for working to bring down the regime and seize power. Indeed, he urged that victory for Russia would be the worst possible thing for their cause: better a shameful defeat for which the Tsar and the Cabinet could be blamed.

Thus urged, the Bolsheviks voted against the Government's war measures whenever they could, and continued to hold inflammatory meetings when all the other parties had ceased. As a result, five Bolshevik deputies were arrested and sent to Siberia. Adishka then had the honour of a visit from Rodzianko, the President of the Duma, who asked if he would consider becoming a deputy.

Adishka stammered in his delight. 'But – but don't I have to be elected? Who would vote for me?'

'There will be no difficulty, I assure you,' said Rodzianko smoothly. 'With so many of our best young men at the front, there is a shortage of people with the right background, and especially of those who are willing to serve. You will be elected unanimously, I assure you. Be a Tribune of the People, Vladimir Nikolayevitch! Your country needs you.'

'In the name of the future I accept, Mikhail Vladimirovitch,' Adishka said. 'It's time there was a Kirov in the Duma. Our family has a history of serving Russia in the old way, as soldiers or statesmen. I shall be the first Kirov to serve her in the new way.'

As a first speech, and unrehearsed, he thought it was pretty good; and it was but the first of many that the President was to hear. Adishka blossomed in his new role. He grew confident, self-possessed, and won himself a reputation as a speaker. He grew a moustache, bought a whole wardrobe of new suits, and even, to Emily's amused eyes, seemed to grow taller and more handsome, especially as he no longer had his brother beside him for comparison.

Anna at first was outraged, for like any good conservative she saw the Duma as a wasps' nest of subversives and revolutionaries. Later, however, seeing Adishka's new dignity, she decided that perhaps his election was a good thing. 'If you're going to be political, better you should do it with a little style.' And besides, though she didn't mention it, Adishka had become devoted to the war effort, and no longer spoke of wishing to remove the Tsar, so it was probably all to the good.

As a deputy, Adishka had never forgotten Alexei's reminder that the shortage of ammunition would not be solved until extra factories could be put to producing it. He had managed to put himself at the head of a committee for involving the business community in war production, which had lately received Government approval. Together with the representative of the businessmen, a man called Guchkov, Adishka and the rest of the committee had just been to Stavka to see for themselves what the situation was.

'So,' Emily said when the tea was poured, 'what are you doing here? I thought you were at Stavka?'

391

'I was,' Adishka said, spooning jam into his cup. He peered at the results. 'Lord, this is dreadful stuff – all pips! I wish we could get decent jam again. Do you remember the *polynika* jam Yenya used to send us each year? I suppose she didn't have the heart to pick the berries last autumn.'

'Oh, never mind the jam, you idiot,' Emily said amiably. 'When did you get back?'

'Today. Just a few hours ago. I went home first of course, but young Petya's bawling his head off, and Anna's in a foul mood because that new footman has been called up, and she's only had him four weeks. So I decided to come out and look for company. And look what I've found,' he said, with another gallant smile at Galina.

'But what's the news from Stavka?' Emily persisted patiently.

'I should have thought you'd have had it by now. Our chaps are doing wonderfully well, smashing the Austrians in spite of all the problems. We've captured all the Carpathian passes and Brusilov is marching the Eighth Army down onto the Hungarian plain. Vienna's only a matter of time now.'

'But we've had such dreadful casualties,' Emily said. 'How can it be worth it?'

Adishka shook his head. 'Just like a woman to ask a silly question like that. Of course no-one likes the high casualty rate, but you can't think we'd just give in and let the Germans walk all over us?'

'No, of course not,' Galina murmured pacifically.

'The problem is,' Adishka explained to her kindly, 'that we're desperately short of artillery shells. Our men are down to three per gun, which means we can't lay down a barrage over the German positions before we charge. Our men have to storm them under heavy artillery fire before they can get close enough for hand-to-hand fighting. Once they get to that stage, they wipe 'em out all right, but obviously the losses are great. That's what our committee's all about – getting civilian factories busy making ammunition and so on. That's what we went to the front to see for ourselves.'

'You went to the front?' Emily exclaimed. 'Not just to Stavka?'

Adishka was flattered by her evident concern. 'Oh, don't worry, we weren't in any danger. Naturally we had our discussions well out of the firing-line.'

'But did you see Alexei?' Emily asked urgently.

'Yes, I saw him. Had dinner with him, as a matter of fact.'

'And is he all right?'

'Of course he's all right. Wouldn't I have told you straight away if he wasn't?' Adishka stared at her. 'Anyway, you get his letters, don't you. Well, Anna gets them, but I'm sure she reads them to you.'

'Yes, of course. I just – hoped you'd have later news of him. He never really talks about himself. Is he well?'

'He was looking a bit tired,' Adishka said with an effort, 'but that's only to be expected. Thinner, too, but then the food isn't up to much right out where he is. He hasn't been wounded, though, if that's what you're worried about.'

'Is he in good spirits?'

Adishka looked puzzled. 'Well, you know, we didn't really talk about him. He's worried about the shortages, of course – not just shells but rifles and boots and spares for gun-carriages and, well, almost everything in that line. He says it's like fighting with one hand tied behind your back. When they attack he has to keep half his men behind the lines waiting for someone to get killed so that they can have a rifle. He says if he'd had the arms and ammunition, they'd have been in Vienna by now.'

'What can your committee do about it?' Galya asked.

'We've got to try to get things organised. Guchkov wants to take it straight to the Tsar, but I think we have to get the Government interested first. The trouble is', he sighed, 'that everyone seems to think the war is his own private war, or ought to be, and that anyone else who tries to get involved is meddling. The Tsar doesn't trust the Government, the Government doesn't trust the Duma; the politicians think the businessmen are hoping to make a profit out of the war, and the businessmen think the politicians don't care if we lose, as long as they keep hold of power. It's a mess.'

Emily nodded. 'I can see your difficulties. But you must do what you can, Adishka. The whole future of Russia may depend on you.'

He frowned at her. 'Are you making fun of me?'

'Only a little,' she smiled. 'Truly, I think this may be your path to greatness. If you and your committee can do something positive about the production of ammunition, you may win the war for us.'

'We'll do our best,' Adishka said. He turned again to Galina and changed the subject. 'What do you angels of mercy do when you're not at the hospital?'

'Mostly we sleep,' Galina said. 'And bathe.'

'But you should have some pleasure, too. A little jollity, to lighten your spirits.'

She smiled. 'It's peace that restores my spirits. I have a day off tomorrow, and I shall spend it sitting in the garden and looking at things that are growing rather than dying.'

'Tomorrow?' Adishka said eagerly. 'Why, that's a coincidence! Anna was telling me that Kschessinska is giving a special performance of *Swan Lake* at her dacha in Strelna for the convalescents. I thought of taking her. Why don't you come along too?'

'Oh well, I don't know,' Galina began doubtfully.

'Oh do say yes! It will be a lovely drive out into the country, with a little culture into the bargain; and dinner afterwards – Kschessinska has a superlative cook. We could make up a little party: you, me, Anna, Emilia, the Duvitskys – '

'Adishka, I can't come. I have so much to do tomorrow,' Emily said. 'And I have to go and see Nina Antonova. The baby hasn't been well, and she's so much alone now that her father and brother have both gone to the front.'

Adishka looked put out. 'I don't see why that should be left to you, for heaven's sake. I mean, don't you *mind*?'

'Why should I? The poor child never meant me any harm.'

'If Emilia isn't going, I don't think I will,' Galina said.

Adishka saw his plan dissolving. 'Oh Emilia, you could go and see Nina the next day, surely? Do come to the ballet tomorrow. It will be such a nice day out – and the proceeds will go to charity. I think you ought to go – both of you.'

Emily consulted Galina's face, and could not be the one to spoil everything. 'Very well, then, I'll go. I expect it will do me good to have a change of scene.'

'Exactly!' Adishka said triumphantly. 'Much more refreshing to the spirit than sitting about doing nothing. You will come, won't you, Galina Arkadievna?'

'Yes, I'd love to. Thank you.'

Emily could think of many ways she would prefer to spend her time than in the company of Anna and Leone Duvitska, but who could resist the lure of playing Cupid? Or would she, rather, be playing gooseberry? Well, perhaps she could persuade them to take the children along. Tatya was growing very fond of the ballet, and was already going through the stage of wanting to be a ballet dancer when she grew up; and Modeste, growing more intelligent every day, was fast replacing Tolya, Yenchik and Tom in her affections.

*

Emily was to look back on that April day at Strelna almost as a pastoral dream. The time soon came when days off were taken only when the frame couldn't bear any more. Russian successes against the Austrians had encouraged Italy to enter the war against her old enemy; and, alarmed in case Austria might crumple and make a separate peace, the German High Command had mounted a huge offensive on the Eastern Front.

It took the Russian troops completely by surprise: the Germans had moved up men and artillery so stealthily that they had no idea they were there. But even had they known, there was nothing they could have done about it, for the Germans were about to demonstrate a kind of warfare against which the Russians had no defence.

One day at the end of April, they opened fire on a Russian position with a massive artillery barrage that went on for several days. Ton upon ton of metal fell on the Russians, and they could do nothing to reply. The Germans had forty guns to their one; but most of all they had limitless ammunition, and the Russians had none. All they could do was to cower in their inadequate, shallow dugouts while the world was torn to pieces around them. And when at last the hellish noise stopped, the German infantry came rushing down on them in an all-out attack. Dazed, battered, exhausted, short of rifles, some of them even without shoes, the Russians could do nothing but retreat.

It was a scene that was repeated again and again along the whole of the Eastern Front. The Russian trenches were obliterated, the soldiers slaughtered by the bombardment. In one sector alone, three-quarters of a million shells fell in a period of four hours, and a Russian division of sixteen thousand men was reduced to five hundred. Fleeing soldiers often lost their rifles, or threw them away, and the shortage grew worse week by week. Rising to their feet when the German guns fell silent, the Russians were meeting the bayonet charges with nothing but their naked hands and undefended breasts.

Day by day the Russian line gave back, yielding all the Galician territory that had been won at such cost, yielding up the bulge of Poland and the fortresses which had been armed at such expense, with the loss of all their precious cannon; yielding now central Poland, Warsaw itself, so that Stavka had hastily to decamp and relocate itself at Mogilev on the Dnieper, well into Russian heartland soil. Still the Germans drove them back. All of Poland was lost, and

Lithuania, Kurland, and much of Latvia besides. Plans were made for the evacuation of Riga and Kiev.

In Petrograd the news was received in desperate silence. Every newspaper brought reports of fresh disaster; shop windows that had displayed flags and pictures of the Tsar now displayed lists of casualties. After the silence came the anger. The Germans were the first target: anyone with a German name was likely to be stoned, his windows broken, his business destroyed. In Moscow there were vicious anti-German riots, shops were looted, houses and factories burned down. Some people speaking French were dragged off a streetcar and beaten by xenophobes who understood no language but Russian. Even the leading piano store of Moscow was attacked and grand pianos were smashed to matchwood because they bore names like Bechstein and Blüthner.

In Petrograd there was a clamouring for scapegoats. The Minister of the Interior and the Minister of Justice were dismissed. Sukhomlinov was sacrificed and replaced by Polivanov, a more vigorous and modern-thinking man, as well as a friend of Guchkov, who might therefore be supposed to be willing to do something about the supply problem. Alarm over the anti-German feeling against the Empress caused the Tsar to persuade Rasputin – whose extraordinary vitality had allowed him to recover from the stabbing of the previous July – to retire to his home village for a time; at least until the Duma, which was to reconvene in July, had been placated.

Amongst Emily's memories of that summer was coming home from the hospital after having coped with another day's influx of wounded, and listening at the supper table to Adishka's fulminations. Weary as she was, her feet sore, her ankles swollen, her head reeling from the sights and smells and miseries of the day, she found his preoccupations so remote as to seem almost ludicrous. His powers of rhetoric had improved, however, she thought.

'We've got to improve our military performance, yes. The war has to be won, and that's the first thing. We're all of one mind about that. But when the war's over, what then? Back to the same old muddle and inefficiency and unfairness? No! We won't allow it! We have the chance now to make changes, to wring some concessions out of the monarchy that will be so embedded in our constitution by the time the war's won, they'll be part of it for ever. Never again will the Duma be trampled underfoot by one man's love of power.'

'Now what is it you mean to do this time, Adishka?' Anna asked severely. 'I hope it's not more revolutionary nonsense about removing the Tsar, because I warn you, I won't have it.'

'No, no, it's not that. We *want* the Tsar at the head of the Government; but there've got to be changes. He's not to think he can go on running Holy Russia like the Romanov family estate, or that we're going to run about like lackeys, obeying orders without question. We want accountability; we want consultation. Most of all, we want the Duma to appoint the ministers, not the Tsar. That way we'll have control over the bureaucracy at last. Maybe then we can start to get things organised efficiently.'

'Oh dear, there's going to be more fuss and bother, I can see it coming,' Anna said peevishly. 'It's always the same in Peter in August – everyone gets so bad-tempered. If it weren't for this war, we could have gone down to the country, or the seaside. Think of Livadia now! But of course one would never be able to get a train. They're always full of soldiers.'

One day towards the end of August, Emily was at the Anatoli helping Galina to change a dressing, when she said, 'I wonder what on earth he's doing here? There's a little boy wandering up the ward, Milya, looking as though his eyes are going to fall out of his head.'

'Looking for his father, perhaps,' Emily said, straightening up. 'They shouldn't have let him in.'

'I'll finish this. You go and see what he wants,' Galina said.

Emily caught the child halfway down the ward, and he looked up at her with terrified eyes, his mouth trembling as he tried not to cry. It was rather an overpowering place at first acquaintance, she thought, as she turned him about and began to steer him back the way he had come. 'Out you go, little one. You shouldn't be in here. Who are you looking for?' He was too frightened to answer. 'Your father is it, or your brother?'

'No, *barina*,' the boy managed to whisper. 'I want Princess Narishkina.'

Emily's heart performed a somersault: news in wartime is hardly ever good news. Then she thought that by his style it was much more likely that he had come from Nina Antonova.

'I'm Princess Narishkina,' she said. 'What do you want with me? Speak up, child, I won't bite you.'

'I was to give you this, highness.' His voice had sunk almost to

397

inaudibility, but he held out his hand, in which was a folded and very grubby piece of paper. Emily took it and opened it. It was brief.

I am at the apartment. I haven't long, and I must see you. Can you come now?

A.

At the apartment? That meant he had come back to Peter, but hadn't been home yet. Anna was not meant to know: this visit was for her alone. She folded the note again and looked sharply at the child.

'Did you read this?'

He looked bewildered, which was her best surety. 'No, highness.'

'Go back to the man who gave you this and tell him *yes*. That's all.' She felt in her pocket for a coin. 'Here. He'll give you another when you give him my message. Go on now.'

He scuttled away. Emily went back to Galina, wondering what excuse she could possibly give. Her friend had finished the dressing and was walking towards the sluice. Emily caught up with her and drew her into the room.

'What's the matter, Milya? You look as though you've seen a ghost.'

'I have to go, now, this minute, but I don't want anyone to know,' Emily said.

Galina wasted no time on useless exclamations. There was no better friend, Emily thought, than a war nurse. 'You could climb out of the window.'

'But I'm in uniform.'

'A grey dress is a grey dress. Take off your apron and veil, and no-one will notice.'

'Bless you! Of course they won't. I'm sorry to leave you with all the work, but I can't help it. There's someone I have to see.'

Galina studied her face for a moment. 'It's not bad news, I can see that. I'm glad. When will you be back?'

'I don't know. If anyone asks for me – '

'I'll think of something.'

He opened the door of the apartment to her and said, 'Thank God! I was afraid you might not be able to get away.'

398

He stepped back, letting her pass him into the hall, and closed the door behind her. Then they stood staring at each other for a moment. Almost ten months, she thought, since she had last seen him. He was certainly thinner, as Adishka had warned her; but Adishka hadn't said that he also looked older. His hair had receded noticeably from his temples, and there were lines in his face and about his eyes that had not been there before. She could see in the changes in him what it had been like at the front.

He smiled wryly, reading her expression. 'I know I don't smell very good, but I did stop off to get myself deloused before I came here.'

She shook her head. 'I didn't realise', she said slowly, 'that it was so very bad. Stupid of me. After all, I see the results here. Oh Alexei – '

'My love,' he said, and opened his arms. She stepped close to him, wrapped her arms around him and felt with a pang of pity how thin he was. She had dreamed often and often of this moment, and in her dreams they had flung themselves together, kissed each other passionately, torn at each other's clothing in a frenzy of desire. But now it had come, she wanted only to hold him and be held, to be quiet and feel his closeness.

At last he said, 'You've changed too. You're not a girl any more.'

'I spent my twenty-first birthday at the hospital,' she said. 'It was one of the worst days. The shelling casualties were at their peak.'

He held her a moment longer, and then they separated, just enough to talk.

'How long have you got?' she asked: the inevitable first question.

'A few hours. I have to go to the palace – a special meeting. I've brought a personal message from General Nikolasha for the Tsar, one that he hopes will go down better from my lips, since the Emperor knows me and, I hope, trusts me. Then I have to go back to Stavka, and then, I suppose, to the front.'

'You haven't told anyone you're here?'

'I haven't been home.' He interpreted the question correctly. 'I wanted the time with you. Now I have to bathe and shave. Marfa is heating water. And while I bathe, she's going to sponge and press my uniform, in the vain hope of making me presentable. If I have time, I'll have something to eat as well. One can't rely on being fed at the palace. But first of all, my splendid, beautiful star . . . ' He took her by the hand and led her towards the bedroom, and she felt her heart beating in all the wrong places. 'First of all, I have to take my uniform off. I wonder if you could help me with it?'

Afterwards he talked to her seriously, while he sat in the bath soaping himself with the meticulous attention of one who has long been rationed of soap and hot water, and she sat on the floor beside him, still tingling from their lovemaking.

'You've had the casualties through your hands,' he said. 'You know something of the scale of them.'

'But I imagine it's only the tip of the iceberg. One hears numbers tossed around – it's hard to know the truth of it.'

'Numbers start not to make sense after a while, but dead and wounded we've lost about a million and a half men. Perhaps another million taken prisoner. Half the army is gone. The lines are so thin now.' He soaped carefully between the toes of his left foot. 'One of the staff officers came down to my sector to bring me the message from Stavka, and he asked to inspect my men, hoping to cheer them up a little. They like the attention. He walked along the lines in the usual way, and then he called out, "How many of you have been in arms since the beginning of the war?" Not a single hand went up. It made me wonder how many of the original army of August 1914 is left, officers and men. Precious few, I'm sure of that.'

'There's Basil,' Emily said. The pain of such thoughts was too great for pity; one could only joke. 'He's having a wonderful time in the Caucasus, thrashing the Turks.'

'Not for much longer, I'm afraid,' Alexei said, turning to look at her seriously. 'We're desperate for men and officers. Two in three units are being transferred from the Caucasus to the Eastern Front, with every experienced officer they can lay their hands on.'

Emily nodded slowly. 'I see.'

'The National Militia's being called up, and the older reservists who've been spared until now. Valya will have to go,' he added. 'That will be a blow to Yenya. Thank God Yenchik's too young still. There are villages I've heard of where there's no-one left to get the harvest in but women, children and blind old men.'

'It's all they talk about, the wounded soldiers – going home. The village is everything to them. I think they hardly know they're Russian. They worry about who's tending the crops and minding the cows – men lying dying, with half their bodies shot away.'

'Their courage is astonishing,' Alexei said. 'Even to me, and I've

400

known them long enough now. But they're beginning to be afraid. They're starting to believe that the Germans are invincible, and that's dangerous. If the time comes when they won't obey the order to advance, or stand fast, when they run at the sight of a German, we're lost.'

'Is it really that bad?'

'Not yet. It need never come to that, with proper management. But now, of all times, the Tsar is about to make the worst decision of his reign, and I don't know that anyone's going to be able to stop him.'

'What is it?'

He put down the soap. 'What I tell you must be in the strictest confidence.'

'Of course. Whatever you say. Is it something to do with why you're here?'

'Yes, that's right. The Tsar is thinking of taking the supreme command away from Nikolasha, and assuming it himself. He wants to leave Petrograd and come down to Stavka on a permanent basis. Nikolasha has sent me to see if I can beg the Tsar on his behalf to reconsider.'

'But why?' Emily exclaimed. 'I mean, why does the Tsar want to take command?'

'He wanted to in the very beginning, but the Cabinet managed to dissuade him. Now he feels that Russia needs him in her hour of trial. Oh, it's that imbecile Empress, of course, feeding him images of glory and holy dedication and all the sentimental claptrap about his vocation! And behind her is Rasputin, who knows that with the Tsar out of the way he can make the Empress do exactly as he pleases. He'll pull her strings, and the whole of Petersburg will dance for him!'

She had rarely heard him so roused. 'Perhaps he might do some good at the front – raise the morale of the men at least?'

'He lost the Japanese war; he was born on Job's day; and at his coronation there was a horrible accident which resulted in thousands of deaths. The men may still venerate him as the Little Father, but they know he's unlucky. They won't want him leading them. And if there are further reverses, he'll bear personal responsibility for them, which will rebound on him politically. It could precipitate a real disaster.'

'You mean – revolution?'

He grimaced. 'It's coming to the point when I wonder whether it

401

wouldn't be a good thing – a Court revolution. We've always been loyal, the Kirovs. But there are other members of the imperial family who could lead the country into an orderly reconstruction: Nikolasha, for example, or the Tsar's brother. But Nicholas himself – ' He shook his head. 'He won't listen to reason; he's blinkered, stubborn, obsessed with mysticism and symbolism; and worst of all, he allows himself to be ruled by the Empress, who is, without a doubt, the stupidest woman I have ever met. I can't see how we're ever going to get a programme of reform past him.'

The clock in the drawing-room struck the hour, distant but clear in the silence. 'Hand me the towel, will you?' he said, rising up from the water.

She did so without comment. His words had struck her with a feeling of foreboding. Political changes – whatever Uncle Westie might have said about the tides of history – always seemed to be accompanied by suffering and bloodshed. And she didn't want it to be Alexei's blood. The woman in her wanted instinctively to hide what she loved, and keep very still until the danger had passed. Let someone else carry the banner and die on the barricades. She wanted only to live and have what she had.

'It needn't be you, need it?' she asked as he dried himself. 'It needn't be any of us. Our lives aren't so uncomfortable under the present system. If things need changing, let the next generation change them. Perhaps it won't hurt by then.'

He stepped out of the bath and stood naked before her. 'A very feminine conclusion,' he said, drying the last bits and dropping the towel. She eyed his body with interest, and seeing her expression, he laughed. 'But you see, *doushka*, the next generation will be our children. We can't leave them a bitter inheritance like that, can we?'

'Our children?' she said, watching the fascinating changes come over him. How flattering it was, she thought, that all of that was for *her*.

'You question the possibility, or the method? Come with me, my dear child, and I will give you a practical demonstration.'

He took her hand and she laughed, pretending reluctance. 'You haven't really got time, have you? I mean, you mustn't keep the Tsar waiting.'

'Don't you know I can make time stop at will? Come here – '

*

402

Alexei's mission did not succeed. Along with the whole of the Cabinet, except for the aged Prime Minister Goremykin and several members of the imperial family, he entirely failed to change the Tsar's mind. The urgings of the Empress prevailed, and on the 22nd of August, Tsar Nicholas left his capital to take the train to Stavka.

He left behind him a political storm. The Duma was still in session, and still pressing for constitutional reform. Through the newspapers, which grew more vocal as the Tsar travelled further away, and through Adishka, Emily heard the details of the extraordinary events of that August. Three hundred of the four hundred and twenty deputies had formed a coalition called the Progressive Bloc, having managed to moderate their ambitions so as to achieve a consensus. Only the most extreme elements of the revolutionaries on one side and the monarchists on the other were excluded. A few days after the Tsar's departure, the Progressive Bloc published a nine-point plan for reforming the system of government.

'It's more moderate than some of us wanted,' Adishka told Emily on that first, exciting day. 'We had to tone it down a little, out of deference to some of the Nationalists, so we're not actually demanding the right to choose the ministers ourselves. But we have demanded a ministry which will enjoy the confidence of the nation – that means us, of course – and which will at once agree to a definite programme of reform.'

'What sort of reforms?' Emily asked. If they wanted to get rid of the Tsar, they would never get any further.

'Oh, pretty straightforward things. The bureaucracy to be subject to legal restraints. An end to the army's automatic authority over civilian administrations. Freedom of religion. Release of all political prisoners. Freedom of speech and association.'

'Very reasonable,' Emily agreed, 'but how will you get it past the Cabinet?'

'I think they may be on our side already,' Adishka said shrewdly. 'They didn't like the Tsar's ignoring their advice and taking command of the army. They don't like everything they decide having to be ratified by the Empress. They don't like the tenure of their jobs depending on the whim of a debauched peasant mystic. Have you seen the newspapers today?'

'No. I've been at the hospital all day.'

'They're calling for Goremykin to be dismissed and replaced by a prime minister chosen by us – by the Duma. And they've published a list of ministers in an ideal Cabinet – all names supplied by us, of course. We're going to do it this time, I can feel it in my blood. If we present a united front, Nicholas will have to listen to us.'

He was right in the first part of his surmise. The Council of Ministers, with the exception of watery-eyed old Goremykin, voted in favour of starting negotiations with the Progressive Bloc to decide on a programme of reform to put before the Tsar; and most of them also pronounced themselves ready to stand down in favour of a new cabinet more to the Duma's taste.

There was euphoria in the drawing-rooms of Petrograd's intelligentsia. If the elected deputies of the Duma had actually managed to get an agreement with ministers personally chosen by the Tsar, they reasoned, then the Tsar must listen. The whole educated class of his people wanted reform: he must now agree to a parliamentary democracy.

On the 28th of August Goremykin took train for Stavka to warn the Tsar what was happening, and advised him to prorogue the Duma, so as to take away its platform for opposition. Nicholas thought the advice good. The Duma was dismissed, and all ministers ordered to remain at their posts until further notice.

Adishka was dazed. 'How could he do it? How could he go against the wishes of the whole Duma and the entire Cabinet? He must be mad, that's all. I mean really, genuinely mad.'

'You really thought he would agree, then,' Emily said, 'despite all he's said in the past about swearing to uphold autocracy and hand on his power intact to his son?'

Adishka wasn't listening. 'Goremykin did this – and we all know he's the lapdog of the Empress. It's that German woman who's ruining this country! Her and that filthy *starets* of hers! They poison the Tsar's mind against everyone who doesn't fawn on them. Well, we've tried being reasonable. Whatever happens next is on his own head.'

But what happened next was that in September the German offensive ground to a halt, and the fronts stabilised again. The threat to the Russian homeland was lifted, and with the Duma out of session, the steam went out of the situation. The newspapers and the Progressive Bloc began to argue that everything possible had been done for the time being, and that there was no point in pressing further. The important thing was to win the war, and the order of things had best not be disturbed until that was achieved. It was decided to postpone demands for reform until after the war.

'I do see the point,' said Adishka, reluctant but fair. 'I mean, if you're in a car going along a steep, narrow road above a crevasse, however incompetent the driver is, you don't wrench the wheel out of his grip until you've got down onto level ground again.'

'Very nicely put,' said Emily.

'Oh, well – I didn't actually think of that myself,' Adishka admitted. 'It was Maklakov said it first – but I think he's absolutely right.'

Chapter Twenty-Three

Emily stood in the vast marble hall of Anna's house putting on her gloves, very conscious of Modeste's eyes on her. He didn't want her to go. He was a strange child, intelligent, but far too sensitive and given to fits of inexplicable melancholy. Lately he had begun suffering from nightmares – something he had gone through before, but which Emily hoped he had outgrown. He could never say what they were about when he woke, but he would clutch Emily – it was usually she who reached him first – and sob as though he were weeping for the whole world.

Anna had no patience with him. She preferred lively, rosy, boisterous children. Her pale and quivering son was a mystery and an irritation to her. When he was presented to friends in the drawing-room, she was able to find things to be proud of – his intellectual prowess, so advanced for a seven-year-old, his growing skill on the violin – but meeting him at any other time she would be likely to tell him to run along, or to go and find Emily. Petya she enjoyed – he was still the property of the nursery maid and brought to her clean and chubby to be played with for half an hour – and Tatya, who was growing ravishingly pretty and knew it, she really loved. But Modeste made her shiver, and his spindly limbs, which seemed all knee and elbow, reminded her of spiders. Privately she was sure he was a changeling, swapped in the cradle by elves.

This morning Modeste had appeared in Emily's room in his night-shirt, very early, and obviously upset about something. There were blue stains under his eyes. His skin was very fine and almost colourless, and at times like these he looked as though he were made of the finest Chinese porcelain, so eggshell-thin that the shadow of what was within could be seen through it.

He didn't speak, but stood just inside the door, rubbing one bare foot on top of the other, and looking at her with a mixture of dread and appeal.

'What is it, little one?' she asked, immediately concerned.

'You're going away,' he said.

'Only for the day. You know that – I told you yesterday. I'm going to see Great-aunt Natasha.' He only stared. 'What is it, *galub-chik*? What's wrong?'

'Don't go,' he said. The words seemed to burst out of him against his will.

'Come here,' Emily said, and he came to stand between her knees and put his arms round her neck – his favourite position for comforting. He was a tall little boy, and she could hold him easily like that. His thin body in her arms seemed unnaturally hot through his cotton shirt, as though the flame of his life burned more fiercely than other children's. 'What's the matter?' she asked, kissing the top of his head. The shape of his skull and the texture of his hair were very like his father's. It tore at her every time, knowing he was not hers.

'I don't want you to go,' he said at last.

'But why?' No answer. '*Mylenkaya*, you must tell me why, or how can I help you?'

He shuddered and pressed himself closer to her, nudging his head into her shoulder as though he were trying to climb inside.

'Did you have a dream?' she tried. His shadowed eyes looked as though he had not slept well.

'No,' he said. 'I just know.'

'What? Know what, Modeste? Tell me.'

He lifted his head then and looked at her seriously, and the look did not seem to come from a child. It might have been Alexei there, looking out of Modeste's eyes, warning her.

'What is it?' she asked again, stifling the fear.

'Bad things,' he said. 'Lots of people shouting. Being bad. Hurting each other.' He began to cry, the words coming out in bursts between the hitching of his narrow chest. 'Noise – and bangs – and blood. Someone's *dying*!'

She held him tightly, cradling his head against her. 'No, my star, my soul, no, little one! It's just a dream. Nothing bad is going to happen. You see, you're safe at home with me. Safe. No-one's going to hurt you.'

It had taken a long time to soothe him. Now, as she came down to the hall, he appeared silently beside her, and stared at her with those disturbing eyes. She thought he would renew his pleas for her not to go, but instead he said, quite steadily, 'Take me with you, Milya, please.'

'I can't, love. You have to go to school.' He attended a special, very exclusive and very expensive school for musically talented children, and Emily knew that Anna would never countenance his missing a day. Her one consolation for Modeste's unprepossessing strangeness was that he might turn out to be a world-famous musician.

To Emily's surprise, Modeste said no more, only watched her in brooding silence. She thought of the backstreet unrest that had muttered and rumbled like distant thunder all that summer of 1916 in Petrograd, of the strikes and protests over the bitter and inexplicable shortages of food, and wondered suddenly about the safety of the streets. Perhaps Modeste had had a premonition. Four years in Russia had given her a certain respect for some aspects of the supernatural.

She turned to the butler. 'I wish Modeste to be taken to school and brought back in my motor car,' she said. 'Make sure it is done.'

'Yes, highness,' he said.

'And have Nikita fetch me a taxi-cab, please, to take me to the station.'

He bowed and went away, and Emily turned to Modeste, expecting to see some relief in his face. But he only looked at her with those disturbingly grave eyes, as though they were to be parted for ever.

'You'd better go upstairs and get ready. Katya will be looking for you,' Emily said.

He turned and went – no kiss, no goodbye. He ran up the stairs as if escaping.

All of which was quite unsettling, Emily thought as she climbed into the taxi-cab. It was a fine day, one of Peter's best, azure and gold like an heraldic device, the trees touched with splendour, the sky as rich and dense as if cream could be blue. In the old days, she thought with a sigh, she would have gone out in the open carriage on a day like this. But her horses had long since gone, requisitioned by the Government, and Seva had died at Pinsk in June.

The war had been going well this year, thanks largely to Polivanov, who seemed to have been an inspired replacement for the old sybarite Sukhomlinov. Polivanov had already been in discussion with Guchkov even before his advancement. Once given his ministry, he had brought forward the idea of joint committees of government officials and businessmen to solve Russia's supply problems, and had actually managed to get it implemented.

They were called Special Councils, and were made up of a mix of Duma deputies, ministry representatives, and private entrepreneurs. Polivanov himself had been chairman of the Defence Council, of which Adishka was still a member, and it had succeeded in eliminating the shortages of ammunition, artillery and manpower to the extent that the offensive in Galicia had been able to be resumed, with great success.

There had followed three other Councils, for Transport, Food Supply, and Fuel Supply, and their efforts, although still in the early stages, were increasingly effective. But Adishka had been anxious to impress on Emily that their real importance was in their absolute innovation: it was the first time in Russian history that ordinary citizens had taken part in the administration of the country on equal terms with government functionaries.

But though things were better, they were also worse. The Austrians had been so beaten they were virtually out of the war, and the Germans had had to withdraw valuable troops from the Western Front to stiffen them. This meant that by September the front had ceased to advance, and it had now dug in for another of those periods of stalemate that always made the casualties brought in daily by the Red Cross trains seem so particularly wasteful.

On the other hand, things in Peter had deteriorated. Old Goremykin, who was showing plain signs of senility, had been dismissed back in February, only to be replaced by a minor bureaucrat called Sturmer, who in addition to having a German name – which was considered dangerously tactless – had no ministerial experience and no talent discernible to the minutest examination.

'A petty-fogging, pen-pushing clerk,' Adishka said bitterly. 'It's an insult to the Duma to promote someone like that. Prime Minister? I doubt if he could blow his own nose without instructions in triplicate from the palace.'

'Then why – ?'

'Need you ask? He's the Empress's choice – beef-wittedly loyal to her and the Tsar, and a friend of that bloody Rasputin. That's all that counts.'

But worse was to come. In March Polivanov was dismissed, in spite of his notable successes, to be replaced by the harmless but unqualified General Shuvayev, a solid monarchist with a comprehensive expertise in, and passion for, footwear. It was said of him that he could turn any conversation round to the topic of boots within five minutes.

'*Her* again!' Adishka raged. 'She's always hated Polivanov because he made no secret of his contempt for Rasputin. So Rasputin whispers to her that Polivanov is their enemy, and she tells the Tsar he isn't to be trusted. Of *course* the Tsar believes her, rather than the evidence of his own senses. It doesn't matter to him that Polivanov was the most capable, successful minister he's ever – '

'Don't you think that was really the problem?' Emily interrupted thoughtfully. 'If the Empress is anxious that the Tsar should keep his power intact, that nothing should be done other than by his express command, then perhaps the very fact that Polivanov was doing well seemed like a threat to her. If things could be run well without the Tsar, then it might occur to people to wonder why they need him.'

'You don't think she has wit enough to think of that?' Adishka said contemptuously.

'No, not consciously. But there's no doubt she loves the Tsar with a single-minded passion, and she probably has strong instincts – like an animal, you know – for what affects him.'

He shrugged. 'You could be right. But it makes no difference to the outcome.'

'I'm sure she means no-one any harm. It's just unfortunate that she combines strong passions with a weak intellect.'

Adishka grinned unwillingly. 'You could say the same about a great many of our best friends, if it comes to it.'

'But not about Galina Arkadievna,' Emily said innocently.

'No. She's perfect in every way,' he said seriously.

'How are you getting on with her?'

He shrugged. 'She lets me take her out now and then, but I don't think she sees me as a potential husband.'

'Oh dear, poor Adishka. Is it that serious, then?'

'I'm in love with her. I've never felt like this about a woman before. Mostly they've frightened me, but she – she's so calm, and strong, and good. I don't wonder she doesn't think anything of me: I could never be worthy of her. And then there's this wretched leg of mine – '

'No, Adishka, that's nonsense,' Emily said firmly. 'Let me tell you two things: firstly, no-one but you ever notices that you limp, at least not after the first time they meet you. The rest of you takes up far too much attention! And secondly, when a woman falls in love she never questions what it is she's in love with. And thirdly – '

'You said two things.'

'Be quiet! Thirdly, if Galina goes out with you, it's because she likes you. I assure you, a nurse's hours of leisure are too precious to be wasted on people she doesn't care for.'

With his fair skin blushing, he looked very much less than his twenty-six years, and far too young to be a Tribune of the People. 'Are you sure?'

'Of course I am. Just court her. She's probably wondering what's taking you so long.'

The favourable advance of his private affairs could not take Adishka's mind entirely away from the state of the nation, however. In July the Foreign Minister, Sazonov – a man universally respected in every country in Europe – was dismissed. His portfolio was given to Sturmer to hold in addition to that of Prime Minister and Minister of the Interior, which would have been a formidable load even for a man of ability. Sturmer was delighted, but the change was badly received in diplomatic circles. The ambassadors of Britain and France said privately that it was an insult to expect them to deal with such a man.

The Duma was to assemble again in November, but such was the situation that the Progressive Bloc had recently called for the deputies to meet before the opening session to decide on a plan of action. Things could not go on the way they were. Worst of all from the deputies' point of view, there were signs that the masses were beginning to lose faith in the Duma, for not acting with enough resolution. So now the Tsar must be persuaded to replace the inefficient, lapdog ministers, and to place significant power in the hands of the Duma. They were going to demand the dismissal of Sturmer, to begin with; and if the Tsar wouldn't dismiss him, they were going to indict him for treason.

The taxi-cab was only halfway along Fourstatskaya Street when Emily saw a figure hurrying along the pavement in the other direction and called to the driver to stop. She let down the window and called out.

Nina Antonova, smartly dressed and holding little Olga Vassili-evna by the hand, stopped, stared around her, and then came hurrying across the street.

'Oh, your highness, I was coming to see you!'

'You almost missed me,' Emily said.

She looked helpless. 'I couldn't get a taxi-cab. I took the streetcar to the end of the street, but Olga can't walk very quickly. I wouldn't have brought her, but the girl didn't come in today and I didn't want to leave her with any of the neighbours. They don't like me very much.'

Emily wondered, as she had wondered before, why Basil had fallen in love with this pathetic creature, who for all her smart prettiness always gave Emily the bedraggled impression of a drowned mouse. It must be something about legs, she thought. Her own father had fallen in love with a ballet girl, after all. Perhaps her mother had been just like Nina. She ought to be kind to her.

'It must have been something serious, if you were coming to my house,' she said genially.

Nina paled a little. 'Oh, I'm sorry, highness!' she whispered. 'I know I shouldn't – it isn't seemly – but you see, I didn't have anyone to send with a note, and the telephone in the hall hasn't worked for days, although I suppose I oughtn't to telephone either – '

'Nina, why don't you get in, and you can talk to me while we drive you home. I'm sure Olga has walked enough for today.'

It took a tedious amount of repetition and reassurance before mother and child were safely inside, the driver reinstructed, and his sliding panel closed. The taxi-cab drove off, and Nina fluttered about, settling Olga in the corner with instructions to look out of the window – which she was already doing, being a perfectly placid child, perhaps in compensation for her mother – and straightening her own clothes with long, nervous fingers.

'Now, Nina, tell me what the problem is,' Emily said at last. The journey to Nina's apartment was not long, and she had no desire to have to go inside to finish the conversation. Probably it was just a demand for more money – Nina was not a good manager, and prices were going up all the time.

'Well, highness, it's just that – I don't know if it's proper, but I don't know what else to do, and if I could write to Vasska – his highness – I would do, but – '

'What do you want to do?'

'Go away. Out of Petersburg – Petrograd, I mean.' She blushed at her mistake. Probably amongst the people she lived with such a slip of the tongue was frowned upon. 'You see, now that Senka's dead, and we don't know where Papachka is – Mama says she thinks he's a prisoner of war, but they say the Germans do frightful things to prisoners – '

'They usually put them to work in the fields, Nina,' Emily said firmly. 'Just as we do our prisoners. Where do you want to go?'

'Mama wants to take Lisa and go back to her village until the war's over, and live with Dedushka, and I'd like to go with her. They say there's plenty of food and everything in the country, and it's horrible here in Peter. You have to queue for hours for a loaf of bread, and the milk's all full of black bits, and you can't get any coal. Everything costs so much, it's frightening.'

'If you need more money, you only have to ask. You know that Basil – Vasska – has told me you are to have anything you want.'

Nina blushed yet more painfully. 'I know. He's very good to me. And you are too, highness. I don't know why you're so kind to me, because if it was me – ' She stopped, as it penetrated even her woolly brain that this was a tactless path to be wandering down. Her eyes began to fill with tears.

'Never mind why,' Emily said hastily. 'I have nothing but goodwill towards you, Nina, you can be sure of that. So you want to go with your mother and sister?'

Nina nodded slowly, dabbing at the end of her little nose with a lace-edged handkerchief. She had the rare talent of continuing to look pretty even when she cried. 'I don't like it here any more. The neighbours are horrid to me, because of my connection with the nobility. Jealous, that's what Mama says. And I worry about Olga. It's so hard to get the things she needs, and it isn't just money, highness. Even if you have the money, you can't get things. And I'm sure the shopkeepers cheat me. Mama says they put the prices up when they see me coming.'

I'm sure they do, Emily thought.

'I don't know why it's got like that. Everyone says the last two harvests have been the best ever. And they say in the country you can get all the food you want.'

'There are problems of transport,' Emily said. 'All the trains are being used for the army, so there aren't enough to bring food and other things into the city.'

It wasn't only that, of course; there was also the problem of inflation. When prices rose all the time, the producers held back their goods in the hope of better and better prices. As for inflation, she understood that it had been caused largely by the Government's issuing huge quantities of paper money. Before the war, 98 per cent of Russian currency had been backed by gold, and it had been considered the most stable currency in the world. Now the figure was 25 per cent, and falling. But Emily would as readily have tried to explain all that to a giraffe as to Nina.

'Well, I'm sure you are doing the right thing,' Emily said, hoping

413

to move the conversation along a bit. 'It will be much nicer for Olga too, having her relatives around her. But what did you want to ask me?'

'If it would be all right,' Nina said. 'I don't know if Vasska – his highness – would think it right of me. Maybe he'd expect me to wait for him? Only no-one seems to know how long the war will go on, and I could always come back when it was over. And he never seems to get any leave, and I get so lonely, all on my own, and Mama such a long way away, and everything horrid – ' More tears.

'I'm quite sure he would be glad to think of your being safe and happy in the country. He would agree with me that it's the best thing you could do.'

'But – after the war? When he comes back – ?'

Emily felt a sudden pang of pity, seeing clearly what she feared. Out of sight could so easily be out of mind. What if Basil, returning to find her gone, washed his hands of her?

'If you give me your address, I'll make sure he gets it as soon as he comes back. And if you need anything, you have only to write to me.'

'Thank you, highness,' she said. She seemed depressed. Perhaps she had wanted to be persuaded not to go? What a trial it must be, always to be in two minds about everything!

'Do you need anything immediately, for the journey?'

'No thank you, highness.'

They were passing the end of the Nevsky Prospekt now, and Emily thought of a way to be rid of her. She took out her purse, and found a reasonably large banknote.

'Why don't you take little Olga shopping, and buy her something pretty to wear for when she meets her great-grandfather? A nice blue velvet dress, perhaps. And then you could take a taxi-cab home.'

Nina took the money and the instructions with docility. The taxi was stopped, the little girl handed out, and as Emily drove on again she could see them walking off obediently towards the shops. It was quite absurd, she told herself, for the sight to make her feel she had been unkind.

She found her grandmother rather distracted. Natasha greeted her with all her usual warmth and affection, but she looked worried, and there was obviously something on her mind. In the last year or so she had aged suddenly, and now, although she was still only sixty, she looked definitely a grandmother. The death this year of her lover, Count Obrovitch, Emily thought, must have been a blow to her. Certainly after it she had ceased to interest herself in the hospital beyond paying the bills, and she now hardly ever came to Petrograd.

To entertain her, Emily told her of the encounter with Nina, and she smiled obediently, though without much amusement.

'You will be glad to have her out of the way,' Natasha said. 'And probably when he comes back, Vasya will never think of her again.'

'He didn't seem much interested in her last time he was home, but he must continue to support her. It isn't her fault, poor child, that she's fallen from favour.'

'You're very generous about it, *mylenkaya*,' Natasha said mournfully. 'I have to admit I was mistaken about Vasya. He isn't all I expected him to be. He shouldn't have been wasting himself on little chits like her when he hadn't even given you a child. It would be such a comfort to you now, if you had a little one to take care of.'

'I have Modeste, and Tatya and Petya,' Emily said.

'Someone else's babies', Natasha said with uncomfortable penetration, 'are never the same.' She sighed. 'I'm afraid I have shown bad judgement about more than one person.'

'What do you mean? Has someone let you down?' Emily asked. Natasha sat down and stared at her granddaughter across the table.

'I'm worried, Emilusha. Very worried. Things at Court are going from bad to worse. Of course, I always knew the Empress had her faults, but she's interfering now where she has no business, and where she does great harm. And it's all at the instigation of Rasputin. He and Anna Vyrubova manipulate her like a string puppet.' She tapped the table in an irritated way. 'Why on earth the Empress chose the Vyrubova as her intimate friend I'll never know! She has nothing – no brain, no wit, no beauty, no breeding. Certainly no judgement. I'm sure if she didn't endorse everything Rasputin says, the Empress wouldn't have come so far under his influence.'

'But he saved Vyrubova's life, didn't he, after that train crash, when she was on the point of death?' Emily said.

'Do you believe that?' Natasha asked sharply.

Emily shrugged. 'I only know what you told me, that she was so badly injured the doctors had given her up, and that he just came in and looked at her, and she made a miraculous recovery.' Natasha

415

didn't speak, watching her drumming fingers with a distracted frown. 'Anyway, the Empress believes it, and that's all that matters.'

'They're ruining the country,' she said suddenly. 'Ministers of the Crown are dismissed on the decision of an ignorant peasant. I know what the Empress writes to the Tsar: "Our Friend says you should take Sturmer because he is a good, loyal man". And then when he's apppointed, she writes, "Sturmer completely believes in our Friend's wonderful, God-sent wisdom, which proves you were right to take him". Rasputin whispers to Vyrubova, Vyrubova murmurs to the Empress, and she speaks out firmly to the Tsar. It's utter madness. I don't know where it will end.'

'Do you think Rasputin wants to rule the country?'

Natasha looked up impatiently. 'No, no! He hasn't the intelligence or the ambition. He's a little, stupid, vain man, who likes being important and having lots of money and having everyone fawn on him. Besides, he has so many enemies now that if the Empress dropped him, he'd be picked up by the Okhrana within the hour and probably hanged. So he defends himself. If a person in power shows he dislikes Rasputin, Rasputin gets rid of him. That way he ensures he'll be left alone to enjoy himself.'

'You really think that's what he's doing?' Emily asked. 'I thought perhaps he genuinely believed he was doing what was right for Russia.'

'So did I, at first. But if you knew of his lifestyle, Emilusha – the drink and the drugs – I doubt whether his mind is ever completely clear.'

'But what about Protopopov? Wasn't it Rasputin's idea to have him made the new Minister of the Interior? That sounds like a step in the right direction. I mean, since Protopopov is vice-president of the Duma, he must surely bring the Duma and the Government closer together?'

'Is that what Adishka told you?' Natasha asked with stark disbelief.

'Well, no. I haven't spoken to Adishka about it. It's only just been announced, and I haven't happened to see him yet.'

'You don't know Protopopov?'

'No, I've never met him. But he's been vice-president for years, so he must be a Duma man.'

'He's anybody's man. I saw him at the palace yesterday, and he was rubbing his hands with glee over his promotion, wagging his tail and writhing with adoration of the Empress, Rasputin, and all

416

their ways. Whatever he was before, he's an ardent monarchist now, ready to do anything Alexandra tells him, and looking forward to putting those interfering, impertinent deputies in their place. As he went past me, I heard him say, "Now Rodzianko will have to do what *I* say for a change".'

'Oh Grandmama, is it really that bad?'

'Adishka will tell you.' She stood up restlessly and walked to the window. 'I've never felt afraid before, but I'm afraid now. The Duma thinks it has all the answers, but none of them knows how to run the country. For that they need the co-operation of experienced ministers. And both need the authority of the Tsar. But they don't seem to realise it. I'm afraid things are going to the bad. I don't know what's going to happen.'

Emily didn't know what to say. She went over to her, and put her hand on her grandmother's shoulder. 'It will probably be all right,' she said. 'Things usually sort themselves out.'

Natasha placed her hand on top of Emily's. 'It isn't for myself I mind. I've had my life, and it's been a good one. But what about you, and your children? It isn't fair on you. I don't know what sort of world we're going to be leaving you.'

'You won't be leaving for a very long time,' Emily said, 'so the question doesn't apply.'

Natasha didn't answer, and Emily could only offer silent comfort.

The taxi-cab that took her from the station was brought to a halt by a crowd which had spilled out of a side-street and spread across the road.

'What's going on?' Emily asked.

'I don't know, *barina*,' the driver said. 'It may be to do with the strike at the Puchikov factory — that's over that way. They were having a demonstration today. Maybe the crowds have gathered to watch.'

'Can you go another way round? It doesn't look as though they're going to move.'

'If I could get a few blocks further on I could cut through, *barina*, but we've got the railway lines to that side of us now.'

Emily looked over her shoulder and saw that the road behind was blocked by held-up traffic and an increasing crowd. They could go neither forward nor back. 'Perhaps I'd better get out and walk.'

'I wouldn't advise that, *barina*. These crowds can get a bit rough, and you're not dressed for it.'

Emily's clothes were quite plain, but there was no mistaking their quality, and she was wearing a fur tippet and several rows of pearls. No-one would take her for a worker.

'Best sit tight, *barina*. I'll get you through as soon as I can.'

Emily sat, not particularly worried. There had been strikes and demonstrations before in Petrograd, and where there was violence, it was usually directed towards shop windows and policemen. She rather wished she had been wearing her nurse's uniform, though: she could have walked through the crowd then, like Moses parting the Red Sea, and picked up another taxi-cab on the other side.

The crowd seemed to grow thicker all around, and other vehicles nearby disappeared as though overwhelmed with bodies. Shortly afterwards some mounted police arrived and began forcing their way through; but the density of the crowd was too much for them, and despite the natural dislike of the pedestrian to coming too close to a horse, they were soon locked in and immobile.

One of them was a few feet away from Emily's taxi-cab. He leaned down from his saddle and peered in at her, and then waved urgently to attract her attention. She put down her window.

'You'd better get out of there, *barina*, before things get rough.' He pointed with his stick towards the side of the road. 'See that doorway? Get yourself inside that building until this lot disperses.'

Emily was not sure she cared for the idea of launching herself into that sea of bodies, but the people nearest the taxi-cab seemed quite docile and friendly, more amused at having got themselves wedged in than angry or frustrated. She guessed they were not demonstrators, but onlookers, mere passers-by who had wandered up to see what was happening and now couldn't get away. When they understood what the policeman was about, they became helpful.

'That's right, *barina*, out you come! Oy, you there, make way, can't you?'

'Let her through, let her through.'

'Come on then, madame, let's get you out of there!'

Passed from hand to hand like a parcel, Emily reached the doorway with no greater injury than a rumpling of her clothing and a knocking askew of her hat. Once in the doorway, however, she found herself in no better case, for the door was locked fast, and ringing at the bell produced no answer. If there was anyone in there, they obviously preferred not to open it for the moment. Still, the doorway was large and deep, perfectly adequate to shelter her.

Now something was happening. Everyone was suddenly looking away down the street, and there was a lot of distant shouting. Emily took the opportunity to slip off her triple strand of pearls and slip it into her purse, just in case. Then she went to the edge of her shelter and looked out.

'Soldiers!' shouted someone nearby. 'They've called out the army!'

She couldn't see the soldiers over the heads of the crowd, but she could see the tops of their bayonets, and the mounted officers.

'Bastards!' someone shouted, and, 'Let's get out of here!'

Now there was a muted roaring sound, mingled with the shouting of the crowd, which resolved itself after a moment into a human voice speaking through a megaphone. It was indecipherable at first. Then, presumably as the mouth of the instrument was swung round, it became clear.

'. . . minutes! This is an official warning. You must disperse at once. If you do not disperse, the troops will begin firing in two minutes!'

The crowd began to leak at the edges, as the mere onlookers decided to embrace the better part of valour. The pressure in this part of the street seemed to ease; Emily could tell that the crowd was thinning, because she could see the police horse swing its hindquarters, which it couldn't have done before.

And then something happened. The people nearest her reeled backwards, and further up the street towards the soldiers a roar went up, mixed with the screams of women. From a side-street a body of men had rushed out, locked together in a mass, some of them carrying banners. Even as she watched, the pole on one side of a two-handed banner snapped, and the white cotton went flapping down like a shot bird. Men in caps, with a few women in scarves on the flank. She guessed that the strikers themselves had been driven away from their original place of demonstration, and had erupted into the crowded street.

Their impetus was such that they drove forward some distance before being brought to a halt. Emily could see the army officer's horse waltzing in fear on the far side of the crowd. The megaphone again, exhorting the demonstrators to go back, the crowd to disperse.

'Very well, you've had your warning. I am giving the order to fire!'

419

Emily caught her breath. For a second nothing happened; and then her heart bounced against her ribs as the brattle of rifle-fire echoed up the street. It was a scattered sound, not a complete volley. There were screams, and then from the crowd a hoarse, communal shout went up, which changed into an ugly kind of cheer.

She couldn't help herself. She reached out and tugged at the nearest sleeve. 'What happened? What happened?'

The man barely glanced round, certainly not enough to take in who she was, only what she asked. Perhaps that was just as well. His mouth was wide open, ready to yell. Emily saw with the dispassion of a moment of danger that he had only two teeth, one in the top jaw and one in the bottom. Perhaps because of that, she couldn't understand what he was saying.

'What?' she screamed over the roar of the crowd. 'What did you say?'

'The sojers wouldn't fire at us! They shot a —ing p'liceman instead!' he bellowed with unholy glee, and his words merged into a triumphant cheering.

'Up the strikers! Down with the Government!'

I'm in danger now, Emily thought, quite dispassionately. She drew back into the doorway, wondering what would happen if they noticed her. Most of them at this end of the street were probably decent people who had merely stopped to look, but discontent was widespread amongst the masses, and it wouldn't be hard for something to set them off.

I'll tell them I'm a nurse, she thought. Some of them will know about the Anatoli. They won't hurt me – if I can make them listen. I must take off this hat. A hat is like a banner proclaiming class. Women of the people wore scarves or shawls on their heads, never hats. She slid her hands cautiously up to take out the pins, trying not to draw attention to the movement; and thought that the pins might be useful weapons if she had to fight for her life. She realised with surprise that she wasn't at all afraid. Her blood seemed to be surging round her veins in the most extraordinary way. If I have to fight, she found herself thinking, I'll leave a few marks on a few faces.

But then the shouting faltered and changed its note. It had been hard and hostile and greedy; now it lost its rhythm and fell away, like a spinning-top losing momentum; and when it resumed, it was different – urgent, but frightened. The people in her segment of vision craned up to try to see what was happening, and then whipped round as fast as they could, even before the one word was spoken and passed from mouth to mouth like forest fire.

'*Cossacks!*'

No-one waited to see what the Cossacks would do. They turned and ran, shoving those in their way, trampling the weak or unready in their desperation to get away. Emily saw the police horse rear, its officer slide helplessly off and disappear like a fragment of river-bank torn away by a flood. Hands grabbed the bridle, the horse screamed and tried to escape. A man scrambled up into the saddle and kicked it forward, and it went rather from the pressure of the crowd than its own volition, with half a dozen people hanging off it like monkeys and trying to scramble up as though it were a streetcar.

A woman reeled into the doorway and collapsed at Emily's feet, bleeding at the mouth. Instinctively Emily crouched over her, used now to the reek of poverty which once would have made her retch.

'I'm a nurse!' she shouted over the noise of the fleeing multitude. 'Where are you hurt? Can you tell me?'

The woman groaned, seeming only half conscious. A head wound, perhaps? Emily bent closer and caught the smell of alcohol on her breath, and at the same moment saw the small bottle that the woman still clutched in one filthy hand. *Khanza*, she thought resignedly. The sale of vodka had been banned since the beginning of the war in an effort to check drunkenness, with the result that black-market vodka, while readily available, had become too expensive for the masses. They had taken to drinking home-made *khanza*, a delightful brew made from fermented bread freely mixed with metal-polish.

Emily slid a cautious hand under the woman's head and felt about in the stringy hair until she found, as she expected, a head wound. It was a vertical cut, and bleeding freely. Probably reeled against the corner of a building or a lamppost. It was superficial, though, and drunk as she was, the woman was unlikely to be concussed. Emily wiped her sticky hand on the woman's coat, and stood up.

A woman paused in flight just long enough to snatch Emily's fur piece from her as she passed. Emily felt the jerk at her neck as the clip broke, and then woman and fur were gone. It happened so fast she had no time even to be afraid, only to register that the woman's face had been completely blank: she had grabbed the fur in the purest automatic reaction.

Another shape staggered in, falling out of the stream into the doorway to sag, panting, against the wall: an elderly man, undersized

421

and horribly dirty. Most of all, he was thin, so thin that the skin was tight and shiny over his nose and cheekbones, and his ears stood out from his head as if on columns. She had seen many malnourished men passing through the hospital, but never before a man who was literally starving to death.

Before she could move or speak to him, there was a clatter of hooves, and a Cossack appeared, whirling his pony in the doorway. There was a sensation of movement, colour and hostility, the smell of horse and garlic, a menace of hooves and bright metal and white teeth under a gash of moustache. The Cossack was grinning with battle fever; he whirled his sabre round his head and made an incoherent sound like an enraged animal. In the same instant the thin man cried out and shrank back against the wall, and Emily knew, the man knew, they all knew that the Cossack was going to kill him.

It was the old man's cry that made her move: there was no defiance in it; just the lost and submissive sound a bird makes from between the teeth of a cat. It was the cry, and the fact of the pony. Unlike almost any member of the proletariat, Emily had no fear of horses, in whatever circumstance. Since before she could walk she had been amongst, on top of and occasionally underneath horses, and they were her friends. As the whirling sabre went up, Emily went forward, caught the pony's bridle, and shouted, '*No!*'

The Cossack's eyes widened as he focused on her. 'Put it down!' she commanded. 'Where is your officer?'

It didn't really matter what she said. His eyes had taken in her clothing as his ear took in her accent. His sabre came down to the ready, he whirled his pony round and was gone.

It was late when she got home. When the street had cleared there remained a number of fallen whom she could not, as a nurse, walk away from. The injuries were mostly slight, and there were soon plenty of helpers gathering to her with an instinctive desire for authority, to be directed to the tending and carrying-away. Astonishingly no-one had been killed, though she learned from the chatter of the helpers that three policemen had been hit by the bullets of the infantry, and several others had been injured by the crowd.

'There'll be trouble over it,' someone said with relish. 'Executions! Bound to be – it was mutiny, plain and simple.'

Emily didn't want to think about that part of it as she walked back to Fourstatskaya Street. She managed to pick up a taxi-cab at last in Znamenskii Square, and was glad to ride the rest of the way. It had been a long and exhausting day.

The butler Rajek's eyes widened at the sight of her as he opened the door, but before he could speak Adishka was there.

'Emilia, where have you been? There's been the most awful trouble!'

'Yes, I know, I was in it,' Emily said. Adishka took in for the first time her appearance – dirty, rumpled, gloveless and bareheaded.

'In it?' he said blankly. 'What are you talking about?'

'The riot. Haven't you heard? I got caught up in a demonstration by some strikers. The infantry were called, but they refused to act and fired on the police instead. It wasn't until the Cossacks charged that the crowd dispersed.'

Adishka was shaking his head slowly, as if unable to understand what she was saying. Then Anna appeared, running down the stairs with her hands out in supplication.

'Emilia! Thank God you've come. You must come upstairs at once! Modeste has had a fit.'

Emily was on the move at once. 'A fit? Have you called the doctor?'

'Yes, yes, he's on the way. But Modeste always wants you. Please hurry!'

They started up the stairs. He had been so upset that morning, Emily remembered. 'I shouldn't have left him,' she muttered.

Adishka was behind her. 'It was the telegram that did it. It was the unluckiest thing. He was in the room when Rajek brought it in, and Anna read it out before she realised what it said.'

'What telegram?'

'Valya's dead. His regiment was on the way from Archangel to Greece. They mutinied in Marseilles, and Valya and another officer were shot. The French Army had to be called in to get them under control again.'

Chapter Twenty-Four

The weather at the beginning of 1917 was bitter, with temperatures dropping to fourteen below. Blizzards and deep ice on the tracks made it difficult for trains to move, and the food and fuel shortages in Petrograd grew more severe. But on the 22nd of February the temperature had suddenly started to rise, and now, four days later, it was a pleasant 48° Fahrenheit. The sun was melting the ice on palace rooftops and glinting off gilded domes. It was Sunday, and everywhere the faithful were communicating amongst the glittering candles and swirling clouds of incense, chanting the lovely liturgy of the Orthodox Mass.

On her way home, Emily stopped at the butcher's shop along the road. It was not open, but the owner, Volkov, opened the side-door to her and welcomed her in with a broad smile.

'Yes, yes, come in, your highness. Yes, I have something for you, something rather special. I'm sure you will be pleased.'

He led her through to the dark, cold cave of the shuttered shop. In the dim light filtering in from the door she saw a carcase on the slab, and her heart sank a little. It was too small – about the size of a lamb, but it was certainly not lamb. She had become over the last few months something of an authority on carcases, but she couldn't identify this one.

'What on earth is it?' she asked.

Volkov, who was ahead of her in the shadows, turned and smiled under his thick, bushy moustache.

'Beaver, your highness.'

'Beaver?'

'From the tannery. The trappers bring it in, the furriers take off the pelt, and what is left – well, someone must have it. Why not? It makes no difference to the beaver.'

'But what does it taste like?'

He shrugged. 'Like beaver. Quite nice, really, with a little cranberry sauce. A little like wild boar, I believe.'

Emily shook her head, not so much in refusal as disappointment. 'It's awfully small.'

Now the teeth showed under the fur in greater amusement. 'No, no, your highness, this is not what I had in mind for you. For you – ' He pulled a piece of sacking off something further along the slab, a large something. 'Venison. A whole deer.'

'Good heavens!' Emily leaned forward. In that dim light, it could have been anything. 'Where did it come from? It looks a bit knocked about.'

He coughed discreetly. 'My source, I fear, must remain unnamed. And as for the condition of the carcase, I understand it was involved in a slight accidental collision with a motor vehicle.'

Emily smiled, supplying the rest for herself. A young officer, she imagined, knocking down a stray deer escaped from an ornamental park, and wanting to cover up his deed. The Tsar kept deer at Tsarskoye Selo. What was the punishment for that, she wondered? Probably death. Perhaps it wasn't even accidental.

'Well, as long as you're not trying to sell me horse,' she said, 'I don't care.'

Volkov spread his hands. 'Would I dare, highness? Would I even think of offering horse to an English lady?'

'You forget. I'm not an English lady any more. I'm a Russian princess.'

Volkov looked at her seriously for a moment, all playfulness gone. 'If the present disturbances should continue to their logical end, better you should be an English lady.'

'What do you mean?' Emily was startled. 'It's only the usual winter strikes and bread riots, isn't it?' Volkov said nothing. 'With this warm weather, the trains will begin to come in again, and once the people have bread they'll be content.'

'I shall say no more, highness. I'm a simple butcher, not a politician. But I saw two proclamations pasted up on the corner of the street this morning. One, that by order of the Tsar street gatherings are forbidden and troops will fire on crowds. The second, that all strikers must return to work, and any who do not will be shipped straight to the front.'

Emily looked uneasy. 'I'm sure it wouldn't come to that. Surely the threat alone will be enough. It won't be necessary to carry it out.'

He smiled, retreating behind his shopkeeper's façade. 'Shall I have the carcase sent round then, your highness?'

'Yes – yes, if you please,' said Emily, somewhat distracted.

On the rest of her journey home, she looked about her with new eyes. There were armed soldiers posted at street corners, and the Troitsky Bridge had been raised, with a patrol at either end, heavily armed. The city was quiet and there was little traffic, but she saw a number of armoured cars rattling past on some or other urgent mission.

Was it possible that Volkov was right, and that the bread riots might turn into something else? It didn't seem possible. Last night they had all gone to the Alexander Theatre in the most normal way, and the audience, in evening dress and jewels, had seemed just as usual. There had been one or two clashes during the day between demonstrators and soldiers, but everything had been quiet by nightfall.

And yet . . . She remembered what Alexei had said when he came home for three days' leave just before Christmas. Indeed, she remembered everything about that visit: she had been living on it ever since. She had gone down alone to the hall to meet him: Adishka was out on Council business, and Anna was still in bed. Under the eyes of the servants he had been able only to kiss her formally, but he held her hand a moment and said, 'You look tired.'

'It's the black clothes, I think,' she said. 'Black doesn't really suit me.'

'No. I'm sorry about Basil.'

'It's strange, but I can hardly feel it. There've been so many now, and after a while you begin to forget who's gone and who hasn't. Poor Basil. They should have left him in the Caucasus. He was happy there.'

'Yes. I don't suppose he enjoyed trench warfare very much.'

They began to walk towards the stairs. 'I suppose one should be surprised he lasted so long, really.'

'He was always good at taking care of himself. How's Anna?'

'As I wrote to you – did you get the letter? – she took it very badly. It was the one death I think she really felt. They were very close, of course.'

He glanced around. 'Where is she now?'

'Still in bed. She doesn't get up until luncheon – sometimes later. I think she's very depressed. She says she hasn't anything to get up for, and I can see her point. I wish she'd interest herself in something.'

They entered the small sitting-room on the first floor and closed the door, and then he was able to take her in his arms. They held each other for a while, and then she pulled back.

426

'I'm sorry,' she said. 'I don't seem to be able to feel things properly.
I *am* glad to see you. I know that I am, but I can't feel it.'

'I know.'

'Do you?'

'It's as though you touch everything through a thick layer of wool.
All your senses are blunted. A sort of numbness.'

'Yes! Yes, just like that.'

He smiled. 'Do you think you're the only one, my little star?'

The endearment reached her. 'Oh Alexei! I wish all this were over.
It seems just to go on for ever.'

'You are tired. Have you been working long hours at the hospital?'

'No, not really. We're getting hardly any casualties now. The beds
are mostly full of convalescents, so there's not so much to do for
them. What does come in is frostbite and gangrene, and a certain
number of self-inflicted wounds. Fingers and toes shot off. The silly
creatures do it to get away from the front.'

Alexei nodded. 'It doesn't occur to some of them they could just
walk away. I suppose they think they'd be caught and sent back.'

'Is there much desertion?'

'Not yet. Not in my sector, anyway. We keep pretty sound, though
there's been a lot of grumbling. But I keep my young officers in
order, and don't let them throw their weight around, so we all get
on pretty quietly. The trouble is we don't have enough for them to
do to keep them from thinking and talking. What are things like
here?'

'Terrible,' she said succinctly. 'Food and fuel shortages have been
getting worse all the time. Protopopov doesn't seem to do anything
about anything, and the Tsar won't get rid of him because he's the
Empress's favourite.'

'So the murder of Rasputin hasn't made any difference?'

'None at all that I can see. People thought at first that once he
was gone the Tsar would become his own man, but he's just shut
himself up with the Empress at Tsarskoye Selo, and makes no
decisions. Natasha Petrovna says they see no-one and never go
beyond the palace railings.'

'It can't be grief on his part,' Alexei said. 'He never really cared
for Rasputin – just tolerated him for the Empress's sake.'

'Grandmama thinks he believes that Rasputin was struck down
just as a way of striking at him; that anyone loyal to them is
automatically a target.'

'Yes, that's always been part of the problem. It's an attitude that makes him impossible to reason with. "I like X, therefore he is the right man for the job. You think X is the wrong man, therefore you must hate me." It's watertight logic: the original circular argument.'

'So what can be done?' she asked anxiously.

'I really don't know. I feel now – and I know most of the senior officers feel – that there's no way to save him. Sooner or later he must be made to abdicate so that we can break this deadlock and start to build a new constitution. And sooner would be better than later. I don't think he has any friends left. If he were to go, there'd be no-one to regret him.'

'Yes,' Emily said sadly. 'I've heard some people saying – the Kovanins and Duvitskys, for instance – that they believe the Tsar wants to make a separate peace with Germany, that he and the Empress are secretly German sympathisers. It's nonsense, of course, but it shows how people think.'

Soon he had to leave her to go and see Anna and spend some time with her, and the rest of the day was spent with the children and Emily. Later, Adishka came home, and what Emily remembered best about the evening was the argument between the two brothers about the political situation.

Adishka, growing excited with his enlarged audience, had gone from talking about the Duma's present plans to describing what they would do when they had power.

After listening for a while, Alexei said, 'It's all very well to say you'll do this and you'll do that, but none of you has the first idea of administration. It isn't enough just to sit in session passing laws, you know – you have to make them work too.'

'That's the old way, the way the Tsar thinks. That's not for us,' Adishka said firmly. 'He reduces everything to matters of administration, and to hell with first principles. We believe principles must come first.'

'Mirabeau said "To administer is to govern, and to govern is to reign",' Alexei began, but Adishka interrupted.

'Oh, we've had enough in this country of governing and reigning! Three hundred years of it! People have had enough. Give them fair laws, freedom and good principles, and they'll rule themselves, you'll see. We're not going to get rid of one oppressive regime just to institute another.'

'Dear God, I do believe you're serious! Adishka, listen to me, this is important. The Duma at the moment commands a lot of respect

428

and trust, and it must act responsibly. That means you must co-operate with the ministers and the bureaucracy to – '

'Our mandate comes from the people.'

'What, the masses whom you're so busy trying to incite to riot? And what happens when you've got your riot? Civil disorder, loot-ing, burning, bloodshed on the streets. How do you restore order then?'

Adishka looked uncomfortable. 'Well, if it came to it, I suppose we'd have to call out the army.'

'The army,' Alexei said flatly. 'That would be to put a match to a bonfire. Don't you realise, you and the rest of your deputy friends, that you are all in the situation of a man blithely smoking a cigar in a powder store? In this city alone you have three hundred and fifty thousand armed and disaffected men who would love an excuse to riot.'

'What are you talking about? What's that got to do with the army?'

'That *is* the army. Owing to a lunatic decision by the Government, the new intakes of soldiers are housed in city barracks, waiting to replace the casualties at the front. They bear the names of the great Guard regiments – the Semyonovsky, the Preobrajensky – but that's not who they are. The real soldiers are with me in the trenches. What you have here is a group of largely middle-aged civilians straight from the plough who believe they were unfairly inducted and that if they're sent up to the front they're doomed to die.'

'But that's not – '

'Their officers are raw, newly commissioned boys in their early twenties who can't command their respect or obedience. They are subjected daily to a diet of lies and propaganda from agitators, and stories of horror and death in the trenches from old soldiers and convalescents. They're in constant touch with the workers and peas-ants in the streets of Petrograd, from whom they differ in no signifi-cant way. And when the Duma calls on these civilians-in-uniform to fire on their demonstrating brothers with whom they're entirely in sympathy, what do you think will happen?'

'Exaggeration is no argument,' Adishka said, falling back on dig-nity. 'It wouldn't happen like that. And anyway, there wouldn't be riots on the streets if we were in power, because we are the people's choice. They'd have no reason for it.'

Alexei looked tired. 'No, of course you're right. I was only sketching the very worst scenario to show you that governing a country is not a stroll down a country lane.'

'Well we know *that*,' Adishka said kindly. 'And we know our people. The Russian worker isn't a political creature. He only riots when he hasn't enough to eat. Give him a pound of bread and he'll go off home quite happily.'

Emily and Alexei were able to snatch a little time together in his private room on the eve of his return to the front.

'I wish I didn't have to go,' he said.

'Don't go then,' she said. 'Just stay here. Others do it. The Astoria's full of officers drinking champagne who should be elsewhere. They come home on leave and just don't bother to go back. Nobody seems to think anything of it now, though at the beginning of the war they'd have been spat upon, if not lynched.'

'But you know I can't do that,' he said gently.

'I don't see why not,' she said stubbornly. 'You don't have any loyalty to the Tsar now, surely?'

'To Nicholas, no. But to the monarchy – that's a different thing. I swore to serve it, and you wouldn't want me to be the sort of person who could ignore an oath, would you?'

'Circumstances change. If what you swore loyalty to proves not to be worthy . . . '

'Yes, I understand. But that time hasn't come yet. I have a duty to my country, and to my soldiers at the front. My presence is needed there to maintain order and decency.'

'And order and decency are worth serving,' she said.

'They're the only things. It doesn't matter how they're dressed.'

'Yes, I know.' She sighed. 'I miss you so much. I get so lonely, and start to wonder what will happen to us – '

'Don't. Everything will be all right. Haven't I promised you?'

'That seems so long ago.' She lifted his hand, which was clasped in hers, and kissed it. 'I was so afraid, you know, that I would feel glad that Basil had died, but at least I've been spared that. I'm so very, very sorry. It's made me much fonder of Anna, too.'

'I'm glad of that, because I have to ask you something. I hesitate to say it, but if anything should happen while I'm away – if there should be any trouble – '

'I'll look after her,' Emily said. 'You don't need to ask. I'll take care of her and the children until you come home.'

'I knew I could rely on you.' He kissed her. 'Bless you, Emilia Edvardovna. You are a rock.'

'So it seems.' She smiled faintly. 'When you come home for good and we're finally married, I'm going to celebrate by turning into jelly. I shall lie on a sofa all day and suffer from my nerves and give everybody as much trouble as I possibly can.'

Emily went over these memories all afternoon as she played with the children and read aloud to Anna, who had decided reading gave her a headache. The present trouble had begun on Thursday with the International Women's Day march, when the demonstrating women had been joined by the workers from a number of factories that had been on strike.

It had been the first day of the warmer weather, which probably accounted for the numbers out in the streets. The procession passed down the Nevsky Prospekt to the Municipal Council, shouting for equality for women and occasionally clamouring for bread. Cossacks and police had kept order, keeping the onlookers moving, and it had all passed off peacefully.

On Friday and Saturday there had been more demonstrations, this time by strikers demanding bread, and the numbers had swollen each day. By Saturday virtually every factory in the city had closed down. The Nevsky Prospekt was packed from side to side, and there had been some shouting of slogans such as 'Down with the Autocracy' and 'Down with the German Woman'. In Kazan Square students and workers had sung the 'Marseillaise'.

But each day, by the evening, the streets were quiet, and it had been pointed out in the newspapers that these disorders were confined to Petrograd, which proved they were only *golodnyi bunt* – hunger riots. She had seen for herself this morning that the streets were quiet, everyone going to church in the normal way. But in the afternoon Adishka went out, and returned some time later to say that since midday the crowds had been building up, and that now thousands of workers were milling about in the public places, waiting for something to happen.

'I met old General Martinov, and he says the mood is getting ugly,' Adishka said. 'He says the Government ought to have acted more firmly yesterday, that the mob thinks it can get away with anything, and that the Government won't do anything to stop them. Of course,' he added triumphantly, 'that's just like the Government. The ministers are a bunch of lily-livered, spineless placemen, we all know that!'

'You won't go out again, Adishka?' Anna said peevishly. 'I don't like to have you wandering about the streets at a time like this. Remember what happened to Emilia that time she got mixed up with strikers.'

'Nothing happened to her, as I recall,' said Adishka, annoyed at being told what to do.

'She lost her beautiful mink tippet,' Ann said severely, 'and was horribly jostled. She might have been killed.'

Modeste looked up from his jigsaw puzzle. 'Is it going to be bad again, Milya?' he asked. 'Is there going to be blood?'

'No, of course not,' Emily said hastily, going over to comfort him.

'You see what you've done now?' Anna said triumphantly. 'Really, Adishka, I expect you to be more responsible around the children.'

Through that uncomfortable afternoon they heard distant bouts of gunfire. Lorries and armoured cars went past very fast under the windows, making them rattle, and sometimes there was the sound of running feet in the street, and shouting. But by nightfall all was quiet again, and nothing had come to disturb them. Late in the evening a telephone call came through for Adishka.

'That was Godnev,' he said when he came back into the drawing-room. 'The troops were out, firing on the crowds. Well, we guessed that, didn't we? The worst incident was in the Znamenskii Square – there was a huge crowd, and inflammatory speeches being made by agitators standing on the plinth of the statue. The police asked them to disperse, and when they refused, a company of the Volinsky Guard opened fire. They're saying forty dead, I don't know how many wounded.'

Emily was silent. Anna said, 'But they've restored order, haven't they? That's the main thing.'

'Oh yes. It's all quiet now. There was just one thing, though, that's a bit worrying.' He hesitated. Emily looked up. 'Apparently there was a mutiny at the Pavolvsky. Some workers went there, stirring up trouble, and a company broke into the arsenal, stole some rifles, and marched out to stop the Volinsky firing on the crowds. They met up with a detachment of mounted police, some fire was exchanged, and they went back to barracks. They've arrested the ringleaders, though, and it's all quiet there now.'

'An isolated incident, then,' Anna said.

'So it seems,' said Adishka. He didn't meet Emily's eye, but they were both thinking of Alexei's warning.

*

432

The next morning, early, Emily started out for the hospital, but when she reached the Troitsky Bridge she found a platoon of soldiers there, guarding it. They watched her approaching with wary expressions, and finally one stepped out in her path and said, 'Where are you going?'

He was not an officer, just a common soldier, but his accent was quite good. The others closed up behind him, and there was something about their expressions she didn't like. She drew herself up.

'To the Anatoli Hospital, on Kronversky,' she said. They exchanged glances. 'I'm a nurse,' she added, pulling back the flap of her coat and showing them the medal on her bib. 'You see? I nurse the wounded soldiers there.'

'You'd better get back home as quick as you can, that's my advice,' the soldier said. 'The streets won't be safe for the likes of you today. Go on back, madame.'

'But I have to get to work,' she said.

One of the others spoke up now. 'The Anatoli's been taken over. There's nothing for you to do there now.'

'Taken over by whom?'

A third one said, 'Never mind. You'll find out. Go on home, before you get shot.'

She didn't argue any more. The expression on the face of the third speaker was not pleasant. As she walked away she made herself walk slowly until she turned the corner. She had the oddest feeling that if she broke into a run, they'd shoot her in the back.

She had just reached the courtyard of the house when a truck came roaring down the street, the back filled with soldiers and one or two women. They were waving rifles, and as it passed her she could hear they were singing the 'Marseillaise'. She pressed herself back to the wall. Another followed it, and another. As the first reached the end of the road there was a sound of shots, and she realised they were firing into the air.

As if it had been a signal, a torrent of soldiers in grey overcoats poured out of the barracks which the trucks had just passed, cheering and waving red flags or handkerchiefs. Emily waited no longer. She ran across the yard and got indoors as quickly as possible, ran upstairs, and from the window of the drawing-room, looked down into the street.

They went past in a torrent of sand-coloured uniforms and ash-coloured greatcoats, cheering, singing, waving their rifles or carrying them slung loosely over their shoulders like farm implements. The

433

faces were grinning, the voices jubilant. She had lived in the area long enough now to recognise the shoulder-flashes of the regiments: the Preobrajensky, the Semyonovsky, the Volinsky, the Litovsky.

A movement made her turn her head. Adishka was there, still in his dressing-gown, with his hair disordered. He stared past her down into the street with wide eyes.

'What's happening?' he asked in a frightened voice.

Emily continued to look at him, and after a moment he turned to meet her eyes.

'You know what's happening,' she said flatly.

He spent all day on the telephone, talking to fellow deputies and other friends. The first call of the day revealed to him that the Tsar had sent a telegraph late last night proroguing the Duma. Most of the other conversations were rambling discussions of what could be done, and whether the Government was going to be able to restore order.

He told what he had seen, and heard reports from other parts of the city. Mutinous soldiers had crossed the bridge to the Vyborg district to join the striking factory hands. They had commandeered cars, broken into the Peter and Paul Fortress and released the prisoners, sacked the Okhrana and police headquarters. The Cossacks had sheathed their sabres and let them pass unhindered. Shops had been looted, policemen had been lynched.

'But what *can* we do? If we've been prorogued, we don't officially exist . . . Well, what does Rodzianko say?'

Emily spent most of the day watching from the windows. It was impossible to keep the children away from them – they thought the whole thing was a carnival put on for their amusement, and even Modeste was more excited than nervous. In the afternoon the soldiers who had gone streaming away towards the river came streaming back again, reinforced this time by the civilian crowd which had been demonstrating on previous days.

They went past in a torrent, soldiers sporting scraps of red material on their bayonet tips, women in heavy *shoobas* and headscarves, factory workers, students in their green and blue caps, sinister-looking men who were not soldiers or workers or students, and who marched in silence with grim faces. They were heading now for the Duma, looking for someone to tell them what to do.

Adishka received another telephone call, summoning him to a

434

special meeting at the Tauride Palace. 'We can't really use the Chamber, can we? It wouldn't be legal . . . Oh, I see. The Semicircular Hall? Yes, as a private body, I understand . . . Well, will I be able to get through? Yes, well I can see them from my window here . . . '

He put on his greatcoat, hat and gloves and hurried away, half elated, half nervous.

The early winter darkness closed in, and still the mob streamed past the windows. Emily got the children to bed at last, and went back to the windows, fascinated. There was a massive crowd in front of the Duma, lit by flaming torches, still indefatigably waving their red flags and singing. The snow of the street outside had been trampled to mush by the multitude of footsteps, and was scattered with the debris of the mutiny – broken poles and lost scarves and discarded handbills. Now and then an army vehicle roared by, or a private car loaded to the gunwales with hilarious soldiers; people still scurried past in both directions, singly or in groups. Two blocks away the Courthouse burned briskly, its upper storey a red blaze with black outlines drawn on it, and ash from the pyre fell from the dark sky onto the remnants of snow on the rooftops opposite.

It was very late when Adishka returned, but Emily was still up. She thought it was a little like the time Petya was born: it was impossible to go to bed when the world was in labour of a new order.

'Well, that decides it,' he said, but he didn't sound decided, or particularly happy.

'What have you decided?'

'To form a de facto Provisonal Government. There was no choice. We did everything we could to keep things proper and legitimate, but the Tsar wouldn't play ball. We formed a committee – making it plain that it was simply a committee of private individuals. I mean, you can't just *take* power, can you? That makes you no better than them.' He jerked a thumb towards the window. Outside in the street there were still parties going by, sounding more like late-night revellers now than revolutionaries.

'We telegraphed the Tsar, telling him the situation, and begged him to let us form a Duma ministry. He refused. Absolutely refused. Told the present Government ministers to remain at their posts and said he was coming back to Petrograd immediately. Well, I ask you!'

'He doesn't believe things are out of control,' Emily said slowly.

'That's it! That's it exactly! I suppose the Empress, miles out of town at Tsarskoye Selo, is telling him it's just a bit of a bread riot, and that he only needs to be firm. Of course Rodzianko told him what was what, but he doesn't like Rodzianko, so he never believes anything he says.'

'But if he's coming back, he'll see for himself, and then he'll have to give you the authority you want.'

'It's too late for that. For one thing, I don't suppose for a moment his train would get through; and that mob out there would never settle for the old order again. And for another thing, when it came to it, it was either we formed a Government, or the other lot did.'

'The other lot?'

'The factory workers' representatives. They set up in another hall of the Duma as soon as their leaders had been let out of prison. They're calling themselves the Provisional Committee of the Soviet of Workers' Deputies, and they're all as mad as hatters. If we let them steal a march on us, God knows what will happen to Russia!'

Over the following days, deputation after deputation went to the Tauride Palace to beg the Duma to take power, and to pledge their allegiance. There were workers and soldiers, of course, but as it became clear that the official Government had given up and gone into hiding, other less expected groups turned up: officers, previously loyal military units like the Palace Guard, even a detachment of the Corps of Gendarmes, who marched up singing the Marseillaise and carrying a red banner to prevent their being lynched by the mobs who hung around the Tauride night and day.

Rodzianko sent telegraphs to all the commanders of the armed forces, telling them that the Duma had assumed power from the former Cabinet and that order would soon be restored, but it soon became clear that there was no dissent anywhere to the new order of things. Friends of Anna's from the rich and titled section of society, telephoning when they could get a clear line, said it was the best thing that could happen, and that a constitutional monarchy was what they had always wanted. Even the Petrograd Soviet meeting in the other hall of the Tauride, which might have challenged the Duma for authority, agreed to acknowledge it and work with it.

As soon as the streets were relatively safe, Emily proposed going to the Anatoli Hospital to find out what had happened to the remaining patients. The telephone seemed to have been cut off, and remembering what the soldiers at the bridge had said, she was worried. She was almost out of the house when Adishka found out her purpose, and rushed to stop her.

'You're mad! Don't you know how dangerous it is?'

'Bosh! Why would anyone hurt me?' she said, though uneasily.

'That's the very heartland of the most extreme agitators over there. They'd hurt anyone,' Adishka said. 'And the streets are still full of drunken soldiers. If you weren't murdered, you'd certainly be robbed, and probably raped.'

Emily blanched a little at his direct language. 'All the same,' she said, 'I would be failing in my duty to my patients if I didn't find out what had happened to them.'

'I'll make some enquiries,' Adishka said, 'but only if you promise not to go out.'

Emily agreed reluctantly. He came back eventually with the news that the Anatoli had been taken over by a radical group as their headquarters, and the convalescent soldiers had been moved to the military hospital which had been set up in one wing of the Winter Palace.

'So you see they'll be well looked after. And it's just as well you didn't go up there. I'm all right – being a Duma deputy at the moment is the best passport a man could have – but they're a rough bunch of men over on the Vyborg side. There's been a terrible lot of looting, and buildings burned down. The Bolsheviks have taken over Kschessinska's house, of all places! You should see the mess. Destructive beasts, they are.'

'But what's this radical group?' Emily asked. 'And why my house? Especially when they could see it was a hospital.'

'I suppose because it was near the Bolsheviks,' Adishka said with a shrug. 'I don't know who they are – runaway soldiers, radical workers, prisoners released from the Peter and Paul, I shouldn't wonder. Certainly not people you ought to go near.'

He didn't tell her of the mess in the house, surpassing that in Kschessinska's. It had obviously been looted during that day of fierce rioting, and when little of value had been discovered, frustration had turned to mindless violence. The present occupants had had to stuff the windows with mattresses, for there was not a pane of glass in the ground floor. He didn't tell her either about her garden, where trees had been hacked down for fun, the pleached walk she had tended so lovingly ripped and smashed to splinters; and where he had seen, in a brief and horrified glance, one of the convalescents lying sprawled across a rose-bush with a neat bullet-hole in his forehead.

As Adishka predicted, the Tsar's train from Stavka could not get through. Mutinous troops to the south of the city blocked the line, and were not in a monarchist mood. The train was diverted to Pskov, the military headquarters of General Ruzsky, where there was a telegraph. The Duma deputies, having finally publicly formed a Provisional Government, sent Guchkov and Shulgin to the Tsar there with the formal request that he abdicate, in order to give them the authority they needed to govern peaceably. The crown was to go to the Tsarevitch, with the Tsar's brother Michael as regent during the boy's minority.

The two-man deputation expected to have to argue their case, but when they came before the Tsar they discovered that the work had already been done, and the Tsar had already begun drafting an abdication document. On the 3rd of March the sensational news was brought back that the Tsar had abdicated not only for himself but for his son, and that he wished the throne to pass to Grand Duke Michael.

'He can't do that,' Anna said indignantly.

'Yes, I know,' Adishka said. 'There's certainly no precedent for it, and I doubt whether it's valid legally. I mean, the instant Nicholas abdicates, by the law of succession his son becomes tsar, and minor or no minor, no-one can abdicate on his behalf.'

'Never mind that,' Anna said. 'You can't possibly accept Michael as tsar. He married a twice-divorced commoner, and that puts him out of the succession for ever.'

'We don't really want him anyway,' Adishka said. 'As regent to the boy, and with the boy as a figurehead, an untainted symbol of power – but I can't see Grand Duke Michael attracting any great loyalty from the mob. Still, I suppose we'll have to talk to him. We must do everything properly, if we're to remain above reproach.'

Later that day a deputation went to see the Grand Duke at his home. He was horrified at the thought of having to take up the burden his brother had just put down. At six o'clock that afternoon he signed a document refusing the throne and exhorting all his fellow countrymen to obey the Provisional Government until such time as a Constituent Assembly could be formed to decide the ultimate shape of future government according to the general will of the people.

'Well, legal or not, that's the end of the Romanovs. Kerensky says Grand Duke Michael burst into tears afterwards,' Adishka said at supper that evening. He was in jubilant mood.

'I should think he would,' said Anna. 'It was a solemn moment – and he must wonder what will happen to him now.'

'Oh, he'll be safe enough with us,' said Adishka. 'We want no blood – we'll leave that to the tsars of this world!'

'I suppose the Empress must know by now,' Anna said thoughtfully. 'I wonder what she thinks of it all.'

Emily thought of the Grand Duchesses, who would never now have to marry princes and go away from home. Their lives would change very little, she thought, and probably for the better. As the daughters of a private country gentleman they would do very well.

'Where will they go, the Tsar and his family?' she asked.

'He said he wanted to live at Murmansk until the war's over, and then to go and live on his estate at Livadia. We've agreed to that for the time being.'

'Very nice,' Anna said approvingly. 'The climate in the Crimea is perfect.'

'Grandmama said they always liked Livadia best,' Emily said.

On the following day, the 4th of March, the two abdication documents were published on the same broadsheeet and pasted up all over Petrograd. The *dvornik* brought one in to show the servants, and it gradually made its way up to the drawing-room. Emily looked at the smudgy printing and thought what a strange thing it was, that an isolated bread riot in a single city had turned into a mutiny, and then into a revolution. In the matter of a week, and almost without bloodshed, the last and greatest autocracy in the world had become a republic: just like that.

What it would mean for them all she couldn't begin to guess.

Chapter Twenty-Five

In retrospect, Emily thought it ought to have been possible to see what was going to happen. From the very beginning, there was not one government, but two. The Provisional Government had the authority, to which, with remarkably few exceptions, everyone in the country swore loyalty; but though it made legislation by the ream from its very first day, it soon proved to have no power to enforce its decisions.

One of its first acts was to abolish the police, the Okhrana, and the Corps of Gendarmes, thus leaving itself with no civil force in a country which had always been ruled by force. All regional governors and deputy governors were also dismissed, and their administrative powers transferred to the *zemtsva*, the elective town councils already in existence that dealt with such local matters as drainage and street-lighting. The *zemtsva* were ordered to form their own police forces, called citizens' militias, which were to be chosen by election.

In Petrograd the only real power was that of the soldiers who had created the revolution, and the first essential was to get them back under control. This was done by the Petrograd Soviet, who claimed to represent them, and who offered them amnesty for having revolted provided they returned to their barracks immediately and swore to obey the Soviet's orders. This they did willingly; and the Soviet then pledged itself to support the Provisional Government. All the same, it meant that while the Government had the nominal authority, it was the Soviet which had the real power.

It was not long before it began to use that power, and, not content with merely ratifying the decisions of the Provisional Government, began to promulgate laws of its own. Its first decrees were ominously repressive: members of the imperial family and those closely associated with it were arrested, and the Provisional Government's plan to send Nicholas, Alexandra and the children into exile in England were vetoed. They were to remain under close guard at Tsarskoye Selo, to make sure there was no counter-revolutionary plot hatched about them.

The Soviet further extended its influence by placing all postal and telegraph services under 'surveillance' by its agents, and placing 'commissars' in every military headquarters to ensure that no military action was taken without ratification by the Petrograd Soviet. It then instituted press censorship by confiscating and banning any publication that had not previously obtained Soviet approval.

Yet these things affected few people, and where they were noticed at all, they were shrugged off. The people of Russia were used to arbitrary actions on the part of Authority; and the only measure which directly affected the intelligentsia – the press censorship – caused such a storm of protest that it quickly had to be modified. Life, on the whole, returned to normal. Almost everyone accepted the end of the imperial regime with relief, and in towns all over Russia, middle-class intellectuals took over the soviets and the *zemtsva* with well-received enthusiasm.

But April and the thaw brought changes. One event which Adishka reported with mild amusement did not seem at the time particularly important. The Provisional Government, anxious to dismantle all forms of oppression, had not only got rid of all the tsarist agencies of enforcement, and abolished the death penalty, but had also declared an amnesty for all political prisoners and exiles. This meant that the leader of the Bolsheviks, Vladimir Ulyanov, was able to return to Petrograd.

He was now calling himself Lenin, after a famous incident at the Lena gold-mine when striking workers had been shot down by troops and had been declared martyrs of socialism. His arrival was celebrated by the Bolsheviks, who organised a welcoming party at the Finland Station, with flags and a brass band and speeches from the top of an armoured car.

'I think they were aiming at grand theatre, but it turned out more like burlesque,' Adishka said. 'Apparently he called for revolution, not realising that we've already had it. He's obviously out of touch. All those years in Switzerland have softened his brain!'

But very soon after Lenin's arrival, it became apparent that there were not two forces in Petrograd, but three. The Bolsheviks began to intrude themselves into everyday life, putting out leaflets and newspapers, addressing meetings, formenting discontent, organising street disorders. From a minor irritation, they became a regular and serious nuisance.

'What is it they want?' Emily asked Adishka once, and he shrugged.

'Lenin wants to be tsar. But don't worry, they're very much a minority; no-one supports them. They claim to be acting on behalf of the masses, but the masses hate them for wanting to make peace with the Germans. They regularly get thrown out of soviets all over the country for their ridiculous policies.'

But May brought other troubles, nearer to home, which put the minor matter of the Bolsheviks firmly in perspective in the Kirov household. One evening while they were sitting at dinner there were sounds of a disturbance downstairs in the hall, and after straining his ears for a moment, Adishka threw down his napkin and stood up.

'I suppose it must be someone for me,' he said, and headed for the door. As the footman opened it for him, the butler appeared, looking anxious.

'It's Olevsky, your excellency, from the estate. He demands to see you. I've told him it isn't convenient, that he should come back in the morning, but he says it's urgent.'

'All right, Rajek, I'll see him.'

'You mustn't let these people impose,' Anna said firmly, getting to her feet. 'I'll soon put him in his place!'

'I'm acting head of the family, while Alyosha's away,' Adishka said, and there was a hint in his voice of the old Adishka, the resentful younger brother always pushed into the background.

'Maybe so, but this is my house,' Anna said, 'and so, for that matter, is Schwartzenturm. It's for me to decide.'

'If Olevsky says it's urgent, someone ought to see him.'

'Why don't we all see him,' Emily suggested, tiring of the wrangling. 'Invite him to dinner while we're at it.'

Anna ignored the second part, but said to Rajek, 'Show him into the ante-room next door. We'll see him there.'

Olevsky was the steward at Schwartzenturm. Emily had only seen him twice, and from a distance: his business was always with the master, and the interviews were conducted away from the family rooms. Reflecting on this, Emily thought that the matter must be serious indeed for him to travel all this way and thrust himself into the house. The first sight of him – she went with Anna and Adishka into the ante-room, seeing no reason why she should miss the fun – confirmed it. Olevsky was looking almost wild. His clothing and hair were disordered, there was mud on his boots and his trousers, and a large, ugly bruise was spreading across the side of his face from a cut on the cheekbone.

'You're hurt!' she exclaimed before anyone else could speak. 'Let me look at it.'

Olevsky seemed put out by the attention. 'No, your highness! I mean, it's nothing, I assure you. I was hit by something, that's all.'

'A brick, I should think,' Emily said.

He stepped back from her and lifted his hands to fend her off. 'I have urgent news for the master,' he said, 'but I know he's at the front, so I thought it best to come here.'

'Leave him alone, Emilia,' Anna commanded. 'Let him speak. What is it, Olevsky? Why are you here, and in this condition? Why could you not telephone?'

Her manner seemed to soothe him. He knew what he was dealing with here.

'The telephones are gone, madame, and I believed my life to be in danger. I could not send a message. I didn't know who to trust.'

'Trust with what? What are you talking about?'

'There's been an uprising in the Kirishi district. Schwartzenturm was attacked by an army of peasants, looted, and set on fire. One or two of the servants remained loyal, but there was little we could do in the face of the mob. In the end we had to flee for our lives and hide in the woods.'

It was Adishka who asked, 'What's the damage?' Anna seemed to be struck dumb with disbelief.

'I crept back at dawn for a look, and by then the main house was in ruins. The roof falling in partly smothered the fire, but since it is largely built of wood, I doubt whether any of it will survive. The two towers were still standing. Some armed peasants seemed to be occupying the White Tower. The Black Tower of course was untouched.'

'I'm not interested in the Black Tower,' Anna snapped. 'Do you mean to tell me that nothing was saved?'

He shook his head, looking down at his feet. Emily saw he was trembling, though whether with exhaustion or fear or shame she couldn't know.

'How did you get her?' Adishka asked. 'You've very muddy.'

'If they'd found me, they would have killed me. I had to walk a long way until I was able to get on a train.'

'But who were these people?' Anna demanded, still perplexed. 'Not our own peasants?'

Now he looked up. 'They heard about the revolution. They believed it meant that all the land would be theirs, and that they simply had to take it and divide it up between them. They went to Grubetskaya first, but the servants there were ready to defend the house, so the peasants began to arm themselves. More and more joined them, until they were like an army. I don't know where they got the guns. I suppose they looted them from somewhere. But they couldn't take Grubetskaya. Well, it's built like a fortress. With the gorge at the back, and the curtain-walls at the front, they couldn't get in without artillery. So they came to Schwartzenturm.'

He sighed unconsciously with weariness. 'They only want the land, of course, but you know what peasants are like when they get excited. They smashed everything they could see, and then raided the cellar, and the drink maddened them. I think they set fire to the house for the sheer fun of it.'

Anna seemed ready to question him further, but Emily could see that his legs were buckling with exhaustion, and she flung an appealing look at Adishka. 'Surely tomorrow? This man is ready to drop.'

'Yes, of course,' Adishka said, coming to attention. 'It seems you did everything possible, Olevsky. We'll talk more about this tomorrow. For now you had better go and get cleaned up and have something to eat. Tell Rajek to find you a bed for the night.'

'Yes, your excellency.'

'And keep your mouth shut about this. I don't want the servants discussing it amongst themselves.'

When he had gone, Anna rounded on her brother-in-law furiously. 'You should have sent him away. You don't really believe he won't talk, do you?'

'I couldn't send him away in that condition. He's been a good employee.'

'If you couldn't, I could! What right have you to interfere in domestic matters?'

Adishka drew himself up. 'It's what Alyosha would have done,' he said, facing Anna down; and since she knew that it was true, she could only subside into silent grievance.

It soon became clear that what had happened at Schwartzenturm was happening all over Russia. As the thaw came, releasing the peasantry from their winter immobility, they swarmed joyously outwards from their villages, taking the land they believed had been promised to them two hundred years before. The first victims were those peasants who had left the communes under Stolypin's scheme: they had always been particularly resented by those left behind, and they made easier targets. But the great houses came next, and there was an orgy of looting and burning. It was dubbed the Black Repartition.

It marked the beginning of Anna's alienation from the new order. She demanded that Adishka *do* something about it, and he went naturally to Kerensky, as both an old colleague and the present Minister of Justice, to ask him to force the peasants to return the land. Kerensky's reply was not propitious.

'He says that the Government intends to issue an appeal to the peasants to desist from illegal seizures.'

Anna's eyes bulged alarmingly, '*What?* Is that all?'

Adishka looked uncomfortable. 'Not quite. The Minister for Agriculture – Shingarov – is to draft a programme of agrarian reform for submission to the Constituent Assembly, when it convenes, and delegates from the Peasants' Union are to be consulted. Once they approve the plans, they ought to be able to quiet the peasants down.'

'But what about *my* land? What about Schwartzenturm? How does he propose to get it back for me?'

Adishka shrugged, trying to slide his eyes away, but Anna in a rage was hard to evade. 'They meant to repartition the land anyway, you know.'

'You mean he won't do *anything*? Why didn't you make him? You are the most pusillanimous, weak-kneed, craven – ! Do you think your brother would stand idly by and let this happen? I'll go to him myself! I'm not going to be robbed by my own peasants!'

She began a campaign that started with irate telephone calls and letters, and culminated in personal visits to the offices and even the homes of the ministers – Kerensky, Shingarov, even Prince Lvov, who as chairman was also Minister of the Interior. He was the most sympathetic, but his answers infuriated her most.

'We are the Government of the people, we are here to reflect the will of the people . . . We are not here to impose decisions on them – that was the old way, the oppressive way . . . Our business is to remove the restraints and allow the goodness and wisdom of the people free reign. That is true democracy.'

'Never mind all that nonsense, how am I to get my land back?'

'Adjustments always take time. They may be painful at first, but ultimately our great Russian people will embrace order and beauty of their own free will . . . '

Kerensky was more direct. 'I'm sorry, madame. I can only tell you what I told Vladimir Nikolayevitch: we dare not enrage the peasants. They believe the land is theirs, and until we can come to a voluntary

445

agreement with them, we must leave things as they are. Besides,' he added, cutting short her protests, 'what would you have me do? March a company of Guards down there and shoot them all?'

'Why not!'

'Because we don't do things that way any more,' Kerensky said coolly.

'It seems to me you don't do anything any more!' Anna said, furious.

'Even if I wanted to order soldiers to fire on civilians – which I don't – I couldn't do it. I don't have that authority. And they wouldn't obey the order anyway.'

Anna at last saw the futility of arguing, and drove her rage down hard inside her. 'We were better off under Bloody Nicholas,' she said, her parting thrust. 'This isn't government, it's anarchy.'

The aftermath of the event puzzled Emily. Anna, she knew, had never been particularly fond of Schwartzenturm, but its loss, and more particularly the failure of the Government to get it back, or even to want to get it back, seemed to take something out of her. When the rage subsided, she lapsed into an apathy which disturbed Emily. Basil's death had grieved Anna, but it had been an active grief, a positive, living feeling. Now she seemed to lose interest in everything. News, friends' gossip, letters from Alexei – nothing seemed really to impinge on her. Only occasionally when Adishka talked about Government meetings or proposals would she be roused to a spark of anger.

'To think I should live to see the day when Russia is ruled by men like that!' she would say.

Natasha was more personally upset by the loss of Schwartzenturm than Emily would have expected.

'It's our ancestral home,' she said. 'I suppose it's the English blood in me – Russians move house without thinking about it. But I loved it. I was always happy there, and it held so much of our history. It makes me wonder what else is going to change. What is the Provisional Government *doing*?'

'Very little, it seems,' Emily said. 'How are things in Tsarskoye Selo?'

'Not good. The palace is sealed off, and no-one is allowed to visit. I worry so about those poor girls. They're at the time of life when they should be enjoying themselves, dancing and falling in love. I always thought they were brought up in too much isolation, but now what chance have they?'

'Perhaps the Government will relent and allow them to go to England.'

Natasha's expression hardened. 'There's no chance of that now. England has refused to have them. The invitation has been withdrawn, except towards the Dowager Empress.'

'But why?' Emily was astonished. 'King George is the Tsar's cousin. Why would he refuse to have him?'

'It's my belief he's afraid for his own skin,' Natasha said. 'There are socialists everywhere – London's a hotbed of them, you know that. He's afraid the Tsar's presence will spark off a protest and topple him from his own throne. I always *said*', she finished, 'that he wouldn't do. His father would have stood by his own family and damned the revolutionaries!'

Emily nodded sympathetically. The fire went out of her grandmother, and she said more quietly, 'There's something I want to talk to you about, little one.'

'Yes, Grandmama.'

'Things are getting bad here. Most of the Guards are decent enough, just plain soldiers obeying orders. But there are others – they're increasingly insolent, and they look at one in such a way! I'm told they are Bolshevik agitators. There's a colonel of the Palace Guard, Belinsky, a very decent man, one of the old school – he's been here to supper once or twice. He tells me that these agitators are infiltrating everywhere, with the intention of destroying the Government. I don't understand why. You'd think they had what they wanted, wouldn't you?'

Emily made no comment.

'At all events, he says this is a very sensitive area, and that everyone who had to do with the imperial family is in danger. Poor old Count Fredericks's palace was burned down, you know, and there could hardly be a more harmless old man – irritating though he was on occasion. Well, at the moment Belinsky says he can keep order, but if these agitators can persuade enough of his men to disboey him, it will be open season on anyone with a title, or wealth, or a connection with the palace. He recommends that I leave here immediately.'

'Leave, Grandmama? You mean, come back to Petrograd?'

'No. He doesn't think that would be safe either. Besides, my house on Kronversky had been "requisitioned", and I don't suppose I'll ever get it back now, even if it were in a habitable condition, after the socialists have been living in it for two months! No, I'm going to leave Petrograd altogether, and go to live with Yenya in Archangel. That should be safe enough; and she needs me, poor child, with Valya and Tolya both gone. It hasn't been a good war for her.'

'When will you go?'

'Immediately. I shall put my furniture in store and shut the house. I may even instruct my solicitor to sell it. There's nothing here for me now. When things have settled down again, I may come back to Petrograd, but Tsarskoye Selo can hardly be the same again, can it?'

'No, I don't think so.'

'Why don't you come with me?' Nastasha said, as though it were a sudden thought; but Emily felt she had been building up to it.

'I can't,' she said at once, before she had even thought why not. 'Anna's children need me; and I promised Alexei I'd take care of her, too.'

She said it without thinking, but something in her voice or expression seemed to catch Natasha's attention. She looked at Emily keenly for a moment, and then said, 'Yes, I see. You're quite right, of course. You must do your duty.'

Guchkov, one of the architects of the revolution, resigned, and Kerensky took over as Minister of War. His design was to reopen the war offensive, which had languished through all the internal upheavals. Every agency from the Provisional Government down to local committees of workers' soviets wanted the war to be fought to a conclusion: the Germans were still violently hated and feared. Only the Bolsheviks wanted peace.

General Alekseyev, who had been commander-in-chief since the dismissal of Grand Duke Nikolasha, was now himself dismissed as having supervised the many failures of the war. Brusilov was appointed in his place, and Kerensky departed on an extended tour of the fronts to heighten morale and ensure loyalty to the new regime.

Alexei's letters were optimistic.

'It's much better the men should have something to do. We're still pretty sound here, though I hear things are bad on the Northern Front, with mass desertions and officers being murdered by their men. We have to have soldiers' councils now, with elections, and there's a certain amount of discussion of orders at times. It annoys

448

some of the junior officers but I make them keep their tempers. These discussions ramble and spread out like water on a plate, until the men begin to falter and look for someone to tell them what they mean. Then I, or one of my faithfuls, step in and tell them. Better that than confrontation, as I tell the officers. The poor fellows only want to feel that they are respected, and I don't know why they shouldn't be. God knows they have little else in their lives.'

Emily usually opened these letters now, and read them aloud to Anna. Occasionally he wrote a separate letter to her, which he sent addressed to old Marfa at the apartment and which she or Mischa brought to Emily. In those letters his official, cheerful mask dropped.

'What is happening in Petrograd? We hear such things – riots on the streets, an attempted coup by the Bolsheviks. What in God's name is the Government doing? This Lenin is a dangerous madman. Why wasn't he arrested? Why did they ever let him into the country? I've read some of his outpourings over the years. If it ever came to a conflict between him and the Government, they would be hampered because they care what happens to Russia and he does not. Warn Adishka if you can. I dare not write to him. Official mail is read by *many eyes.*'

And another time: 'The replacement troops from the city garrisons are highly politicised, and talk to my men about a workers' revolution – encourage them to disobey orders – tell them to refuse to fight the "imperialist" war. And I'm not allowed to shoot the bastards! Well, we go into battle soon, and Uriah the Hittite comes to mind. I won't let my men be corrupted.'

Emily did as she was asked, and tried to warn Adishka about the Bolsheviks. But Adishka was blithe, revelling in his new advancement to chief secretary of the Ministry of Transport. To conceive of his Government's being in danger was to believe he might lose his newly enhanced status. He shut his eyes to what he did not like to see.

'You needn't worry about the Bolsheviks. They're just a handful, and no-one likes them. The troops are loyal to us – Kerensky says so, and he should know. The Bolsheviks can't do anything about that.'

The new offensive was launched on June the 16th, 1917. Well prepared and well provided with shells and ammunition, the Russian Army opened a major attack on the Galician front and lesser operations on the Central and Northern Fronts. For a few days it went well, the Russians advanced, prisoners were taken. But then the engine of war began to run out of steam. The Germans counterattacked, and the Russian soldiers wondered what was keeping them there, miles from home, to be shot at. Some units refused to obey the order to attack; some attacked, but half-heartedly; others threw down their guns and ran.

The campaign was a failure. Throughout July the German armies reversed the trend and drove the Russians back further and further. News of the defeats caused discontent in Petrograd, which was again suffering from food and fuel shortages, owing to the breakdown of the transport system.

'It's not our fault!' Adishka wailed, almost tearing his hair. 'There are mass desertions at the fronts. The troops just commandeer a train and make the driver take them home – and then, of course, it's simply abandoned. I'm losing rolling-stock all over the place, and we were short of trains from the beginning!'

There was another serious street riot, initiated by Bolshevik agitators. Kerensky came back from the front and took over the premiership from the ineffectual Prince Lvov, which made him virtual dictator. To enhance his standing he moved into the Winter Palace, where the Provisional Government now operated, and slept in Alexander III's bed. He declared martial law and restored order with the help of the loyal troops and the Petrograd Soviet, who hated the Bolsheviks as much as anyone, and he reinstated the death penalty in the army only. Things quietened down again.

But the system was breaking down. Food, clothing and shoes were in short supply. Most manufactured goods had disappeared from the shops, and a brisk black-market trade was flourishing in almost every commodity, which made for rampant inflation. Factories and offices were disrupted by strikes and lack of fuel. Streetcars operated only intermittently. Telephone services from outside the capital were frequently disrupted by peasants and soldiers cutting down the telegraph poles for firewood. Postal services, other than the military couriers, operated only within Petrograd.

And yet, Emily reflected, such was the human propensity to adapt to circumstances that the chaos was glimpsed only through the gaps in normality. People went to work, children went to school, shops opened with their depleted stocks. In the evenings the restaurants were thronged with well-dressed people, the Conservatoire gave its usual series of concerts by summer-school pupils, and the ballet companies were in rehearsal for the new season to begin in September.

It seemed to Emily like one of those nightmares where everything seems normal, except that there is something utterly sinister and horrible about it that one cannot put one's finger on. She missed her work at the Anatoli, which had never reopened, and although she loved the children and devoted much of her time to teaching and playing with them, she found Anna an increasingly onerous burden. Many wealthy Petrograd families had left for the Crimea and the Caucasus, their usual summer destinations, which meant that there were few of Anna's friends in town to visit her or be visited. Emily's only real friend, Galina Strakova, had left in May with a Red Cross team to nurse at the front, and God knew when she would be back.

Never had Emily felt so alone. She longed ceaselessly for Alexei, and cursed the futile war which kept him from her. It seemed to her that it could not possibly be won; why then go on sacrificing lives to it? War-weariness afflicted everyone as summer turned to autumn and the prospect had to be faced of another winter of shortages.

Alexei wrote to her. 'Oh my dear one, my soul, I wish I were with you! I am so tired of all this. I keep my men together with difficulty. Food and fuel are so short I have to send out foraging parties every day. A great many of them never come back, of course.

'We hear rumours all the time of a coming Bolshevik coup. If that should happen, if it should succeed, I don't know what kind of regime would follow. I worry for you. I will come as soon as I can. Meanwhile, hold on. I know you are strong. If there should be danger, go to Mischa – he will help you. I wish I could trust Adishka to take care of you, but his head is too easily turned. My fault! But that's no good now. I can't conceive that anyone would willingly hurt you, but mobs can be indiscriminate. If Peter becomes too dangerous, get away – to England if necessary. I will follow you.'

As time passed, and the Bolsheviks grew bolder and the Soviet more openly contemptuous of the Provisonal Government, Anna's servants slipped from carelessness to insolence, and then to absence. Their numbers had already been depleted by the war: able-bodied men were all either at the front or in hiding; female servants either didn't want domestic work, or took on the position only as an opportunity to steal.

It was becoming in any case 'unacceptable' to have servants at all. Anna fulminated bitterly about it. 'What's wrong with these people? We've given them work and wages and a home all these years – easier work and a better home than if they'd gone to a factory or lived in a commune. Now suddenly that makes us worse than criminals!'

Rajek, who was a Cossack, stayed on. Like all Cossacks, he resented as a mortal insult any suggestion that he was not his own man. He had chosen to work for the Kirovs of his own free, independent will, and he would not be talked out of it by any political agitator, especially one he regarded as inferior to himself – which category embraced almost all of mankind. And any agitator who was so foolish as to suggest that Rajek was a slave or a lackey or one of the exploited masses was likely to go home with radically rearranged features.

He did his work now with the help of two teenage boys who were still too young to be called up, two housemaids who had remained faithful to the family, and the second cook, who had a speech impediment and felt safer in the kitchen where the pots and pans would never mock him. Nikita, the old *dvornik*, and the boilerman also stayed – indeed, it was doubtful whether the boilerman, living his entire life between his subterranean cave and the woodshed across the backyard, actually knew the revolution had taken place. He belonged to the house rather than to the family. Two of the nursery maids left, under pressure from their parents, but one remained, and Anna's personal maid stayed too.

As a result the house was gradually assuming an air of neglect, in spite of Rajek's proud efforts, and Anna, Emily and the children took to using the same few rooms all the time to ease the workload. Adishka was no longer with them. He had gone to share the apartment of a friend, Godnev – a fellow deputy – which was more convenient for the Winter Palace, where the sessions often went on through the night. Anna had been resentful of that, too, accusing him of leaving them without male protection.

Adishka was glumly realistic. 'I don't see what sort of protection I could have offered you anyway. If it came to it, you'd be better off relying on Rajek – he's twice my size.'

'That's true,' Anna said contemptuously. 'You didn't manage to stop them taking my motor cars, did you?'

'They were requisitioned officially – ' Adishka began.

'By the Soviet. I didn't realise *they* were the Government of this country.'

452

'They aren't, but we work together. They've a right to requisition things if they need them. We are at war, you know.'

'They only have the right of force', Anna said with unusual penetration, 'because *you* won't keep them in order.'

'The cars were no use to you anyway,' Adishka said. 'You haven't got a driver.'

'Emilia can drive,' Anna said, revealing how far her standards had already fallen. To have thought of allowing Princess Narishkina to be her chauffeur would once have been beyond her.

In August, the cracks in the face of normality opened wider. It happened one hot evening, after the children were in bed. Emily was worried about Modeste: the heat seemed to trouble him, and he had been restless and depressed all day. The women sat in the drawing-room, Emily reading, Anna sewing. The room seemed airless: Petrograd was beginning not to smell too good, and it was necessary to keep the windows closed.

There was a thunderous knocking on the main door downstairs, startling them both. It had a perilous, splintery sound to it, as though the door were being struck with something very heavy, with a view to smashing it in. Emily met Anna's eyes, and saw the same apprehension in them.

Fourstatskaya Street, which had once been so quiet, leafy and secluded, was uncomfortably placed as a highway between the various rivals for power. The Tauride was only two blocks away; the Petrograd Soviet had set themselves up in the Smolny Institute, more or less at one end of the road; and at the other end of the street was the Troitsky Bridge, which was the way to the Bolshevik headquarters in Kschessinska's house. Fourstatskaya had become a revolutionary highway; and the presence in the nearby garrisons of the soldiery, with their new freedoms and shaky loyalties, was not at all reassuring.

There was the sound downstairs of altercation, loud male voices, amongst which Emily could easily distinguish Rajek's.

'I'd better go down,' Emily said. 'If Rajek kills anyone, there'll be the devil to pay.'

Anna's eyes seemed to brighten at the mention of killing. 'I'll come with you.'

Emily misgave. 'No, really, I'll deal with it.'

'It's my house,' Anna said unassailably, and led the way.

When they reached the top of the stairs, they could see a group of men, a mixture of soldiers and civilians, perhaps a dozen in all.

All were armed, though their rifles were slung over their shoulders in a variety of unprofessional but at least unready ways. Rajek was facing them furiously, evidently barring their way by sheer force of indignation.

Anna spoke first, walking down the stairs. 'What's going on here? Rajek, who are these people?'

Rajek turned to her, but another man spoke first, a man in an officer's greatcoat and hat, but without any regimental flashes or marks of rank.

'Are you the Countess Kirova?' he asked. His voice was educated, but his manner was without either hostility or ingratiation. He sounded indifferent, like a schoolteacher asking for the date of a famous battle.

Anna did not look at him. 'Rajek, who are these people?' she asked again.

'Red Guard, *barina*. They forced their way in. If you say the word, I will have them thrown out into the gutter where they belong.'

Emily saw the officer frown. Anna reached her butler and touched his arm very slightly, warningly. Emily knew then how dangerous the situation was. Never in her life before had Anna voluntarily touched a servant.

'Who are you?' she asked the officer.

'I am Malinov, Commander of the Tauride section of the People's Defence Corps of the Petrograd Red Guard.'

'The titles you people invent for yourselves!' Anna interrupted him. 'What do you want?'

'I have come to give you warning, madame, that this house has been requisitioned for immediate occupation. You will have to vacate the premises by ten o'clock tomorrow morning. Here is the order, as you see – '

'Requisitioned? What are you talking about? This is my house. You have no authority that I know of.'

'The order,' Malinov continued calmly, 'as you see, was issued and duly signed by the Commissar of the Housing Requisition Committee of the Petrograd Soviet of Workers' and Soldiers' Deputies. It's all in order.'

'You're mad,' Anna said. 'Get out of my house. And take this filthy rabble with you. Red Guard indeed! I wouldn't let you guard my chicken-house. Look at you – slovenly, dirty, undisciplined, don't even know how to stand up straight! The men were soldiers in my family, generation after generation. My father would have been

454

ashamed to stand in the same street as you! My brother died fighting the Germans on the Polish front. I don't suppose any of you has ever seen a German!'

It was splendid, Emily thought, with a mixture of admiration and dismay. The officer remained utterly unmoved, but some of the others were fidgeting and muttering, and there was one in particular she feared. He was short and squat, with the typical peasant's broad face, wide nostrils and loose mouth, and his small eyes seemed the epitome of greedy hatred. She saw them rove around the hall, taking in the trappings of wealth, before resting again on Anna. He wants to kill her, Emily thought, and only this Malinov stops him.

'Anna, don't,' she said very softly.

Malinov turned on her. 'Wise advice, madame. You are . . . ' He pretended to consult the document. 'Princess Narishkina, I take it?'

'You know perfectly well who I am,' Emily said. 'What do you want this house for?'

'It is not for me to question that. I am the requisitioning officer. What the Soviet needs the house for is its business.'

'And where are we supposed to go? Is that the Soviet's business?' Emily asked. 'Don't you know we have three small children, to say nothing – ' She stopped short of mentioning the servants.

'Alas, madame, the Soviet cannot concern itself with individual cases. Its task is to work for the common good of all Russian people. I'm sure you won't have any difficulty in finding accommodation, however. There are some excellent hotels in Petrograd. A little expensive, perhaps, but – ' He shrugged significantly, and the other men laughed.

Anna roused herself. She had seemed almost in a daze through the last few exchanges. 'Perhaps you do not realise that my brother-in-law is a member of the Provisional Government – '

'Yes, quite,' Malinov said. 'If you'll take my advice, madame, you'll keep quiet on that score in future. The so-called Provisional Government are bourgeois lackeys, the lapdogs of capital who bleed the workers white and are in the process of betraying the glorious revolution for their own selfish ends. Their time of reckoning is coming!'

A growl of assent from behind him. Emily stared at him in amazement. 'Do you believe that?' she asked. He looked at her, startled for a moment. 'You sound like an educated man: do you really believe that nonsense?'

For a moment a real person looked out of his eyes, and then the mask came down again. 'I am not here to educate you, however much you may need it. You will leave this house by tomorrow morning. If you do not, we will have to evict you by force. I would not recommend that process to you.'

'We can't be ready by the morning. It's unreasonable. What about all the furniture?'

'The house is requisitioned *with* its furnishings. You may take your personal belongings, of course. A receipt will be issued for everything else.'

He wheeled around, barked an order, and marched out with his men slouching and shuffling behind him.

Anna stood in the centre of the hall as though she'd been turned to salt. Rajek stood nearby, quivering with the effort of holding himself still. Emily put out her hand to Anna, but at the last minute dared not touch her.

'It's come to this,' she said. 'I can't believe it. I was born Princess Narishkina, and it's come to this, that a – a common soldier should speak to me like that, and order me out of my own house.'

'You should have ordered me to kill him, *barina*,' Rajek said simply.

Anna didn't heed him. 'I should never have married below me,' she mourned softly. 'The Kirovs have bad blood. One of them was exiled for treason once. I should have married Sapetsky when he asked me.'

'Anna, come upstairs,' Emily said. 'Come, we'll talk about it.'

'Talk about it?' Anna turned on her. 'What is there to talk about? I won't be ordered out of my own house.'

'We'll have to go,' Emily said. 'You've seen those men – and heard them. They wouldn't have come here if they didn't know they could do what they threatened.'

'Adishka won't let it happen. He will make Kerensky act,' Anna said, but even as she spoke, Emily could see recollection in her eyes.

'As he did over Schwartzenturm?' Emily said. 'And the cars?'

Anna stared at her with growing helplessness. 'Ten o'clock tomorrow? How can we be ready in time? How will we take everything? What about the children?'

'The children will think it all a great adventure,' Emily said. She tried to smile. 'You know you've never liked this house. It was almost the first thing you told me, the day I first came here. And it hasn't been so comfortable here lately, has it?'

Anna did not smile. She looked through Emily at some other vision, perhaps at a world lost. 'I can't,' she said in defeat.

'Yes you can. I'll help you. We'll get everything done in time.'

'But where will we go? If they've moved us out of here, they'll move us on wherever we go. I can't bear it. I'm so tired of all this – this hatred.'

The thought came to Emily like sweet relief. It would be like going home. 'It's all right,' she said. 'I know a place where we'll be safe.'

Chapter Twenty-Six

The end, when it came, was sudden, and almost without resistance, as though the will of the population had been worn down by the struggles of the last year to the point where they wanted only for it to be over. One day in October, Lenin smuggled himself heavily disguised into the Smolny, gave his orders, and Bolshevik soldiers took possession of Petrograd.

They took the railway stations, the National Bank, the electrical station, the sewage works, the bridges. They took the telephone exchange, and seized every printing works in the city. All but four regiments had already been subverted, and the loyal four hesitated to act, remaining in their barracks, hoping for someone to tell them what to do.

By eleven o'clock bills were being plastered up all over Petrograd. 'TO THE CITIZENS OF RUSSIA!' they proclaimed. 'The Provisional Government has been deposed. Government authority has passed into the hands of the organ of the Petrograd Soviet of Workers' and Soldiers' Deputies.'

The citizens of Russia who read it seemed only mildly interested. The Government had been deposed? Well, it had done nothing for the last two months. Did one even know the names of the ministers? And what was this organ? Everyone knew it was the Bolsheviks who had seized power. Well, what did it matter? Things couldn't possibly be worse. Let the Bolshies have a try. And if they were acting on behalf of the Soviet, it must be all right, mustn't it?

People went to their offices and factories, the shops filled up, the cafés and restaurants served coffee and then luncheon. Now and then an armoured car raced past, or a platoon of soldiers marched quickly out of one street and down another. There was no sound of gunfire. It seemed a normal day.

Emily took a handbill home to the apartment. 'What does it mean? I don't understand. The Government is meeting today in the Winter Palace, as usual. And Adishka told me yesterday that Kerensky knew all about the Bolshevik plot, and that he would move to crush it as soon as it began.'

Emily remembered the conversation. 'Why not arrest them now, before it begins?' she had asked in frustration.

'We don't do that kind of thing,' Adishka had said loftily. 'We have laws now. We can't arrest people for being suspected of planning an illegal act. That's the old way, the oppressive way. In our new democracy, a man is not arrested until he has committed a crime.'

'I'm sure Lenin and his friends won't offer you the same courtesy,' Emily had retorted.

'Well, we aren't going to descend to their level, or we'd be no better than them, would we? Anyway, there's nothing to worry about. The troops are loyal to us. As soon as the Bolshies move, we'll have them.'

Anna read the handbill through. 'It says it's already been done. Do you think they could have arrested the Government? Try telephoning Godnev.'

At first she could not get a line. Then at last the telephone exchange answered, and a very rough male voice said only official calls were being put through.

'This is official government business,' Emily said sternly.

'That number is not a government number.'

'Then put me through to the Winter Palace, Department of – ' The line went dead.

They waited for news, trying the telephone at intervals. Mostly the telephone was dead, but when they got a line the call was always intercepted and cut off. In the afternoon, however, Godnev managed to ring them.

'Is Adishka there?'

'No. We hoped he was with you,' Emily said.

'He must be inside the Winter Palace, then. I told him this morning it was madness. The Bolsheviks took all the bridges last night, so we knew it would be today. But he would go. "Business as usual," he said when he left.'

'He went to the Winter Palace?'

'The Government's in session in the Malachite Room. God knows what they're doing in there. The whole place is surrounded by Soviet troops and Bolshevik sailors froom Kronstadt. Kerensky got out before they arrived and drove off in a motor car, I don't know where or why.'

'Is there fighting?' Emily asked anxiously.

'No, they're just sitting there. There's a troop of Cossacks in the yard, and I suppose they don't know what forces the Government has inside. But everything's quiet. It's all so strange.'

'Perhaps Adishka isn't in there,' Emily said. 'He may have left earlier, too.'

'Maybe. If he arrives there, will you let me know?'

'Yes, of course, and if he arrives with you – ' They were cut off again.

There was no more news. The day dragged on. At about nine o'clock there was a distant sound of heavy guns, just one salvo, followed by silence. Some time later there was a longer burst, and then again silence. The telephone was obstinately dead. Emily got up.

'I'm going out. I must find out what's happening.'

'You mustn't! It's dangerous. For God's sake, Emilia!' Anna protested.

'But Adishka – '

'What good could you do him if you went up there?'

In the early hours of the morning, Emily managed to get Godnev's number to ring. He was a long time answering, and when he did he was out of breath. 'Oh, it's you, Princess! I was out on the leads, watching. Any word from Adishka?'

'No. And you?'

'I think he must have been inside. He would surely have contacted me otherwise. You know the Winter Palace has been taken?'

'No, we didn't know. We heard heavy guns – '

'Oh, that was nothing. The *Aurora* came up the Neva and fired a few shots, didn't even score a hit. Then the Peter and Paul lobbed a few shells over and knocked a few bits of plaster off. Nothing at all, really.'

'So how was it taken?'

'It was a bit of a farce in the end,' Godnev said sadly. 'The shellfire unnerved the Cossacks in the yard, and they sloped off under cover of darkness. Eventually the Bolshies decided it was safe to go in. Some of the sailors climbed through the open windows on the Hermitage side. They opened the side-doors, and the Red Guard crept in looking frightened as rabbits, ready to run at the first bang. The word's going round that when they got to the Malachite Room they found it was only guarded by a few young cadets and a company of the Women's Death Battalion.'

'The Government was there?'

'Yes, they surrendered at that point to avoid bloodshed. But I

460

don't know what's happened to them, whether they've been taken away or what.'

After remaining sleepless for the rest of the night, Emily would not be talked out of it any more. She dressed in her plainest skirt and jacket, borrowed an old *shooba* from Marfa, and went out to make her way to the Winter Palace.

'You heard how quiet it was,' she reassured Anna. 'Nobody seems to have resisted at all. Why would they harm me?'

Petrograd seemed normal, or what passed for normal nowadays. People were going to work, the streetcars were overloaded, and there were few private motor cars. Such as there were, they were all flying red pennants this morning, and were carrying serious-looking men in dark overcoats or military men reading important documents. Emily didn't care for the idea of struggling onto a streetcar, and decided to walk.

As she neared the Winter Palace, she came up against the tail of a crowd. They were obviously sightseers, not demonstrators, so she began cautiously wriggling her way through them. They seemed not at all depressed or afraid; in fact, as she made her way forward, the mood became frankly hilarious.

'What's happening?' she asked at last, when she could get no further. 'I can't see. What's happening?'

The nearest man, a young bank clerk by the look of him, turned to her, grinning. 'Drunks,' he said. 'You never saw such a thing – reeling about sozzled, half of them passed out cold.'

'Drunks? Who's drunk?'

'The mob,' he said succinctly. 'Factory workers from across the river. Came down here last night to cheer their precious Bolshies on. Then some bright spark remembered the old Tsar's cellars must be full of wine.'

Another man joined in. 'That's right. They broke in and boozed themselves silly. I wish I'd been here earlier! It must have been some sight, factory workers and coal-heavers pouring back fifty-year-old port and old Nicholas's best champagne!'

Emily smiled too. They would undoubtedly have preferred *khanza*, she thought. What a waste! 'Didn't anyone try to stop them?'

The first man grinned. 'Yes, they sent in the Red Guard, but one sight of all that booze and they chucked their rifles and joined in.

461

So then they sent in the fire brigade to flood the cellars, and now *they're* dead drunk as well.'

Emily managed to work her way further forward, and got a view at last. It was certainly an odd one. Hundreds of men and not a few women were sitting and lying around the Winter Palace courtyard in various attitudes of stupor. Yet others were sitting in groups jealously guarding small heaps of bottles which they were methodically opening by the simple means of breaking off the necks and up-ending them over their mouths. There was some more organised military activity going on by the main entrance, and some perplexed-looking soldiers were trying to persuade a group of dead-drunk firemen to move their tender out of the way.

The onlooking crowd was being held at bay by a cordon of soldiers of the Pavlovsky. Emily wriggled her way through to the nearest one.

'Where is your officer?' she asked him. 'I want to speak to him.'

'Get back, will you,' he said automatically, lifting his rifle across his chest ready to push her.

She lifted her hand a little, trying to engage his attention. 'Who's in charge here?'

'What's it to you?' he demanded crossly. He had been on duty all night, and not a single bottle had come his way.

Emily kept her patience. 'I want to speak to your officer. Where is he?'

'Over there, in that car. But you can't see him.'

'Yes I can,' she said, ducked under his arm, and walked towards the car.

'Oy, you, stop!' the guard shouted. The two officers in the car looked up from their consultation, and jumped hastily out.

'What the devil are you doing? It's all right, Popov, we've got her! I don't think she's dangerous. Now, miss, you can't come in here. Just you go back where you came from,' the older of the two said kindly.

'Are you the officer in charge here?' Emily asked.

At the sound of her voice his eyes narrowed, and he took her by the elbow and led her further from the crowds and the sentries.

'What do you want, madame? You shouldn't be here. Don't you know you could have got yourself shot just then?'

She smiled. 'I don't think so. You don't want any corpses to mar this glorious day, do you?'

462

They exchanged an impatient glance. 'What do you want?' the younger one asked tersely.

'Just some information. The members of the Government who were in the Malachite Room last night – I want to know where they've been taken.'

'To the Peter and Paul Fortress,' the older one answered.

'On what charge?'

'Oh, just for their own safety,' he said. 'No charge as yet.'

'They are dangerous counter-revolutionaries, pledged to destroying the new Socialist order,' said the younger. 'They'll be charged with crimes against the people.' He narrowed his eyes. 'Don't I know you?'

'No,' Emily said calmly, though her heart was beating fast. 'I'm no-one. No-one at all.'

At the fortress she eventually saw a lieutenant of the guard, who eyed her in a most unpleasant way but confirmed that the former Provisional Government had been brought there. After much patient insisting on her part, he agreed that there was a list of their names in existence, and finally brought it out and said yes, there was a Vladimir Nikolayevitch Kirov amongst them.

Relief flooded her. 'Can I see him?'

'No.'

'Why not?'

'Orders. They can't have any visitors. Got to protect them against assassination. They almost got lynched on the way here.'

'I'm not an assassin,' Emily said. 'I'm his cousin.'

'Bad luck on you then. I wouldn't tell anyone if I were you.' And he laughed at his own humour.

'Is there a senior officer here?' she asked impatiently.

'Wouldn't make any difference if there was. The order's quite clear – no visitors. I could show it to you, if you like.' He didn't, however. 'Comes right from the top, that does – no argument.'

'What's going to happen to them?'

'*I* don't know. Why would they tell me?'

It was the beginning of a long and fruitless campaign. Every day she visited the fortress, to be told the same thing: yes, he was there; no, she couldn't see him. In between, she tried every new department of the new Government she could gain access to. The days went by in a confusion of long waits in crowded corridors; of the smell of sweat and boots and *makhorka*; of weary and irritable faces, always saying no.

'We haven't time for that sort of thing! Who let you in anyway?'

'There's no-one here to answer that sort of question. Try next door.'

'Don't come troubling me with nonsense at a time like this!'

And once a narrow-eyed suspicion. 'Who are you? Why are you so interested in counter-revolutionaries?'

Her task was made impossible by the fact that the entire office workforce of Petrograd had gone on strike. It had been a spontaneous protest by the better-educated sector of the employed. Lenin had taken power in the name of the Petrograd Soviet and had promised to form a coalition government of all the socialist parties; but despite the fact that the Bolsheviks were only a tiny minority of the Soviet, every single member of his new Government was a Bolshevik.

The strike spread rapidly from typists, clerks and telephonists to bank staff, shop assistants and even janitors. The revolutionaries had to type their own letters and stoke their own boilers, and it didn't improve their tempers. No-one had time to answer her questions; and the more she asked them, the angrier they got.

Then, one day in the middle of November, the answer at the fortress was different. A captain came out into the guardroom and stood before her, his eyes fixed on a space over her shoulder.

'He's not here,' he said.

Emily felt a chill of foreboding. 'Where has he been taken?'

The captain cleared his throat. 'There was an incident last night. Kirov and three other prisoners were shot while trying to escape.'

Emily stared at him, and still he refused to meet her eyes. 'Shot? Where were they wounded?' she asked in a hard voice. 'You must let me see them — I am a trained nurse.'

'They were not wounded. They were shot dead,' he said at last.

The new Government had already shown its colours. Censorship of the press was reintroduced and rigorously enforced. It was forbidden for any private citizen to possess firearms or even ammunition. Private ownership of property was to be abolished, and the Government could confiscate anything it needed without notice. The death penalty was reintroduced for a wide variety of crimes, including the blanket terms 'crimes against the State' and 'counter-revolutionary activities'. A new secret police force called the Cheka was instituted to replace the abolished Okhrana of tsarist days, and its agents operated undercover in every area of everyday life.

Life at the apartment became harder. When they moved house they had parted with most of the servants. Nikita and the boilerman had stayed on under the new occupiers; Rajek had accepted a handsome gift and returned to his own people; and the boys, one of the housemaïds and the cook had taken their wages and gone to look for other work. To the apartment they had taken only Anna's French maid, the other housemaid to help Marfa, and the nursery maid.

The French maid left immediately after the Bolshevik coup, saying she wanted to go home to France before things got worse. The housemaid they had to dismiss when it was discovered she was stealing their clothes and selling them. Now, after Adishka's death, the nursery maid simply disappeared, presumably going home to her family. Anna had never had to cope with dressing herself, and with the loss of her maid she stayed more and more in bed. Mischa's wife, Fima, came in each day to help Marfa, and Emily took charge of the children, and so they managed.

It was while Emily was still going daily to the fortress that they were first searched. A platoon of soldiers arrived, looking for weapons and ammunition – the penalty for possession being death. Emily was not concerned about that – they had never had so much as a pistol between them – but there was a thick roll of banknotes and both women's jewellery hidden in the piano, which they would certainly take if they found them. However, the soldiers seemed in a hurry, didn't search very thoroughly, and went away empty-handed.

'They'll be back, *barina*,' Marfa warned. 'And next time they'll look everywhere.'

'We'll have to find a better hiding-place,' Emily said. 'Somewhere they'll never think of looking.'

In the end, with Mischa's help, they hid the jewellery beneath the floorboards under Emily's bed, and the roll of banknotes in a recess Mischa cut for the purpose in the skirting-board in the kitchen. It was fortunate that they did, for a few days later another armed party came to search again.

This time they went through everything, and when they had failed to find anything of value, the officer said, 'There is too much furniture in this apartment. No-one in the land needs more than one chair and one bed each, and a table to eat off. We will take the excess away.'

They removed chairs, sofas, ornaments, tables, mirrors and rugs. They took the piano. Emily was distressed when she saw the soldiers deliberately drop it in the stairs so that it smashed, and along with Marfa she wished the revengeful ghost of old Madame Blavatsky onto them. 'May she never give them a quiet moment,' Marfa said fervently. The party didn't quite strip the apartment bare, but they left it looking very much more Spartan.

'That's how other people live, *bourgeoises*,' the officer said spitefully as he left. 'Get used to it!'

Now there was only a kitchen table to dine off, Anna took to taking her meals on a tray in her room. No-one questioned the decision. As Emily sat down in the kitchen with Marfa and the children, she reflected that Anna would never be able to adjust to the new regime. To eat in the kitchen, or to share her table with a peasant, were actions simply impossible for her.

After she was told of Adishka's death, Emily thought things could not be worse, but they very soon were. One day there was a hammering on the apartment door early in the morning. Marfa started automatically down the hall, but Emily, who was supervising the children's breakfast, was nervous.

'I'll open it,' she said. 'Stay with the children, Marfa.'

Outside there were soldiers. The familiar sinking of heart as their smell entered the hall ahead of them: feet and tobacco, dirty bodies and nervous sweat. Four of them – a corporal and three privates. The corporal pushed her back roughly and they crowded in. The physical contact was unusual: so far, though they had been brusque, they had remained polite. There was no officer with them this time. She was afraid. The house was behind her – no escape that way – with the children to be protected and Anna to bring her trouble. Four of them and her in a narrow hall. Her hands were damp, her mouth dry.

'What do you want?' Her voice sounded astonishingly calm. At this moment of great peril she had a strange, involuntary flash of memory of the kitchen at The Lodge, with Penny standing at the range making cheese sauce. Could such things exist in the same world as this brutish scene? She shook the vision away.

'You are Anna Kirova?' the corporal said harshly.

'No, I'm not. What – '

He consulted a dirty piece of paper. 'Then you are Emilia Narish-kina. Where is the other one?'

'She's asleep. She is unwell.'

'Wake her. You, old woman, make her get up and dressed. You are both to come with us immediately.'

'Why? On whose orders?'

'Commissar of this Section. Standing orders of Citizen Lenin and the Central Committee. Every citizen has an obligation to work for the good of all. Those who do not work are enemies of the people and will be shot. We have come to take you to your work detail.'

Emily listened in dull relief. They were not going to rape her or take her to prison, then – only a forced work party. She had heard of them recently, but had not thought – stupidly! – that they would apply to her. But of course, it was all part of the policy of humiliating the middle and upper classes.

'Very well, I will come. But Madame Kirova cannot come. She is ill, as I have already told you. We have been recently bereaved, and she – '

'*Citizen* Kirova had better come, or she will be sorry.'

'I am a trained nurse, and I assure you she cannot work.'

'I will decide that.'

Anna appeared, looking dishevelled and swollen-eyed, half drug-ged with sleep, her clothes scrambled on; but the sight of the soldiers kindled something in her. 'What is the meaning of this? How dare you burst into my house like this?'

'She's well enough to work,' said the corporal with a kind of spare humour. 'Get your coat on, citizen. You're both on street-sweeping detail this morning.'

Anna looked ready to explode. Emily took advantage of her temporary speechlessness to say quickly, 'Let her stay. Someone has to look after the children.'

'The old woman can take care of them. We've wasted enough time. Come.'

Emily gave Anna an expressive look, and she allowed Marfa to help her into her coat, scarf and gloves, and followed Emily out of the house. It was a raw, unpleasant day, the skies heavy with snow. Downstairs they passed the concierge's room, and he looked out at them with an expression of satisfaction and malice. He was a new concierge since the coup, not the one Emily had known when she

467

first went there. She wondered if he had given their names to some local jack-in-office as suitable candidates.

There was a group waiting patiently in the snow, four elderly people, well dressed but looking bewildered and frightened, guarded by two soldiers with rifles. A bulging sack lay at their feet. Anna and Emily were directed to fall in behind, and they were marched off through the snowy streets by their armed guard.

They stopped at last in a broader boulevard, where streetcars passed and people hurried by on their way to work. Here shovels were produced from the sack and handed out, and they were told to clear the snow from the pavements. An audience, Emily thought dully. Ex-aristocrats are to be humiliated in public for the purposes of education. She took a shovel and began to work. There were worse things, she thought; and at least one kept warm.

There were only four shovels. Anna and an old man with a thin, beaked nose and blue-veined hands had none. The corporal pointed at them. 'You – and you – why aren't you working? You have no spade? Then use your hands! Get down on your knees and dig!'

The old man stared in amazement as if he could not understand what was being said to him, and the corporal shoved him roughly so that he slipped and fell to his knees. 'That's right, and now you are down there, dig! Dig, old man!'

Anna was trembling with rage, and Emily, in fear for her, intervened. 'Is it necessary to be so rough? Everyone must work, but they need not be humiliated.'

'Mind your own business,' he snapped. He turned on Anna. 'You heard me. On your knees, woman! Dig!'

He reached out and seized her arm to push her down. Anna reacted without thought, wrenching her arm back and striking the corporal across the face in the same movement.

What followed happened all in the same second: the corporal reached for his pistol in automatic reaction and Emily cried out; Anna shouted something at him and put her hands out to stop him; there was the crack of a rifle-shot, and she fell, her words cut off in a grunt.

Emily flung her spade away and rushed forward. She felt rather than saw the rifles come round on her. The corporal barked, 'Stand still!' Emily was on her knees in the snow beside Anna: pale face, greying fair hair tumbled on the grimy snow. Where was she hit? A hand seized her arm to pull her away. She jerked her head round. 'I'm a nurse, let me alone.'

468

The hand released her. Emily began unbuttoning the *shooba*. Was she dead? One hand at the buttons, the other feeling under the jaw for the pulse. Then Anna coughed, and a froth of blood sprayed from her mouth. Behind her someone said dispassionately, 'She's had it.' There were legs coming in on all sides, civilian boots – interested passers-by, enough of them not to fear the guns. A little murmur of comment and question bubbled in the background.

Emily's fingers encountered warm stickiness. Yes, here it was, the black, leaking hole in the chest. Anna's eyes opened. She frowned.

'Anna? It's all right, I'm here.'

Anna seemed to be trying to speak, but instead of words came a cough. The violence of it pulled her head up off the ground, and a gout of blood shot out, splattering Emily's face and chest. The head thumped back onto the snow, a hand twitched, and she was gone.

She had written to Alexei when Adishka died, a carefully phrased letter, remembering his warning that his letters were read by many eyes. There had been no reply or acknowledgement, and she thought that probably the letter had been intercepted, since it dealt with the death of a 'counter-revolutionary'. Now she wrote again to tell him that Anna was dead. Surely they would allow that letter through? She said nothing about the circumstances of the shooting, simply that Anna had died in an accident. There was no reason to hold that back. And when he received it, surely, *surely* he would come home.

She waited, comforting the children, giving them their lessons. Fima took them out to the park each day for fresh air. Emily remained in the apartment, dreading the knock on the door and another search, another seizure, another work party. But they left her alone, and nothing disturbed the silence but the small sounds of Marfa going about her tasks.

'They've stopped the letter reaching him,' Emily said to her. 'Or they've intercepted his reply.'

'Will you write again, *barina*? He will surely come home when he knows.'

She wrote another letter, and this time addressed it to him care of Stavka, thinking that they might not interfere with letters going directly to headquarters. This second letter provoked a response, but not the one she was expecting: a few days after she had sent it, an

469

armed guard arrived to take her before the Military Revolutionary Committee for questioning.

There was a long wait in a small room, completely bare except for two wooden chairs. She wondered what the room had originally been used for. It had two small windows, high up and glazed with frosted glass, and there were a number of holes in the walls, and ragged patches of plaster where some kind of fitments had been ripped out. A washroom perhaps, she decided in the end. The building had once been a school. Yes, there were four symmetrical holes and a lighter patch on the wall where a looking-glass might once have been fixed; and over there, that was where there had been coathooks. She was keeping her mind well away from what might lie before her. A few weeks ago she would not have believed that they would harm her; but that had been before she had seen Anna shot down in front of her.

They came for her at last, and she was ushered by two armed guards along a corridor and finally into another room, stiflingly warm and full of cigarette smoke. There was a stove in the corner, carpet on the floor, albeit rather ragged, a large and handsome desk, somewhat scarred, a hard chair facing it, and on the other side, three men in civilian suits, smoking rapidly and adding their ash to an already overflowing ashtray.

The men on either side looked up as she came in; the man in the centre continued to write. He was neatly dressed, with carefully manicured hands, except that his right fore- and middle fingers were stained yellow with nicotine. His hair was brushed back from a high forehead, and he wore gold-rimmed pince-nez on a filagree chain. Emily stood waiting for him, aware that his ignoring her was meant to unnerve her, like the long wait in the empty room. In Papa's stories, the captured hero was always made to wait before being taken before the bad men.

He looked up at last. 'Sit down, citizen,' he said. Emily sat. Aunt Maud would have been proud of her. Her back was straight, and no part of it touched the chair. She met his eyes levelly. 'My name is Nasvikev,' he said. 'This Committee has been directed to consider the implications of certain letters you have been writing.'

He moved to one side the paper on which he had been writing. Underneath Emily saw what looked like one of her letters to Alexei.

'Implications?' she said. 'I don't understand.'

'Do you deny you wrote to Colonel Alexei Nikolayevitch Kirov last week?'

'Of course not. I suppose that is the letter there,' Emily said. 'I wrote to tell him that his wife is dead.'

'You addressed it to him at Mogilev.'

'He did not reply to my first letter. I thought perhaps it had gone astray. I hoped Stavka would forward it to him.'

'Ah! So you believed that at Stavka they would know where he was.'

Emily was puzzled. 'Yes, of course. Why not? Surely headquarters must know where everyone is?'

'Do you pretend you do not know that Stavka is in the hands of anti-Bolshevik generals, pledged to destroying the revolution?'

Emily's heart leapt, but she remained steady. 'Of course I didn't know that. How could I?'

'You want us to believe you knew nothing of their counter-revolutionary activities? That this letter does not contain coded instructions concerning subversive actions being planned against the people's Government?'

Emily's incredulity could not be doubted. 'You have the letter there, you can read for yourself. I wrote simply to tell him that his wife is dead. What is wrong with that?'

'You also wrote to him concerning a member of the former so-called Provisional Government – '

'His brother.'

'And your cousin. You are unfortunate in your choice of relatives, are you not?'

'One does not choose one's relatives,' she pointed out.

'One may choose to ignore them, if they prove unworthy of notice.'

She made no answer.

'You also chose your husband, Citizen Narishkina,' Nasvikev said silkily.

'My husband was killed at the front fighting the Germans. He was awarded a medal. You can have no reason to doubt his loyalty.'

'His loyalty to the tsarist state! His dedication to the imperialist war!'

Emily felt a sudden, suicidal desire to laugh. 'But that was all there was at the time! You can't really expect him to have been loyal to a Bolshevik government before it existed! Do try not to talk nonsense.'

Her interlocutor did not alter his expression, though his two silent companions puffed more rapidly at their cigarettes and flicked

471

glances at each other. Emily wondered what they meant. She hoped approval for her logic; she feared otherwise.

Nasvikev did not pursue the line. Instead he said evenly, 'You do not say in your letter how Anna Kirova died.'

Emily grew angry, and anger overcame her personal apprehension. 'She was shot, sir, in cold blood on the street by a brute of a soldier – an unarmed woman in poor health. That is not the sort of thing to tell a man by letter when he is far from home and serving his country. I hoped and expected that he would be given compassionate leave to come home and comfort his grieving children. Time enough then to tell him how his wife died.'

For the first time Nasvikev's composure wavered. His eyes slid away. 'The manner of her death was unfortunate,' he acknowledged. 'However, accidents can happen at the best of times – '

'And this is not the best of times,' Emily said. 'Will you pass the information to him, sir? If you still have some reservation about my letter, you could send an official notification, could you not? Will you at least do that?'

Nasvikev paused only a moment to consult with his colleagues by an exchange of glances. Then he said, 'It will not be necessary. Colonel Kirov, though perhaps an excellent soldier in some ways, had some unfortunate opinions about the people's revolution. He tried to impose them on his troops, but they were true revolutionaries, and refused to be subverted.'

Emily felt the hair rising on the back of her neck. 'What are you talking about?'

'He was forcing his troops to march to join the rebel generals. Before they reached Stavka they heard the news that it had been liberated by our General Krylenko and the rebel generals arrested. Colonel Kirov's men turned on him and expressed their loyalty to the revolution in the most practical way: they convened a soldiers' court martial, and shot him.'

They let her go, and she walked out into the street. She had not been harmed in any way, but she felt she had been dealt a deathblow. Something critical had been broken inside her, though as yet there was no pain or dissolution, only the knowledge that the blow could not be survived. She had nursed men in hospital who lay patient and wordless under desperate wounds, feeling nothing, waiting to die.

People going in and out of the building brushed past her, some glancing at her curiously, others ignoring her in their urgent concerns. One pushed her quite roughly out of his way, and the shove started her walking, one foot in front of the other, through the trodden snow, wandering blindly.

He was dead, she thought. She tried to make it make sense, but her mind wouldn't grasp it. She had had experience enough by now of the deaths of those close to her; she ought to have known how it felt. She had been afraid for him often, and often since he had first gone away to the front; yet she discovered now that she had never really thought he would be killed, not *really*. She didn't know how to think about it; she didn't know what to feel.

How could she not have known? That was one question she could ask herself. She would have expected some place inside her, some extra sense that was connected to him, to have felt it. When the bullets struck him, when his spirit and body parted, she ought to have felt the wrench. But she hadn't felt him go. Now she felt cheated, as though he had gone without saying goodbye to her. If she had known the last time she saw him that it *was* the last time, she could have said and done many things that were now denied her.

She found herself by the river, and turning away from the bridge, wandered along the quayside. The noble façades along the Neva looked just the same, mocking the new regime with their vastness, their magnificence. How long before they began to show signs that things had changed? She turned her back on them and stared out over the river. Dead. Alexei dead. She clenched her fists in a strange access of anger. He had gone, leaving her alone, leaving her to carry on uselessly, trapped in a world that no longer held him, held no reason for anything. *Why did you leave me? You promised to come back! How could you do this to me?*

His face came before her imagination, and she grasped at it eagerly, wanting him so badly, wanting his presence, his arms around her, now, this minute! But she would never see him again. Now at last the full realisation struck her sickeningly. *Never see him again.* It filled her blackly in its absoluteness, so that she could only stand still and endure it, like pain. But pain at least goes away, in the end, one way or the other. This would never go away. She would have to live with it every moment of every day until the end of her life.

*

The short December day closed in. Lights began to come on, and at once dusk turned to dark, and the darkness was cold. She came to herself feeling chilled and desperately tired in a sidestreet she didn't at first recognise. Looking around her, she turned in the direction of what was obviously a main street: brighter lights, traffic passing, and the sad clanging of the streetcar bell. She came out onto it, found it was the Litieny, and turned in the direction of home. From the aching of her legs, she knew she must have walked a long way.

She would have to tell them, of course. Marfa would mourn him with that simple dignity of hers, born of her special love for him – the nurseling she had fed at her breast, whom she could never call her own. In a sense she had mourned him all her life, her stolen child. In death he would be no less hers.

And the children: Tatya had been her mother's child, and was grieving for her, still having fits of weeping and tantrums of bewilderment. She hardly remembered her father, away at the war; probably she would hardly miss him. Petya, just three, had never known him.

But Modeste – how would she tell Modeste? She was afraid he might have another of his fits. She imagined his fragile face blue-white, his eyes too large for it as he fought for breath, his thin body held in her arms, and the shape of his skull under her fingers, which was so disturbingly like his father's. Her child now, though not her son. A wave of fierce tenderness swept through her. Hers to protect, nourish, care for, bring to adulthood – a frail fledgeling cast out from the nest. More even than the little ones, she must care for him, the child of Alexei's that should have been hers.

She found herself hurrying, one tired foot in front of the other, desperate to get home. They were all that was left of him, and he had left them to her when he went away. She could not die to escape her loss; she must not even sleep. She had a duty: she must survive and be strong for the children's sake.

Chapter Twenty-Seven

The bitter winter set in, and Petrograd starved. The clerical strike went on, paralysing commerce; industry was paralysed by lack of fuel and raw materials, and the inability of the new managers, put into factories for political rather than practical reasons, to run them. Black marketeers set up on street corners to sell sugar, soap, cotton thread, shoes, knitting-wool, butter, meat. Black marketeering was decreed punishable by death, but when the Red Guard tried to pounce on them, they would melt away into the crowds; and the next day they would be back at the same site. To eliminate them, it would have been necessary to execute the entire population.

That population was getting smaller. Peasants and workers were leaving the city, streaming out into the countryside where they hoped to take part in the unofficial repartitioning and at least grab enough land to feed themselves and their children. People were dying, too: not only being shot by the Bolshevik soldiers and the Red Guard – though that was becoming such an everyday occurrence that it hardly caused a stir any more – but murdered by looters, and wiped out by disease. Cold, hunger, influenza and pneumonia took their toll; when the water supplies failed, toilets did not work, and cholera and typhoid began to appear.

The educated pinned their hopes on the result of the election. The Provisional Government had pledged itself at the time of the February Revolution to free national elections and a Constituent Assembly to determine the exact form of the democratic republic which was to replace the old regime. When the Bolsheviks had taken power, they had done so under a mantle of respectability, claiming that they were acting on behalf of the Petrograd Soviet; and that same respectability demanded that they went ahead with the elections and the Assembly, too.

The elections duly, and fairly freely, took place. Every man and woman over twenty could vote, and country-wide about forty-one million did, of whom only a quarter voted for the Bolsheviks. It was a shattering defeat for Lenin. His opponents now looked forward to the Constituent Assembly's expressing their will and finally establishing a proper democratic order. Of the 704 seats on the Assembly, the Socialist Revolutionaries had a clear majority of 410. The Bolsheviks had only 175. There was no possibility that they could outvote the other delegates.

The Assembly met on the 5th of January in the Tauride Palace. Lenin and the Bolshevik delegates made an appearance, but soon walked out. Some time later the commander of the Tauride Guard entered, walked up to the podium and interrupted the chairman to order the Assembly to disperse because 'the Guard was tired'. Bolshevik troops were crowding in at the back of the hall, and an ugly clash was threatening. The delegates had no choice but to adjourn until the next day.

In the morning, however, they found the Tauride Palace closed and heavily guarded. The delegates were told that by order of Comrade Lenin and the Central Committee, the Assembly had been dissolved permanently.

Pravda that day carried large headlines:

THE HIRELINGS OF CAPITALISTS AND LANDLORDS, THE SLAVES OF THE AMERICAN DOLLAR DEMAND IN THE CONSTITUENT ASSEMBLY ALL POWER FOR THEMSELVES AND THEIR MASTERS, THE ENEMIES OF THE PEOPLE. THEY PAY LIP-SERVICE TO POPULAR DEMANDS, BUT IN REALITY FASTEN A NOOSE ABOUT THE NECK OF THE REVOLUTION. BUT THE WORKERS, PEASANTS AND SOLDIERS WILL NOT FALL FOR THE BAIT OF LIES OF THE MOST EVIL ENEMIES OF SOCIALISM . . .

There was a great deal more of the same, and reading it, the educated classes felt the last of their hope drain quietly away. Two days later, the Bolsheviks convened their own alternative assembly, the Third Congress of Soviets, in which they reserved for themselves 94 per cent of the seats, leaving just enough seats for opposition socialists to provide them with a captive target for abuse and ridicule.

There would be no democratic solution; the Bolsheviks would never be talked into abandoning power. Lenin could only be displaced by violence and blood, and even if his opponents had had the stomach for it, there was no organised agency of force which was not already in his control. The clerical workers' strike ended that same day, for there was no longer any point to it. They drifted back to work, exhausted by the ruthlessness and brutality of those who wanted power at any cost.

As to the peasants and workers, they made blank their faces and endured, as so often before; patient as the earth itself. They had a saying: *He who grabs the stick is corporal.* Someone must rule, and it would never be them, so what did it matter?

They lived most of the time in the kitchen now, and life centred on the kitchen table where they ate, worked and played. Emily gave the children lessons, devised games, read with them and to them, set them puzzles. Marfa sewed and mended, watched the children broodingly, prepared meals and did what little work was left in this depleted household.

She and Emily took turns to join the queues for bread and essentials. Prices rose daily, and the roll of banknotes grew thinner. Mischa foraged for them, too, when he foraged for his own family, and sometimes brought them firewood. Old wooden buildings around the city were disappearing, for as they fell empty they were dismantled piece by piece for fuel. When they could get nothing else, Emily and Marfa broke up the furniture and began lifting the floorboards in the unused rooms. Tatya and Petya thought it great fun to break up a chair and feed a leg into the stove; Modeste only stared, wide-eyed and unsmiling, as though watching a hostile army marching ever nearer.

Occasionally there was meat: usually bacon, sometimes rather bitter-tasting rabbit. Emily once had the thought cross her mind that it might not be rabbit at all but rat, but she hastily dismissed it. When there was meat, everyone felt better and stronger, and she worried almost constantly about Modeste, who seemed to be growing somehow transparent. The rest of the time they lived on a peasant diet of potatoes, onions, pickled cucumbers, cabbage, and occasionally lentils or a few bony fish. What milk they could get – blueish and suspiciously speckled – went to the children. Tea was a luxury, bread strictly rationed.

With less food and less fuel to burn, they wore more and more layers of clothes to keep warm. Washing was difficult with the water-supply constantly interrupted, and drinking- and cooking-water having to be boiled for safety. Emily supposed that they must all smell by now, but as long as they all smelled the same, none of them would notice. Her greatest fear was of lice, which were rife amongst the soldiery and the poor, and were known to carry cholera.

When the Bolsheviks dissolved the Constituent Assembly, Emily began to wonder what the future held for her in Russia, and how the children would ever have the chance of a normal life. She had her own and Anna's jewellery – what was not deposited in the banks – still hidden, but under the present regime there was little chance of selling it, and none at all of using the proceeds for the children's benefit. Would they go on like this for ever, living like peasants, keeping hidden away from the eyes of authority, afraid of drawing attention to themselves?

One day she voiced these thoughts to Mischa, who had brought her some more firewood, and had stayed to keep her company until Marfa came back from the bread queue.

'I'm glad you brought the subject up, because I've been wondering how to broach it with you,' he said.

'Come, you can speak to me about anything, surely,' Emily said. 'We wouldn't be able to survive without you, and Alexei – ' She faltered, and then made herself go on. 'Alexei told me that I should always come to you if I were in trouble.'

Mischa looked pleased. 'He was right. That's why I've been wondering whether you realise quite that you might be in danger.'

Emily almost laughed. 'We've all been that, ever since October.'

'Not you. Don't you understand that you are English, and there is a great deal of goodwill for the English in our country? Not only that, but they are our allies, and even the Bolsheviks wouldn't dare harm an Englishwoman, for fear of British reprisals.'

'But what about when I was taken for forced labour? I'm sure they would have shot me then, if I had resisted like Anna.'

'They would never have taken you if you'd told them you were English,' Mischa said impatiently. 'Why do you think they've been leaving you alone since then? I told the concierge downstairs – it was the quickest way to alert the authorities. You haven't even been searched since then, have you?'

'No,' said Emily thoughtfully. She went back over the interview with the Military Revolutionary Committee, and remembered the chairman's brief discomfort. Had he been afraid she was going to make a complaint about her own treatment? 'But surely they must regard me as Russian, because of my marriage to Prince Narishkin?'

'If he were still alive, they might,' Mischa said succinctly.

Poor Basil, Emily thought, if the best thing he could ever do for me was to get himself killed. 'Well then,' she said, 'if I am safe – '

'Ah, but that's the point I'm trying to make. You're safe from the Bolsheviks as long as the war lasts. But once they make peace with

478

Germany – and that could be at any time – being English won't help you. It might even be a danger to you. If the Allies become the enemy – '

'Yes,' said Emily. 'I see.'

There was a silence as they both pursued thoughts. The Bolsheviks had begun peace talks with Germany at the beginning of December, but they had not yet been able to agree terms. The Germans had stated categorically that the Russian provinces they already occupied – Lithuania, Poland, the Baltics – must remain under German rule, and any others, like the Ukraine, who wished to do so must be free to leave Russia and join Germany. Peace on those terms would leave Lenin ruling a country very little larger than the mediaeval duchy of Moscow – a severe blow to Russian pride and the prestige of the Bolsheviks.

Yet it could only be a matter of time. Russia was plainly unable to continue fighting a war and the Germans were on the doorstep, deeply anxious to have the matter settled so that they could concentrate on the Western Front. If Germany grew tired of Russian prevarication and threatened to resume hostilities, the Bolsheviks would have no choice but to sign.

'You think I ought to go?' Emily said. 'Leave the country?'

'Yes. And the sooner the better. Once the treaty's signed, the news will be everywhere within days. It will be much harder for you to get away.'

'What about the children? I can't leave them.'

'Take them with you.' Mischa shrugged, and repeated her own frequent thought: 'What kind of a life will there be for them in this Russia, the children of aristocrats? For any children, come to that. If I could leave and take my family, I would; but there's nowhere for us to go. But you – you can give them something.'

'But where would I go?' She knew the answer he would give even as she said it.

'To England, of course,' he said simply.

At the words, a flood of images rushed through her mind: of small green fields grazed by placid brown cows; of rolling downland dotted with sheep; of deep country lanes in May, frothed with the green-white lace of hawthorn and kex; of orchards heavy with scented English apples, green flecked with russet among pale leaves; of grey English churches, and the Sunday sound of change-ringing.

And such a homesickness swept over her that just for a moment she thought she would die of it. What am I doing here, she wondered desperately, in this country of huge emptiness, vast plains and dark, jewelled caves of churches, of violent passions and brutal, brilliant beauty? She had come here, tugged by her wandering Russian blood, in search of wider horizons, but now her English blood was calling her home.

'England,' she said. 'Home.'

'Yes, *barina*,' said Mischa, and in his dark, bright eyes there was understanding of all she was feeling. Whatever else she had learned about Russia, she knew at least there was nothing about love of country that they did not know. 'I think you should go home.'

Marfa came back, and approved the decision, though there was sadness in her eyes. She was old, and life could only take away from her. If they went, she would probably never see them again – Emilia and the images of her nurseling, her stolen child.

They talked long into the night about how it should be done.

'Should I go to Archangel? My grandmother is there, and my aunt. They would help me, and I could get a boat from there, if not straight to England at least to Sweden.'

Marfa thought it a good idea, but Mischa was against it.

'Archangel has a very strong local Bolshevik party. They love nothing better than searches and seizures, and they're ruthless about it.'

Emily frowned. 'Mischa, how can you know that?'

'I read. And I hear things. One of the men I work with has family in Archangel. He went to visit them at Christmas, and he told me. He says the Bolshies get nervous, being so close to Finland, and that makes them mean. Besides,' he added as the clinching argument, 'it's still iced in. There'll be no ships there for another month or six weeks, and by then it may be too late.'

'What should I do then?'

'Go south. If you can get to the Black Sea, you can get a ship there. And from what I hear, they're less friendly to the Bolshies down there.'

'*If* I can get to the Black Sea,' Emily said.

'You must become completely English again,' Marfa said. 'Then no-one will trouble you.'

'I still have my British passport somewhere,' Emily mused.

'Yes, you must travel on a British passport,' said Mischa, nodding approval. 'That's good.'

'But it's out of date.'

Mischa shrugged. 'I don't see that it matters. All you need is to prove that you are English. And the children must be your children. They will have to learn to call you Mother.'

Mischa went with the remaining roll of banknotes to find out about trains and to purchase tickets. Emily and Marfa sat at the kitchen table laboriously sewing jewels into Emily's and the children's clothing.

'Thank God it's winter,' Emily said. 'We wouldn't be able to hide much in thin summer clothing, but these padded waistcoats and thick coats are a boon.'

'You won't be able to take it all, *barina*,' Marfa said, wrapping kapok around a diamond brooch.

'No, I know. I'll have to pick the most valuable, I suppose – which means leaving my pearls, and they're the things I loved best.'

'What will you do with the rest?' Marfa asked.

'You shall keep them for me,' Emily said. 'Well, for the children, really. One day perhaps things will be different. We may be able to come back – or you may be able to come to England. In the meantime – '

'They will be safe with me,' Marfa said.

'I know.' She put down her needle and reached out to touch Marfa's skinny, freckled hand. 'If there should be anything you need, or Mischa, or Fima and the children, you have my authority to sell whatever is necessary.'

'That wouldn't be right,' Marfa said, frowning as she tried to imagine herself doing it. The picture wasn't convincing.

'Yes, you must,' Emily insisted. 'If Count Alexei were alive, he would say the same thing. Do you think he would ever have let any of you suffer for want of money? And if none of us can be here and it's money you need, you must take the jewels and sell something. Promise me, Marfa.'

Marfa looked a moment longer, and then bent her head over her work again to hide her eyes. 'Yes, I promise,' she said.

Tatya was wildly excited. 'Is it an adventure?'

'A sort of adventure. But it's also very serious. You must be very good and do exactly as I say, and never argue. And when we are on the journey, you must not speak unless I say so.'

'It doesn't sound like an adventure,' she pouted.

'Oh, it will be – the greatest one you will ever have, I hope. We are going on a long, long journey to another country, the country where I was born. But to get there, we have to go through great danger.'

'Are we really going to England, Milya?' Modeste asked quietly.

'Yes,' she said. She met his eyes and saw that there was very little she needed to tell him. He understood it all in a very few words – his father's son. 'It will be dangerous, but I think we can get through.'

'I'll make Tatya understand,' he said. 'Don't worry.' She reached out and brushed his hair from his eyes, unable to bear not to touch him just then: her good, serious little boy, already taking on the man's burden.

'And, Modeste, you will all have to pretend that I am your mother. That means you must call me Mama instead of Milya. I think you all ought to begin now, so as to get into practice.'

'Yes, Mama,' Modeste said with a faint smile.

'Tatya, do you understand?'

'Yes, Milya, I suppose so. Like a play.'

'Yes, like a play. But say "Yes, Mama".'

'Yes, Mama,' Tatya said, and giggled.

'I'll explain it,' Modeste said; then he and Emily looked at Petya. If only he were a little younger or a little older, Emily thought. 'We'll have to try and make sure he doesn't say anything at all,' Modeste said.

'I think it's going to be too difficult going from the station here,' Mischa said. 'The Red Guards check everyone and everything, and in Peter the Bolshies are mostly able to read and write. They'd be bound to question you.'

'What can we do, then?' Emily asked.

'The only way I can think of is for you to hire a sledge and horses and go across country to a station further down the line where they won't be so fussy. If I can find something that will do, I can drive you myself and buy the tickets for you and make sure you get on the train.'

'But can you find a vehicle? I didn't think there were any horses left in Petrograd.'

'I have an idea where I may get one, but it's going to be expensive. More than the roubles you have left.'

'I have lots of jewels to sell. Can that be done?' Emily asked. She had no idea how one could go about selling jewels in the Petrograd of 1918.

Mischa nodded. 'The man I'm thinking of would probably prefer jewels to roubles, especially the way things are going. In a few weeks banknotes will be useful only for lighting fires, but jewels will always keep their value.'

'Take whatever you need, then,' Emily said. 'Mischa – I'm very grateful to you. You won't get yourself into trouble, will you?'

He grinned suddenly. 'No, trust me! I don't mean to make myself a martyr. It's rather fun, though, beating the Bolshies at their own game.'

He came back in the evening. 'It's done. A sledge and troika. We'll have to get the tram out to the suburbs and then walk a bit, but it can't be helped. I'll help you with the luggage.'

'Is it safe? Will he really be there?'

'Yes. I know this man – we can trust him. Besides, he'd do almost anything to get his hands on the Polotski sapphires – that's what I promised him. He's a connoisseur, you see, and he covets them as a work of art. He says he's actually seen you wear them at the Maryinsky.'

It would be the most expensive horse and cart in the history of the world, Emily thought. 'When do we leave?'

'We'll have to catch the first tram in the morning – '

'Tomorrow morning?' Emily said, startled. She hadn't expected it to be so soon. All at once from being a plan it had become a reality, and an unpleasant feeling rolled in the pit of her stomach.

'Yes. Can you be ready in time? We dare not delay in case he changes his mind or tells someone.'

'I thought you said you could trust him.'

'As much as I can trust anyone these days,' Mischa said grimly.

Packing was easy enough. The Bolsheviks had made a rule that no-one was allowed to have more than two of anything – trousers, shirts, skirts – so a leather Gladstone bag was enough to hold a change of clothes each for Emily and the three children. More perma-

483

nent possessions could not be taken for fear of making it look like an escape, but she told the children they could take one toy each. Petya, of course, had to take Bobo, his bear with the well-sucked ears. Modeste chose a book; Tatya, growing more excited by the minute, flitted between a doll, a puzzle and a solitaire set, and wanted to know why she couldn't take all three.

It was Modeste who took her to one side and explained the realities to her; and when she finally realised that they were going away for ever and that she would never see the apartment or Marfa or any of her things again, she burst into tears and the choice became unimportant. Marfa took her on her lap and rocked her until she fell asleep; Modeste chose the doll on her behalf.

Emily and Marfa worked through the night with the children sleeping around them where they had finally fallen, finishing the sewing, and packing a second bag with food for the journey. Mischa went back home for a while to explain to Fima where he was going, and came back with a contribution of food from her, which was likely to prove invaluable. Certainly while they were in the north there would be little to be bought on the way, and it would be a long journey.

In the dead darkness of four o'clock on a winter morning, they said their last goodbyes to Marfa, and with the children stumbling with weariness from their sleepless night they went out into the silent, snowbound street. It was a moment of strange unreality to Emily, as though she had become part of a photograph: everything was black and white, the black sky above, the white snow crunching underfoot, the grey buildings with their darkened windows. There was no-one about yet. She held Tatya's hand, and carried the Gladstone bag on the other side. Mischa carried Petya, clutching Bobo, and carried the food bag. It was a moment of awesome momentousness, but there seemed to be nothing to say or even to think about it.

At the tram-stop they joined the queue of early workers, sunk in the silence of before-dawn. After a while the tram came rattling and clanging out of the darkness, its yellow lights spilling onto the snow like melted butter, its stuffy chilliness a relief after the bitterness of the morning air. Once they had their seats, the children fell asleep, lolling against them. Emily worried about what their fellow travellers might be thinking about them all, but it was soon clear that they weren't thinking anything. One or two unfolded newspapers, but mostly they sat staring at nothing in incurious morning numbness.

Emily, exhausted, sat dozing and waking as the streetcar trundled her out of Petrograd.

Twenty-six hours later they stood on a country platform and watched the train steam slowly in, and the sense of unreality had not lessened. Mischa, standing beside her, looked grey with fatigue. He had driven them here, purchased their tickets, acquired cups of hot tea for them all, taken care of Petya like a mother while they waited for the train; now, when he had seen them off, he had to get back to Petrograd in time to be at work the following day.

Time was running out, and how could she ever thank him? 'Mischa,' she said urgently, turning to him as the engine dragoned past her breathing smoke and spitting fire. He looked down briefly, met her eyes, and merely shook his head slightly. There was nothing to say that would cover the occasion. He looked away again.

'Christ alive, it's full,' he muttered. The waggons seemed packed tight already. Emily felt despair. How would they ever get on? And yet they must, they must! An empty carriage – oh no, it was the first-class, which meant that only Bolshevik officials and soldiers could use it. The rest of the waggons were third-class – peasant waggons, fitted with bare plank shelves in tiers on which the passengers lay when they were not standing.

Emily looked about her, as she knew she would look a thousand times, to gather with her eye her children and her luggage, and to check for danger. The train shuddered to a halt, the people on the platform surged forward. No-one was getting off.

Mischa put Petya into her arms. 'Get on any way you can. Just shove. I'll push the children up behind you.'

Impossible, she thought, looking at the press of bodies. Despair sank and determination rose, giving her strength: these others were fighting for a place on the train, but she was fighting for their lives. She wedged herself in the doorway, thrashing like a fish against solid obstructions. A hand – Mischa's? – shoved her in the small of the back and then someone in front of her slid sideways, and the obstruction yielded.

'Come on, mother, in you come,' said someone cheerfully – the first kind word from a stranger she had heard in months, and it cheered her like hot coffee. 'Make way for the little 'uns, there!'

Mischa's voice. 'They're on, they're behind you.'

She wanted to turn to call out to him, to say goodbye, to see his face for the last time, but she could not move. She and Petya and the bag were lodged in an angle between two bodies, and she couldn't stir at all.

'Modeste!' she cried out.

A small hand tugging her sleeve. 'We're here. It's all right, Mama.'

God bless the child, at such a moment even remembering to call her Mama!

'Don't worry, mother, they're safe on board,' said the cheery one. There was a sound of doors slamming, and the guard's whistle; and then the train jerked so hard that if she had not been wedged she would have fallen. Jerked again, and then chug, chug, chug, gathering speed. Emily felt her arm going dead under the weight of Petya, and despite the winter day outside, the press of bodies inside the waggon made the heat almost unbearable. Four days of this, she thought, before they reached their destination.

The train trundled slowly across snowbound Russia, stopping from time to time to take on fuel and water. At the stations, tea-sellers would come up under the windows with their trolleys. In the old days there would have been hot *pirozhkis*, soup, bread and cakes to buy as well; now there was little more than hot water.

Inside the stifling carriage the passengers had rearranged themselves somewhat. Room had been found on two shelves for Petya and Tatya, and Emily was able to lean up against the wall beside them, with Modeste leaning against her. The bags were at her feet, and sometimes Modeste was able to sit on them as a change from sleeping standing up. Next door was an almost empty carriage containing only the railway officials. They insisted that the door must be kept shut, even though a little air from that direction would have been a boon.

Days and nights, light and dark; stifling, cramped, uncomfortable, bad-smelling conditions. The children so very, very good. Eking out their food, buying tea and sometimes bread at the stations, getting out at the long stops to use the facilities – oh primitive! And thank God it was winter! At the larger stations Bolshevik guards got in to search, to question, to harry. Emily's luggage was rifled through by dirty, acquisitive paws, and many a speculative eye was cast over her person and clothing, but she was not touched.

Others were not so lucky. At one search three soldiers discovered three shirts in a man's luggage. In vain he protested that two were

486

presents for his father and brother whom he was going to visit. One spare was what was allowed, they said, and to show him he must not try to cheat the new order, they would take all three as a punishment.

'Leave me one! My wife made them. Please leave me one!' he cried over and over, but they tore them out of his hands. In desperation as they were moving off he offered them money in exchange for one of the shirts.

The soldiers stopped and looked at each other.

'How much?' asked one of them.

'A hundred roubles,' the passenger said wildly.

'You haven't got so much!' they scoffed.

'I have, I have!' the man protested, fumbling for his purse, and opening it to show a roll of banknotes. With trembling hands he pulled out a hundred, but there was many times more than that amount in the purse.

The boldest of the three soldiers snatched the purse and the hundred roubles, and shouted, 'Don't you know a true revolutionary is not to be bought? You could get into serious trouble, my friend, trying to bribe us! You could get yourself shot.' And the three of them made off with all the money, and the shirts. Emily heard them laughing in the next waggon.

It grew hotter as they moved south, and the children, cramped on the shelves, sweated in silent misery. The men in the carriage smoked and spat on the floor. There was a little more room, now that a few people had got out, and from time to time Emily was able to sit down and rest her back against the wall of the waggon and doze a little. Modeste, she knew, was suffering, but he never complained; only sometimes when she looked at him she saw his eyes fixed and staring with distress.

'What it is, my love?' she asked him once or twice; but he said it was nothing. She touched his forehead and it was burning hot, and she wondered whether he were sickening with something, or if it were only the heat in the carriage, or his spiritual unease.

'Are you afraid?' she asked him. He looked at her slowly, and then nodded.

'Bad things,' he whispered. 'I dreamed about bad things.'

It was to comfort him, and to ease the tedium for the little ones that she began to tell them stories, beginning with the famous ones

487

like 'The Three Bears' and 'Cinderella' that exist in every language. After a while, she noticed that it had grown quiet in her immediate vicinity. She looked around, and saw that she had the attention of the whole compartment: even the grown men, some of them rough-looking and dirty, were listening.

'Go on, *barina*,' someone said. 'Don't stop. Tell us another one.'

'Do you know "The Tinder Box"?' the cheerful man asked. Emily smiled. It had been one of Roxane's favourites. She told it, going through the rigmarole of threes and the magic dogs with eyes as big as teacups, mill-wheels and towers respectively, for her rapt audience. Then, on request, she told some Russian stories, 'The Soldier of Fortune' and 'Lieutenant Bubnov and the Devil'. Tatya had fallen asleep again, and Petya was sucking Bobo's ear with his eyes half open, but Modeste was listening as though his life depended on it. He was leaning against her, and she could feel him move and quiver with the words as though he were acting it all out.

She had just got to the part where the Devil's daughter proposes to Bubnov when the train jerked violently, the brakes screamed, and they shuddered to a halt. Someone peered out and said tersely, 'Red Guards, looks like. On the track.' No-one had spoken before on their journey other than to their own companions and in an undertone. Emily realised that her story-telling had welded them together as a group, and she wondered suddenly and nervously whether that was a good idea.

The Red Guard entered the compartment, three men heavily armed and looking aggressive. Emily saw with a mixture of pity and fear that they were only about nineteen or twenty. They began the usual routine of searching luggage and pockets; but this time, when they came to the man who had lost the shirts, he said loudly, 'You'll find nothing here. Your lot have searched us ten times already on this line. They've had anything worth having.'

And the cheerful man said, 'Yes, can't you just leave us alone? It's bad enough crammed in here together like cattle.'

The Red Guard said nothing, but they looked annoyed – or was it uneasy? Modeste pushed his hand into Emily's. Despite the heat, it was icy cold.

'Let's see your passports,' they said. One of them came up to Emily, stood before her, eyed her clothing. 'What have you got in your pockets?' he demanded.

'Nothing,' she said, forcing herself to look him levelly and unconcernedly in the eye.

'If you say nothing and then we find something, it will be much worse for you,' he said.

'I have nothing,' Emily said.

'And in the bags?'

'Nothing.'

He stared at her so long she thought he might search her, but eventually he said, 'Passport.' She brought it out, and he looked at it for a long time, turning pages and scrutinising it closely. She felt the worm of fear in her stomach, but stood still and straight. I am a British subject, she thought. They cannot hurt me.

'Is this yours?' he asked her, and then, 'What's your name?'

For the fraction of a second, the question puzzled her: the name was on the passport in both English and Cyrillic characters. Was he trying to catch her out? And then she saw that he was holding it upside down. His close scrutiny was simply a pose, to intimidate her or to boost his own morale; in fact he couldn't read.

'I am Emilia Edvardovna Paget,' she said firmly. 'I am a British subject.'

He seemed impressed and began to hand the passport back; then a thought struck him, and he asked, 'Are these children yours? Are they on this passport?'

It was a point on which she had hoped to avoid close questioning; but at that moment the boy's attention was distracted by an altercation on the other side of the compartment. It had begun with the shirt man, whose sense of grievance had evidently overcome his common sense.

'It's not right, treating us like this! What gives you the right to shove us around?'

'That's right,' said the cheerful man. 'We're not animals, you know. This man had his clothes and money stolen.'

'Nothing to do with us,' said one Red Guard, but the other said, 'How much money?'

'It was over five hundred roubles,' the shirt man said indignantly. 'I offered them a hundred to give me one of my shirts back, and they took the lot. Well, I'm allowed one, aren't I?'

'One? It's a disgrace,' someone else said. 'Why can't a man have as many shirts as he wants? How is that going to destroy the revolution?'

Emily's Guard thrust her passport back into her hand and went to join his companions. They could feel that they were growing unpopular.

'What are you saying, that you tried to buy your own shirt back?'

'A hundred roubles,' the man grumbled. 'Well, my wife made it for me. I said here's a hundred roubles if you'll just leave me one, and he took the lot, *and* all my money.'

'It's not right,' said someone else. The atmosphere was growing tense, and Emily could see one of the boys fingering his rifle in a nervous way. Ought she to intervene? Or would that only make things worse?

But the third Guard had decided to act. 'You tried to bribe a Red Guard, to stop him doing his duty?' he said menacingly.

There was an electric tension. The temperature in the compartment seemed to drop ten degrees in a second. The shirt man paled, seeing at last where his protests had led him. 'Well, no, no, not bribe exactly – ' he began to mumble. He looked around, but the other passengers were suddenly not there, looking anywhere but him, never having seen him before in their lives. 'I didn't do anything wrong.'

'Bribery's a very serious crime,' said the Guard, and took hold of the shirt man's arm. Immediately he began to scream, very thin, faint screams of fear. Behind her, Emily heard Tatya whimpering; Modeste was pressed so hard against her his bones hurt her.

'No, no, I didn't!' the man shrieked. The three soldiers hustled him out of the compartment and down off the train, the last one picking up his bag as he left. A few moments later they stood the shirt man up against a tree opposite the compartment window and shot him.

After that, a sullenness settled over the compartment. No-one spoke or looked at anyone else. Emily drew herself into her corner with the children, feeling miserable and guilty. If she had not told her stories, drawing them all together, the shirt man would never have had the courage to complain. He would have kept his mouth shut and still be alive. She was afraid that others in the compartment might come to the same conclusion, and though they had all been in the palm of her hand before, she knew better than to rely on that. She feared some unpleasantness, and thought it best to draw no attention to herself for the rest of the journey.

When they arrived at last in Novorissisk, they were all exhausted beyond fear from the long journey and the heat. There was a cold rain falling when they emerged from the station, and as they turned

490

the corner, they felt the full force of an icy wind. Beyond the harbour the Black Sea was squally and dangerous-looking. The children shivered, and Emily hurried them along the street in the direction pointed out to her by a station porter to the haven of the Nicholas Hotel.

The lobby was crowded, and when she managed to fight her way up to the desk, she was told that there were no rooms available, now or for the foreseeable future.

'You see for yourself, madame,' the clerk said waving an arm. He was not unfriendly, but what could he do?

'Is there another hotel you could recommend?' she asked, trying to remember how to smile seductively.

He shrugged. 'They are all full just like this, I know, madame. There is no bed to spare in the whole town.'

'But I have three small children,' she said. 'I hope not to be here for long,' she added temptingly. 'Is there nothing you can do for me?'

'Nothing, nothing, I am so sorry. But if you wish, you can remain here in the lobby for a while. I would not throw out a dog into such weather as this, madame, I assure you.'

He smiled whitely under his short, black moustache, and she smiled back. 'You are very kind. Perhaps we could have some tea, as well. It has been a long journey.'

'Of course. And anything else I can do for you, madame, please ask. My name is Kamud, and I am at your service.'

She was never sure afterwards whether Kamud helped her purely out of the kindness of his heart, or whether he hoped for something from her by way of returned favours; but she knew she could not have managed without him. He kept an eye on the children for her when she went out of the hotel; it was he who, after she had retired to the ladies' room to retrieve one of her jewels, told her exactly where to go to dispose of it, and how much not to accept less than. Thus provided with some ready cash, she was able to buy food for them all – sausage, bread and dried figs – and a change of stockings.

They spent the night sleeping in chairs in the hotel foyer: a strange night, alternating between the dead, dreamless sleep of exhaustion, and sudden wakings in cold fright, not knowing where they were. Emily was having to fight against feelings of despair, which she knew were caused partly by tiredness and partly by the strangeness of her surroundings. Being so alone and lost in a strange place, with no sure knowledge of where she would be going next, made her long for the reassurance of home, and many times she wished herself back in the apartment with Marfa.

The next day the rain had stopped, but the skies were threatening and the icy wind had hardly moderated. Emily breakfasted on bread and Turkish coffee – a wonderful luxury – and leaving the children under the joint care of Kamud and Modeste, went out to the harbour to look for a ship. It proved easier than she had expected. There were several fishing-trawlers in the harbour, sheltering from the storm; and with an eye to the roughness of the sea, and remembering the legends about their seamanship, Emily chose to approach a Greek one first.

The captain proved most amenable. The diamond brooch, earrings and bracelet that Emily laid on the table in his tiny cabin took his fancy very much, and he agreed to take her and the children to Constantinople as soon as the sea moderated.

'But how will you get on from there?' he asked. 'Have you more jewels to sell, to get you to England?'

Emily sensed a disingenuous question, and shook her head. 'No, these are the last of my things. I've had to sell everything else to get this far. But I have relatives in Constantinople, a great-aunt whose husband is in the French Embassy. They will help me.'

Captain Kostaki nodded and smiled so pleasantly that Emily felt she had probably misjudged him. 'Good, good, I was worried for you. Well, I should think by the way the wind is dropping, we can probably sail tomorrow. I will send word to the hotel if things don't look good. Otherwise we'll sail at dawn.'

Kostaki's idea of moderation was not hers, but she would not have wanted to delay any further. Kamud had told her there was cholera in Novorissisk, and she was desperate now to get back to England and things familiar. All the same, the Black Sea when in a rough mood was no place for the weak-spirited, and for forty-eight hours the little ship was tossed like a cork on the huge waves. For the passengers it was like being trapped in a malfunctioning lift that was going up and down at high speed and completely at random.

When they entered the Bosphorus at last the captain allowed them up on deck for a breath of fresh air. They clambered up, pale and puffy-eyed and shimmering slightly from the fine coating of fish-scales they had acquired down below. A watery sun broke through the clouds at last, and the white summer residences up on the cliffs above them looked suddenly beautiful and peaceful in their wreaths of greenery. There was sense and order in the world somewhere, Emily thought, with a renewal of hope. Her Great-aunt Tatiana, for whom Tatya had been named, was not far away now, and from here everything would be straightforward. She had brought the three children and a large part of her jewellery safe out of Russia. Now it was only a matter of time before they would all be home in England.

A white cutter appeared, travelling very fast towards them, and flying both the Tricolor and the Union flag. Emily's heart rose at the sight of the familiar standard.

'Intelligence agents,' Captain Kostaki growled, but resignedly. 'Well, they should be pleased enough with what I've brought them this time.'

The cutter pulled up alongside, and there was some conversation with the captain, and then a clear young English voice called out, 'What is your name, madam? I understand you are British?'

'My name is Emily Paget. My uncle is the Marquess of Westinghouse. I also have a great-aunt in Constantinople, the wife of the Comte de Zibeline.'

The French officer spoke. 'Yes, of course, I know him well. You are intending to seek asylum with them?'

'Yes, until passage can be arranged for me to return to England.'

The cutter preceded them into Constantinople harbour, and the two officers were waiting for Emily when, having thanked Captain Kostaki, she stepped down onto solid ground at last. She had Petya in her arms, Tatya by the hand, and Modeste was behind her, carrying the Gladstone bag.

'Oh, I am so glad to be here,' she said. 'It has become a nightmare in Russia.'

'So we understand,' the English officer said kindly. 'Look here, I'm afraid you'll have to go through a few formalities, but we'll telephone ahead and let your uncle the Count know you're here. I'm sure he'll send transport down for you.'

'Thank you, you're very kind.'

'Oh, not at all, ma'am. I'm sure you've been through a great deal. The MO will have to give you the once-over as well, I'm afraid. We hear there's cholera in Novorissisk as well as typhoid and typhus,

493

but I'm sure – I say!' He broke off, looking past her. 'Is your little boy all right?'

Emily turned to see that Modeste had stopped and put down the bag he was carrying. His face was flushed, his eyes half closed, and he swayed a little on his feet.

'Modeste, what is it?' she said, putting down Petya and going to him. His face was stinging hot, but he was shivering violently.

'I don't feel well, Milya,' he whimpered softly.

She gathered him to her, burning and shivering, bony and fragile child, her darling boy, and inwardly offered up a cry of anguish, like a driven and cornered animal. Not Modeste too, God! How much more do you want from me? *Not Modeste!*

Chapter Twenty-Eight

Victoria Station! How deliciously familiar and utterly alien it looked, different not only from Russia, but from its remembered self. To begin with, everyone male was in uniform. There were soldiers, sailors and airmen, setting out and coming home on leave. The entire rear half of the train they came in on was taken up by the Red Cross, and when the walking wounded had helped each other down, the stretchers began appearing – surely more than the train could have held, like handkerchiefs being pulled out of a conjuror's hat. Nurses in their stiff veils and white aprons pattered round efficiently, volunteer ladies wheeled tea trolleys, and ambulances were backed up the platform with women drivers hanging out of the cab windows.

Everywhere women were doing men's jobs: porters in strange hermaphroditic uniforms, top half male, bottom half female, heaved trunks about as though they were featherweights and trotted along pushing laden trolleys. Women were loading and driving the railway baggage waggons, manning the ticket office and the platform barriers.

Emily secured a cab, bundled the children in, and gave the address of Lady Hamilton's house. More working women outside: there was a lady policeman directing the traffic, and a woman in a brown dust-coat perched up a ladder posting advertising bills on the station wall. Emily spotted postwomen and a milkwoman, women driving the motor buses – and, strangest sight of all, down a side-street a coal dray with three diminutive blackened females in leather helmets shifting sacks of coal hardly smaller than themselves.

The war had achieved in four years what the Suffragists and the WSPU could not manage in fifty. The war could not have been waged without women taking over the vacated jobs, working in munitions factories, farming the land, running the offices. Women had formed their own branches of the army and navy, too; and when the question arose again of the universal franchise for men, it was seen that as men who had served their country could not be excluded, neither could women.

Emily had still been in Constantinople when the Representation of the People Bill passed its third reading in the Commons, but the English papers were sent over there, and she had read about it in *The Times*. So women had the vote at last! Of course, it was not *all* women: the die-hard old reactionaries had pointed out, in tones of horror, that if all women over twenty-one were enfranchised, there would be more female voters than male. So it was finally agreed that to qualify, women must be over thirty and either rate-payers, or the wives of rate-payers. Still, the principle had been admitted, and surely it would be only a matter of time before the detail was finally adjusted.

She had had little opportunity at the time to feel glad about it, and little heart later. Modeste had proved to be suffering not from cholera or typhoid, but from influenza, which was beginning to be rife all around the Black Sea. She guessed that he had been sickening for it for some time, but had hidden it from her while their situation was so uncertain. Such courage from a small child was remarkable; when he collapsed on the harbour front, she realised how much she had relied on him since they had left Petrograd.

It was a particularly virulent kind of sickness, which the English papers had already noted and were calling the Spanish flu. Within two days of their arrival all three children were down with it. Eight days later they buried Modeste in a quiet corner of the British Military Cemetery.

She had not believed until the very end that he was going to die: she could not bear to believe it. She stayed with him all the time, sleeping in his room at night, and after the first violent fever had abated, she had thought he would recover. But his breathing got worse, and he developed irregular heart sounds. Finally the fever returned, and he had no strength left to fight it. He burned up and was consumed like a piece of paper.

It seemed in the last feverish stage that he had known he was dying. He had come to himself near the end and looked up at Emily, who was sitting by him holding his hand, with recognition.

'Yes, my darling,' she said. 'How do you feel?'

'My head hurts,' he said. Then, 'My chest, too.'

She raised him a little and fed him a few sips of water. When she lay him down again he continued to look at her attentively. 'Milya, if I die, will it stop hurting?' His voice was a thread, his face as delicate as a painting on transparent ivory.

'Yes, my star. But I don't think you're going to die.'

496

He closed his eyes. 'I think I will,' he said, and he sounded drowsy, almost content. 'It will be nice to be with Mama again.'

'And Papa.'

She hadn't realised she had said it aloud, but Modeste, his eyes still closed, murmured, 'Not Papa. Papa's still with you.'

'What do you mean, my soul?' she asked, but he didn't answer. He died, very quietly, about half an hour later.

Tatya and Petya had had the influenza lightly, but even so it had left them very weak and suffering from the lassitude typical of the disease. Natasha's sister and brother-in-law were everything kind, and suggested that Emily should make her permanent home with them; at the very least, she should stay for the summer, until she had had time to think what she wanted to do. But she had a desperate longing for home now, and had begged their help to get back to England.

It had been a long journey. They set off by ship, a French cargo vessel which left Constantinople in mid-April for Marseilles. From there a long train journey took them to Paris, and then to Calais, where after considerable delay they were able to get on a boat for England.

Now here they were in mid-May in London, feeling very alone and bewildered. In the ten weeks of her escape journey, Emily had looked round a thousand times to check that the luggage and the three children were near her and safe. She had not yet learned to stop looking for Modeste: his absence nagged at the corner of her attention all the time, and she mourned for him as ceaselessly as for his father. At least she knew where his narrow grave lay; she would never know what strip of earth sheltered the poor bones of the man she loved.

London looked strange to her. The streets were so narrow, the buildings so small and grey. There was an air of dilapidation about everything, though she didn't know if that was because of the war, or whether it had always been like that without her noticing. The traffic seemed beyond any reason: surely it was not possible to cram so many motor vehicles into such narrow arteries? Surely no-one with any sense would try? But the trees were lovely, beginning to be full-leafed, and there were glimpses here and there of the parks and squares and gardens which had always made London special.

Tatya began to cry. 'I don't like it. It's ugly and dark! I want to go home!'

Emily was perplexed. 'Home where, *mylenkaya*?' Did she mean to the apartment, or the house in Fourstatskaya Street? Or even to Constantinople, her most recent 'home'?

'I don't know!' Tatya cried harder, while Petya sucked Bobo's ears and watched her roundly over the top of them, wondering whether to join in.

'We'll have a new home soon, and then we'll settle down and stay for ever and ever. Don't cry any more. Look, see there? That's where the King of England lives.'

They pulled up in front of Lady Hamilton's house at last, and the taxi-driver – an old man with the splendid whiskers of a Boer War veteran – craned round to say, 'Are you sure this is it, miss?'

'Yes,' she said. She saw what he meant. It had a raffish air about it. There was a large piece of coping missing from the false parapet at the top, and Emily remembered that there had been some strategic bombing on London in 1916 and '17. Apart from that, the windows were dirty, the steps hadn't been whitened in a very long time, the front door stood open, and the paint was peeling off it. A bicycle was propped against the railings, and as Emily helped the children out of the taxi, a very tall young man in bicycle-clips ran down the steps, swung himself onto the bicycle, and with only a curious glance at her rode briskly away.

She took up the bags, and ushering the children ahead of her, went in. The hall was empty of its usual furnishings and paintings, but there was a very large desk to one side, with a lamp on it, a visitors' book, and a black telephone apparatus. From somewhere upstairs came a distant sound of music – it sounded like a phonograph. Emily put down the bags and looked around her, with the dislocated feeling of having gone up a step that wasn't there.

'What's this place called?' Tatya asked, and Petya removed Bobo from his mouth for long enough to say, 'I'm hungry, Mama.'

There were footsteps, and another young man appeared from the passage that led to the servants' entrance. He stopped short when he saw them, and gave them a wide, shy grin.

'I'm sorry, have you been waiting long? I just went to close the back door – someone must have gone out that way and left it open. Can I help you in some way? You kinda look as though you're lost.'

'I think I'm having a dream,' Emily said. 'My name is Emily Paget, and this is my house. Who are you, and what are you doing here?'

The young man stared for a moment, and then snapped his fingers, laughing. 'I get it! You must be our absent landlady! Well, it really is a pleasure to meet you, ma'am. I guess you must be puzzled by all this.'

'Not really,' Emily said, smiling in return. It was impossible to do otherwise in the face of his infectious goodwill. 'No-one who lived through 1917 in Russia could be ignorant of the word "requisition".'

'There you have it, ma'am, in a nutshell. Your own British Government couldn't bear to see a good building like this stand empty, so the War Office took it over. Some kind of administration office. Then last year they leased it to the United States Army as a billet for headquarters staff officers – there seem to be more of us all the time, I'm afraid. But that's war for you! We try to take good care of it for you, ma'am.'

'I'm sure you do, but where does that leave me?' Emily said, and made a small gesture towards the children, who were fascinated by his accent and were staring at him almost open-mouthed.

The young man looked lost. 'I guess nobody knew you were coming back, ma'am. I'm sure you'll get your house back after the war, but that's no use to you now, of course.'

'What happened to my staff, Katya and Lovibond? I understood they were to live here and keep the house for me.'

He looked relieved. 'Oh, yes, Lovibond's still here! He acts as our caretaker. He has his quarters in the basement. I don't know any Katya, though. I guess she must have been before my time.'

'Perhaps I'd better go and see Lovibond,' Emily said.

'That might be best. Let me help you with your bags, ma'am.'

Lovibond cried, which upset Emily; but he soon pulled himself together, saw them comfortable in his tiny sitting-room, and set about making tea and sandwiches.

'I didn't think I'd ever see you again, Miss Emily – your highness, I should say – '

'No, please, I like Miss Emily better. It's all right, you can speak English to the children. They've learned it since birth.'

'Thank you, miss. That's right then, my little dears, you make yourselves comfy. My, the little boy has such a look of you, Miss Emily! Oh miss, we thought you was dead, murdered by them wicked Bolshies!'

'I nearly was. I'll tell you about it later, but for now, you tell me everything. What's happened to my house?'

'Her ladyship was right about you needing it, wasn't she?' Lovibond said cannily. 'She said you'd be back, though I think she half expected to see you herself before she died. But she made a good end, miss, as peaceful as you could wish, and Katya was with her right to the end, and the doctor.'

'Where's Katya now?'

'She's dead too, miss. Pneumonia, January 1917. There's just me now – you can't kill an old horseman, miss!' He looked suddenly upset. 'I tried to look after your house, but when the Government came and asked for it, what could I say? They took it over, and said I could stay on in the basement. But they never hardly used it; and then the Yanks came along and the War Office leased it to them. I don't know rightly how that works. They ought to pay the money to you really, you being the legal owner.'

'I don't think I feel much like taking them on at the moment. Perhaps I'll get my uncle to tackle them.'

'That'd be best, miss, I'm sure. Now, here's your cup of tea. You have your bite of luncheon while I take care of the little ones and you tell me everything that's happened to you.' He gave her a watery smile. 'I wish Katya could have been here to see how you've turned out. She was so pleased when you married a prince! Always knew you were destined to be a princess, she used to say.

The children took to Lovibond, especially after he had told them some of his horse stories, and after luncheon they all went out into the garden to let the children run about and play.

'It's a bit overgrown,' Emily said, 'but I think the children like it that way.'

Lovibond sighed. 'I do my best, miss, but it's all a bit much for me, with the boiler and the dustbins and everything. I'm not as young as I was.'

'I didn't know you had to do the garden as well!'

'Oh, well, there's a girl comes in now and then for the heavy work, but she doesn't hardly do more than mow the lawn and cut the hedges. I can't get used to all these slips of girls doing such rough work. Of course, you were always mad to be a typewriter, miss, but that's quite ladylike when all's said and done. We have girls delivering the coal and everything now.'

500

'Things have changed a lot, haven't they?' Emily said sympathetically.

'They have and all! Some of it's for the better, of course. But it seems almost as if the old world's passed away. If the old Queen was to come back now, I don't think she'd know the place.'

He told her about old friends. Sylvia and Frances had trained as war nurses and gone to France, where both had distinguished themselves. Sylvia had died over there, of typhoid in the winter after Passchendaele. Fanny was still there, nursing at the front, and had recently been awarded the George Cross. Lady Ongar, Lady Frances's mother, was so kind as to telephone Lovibond and tell him about it. Pleased as Punch, she was.

The war had been hard on her ladyship, what with all the horses and motor cars being requisitioned, so she was pretty well stuck out at Greenlands. It was hard on her Lady Frances being away, too, what with Mr Harry being killed at the Somme. But Mrs Partridge went to visit her quite often, he believed. The Partridges had done their bit, too, all in all, what with Sylvia dying, and her brother Perry at Ypres, and young Algie at Gallipoli . . .

'Is it all deaths, Lovibond?' Emily asked him at last.

'That's what wars are about, Miss Emily.'

'Yes. Yes, I suppose you're right. I wish the generals and politicians who started them knew that, though.'

And there was one more to tell her about – her cousin Tom, who had died only two months earlier when his ship was torpedoed by a German U-boat in the northern approaches. 'He'd made lieutenant, one of the youngest ever,' Lovibond told her, as though that were some compensation. 'They said he was very promising. I read about him in *The Times*. I kept the piece – I've got it somewhere. I started keeping cuttings of all the ladies and gentlemen I knew, after the first one got mentioned in the war. Her ladyship always had a lot of young people around her. Very lively-minded, her ladyship was.'

And now they were all dead, Emily thought. She cried a little when he told her about Tom. She had been looking forward almost more than anything to a reunion with him, to telling him her adventures and introducing his little cousins to him. When she thought back, the road from Bratton to the present was marked as though by a row of crosses with the deaths of everyone she cared for. It was as if she were being cast off from every association: being made almost into one of those refugees who no longer had anywhere they could call home.

All she had was the children, Tatya and Petya. Lovibond asked her what she meant to do about them, and she answered unhesitatingly. 'I want to adopt them as my own. I've been more or less a mother to them for years now, and their father left them to my special charge when he went away. He said if anything happened, I was to take care of them.'

'Poor gentleman,' Lovibond said. 'That's a rotten way to go, to be killed by your own side.'

He meant it kindly, but it seemed to her that when someone was dead, it didn't matter to them any more how they died; and as for her, there was no comfort in anything about his death.

'At least in England I can see that they have a decent upbringing and a proper education, not all those awful Bolshevik lies and brutalities,' she went on. 'And with the jewellery I've managed to bring out, I should have enough money to live respectably.' She smiled suddenly. 'If not, I can always get myself a job as a motor-bus driver, can't I?'

He laughed. 'Lord, Miss Emily, do you remember me teaching you young ladies round and round that field, and Miss Angela, God rest her soul, with such a determined look on her face! Oh dear, they were good days!' He wiped his eyes. 'Look at those blessed children, running about. They'll be getting up an appetite for their tea. What', he asked delicately, 'was you wanting to do about that, Miss Emily?'

'Yes, I know,' she sighed. 'I've got to find somewhere to live for the time being, haven't I? Obviously I can't live here until the war's over – if it ever is.'

'Why don't you go home, miss?' Lovibond said after a moment.

'Home?'

'To your father's, miss – to Bratton. Just for the summer, like. Get the little ones out into the fresh air and everything. Then you could have time to think what to do. I'm sure you'd want to see him anyway, after all this time.'

'I hardly dared ask you about Papa,' she said, 'with the list of deaths you were giving me. But then Papa's the last person who'd get himself killed. He's all right, is he?'

'As far as I know, Miss Emily. I did see Lord Westinghouse outside the In-and-Out a few weeks ago, and he was kind enough to stand and chat with me a while, and tell me how everyone was. He'd been to collect Tom's medal – showed it to me. Proud of him, he was. Of course it's an extra sad thing for him, because he and the new

Lady Westinghouse have only got the three girls, though I suppose there's always time for more, but if he doesn't have a boy, the title will go to some cousin out in Australia that he's never seen, from what he was telling me, and a sad thing that would be for Bratton . . . '

And so the next day, Emily and the children took a taxi-cab to Waterloo and caught the Salisbury train. It was a neat ending, she thought, to her long, long journey – really coming home, with a vengeance!

There was something very healing about the English countryside, Emily thought, as she took her accustomed stroll through the park, up to the poplars, across as far as the dew-pond, and back through the spinney and the old white road. She had expected to find Bratton claustrophobic, but it seemed to have grown bigger since she had been away; large enough, anyway, to accommodate her much smaller dreams. She had come meaning to stay perhaps a few weeks at most, but she had been here a year already. She thought she would probably stay. There seemed no reason any more to leave.

The first sight of The Lodge had tugged at her in a number of painful ways, awakening tender memories and sad ones, and echoing old feelings of frustration and imprisonment. Yet by some strange alchemy, the inside of the tiny house no longer seemed dark and cramped but cosy and welcoming; and the glorious greenness of the park and the open countryside seemed to flow around it and through it and lap it with beauty and healing.

The sight of her father was a shock to her, for he seemed to have aged more than was right in the time she had been away. Afterwards she thought she had probably made him younger in memory. He was expecting her. She had meant at first to surprise him, but had then reconsidered that in view of all that had happened, surprises were probably not fair on anyone. So she telephoned him from London.

He greeted her vaguely and affectionately, looked her over, pronounced her grown beautiful but rather too thin. He greeted the children in exactly the same way. He did not distinguish between people by age or rank – probably not much by sex any more. After being with him for a while, she began to think he didn't really distinguish real people from fictional ones either. Having greeted them all, he began telling them about his latest story, a thrilling war adventure of his newest hero, Sergeant 'Ironjaw' Morris, and it was plain that Ironjaw was as real to him as they were – if not more so.

The domestic arrangements inside The Lodge left something to be desired. Mrs Vicar had long since left, and the cleaning and cooking were done by a woman from the village who came up every other day.

'Every other day? What do you eat in between, then?' Emily asked, perplexed.

'I eat up at the Big House sometimes. Or I heat something up. Mrs Maddock leaves me stews and things. Not very appetising, but everyone has to make sacrifices. There's a war on, you know.'

Emily found a sample of Mrs Maddock's stew in the kitchen, and hastily threw it out. Judging by the state of the house, she was not much of a cleaner, either. Emily decided that she had made her last call.

'I'll keep house for the time being, until I can find a suitable replacement,' she told her father.

'You?' he said, perplexed. 'What can you do?'

'Dear old Pa, I've been keeping house for myself and three children for a long time now. You'd be surprised what a good cook I've become. Better than Mrs Maddock, anyway.'

'Lucretia Borgia was probably a better cook than Mrs M,' he said sadly.

His secretary, Miss Foston, had long gone, too. 'She went off to work for the War Office. I think she disapproved of me because I didn't volunteer when the war broke out. I told her my work was essential to the war effort too, but she didn't believe me. Well, I was proved right, because when they called up the men between forty-one and fifty, they let me off. My war stories are important for morale. I had an official letter saying so. I've got it somewhere . . . '

Emily had a busy few days setting things to rights, but was satisfied in seeing the children cheerful and lively, enjoying having the freedom to run about after so many and such long confinements. They loved the park and the hedgerows, and were always bringing things in to show her – an eggshell, a flower, a mushroom. They had true Russian instincts when it came to foraging, and she put them on permanent mushroom patrol. It was wonderful, she thought, as she beat rugs and watched through the resultant fog her children running off into the park to play, to know that they would not be stopped by an illiterate soldier with a gun and terrorised or murdered.

The children slept in Penny's old room; Emily had her childhood room back. There were many strange things to feel about that, especially as it had not been touched in the intervening years. There had been no need for Edward to throw away her things, and so there they all were, to divert and haunt and sadden her. Coming home, as far home as one could possibly come, she thought.

There was a little awkwardness about going up to the house for the first time, but the new Lady Westinghouse was as nice as could be, though shy and not a little embarrassed. She was horrified to learn that Emily was doing her own housework, and insisted on sending someone from the house in every day at least to do the cleaning.

'If the arrangement suits you, it can stand for as long as you like. If I'd only known, if Edward had only told me, I'd have done something long ago. But he never talks about domestic matters. Now what about cooking?'

'I'm quite happy to cook,' Emily said.

'Oh no!' said Lady Westinghouse, and eventually, 'Well, if I send Betty up to you every day – she's one of my housemaids, a very reliable girl – she can do all the cleaning, and the heavy work in the kitchen, too, preparing things and peeling vegetables and so on. You won't want to do all that. And if you tell her in the afternoon what you want to cook the next day, she can bring it up with her. We've plenty of vegetables and so on, and milk, eggs and cheese from the Home Farm – well, you know all that anyway, of course, having been born here.' She laughed nervously.

Emily grew quite to like her, and oddly enough, felt sorry for her. She got the impression that Lady Westinghouse felt guilty about Aunt Maud's death, and about stepping into her shoes so soon. She also gathered, though it was never said, that the marriage itself had disappointed her. Uncle Westie was not nearly so exciting or attentive a husband as he had been a lover. He didn't come to Bratton much, and when he did he was hearty and impenetrable towards Emily. He lived an Edwardian life of clubs and house parties, and was probably – though Emily of course never discussed it with Pamela – running around with other women.

Emily also guessed his three daughters were a bitter disappointment to him now that Tom was dead. They were four, three and two years old, and quite painfully well behaved, shy and polite like their mother. When approval had been given on both sides, they and Tatya and Petya were allowed to play together, and a new generation of children went up from The Lodge to the Big House to play in the nursery, where Emily had told stories to Tom, Lexy, Vick and Maudie.

Tatya soon licked her cousins into shape, and emerged as triumphant leader, organiser – virtual dictator – with Petya her loyal lieutenant. Tatya was turning into quite a storyteller herself, Emily noted. She had elaborated her memories of life in Russia and her Great Escape until they bore little resemblance to the truth; but the cousins lapped it up, each new version being accepted alongside the old with a child's easy lack of criticism.

Once they had settled in at The Lodge, and Emily began to feel that she would not necessarily want to go away again at once, she had to find something to do to keep herself occupied, beyond cooking and caring for the children.

'Why don't you write down some of your experiences?' Edward suggested one day at dinner. 'A history of the revolution, from the inside. I dare say lots of people will write down the politics and the battles, but who will know what it was like to be an ordinary person through the war and the revolution and afterwards?'

So she did it. She purchased a second typewriter, and her father pronounced himself perfectly agreeable to sharing his room, so they turned the desk round and worked one on either side of it. It proved a successful and companionable scheme. There was always someone on hand to consult on spellings and the date of the Battle of Tannenberg. Emily found her father's professional expertise invaluable, and he fed unashamedly on her experiences and her fresh imagination. Writing being such an utterly solitary occupation, it was pleasant for each of them to have another writer on hand to whom to read out a particularly pleasing passage, or consult over a difficulty of phrasing. Edward came some distance out of his shell as a result of the arrangement, and Emily felt she had never been so close to him, or liked him so much.

In the autumn Emily felt it would be a good thing for Tatya to go to school. She enrolled her in the village school for the time being, for it had a good reputation and Emily knew the head teacher personally as a friend of *her* old friend, the vicar. So that brother and sister could be together, Miss Elmbridge agreed to take Petya into the infant class, although he was only four; and after a week or two, when she was invited to tea at The Lodge, she proclaimed him to be so advanced that the year's difference in age didn't trouble him at all.

'In fact, he's ahead of the others in some respects. He has obviously been well taught.'

'Thank you. I taught him!' Emily laughed.

Miss Elmbridge smiled. 'He's very lucky to have a mother like you.'

It was innocently said, but it pained Emily, and reminded her that she must put matters in hand if the children were to be legally adopted and given the security they needed. She went up to London to consult a solicitor, and spent the rest of the day shopping for clothes for herself and the children and presents for everybody. It was a delightful experience, reminding her of her early days in Petersburg when she had gone shopping with her grandmother; but this was better, because the things were needed, not just bought because they were there.

In November came the Armistice, and the war seemed to be all but over at last. The village erupted with joy. A bonfire was hastily built at the end of the village green, and a party was held to which everyone was invited. The two public houses set out trestles and served beer far into the night in safe defiance of the licensing laws. The vicarage, which was the nearest big house to the bonfire, also opened its doors: the vicar's wife provided hot punch for those who didn't care for beer, and the vicar a polite ear and a comforting word for all those who wanted to remember their fallen.

Potatoes and apples were roasted in the embers and eaten. Children ran about shrieking, completely out of control, until far past their bedtimes. Several local musicians brought their instruments out in unrehearsed harmony of intention, and there was singing and dancing and a great deal of indiscriminate kissing in the firelight; probably an unfortunate amount of copulation away from it, too.

But for Emily the real Armistice celebration came the next evening, after the children were in bed, when her father suddenly put down his book and got up from the fireside. He went out and returned a little while later with a bottle and two glasses on a tray.

'Champagne?' Emily said, putting her book aside. 'What a pleasant surprise.'

'I've been saving it for the end of the war – God knows why. I never expected to have anyone to drink it with. It hasn't been chilled, of course, but it's quite cold. It's been in the bottom of the cheese pantry, and that's like the Antarctic at the moment.'

She watched him while he opened the bottle and poured, and then received her glass from him.

'Well,' he said. 'To Peace!'

'To Peace,' she said, and they both drank.

He lowered his glass and looked at her keenly. 'I'm so glad you've come home, Emily,' he said. 'I would never have guessed before you went how much I'd miss you. I've been lonely these last six years. Since you've come back, it's been – ' His vocabulary failed him. He waved his glass helplessly. 'Really nice.'

Emily stood up and went to put her arm round his neck and kiss his cheek. 'Thank you, Papa. That's the nicest thing you've ever said to me. I'm glad to be home, too.'

'And the children,' he said, sitting down in the chair opposite hers. 'I've never really asked you what happened in your personal life. I don't want to pry. But if ever you want to tell me – well, here I am.'

'Thanks,' she said painfully. 'I don't think I do yet. One day I will, but not yet. But thank you.'

He nodded and sipped again. When next he looked up, she saw with painful surprise that there were tears in his eyes. She had never seen her father cry. It was a reversal of the natural order of things that made her afraid. 'So many people,' he said. 'Maud – Tom – well, your list is probably longer than mine. Must be so, indeed. I'm not expressing myself very well tonight, am I?'

She shook her head, unable for the moment to speak.

'But we're alive, and that's important. It's all we can do for them, now – to live, and know we're alive, and make the most of it.'

'Yes,' she said. 'Yes. It's what I mean to do.'

'I'm fond of you, Emily. I don't know if I've ever said it properly to you before.'

'And I of you, Papa. And the children – they already think of you as their grandfather.'

'Yes, the children. Thank you for bringing me them. I suppose they're what it was all for. I hope to God they never make the same mistakes as our generation did.'

'I don't think they will,' Emily said. 'Let's drink to them, Papa – the new generation.'

He smiled, and drank the toast.

*

And now it was May again – May 1919. Her long ramble had been spent partly in reminiscing, partly in planning the next part of her book – which was much the same thing. Coming to the end of a train of thought, she became aware again of her surroundings, and looked about her at the lush pasture, the line of poplars, stiff and comical over to her left, the white road to her right leading down to the small Gothic shape of The Lodge, with the quiet smoke rising from its kitchen chimney.

The most surprising thing, she thought, was that she felt content, and she hadn't ever experienced that before. All her life she had been longing and fretting and striving, wanting things she hadn't got, and quite often not wanting what she had got. She had been through great unhappiness, and danger, and loss, and now that she had come full circle, she had suddenly found contentment where she would least have expected it. It was not exactly happiness – that was too positive a word, something she associated with Alexei, and which therefore she could not expect to feel again; but it was a quietness. She had escaped with her life, her health, and the children to take care of and bring up in his remembered image. Things could have been very much worse.

She started down the slope towards the house, feeling suddenly hungry. Her stomach was a good timekeeper, and if it told her it was time for luncheon, it meant that the children would be home at any moment. She had left Betty in the early throes of a steak and kidney pie – she was proving to be a very reliable cook, and her pastry was as good as Penny's had been.

As she came nearer, she saw that there was someone standing outside the gate looking in, someone in what seemed to be a military greatcoat. Well, khaki anyway. It was a good job, she thought, that Betty always did a large enough pie for second helpings, because if that was a discharged soldier making his way home, he would have the appetite of the Big House boiler for coke.

They got quite a few of them these days, walking home because they had spent their demobilisation money on celebrations, or sometimes on presents for the wife and children at home. They stopped at the gate of The Lodge and asked for a drink of water, but they were always invited to stay for whatever the next meal happened to be, and usually left with half-a-crown and a pocket full of bread and cheese for their onward journey. They told their stories and Emily told hers, and it was hard to say which enjoyed the other more.

She wondered sometimes if there were some secret means by which

509

they communicated with each other where there was a meal to be had, as tramps were supposed to do. She began to walk more briskly, already slipping into place the welcoming smile so as not to frighten the poor chap away. 'Hello,' she called from a few yards off. 'Come in, if you like. The little gate's not locked. I suppose you're – '

She stopped, and everything inside her went still with disbelief and terror: terror that what her senses told her would turn out not to be true – as indeed it couldn't be. The soldier moved at last, stepped aside and opened the small wicket-gate, came through, closed it carefully behind him. He came a step or two nearer, and then he stopped, looking at her questioningly; looking as though he, too, was afraid of waking from whatever dream they had both strayed into.

It seemed a very long time – two or three centuries perhaps – before she was able to speak.

'How did you find me?'

'I went to your London house and they told me where you were. Thank God you got out! I hoped you had. I could never have got to you in Petersburg – *doushka*, what is it?'

'I thought you were dead,' she whispered. 'They told me you were dead.'

He seemed dazed. 'Who told you?'

'The Bolsheviks.'

'But why did you believe them?'

That was real. She could never have imagined that question, which, fool of all fools that she was, had never occurred to her before. And it was his voice. In all her memories and dreams and longings she had never been able to recreate that. 'Alexei?'

'Yes, it's me.' He moved his hands, and an urgency came into his expression. 'For God's sake, come here.'

In his arms; oh God, in his arms, as she had never thought to be again. Too much joy. She didn't know how to cope with it. 'Can you die from this?' she muttered.

'I think so. God, I hope so!'

'Not yet though. Alexei, is it really you? I'm not dreaming?'

'I don't think so. Emilia, I've thought about this – '

After a moment she pushed herself away from him, but only to feed another sense. She gazed at him greedily. There was a healed scar on his forehead, he was thin, and he had about him the undefined seediness she had grown used to in soldiers coming back from the front. He looked older. His hair had turned grey at the temples.

510

That upset her. It wasn't fair for time to have done that to him. She had lost years of his life. He ought to have come back exactly as he went away.

'Where have you been? They told me your own men had mutinied and shot you,' she said.

'Perhaps that's the way they'd have liked it to be – wishful thinking. My men were sound. We joined the other loyal troops fighting for the Provisional Government; then when that turned out to be no good, we went south and joined the Whites in the Caucasus. But I don't think now that the Whites can win without real help from Britain and America, and they won't play. It was turning sour, too. The things I've seen . . . They were doing worse things than the Reds, and I started to wonder if there was a right side any more. So I got out. I think', he concluded with an unconscious sigh, 'I've done enough.'

'I thought you were dead,' she said. 'All this time . . . '

'I'm sorry. I'm so sorry. But I told you, didn't I, that it would be all right. I promised you. You should have trusted me.'

She smiled, perilously close to crying. 'Oh you fool!'

He took her in his arms again. 'I'm never going to let you out of my sight again. I've missed you so much, my Emilia.'

She held him, crying a little into his collar. After a while he said hesitantly, 'Is Anna in England?'

She couldn't think of a way to cushion it. 'She's dead. The Bolsheviks shot her. And Adishka. Mischa helped us get out. He did everything.'

After a moment, 'Are the children here with you?'

'Yes. They're at school. They'll be back any time.'

He drew back to read her face. 'They said – in London – that there were only two.'

She licked her lips. 'Modeste – at Constantinople, the influenza. They all had it, but he – Oh Alexei, I'm sorry. I tried to save them all!'

She saw age and death in his face; and then the terrible courage, the regathering for one more effort. So must they have done as soldiers, she thought: exhausted and afraid, gathered themselves to fight on a little longer. 'No, I'm sorry,' he said. 'It's you who've had to carry the burden.'

They seemed to have come to the end of all they could say for the moment, and simply stood, their hands linked, looking at each other. She had been braced so long to go on living without him it was hard to let herself yield to joy; and she saw that something of the same kind was happening to him. She ought to say something, to take him inside – the children would be home soon, they must prepare for that. But it simply wasn't possible yet to move from this spot. A kind of superstitious dread had her, that if she did or said the wrong thing, the spell would be broken, and she would lose him again.

Two days later, in the evening, they went for a stroll. It was a warm, still, moonlit night, the very essence of romance.

'How they lay it on for us!' she said. 'Just like the end of a moving picture. Do you remember that first night at Schwartzenturm, how you took me out on the terrace to make a wish?'

'Mine came true,' he said.

'Did it? I think mine will, now.'

His arm was wound round her waist, they walked hip to hip. They could never have enough of touching each other. Last night by the fire she had sat on the floor, leaning against his knees, and he had stroked her head over and over as they talked.

'Will we ever go back?' she had asked. 'You say that the Whites can't win?'

'Not this time. But I can't believe that our people will tolerate the Bolsheviks for long. There'll be another revolution – there'll have to be. Then we – people like us – will fight again. Russia is ours. We have to get it back – for our children if not for ourselves.'

She didn't believe it. It sounded like a fairy story, and she had become expert now at telling them apart from reality. This was reality: the small room, the firelight, Alexei's hand on her hair; the children asleep upstairs, her father reading in the armchair opposite, with his glasses slipping to the end of his nose.

'I wish I knew what had happened to the people we left behind, though. Grandmama and Aunt Yenya and the children, and Mischa and Marfa,' she said. 'I feel as though we let them down, leaving them behind.'

'Do you think I don't feel it too? I left you to cope alone. If I had been there we might have got out earlier. They might not have died, Anna and Adishka – '

He didn't say Modeste's name, but they both thought of him. She had tried to tell Alexei about his courage in the last weeks and on the journey, but it still made her cry too much. One day. They had time now, thank God, time to be together; and nothing any more to keep them apart.

'I think your father is beginning to suspect,' Alexei said now as they came through the poplars into the open meadow. 'I'll have to make an honest woman of you. How quickly do you think we can get married?'

She smiled. 'Do you feel that if we're properly married, nothing will be able to part us again?'

'Yes, of course. Don't you?'

'Yes, but I thought I was the only superstitious fool.'

'All Russians are superstitious. I told you that.' He turned his head and kissed her. 'I love you, Emilia Edvardovna.'

'I love you, too, Alexei Nikolayevitch.'

They walked on. 'The children have grown so much. Tatya's becoming quite a lady.'

'You wouldn't say that if you saw her bullying her cousins. She's as ladylike as a Don Cossack.'

There was pain in his face. 'I've missed so much of their lives. Petya didn't even know me.'

'They'll find you again.'

'But will I find them? Will I find you?'

Pain struck at her. 'I'm here.'

'I've seen such things – a lifetime of horror in just a few years. Sometimes I feel as if I can't get back, as though there's a wide river – '

She stopped and turned to face him in the moonlight. 'You'll find a way to cross it. It's just another part of the journey. It will be all right.' She saw she hadn't convinced him yet. She realised suddenly that since he had reappeared beside the gate, she had hardly seen him smile, and never in that full and easy way she remembered, which had first made her love him.

She had lost him into death, and gone on living without him, and that was the river she had to cross. But he had actually *been* there: he had lived with death and looked into its face day after day, and it was a much longer way back from there.

'We must give it time,' she said.

'Time,' he repeated, as though she had asked for Roc's eggs.

'You once told me you could make it stop,' she said. Still there was no response in his face. How to reach him? How to get closer? 'I love you,' she said, looking up searchingly into his face. 'We've survived, we're together, and it will get better and better all the time.

Every time you lie with me in your arms, the past will fade a little more.'

'Yes,' he said. 'I know you're right.'

Knew it but didn't feel it yet. 'And when we have children of our own,' she began lightly.

'Children?' He seemed startled.

'Yes, children. I only have two of yours,' she said, looking stern. 'I want at least three more, and I want to know what you intend to do about it.'

'Would you like me to tell you,' he invited slowly, 'or show you?'

'Yes,' she said comprehensively.

'I love you, Emilia,' he said. He was looking down at her intently, searchingly, and with the beginning of joy in his face. Not smiling: better than that.